WESTERN CANON SERIES

The Western Canon's value is self-evident. Its status, however, has been under threat since the middle of the 20th century. Feminists, Marxists, intersectionalists, and others deny the Canon's existence by refusing to observe its traditional boundaries, throwing the borders open to invite all manner of second- and third-rate material. They intentionally misread the Canon, deconstructing it and looking for incoherence where men have only ever found genius.

Imperium Press' Western Canon series reclaims the Canon from the forces hostile to it. The series offers not only definitive versions of these works, but also supplementary material placing them at the centre of our aesthetic, intellectual, and spiritual life—where they belong.

FOLKTALES IN THE INDO-EUROPEAN TRADITION

Compiled and with foreword by
EDWARD MAXWELL III

Illustrations by
GRAMAN

PERTH
IMPERIUM PRESS
2021

Published by Imperium Press

www.imperiumpress.org

Foreword © Edward Maxwell III, 2021
Illustrations © Graman, 2021
The moral rights of the artists and authors have been asserted
All translations and illustrations used under license
to Imperium Press

© Imperium Press, 2021

FIRST EDITION

A catalogue record for this
book is available from the
National Library of Australia

ISBN 978-1-922602-26-8 Paperback
ISBN 978-1-922602-27-5 EPUB
ISBN 978-1-922602-28-2 Kindle

CONTENTS

APPENDICES

ILLUSTRATIONS

FOLKTALE AND THE
INDO-EUROPEAN FOLK-SOUL

Folktale and fairy tale are pejorative terms today. They have a musty, antiquated smell. For many curators of high culture, they are little more than childish fantasies, and maybe far less. And yet somehow, folktales persist. This is no accident—nothing persists so long for no reason at all. The fact is that if folktales lacked significance, they would have died out long ago.

Tolkien understood the significance of the folktale. In his 1936 lecture *Beowulf: The Monsters and the Critics*, he lamented what he saw as the undue emphasis Beowulf scholars of his time had placed on the factual and historical dimensions of the poem, giving short shrift to the "mere" story of a dragon slaying. In expressing his frustration with them, he captures something of the literary scholar's attitude toward the folktale:

> Yet this poetic talent, we are to understand, has all been squandered on an unprofitable theme: as if Milton had recounted the story of Jack and the Beanstalk in noble verse. Even if Milton had done this (and he might have done worse), we should perhaps pause to consider whether his poetic handling had not had some effect upon the trivial theme; what alchemy had been performed upon the base metal; whether indeed it remained base or trivial when he had finished with it.[1]

We should pause over "and he might have done worse". Tolkien took folklore very seriously, and in this he was following a centuries old tradition.

---

1 Tolkien, J. R. R. *Beowulf: The Monsters and the Critics* (London: Oxford University Press, 1963).

INTRODUCTION TO TALE TYPES

Folktales have been collected in earnest since at least the 17th century, but it was not until the 19th century that *folkloristics*, the study of folklore, became a serious and systematic discipline. The revival of interest in folklore was driven in part by Romantic nationalism with its focus on the organic unity of the *folk*, and this revival was never better embodied than in Jakob and Wilhelm Grimm. The Brothers Grimm studied law under Friedrich Carl von Savigny, an important figure in German jurisprudence whose historicism deeply impressed the Grimms with the concept of law as the organic expression of a national consciousness, or *volksgeist*.[2] Savigny awakened in the Grimms a passion for "the investigation of our earlier language, poetry and laws",[3] whereupon they took up the study of medieval German literature. The Grimms eventually found work as court librarians to the King of Westphalia, during which they published their collection of folktales *Kinder- und Hausmärchen* to much celebration. The Grimms, linguists by trade, were always keenly aware of the deep history lurking below the surface of these "children's tales", as Wilhelm explains by reference to the Indo-Germanic:[4]

> The outermost lines [of common heritage in stories] [...] are coterminous with those of the great race which is commonly called Indo-Germanic, and the relationship draws itself in constantly narrowing circles round the settlements of the Germans [...] It is my belief that the German stories do not belong to the northern and southern parts of our fatherland alone but that they are the absolutely common property of the nearly related Dutch, English and Scandinavians.[5]

The Romanticism of the time proved fertile ground for the Grimms' efforts. Asbjørnsen and Moe in Norway, Alexander Afanasyev in Russia, Joseph Jacobs in England, and many others soon embarked on the quest for their own *volksgeist* along the same lines, and many saw similarly archaic elements within their own folklore:

> The subject-matter of "Childe Rowland" has also claims on our attention especially with regard to recent views on the true nature and origin of elves, trolls, and fairies. I refer to the recently published work

---

2 Literally "folk spirit". The closest colloquial English term is "folk-soul", in German, *volksseele*.

3 Sweet, Henry. *Encyclopaedia Britannica*, 11th ed., s.v. "Grimm, Jacob Ludwig Carl" (1911).

4 What we now call Indo-European, the last common ancestor people of, among others, the Indians, Iranians, and most European peoples.

5 Grimm, Wilhelm. Preface in *Children's and household tales,* 3rd ed. (London: George Bell, 1856).

of Mr. D. MacRitchie, "The Testimony of Tradition" (Kegan Paul, Trench, Trübner & Co.)—i.e., of tradition about the fairies and the rest. Briefly put, Mr. MacRitchie's view is that the elves, trolls, and fairies represented in popular tradition are really the mound-dwellers, whose remains have been discovered in some abundance in the form of green hillocks, which have been artificially raised over a long and low passage leading to a central chamber open to the sky. Mr. Mac-Ritchie shows that in several instances traditions about trolls or "good people" have attached themselves to mounds, which have afterwards on investigation turned out to be evidently the former residence of men of smaller build than the mortals of to-day.[6]

By the early 20th century, folkloristics had developed still further—the massive corpus of European folktales was catalogued according to *tale type* by Finnish folklorist Antti Aarne in 1910, and substantially revised and expanded by Stith Thompson and Hans-Jörg Uther in 1961 and 2004 respectively. Over the course of nearly a century, these men sifted "some 2500 basic plots from which, for countless generations, European and Near Eastern storytellers have built their tales"[7] into the useful but rather cumbersomely named *Aarne–Thompson–Uther (ATU) Index.*

Each ATU tale type is the kernel of a story, some with pre-determined variations. Tale types rarely appear in their "pure" form, but parts can be expanded or omitted. Some tale types are more flexible than others—*314A: The Shepherd and the Giants* exhibits great variation, *361: Bear Skin* much less. Very often folktales will include more than one tale type, sometimes alongside original elements not answering to any tale type at all. The modular nature of the folktale is seen in Grimms' *The White Snake*, which exhibits tale types *673: The White Serpent's Flesh, 554: The Grateful Animals,* and *736: Luck and Wealth* all in the same tale. By this process of accretion, some folktales reach mini-epic proportions, such as *The Story of Little Tsar Novishny, the False Sister, and the Faithful Beasts.* This tale runs to some 7,500 words and includes the following types:

314A*: Animal Helper in the Flight – The Bullock-savior. A bullock helps children escape from their kidnapper (bear, witch).

315: The Treacherous Sister – The children promised to the water-spirit. The maiden wife of the water-spirit (devil). At his advice she feigns sickness and sends her brother for a remedy (or the like). Imprisoned animals break loose and save the boy.

565: The Magic Mill – Grinds an enormous amount of meal or salt

---

6 Jacobs, Joseph. *English Fairy Tales* (London: David Nutt, 1890).
7 Ashliman, D. L. *A Guide to Folktales in the English Language: Based on the Aarne–Thompson Classification System* (New York: Greenwood Press, 1987).

when the man who has stolen it cannot stop it.[8]

Folkloristics had come a long way, but as the 20th century wore on and the structural conflict of its prevailing ideology unfolded, folklore inevitably came in for a "reappraisal". In the tireless search for hot takes, academics, mostly outside of folkloristics, grew dissatisfied with folklore as the lore of the folk and sought to recast it as something else. Something that could be reinvented guilt-free out of whole cloth—something, perhaps, a little less "problematic", that could embody a new morality for a new age. Anderson's law of auto-correction, the well-worn mechanism whereby audience-driven censorship creates a novelty-suppressing feedback loop,[9] was put into the balance and found wanting. Scholarship is no less prone to fashion than anything else, and a field that had begun as genuinely scientific had evolved into something else. The problematic had to be itself problematized, and a new history had to be written. See Ruth B. Bottigheimer's *Fairy Tales: A New History*:

> It has been said so often that the folk invented and disseminated fairy tales that this assumption has become an unquestioned proposition. It may therefore surprise readers that folk invention and transmission of fairy tales has no basis in verifiable fact. Literary analysis undermines it, literary history rejects it, social history repudiates it, and publishing history (whether of manuscripts or of books) contradicts it.[10]

The reactionary *volksgeist* had been replaced by centralized media as the author of folk culture, opening the door for the progressive impulse to overwrite this culture. While no contortion of any traditional fairy tale had any staying power beyond its initial popularity, this was not a problem for the theory that folklore is mainly a literary enterprise, as the theory generally did not concern itself with empirical confirmation. This was shrewd because empirical disconfirmation was not long in coming. In 2015, Sara Graça da Silva and Jamshid J. Tehrani published a paper that

---

8 Thompson, Stith. *The Types of the Folktale: A Classification and Bibliography* (Indiana University, 1961).

9 "...the law of folkloric feedback, (or self-regulation, or stability), *das Gesetz der Selbstberichtigung*, which, in essence, is briefly the following. Variations of folk tales are surprisingly undeviating from certain limits and the story will never change beyond recognition, even if its lifespan is very long and its circulation wide. According to Anderson, it is caused by the fact that the narrator has generally heard the tale from not one but from many different narrators, and has also heard it on various occasions from the same narrator; all random fluctuations which might drastically differ from the basic story are thereby suppressed, and the tale reassumes its basic form, 'flows back to its original streambed'." Krikmann, Arvo. *Proverbs on Animal Identity: Typological Memoirs*, tr. Realo, Kait. In *Folklore: Electronic Journal of Folklore* (Tartu: Estonian Folklore Institute, 2001).

10 Bottigheimer, Ruth B. *Fairy Tales: A New History* (SUNY Press, 2009).

shocked the world, but would not have shocked Indo-Europeanist Jakob Grimm, who anticipated it some 150 years before:

> In this study, we introduce new methods for tackling [the problem of lack of historical data in folklore studies] by applying comparative phylogenetic methods and autologistic modelling to analyse the relationships between folktales, population histories and geographical distances in Indo-European-speaking societies. We find strong correlations between the distributions of a number of folktales and phylogenetic, but not spatial, associations among populations that are consistent with vertical processes of cultural inheritance. Moreover, we show that these oral traditions probably originated long before the emergence of the literary record, and find evidence that one tale ('The Smith and the Devil') can be traced back to the Bronze Age.[11]

In their study, Silva and Tehrani used phylogenetic comparative methods developed in biology to study genetic similarity, methods that had already been used to study other cultural phenomena such as languages, marriage practices, political institutions, material culture, and music. Applying these methods, they established how far back shared folktales can be traced in Indo-European oral traditions, finding that many folktales that literary studies trace no further back than a few centuries can in fact be traced well into the deep past.

The study analyzed a large dataset of folktales to determine the approximate time of origin for ATU tale types. They restricted their study to fairy tales since these are the largest and most widely dispersed group of tales, and because they have most often been the subject of debate over their antiquity and origin. The results were striking—Silva and Tehrani found that 50 ATU tale types were more than 50% likely to have originated in the last common ancestor of at least one major Indo-European sub-family, and 31 tale types were more than 70% likely to have originated thus. In other words, some of these folktales are more likely than not to go back even as far as Proto-Indo-European culture, and some with a higher likelihood still. The researchers also found that most of these tales were transmitted vertically—passed down through a lineage or tradition—rather than horizontally—transplanted from one tradition to another. Moreover, they found that not only were most tales transmitted vertically, but that horizontal transmission was negatively correlated with spatial proximity. In other words, the closer your neighbour is, the *less* likely you are to adopt his folklore into your own tradition. Culture is shaped in large part by folklore, and at the heart of folklore is *bias*—es-

---

11 Silva, Sara Graça da, and Tehrani, Jamshid J., *Comparative phylogenetic analyses uncover the ancient roots of Indo-European folktales,* in *Royal Society Open Science* (The Royal Society Publishing, 2015).

pecially transmission biases such as neophobia, conservatism, conformity, and the endowment effect—which tends to "inhibit the exchange of information between groups and preserve local distinctions".[12] Cultural formation and diversity is driven by the *volksgeist* in what Joseph de Maistre calls the *work of circumstances*, the working of these parochial biases in the world unconsciously and according to no human plan. This mechanism of particularized cultural formation goes back further than the historical record, as do most of the folktales in the study—these tales are so old that they antedate any written evidence of European myth:

> Our findings [...] suggest that a substantial number of magic tales have existed in Indo-European oral traditions long before they were first written down. For example, two of the best known fairy tales, ATU 425C 'Beauty and the Beast' and ATU 500 'The Name of the Supernatural Helper' ('Rumplestiltskin') were first written down in the seventeenth and eighteenth centuries. While some researchers claim that both storylines have antecedents in Greek and Roman mythology, our reconstructions suggest that they originated significantly earlier. Both tales can be securely traced back to the emergence of the major western Indo-European subfamilies as distinct lineages between 2500 and 6000 years ago, and may have even been present in the last common ancestor of Western Indo-European languages.[13]

These folktales are not late, distorted cultural expressions, and certainly not the literary expressions of individuals, but are themselves generative of culture, no less than myth, being born of the same stock, at the same time. Folktales, far from being mere trifles, are serious business, and yet many lovers of high culture still do not take them seriously. Tolkien again sums up this attitude (emphasis added):

> The term 'folk-tale' is misleading; its very tone of depreciation begs the question. Folk-tales in being, as told—for the 'typical folk-tale', of course, is merely an abstract conception of research nowhere existing—do often contain elements that are thin and cheap, with little even potential virtue; but they also contain much that is far more powerful, and that *cannot be sharply separated from myth*, being derived from it, or capable in poetic hands of turning into it: that is of becoming largely significant—as a whole, accepted unanalysed.[14]

12 Collard, Mark et al. *Branching, blending, and the evolution of cultural similarities and differences among human populations*. In *Evolution and Human Behavior* (Amsterdam: Elsevier, 2006).
13 *Comparative phylogenetic analyses uncover the ancient roots of Indo-European folktales.*
14 Tolkien. *Beowulf: The Monsters and the Critics.*

THE ENTANGLEMENT OF
MYTH, LEGEND, AND FOLKTALE

Alan Dundes typifies the modern scholarly outlook on myth in his definition of myth as "a sacred narrative that explains how the world and humanity came to be in their present form".[15] Putting aside the need for a myth to *explain* something, which seems to rule out much of what we commonly think of as myth,[16] even the aspect of myth as sacred can be called into question. This is not to say that myth is not sacred, only that it is not *uniquely* so. Why should myth be sacred and folklore (or legend) be secular? Pre-modern peoples did not observe a neat distinction between the sacred and secular,[17] and so this definition has a flavour of anachronism. If by "sacred" we simply mean "concerning the *other* world" and by secular we mean "concerning this world", this still does not draw a useful line between myth and folklore, as folklore so often concerns the magical and supernatural, as all the folktales in the Silva/Tehrani study do. The distinction between the magical and the sacred is itself a novel development in the history of Indo-European peoples, and so is wholly inappropriate for tales which reach back some 6,000 years, erasing any border between myth and folktale according to this definition. It seems that, even at first glance, myth, legend, and folktale are hopelessly entangled.

Indo-Europeanists tend to take a more holistic approach. Jan de Vries, an important philologist in the first half of the 20th century, "published on fairy tales—which according to him should be seen as an extension of myths".[18] Georges Dumézil, perhaps the foremost Indo-Europeanist of the 20th century, saw folklore as important for comparativism[19]—the method of reconstructing the language, beliefs, religion, and practices of cultures which have left no historical records. In his *Gods of the Ancient Northmen*,[20] Dumézil makes extensive use of folklore to reconstruct aspects of the Germanic deities, and in his 1955 article *Njordr, Nerthus et le folklore scandinave des génies de la mer*, he identifies the sea god Njorðr

---

15 Dundes, Alan. *Sacred Narrative: Readings in the Theory of Myth* (University of California Press, 1984).

16 It is hard to see how the myths of Orpheus and Eurydice, the labours of Herakles, Cupid and Psyche, Carna and Janus, Baldr's death, Sigurd the dragon slayer, and the voyage of Bran explain how the world or mankind came to be as they are.

17 Cavanaugh, William T. *The Invention of Religion*. In *The Myth of Religious Violence: Secular Ideology and the Roots of Modern Conflict* (Oxford University Press, 2009).

18 *Bio- en bibliografisch lexicon van de neerlandistiek*, s.v. "Vries, Jan Pieter Marie Laurens de" (Retrieved Nov. 2021) https://www.dbnl.org/tekst/anro001bioe01_01/vrie031.php

19 Allen, N. J. *Debating Dumézil: Recent Studies in Comparative Mythology*. In JASO 24/2 (1993).

20 Dumézil, Georges. *Les Dieux des Germains*, (Presses Universitaires de France, 1959).

with the archaic Germanic earth goddess Nerthus largely by way of comparative folklore, concluding that "it will be possible, as much for Njordr as for other deities and for several rituals of the pagan Scandinavians, to ask similar confirmations of modern folklore: all has not yet been said."[21] This raises exciting possibilities for Indo-European reconstruction, but we might start by asking for more modest confirmations.

The *Poetic Edda* was written down centuries after Christianization, and the degree of Christian influence on it has long been the subject of scholarly controversy. In his doctoral dissertation,[22] Danish scholar Henry Petersen proposed that the *Poetic Edda* was not only written down late but was composed late given its emphasis on Odin, which he argued "was a kind of court mythology" imposed by elites in the transition to Christianity, as opposed what he took to be the original worship of Thor, who "appears on the whole rather blurred and withdrawn in [the Odinic] poetry". This was later supported by Sophus Bugge who produced an important critical edition of the *Poetic Edda*, arguing that the Eddic lays were composed around the 9th century CE.[23] Through the 20th century, evidence, mostly linguistic, began to mount suggesting that the *Poetic Edda* is in fact more archaic than was previously thought, with John McKinnell listing the *Poetic Edda* as among the "genuinely heathen voices", and stating that "if we wish to study Norse myth through the eyes of those for whom it was a living faith [...] the evidence of Eddic poetry is likely to be the most useful."[24] Let us turn to folklore to mediate this dispute.

Several folktale types show up in various lays of the *Poetic Edda*. Perhaps the most marked example is in *Grottasöngr*, where ATU tale type *565: The Magic Mill* can clearly be seen. In a typical folktale of this type, *Why the Sea is Salt*, a poor man is sent to Hell where he finds a mill that will magically grind out whatever he wishes, which he exploits to his great advantage. Eventually a sailor comes into possession of the mill and brings it with him on a sea voyage; having ordered the mill to grind out salt, the sailor cannot stop it, at which point the ship sinks, sailor, mill and all—we are then given an etiology as to "why the sea is salt". In *Grottasöngr*, king Fróði commands two slave women to grind out gold, peace, and happiness with a similarly magic mill. Owing to Fróði's cruelty, the women (revealed to be descended of mountain-giants) grind out an army against him. Snorri further relates in the *Prose Edda* that Fróði is defeated

21 Dumézil, Georges. *Njordr, Nerthus et le folklore scandinave des génies de la mer.* In *Revue de l'histoire des religions* (Collège de France, 1955).
22 Petersen, Henry. *Om nordboernes gudedyrkelse og gudetro i hedenold : en antikvarisk undersøgelse* (C. A. Reitzels Forlag, 1876).
23 Bugge, Elseus Sophus. *Forhandlinger paa det fjerde nordiske filologmøde i København den 18–21 juli 1892* (Copenhagen, 1892).
24 McKinnell, John, and Ruggerini, Maria Elena. *Both One and Many: Essays on Change and Variety in Late Norse Heathenism* (Il calamo, 1994).

by a sea king who takes possession of the women and the mill and then orders them to grind salt, whereupon they all meet the same fate as the sailor in our folktale—even the same etiology is given.

Further examples of folktale types in the *Poetic Edda* are found in the lays concerning the Niflung Cycle. To win the hand of Gunnar's sister, Sigurð must help Gunnar woo the strong woman Brynhild, which he does by way of subterfuge. Gunnar, unable to perform the three tasks set by Brynhild in order to marry her, trades appearances with Sigurð who performs them on his behalf, winning her hand for Gunnar and setting off a tragic chain of events. This matches up with tale type *519: The Strong Woman as Bride* to such a degree that the type is sometimes called *519: Brunhilde the Strong Bride*.[25] And sure enough, in the folktale *The Snow, the Crow, and the Blood*, the hero Jack must court the Princess of the East who sets him three tasks to perform in order to win her as bride. This tale type is so widespread in the Indo-European world that it is found even in the *Panchatantra*,[26] an ancient Indian collection of folktales.

We also find in the heroic lays of the *Poetic Edda* the tale type *673: The White Serpent's Flesh*, well expressed in *The Story of Michael Scott*. The titular character learns from an old wise woman how to slay a mythical white serpent that can regenerate itself, which he does by fetching and cooking the snake's middle part after hewing it in three. While the snake's flesh is cooking, Scott touches the broth, which burns him, and puts his finger into his mouth—this magically confers on him the power "to foretell events, to work magic cures, and to read the minds of other people." (p. 486) And so we find in the Eddic lay *Fafnismal* that after Sigurð slays the serpent Fafnir, he roasts his heart on a spit. Testing to see whether the heart was ready to eat, he burns his finger and puts it into his mouth, which magically confers on him the power to understand the language of birds.

All this would be interesting enough for its own sake, but the presence of these ATU tale types in these lays has bearing on the question of how genuine the heathen voice of the *Poetic Edda* is. The Silva/Tehrani study traces all three tale types here cited to the Proto-Balto-Slavic era of the Indo-European migrations, so we can be confident that these plot elements of the *Poetic Edda* go back not just to the 9th century CE, but to the 8th century BCE[27]—comparative folklore enables us to trace the heathen voice of these passages a full millennium and a half earlier than pre-

25 cf. Ashliman, *A Guide to Folktales in the English Language.*
26 Shedden-Ralston, William Ralston. Footnote to *The Blind Man and the Cripple*. In *Russian fairy tales: a choice collection of Muscovite folk-lore* (New York: Pollard & Moss, 1887).
27 See p. 760 for references on the calculation of dates for the various Indo-European sub-family migrations in the study.

viously thought.

Celtic myth is not without its folklore antecedents. In the *Voyage of Bran*, the hero and his men set off to find the wondrous Land of Women. Finding it, they spend a year feasting until one of the men becomes homesick and the crew returns, only to find that no one recognizes them and that their name has passed into ancient legend. This is the exact motif of tale type *470: Friends in Life and Death*. In the folktale of the same name, a man seeks out his dead friend to stand as best man at his wedding, which the dead man agrees to, but only after the two embark upon a journey through the underworld. When the two emerge, they find that the live man's kinsmen, bride, and friends have all been dead for four hundred years. This major plot element of an Irish myth written down in the 8th century CE can be traced back to the Proto-Germanic-Italo-Celtic era ca. 2250 BCE, an astonishing survival of some three millennia. In the Welsh *Culhwch and Olwen*, ants come to Gwythyr's aid after he rescues them from a fire, later helping him perform the impossible task of recovering "nine hestors of flax seed" demanded by Ysbaddaden, a motif found in type *554: The Grateful Animals*. This plot element is of less consequence to the story than that found in the *Voyage of Bran*, but it is still compelling, and all the more so for how old it is—this type goes back all the way to the Proto-Indo-European urheimat ca. 4500 BCE.

Even classical and biblical narrative cannot escape entanglement with folktale. Among the many anecdotes in Herodotus' *Histories* is that of king Polycrates where the king is advised by pharaoh Amasis II to give up his greatest treasure so as not to incur the gods' wrath by his unblemished good fortune. He chooses to sacrifice his gold ring which is then cast away far out to sea at his command. Later, a fisherman presents to the king his prized catch, and on cutting open the fish, Polycrates is stunned to find his gold ring returned to him in the fish's belly. This of course ahistorical, but because it is a clear example of ATU tale type *736: Luck and Wealth*—traceable back to Proto-Balto-Slavic times—we can push it back some three centuries before Herodotus, and two centuries before even the reign of Polycrates. We also find in various Balkan folktales the motif of the man desired by another man's wife whom he rejects, and who then goes on to falsely accuse him of rape. This is one variant of *318: The Faithless Wife*,[28] and is clearly cognate with the story of Joseph and Potiphar's wife in Genesis 39:7–20. This tale type is traced in European folklore to Proto-Balto-Slavic, which puts it ca. 750 BCE—we cannot be sure which of these tales came first.[29] And yet this tale is found outside

---

28 A folktale type exhibiting great variety.

29 "The first major comprehensive Pentateuchal narrative was composed either late in pre-exilic times or in the Babylonian exile (7th or 6th cent. BCE), rather than in the early monarchy. Some prefer to speak of a 'late Yahwist' (Schmid, Van Seters), some of a Deuterono-

of Europe in much older form, as in the *Tale of Two Brothers* from the Egyptian New Kingdom, where Anubis and Bata take the place of Potiphar and Joseph respectively, pushing the authorship of the tale still further back to ca. 1200 BCE.

Comparative folkloristics sheds important light on chronologies, the authenticity of late-recorded European myth, and original authorship of these tales, and many more examples could be cited.[30] Moreover, it is clear that folklore cannot be sharply distinguished from legend and myth—perhaps not at all, except to say, as Dundes does, that myth is the vessel of the sacred. Folklore, then, must be the vessel of the secular. This is historically not far from how folklore has been perceived. And yet, it is just because of this superficial secularity that folklore has served as an ideal vessel for the transmission of some of our most ancient and most sacred treasures.

Dumézil's oracular pronouncement that all has not yet been said for folklore's use in Indo-European reconstruction has proven true.

FOLKTALES AS PRESERVATIVE
OF THE INDO-EUROPEAN SACRA

The transition from paganism to Christianity is popularly thought of as a simple supersession, but under closer historical examination it becomes clear that the two mutually influenced each other wherever Christianity set down roots,[31] and this mutual influence was never stronger than in folklore. It was only when European peoples had been sufficiently Christianized that it was permitted to write down what remained of their native myths, as these had persisted in purely oral form, recited usually for the entertainment of the warlike nobility who were slow to lose interest in the traditional stories of their ancestors.[32] In some cases, stories of the gods were *euhemerized*, interpreted as the historical deeds of great men that had become distorted in the telling, tall tales growing ever taller to where these men had attained the status of gods. Such interpretation served to delegitimize and debase the myths without wholly eras-

mistic narrative (Johnstone, Blum), but they are largely talking about the same thing and using the same arguments." *The Oxford Bible Commentary* (Oxford University Press, 2013).
30 Among them, *Cupid and Psyche* vs. ATU 425, *Pururavas and Urvasi* vs. the same, and many aspects of Thor's mythos vs. ATU 650A.
31 James C. Russell's *The Germanization of Early Medieval Christianity* (Oxford University Press, 1996) documents this process in detail as it occurred in the Germanic world, showing that the Christianity of the primitive church differed in important ways from that later accepted by the Germanic peoples, which had accommodated itself to their native character and worldview.
32 *Encyclopaedia Britannica*, 11th ed., s.v. "Beowulf." (1911).

ing them, and served as a useful compromise especially in the Germanic world where royal houses traditionally traced their descent from Odin. In this way, a certain amount of native European mythos survived, but much was lost.

Not so with folklore. The ostensible "secularity" of the folk tale posed little threat to sacred doctrine; as the lore of the unlettered folk, folktales were seen as being of little concern to the curators of high culture and theological orthodoxy. While the line between sacred and secular was less clear in pre-modern times, and while freedom to depict heathen practices was certainly not boundless, in the folktale traditional (Indo-)European stories enjoyed a wider latitude under a less watchful eye—folklore could act as a sort of "permafrost" beneath which the changing winds of theology could penetrate but little. In many cases, traditional narrative was overlaid with Christian elements to produce a kind of hybrid, the Christian elements making acceptable what was otherwise ambiguously heretical. An example is found in *The Legend of Paracelsus*, the tale of a medieval alchemist with ancient Indo-European roots as ATU type *331: The Spirit in the Bottle*. In it, Paracelsus finds a land spirit trapped within a tree whom he frees, receiving those remarkable powers for which he would later be known, and then by his cunning traps the spirit again within the tree. This tale bears the stamp of heathenry with its positive depiction of magic and theurgy, but also has Christian elements in that the spirit is identified with "the Evil One". However, we know by the antiquity of this tale[33] that this Evil One originates no later than the 8th century BCE.

This dressing up of old beliefs and usages in new clothes is what anthropologists call a "survival":

> Among evidence aiding us to trace the course which the civilization of the world has actually followed, is that great class of facts to denote which I have found it convenient to introduce the term 'survivals.' [...] The ordeal of the Key and Bible, still in use, is a survival; the Midsummer bonfire is a survival; the Breton peasants' All Souls' supper for the spirits of the dead is a survival. The simple keeping up of ancient habits is only one part of the transition from old into new and changing times. The serious business of ancient society may be seen to sink into the sport of later generations, and its serious belief to linger on in nursery folk-lore, while superseded habits of old-world life may be modified into new-world forms still powerful for good and evil.[34]

Many such survivals persist in Indo-European folklore, in some cases sur-

---

33 Proto-Balto-Slavic.

34 Tylor, Edward Burnett. *Primitive culture: researches into the development of mythology, philosophy, religion, language, art, and custom, vol. I* (London: John Murray, 1920).

vivals of elements remarkably archaic and, as Tylor points out, of great significance to ancient peoples.

In *The Princess Frog*, ATU type *402: The Animal Bride*, the prince marries an enchanted princess in the form of a frog, and when she temporarily takes her human form, the prince burns and discards the frog skin, leading to dire consequences. The wearing and burning of an animal skin was highly significant to ritual across the various branches of the Indo-European world. In 2017, researchers discovered evidence for Indo-European initiation rituals in Krasnosamarskoe, Russia, which they linked to wintertime coming of age rituals ca. 1900–1700 BCE. These rituals involved dog sacrifice, which is linked to the Greek *koryos*, the Roman Lupercalia, the Germanic *Männerbund*, and to other cognates elsewhere in the Indo-European world:

> In Germanic traditions, these bands of young warriors thought of themselves as wolf packs. A famous myth about the hero Siegfried has him donning a dog skin to go raiding with his nephew, whom he is training to become a warrior. In the Rigveda, an ancient Sanskrit text composed sometime before 1000 B.C., young men can only become warriors after sacrificing a dog at a winter ceremony and wearing its skin for four years, which they burn upon their return to society.[35]

The ritual significance of the burning and discarding of the animal skin is in the transition from one form of life to another, as it is in *The Princess Frog*. At the midwinter ritual, death came both to the old year and to the boyhood identities of the initiates. So, too, in *The Dog Bride*,[36] an Indian folktale where a man takes for his bride an enchanted woman in the form of a dog and throws the dog skin into the fire to enable the consummation of the marriage—the liminal aspect of both the folktale and the ritual are eminently clear. David Anthony in *The Horse, the Wheel, and Language* tells us that the Krasnosamarskoe site contains archeological evidence that matches evidence from Indo-Iranian ritual, "and perhaps even Proto-Indo-European".[37] Given that a) the liminal element of the burning of the skin carries an explicit ritual significance across a wide swathe of the Indo-European world, that b) ATU 402 often contains this element, and that c) per Silva/Tehrani ATU 402 hearkens back to Proto-Indo-European times, we may feel that Anthony's intuition of the deep antiquity

35 *Wolf Rites of Winter. In Archaeology Magazine* (Archaeological Institute of America, 2017). https://www.archaeology.org/issues/102-1309/features/1205-timber-grave-culture-krasnosamarskoe-bronze-age
36 Another example of ATU 402.
37 Anthony, David W. *The Opening of the Eurasian Steppes. In The Horse, the Wheel, and Language: How Bronze-Age Riders from the Eurasian Steppes Shaped the Modern World* (Princeton University Press, 2007).

of this rite is more than just an intuition.

Occasionally particular folktales, as opposed to a broader tale type, will contain ancient elements. At the end of the Russian folktale *Never-Wash*, the character asks the devil to turn him into a youth for his betrothal and he undergoes the following procedure:

> So the devil cut him up into little bits, threw them into a cauldron, and began to brew him—brewed him, washed him and collected all his bones, one by one, in the proper way, every bone with every bone, every joint with every joint, every nerve with every nerve: then he sprinkled them with the water of life, and the soldier arose, such a fine young man as no tale can tell and no pen can write.

This recalls the Second Merseburg charm, a magic spell recorded in Old High German in the 9th century:

> *Phol and Wodan were riding to the woods,*
> *and the foot of Balder's foal was sprained*
> *So Sinthgunt, Sunna's sister, conjured it;*
> *and Frija, Volla's sister, conjured it;*
> *and Wodan conjured it, as well he could:*
> *Like bone-sprain, so blood-sprain,*
> *so joint-sprain:*
> *Bone to bone, blood to blood,*
> *joints to joints, so may they be glued.*

While the charm dates back over a millennium, it was rediscovered only in 1841 in a long-forgotten manuscript. *Never-Wash* was collected in the 1850s by Alexander Afanasyev, mostly from illiterate Russian peasants who tended not to keep up with recent developments in German historiography. The odds of this spell making its way into the oral folklore tradition of a foreign people in a decade are essentially zero, so we may regard this as a survival of great antiquity. And since the charm refers to pre-Christian beliefs, we may infer that the spell itself dates back further than the 9th century, after Germany had been Christianized. Given the transmission biases noted in the Silva/Tehrani study, it seems likely that the charm was carried into Russian traditional culture by the Varangians, a Germanic people who migrated into the Volga area around the time the charm was set down in writing in what is now central Germany. The fidelity with which the ritual utterance has been preserved across two languages is impressive and shows what a faithful medium folklore can be for the transmission of culture across time and irrespective of the broader religious environment.

In some cases, folklore can influence that religious environment as much as vice versa. The traditional Russian spiritual verse concerning the

Book of the Dove, while not exactly a folktale, is a piece of folk culture offering a tantalizing glimpse at the truly archaic and illustrates the dialectical relationship between Christianity and European paganisms.

The verse varies in length and content among different folk traditions, but can be summarized as follows: An immense book has fallen from heaven, inviting the curiosity of kings from all over the world, among whom is King David. The kings ask David who wrote the book, and he answers, "Jesus Christ, the Lord of Heaven. Isaiah tried to read it but could read only three pages in three years." As such, the kings ask David to relate the book's contents by heart, and to answer the questions, "how did the world begin? how did the sun, the moon, and stars start shining? where did the winds, thunder, tsars, boyars, and peasants come from?" David's answer:

> The whole world was begotten by the Holy Spirit of Sabaoth; the red sun is from God's face; the moon from God's breasts; the stars from God's vestments; the dawn and dusk are from God's eyes; the winds from the breath of Sabaoth; thunder from God's speech; the Tsars from the holy head of Adam, the boyar-princes from the holy relics of Adam, the orthodox peasants from the holy knee of Adam.

This bears an uncanny resemblance to a number of Indo-European cosmogonies which resemble each other so closely that it has been possible to reconstruct a Proto-Indo-European cosmogony. David Anthony gives us a précis:

> At the beginning of time there were two brothers, twins, one named Man (**Manu*, in Proto-Indo-European) and the other Twin (**Yemo*). They traveled through the cosmos accompanied by a great cow. Eventually Man and Twin decided to create the world we now inhabit. To do this, Man had to sacrifice Twin (or, in some versions, the cow). From the parts of this sacrificed body, with the help of the sky gods (*Sky Father, Storm God of War, Divine Twins*), Man made the wind, the sun, the moon, the sea, earth, fire, and finally all the various kinds of people. Man became the first priest, the creator of the ritual of sacrifice that was the root of world order.[38]

The Russian Orthodox Church eventually banned the verse as heretical, and it shows the deep entanglement between folk custom and myth that can persist through immense spans of time. Since the 19th century there has been a concerted effort to reconstruct the beliefs and practices of the Proto-Indo-Europeans, and the voice of comparative folklore has been

---

38 Anthony, *First Farmers and Herders: The Pontic-Caspian Neolithic.* In *The Horse, The Wheel, and Language.*

relatively silent in this project. Dumézil was right: not all has yet been said on its behalf.

FOLKTALES AND
PROTO-INDO-EUROPEAN
RECONSTRUCTION

Proto-Indo-European (PIE) reconstruction is surely a science, but there is an uncommon degree of art in it. While it is based on hard laws of linguistic change, painstaking analysis of material evidence, and cutting-edge developments in genomics, reconstructing the beliefs and practices of this ancestor people requires a great deal of something that cannot be quantified: intuition. Given the difficulty of the subject and the necessarily interdisciplinary nature of the work, it does not enter into the scope of this essay to offer original reconstructions of PIE life, only to offer hints at what may be achieved by way of comparative folkloristics.

Mention the name of Georges Dumézil and one word will be conjured in the mind of anyone familiar with him: *trifunctionality*. The *trifunctional hypothesis* was Dumézil's idea that PIE society was based upon a tripartite ideology which at the political level produced three castes: priests, warriors, and producers. Dumézil later walked back this hypothesis somewhat since it proved difficult to establish tripartition in all the major Indo-European branches, but he continued to maintain the soundness of a threefold supernatural ideology, if not necessarily a threefold social system. In any case, Indo-European thought is strongly marked by triplicity. It runs through its theology (Hindu *Trimūrti*, Capitoline Triad, three *Norns* and *Moirai*), its languages (three genders, three basic tenses, three grammatical numbers), and its ritual praxis (*confarreatio*, threefold invocations of gods, *suovetaurilia*). We even get the Latin proverb *omne trium perfectum*—all that comes in threes is perfect.

In modern times, and in a much more secular idiom, we know this as the *rule of three*, stating that a trio of verbal elements—be they examples, characters, repetitions, events, rhymes, concepts, etc.—is more aesthetically pleasing than any other grouping, and folktales are prime examples of the ubiquity of the rule. We get three children born in *The Lassie and Her Godmother*, three dogs in *The Tinder-Box*, three Yezinkas in *Grandfather's Eyes*, three riding trials in *Princess on the Glass Hill*, three apples in *Fortunio and the Siren*—hardly a tale is told without some element of triplicity in it. Being oral in nature, folktale tends to be more formalist than other narrative forms, and this lends itself to such structural regularity.[39] This almost *obsession* with threes, along with the antiquity of many folktale types, lends weight to the already strong case for some sort of tripartite ideology animating the Indo-European folk-soul.

Folklore can tell us about more material aspects of culture too; we find in the ATU tale type *330: The Smith and the Devil* evidence for metallurgy among the PIEs. As noted by Silva and Tehrani:

> The likely presence of this tale [ATU 330: The Smith and the Devil] in the last common ancestor of Indo-European-speaking cultures resonates strongly with wider debates in Indo-European prehistory, since it implies the existence of metallurgy in Proto-Indo-European society. This inference is consistent with the so-called 'Kurgan hypothesis', which links the origins of the Indo-European language family to archaeological and genetic evidence of massive territorial expansions made by nomadic pastoralist tribes from the Pontic steppe 5000–6000 years ago. [...] By contrast, the presence of this story in PIE society appears to be incompatible with the alternative 'Anatolian hypothesis' of Indo-European origins.

In 2015 a genetic study from the Universitat Autònoma de Barcelona[40] was published that strongly favoured the Kurgan hypothesis.[41] This along with the Silva/Tehrani study was essentially the final nail in the coffin of the Anatolian hypothesis and shows that comparative folkloristics undergoing rigorous quantitative analysis can be as powerful as genomics in explaining the deep past.

Folklore can also be helpful in fleshing out the content of ritual praxis. In the 19th century, Numa Denis Fustel de Coulanges made a strong case that the core of PIE theology was ancestor worship;[42] these people likely did not draw a sharp distinction between the gods and the ancestors. The devotional life of PIE man consisted largely in the domestic cult of ancestor worship, where each family, each clan, worshipped deities particular

---

39 Structural regularity also shows up in phrases bookending folktales, colloquially in English "Once upon a time [...] and they lived happily ever after." This formulaic phrase finds a tautological variant in Czech, Danish, Estonian, German, Luxembourgish, and Slovak, "...and if they're not dead, they are still alive." A variant in Faroese, Norwegian, Swedish appears as "...snip, snap, snout, this tale's told out." A variant in Lithuanian, with similar variants in Polish and Russian, is "...and I was there, drank some mead ale, it dribbled through my beard, but none got in my mouth." There is a formalism here which recalls the invocations, prayers, and the overall structure of ritual observance in many Indo-European branches.

40 *Massive migration from the steppe was a source for Indo-European languages in Europe.* In *Nature 522 (2015).*

41 The Kurgan hypothesis claims that the PIEs migrated from the Pontic steppe roughly 6,000 years ago, the Anatolian hypothesis claims that they migrated out of Anatolia some 8,000–9,000 years ago.

42 Fustel de Coulanges, Numa Denis. *The Ancient City* (Perth: Imperium Press, 2020).

to itself—its agnatic line of ancestors, which when traced back far enough reached unto the high gods themselves. Because this archaic form of worship was so strongly domestic, so tied to a particular place, the tutelary spirits inhabiting that particular place figured significantly in the worship—they later came to be called by various names: *lares, penates, daimones, domovoi, aos sí, landvættir, álfar, brownies, fairies*, etc. depending on the tradition in question. Often these land or domestic spirits took the form of animals, among the most ancient forms of which is the snake. As late as the 17th century, Ján Lasiczki noted:

> Furthermore, the Lithuanians and the Samogytians keep serpents in their houses, beneath the furnace or in the corner of the drying oven, where the table is. At certain times of the year, they honour them like gods, inviting them to their tables with sacrificial prayers. Leaving their lairs, these reptiles climb upon the table with the help of a clean sheet and settle in. After having tasted a little of each dish, they then go back down into their holes. After they leave, the people gaily eat the dishes they tasted, hoping that the year will be a fortunate one.[43]

The ritual performance is sketched out in more detail by August Wilhelm Hupel, who in the 18th century supplied the offering in his description of Livonia and Estonia: "The ancient custom, introduced even into numerous German homes, of keeping domestic snakes, feeding them milk, and giving them a home in the stables so the livestock will be happier, appears, it seems, to have stopped."[44] Going back much further, we find Zeus Ktesios[45] worshipped among the ancient Greeks, a tutelary spirit who took the form of a snake and presided over the prosperity of the household.

This ritual element of the tutelary snake is of great antiquity, but we can push it back still further by observing it in ATU type 672: *The Serpent's Crown*. In this tale type we often see that the snake is fed milk as an offering, as in the Austrian tale of *The Grass Snake of the House*, and moreover that the snake usually presides over a crown, upon the loss of which the snake deserts the family, as in the Grimms' *Second Tale of the Snake*. This matches up neatly with the function of a tutelary deity concerned with the material prosperity of the family which is propitiated with milk offerings, and it is all the more striking that this tale type can be traced back to the Proto-Balto-Slavic era, earlier than any Greek attestation. We have here a Greek household spirit corroborated in German oral folklore, traceable back to the last common ancestor of the Slavic and

---

43 Lasicius, Johannes (Ján Lasiczki), *De diis Samagitarum libellus* (Basel, 1615).

44 Paulson, Ivar. "Die Hausgeister und ihre idole in Norderasien." In *Tribus 12* (1963): 125–58.

45 An epithet of the high god Zeus mentioned in Aeschylus and appearing on many altars and reliefs. His ritual praxis is preserved in a fragment of Anticleides of Athens.

Baltic Indo-European branches. If we make the reasonable assumption of no horizontal transmission of domestic cultic practices between the Slavs, Balts, and Greeks ca. 750 BCE, we must posit the source of this rite as the last common ancestor of all three, which is the PIEs themselves. In *Hellenic Polytheism*,[46] a manual of Hellenic ritual praxis, we are told that "it is possible to say that the worship of Zeus Ktesios remained unbroken in the rural areas where the house snake continued to play a dominant role in household worship and folk tales"—we have a significant rite perpetuated across 6,000 years down to the present day. Such is the power of folk culture as a medium for the preservation of the Indo-European *volksgeist*.

Considering what a rich source of Indo-European sacra folklore is, comparative folkloristics represents one of the most exciting branches of Indo-European reconstruction—all the more exciting because it has been so underexplored. Three centuries ago, the Proto-Indo-Europeans were unknown; today, a great part of their worldview, language, and culture has been reconstructed, and much more yet remains to be done. The folk-soul of a people never dies—not until the last of those people dies. Two in five human beings alive today speak a dialect of their language, this success owing in large part to their folk culture, which remains substantially intact. The Proto-Indo-Europeans still have much to teach us, and the humble folktale, musty though it may be, will no doubt play a significant role in our edification, as it has since our ancestors all dwelt together in Bronze Age Central Asia.

46 *Hellenic Polytheism: Household Worship* (Athens: Labrys, 2014).

NOTE ON THE TEXT

This anthology includes three folktales of each of the 50 tale types in the Silva/Tehrani study referenced in the introduction.[1] Three examples of each type were included not only because three is a number significant to Indo-European theology[2] but because, concerned as this anthology is with the comparative method, three is the minimum number of elements needed to establish a pattern. It is hoped that the reader can glean something of each tale type by comparing the different examples. Generally, the most representative tale comes first, but not always.

The text has been very lightly corrected wherever errors have crept in, but no attempt has been made to harmonize the spelling or punctuation style between the tales. Folktales from the Indo-Iranian world have not been included because all but the first four tale types in the anthology concern Western Indo-European migrations, and all of the types that concern the Proto-Indo-Iranian migration show up elsewhere.

Tale types have generally been placed in the earliest branch they appear in, but not always. For example, all tale types in Proto-Celtic show up in earlier branches, so some have been placed under this category rather than earlier ones so that Proto-Celtic is not empty of content. Tale type 315 falls under Proto-Italo-Celtic but would be the only one in this category not seen earlier, so it has been placed under Proto-Romance where it also shows up, and Proto-Italo-Celtic has been omitted. See *Tale Types by Migration* (pp. 759–60) which reproduces the full list of tale types for each branch.

The Three Gold Hairs of Old Vsevede was wrongly labelled as a Serbian folktale in the original publication,[3] but has been corrected to Czech.

1 See pp. xiv–xvi.
2 See pp. xxvi–xxvii.
3 See p. 764.

FOLKTALES
IN THE
INDO-EUROPEAN
TRADITION

PROTO-INDO-EUROPEAN

328: The Treasures of the Giant

Jack and the Beanstalk
(*England*)

There was once upon a time a poor widow who had an only son named Jack, and a cow named Milky-white. And all they had to live on was the milk the cow gave every morning which they carried to the market and sold. But one morning Milky-white gave no milk and they didn't know what to do.

"What shall we do, what shall we do?" said the widow, wringing her hands.

"Cheer up, mother, I'll go and get work somewhere," said Jack.

"We've tried that before, and nobody would take you," said his mother; "we must sell Milky-white and with the money do something, start shop, or something."

"All right, mother," says Jack; "it's market-day today, and I'll soon sell Milky-white, and then we'll see what we can do."

So he took the cow's halter in his hand, and off he starts. He hadn't gone far when he met a funny-looking old man who said to him: "Good morning, Jack."

"Good morning to you," said Jack, and wondered how he knew his name.

"Well, Jack, and where are you off to?" said the man.

"I'm going to market to sell our cow here."

"Oh, you look the proper sort of chap to sell cows," said the man; "I wonder if you know how many beans make five."

"Two in each hand and one in your mouth," says Jack, as sharp as a needle.

"Right you are," said the man, "and here they are the very beans themselves," he went on pulling out of his pocket a number of strange-looking beans. "As you are so sharp," says he, "I don't mind doing a swap with you—your cow for these beans."

"Walker!" says Jack; "wouldn't you like it?"

"Ah! you don't know what these beans are," said the man; "if you plant them over-night, by morning they grow right up to the sky."

"Really?" says Jack; "you don't say so."

"Yes, that is so, and if it doesn't turn out to be true you can have your cow back."

"Right," says Jack, and hands him over Milky-white's halter and pockets the beans.

Back goes Jack home, and as he hadn't gone very far it wasn't dusk by the time he got to his door.

"What back, Jack?" said his mother; "I see you haven't got Milky-white, so you've sold her. How much did you get for her?"

"You'll never guess, mother," says Jack.

"No, you don't say so. Good boy! Five pounds, ten, fifteen, no, it can't be twenty."

"I told you you couldn't guess, what do you say to these beans; they're magical, plant them over-night and——"

"What!" says Jack's mother, "have you been such a fool, such a dolt, such an idiot, as to give away my Milky-white, the best milker in the par-ish, and prime beef to boot, for a set of paltry beans. Take that! Take that! Take that! And as for your precious beans here they go out of the window. And now off with you to bed. Not a sup shall you drink, and not a bit shall you swallow this very night."

So Jack went upstairs to his little room in the attic, and sad and sorry he was, to be sure, as much for his mother's sake, as for the loss of his supper.

At last he dropped off to sleep.

When he woke up, the room looked so funny. The sun was shining into part of it, and yet all the rest was quite dark and shady. So Jack jumped up and dressed himself and went to the window. And what do you think he saw? why, the beans his mother had thrown out of the window into the garden, had sprung up into a big beanstalk which went up and up and up till it reached the sky. So the man spoke truth after all.

The beanstalk grew up quite close past Jack's window, so all he had to do was to open it and give a jump on to the beanstalk which was made like a big plaited ladder. So Jack climbed and he climbed and he climbed and he climbed and he climbed and he climbed and he climbed till at last he reached the sky. And when he got there he found a long broad road going as straight as a dart. So he walked along and he walked along and he walked along till he came to a great big tall house, and on the doorstep there was a great big tall woman.

"Good morning, mum," says Jack, quite polite-like. "Could you be so kind as to give me some breakfast." For he hadn't had anything to eat, you know, the night before and was as hungry as a hunter.

"It's breakfast you want, is it?" says the great big tall woman, "it's breakfast you'll be if you don't move off from here. My man is an ogre and there's nothing he likes better than boys broiled on toast. You'd bet-ter be moving on or he'll soon be coming."

"Oh! please mum, do give me something to eat, mum. I've had nothing to eat since yesterday morning, really and truly, mum," says Jack. "I may as well be broiled, as die of hunger."

Well, the ogre's wife wasn't such a bad sort, after all. So she took Jack into the kitchen, and gave him a junk of bread and cheese and a jug of milk. But Jack hadn't half finished these when thump! thump! thump! the whole house began to tremble with the noise of someone coming.

"Goodness gracious me! It's my old man," said the ogre's wife, "what on earth shall I do? Here, come quick and jump in here." And she bundled Jack into the oven just as the ogre came in.

He was a big one, to be sure. At his belt he had three calves strung up by the heels, and he unhooked them and threw them down on the table and said: "Here, wife, broil me a couple of these for breakfast. Ah what's this I smell?

> *Fee-fi-fo-fum,*
> *I smell the blood of an Englishman,*
> *Be he alive, or be he dead*
> *I'll have his bones to grind my bread.*

"Nonsense, dear," said his wife, "you're dreaming. Or perhaps you smell the scraps of that little boy you liked so much for yesterday's dinner. Here, go you and have a wash and tidy up, and by the time you come back your breakfast'll be ready for you."

So the ogre went off, and Jack was just going to jump out of the oven and run off when the woman told him not. "Wait till he's asleep," says she; "he always has a snooze after breakfast."

Well, the ogre had his breakfast, and after that he goes to a big chest and takes out of it a couple of bags of gold and sits down counting them till at last his head began to nod and he began to snore till the whole house shook again.

Then Jack crept out on tiptoe from his oven, and as he was passing the ogre he took one of the bags of gold under his arm, and off he pelters till he came to the beanstalk, and then he threw down the bag of gold which of course fell in to his mother's garden, and then he climbed down and climbed down till at last he got home and told his mother and showed her the gold and said: "Well, mother, wasn't I right about the beans? They are really magical, you see."

So they lived on the bag of gold for some time, but at last they came to the end of that so Jack made up his mind to try his luck once more up at the top of the beanstalk. So one fine morning he got up early, and got on to the beanstalk, and he climbed and he climbed and he climbed and he climbed and he climbed and he climbed till at last he got on the road again and came to the great big tall house he had been to before. There, sure enough, was the great big tall woman a-standing on the door-step.

"Good morning, mum," says Jack, as bold as brass, "could you be so good as to give me something to eat?"

"Go away, my boy," said the big, tall woman, "or else my man will eat you up for breakfast. But aren't you the youngster who came here once before? Do you know, that very day, my man missed one of his bags of gold."

"That's strange, mum," says Jack, "I dare say I could tell you something about that but I'm so hungry I can't speak till I've had something to eat."

Well the big tall woman was that curious that she took him in and gave him something to eat. But he had scarcely begun munching it as slowly as he could when thump! thump! thump! they heard the giant's footstep, and his wife hid Jack away in the oven.

All happened as it did before. In came the ogre as he did before, said: "Fee-fi-fo-fum," and had his breakfast of three broiled oxen. Then he said: "Wife, bring me the hen that lays the golden eggs." So she brought it, and the ogre said: "Lay," and it laid an egg all of gold. And then the ogre began to nod his head, and to snore till the house shook.

Then Jack crept out of the oven on tiptoe and caught hold of the golden hen, and was off before you could say "Jack Robinson." But this time the hen gave a cackle which woke the ogre, and just as Jack got out of the house he heard him calling: "Wife, wife, what have you done with my golden hen?"

And the wife said: "Why, my dear?"

But that was all Jack heard, for he rushed off to the beanstalk and climbed down like a house on fire. And when he got home he showed his mother the wonderful hen and said "Lay," to it; and it laid a golden egg every time he said "Lay."

Well, Jack was not content, and it wasn't very long before he determined to have another try at his luck up there at the top of the beanstalk. So one fine morning, he got up early, and went on to the beanstalk, and he climbed and he climbed and he climbed and he climbed till he got to the top. But this time he knew better than to go straight to the ogre's house. And when he got near it he waited behind a bush till he saw the ogre's wife come out with a pail to get some water, and then he crept into the house and got into the copper. He hadn't been there long when he heard thump! thump! thump! as before, and in come the ogre and his wife.

"Fee-fi-fo-fum, I smell the blood of an Englishman," cried out the ogre; "I smell him, wife, I smell him."

"Do you, my dearie?" says the ogre's wife. "Then if it's that little rogue that stole your gold and the hen that laid the golden eggs he's sure to have got into the oven." And they both rushed to the oven. But Jack wasn't there, luckily, and the ogre's wife said: "There you are again with your fee-fi-fo-fum. Why of course it's the laddie you caught last night that I've broiled for your breakfast. How forgetful I am, and how careless you are not to tell the difference between a live un and a dead un."

So the ogre sat down to the breakfast and ate it, but every now and then he would mutter: "Well, I could have sworn——" and he'd get up and search the larder and the cupboards, and everything, only luckily he didn't think of the copper.

After breakfast was over, the ogre called out: "Wife, wife, bring me my golden harp." So she brought it and put it on the table before him. Then he said: "Sing!" and the golden harp sang most beautifully. And it went on singing till the ogre fell asleep, and commenced to snore like thunder.

Then Jack lifted up the copper-lid very quietly and got down like a mouse and crept on hands and knees till he got to the table when he got up and caught hold of the golden harp and dashed with it towards the door. But the harp called out quite loud: "Master! Master!" and the ogre woke up just in time to see Jack running off with his harp.

Jack ran as fast as he could, and the ogre came rushing after, and would soon have caught him, only Jack had a start and dodged him a bit and knew where he was going. When he got to the beanstalk the ogre was not more than twenty yards away when suddenly he saw Jack disappear like, and when he got up to the end of the road he saw Jack underneath climbing down for dear life. Well, the ogre didn't like trusting himself to such a ladder, and he stood and waited, so Jack got another start. But just then the harp cried out: "Master! master!" and the ogre swung himself down on to the beanstalk which shook with his weight. Down climbs Jack, and after him climbed the ogre. By this time Jack had climbed down and climbed down and climbed down till he was very nearly home. So he called out: "Mother! mother! bring me an axe, bring me an axe." And his mother came rushing out with the axe in her hand, but when she came to the beanstalk she stood stock still with fright for there she saw the ogre just coming down below the clouds.

But Jack jumped down and got hold of the axe and gave a chop at the beanstalk which cut it half in two. The ogre felt the beanstalk shake and quiver so he stopped to see what was the matter. Then Jack gave another chop with the axe, and the beanstalk was cut in two and began to topple over. Then the ogre fell down and broke his crown, and the beanstalk came toppling after.

Then Jack showed his mother his golden harp, and what with showing that and selling the golden eggs, Jack and his mother became very rich, and he married a great princess, and they lived happy ever after.

Thirteenth
(*Italy*)

There was once a father who had thirteen sons, the youngest of whom was named Thirteenth. The father had hard work to support his children, but made what he could gathering herbs. The mother, to make the children quick, said to them: "The one who comes home first shall have herb soup." Thirteenth always returned the first, and the soup always fell to his share, on which account his brothers hated him and sought to get rid of him.

The king issued a proclamation in the city that he who was bold enough to go and steal the ogre's coverlet should receive a measure of gold. Thirteenth's brothers went to the king and said: "Majesty, we have a brother, named Thirteenth, who is confident that he can do that and other things too." The king said: "Bring him to me at once." They brought Thirteenth, who said: "Majesty, how is it possible to steal the ogre's coverlet? If he sees me he will eat me!" "No matter, you must go," said the king. "I know that you are bold, and this act of bravery you must perform." Thirteenth departed and went to the house of the ogre, who was away. The ogress was in the kitchen. Thirteenth entered quietly and hid himself under the bed. At night the ogre returned. He ate his supper and went to bed, saying as he did so:

> *I smell the smell of human flesh;*
> *Where I see it I will swallow it!*

The ogress replied: "Be still; no one has entered here." The ogre began to snore, and Thirteenth pulled the coverlet a little. The ogre awoke and cried: "What is that?" Thirteenth began to mew like a cat. The ogress said: "Scat! scat!" and clapped her hands, and then fell asleep again with the ogre. Then Thirteenth gave a hard pull, seized the coverlet, and ran away. The ogre heard him running, recognized him in the dark, and said: "I know you! You are Thirteenth, without doubt!"

After a time the king issued another proclamation, that whoever would steal the ogre's horse and bring it to the king should receive a measure of gold. Thirteenth again presented himself, and asked for a silk ladder and a bag of cakes. With these things he departed, and went at night to the ogre's, climbed up without being heard, and descended to the stable. The horse neighed on seeing him, but he offered it a cake, saying: "Do you see how sweet it is? If you will come with me, my master will give you these always." Then he gave it another, saying: "Let me mount you and see how we go." So he mounted it, kept feeding it with cakes, and brought it to the king's stable.

The king issued another proclamation, that he would give a measure of gold to whoever would bring him the ogre's bolster. Thirteenth said: "Majesty, how is that possible? The bolster is full of little bells, and you must know that the ogre awakens at a breath." "I know nothing about it," said the king. "I wish it at any cost." Thirteenth departed, and went and crept under the ogre's bed. At midnight he stretched out his hand very softly, but the little bells all sounded. "What is that?" said the ogre. "Nothing," replied the ogress; "perhaps it is the wind that makes them ring." But the ogre, who was suspicious, pretended to sleep, but kept his ears open. Thirteenth stretched out his hand again. Alack! the ogre put out his arm and seized him. "Now you are caught! Just wait; I will make you cry for your first trick, for your second, and for your third." After this he put Thirteenth in a barrel, and began to feed him on raisins and figs. After a time he said: "Stick out your finger, little Thirteenth, so that I can see whether you are fat." Thirteenth saw there a mouse's tail, and stuck that out. "Ah, how thin you are!" said the ogre; "and besides, you don't smell good! Eat, my son; take the raisins and figs, and get fat soon!" After some days the ogre told him again to put out his finger, and Thirteenth stuck out a spindle. "Eh, wretch! are you still lean? Eat, eat, and get fat soon."

At the end of a month Thirteenth had nothing more to stick out, and was obliged to show his finger. The ogre cried out in joy: "He is fat, he is fat!" The ogress hastened to the spot: "Quick, my ogress, heat the oven three nights and three days, for I am going to invite our relatives, and we will make a fine banquet of Thirteenth."

The ogress heated the oven three days and three nights, and then released Thirteenth from the barrel, and said to him: "Come here, Thirteenth; we have got to put the lamb in the oven." But Thirteenth caught her meaning; and when he approached the oven, he said: "Ah, mother ogress, what is that black thing in the corner of the oven?" The ogress stooped down a little, but saw nothing. "Stoop down again," said Thirteenth, "so that you can see it." When she stooped down again, Thirteenth seized her by the feet and threw her into the oven, and then closed the oven door. When she was cooked, he took her out carefully, cut her in two, divided her legs into pieces, and put them on the table, and placed her trunk, with her head and arms, in the bed, under the sheet, and tied a string to the chin and another to the back of her head.

When the ogre arrived with his guests he found the dishes on the table. Then he went to his wife's bed and asked: "Mother ogress, do you want to dine?" Thirteenth pulled the string, and the ogress shook her head. "How are you, tired?" And Thirteenth, who was hidden under the bed, pulled the other string and made her nod. Now it happened that one of her relatives moved something and saw that the ogress was dead, and only half of her was there. She cried in a loud voice: "Treason! treason!" and all hastened to the bed. In the midst of the confusion Thirteenth escaped from under the bed and ran away to the king with the bolster and the ogre's most valuable things.

After this, the king said to Thirteenth: "Listen, Thirteenth. To complete your valiant exploits, I wish you to bring me the ogre himself, in person, alive and well." "How can I, your Majesty?" said Thirteenth. Then he roused himself, and added: "I see how, now!" Then he had a very strong chest made, and disguised himself as a monk, with a long, false beard, and went to the ogre's house, and called out to him: "Do you know Thirteenth? The wretch! he has killed our superior; but if I catch him! If I catch him, I will shut him up in this chest!" At these words the ogre drew near and said: "I, too, would like to help you, against that wretch of an assassin, for you don't know what he has done to me." And he began to tell his story. "But what shall we do?" said the pretended monk. "I do not know Thirteenth. Do you know him?" "Yes, sir." "Then tell me, father ogre, how tall is he?" "As tall as I am." "If that is so," said Thirteenth, "let us see whether this chest will hold you; if it will hold you, it will hold him." "Oh, good!" said the ogre; and got into the chest. Then Thirteenth shut the chest and said: "Look carefully, father ogre, and see whether there is any hole in the chest." "There is none." "Just wait; let us see whether it shuts well, and is heavy to carry."

Meanwhile Thirteenth shut and nailed up the chest, took it on his back, and hastened to the city. When the ogre cried: "Enough, now!" Thirteenth ran all the faster, and, laughing, sang this song to taunt the ogre:

"I am Thirteenth, Who carry you on my back; I have tricked you and am going to trick you. I must deliver you to the king."

When he reached the king, the king had an iron chain attached to the ogre's hands and feet, and made him gnaw bones the rest of his miserable life. The king gave Thirteenth all the riches and treasures he could bestow on him, and always wished him at his side, as a man of the highest valor.

How the Dragon Was Tricked
(*Greece*)

Once upon a time there lived a man who had two sons but they did not get on at all well together, for the younger was much handsomer than his elder brother who was very jealous of him. When they grew older, things became worse and worse, and at last one day as they were walking through a wood the elder youth seized hold of the other, tied him to a tree, and went on his way hoping that the boy might starve to death.

However, it happened that an old and humpbacked shepherd passed the tree with his flock, and seeing the prisoner, he stopped and said to him, 'Tell me, my son why are you tied to that tree?'

'Because I was so crooked,' answered the young man; 'but it has quite cured me, and now my back is as straight as can be.'

'I wish you would bind me to a tree,' exclaimed the shepherd, 'so that my back would get straight.'

'With all the pleasure in life,' replied the youth. 'If you will loosen these cords I will tie you up with them as firmly as I can.'

This was soon done, and then the young man drove off the sheep, leaving their real shepherd to repent of his folly; and before he had gone very far he met with a horse boy and a driver of oxen, and he persuaded them to turn with him and to seek for adventures.

By these and many other tricks he soon became so celebrated that his fame reached the king's ears, and his majesty was filled with curiosity to see the man who had managed to outwit everybody. So he commanded his guards to capture the young man and bring him before him.

And when the young man stood before the king, the king spoke to him and said, 'By your tricks and the pranks that you have played on other people, you have, in the eye of the law, forfeited your life. But on one condition I will spare you, and that is, if you will bring me the flying horse that belongs to the great dragon. Fail in this, and you shall be hewn in a thousand pieces.'

'If that is all,' said the youth, 'you shall soon have it.'

So he went out and made his way straight to the stable where the flying horse was tethered. He stretched his hand cautiously out to seize the bridle, when the horse suddenly began to neigh as loud as he could. Now the room in which the dragon slept was just above the stable, and at the sound of the neighing he woke and cried to the horse, 'What is the matter, my treasure? is anything hurting you?' After waiting a little while the young man tried again to loose the horse, but a second time it neighed so loudly that the dragon woke up in a hurry and called out to know why the horse was making such a noise. But when the same thing happened the third time, the dragon lost his temper, and went down into the stable and took a whip and gave the horse a good beating. This offended the horse and made him angry, and when the young man stretched out his hand to untie his head, he made no further fuss, but suffered himself to be led quietly away. Once clear of the stable the young man sprang on his back and galloped off, calling over his shoulder, 'Hi! dragon! dragon! if anyone asks you what has become of your horse, you can say that I have got him!'

But the king said, 'The flying horse is all very well, but I want something more. You must bring me the covering with the little bells that lies on the bed of the dragon, or I will have you hewn into a thousand pieces.'

'Is that all?' answered the youth. 'That is easily done.'

And when night came he went away to the dragon's house and climbed up on to the roof. Then he opened a little window in the roof and let down the chain from which the kettle usually hung, and tried to hook the bed covering and to draw it up. But the little bells all began to ring, and the dragon woke and said to his wife, 'Wife, you have pulled off all the bed-clothes!' and drew the covering towards him, pulling, as he did so, the young man into the room. Then the dragon flung himself on the youth and bound him fast with cords saying as he tied the last knot, 'To-morrow when I go to church you must stay at home and kill him and cook him, and when I get back we will eat him together.'

So the following morning the dragoness took hold of the young man and reached down from the shelf a sharp knife with which to kill him. But as she untied the cords the better to get hold of him, the prisoner caught her by the legs, threw her to the ground, seized her and speedily cut her throat, just as she had been about to do for him, and put her body in the oven. Then he snatched up the covering and carried it to the king.

The king was seated on his throne when the youth appeared before him and spread out the covering with a deep bow. 'That is not enough,' said his majesty; 'you must bring me the dragon himself, or I will have you hewn into a thousand pieces.'

'It shall be done,' answered the youth; 'but you must give me two years to manage it, for my beard must grow so that he may not know me.'

'So be it,' said the king.

And the first thing the young man did when his beard was grown was to take the road to the dragon's house and on the way he met a beggar, whom he persuaded to change clothes with him, and in the beggar's garments he went fearlessly forth to the dragon.

He found his enemy before his house, very busy making a box, and addressed him politely, 'Good morning, your worship. Have you a morsel of bread?'

'You must wait,' replied the dragon, 'till I have finished my box, and then I will see if I can find one.'

'What will you do with the box when it is made?' inquired the beggar.

'It is for the young man who killed my wife, and stole my flying horse and my bed covering,' said the dragon.

'He deserves nothing better,' answered the beggar, 'for it was an ill deed. Still that box is too small for him, for he is a big man.'

'You are wrong,' said the dragon. 'The box is large enough even for me.'

'Well, the rogue is nearly as tall as you,' replied the beggar, 'and, of course, if you can get in, he can. But I am sure you would find it a tight fit.'

'No, there is plenty of room,' said the dragon, tucking himself carefully inside.

But no sooner was he well in, than the young man clapped on the lid and called out, 'Now press hard, just to see if he will be able to get out.'

The dragon pressed as hard as he could, but the lid never moved.

'It is all right,' he cried; 'now you can open it.'

But instead of opening it, the young man drove in long nails to make it tighter still; then he took the box on his back and brought it to the king. And when the king heard that the dragon was inside, he was so excited that he would not wait one moment, but broke the lock and lifted the lid just a little way to make sure he was really there. He was very careful not to leave enough space for the dragon to jump out, but unluckily there was just room for his great mouth, and with one snap the king vanished down his wide red jaws. Then the young man married the king's daughter and ruled over the land, but what he did with the dragon nobody knows.

330: The Smith Outwits the Devil

The Master-Smith

The Master-Smith
(*Norway*)

Once on a time, in the days when our Lord and St. Peter used to wander on earth, they came to a smith's house. He had made a bargain with the Devil, that the fiend should have him after seven years, but during that time he was to be the master of all masters in his trade, and to this bargain both he and the Devil had signed their names. So he had stuck up in great letters over the door of his forge: "*Here dwells the Master over all Masters.*"

Now when our Lord passed by and saw that, he went in.

"Who are you?" he said to the Smith.

"Read what's written over the door", said the Smith; "but maybe you can't read writing. If so, you must wait till someone comes to help you."

Before our Lord had time to answer him, a man came with his horse, which he begged the Smith to shoe.

"Might I have leave to shoe it?" asked our Lord.

"You may try, if you like", said the Smith; "you can't do it so badly that I shall not be able to make it right again."

So our Lord went out and took one leg off the horse, and laid it in the furnace, and made the shoe red-hot; after that, he turned up the ends of the shoe, and filed down the heads of the nails, and clenched the points; and then he put back the leg safe and sound on the horse again. And when he was done with that leg, he took the other fore-leg and did the same with it; and when he was done with that, he took the hind-legs—first, the off, and then the near leg, and laid them in the furnace, making the shoes red-hot, turning up the ends; filing the heads of the nails, and clenching the points; and after all was done, putting the legs on the horse again. All the while, the Smith stood by and looked on.

"You're not so bad a smith after all", said he.

"Oh, you think so, do you?" said our Lord.

A little while after came the Smith's mother to the forge, and called him to come home and eat his dinner; she was an old, old woman with an ugly crook on her back, and wrinkles in her face, and it was as much as she could do to crawl along.

"Mark now, what you see", said our Lord.

Then he took the woman and laid her in the furnace, and smithied a lovely young maiden out of her.

"Well", said the Smith, "I say now, as I said before, you are not such a bad smith after all. There it stands over my door. *Here dwells the Master over all Masters*; but for all that, I say right out, one learns as long as one lives"; and with that he walked off to his house and ate his dinner.

So after dinner, just after he had got back to his forge, a man came riding up to have his horse shod.

"It shall be done in the twinkling of an eye", said the Smith, "for I have just learnt a new way to shoe; and a very good way it is when the days are short."

So he began to cut and hack till he had got all the horse's legs off, for he said, I don't know why one should go pottering backwards and forwards—first, with one leg, and then with another.

Then he laid the legs in the furnace, just as he had seen our Lord lay them, and threw on a great heap of coal, and made his mates work the bellows bravely; but it went as one might suppose it would go. The legs were burnt to ashes, and the Smith had to pay for the horse.

Well, he didn't care much about that, but just then an old beggar-woman came along the road, and he thought to himself, "better luck next time"; so he took the old dame and laid her in the furnace, and though she begged and prayed hard for her life, it was no good.

"You're so old, you don't know what is good for you", said the Smith; "now you shall be a lovely young maiden in half no time, and for all that, I'll not charge you a penny for the job."

But it went no better with the poor old woman than with the horse's legs.

"That was ill done, and I say it", said our Lord.

"Oh! for that matter", said the Smith, "there's not many who'll ask after her, I'll be bound; but it's a shame of the Devil, if this is the way he holds to what is written up over the door."

"If you might have three wishes from me", said our Lord, "what would you wish for?"

"Only try me", said the Smith, "and you'll soon know."

So our Lord gave him three wishes.

"Well", said the Smith, "first and foremost, I wish that anyone whom I ask to climb up into the pear-tree that stands outside by the wall of my forge, may stay sitting there till I ask him to come down again. The second wish I wish is, that anyone whom I ask to sit down in my easy chair which stands inside the workshop yonder, may stay sitting there till I ask him to get up. Last of all, I wish that anyone whom I ask to creep into the steel purse which I have in my pocket, may stay in it till I give him leave to creep out again."

"You have wished as a wicked man", said St. Peter; "first and foremost, you should have wished for God's grace and goodwill."

"I durstn't look so high as that", said the Smith; and after that our

Lord and St. Peter bade him "good-bye", and went on their way.

Well, the years went on and on, and when the time was up, the Devil came to fetch the Smith, as it was written in their bargain.

"Are you ready?" he said, as he stuck his nose in at the door of the forge.

"Oh", said the Smith, "I must just hammer the head of this tenpenny nail first; meantime, you can just climb up into the pear-tree, and pluck yourself a pear to gnaw at; you must be, both hungry and thirsty after your journey."

So the Devil thanked him for his kind offer, and climbed up into the pear-tree.

"Very good", said the Smith; "but now, on thinking the matter over, I find I shall never be able to have done hammering the head of this nail till four years are out at least, this iron is so plaguey hard; down you can't come in all that time, but may sit up there and rest your bones."

When the Devil heard this, he begged and prayed till his voice was as thin as a silver penny that he might have leave to come down; but there was no help for it. There he was, and there he must stay. At last he had to give his word of honour not to come again till the four years were out, which the Smith had spoken of, and then the Smith said, "Very well, now you may come down."

So when the time was up, the Devil came again to fetch the Smith.

"You're ready now, of course", said he; "you've had time enough to hammer the head of that nail, I should think."

"Yes, the head is right enough now", said the Smith; "but still you have come a little tiny bit too soon, for I haven't quite done sharpening the point; such plaguey hard iron I never hammered in all my born days. So while I work at the point, you may just as well sit down in my easy chair and rest yourself; I'll be bound you're weary after coming so far."

"Thank you kindly", said the Devil, and down he plumped into the easy chair; but just as he had made himself comfortable, the Smith said, on second thoughts, he found he couldn't get the point sharp till four years were out. First of all, the Devil begged so prettily to be let out of the chair, and afterwards, waxing wroth, he began to threaten and scold; but the Smith kept on, all the while excusing himself, and saying it was all the iron's fault, it was so plaguey hard, and telling the Devil he was not so badly off to have to sit quietly in an easy chair, and that he would let him out to the minute when the four years were over. Well, at last there was no help for it, and the Devil had to give his word of honour not to fetch the Smith till the four years were out; and then the Smith said:

"Well now, you may get up and be off about your business", and away went the Devil as fast as he could lay legs to the ground.

When the four years were over, the Devil came again to fetch the Smith, and he called out, as he stuck his nose in at the door of the forge:

"Now, I know you must be ready."

"Ready, aye, ready", answered the Smith; "we can go now as soon as you please; but hark ye, there is one thing I have stood here and thought, and thought, I would ask you to tell me. Is it true what people say, that the Devil can make himself as small as he pleases?"

"God knows, it is the very truth", said the Devil.

"Oh!" said the Smith; "it *is* true, is it? then I wish you would just be so good as to creep into this steel purse of mine, and see whether it is sound at the bottom, for to tell you the truth, I'm afraid my travelling money will drop out."

"With all my heart", said the Devil, who made himself small in a trice, and crept into the purse; but he was scarce in when the Smith snapped to the clasp.

"Yes", called out the Devil inside the purse; "it's right and tight every-where."

"Very good", said the Smith; "I'm glad to hear you say so, but 'more haste the worse speed', says the old saw, and 'forewarned is forearmed', says another; so I'll just weld these links a little together, just for safety's sake"; and with that he laid the purse in the furnace, and made it red-hot.

"AU! AU!" screamed the Devil, "are you mad? don't you know I'm inside the purse?"

"Yes, I do!" said the Smith; "but I can't help you, for another old saw says, 'one must strike while the iron is hot'"; and as he said this, he took up his sledge-hammer, laid the purse on the anvil, and let fly at it as hard as he could.

"AU! AU! AU!" bellowed the Devil, inside the purse. "Dear friend, do let me out, and I'll never come near you again."

"Very well!" said the Smith; "now, I think, the links are pretty well welded, and you may come out"; so he unclasped the purse, and away went the Devil in such a hurry that he didn't once look behind him.

Now, some time after, it came across the Smith's mind that he had done a silly thing in making the Devil his enemy, for, he said to himself:

"If, as is like enough, they won't have me in the kingdom of Heaven, I shall be in danger of being houseless, since I've fallen out with him who rules over Hell."

So he made up his mind it would be best to try to get either into Hell or Heaven, and to try at once, rather than to put it off any longer, so that he might know how things really stood. Then he threw his sledge-hammer over his shoulder and set off; and when he had gone a good bit of the way, he came to a place where two roads met, and where the path to the kingdom of Heaven parts from the path that leads to Hell, and here he overtook a tailor, who was pelting along with his goose in his hand.

"Good day", said the Smith; "whither are you off to?"

"To the kingdom of Heaven", said the Tailor, "if I can only get into it"—"but whither are you going yourself?"

"Oh, our ways don't run together", said the Smith; "for I have made up my mind to try first in Hell, as the Devil and I know something of one another, from old times."

So they bade one another "Good-bye", and each went his way; but the Smith was a stout, strong man, and got over the ground far faster than the tailor, and so it wasn't long before he stood at the gates of Hell. Then he called the watch, and bade him go and tell the Devil there was someone outside who wished to speak a word with him.

"Go out", said the Devil to the watch, "and ask him who he is?" So that when the watch came and told him that, the Smith answered:

"Go and greet the Devil in my name, and say it is the Smith who owns the purse he wots of; and beg him prettily to let me in at once, for I worked at my forge till noon, and I have had a long walk since."

But when the Devil heard who it was, he charged the watch to go back and lock up all the nine locks on the gates of Hell.

"And, besides", he said, "you may as well put on a padlock, for if he only once gets in, he'll turn Hell topsy-turvy!"

"Well!" said the Smith to himself, when he saw them busy bolting up the gates, "there's no lodging to be got here, that's plain; so I may as well try my luck in the kingdom of Heaven"; and with that he turned round and went back till he reached the cross-roads, and then he went along the path the tailor had taken. And now, as he was cross at having gone backwards and forwards so far for no good, he strode along with all his might, and reached the gate of Heaven just as St. Peter was opening it a very little, just enough to let the half-starved tailor slip in. The Smith was still six or seven strides off the gate, so he thought to himself, "Now there's no time to be lost"; and, grasping his sledge-hammer, he hurled it into the opening of the door just as the tailor slunk in; and if the Smith didn't get in then, when the door was ajar, why I don't know what has become of him.

Brother Lustig
(*Germany*)

There was once on a time a great war, and when it came to an end, many soldiers were discharged. Then Brother Lustig also received his dismissal, and besides that, nothing but a small loaf of contract-bread, and four kreuzers in money, with which he departed. St. Peter had, however, placed himself in his way in the shape of a poor beggar, and when Brother Lustig came up, he begged alms of him. Brother Lustig replied, "Dear beggar-man, what am I to give you? I have been a soldier, and have received my dismissal, and have nothing but this little loaf of contract-bread, and four kreuzers of money; when that is gone, I shall have to beg as well as you. Still I will give you something." Thereupon he divided the loaf into four parts, and gave the apostle one of them, and a kreuzer likewise. St. Peter thanked him, went onwards, and threw himself again in the soldier's way as a beggar, but in another shape; and when he came up begged a gift of him as before. Brother Lustig spoke as he had done before, and again gave him a quarter of the loaf and one kreuzer. St. Peter thanked him, and went onwards, but for the third time placed himself in another shape as a beggar on the road, and spoke to Brother Lustig. Brother Lustig gave him also the third quarter of bread and the third kreuzer. St. Peter thanked him, and Brother Lustig went onwards, and had but a quarter of the loaf, and one kreuzer. With that he went into an inn, ate the bread, and ordered one kreuzer's worth of beer. When he had had it, he journeyed onwards, and then St. Peter, who had assumed the appearance of a discharged soldier, met and spoke to him thus: "Good day, comrade, canst thou not give me a bit of bread, and a kreuzer to get a drink?" "Where am I to procure it?" answered Brother Lustig; "I have been discharged, and I got nothing but a loaf of ammunition-bread and four kreuzers in money. I met three beggars on the road, and I gave each of them a quarter of my bread, and one kreuzer. The last quarter I ate in the inn, and had a drink with the last kreuzer. Now my pockets are empty, and if thou also hast nothing we can go a-begging together." "No," answered St. Peter, "we need not quite do that. I know a little about medicine, and I will soon earn as much as I require by that." "Indeed," said Brother Lustig, "I know nothing of that, so I must go and beg alone." "Just come with me," said St. Peter, "and if I earn anything, thou shalt have half of it." "All right," said Brother Lustig, so they went away together.

Then they came to a peasant's house inside which they heard loud lamentations and cries; so they went in, and there the husband was lying sick unto death, and very near his end, and his wife was crying and weeping quite loudly. "Stop that howling and crying," said St. Peter, "I will make the man well again," and he took a salve out of his pocket, and healed the sick man in a moment, so that he could get up, and was in perfect health. In great delight the man and his wife said, "How can we reward you? What shall we give you?" But St. Peter would take nothing, and the more the peasant folks offered him, the more he refused. Brother Lustig, however, nudged St. Peter, and said, "Take something; sure enough we are in need of it." At length the woman brought a lamb and said to St. Peter that he really must take that, but he would not. Then Brother Lustig gave him a poke in the side, and said, "Do take it, you stupid fool; we are in great want of it!" Then St. Peter said at last, "Well, I will take the lamb, but I won't carry it; if thou wilt insist on having it, thou must carry it." "That is nothing," said Brother Lustig. "I will easily carry it," and took it on his shoulder. Then they departed and came to a wood, but Brother Lustig had begun to feel the lamb heavy, and he was hungry, so he said to St. Peter, "Look, that's a good place, we might cook the lamb there, and eat it." "As you like," answered St. Peter, "but I can't have anything to do with the cooking; if thou wilt cook, there is a kettle for thee, and in the meantime I will walk about a little until it is ready. Thou must, however, not begin to eat until I have come back, I will come at the right time." "Well, go, then," said Brother Lustig, "I understand cookery, I will manage it." Then St. Peter went away, and Brother Lustig killed the lamb, lighted a fire, threw the meat into the kettle, and boiled it. The lamb was, however, quite ready, and the apostle Peter had not come back, so Brother Lustig took it out of the kettle, cut it up, and found the heart. "That is said to be the best part," said he, and tasted it, but at last he ate it all up. At length St. Peter returned and said, "Thou mayst eat the whole of the lamb thyself, I will only have the heart, give me that." Then Brother Lustig took a knife and fork, and pretended to look anxiously about amongst the lamb's flesh, but not to be able to find the heart, and at last he said abruptly, "There is none here." "But where can it be?" said the apostle. "I don't know," replied Brother Lustig, "but look, what fools we both are, to seek for the lamb's heart, and neither of us to remember that a lamb has no heart!" "Oh," said St. Peter, "that is something quite new! Every animal has a heart, why is a lamb to have none?" "No, be assured, my brother," said Brother Lustig, "that a lamb has no heart; just consider it seriously, and then you will see that it really has none." "Well, it is all right," said St. Peter, "if there is no heart, then I want none of the lamb; thou mayst eat it alone." "What I can't eat now, I will carry away in my knapsack," said Brother Lustig, and he ate half the lamb, and put the rest in his knapsack.

They went farther, and then St. Peter caused a great stream of water to flow right across their path, and they were obliged to pass through it. Said St. Peter, "Do thou go first." "No," answered Brother Lustig, "thou must go first," and he thought, "if the water is too deep I will stay behind." Then St. Peter strode through it, and the water just reached to his knee. So Brother Lustig began to go through also, but the water grew deeper and reached to his throat. Then he cried, "Brother, help me!" St. Peter said, "Then wilt thou confess that thou hast eaten the lamb's heart?" "No," said he, "I have not eaten it." Then the water grew deeper still and rose to his mouth. "Help me, brother," cried the soldier. St. Peter said, "Then wilt thou confess that thou hast eaten the lamb's heart?" "No," he replied, "I have not eaten it." St. Peter, however, would not let him be drowned, but made the water sink and helped him through it.

Then they journeyed onwards, and came to a kingdom where they heard that the King's daughter lay sick unto death. "Hello, brother!" said the soldier to St. Peter, "this is a chance for us; if we can heal her we shall be provided for, for life!" But St. Peter was not half quick enough for him, "Come, lift your legs, my dear brother," said he, "that we may get there in time." But St. Peter walked slower and slower, though Brother Lustig did all he could to drive and push him on, and at last they heard that the princess was dead. "Now we are done for!" said Brother Lustig; "that comes of thy sleepy way of walking!" "Just be quiet," answered St. Peter, "I can do more than cure sick people; I can bring dead ones to life again." "Well, if thou canst do that," said Brother Lustig, "it's all right, but thou shouldst earn at least half the kingdom for us by that." Then they went to the royal palace, where everyone was in great grief, but St. Peter told the King that he would restore his daughter to life. He was taken to her, and said, "Bring me a kettle and some water," and when that was brought, he bade everyone go out, and allowed no one to remain with him but Brother Lustig. Then he cut off all the dead girl's limbs, and threw them in the water, lighted a fire beneath the kettle, and boiled them. And when the flesh had fallen away from the bones, he took out the beautiful white bones, and laid them on a table, and arranged them together in their natural order. When he had done that, he stepped forward and said three times, "In the name of the holy Trinity, dead woman, arise." And at the third time, the princess arose, living, healthy and beautiful. Then the King was in the greatest joy, and said to St. Peter, "Ask for thy reward; even if it were half my kingdom, I would give it thee." But St. Peter said, "I want nothing for it." "Oh, thou tomfool!" thought Brother Lustig to himself, and nudged his comrade's side, and said, "Don't be so stupid! If thou hast no need of anything, I have." St. Peter, however, would have nothing, but as the King saw that the other would very much like to have something, he ordered his treasurer to fill Brother Lustig's knapsack with gold. Then they went on their way, and when they came to a forest, St. Peter said to Brother Lustig, "Now, we will divide the gold." "Yes," he replied, "we will." So St. Peter divided the gold, and divided it into three heaps. Brother Lustig thought to himself, "What craze has he got in his head now? He is making three shares, and there are only two of us!" But St. Peter said, "I have divided it exactly; there is one share for me, one for thee, and one for him who ate the lamb's heart."

"Oh, I ate that!" replied Brother Lustig, and hastily swept up the gold. "You may trust what I say." "But how can that be true," said St. Peter, "when a lamb has no heart?" "Eh, what, brother, what can you be thinking of? Lambs have hearts like other animals, why should only they have none?" "Well, so be it," said St. Peter, "keep the gold to yourself, but I will stay with you no longer; I will go my way alone." "As you like, dear brother," answered Brother Lustig. "Farewell."

Then St. Peter went a different road, but Brother Lustig thought, "It is a good thing that he has taken himself off, he is certainly a strange saint, after all." Then he had money enough, but did not know how to manage it, squandered it, gave it away, and when some time had gone by, once more had nothing. Then he arrived in a certain country where he heard that a King's daughter was dead. "Oh, ho!" thought he, "that may be a good thing for me; I will bring her to life again, and see that I am paid as I ought to be." So he went to the King, and offered to raise the dead girl to life again. Now the King had heard that a discharged soldier was traveling about and bringing dead persons to life again, and thought that Brother Lustig was the man; but as he had no confidence in him, he consulted his councillors first, who said that he might give it a trial as his daughter was dead. Then Brother Lustig ordered water to be brought to him in a kettle, bade everyone go out, cut the limbs off, threw them in the water and lighted a fire beneath, just as he had seen St. Peter do. The water began to boil, the flesh fell off, and then he took the bones out and laid them on the table, but he did not know the order in which to lay them, and placed them all wrong and in confusion. Then he stood before them and said, "In the name of the most holy Trinity, dead maiden, I bid thee arise," and he said this thrice, but the bones did not stir. So he said it thrice more, but also in vain: "Confounded girl that you are, get up!" cried he, "Get up, or it shall be worse for you!" When he had said that, St. Peter suddenly appeared in his former shape as a discharged soldier; he entered by the window and said, "Godless man, what art thou doing? How can the dead maiden arise, when thou hast thrown about her bones in such confusion?" "Dear brother, I have done everything to the best of my ability," he answered. "This once, I will help thee out of thy difficulty, but one thing I tell thee, and that is that if ever thou undertakest anything of the kind again, it will be the worse for thee, and also that thou must neither demand nor accept the smallest thing from the King for this!" Thereupon St. Peter laid the bones in their right order, said to the maiden three times, "In the name of the most holy Trinity, dead maiden, arise," and the King's daughter arose, healthy and beautiful as before. Then St. Peter went away again by the window, and Brother Lustig was rejoiced to find that all had passed off so well, but was very much vexed to think that after all he was not to take anything for it. "I should just like to know," thought he, "what fancy that fellow has got in his head, for what he gives with one hand he takes away with the other, there is no sense whatever in it!" Then the King offered Brother Lustig whatsoever he wished to have, but he did not dare to take anything; however, by hints and cunning, he contrived to make the King order his knapsack to be filled with gold for him, and with that he departed. When he got out, St. Peter was standing by the door, and said, "Just look what a man thou art; did I not forbid thee to take anything, and there thou hast thy knapsack full of gold!" "How can I help that," answered Brother Lustig, "if people will put it in for me?" "Well, I tell thee this, that if ever thou settest about anything of this kind again thou shalt suffer for it!" "Eh, brother, have no fear, now I have money, why should I trouble myself with washing bones?" "Faith," said St. Peter, "the gold will last a long time! In order that after this thou mayst never tread in forbidden paths, I will bestow on thy knapsack this property, namely, that whatsoever thou wishest to have inside it, shall be there. Farewell, thou wilt now never see me more." "Good-bye," said Brother Lustig, and thought to himself, "I am very glad that thou hast taken thyself off, thou strange fellow; I shall certainly not follow thee." But of the magical power which had been bestowed on his knapsack, he thought no more.

Brother Lustig travelled about with his money, and squandered and wasted what he had as before. When at last he had no more than four kreuzers, he passed by an inn and thought, "The money must go," and ordered three kreuzers' worth of wine and one kreuzer's worth of bread for himself. As he was sitting there drinking, the smell of roast goose made its way to his nose. Brother Lustig looked about and peeped, and saw that the host had two geese standing in the oven. Then he remembered that his comrade had said that whatsoever he wished to have in his knapsack should be there, so he said, "Oh, ho! I must try that with the geese." So he went out, and when he was outside the door, he said, "I wish those two roasted geese out of the oven and in my knapsack," and when he had said that, he unbuckled it and looked in, and there they were inside it. "Ah, that's right!" said he, "now I am a made man!" and went away to a meadow and took out the roast meat. When he was in the midst of his meal, two journeymen came up and looked at the second goose, which was not yet touched, with hungry eyes. Brother Lustig thought to himself, "One is enough for me," and called the two men up and said, "Take the goose, and eat it to my health." They thanked him, and went with it to the inn, ordered themselves a half bottle of wine and a loaf, took out the goose which had been given them, and began to eat. The hostess saw them and said to her husband, "Those two are eating a goose; just look and see if it is not one of ours, out of the oven." The landlord ran thither, and behold the oven was empty! "What!" cried he, "you thievish crew, you want to eat goose as cheap as that? Pay for it this moment; or I will wash you well with green hazel-sap." The two said, "We are no thieves, a discharged soldier gave us the goose, outside there in the meadow." "You shall not throw dust in my eyes that way! the soldier was here but he went out by the door, like an honest fellow. I looked after him myself; you are the thieves and shall pay!" But as they could not pay, he took a stick, and cudgeled them out of the house.

Brother Lustig went his way and came to a place where there was a magnificent castle, and not far from it a wretched inn. He went to the inn and asked for a night's lodging, but the landlord turned him away, and said, "There is no more room here, the house is full of noble guests." "It surprises me that they should come to you and not go to that splendid castle," said Brother Lustig. "Ah, indeed," replied the host, "but it is no slight matter to sleep there for a night; no one who has tried it so far, has ever come out of it alive."

"If others have tried it," said Brother Lustig, "I will try it too."

"Leave it alone," said the host, "it will cost you your neck." "It won't kill me at once," said Brother Lustig, "just give me the key, and some good food and wine." So the host gave him the key, and food and wine, and with this Brother Lustig went into the castle, enjoyed his supper, and at length, as he was sleepy, he lay down on the ground, for there was no bed. He soon fell asleep, but during the night was disturbed by a great noise, and when he awoke, he saw nine ugly devils in the room, who had made a circle, and were dancing around him. Brother Lustig said, "Well, dance as long as you like, but none of you must come too close." But the devils pressed continually nearer to him, and almost stepped on his face with their hideous feet. "Stop, you devils' ghosts," said he, but they behaved still worse. Then Brother Lustig grew angry, and cried, "Hola! but I will soon make it quiet," and got the leg of a chair and struck out into the midst of them with it. But nine devils against one soldier were still too many, and when he struck those in front of him, the others seized him behind by the hair, and tore it unmercifully. "Devils' crew," cried he, "it is getting too bad, but wait. Into my knapsack, all nine of you!" In an instant they were in it, and then he buckled it up and threw it into a corner. After this all was suddenly quiet, and Brother Lustig lay down again, and slept till it was bright day. Then came the inn-keeper, and the nobleman to whom the castle belonged, to see how he had fared; but when they perceived that he was merry and well they were astonished, and asked, "Have the spirits done you no harm, then?" "The reason why they have not," answered Brother Lustig, "is because I have got the whole nine of them in my knapsack! You may once more inhabit your castle quite tranquilly, none of them will ever haunt it again." The nobleman thanked him, made him rich presents, and begged him to remain in his service, and he would provide for him as long as he lived. "No," replied Brother Lustig, "I am used to wandering about, I will travel farther." Then he went away, and entered into a smithy, laid the knapsack, which contained the nine devils on the anvil, and asked the smith and his apprentices to strike it. So they smote with their great hammers with all their strength, and the devils uttered howls which were quite pitiable. When he opened the knapsack after this, eight of them were dead, but one which had been lying in a fold of it, was still alive, slipped out, and went back again to hell. Thereupon Brother Lustig travelled a long time about the world, and those who know them can tell many a story about him, but at last he grew old, and thought of his end, so he went to a hermit who was known to be a pious man, and said to him, "I am tired of wandering about, and want now to behave in such a manner that I shall enter into the kingdom of Heaven." The hermit replied, "There are two roads, one is broad and pleasant, and leads to hell, the other is narrow and rough, and leads to heaven." "I should be a fool," thought Brother Lustig, "if I were to take the narrow, rough road." So he set out and took the broad and pleasant road, and at length came to a great black door, which was the door of Hell. Brother Lustig knocked, and the door-keeper peeped out to see who was there. But when he saw Brother Lustig, he was terrified, for he was the very same ninth devil who had been shut up in the knapsack, and had escaped from it with a black eye. So he pushed the bolt in again as quickly as he could, ran to the devil's lieutenant, and said, "There is a fellow outside with a knapsack, who wants to come in, but as you value your lives don't allow him to enter, or he will wish the whole of hell into his knapsack. He once gave me a frightful hammering when I was inside it." So they called out to Brother Lustig that he was to go away again, for he should not get in there! "If they won't have me here," thought he, "I will see if I can find a place for myself in heaven, for I must be somewhere." So he turned about and went onwards until he came to the door of Heaven, where he knocked. St. Peter was sitting hard by as door-keeper. Brother Lustig recognised him at once, and thought, "Here I find an old friend, I shall get on better." But St. Peter said, "I really believe that thou wantest to come into Heaven." "Let me in, brother; I must get in somewhere; if they would have taken me into Hell, I should not have come here." "No," said St. Peter, "thou shalt not enter." "Then if thou wilt not let me in, take thy knapsack back, for I will have nothing at all from thee." "Give it here, then," said St. Peter. Then Brother Lustig gave him the knapsack into Heaven through the bars, and St. Peter took it, and hung it beside his seat. Then said Brother Lustig, "And now I wish myself inside my knapsack," and in a second he was in it, and in Heaven, and St. Peter was forced to let him stay there.

Gambling Hansel
(*Germany*)

Once upon a time there was a man who did nothing but gamble, and for that reason people never called him anything but Gambling Hansel, and as he never ceased to gamble, he played away his house and all that he had. Now the very day before his creditors were to take his house from him, came the Lord and St. Peter, and asked him to give them shelter for the night. Then Gambling Hansel said, "For my part, you may stay the night, but I cannot give you a bed or anything to eat." So the Lord said he was just to take them in, and they themselves would buy something to eat, to which Gambling Hansel made no objection. Thereupon St. Peter gave him three groschen, and said he was to go to the baker's and fetch some bread. So Gambling Hansel went, but when he reached the house where the other gambling vagabonds were gathered together, they, although they had won all that he had, greeted him clamorously, and said, "Hansel, do come in." "Oh," said he, "do you want to win the three groschen too?" On this they would not let him go. So he went in, and played away the three groschen also. Meanwhile St. Peter and the Lord were waiting, and as he was so long in coming, they set out to meet him. When Gambling Hansel came, however, he pretended that the money had fallen into the gutter, and kept raking about in it all the while to find it, but our Lord already knew that he had lost it in play. St. Peter again gave him three groschen, and now he did not allow himself to be led away once more, but fetched them the loaf. Our Lord then inquired if he had no wine, and he said, "Alack, sir, the casks are all empty!" But the Lord said he was to go down into the cellar, for the best wine was still there. For a long time he would not believe this, but at length he said, "Well, I will go down, but I know that there is none there." When he turned the tap, however, lo and behold, the best of wine ran out! So he took it to them, and the two passed the night there. Early next day our Lord told Gambling Hansel that he might beg three favours. The Lord expected that he would ask to go to Heaven; but Gambling Hansel asked for a pack of cards with which he could win everything, for dice with which he would win everything, and for a tree whereon every kind of fruit would grow, and from which no one who had climbed up, could descend until he bade him do so. The Lord gave him all that he had asked, and departed with St. Peter.

And now Gambling Hansel at once set about gambling in real earnest, and before long he had gained half the world. Upon this St. Peter said to the Lord, "Lord, this thing must not go on, he will win, and thou lose, the whole world. We must send Death to him." When Death appeared, Gambling Hansel had just seated himself at the gaming-table, and Death said, "Hansel, come out a while." But Gambling Hansel said, "Just wait a little until the game is done, and in the meantime get up into that tree out there, and gather a little fruit that we may have something to munch on our way." Thereupon Death climbed up, but when he wanted to come down again, he could not, and Gambling Hansel left him up there for seven years, during which time no one died.

So St. Peter said to the Lord, "Lord, this thing must not go on. People no longer die; we must go ourselves." And they went themselves, and the Lord commanded Hansel to let Death come down. So Hansel went at once to Death and said to him, "Come down," and Death took him directly and put an end to him. They went away together and came to the next world, and then Gambling Hansel made straight for the door of Heaven, and knocked at it. "Who is there?" "Gambling Hansel." "Ah, we will have nothing to do with him! Begone!" So he went to the door of Purgatory, and knocked once more. "Who is there?" "Gambling Hansel." "Ah, there is quite enough weeping and wailing here without him. We do not want to gamble, just go away again." Then he went to the door of Hell, and there they let him in. There was, however, no one at home but old Lucifer and the crooked devils who had just been doing their evil work in the world. And no sooner was Hansel there than he sat down to gamble again. Lucifer, however, had nothing to lose but his mis-shapen devils, and Gambling Hansel won them from him, as with his cards he could not fail to do. And now he was off again with his crooked devils, and they went to Hohenfuert and pulled up a hop-pole, and with it went to Heaven and began to thrust the pole against it, and Heaven began to crack. So again St. Peter said, "Lord, this thing cannot go on, we must let him in, or he will throw us down from Heaven." And they let him in. But Gambling Hansel instantly began to play again, and there was such a noise and confusion that there was no hearing what they themselves were saying. Therefore St. Peter once more said, "Lord, this cannot go on, we must throw him down, or he will make all Heaven rebellious." So they went to him at once, and threw him down, and his soul broke into fragments, and went into the gambling vagabonds who are living this very day.

402: The Animal Bride

Doll i' the Grass
(*Norway*)

Once on a time there was a King who had twelve sons. When they were grown big he told them they must go out into the world and win themselves wives, but these wives must each be able to spin, and weave, and sew a shirt in one day, else he wouldn't have them for daughters-in-law.

To each he gave a horse and a new suit of mail, and they went out into the world to look after their brides; but when they had gone a bit of the way, they said they wouldn't have Boots, their youngest brother, with them—he wasn't fit for anything.

Well, Boots had to stay behind, and he didn't know what to do or whither to turn; and so he grew so downcast, he got off his horse, and sat down in the tall grass to weep. But when he had sat a little while, one of the tufts in the grass began to stir and move, and out of it came a little white thing, and when it came nearer, Boots saw it was a charming little lassie, only such a tiny bit of a thing. So the lassie went up to him, and asked if he would come down below and see "Doll i' the Grass".

Yes, he'd be very happy, and so he went.

Now, when he got down; there sat Doll i' the Grass on a chair; she was so lovely and so smart, and she asked Boots whither he was going, and what was his business.

So he told her how there were twelve brothers of them, and how the King had given them horses and mail, and said they must each go out into the world and find them a wife who could spin, and weave, and sew a shirt in a day.

"But if you'll only say at once you'll be my wife, I'll not go a step further", said Boots to Doll i' the Grass.

Well, she was willing enough, and so she made haste and span, and wove, and sewed the shirt, but it was so tiny, tiny little. It wasn't longer than so————long.

So Boots set off home with it, but when he brought it out he was almost ashamed, it was so small. Still the King said he should have her, and so Boots set off, glad and happy to fetch his little sweetheart. So when he got to Doll i' the Grass, he wished to take her up before him on his horse; but she wouldn't have that, for she said she would sit and drive along in a silver spoon, and that she had two small white horses to draw her. So off they set, he on his horse and she on her silver spoon, and the two horses that drew her were two tiny white mice; but Boots always kept the other side of the road, he was so afraid lest he should ride over her, she was so little. So, when they had gone a bit of the way, they came to a great piece of water. Here Boots' horse got frightened, and shied across the road and upset the spoon, and Doll i' the Grass tumbled into the water. Then Boots got so sorrowful because he didn't know how to get her out again; but in a little while up came a merman with her, and now she was as well and full grown as other men and women, and far lovelier than she had been before. So he took her up before him on his horse, and rode home.

When Boots got home all his brothers had come back each with his sweetheart, but these were all so ugly and foul and wicked that they had done nothing but fight with one another on the way home, and on their heads they had a kind of hat that was daubed over with tar and soot, and so the rain had run down off the hats on to their faces, till they got far uglier and nastier than they had been before. When his brothers saw Boots and his sweetheart, they were all as jealous as jealous could be of her; but the King was so overjoyed with them both, that he drove all the others away, and so Boots held his wedding-feast with Doll i' the Grass, and after that they lived well and happily together a long long time, and if they're not dead, why they're alive still.

The Princess Frog
(*Russia*)

Long, long ago, in days of yore, there lived a king who had three sons, all of them grown to manhood. One day the king called them to him and said, "My sons, let each of you make a bow for himself and shoot an arrow. The maiden who brings your arrow back will be your bride; and he whose arrow is not returned will stay unwed." The eldest son shot an arrow and a prince's daughter brought it back. The middle son loosed an arrow and a general's daughter brought it back. But young Prince Ivan's arrow fell into a marsh and was brought back by a frog holding it between her teeth. The first two brothers were joyful and happy, but Prince Ivan was downcast and cried: "How can I live with a frog? Marrying is for a lifetime, it isn't like wading a stream or crossing a field!" He wept and wept but there was nothing for it: he had to marry the frog. All three couples were wed together according to the custom—the frog being held aloft on a platter.

Some time passed. One day the king wished to see which bride was the best needle-woman. So he ordered them to make him a shirt. Poor Prince Ivan was again downcast and cried: "How can my frog sew? I'll be a laughing stock." The frog only jumped across the floor croaking. But no sooner was Prince Ivan asleep than she went outside, cast off her skin and turned into a beautiful maiden, calling, "Maids and matrons, sew me a shirt!" The maids and matrons straightway brought a finely-embroidered shirt: she took it, folded it, and placed it alongside Prince Ivan.

Thereupon she turned back into a frog as if nothing had happened. In the morning Prince Ivan awoke and was overjoyed to find the shirt, which he took forthwith to the king. The king gazed at it and said: "Now there's a shirt for you, fit to wear on holy days!" Then the middle brother brought a shirt, at which the king said, "This shirt is fit only for the bath-house!" And taking the eldest brother's shirt, he said, "And this one is fit only for a smoky peasant hut!" The king's sons went their separate ways, with the two eldest muttering among themselves, "We were surely wrong to mock at Prince Ivan's wife; she must be a cunning sorceress, not a frog."

Presently the king again issued a command: this time the daughters-in-law were each to bake a loaf of bread, and bring it to him to judge which bride was the best cook. The other two brides had made fun of the frog, but now they sent a chamber-maid to see how she would bake her loaf. The frog noticed the woman, so she kneaded some dough, rolled it out, made a hole in the stove and tipped the dough straight into the fire. The chambermaid ran to tell her mistresses, the royal brides, and they proceeded to do the same. But the crafty frog had tricked them; as soon as the woman had gone, she retrieved the dough, cleaned and mended the stove as if nothing had happened, then went out on to the porch, cast off her skin and called, "Maids and matrons, bake me a loaf of bread such as my dear father used to eat on Sundays and holidays." In an instant, the maids and matrons brought the bread. She took it, placed it beside Prince Ivan, and turned into a frog again. In the morning Prince Ivan awoke, took the loaf of bread and gave it to his father. His father was receiving the loaves brought by the elder brothers: their wives had dropped the dough into the fire just as the frog had done, so their bread was black and lumpy. First the king took the eldest son's loaf, inspected it and despatched it to the kitchen.

Then he took the middle son's loaf and despatched it thither too. Then came Prince Ivan's turn: he presented his loaf to his father who looked at it and said, "Now this is bread fit to grace a holy day. It is not at all like the burnt offerings of my elder daughters-in-law!"

After that the king thought to hold a ball to see which of his sons' wives was the best dancer. All the guests and daughters-in-law assembled; everyone was there except Prince Ivan, who thought: "How can I go to the ball with a frog?" And the poor prince began to weep bitterly. "Do not cry, Prince Ivan," said the frog. "Go to the ball. I shall follow in an hour." Prince Ivan was somewhat cheered at the frog's words, and left for the ball. Then the frog cast off her skin and turned into a lovely maid dressed in finery. When she arrived at the ball, Prince Ivan was overjoyed, and the guests clapped their hands at the sight of such beauty. They began to eat and drink. But the frog-princess would eat and slip the bones into her sleeve, then drink and pour the dregs into her other sleeve. The elder brothers' wives saw this and followed suit, slipping bones into one sleeve and dregs into the other. When the time came for dancing, the king called upon his elder sons' wives but they insisted on the frog-princess dancing first. And she straightway took Prince Ivan's arm and came forward to dance. She danced and danced, whirling round and round, to the delight of all. When she shook her right sleeve, woods and lakes appeared; when she shook her left sleeve, all kinds of birds flew about. The guests were filled with wonder. When she finished dancing, everything disappeared. Then the wives of the two elder sons began to dance. They wished to do as the frog-princess had done, so they shook their right sleeves and bones flew out hitting folk about them; and when they shook their left sleeves, water splashed all over the onlookers. The king was most displeased and soon called an end to the dancing.

The ball was over. Prince Ivan rode off ahead of his wife, found the frogskin and burnt it. So when his wife returned and looked for the skin, it was nowhere to be seen. She lay down to sleep with Prince Ivan, but just before daybreak she said to him, "Oh, Prince Ivan, if only you had waited a little longer I would have been yours. Now God alone knows when we shall meet again. Farewell. If you wish to find me you must go beyond the Thrice-Nine Land to the Thrice-Ten Kingdom." And the frog-princess vanished.

A year went by, and Prince Ivan still pined for his wife. As a second year began, he made ready to leave, seeking first the blessing of his father and mother. He rode for a long way and eventually chanced upon a little hut facing the trees, with its back to him. "Little hut, little hut," he called. 'Turn your face to me, please, and your back to the trees." The little hut did as he said and Prince Ivan entered. There before him sat an old woman, who cried, "Fie, Foh! There was neither sight nor sound of Russian bones, yet now they come marching in of their own free will! Whither go you, Prince Ivan?" "First give me food and drink and put me to bed, old woman, then ask your questions." So the old woman gave food and drink and put him to bed. Then Prince Ivan said to her, "Grannie, I have set out to rescue Yelena the Fair." "Oh, my child," the old woman said, "you've waited too long! At first she spoke of you often, but now she no longer remembers you. I haven't seen her for a long time. Go now to my middle sister, she knows more than me."

In the morning Prince Ivan set out, came to another little hut, and cried, "Little hut, little hut, turn your face to me, please, and your back to the trees." The little hut did as he said and Prince Ivan entered. There before him sat an old woman, who cried, "Fie, Foh! There was neither sight nor sound of Russian bones, yet now they come marching in of their own free will! Whither go you. Prince Ivan?" "I seek Yelena the Fair, Grannie," he replied. "Oh, Prince Ivan," the old woman said, "you've waited too long! She has begun to forget you and is to marry another. She is now living with my eldest sister; go there now, but beware: as you approach they will know it is you. Yelena will turn into a spindle, her dress will turn to gold. My sister will wind the gold thread around the spindle and put it into a box which she will lock. But you must find the key, open the box, break the spindle, toss the top over your shoulder and the bottom before you. Then she will appear."

Off went Prince Ivan, came to the old woman's hut, entered and saw her winding gold thread around a spindle; she then locked it in a box and hid the key. But Prince Ivan quickly found the key, opened the box, took out the spindle, broke it as he had been told, tossed the top over his shoulder and the bottom before him. All of a sudden, there was Yelena the Fair standing in front of him. "Oh, Prince Ivan," she sighed, "how long you were in coming! I almost wed another." And she told him that the other bridegroom would soon arrive. But, taking a magic carpet from the old woman, Yelena the Fair sat upon it and they soared up and away like birds. The bridegroom set off quickly in pursuit. He was clever and guessed that they had fled. He was within ten feet of them when they flew on the carpet into Rus. Just in time! He could not follow them there, so he turned back. But Prince Ivan and Yelena the Fair flew home to the rejoicing of all; and lived happily ever after.

The Three Feathers
(Germany)

There was once on a time a King who had three sons, of whom two were clever and wise, but the third did not speak much, and was simple, and was called the Simpleton. When the King had become old and weak, and was thinking of his end, he did not know which of his sons should inherit the kingdom after him. Then he said to them, "Go forth, and he who brings me the most beautiful carpet shall be King after my death." And that there should be no dispute amongst them, he took them outside his castle, blew three feathers in the air, and said, "You shall go as they fly." One feather flew to the east, the other to the west, but the third flew straight up and did not fly far, but soon fell to the ground. And now

one brother went to the right, and the other to the left, and they mocked
Simpleton, who was forced to stay where the third feather had fallen. He
sat down and was sad, then all at once he saw that there was a trap-door
close by the feather. He raised it up, found some steps, and went down
them, and then he came to another door, knocked at it, and heard somebody inside calling,

> *Little green maiden small,*
> *Hopping hither and thither;*
> *Hop to the door,*
> *And quickly see who is there.*

The door opened, and he saw a great, fat toad sitting, and round about
her a crowd of little toads. The fat toad asked what he wanted? He answered, "I should like to have the prettiest and finest carpet in the world."
Then she called a young one and said,

> *Little green maiden small,*
> *Hopping hither and thither,*
> *Hop quickly and bring me*
> *The great box here.*

The young toad brought the box, and the fat toad opened it, and gave
Simpleton a carpet out of it, so beautiful and so fine, that on the earth
above, none could have been woven like it. Then he thanked her, and
ascended again. The two others had, however, looked on their youngest
brother as so stupid that they believed he would find and bring nothing
at all. "Why should we give ourselves a great deal of trouble to search?"
said they, and got some coarse handkerchiefs from the first shepherds'
wives whom they met, and carried them home to the King. At the same
time Simpleton also came back, and brought his beautiful carpet, and
when the King saw it he was astonished, and said, "If justice be done,
the kingdom belongs to the youngest." But the two others let their father
have no peace, and said that it was impossible that Simpleton, who in
everything lacked understanding, should be King, and entreated him to
make a new agreement with them. Then the father said, "He who brings
me the most beautiful ring shall inherit the kingdom," and led the three
brothers out, and blew into the air three feathers, which they were to follow. Those of the two eldest again went east and west, and Simpleton's
feather flew straight up, and fell down near the door into the earth. Then
he went down again to the fat toad, and told her that he wanted the most
beautiful ring. She at once ordered her great box to be brought, and gave
him a ring out of it, which sparkled with jewels, and was so beautiful that
no goldsmith on earth would have been able to make it. The two eldest

laughed at Simpleton for going to seek a golden ring. They gave themselves no trouble, but knocked the nails out of an old carriage-ring, and took it to the King; but when Simpleton produced his golden ring, his father again said, "The kingdom belongs to him." The two eldest did not cease from tormenting the King until he made a third condition, and declared that the one who brought the most beautiful woman home should have the kingdom. He again blew the three feathers into the air, and they flew as before.

Then Simpleton without more ado went down to the fat toad, and said, "I am to take home the most beautiful woman!" "Oh," answered the toad, "the most beautiful woman! She is not at hand at the moment, but still thou shalt have her." She gave him a yellow turnip which had been hollowed out, to which six mice were harnessed. Then Simpleton said quite mournfully, "What am I to do with that?" The toad answered, "Just put one of my little toads into it." Then he seized one at random out of the circle, and put her into the yellow coach, but hardly was she seated inside it than she turned into a wonderfully beautiful maiden, and the turnip into a coach, and the six mice into horses. So he kissed her, and drove off quickly with the horses, and took her to the King. His brothers came afterwards; they had given themselves no trouble at all to seek beautiful girls, but had brought with them the first peasant women they chanced to meet. When the King saw them he said, "After my death the kingdom belongs to my youngest son." But the two eldest deafened the King's ears afresh with their clamour, "We cannot consent to Simpleton's being King," and demanded that the one whose wife could leap through a ring which hung in the centre of the hall should have the preference. They thought, "The peasant women can do that easily; they are strong enough, but the delicate maiden will jump herself to death." The aged King agreed likewise to this. Then the two peasant women jumped, and jumped through the ring, but were so stout that they fell, and their coarse arms and legs broke in two. And then the pretty maiden whom Simpleton had brought with him, sprang, and sprang through as lightly as a deer, and all opposition had to cease. So he received the crown, and has ruled wisely for a length of time.

554: The Grateful Animals

The Queen Bee

The Queen Bee
(*Germany*)

Two king's sons once started to seek adventures, and fell into a wild, reckless way of living, and gave up all thoughts of going home again. Their third and youngest brother, who was called Witling, and had remained behind, started off to seek them; and when at last he found them, they jeered at his simplicity in thinking that he could make his way in the world, while they who were so much cleverer were unsuccessful.

But they all three went on together until they came to an ant-hill, which the two eldest brothers wished to stir up, that they might see the little ants hurry about in their fright and carrying off their eggs, but Witling said, "Leave the little creatures alone, I will not suffer them to be disturbed."

And they went on farther until they came to a lake, where a number of ducks were swimming about. The two eldest brothers wanted to catch a couple and cook them, but Witling would not allow it, and said, "Leave the creatures alone, I will not suffer them to be killed."

And then they came to a bee's-nest in a tree, and there was so much honey in it that it overflowed and ran down the trunk. The two eldest brothers then wanted to make a fire beneath the tree, that the bees might be stifled by the smoke, and then they could get at the honey. But Witling prevented them, saying, "Leave the little creatures alone, I will not suffer them to be stifled."

At last the three brothers came to a castle where there were in the stables many horses standing, all of stone, and the brothers went through all the rooms until they came to a door at the end secured with three locks, and in the middle of the door a small opening through which they could look into the room. And they saw a little grey-haired man sitting at a table. They called out to him once, twice, and he did not hear, but at the third time he got up, undid the locks, and came out. Without speaking a word he led them to a table loaded with all sorts of good things, and when they had eaten and drunk he showed to each his bed-chamber.

The next morning the little grey man came to the eldest brother, and beckoning him, brought him to a table of stone, on which were written three things directing by what means the castle could be delivered from its enchantment. The first thing was that in the wood under the moss lay the pearls belonging to the princess—a thousand in number—and they were to be sought for and collected, and if he who should undertake the task had not finished it by sunset, if but one pearl were missing, he must be turned to stone. So the eldest brother went out, and searched all day, but at the end of it he had only found one hundred; just as was said on the table of stone came to pass and he was turned into stone. The second brother undertook the adventure next day, but it fared with him no better than with the first; he found two hundred pearls, and was turned into stone. And so at last it was Witling's turn, and he began to search in the moss; but it was a very tedious business to find the pearls, and he grew so out of heart that he sat down on a stone and began to weep. As he was sitting thus, up came the ant-king with five thousand ants, whose lives had been saved through Witling's pity, and it was not very long before the little insects had collected all the pearls and put them in a heap.

Now the second thing ordered by the table of stone was to get the key of the princess's sleeping-chamber out of the lake. And when Witling came to the lake, the ducks whose lives he had saved came swimming, and dived below, and brought up the key from the bottom.

The third thing that had to be done was the most difficult, and that was to choose out the youngest and loveliest of the three princesses, as they lay sleeping. All bore a perfect resemblance each to the other, and only differed in this, that before they went to sleep each one had eaten a different sweetmeat, the eldest a piece of sugar, the second a little syrup, and the third a spoonful of honey. Now the Queen-bee of those bees that Witling had protected from the fire came at this moment, and trying the lips of all three, settled on those of the one that had eaten honey, and so it was that the king's son knew which to choose.

Then the spell was broken; everyone awoke from stony sleep, and took their right form again. And Witling married the youngest and loveliest princess, and became king after her father's death. But his two brothers had to put up with the two other sisters.

The Sea-Hare
(*Germany*)

There was once upon a time a princess, who, high under the battlements in her castle, had an apartment with twelve windows, which looked out in every possible direction, and when she climbed up to it and looked around her, she could inspect her whole kingdom. When she looked out of the first, her sight was more keen than that of any other human being; from the second she could see still better, from the third more distinctly still, and so it went on, until the twelfth, from which she saw everything above the earth and under the earth, and nothing at all could be kept secret from her. Moreover, as she was haughty, and would be subject to no one, but wished to keep the dominion for herself alone, she caused it to be proclaimed that no one should ever be her husband who could not conceal himself from her so effectually that it should be quite impossible for her to find him. He who tried this, however, and was discovered by her, was to have his head struck off, and stuck on a post. Ninety-seven posts with the heads of dead men were already standing before the castle, and no one had come forward for a long time. The princess was delighted, and thought to herself, "Now I shall be free as long as I live." Then three brothers appeared before her, and announced to her that they were desirous of trying their luck. The eldest believed he would be quite safe if he crept into a lime-pit, but she saw him from the first window, made him come out, and had his head cut off. The second crept into the cellar of the palace, but she perceived him also from the first window, and his fate was sealed. His head was placed on the nine and ninetieth post. Then the youngest came to her and entreated her to give him a day for consideration, and also to be so gracious as to overlook it if she should happen to discover him twice, but if he failed the third time, he would look on his life as over. As he was so handsome, and begged so earnestly, she said, "Yes, I will grant thee that, but thou wilt not succeed."

Next day he meditated for a long time how he should hide himself, but all in vain. Then he seized his gun and went out hunting. He saw a raven, took a good aim at him, and was just going to fire, when the bird cried, "Don't shoot; I will make it worth thy while not." He put his gun down, went on, and came to a lake where he surprised a large fish which had come up from the depths below to the surface of the water. When he had aimed at it, the fish cried, "Don't shoot, and I will make it worth thy while." He allowed it to dive down again, went onwards, and met a fox which was lame. He fired and missed it, and the fox cried, "You had much better come here and draw the thorn out of my foot for me." He did this; but then he wanted to kill the fox and skin it, the fox said, "Stop, and I will make it worth thy while." The youth let him go, and then as it was evening, returned home.

Next day he was to hide himself; but howsoever much he puzzled his brains over it, he did not know where. He went into the forest to the raven and said, "I let thee live on, so now tell me where I am to hide myself, so that the King's daughter shall not see me." The raven hung his head and thought it over for a longtime. At length he croaked, "I have it." He fetched an egg out of his nest, cut it into two parts, and shut the youth inside it; then made it whole again, and seated himself on it. When the King's daughter went to the first window she could not discover him, nor could she from the others, and she began to be uneasy, but from the eleventh she saw him. She ordered the raven to be shot, and the egg to be brought and broken, and the youth was forced to come out. She said,

"For once thou art excused, but if thou dost not do better than this, thou art lost!"

Next day he went to the lake, called the fish to him and said, "I suffered thee to live, now tell me where to hide myself so that the King's daughter may not see me." The fish thought for a while, and at last cried, "I have it! I will shut thee up in my stomach." He swallowed him, and went down to the bottom of the lake. The King's daughter looked through her windows, and even from the eleventh did not see him, and was alarmed; but at length from the twelfth she saw him. She ordered the fish to be caught and killed, and then the youth appeared. Everyone can imagine what a state of mind he was in. She said, "Twice thou art forgiven, but be sure that thy head will be set on the hundredth post."

On the last day, he went with a heavy heart into the country, and met the fox. "Thou knowest how to find all kinds of hiding-places," said he; "I let thee live, now advise me where I shall hide myself so that the King's daughter shall not discover me." "That's a hard task," answered the fox, looking very thoughtful. At length he cried, "I have it!" and went with him to a spring, dipped himself in it, and came out as a stall-keeper in the market, and dealer in animals. The youth had to dip himself in the water also, and was changed into a small sea-hare. The merchant went into the town, and showed the pretty little animal, and many persons gathered together to see it. At length the King's daughter came likewise, and as she liked it very much, she bought it, and gave the merchant a good deal of money for it. Before he gave it over to her, he said to it, "When the King's daughter goes to the window, creep quickly under the braids of her hair." And now the time arrived when she was to search for him. She went to one window after another in turn, from the first to the eleventh, and did not see him. When she did not see him from the twelfth either, she was full of anxiety and anger, and shut it down with such violence that the glass in every window shivered into a thousand pieces, and the whole castle shook.

She went back and felt the sea-hare beneath the braids of her hair. Then she seized it, and threw it on the ground exclaiming, "Away with thee, get out of my sight!" It ran to the merchant, and both of them hurried to the spring, wherein they plunged, and received back their true forms. The youth thanked the fox, and said, "The raven and the fish are idiots compared with thee; thou knowest the right tune to play, there is no denying that!"

The youth went straight to the palace. The princess was already expecting him, and accommodated herself to her destiny. The wedding was solemnized, and now he was king, and lord of all the kingdom. He never told her where he had concealed himself for the third time, and who had helped him, so she believed that he had done everything by his own skill, and she had a great respect for him, for she thought to herself, "He is able to do more than I."

The Grateful Beasts
(*Hungary*)

There was once upon a time a man and woman who had three fine-looking sons, but they were so poor that they had hardly enough food for themselves, let alone their children. So the sons determined to set out into the world and to try their luck. Before starting their mother gave them each a loaf of bread and her blessing, and having taken a tender farewell of her and their father the three set forth on their travels.

The youngest of the three brothers, whose name was Ferko, was a beautiful youth, with a splendid figure, blue eyes, fair hair, and a complexion like milk and roses. His two brothers were as jealous of him as they could be, for they thought that with his good looks he would be sure to be more fortunate than they would ever be.

One day all the three were sitting resting under a tree, for the sun was hot and they were tired of walking. Ferko fell fast asleep, but the other two remained awake, and the eldest said to the second brother, 'What do you say to doing our brother Ferko some harm? He is so beautiful that everyone takes a fancy to him, which is more than they do to us. If we could only get him out of the way we might succeed better.'

'I quite agree with you,' answered the second brother, 'and my advice is to eat up his loaf of bread, and then to refuse to give him a bit of ours until he has promised to let us put out his eyes or break his legs.'

His eldest brother was delighted with this proposal, and the two wicked wretches seized Ferko's loaf and ate it all up, while the poor boy was still asleep.

When he did awake he felt very hungry and turned to eat his bread, but his brothers cried out, 'You ate your loaf in your sleep, you glutton, and you may starve as long as you like, but you won't get a scrap of ours.'

Ferko was at a loss to understand how he could have eaten in his sleep, but he said nothing, and fasted all that day and the next night. But on the following morning he was so hungry that he burst into tears, and implored his brothers to give him a little bit of their bread. Then the cruel creatures laughed, and repeated what they had said the day before; but when Ferko continued to beg and beseech them, the eldest said at last, 'If you will let us put out one of your eyes and break one of your legs, then we will give you a bit of our bread.'

At these words poor Ferko wept more bitterly than before, and bore the torments of hunger till the sun was high in the heavens; then he could stand it no longer, and he consented to allow his left eye to be put out and his left leg to be broken. When this was done he stretched out his hand eagerly for the piece of bread, but his brothers gave him such a tiny scrap that the starving youth finished it in a moment and besought them for a second bit.

But the more Ferko wept and told his brothers that he was dying of hunger, the more they laughed and scolded him for his greed. So he endured the pangs of starvation all that day, but when night came his endurance gave way, and he let his right eye be put out and his right leg broken for a second piece of bread.

After his brothers had thus successfully maimed and disfigured him for life, they left him groaning on the ground and continued their journey without him.

Poor Ferko ate up the scrap of bread they had left him and wept bitterly, but no one heard him or came to his help. Night came on, and the poor blind youth had no eyes to close, and could only crawl along the ground, not knowing in the least where he was going. But when the sun was once more high in the heavens, Ferko felt the blazing heat scorch him, and sought for some cool shady place to rest his aching limbs. He climbed to the top of a hill and lay down in the grass, and as he thought under the shadow of a big tree. But it was no tree he leant against, but a gallows on which two ravens were seated. The one was saying to the other as the weary youth lay down, 'Is there anything the least wonderful or remarkable about this neighbourhood?'

'I should just think there was,' replied the other; 'many things that don't exist anywhere else in the world. There is a lake down there below us, and anyone who bathes in it, though he were at death's door, becomes sound and well on the spot, and those who wash their eyes with the dew on this hill become as sharp-sighted as the eagle, even if they have been blind from their youth.'

'Well,' answered the first raven, 'my eyes are in no want of this healing bath, for, Heaven be praised, they are as good as ever they were; but my wing has been very feeble and weak ever since it was shot by an arrow many years ago, so let us fly at once to the lake that I may be restored to health and strength again.' And so they flew away.

Their words rejoiced Ferko's heart, and he waited impatiently till evening should come and he could rub the precious dew on his sightless eyes.

At last it began to grow dusk, and the sun sank behind the mountains; gradually it became cooler on the hill, and the grass grew wet with dew. Then Ferko buried his face in the ground till his eyes were damp with dewdrops, and in a moment he saw clearer than he had ever done in his life before. The moon was shining brightly, and lighted him to the lake where he could bathe his poor broken legs.

Then Ferko crawled to the edge of the lake and dipped his limbs in the water. No sooner had he done so than his legs felt as sound and strong as they had been before, and Ferko thanked the kind fate that had led him to the hill where he had overheard the ravens' conversation. He filled a bottle with the healing water, and then continued his journey in the best of spirits.

He had not gone far before he met a wolf, who was limping disconsolately along on three legs, and who on perceiving Ferko began to howl dismally.

'My good friend,' said the youth, 'be of good cheer, for I can soon heal your leg,' and with these words he poured some of the precious water over the wolf's paw, and in a minute the animal was springing about sound and well on all fours. The grateful creature thanked his benefactor warmly, and promised Ferko to do him a good turn if he should ever need it.

Ferko continued his way till he came to a ploughed field. Here he noticed a little mouse creeping wearily along on its hind paws, for its front paws had both been broken in a trap.

Ferko felt so sorry for the little beast that he spoke to it in the most friendly manner, and washed its small paws with the healing water. In a moment the mouse was sound and whole, and after thanking the kind physician it scampered away over the ploughed furrows.

Ferko again proceeded on his journey, but he hadn't gone far before a queen bee flew against him, trailing one wing behind her, which had been cruelly torn in two by a big bird. Ferko was no less willing to help her than he had been to help the wolf and the mouse, so he poured some healing drops over the wounded wing. On the spot the queen bee was cured, and turning to Ferko she said, 'I am most grateful for your kindness, and shall reward you some day.' And with these words she flew away humming, gaily.

Then Ferko wandered on for many a long day, and at length reached a strange kingdom. Here, he thought to himself, he might as well go straight to the palace and offer his services to the King of the country, for he had heard that the King's daughter was as beautiful as the day.

So he went to the royal palace, and as he entered the door the first people he saw were his two brothers who had so shamefully ill-treated him. They had managed to obtain places in the King's service, and when they recognised Ferko with his eyes and legs sound and well they were frightened to death, for they feared he would tell the King of their conduct, and that they would be hung.

No sooner had Ferko entered the palace than all eyes were turned on the handsome youth, and the King's daughter herself was lost in admiration, for she had never seen anyone so handsome in her life before. His brothers noticed this, and envy and jealousy were added to their fear, so much so that they determined once more to destroy him. They went to the King and told him that Ferko was a wicked magician, who had come to the palace with the intention of carrying off the Princess.

Then the King had Ferko brought before him, and said, 'You are accused of being a magician who wishes to rob me of my daughter, and I condemn you to death; but if you can fulfil three tasks which I shall set you to do your life shall be spared, on condition you leave the country; but if you cannot perform what I demand you shall be hung on the nearest tree.'

And turning to the two wicked brothers he said, 'Suggest something for him to do; no matter how difficult, he must succeed in it or die.'

They did not think long, but replied, 'Let him build your Majesty in one day a more beautiful palace than this, and if he fails in the attempt let him be hung.'

The King was pleased with this proposal, and commanded Ferko to set to work on the following day. The two brothers were delighted, for they thought they had now got rid of Ferko forever. The poor youth himself was heart-broken, and cursed the hour he had crossed the boundary of the King's domain. As he was wandering disconsolately about the meadows round the palace, wondering how he could escape being put to death, a little bee flew past, and settling on his shoulder whispered in his ear, 'What is troubling you, my kind benefactor? Can I be of any help to you? I am the bee whose wing you healed, and would like to show my gratitude in some way.'

Ferko recognised the queen bee, and said, 'Alas! how could you help me? for I have been set to do a task which no one in the whole world could do, let him be ever such a genius! To-morrow I must build a palace more beautiful than the King's, and it must be finished before evening.'

'Is that all?' answered the bee, 'then you may comfort yourself; for before the sun goes down to-morrow night a palace shall be built unlike any that King has dwelt in before. Just stay here till I come again and tell you that it is finished.' Having said this she flew merrily away, and Ferko, reassured by her words, lay down on the grass and slept peacefully till the next morning.

Early on the following day the whole town was on its feet, and everyone wondered how and where the stranger would build the wonderful palace. The Princess alone was silent and sorrowful, and had cried all night till her pillow was wet, so much did she take the fate of the beautiful youth to heart.

Ferko spent the whole day in the meadows waiting the return of the bee. And when evening was come the queen bee flew by, and perching on his shoulder she said, 'The wonderful palace is ready. Be of good cheer, and lead the King to the hill just outside the city walls.' And humming gaily she flew away again.

Ferko went at once to the King and told him the palace was finished. The whole court went out to see the wonder, and their astonishment was great at the sight which met their eyes. A splendid palace reared itself on the hill just outside the walls of the city, made of the most exquisite flowers that ever grew in mortal garden. The roof was all of crimson roses, the windows of lilies, the walls of white carnations, the floors of glowing auriculas and violets, the doors of gorgeous tulips and narcissi with sunflowers for knockers, and all round hyacinths and other sweet-smelling flowers bloomed in masses, so that the air was perfumed far and near and enchanted all who were present.

This splendid palace had been built by the grateful queen bee, who had summoned all the other bees in the kingdom to help her.

The King's amazement knew no bounds, and the Princess's eyes beamed with delight as she turned them from the wonderful building on the delighted Ferko. But the two brothers had grown quite green with envy, and only declared the more that Ferko was nothing but a wicked magician.

The King, although he had been surprised and astonished at the way his commands had been carried out, was very vexed that the stranger should escape with his life, and turning to the two brothers he said, 'He has certainly accomplished the first task, with the aid no doubt of his diabolical magic; but what shall we give him to do now? Let us make it as difficult as possible, and if he fails he shall die.'

Then the eldest brother replied, 'The corn has all been cut, but it has not yet been put into barns; let the knave collect all the grain in the kingdom into one big heap before to-morrow night, and if as much as a stalk of corn is left let him be put to death.

The Princess grew white with terror when she heard these words; but Ferko felt much more cheerful than he had done the first time, and wandered out into the meadows again, wondering how he was to get out of the difficulty. But he could think of no way of escape. The sun sank to rest and night came on, when a little mouse started out of the grass at Ferko's feet, and said to him, 'I'm delighted to see you, my kind benefactor; but why are you looking so sad? Can I be of any help to you, and thus repay your great kindness to me?'

Then Ferko recognised the mouse whose front paws he had healed, and replied, 'Alas! how can you help me in a matter that is beyond any human power! Before to-morrow night all the grain in the kingdom has to be gathered into one big heap, and if as much as a stalk of corn is wanting I must pay for it with my life.'

'Is that all?' answered the mouse; 'that needn't distress you much. Just trust in me, and before the sun sets again you shall hear that your task is done.' And with these words the little creature scampered away into the fields.

Ferko, who never doubted that the mouse would be as good as its word, lay down comforted on the soft grass and slept soundly till next morning. The day passed slowly, and with the evening came the little mouse and said, 'Now there is not a single stalk of corn left in any field; they are all collected in one big heap on the hill out there.'

Then Ferko went joyfully to the King and told him that all he demanded had been done. And the whole Court went out to see the wonder, and were no less astonished than they had been the first time. For in a heap higher than the King's palace lay all the grain of the country, and not a single stalk of corn had been left behind in any of the fields. And how had all this been done? The little mouse had summoned every other mouse in the land to its help, and together they had collected all the grain in the kingdom.

The King could not hide his amazement, but at the same time his wrath increased, and he was more ready than ever to believe the two brothers, who kept on repeating that Ferko was nothing more nor less than a wicked magician. Only the beautiful Princess rejoiced over Ferko's success, and looked on him with friendly glances, which the youth returned.

The more the cruel King gazed on the wonder before him, the more angry he became, for he could not, in the face of his promise, put the stranger to death. He turned once more to the two brothers and said, 'His diabolical magic has helped him again, but now what third task shall we set him to do? No matter how impossible it is, he must do it or die.'

The eldest answered quickly, 'Let him drive all the wolves of the kingdom on to this hill before to-morrow night. If he does this he may go free; if not he shall be hung as you have said.'

At these words the Princess burst into tears, and when the King saw this he ordered her to be shut up in a high tower and carefully guarded till the dangerous magician should either have left the kingdom or been hung on the nearest tree.

Ferko wandered out into the fields again, and sat down on the stump of a tree wondering what he should do next. Suddenly a big wolf ran up to him, and standing still said, 'I'm very glad to see you again, my kind benefactor. What are you thinking about all alone by yourself? If I can help you in any way only say the word, for I would like to give you a proof of my gratitude.'

Ferko at once recognised the wolf whose broken leg he had healed, and told him what he had to do the following day if he wished to escape with his life. 'But how in the world,' he added, 'am I to collect all the wolves of the kingdom on to that hill over there?'

'If that's all you want done,' answered the wolf, 'you needn't worry yourself. I'll undertake the task, and you'll hear from me again before sunset to-morrow. Keep your spirits up.' And with these words he trotted quickly away.

Then the youth rejoiced greatly, for now he felt that his life was safe; but he grew very sad when he thought of the beautiful Princess, and that he would never see her again if he left the country. He lay down once more on the grass and soon fell fast asleep.

All the next day he spent wandering about the fields, and toward evening the wolf came running to him in a great hurry and said, 'I have collected together all the wolves in the kingdom, and they are waiting for you in the wood. Go quickly to the King, and tell him to go to the hill that he may see the wonder you have done with his own eyes. Then return at once to me and get on my back, and I will help you to drive all the wolves together.'

Then Ferko went straight to the palace and told the King that he was ready to perform the third task if he would come to the hill and see it done. Ferko himself returned to the fields, and mounting on the wolf's back he rode to the wood close by.

Quick as lightning the wolf flew round the wood, and in a minute many hundred wolves rose up before him, increasing in number every moment, till they could be counted by thousands. He drove them all before him on to the hill, where the King and his whole Court and Ferko's two brothers were standing. Only the lovely Princess was not present, for she was shut up in her tower weeping bitterly.

The wicked brothers stamped and foamed with rage when they saw the failure of their wicked designs. But the King was overcome by a sudden terror when he saw the enormous pack of wolves approaching nearer and nearer, and calling out to Ferko he said, 'Enough, enough, we don't want any more.'

But the wolf on whose back Ferko sat, said to its rider, 'Go on! go on!' and at the same moment many more wolves ran up the hill, howling horribly and showing their white teeth.

The King in his terror called out, 'Stop a moment; I will give you half my kingdom if you will drive all the wolves away.' But Ferko pretended not to hear, and drove some more thousands before him, so that everyone quaked with horror and fear.

Then the King raised his voice again and called out, 'Stop! you shall have my whole kingdom, if you will only drive these wolves back to the places they came from.'

But the wolf kept on encouraging Ferko, and said, 'Go on! go on!' So he led the wolves on, till at last they fell on the King and on the wicked brothers, and ate them and the whole Court up in a moment.

Then Ferko went straight to the palace and set the Princess free, and on the same day he married her and was crowned King of the country. And the wolves all went peacefully back to their own homes, and Ferko and his bride lived for many years in peace and happiness together, and were much beloved by great and small in the land.

PROTO-WESTERN-INDO-EUROPEAN

311: Rescue by the Sister

The Old Dame and Her Hen
(*Norway*)

Once on a time there was an old widow who lived far away from the rest of the world, up under a hillside, with her three daughters. She was so poor that she had no stock but one single hen, which she prized as the apple of her eye; in short, it was always cackling at her heels, and she was always running to look after it. Well! one day, all at once, the hen was missing. The old wife went out, and round and round the cottage, looking and calling for her hen, but it was gone, and there was no getting it back.

So the woman said to her eldest daughter, "You must just go out and see if you can find our hen, for have it back we must, even if we have to fetch it out of the hill."

Well! the daughter was ready enough to go, so she set off and walked up and down, and looked and called, but no hen could she find. But all at once, just as she was about to give up the hunt, she heard someone calling out in a cleft in the rock:

> *Your hen trips inside the hill!*
> *Your hen trips inside the hill!*

So she went into the cleft to see what it was, but she had scarce set her foot inside the cleft, before she fell through a trap-door, deep, deep down, into a vault under ground. When she got to the bottom she went through many rooms, each finer than the other; but in the innermost room of all, a great ugly man of the hill-folk came up to her and asked, "Will you be my sweetheart?"

"No! I will not", she said. She wouldn't have him at any price! not she; all she wanted was to get above ground again as fast as ever she could, and to look after her hen which was lost. Then the Man o' the Hill got so angry that he took her up and wrung her head off, and threw both head and trunk down into the cellar.

While this was going on, her mother sat at home waiting and waiting, but no daughter came. So after she had waited a bit longer, and neither heard nor saw anything of her daughter, she said to her midmost daughter that she must go out and see after her sister, and she added:

"You can just give our hen a call at the same time."

Well! the second sister had to get off, and the very same thing befell her;

she went about looking and calling, and all at once she too heard a voice away in the cleft of the rock saying:

> *Your hen trips inside the hill!*
> *Your hen trips inside the hill!*

She thought this strange, and went to see what it could be; and so she too fell through the trap-door, deep, deep down, into the vault. There she went from room to room, and in the innermost one the Man o' the Hill came to her and asked if she would be his sweetheart? No! that she wouldn't; all she wanted was to get above ground again, and hunt for her hen which was lost. So the Man o' the Hill got angry, and took her up and wrung her head off, and threw both head and trunk down into the cellar.

Now, when the old dame had sat and waited seven lengths and seven breadths for her second daughter, and could neither see nor hear anything of her, she said to the youngest:

"Now, you really must set off and see after your sisters. 'Twas silly to lose the hen, but 'twill be sillier still if we lose both your sisters; and you can give the hen a call at the same time"—for the old dame's heart was still set on her hen.

Yes! the youngest was ready enough to go; so she walked up and down, Wanting for her sisters and calling the hen, but she could neither see nor hear anything of them. So at last she too came up to the cleft in the rock, and heard how something said:

> *Your hen trips inside the hill!*
> *Your hen trips inside the hill!*

She thought this strange, so she too went to see what it was, and fell through the trap-door too, deep, deep down, into a vault. When she reached the bottom she went from one room to another, each grander than the other; but she wasn't at all afraid, and took good time to look about her. So, as she was peeping into this and that, she cast her eye on the trap-door into the cellar, and looked down it, and what should she see there but her sisters, who lay dead. She had scarce time to slam to the trap-door before the Man o' the Hill came to her and asked:

"Will you be my sweetheart?"

"With all my heart", answered the girl, for she saw very well how it had gone with her sisters. So, when the Man o' the Hill heard that, he got her the finest clothes in the world; she had only to ask for them, or for anything else she had a mind to, and she got what she wanted, so glad was the Man o' the Hill that anyone would be his sweetheart.

But when she had been there a little while, she was one day even more doleful and downcast than was her wont. So the Man o' the Hill asked her what was the matter, and why she was in such dumps.

"Ah!" said the girl, "it's because I can't get home to my mother. She's hard pinched, I know, for meat and drink, and has no one with her."

"Well!" said the Man o' the Hill, "I can't let you go to see her; but just stuff some meat and drink into a sack, and I'll carry it to her."

Yes! she would do so, she said, with many thanks; but at the bottom of the sack she stuffed a lot of gold and silver, and afterwards she laid a little food on the top of the gold and silver. Then she told the ogre the sack was ready, but he must be sure not to look into it. So he gave his word he wouldn't, and set off. Now, as the Man o' the Hill walked off, she peeped out after him through a chink in the trap-door; but when he had gone a bit on the way, he said:

"This sack is so heavy, I'll just see what there is inside it."

And so he was about to untie the mouth of the sack, but the girl called out to him:

> *I see what you're at!*
> *I see what you're at!*

"The deuce you do!" said the Man o' the Hill; "then you must have plaguey sharp eyes in your head, that's all!"

So he threw the sack over his shoulder, and dared not try to look into it again. When he reached the widow's cottage, he threw the sack in through the cottage door, and said:

"Here you have meat and drink from your daughter; she doesn't want for anything."

So, when the girl had been in the hill a good bit longer, one day a billy-goat fell down the trap-door.

"Who sent for you, I should like to know? you long-bearded beast!" said the Man o' the Hill, who was in an awful rage, and with that he whipped up the goat, and wrung his head off, and threw him down into the cellar.

"Oh!" said the girl, "why did you do that? I might have had the goat to play with down here."

"Well!" said the Man o' the Hill, "you needn't be so down in the mouth about it, I should think, for I can soon put life into the billy-goat again."

So saying, he took a flask which hung up against the wall, put the billy-goat's head on his body again, and smeared it with some ointment out of the flask, and he was as well and as lively as ever again.

"Ho! ho!" said the girl to herself; "that flask is worth something—that it is."

So when she had been some time longer in the hill, she watched for a day when the Man o' the Hill was away, took her eldest sister, and putting her head on her shoulders, smeared her with some of the ointment out of the flask, just as she had seen the Man o' the Hill do with the billy-goat, and in a trice her sister came to life again. Then the girl stuffed her into a sack, laid a little food over her, and as soon as the Man o' the Hill came home, she said to him:

"Dear friend! Now do go home to my mother with a morsel of food again; poor thing! she's both hungry and thirsty, I'll be bound; and besides that, she's all alone in the world. But you must mind and not look into the sack."

Well! he said he would carry the sack; and he said, too, that he would not look into it; but when he had gone a little way, he thought the sack got awfully heavy; and when he had gone a bit farther he said to himself:

"Come what will, I must see what's inside this sack, for however sharp her eyes may be, she can't see me all this way off."

But just as he was about to untie the sack, the girl who sat inside the sack called out:

> I see what you're at!
> I see what you're at!

"The deuce you do!" said the ogre; "then you must have plaguey sharp eyes"; for he thought all the while it was the girl inside the hill who was speaking. So he didn't care so much as to peep into the sack again, but carried it straight to her mother as fast as he could, and when he got to the cottage door he threw it in through the door, and bawled out:

"Here you have meat and drink from your daughter; she wants for nothing."

Now, when the girl had been in the hill a while longer, she did the very same thing with her other sister. She put her head on her shoulders, smeared her with ointment out of the flask, brought her to life, and stuffed her into the sack; but this time she crammed in also as much gold and silver as the sack would hold, and over all laid a very little food.

"Dear friend", she said to the Man o' the Hill, "you really must run home to my mother with a little food again; and mind you don't look into the sack."

Yes! the Man o' the Hill was ready enough to do as she wished, and he gave his word too that he wouldn't look into the sack; but when he had gone a bit of the way he began to think the sack got awfully heavy, and when he had gone a bit further, he could scarce stagger along under it, so he set it down, and was just about to untie the string and look into it, when the girl inside the sack bawled out:

> I see what you're at!
> I see what you're at!

"The deuce you do", said the Man o' the Hill, "then you must have plaguey sharp eyes of your own."

Well, he dared not try to look into the sack, but made all the haste he could, and carried the sack straight to the girl's mother. When he got to the cottage door he threw the sack in through the door, and roared out:

"Here you have food from your daughter; she wants for nothing."

So when the girl had been there a good while longer, the Man o' the Hill made up his mind to go out for the day; then the girl shammed to be sick and sorry, and pouted and fretted.

"It's no use your coming home before twelve o'clock at night", she said, "for I shan't be able to have supper ready before—I'm so sick and poorly."

But when the Man o' the Hill was well out of the house, she stuffed some of her clothes with straw, and stuck up this lass of straw in the corner by the chimney, with a besom in her hand, so that it looked just as if she herself were standing there. After that she stole off home, and got a sharp-shooter to stay in the cottage with her mother.

So when the clock struck twelve, or just about it, home came the Man o' the Hill, and the first thing he said to the straw-girl was, "Give me something to eat."

But she answered him never a word.

"Give me something to eat, I say!" called out the Man o' the Hill, "for I am almost starved."

No! she hadn't a word to throw at him.

"Give me something to eat!" roared out the ogre the third time." I think you'd better open your ears and hear what I say, or else I'll wake you up, that I will!"

No! the girl stood just as still as ever; so he flew into a rage, and gave her such a slap in the face that the straw flew all about the room; but when he saw that, he knew he had been tricked, and began to hunt everywhere; and at last, when he came to the cellar, and found both the girl's sisters missing, he soon saw how the cat jumped, and ran off to the cottage, saying, "I'll soon pay her off!"

But when he reached the cottage, the sharp-shooter fired off his piece, and then the Man o' the Hill dared not go into the house, for he thought it was thunder. So he set off home again as fast as he could lay legs to the ground; but what do you think, just as he got to the trap-door, the sun rose and the Man o' the Hill burst.

Oh! if one only knew where the trap-door was, I'll be bound there's a whole heap of gold and silver down there still!

The Cobbler and His Three Daughters
(*Spain*)

Like many others in the world, there was a cobbler who had three daughters. They were very poor. He only earned enough just to feed his children. He did not know what would become of him. He went about in his grief, walking, walking sadly on, and he meets a gentleman, who asks him where he is going, melancholy like that. He answers him, "Even if I shall tell you, I shall get no relief."

"Yes, yes; who knows? Tell it."

"I have three daughters, and I have not work enough to maintain them. I have famine in the house."

"If it is only that, we will manage it. You will give me one of your daughters, and I will give you so much money."

The father was very grieved to make any such bargain; but at last he comes down to that. He gives him his eldest daughter. This gentleman takes her to his palace, and, after having passed some time there, he said to her that he has a short journey to make—that he will leave her all the keys, that she might see everything, but that there is one key that she must not make use of—that it would bring misfortune on her. He locks the door on the young lady. This young girl goes into all the rooms, and finds them very beautiful, and she was curious to see what there was in that which was forbidden. She goes in, and sees heaps of dead bodies. Judge of her fright! With her trembling she lets the key fall upon the ground. She trembles for the coming of her husband. He arrives, and asks her if she has entered the forbidden chamber. She tells him "Yes." He takes her and puts her into an underground dungeon; hardly did he give her enough to eat (to live on), and that was human flesh.

This cobbler had finished his money, and he was again melancholy. The gentleman meets him again, and says to him, "Your other daughter is not happy alone; you must give me another daughter. When she is happy, I will send her back; and I will give you so much money."

The father did not like it; but he was so poor that, in order to have a little money, he gives him his daughter. The gentleman takes her home with him, like the other. After some days he said to her too, "I must take a short journey. I will give you all the keys of the house, but do not touch such a key of such a room."

He locks the house-door, and goes off, after having left her the food she needed. This young girl goes into all the rooms, and, as she was curious, she went to look into the forbidden chamber. She was so terribly frightened at the sight of so many dead bodies in this room, that she lets the key fall, and it gets stained. Our young girl was trembling as to what should become of her when the master should come back. He arrives, and the first thing he asks—

"Have you been in that room?"

She told him "Yes." He takes her underground, like her other sister.

This cobbler had finished his money, and he was in misery; when the gentleman comes to him again, and says to him, "I will give you a great deal of money if you will let your daughter come to my house for a few days; the three will be happier together, and I will send you the two back again together."

The father believes it, and gives him his third daughter. The gentleman gives him the money, and he takes this young girl, like the others. At the end of some days he leaves her, saying that he is going to make a short journey. He gives her all the keys of the house, saying to her—

"You will go into all the rooms except this one," pointing out the key to her. He locks the outside door, and goes off. This young girl goes straight, straight to the forbidden chamber; she opens it, and think of her horror at seeing so many dead people. She thought that he would kill her too, and, as there were all kinds of arms in this chamber, she takes a sabre with her, and hides it under her dress. She goes a little further on, and sees her two sisters almost dying with hunger, and a young man in the same condition. She takes care of them as well as she can till the gentleman comes home. On his arrival, he asks her—

"Have you been in that room?"

She says, "Yes;" and, in giving him back the keys, she lets them fall on the ground, on purpose, and at the instant that this gentleman stoops to pick them up, the young lady cuts off his head (with her sword). Oh, how glad she was! Quickly she runs to deliver her sisters and that young man, who was the son of a king. She sends for her father, the cobbler, and leaves him there with his two daughters, and the youngest daughter goes away with her young gentleman, after being married to him. If they lived well, they died well too.

Peerifool
(*Scotland*)

There was once a king and queen in Rousay who had three daughters. The king died and the queen was living in a small house with her daughters. They kept a cow and a kale yard; they found their cabbage was all being taken away. The eldest daughter said to the queen, she would take a blanket about her and would sit and watch what was going away with the kale. So when the night came she went out to watch. In a short time a very big giant came into the yard; he began to cut the kale and throw it in a big cubby[1]. So he cut till he had it well filled.

The princess was always asking him why he was taking her mother's kale. He was saying to her, if she was not quiet he would take her too.

As soon as he had filled his cubby he took her by a leg and an arm and threw her on the top of his cubby of kale and away home he went with her.

When he got home he told her what work she had to do; she had to milk the cow and put her up to the hills called Bloodfield, and then she had to take wool, and wash and tease it and comb and card, and spin and make claith[2].

When the giant went out she milked the cow and put her to the hills. Then she put on the pot and made porridge to herself. As she was supping it, a great many peerie[3] yellow-headed folk came running, calling out to give them some. She said:

> *Little for one, and less for two,*
> *And never a grain have I for you.*

When she came to work the wool, none of that work could she do at all.

The giant came home at night and found she had not done her work. He took her and began at her head, and peeled the skin off all the way down her back and over her feet. Then he threw her on the couples[4] among the hens.

The same adventure befell the second girl. If her sister could do little with the wool she could do less.

When the giant came home he found her work not done. He began at the crown of her head and peeled a strip of skin all down her back and over her feet, and threw her on the couples beside her sister. They lay there and could not speak nor come down.

The next night the youngest princess said she would take a blanket about her and go to watch what had gone away with her sisters. Ere long, in came a giant with a big cubby, and began to cut the kale.

She was asking why he was taking her mother's kale. He was saying if she was not quiet he would take her too. He took her by a leg and an arm and threw her on the top of his cubby and carried her away.

Next morning he gave her the same work as he had given her sisters.

When he was gone out she milked the cow and put her to the high hills. Then she put on the pot and made porridge to herself. When the peerie

1   Straw basket.
2   Cloth.
3   Little.
4   Rafters.

yellow-headed folk came asking for some she told them to get something to sup with. Some got heather cows and some got broken dishes; some got one thing, and some another, and they all got some of her porridge.

After they were all gone a peerie yellow-headed boy came in and asked her if she had any work to do; he could do any work with wool. She said she had plenty, but would never be able to pay him for it. He said all he was asking for it was to tell him his name. She thought that would be easy to do, and gave him the wool.

When it was getting dark an old woman came in and asked her for lodging. The princess said she could not give her that, but asked her if she had any news. But the old woman had none, and went away to lie out.

There is a high knowe[1] near the place, and the old woman sat under it for shelter. She found it very warm. She was always climbing up, and when she came to the top she heard someone inside saying, "Tease, teasers, tease; card, carders, card; spin, spinners, spin, for Peerie Fool, Peerie Fool is my name." There was a crack in the knowe, and light coming out. She looked in and saw a great many peerie folk working, and a peerie yellow-headed boy running round them calling out that.

The old woman thought she would get lodging if she went to give this news, so she came back and told the princess the whole of it.

The princess went on saying "Peerie Fool, Peerie Fool," till the yellow-headed boy came with all the wool made into claith.

He asked what was his name, and she guessed names; and he jumped about and said, "No."

At last she said, "Peerie Fool is your name." He threw down the wool and ran off very angry.

As the giant was coming home he met a great many peerie yellow-headed folk, some with their eyes hanging on their cheeks, and some with their tongues hanging on their breasts. He asked them what was the matter. They told him it was working so hard pulling wool so fine. He said he had a good wife at home, and if she was safe, never would he allow her to do any work again.

When he came home she was all safe, and had a great many webs lying all ready, and he was very kind to her.

Next day when he went out she found her sisters, and took them down from the couples. She put the skin on their backs again, and she put her eldest sister in a cazy,[2] and put all the fine things she could find with her, and grass on the top.

When the giant came home she asked him to take the cazy to her mother with some food for her cow. He was so pleased with her he would do

1 Knoll.
2 Basket.

anything for her, and took it away.

Next day she did the same with her other sister. She told him she would have the last of the food she had to send her mother for the cow ready next night. She told him she was going a bit from home, and would leave it ready for him. She got into the cazy with all the fine things she could find, and covered herself with grass. He took the cazy and carried it to the queen's house. She and her daughters had a big boiler of boiling water ready. They couped[1] it about him when he was under the window, and that was the end of the giant.

1 Overturned.

332: Godfather Death

Godfather Death

Godfather Death
(*Germany*)

A poor man had twelve children and was forced to work night and day to give them even bread. When therefore the thirteenth came into the world, he knew not what to do in his trouble, but ran out into the great highway, and resolved to ask the first person whom he met to be godfather. The first to meet him was the good God who already knew what filled his heart, and said to him, "Poor man, I pity thee. I will hold thy child at its christening, and will take charge of it and make it happy on earth." The man said, "Who art thou?" "I am God." "Then I do not desire to have thee for a godfather," said the man; "thou givest to the rich, and leavest the poor to hunger." Thus spoke the man, for he did not know how wisely God apportions riches and poverty. He turned therefore away from the Lord, and went farther. Then the Devil came to him and said, "What seekest thou? If thou wilt take me as a godfather for thy child, I will give him gold in plenty and all the joys of the world as well." The man asked, "Who art thou?" "I am the Devil." "Then I do not desire to have thee for godfather," said the man; "thou deceivest men and leadest them astray." He went onwards, and then came Death striding up to him with withered legs, and said, "Take me as godfather." The man asked, "Who art thou?" "I am Death, and I make all equal." Then said the man, "Thou art the right one, thou takest the rich as well as the poor, without distinction; thou shalt be godfather." Death answered, "I will make thy child rich and famous, for he who has me for a friend can lack nothing." The man said, "Next Sunday is the christening; be there at the right time." Death appeared as he had promised, and stood godfather quite in the usual way.

When the boy had grown up, his godfather one day appeared and bade him go with him. He led him forth into a forest, and showed him a herb which grew there, and said, "Now shalt thou receive thy godfather's present. I make thee a celebrated physician. When thou art called to a patient, I will always appear to thee. If I stand by the head of the sick man, thou mayst say with confidence that thou wilt make him well again, and if thou givest him of this herb he will recover; but if I stand by the patient's feet, he is mine, and thou must say that all remedies are in vain, and that no physician in the world could save him. But beware of using the herb against my will, or it might fare ill with thee."

It was not long before the youth was the most famous physician in the whole world. "He had only to look at the patient and he knew his condition at once, and if he would recover, or must needs die." So they said of him, and from far and wide people came to him, sent for him when they had anyone ill, and gave him so much money that he soon became a rich man. Now it so befell that the King became ill, and the physician was summoned, and was to say if recovery were possible. But when he came to the bed, Death was standing by the feet of the sick man, and the herb did not grow which could save him. "If I could but cheat Death for once," thought the physician, "he is sure to take it ill if I do, but, as I am his godson, he will shut one eye; I will risk it." He therefore took up the sick man, and laid him the other way, so that now Death was standing by his head. Then he gave the King some of the herb, and he recovered and grew healthy again. But Death came to the physician, looking very black and angry, threatened him with his finger, and said, "Thou hast overreached me; this time I will pardon it, as thou art my godson; but if thou venturest it again, it will cost thee thy neck, for I will take thee thyself away with me."

Soon afterwards the King's daughter fell into a severe illness. She was his only child, and he wept day and night, so that he began to lose the sight of his eyes, and he caused it to be made known that whosoever rescued her from death should be her husband and inherit the crown. When the physician came to the sick girl's bed, he saw Death by her feet. He ought to have remembered the warning given by his godfather, but he was so infatuated by the great beauty of the King's daughter, and the happiness of becoming her husband, that he flung all thought to the winds. He did not see that Death was casting angry glances on him, that he was raising his hand in the air, and threatening him with his withered fist. He raised up the sick girl, and placed her head where her feet had lain. Then he gave her some of the herb, and instantly her cheeks flushed red, and life stirred afresh in her.

When Death saw that for a second time he was defrauded of his own property, he walked up to the physician with long strides, and said, "All is over with thee, and now the lot falls on thee," and seized him so firmly with his ice-cold hand, that he could not resist, and led him into a cave below the earth. There he saw how thousands and thousands of candles were burning in countless rows, some large, others half-sized, others small. Every instant some were extinguished, and others again burnt up, so that the flames seemed to leap hither and thither in perpetual change. "See," said Death, "these are the lights of men's lives. The large ones belong to children, the half-sized ones to married people in their prime, the little ones belong to old people; but children and young folks likewise have often only a tiny candle." "Show me the light of my life," said the physician, and he thought that it would be still very tall. Death pointed to a little end which was just threatening to go out, and said, "Behold, it is there." "Ah, dear godfather," said the horrified physician, "light a new one for me, do it for love of me, that I may enjoy my life, be King, and the husband of the King's beautiful daughter." "I cannot," answered Death, "one must go out before a new one is lighted." "Then place the old one on a new one, that will go on burning at once when the old one has come to an end," pleaded the physician. Death behaved as if he were going to fulfill his wish, and took hold of a tall new candle; but as he desired to revenge himself, he purposely made a mistake in fixing it, and the little piece fell down and was extinguished. Immediately the physician fell on the ground, and now he himself was in the hands of Death.

Dr. Urssenbeck, Physician of Death
(*Austria*)

The city of Vienna has always been distinguished by famous physicians, and so at the end of the fifteenth century there were several very distinguished doctors there. Among them, the Rector Dr. Urssenbeck of the University, founded by Duke Rudolf IV in 1365, enjoyed particular fame in 1482, especially because he was said to be the only one who knew for sure whether a patient would get well or die. From this he received the name Doctor Death, and the house in which he lived and which was also his property was known under the name the "Doctor Death House". It stood next to the so-called Basilisk House (in Schönlaterngasse).

No wonder that its name was associated with a variety of miraculous legends, because our ancestors in those still unenlightened times preferred to interpret even the most natural things in supernatural ways. Thus, a very peculiar story was told about Dr. Urssenbeck. According to this story, he was not actually a learned doctor, but in earlier years had been engaged in the honourable weaving trade in the small town of Deckendorf near Straubigen in Bavaria.

He is said to have been quite a poor weaver. It happened that a great famine broke out and he was made to suffer great hardship with his wife and children. Then heaven gave him a twelfth child, which was a great misery for the poor couple. Indeed, the circumstances were so sad that the poor father could not even find a godfather among his acquaintances and relatives in the small town.

Paul Urssenbeck therefore took his walking stick and wished to knock on the door of one of his friends in the neighboring town and ask him to be godfather to his child.

The way there was hard enough, and when he put forth to him his plea, it was kindly but firmly refused.

Again the poor man went on his way without having achieved anything, and was so desperate that he decided not to return to his family at all, but rather to die. When he came to a deep dark forest, he sat down and begged for Death to finally deliver him from his heavy heartache.

Suddenly the darkness of the forest lightened; a tall figure stood before him wrapped in a dark cloak, his face shaded by a large hood. "I am the Death whom thou dost soot, what wilt thou have of me?" he spake. As much as the poor weaver wished to die earlier, he now preferred to live. He fell down before Death and begged him for mercy. He told him how miserable he was, how his poor children had to suffer bitter hardship, how he was unable to care for his own with all his hard work, and how he could not even find a godfather for his smallest child.

Death listened attentively and said at last, "Well, it is not my business to be godfather, but if thou art satisfied, I will help thee out of thy distress and lift thy child from the baptism. Just tell me the place and the hour when thy child is to be baptized and I shall not fail to appear under thy roof."

What could the desperate weaver do but accept the kind offer of Death? If as he had learned people had no mercy, he was obliged to turn to supernatural beings anyway. He therefore thanked his friend, told him what he needed to know and took leave of him. When Urssenbeck came home, he said that he had a godfather, but he did not know who he was.

The day on which the baptism of the child was to take place approached; in the poor house all was decorated as well as could be for the joyful celebration. The hour of the holy sacrament had arrived, everyone was already gathered, only the godfather was still missing. In anxious expectation the father of the house kept an eye on the door—then there were three knocks, the door opened and the sinister godfather entered. Those present could not help feeling a certain horror at the strange figure.

Now they went away to the church where the holy sacrament quickly proceeded. When the ceremony was over and Death had handed the little child back to the father, he beckoned him to join him later. The child was brought home from the church, and trembling, though not without hope, the weaver went to the fine godfather, whom he soon reached.

"My dear friend," Death said to the weaver, "I should like to give thee a gift for thy child, but I have neither gold nor silver, but I can do something for thee—thou canst still become a rich and respected man through me. Listen! I wish to entrust thee with a secret and if thou shouldst use it properly, it will make thee very happy. I am present to every seriously ill person, of course invisible to all; if I sit by his feet, he will recover, but if I sit by his head, he shall die. Now I give thee the gift of seeing me at all times, and so thou canst easily determine whether the sick person shall live or whether he must die. So, use honestly what I have entrusted to thee, and farewell."

With that, Death disappeared and the weaver awoke as if from a dream.

This was a delicious secret indeed, and soon enough the perfect opportunity was found to use it. The poor weaver became a sought-after physician, his former hardship was replaced by great affluence, and finally Urssenbeck took his wife and twelve children and moved with them to the glorious city of Vienna. Soon he made a famous name for himself here as well; "Doctor Death" came into the most distinguished circles and just like that, gold flowed his way.

But howsoever good the poor weaver was, so arrogant was the rich doctor! The greater his wealth became, the greater his greed, and if he had had all the gold in the world, he still would not have been satisfied.

It happened that he was once called to a very rich, highly respected, but also seriously ill man. No sooner had he looked at him than he declared that the sick man must die, for he saw death sitting at his head. He was then offered a great fortune if he would make the sick man well, many thousands and thousands of ducats. The temptation was great and Urssenbeck's greed could not resist it. He then fell for a trick. He went out, fetched four of the handsomest servants, and told them to turn the bed around quickly.

Little sense as it made to them, they went to the hospital and did as they were ordered. Death was now sitting at the feet of the sick man. The rich man was saved.

With a dreadful look at Urssenbeck, Death stood up and moved away. The doctor, not however without some fear, pocketed the money, climbed into his litter, and let himself be borne away. They then came to a narrow pass. Urssenbeck made the bearers halt, got out of the litter, let them go ahead, and slowly followed them.

Suddenly, Death was standing next to him. "Luckless man, what hast thou done?" he said to the terrified Urssenbeck. "Die thou must, and prepare thyself. For the life of the one thou hast saved, I take thine."

To die now, when he had so many riches, was awful for Urssenbeck. He fell at death's feet and begged him for mercy. But he was inexorable. A small door suddenly opened and Urssenbeck saw himself in a large hall with thousands of lights burning. But Death said, "As thou seest these lights burning, each one meaneth the life of a human being; here look thou at thy light, it hath burned down to a small stump, it will soon go out." Then, in his mortal fear, Urssenbeck reached for a second light to take some of its wax and dole it out to his light. But as soon as he touched his stump, its flame went out and Urssenbeck fell to the ground, dead.

In the evening, he was found lying in the narrow pass and was buried in St. Stephen's Cathedral.

Death and the Doctor
(*Norway*)

Once on a time there was a lad who had lived as a servant a long time with a man of the North Country. This man was a master at ale-brewing; it was so out-of-the-way good the like of it was not to be found. So, when the lad was to leave his place and the man was to pay him the wages he had earned, he would take no other pay than a keg of Yule-ale. Well, he got it and set off with it, and he carried it both far and long, but the longer he carried the keg the heavier it got, and so he began to look about to see if anyone were coming with whom he might have a drink, that the ale might lessen and the keg lighten. And after a long, long time, he met an old man with a big beard.

"Good day," said the man.

"Good day to you," said the lad.

"Whither away?" asked the man.

"I'm looking after someone to drink with, and get my keg lightened," said the lad.

"Can't you drink as well with me as with anyone else?" said the man. "I have fared both far and wide, and I am both tired and thirsty."

"Well! why shouldn't I?" said the lad; "but tell me, whence do you come, and what sort of man are you?"

"I am 'Our Lord,' and come from Heaven," said the man.

"Thee will I not drink with," said the lad; "for thou makest such distinction between persons here in the world, and sharest rights so unevenly that some get so rich and some so poor. No! with thee I will not drink," and as he said this he trotted off with his keg again.

So when he had gone a bit farther the keg grew too heavy again; he thought he never could carry it any longer unless someone came with whom he might drink, and so lessen the ale in the keg. Yes! he met an ugly, scrawny man who came along fast and furious.

"Good day," said the man.

"Good day to you," said the lad.

"Whither away?" asked the man.

"Oh, I'm looking for someone to drink with, and get my keg lightened," said the lad.

"Can't you drink with me as well as with anyone else?" said the man; "I have fared both far and wide, and I am tired and thirsty."

"Well, why not?" said the lad; "but who are you, and whence do you come?"

"Who am I? I am the De'il, and I come from Hell; that's where I come from," said the man.

"No!" said the lad; "thou only pinest and plaguest poor folk, and if there is any unhappiness astir, they always say it is thy fault. Thee I will not drink with."

So he went far and farther than far again with his ale-keg on his back, till he thought it grew so heavy there was no carrying it any farther, he began to look round again if anyone were coming with whom he could drink and lighten his keg. So after a long, long time, another man came, and he was so dry and lean 'twas a wonder his bones hung together.

"Good day," said the man.

"Good day to you," said the lad.

"Whither away?" asked the man.

"Oh, I was only looking about to see if I could find someone to drink with, that my keg might be lightened a little, it is so heavy to carry."

"Can't you drink as well with me as with anyone else?" said the man.

"Yes; why not?" said the lad. "But what sort of man are you?"

"They call me Death," said the man.

"The very man for my money," said the lad. "Thee I am glad to drink with," and as he said this he put down his keg, and began to tap the ale into a bowl. "Thou art an honest, trustworthy man, for thou treatest all alike, both rich and poor."

So he drank his health, and Death drank his health, and Death said he had never tasted such drink, and as the lad was fond of him, they drank bowl and bowl about, till the ale was lessened, and the keg grew light.

At last Death said, "I have never known drink which smacked better, or did me so much good as this ale that you have given me, and I scarce know what to give you in return." But, after he had thought awhile, he said the keg should never get empty, however much they drank out of it, and the ale that was in it should become a healing drink, by which the lad could make the sick whole again better than any doctor. And he also said that when the lad came into the sick man's room, Death would always be there, and show himself to him, and it should be to him for a sure token if he saw Death at the foot of the bed that he could cure the sick with a draught from the keg; but if he sat by the pillow, there was no healing nor medicine, for then the sick belonged to Death.

Well, the lad soon grew famous, and was called in far and near, and he helped many to health again who had been given over. When he came in and saw how Death sat by the sick man's bed, he foretold either life or death, and his foretelling was never wrong. He got both a rich and powerful man, and at last he was called in to a king's daughter far, far away in the world. She was so dangerously ill no doctor thought he could do her any good, and so they promised him all that he cared either to ask or have if he would only save her life.

Now, when he came into the princess's room, there sat Death at her pillow; but as he sat he dozed and nodded, and while he did this she felt herself better.

"Now, life or death is at stake," said the doctor; "and I fear, from what I see, there is no hope."

But they said he *must* save her, if it cost land and realm. So he looked at Death, and while he sat there and dozed again, he made a sign to the servants to turn the bed round so quickly that Death was left sitting at the foot, and at the very moment they turned the bed, the doctor gave her the draught, and her life was saved.

"Now you have cheated me," said Death, "and we are quits."

"I was forced to do it," said the doctor, "unless I wished to lose land and realm."

"That shan't help you much," said Death; "your time is up, for now you belong to me."

"Well," said the lad, "what must be must be; but you'll let me have time to read the Lord's Prayer first?"

Yes, he might have leave to do that; but he took very good care not to read the Lord's Prayer; everything else he read, but the Lord's Prayer never crossed his lips, and at last he thought he had cheated Death for good and all. But when Death thought he had really waited too long, he went to the lad's house one night, and hung up a great tablet with the Lord's Prayer painted on it over against his bed. So when the lad woke in the morning he began to read the tablet, and did not quite see what he was about till he came to Amen; but then it was just too late, and Death had him.

425C: Beauty and the Beast

Beauty and the Beast
(*France*)

There was once a merchant that had three daughters, and he loved them better than himself. Now it happened that he had to go a long journey to buy some goods, and when he was just starting he said to them, "What shall I bring you back, my dears?"

And the eldest daughter asked to have a necklace; and the second daughter wished to have a gold chain; but the youngest daughter said, "Bring back yourself, papa, and that is what I want the most."

"Nonsense, child," said her father, "you must say something that I may remember to bring back for you."

"So," she said, "then bring me back a rose, father."

Well, the merchant went on his journey and did his business and bought a pearl necklace for his eldest daughter, and a gold chain for his second daughter; but he knew it was no use getting a rose for the youngest while he was so far away because it would fade before he got home. So he made up his mind he would get a rose for her the day he got near his house.

When all his merchanting was done he rode off home and forgot all about the rose till he was near his house; then he suddenly remembered what he had promised his youngest daughter, and looked about to see if he could find a rose. Near where he had stopped he saw a great garden, and getting off his horse he wandered about in it till he found a lovely rosebush; and he plucked the most beautiful rose he could see on it. At that moment he heard a crash like thunder, and looking around he saw a huge monster—two tusks in his mouth and fiery eyes surrounded by bristles, and horns coming out of its head and spreading over its back.

"Mortal," said the beast, "who told you you might pluck my roses?"

"Please, sir," said the merchant in fear and terror for his life, "I promised my daughter to bring her home a rose and forgot about it till the last moment, and then I saw your beautiful garden and thought you would not miss a single rose, or else I would have asked your permission."

"Thieving is thieving," said the beast, "whether it be a rose or a diamond; your life is forfeit."

The merchant fell on his knees and begged for his life for the sake of his three daughters who had none but him to support them.

"Well, mortal, well," said the beast, "I grant your life on one condition: Seven days from now you must bring this youngest daughter of yours, for whose sake you have broken into my garden, and leave her

here in your stead. Otherwise swear that you will return and place yourself at my disposal."

So the merchant swore, and taking his rose, mounted his horse and
rode home.

As soon as he got into his house his daughters came rushing round
him, clapping their hands and showing their joy in every way, and soon
he gave the necklace to his eldest daughter, the chain to his second daughter, and then he gave the rose to his youngest, and as he gave it he sighed.

"Oh, thank you, father," they all cried.

But the youngest said, "Why did you sigh so deeply when you gave me
my rose?"

"Later on I will tell you," said the merchant.

So for several days they lived happily together, though the merchant
wandered about gloomy and sad, and nothing his daughters could do
would cheer him up till at last he took his youngest daughter aside and
said to her, "Bella, do you love your father?"

"Of course I do, father, of course I do."

"Well, now you have a chance of showing it"; and then he told her of
all that had occurred with the beast when he got the rose for her. Bella
was very sad, as you can well think, and then she said, "Oh, father, it was
all on account of me that you fell into the power of this beast; so I will go
with you to him; perhaps he will do me no harm; but even if he does—
better harm to me than evil to my dear father."

So next day the merchant took Bella behind him on his horse, as was
the custom in those days, and rode off to the dwelling of the beast. And
when he got there and they alighted from his horse the doors of the house
opened, and what do you think they saw there! Nothing. So they went
up the steps and went through the hall, and went into the dining room,
and there they saw a table spread with all manner of beautiful glasses and
plates and dishes and napery, with plenty to eat upon it. So they waited
and they waited, thinking that the owner of the house would appear, till
at last the merchant said, "Let's sit down and see what will happen then."
And when they sat down invisible hands passed them things to eat and
to drink, and they ate and drank to their heart's content. And when they
arose from the table it arose too and disappeared through the door as if it
were being carried by invisible servants.

Suddenly there appeared before them the beast who said to the merchant, "Is this your youngest daughter?"

And when he had said that it was, he said, "Is she willing to stop here
with me?"

And then he looked at Bella who said, in a trembling voice, "Yes, sir."

"Well, no harm shall befall you." With that he led the merchant down
to his horse and told him he might come that day each week to visit his

daughter. Then the beast returned to Bella and said to her, "This house with all that therein is, is yours; if you desire aught, clap your hands and say the word and it shall be brought unto you." And with that he made a sort of bow and went away.

So Bella lived on in the home with the beast and was waited on by invisible servants and had whatever she liked to eat and to drink; but she soon got tired of the solitude and, next day, when the beast came to her, though he looked so terrible, she had been so well treated that she had lost a great deal of her terror of him. So they spoke together about the garden and about the house and about her father's business and about all manner of things, so that Bella lost altogether her fear of the beast. Shortly afterwards her father came to see her and found her quite happy, and he felt much less dread of her fate at the hands of the beast.

So it went on for many days, Bella seeing and talking to the beast every day, till she got quite to like him, until one day the beast did not come at his usual time, just after the midday meal, and Bella quite missed him. So she wandered about the garden trying to find him, calling out his name, but received no reply. At last she came to the rosebush from which her father had plucked the rose, and there, under it, what do you think she saw! There was the beast lying huddled up without any life or motion. Then Bella was sorry indeed and remembered all the kindness that the beast had shown her; and she threw herself down by it and said, "Oh, Beast, Beast, why did you die? I was getting to love you so much."

No sooner had she said this than the hide of the beast split in two and out came the most handsome young prince who told her that he had been enchanted by a magician and that he could not recover his natural form unless a maiden should, of her own accord, declare that she loved him.

Thereupon the prince sent for the merchant and his daughters, and he was married to Bella, and they all lived happy together ever afterwards.

The Enchanted Tsarévich
(*Russia*)

Once upon a time there was a merchant who had three daughters. It so happened he had one day to go to strange countries to buy wares, and so he asked his daughters, "What shall I bring you from beyond the seas?"

The eldest asked for a new coat, and the next one also asked for a new coat; but the youngest one only took a sheet of paper and sketched a flower on it. "Bring me, *bátyushka*,[1] a flower like this!"

So the merchant went and made a long journey to foreign kingdoms, but he could never see such a flower. So he came back home, and he saw on his way a splendid lofty palace with watchtowers, turrets, and a garden. He went a walk in the garden, and you cannot imagine how many trees he saw and flowers, every flower fairer than the other flowers. And then he looked and he saw a single one like the one which his daughter had sketched.

"Oh," he said, "I will tear off and bring this to my beloved daughter; evidently there is nobody here to watch me."

So he ran up and broke it off, and as soon as he had done it, in that very instant a boisterous wind arose and thunder thundered, and a fearful monster stood in front of him, a formless, winged snake with three heads. "How dared you play the master in my garden!" cried the snake to the merchant. "Why have you broken off a blossom?"

The merchant was frightened, fell on his knees and besought pardon.

"Very well," said the snake, "I will forgive you, but on condition that whoever meets you first, when you reach home, you must give me for all eternity; and, if you deceive me, do not forget, nobody can ever hide himself from me. I shall find you wherever you are."

The merchant agreed to the condition and came back home. And the youngest daughter saw him from the window and ran out to meet him. Then the merchant hung his head, looked at his beloved daughter, and began to shed bitter tears.

"What is the matter with you? Why are you weeping, *bátyushka*?"

He gave her the blossom and told what had befallen him.

"Do not grieve, *bátyushka*," said the youngest daughter. "It is God's gift. Perhaps I shall fare well. Take me to the snake."

So the father took her away, set her in the palace, bade farewell, and set out home. Then the fair maiden, the daughter of the merchant, went in the different rooms, and beheld everywhere gold and velvet; but no one was there to be seen, not a single human soul.

Time went by and went by, and the fair damsel became hungry and thought, "Oh, if I could only have something to eat!" But before ever she had thought, in front of her stood a table, and on the table were dishes and drinks and refreshments. The only thing that was not there was birds' milk. Then she sat down to the table, drank and ate, got up, and it had all vanished.

Darkness now came on, and the merchant's daughter went into the bedroom, wishing to lie down and sleep. Then a boisterous wind rustled round and the three- headed snake appeared in front of her.

---

1 Father.

"Hail, fair maiden! Put my bed outside this door!"

So the fair maiden put the bed outside the door and herself lay on the bedstead.

She awoke in the morning, and again in the entire house there was not a single soul to be seen. And it all went well with her. Whatever she wished for appeared on the spot.

In the evening the snake flew to her and ordered, "Now, fair maiden, put my bed next to your bedstead."

She then laid it next to her bedstead, and the night went by, and the maiden awoke, and again there was never a soul in the palace.

And for the third time the snake came in the evening and said, "Now, fair maiden, I am going to lie with you in the bedstead."

The merchant's daughter was fearfully afraid of lying on a single bed with such a formless monster. But she could not help herself, so she strengthened her heart and lay down with him.

In the morning the serpent said to her, "If you are now weary, fair maiden, go to your father and your sisters. Spend a day with them, and in the evening come back to me. But see to it that you are not late. If you are one single minute late I shall die of grief."

"No, I shall not be late," said the maiden, the merchant's daughter, and descended the steps; there was a barouche[1] ready for her, and she sat down. That very instant she arrived at her father's courtyard.

Then the father saw, welcomed, kissed her, and asked her, "How has God been dealing with you, my beloved daughter ? Has it been well with you?"

"Very well, father!" And she started telling of all the wealth there was in the palace, how the snake loved her, how whatever she only thought of was in that instant fulfilled.

The sisters heard, and did not know what to do out of sheer envy.

Now the day was ebbing away, and the fair maiden made ready to go back, and was bidding farewell to her father and her sisters, saying, "This is the time I must go back. I was bidden keep to my term."

But the envious sisters rubbed onions on their eyes and made as though they were weeping: "Do not go away, sister; stay until tomorrow."

She was very sorry for her sisters, and stayed one day more.

In the morning she bade farewell to them all and went to the palace. When she arrived it was as empty as before. She went into the garden, and she saw the serpent lying dead in the pond! He had thrown himself for sheer grief into the water.

"Oh, my God, what have I done!" cried out the fair maiden, and she wept bitter tears, ran up to the pond, hauled the snake out of the water,

1 Horse-drawn carriage.

embraced one head and kissed it with all her might. And the snake trembled, and in a minute turned into a good youth.

"I thank you, fair maiden," he said. "You have saved me from the greatest misfortune. I am no snake, but an enchanted prince."

Then they went back to the merchant's house, were betrothed, lived long, and lived for good and happy things.

The Small-Tooth Dog
(*England*)

Once upon a time there was a merchant who travelled about the world a great deal. On one of his journeys thieves attacked him, and they would have taken both his life and his money if a large dog had not come to his rescue and driven the thieves away.

When the dog had driven the thieves away he took the merchant to his house, which was a very handsome one, and he dressed his wounds and nursed him until he was well.

As soon as he was able to travel the merchant began his journey home, but before starting he told the dog how grateful he was for his kindness, and asked him what reward he could offer in return, and he said he would not refuse to give him the most precious thing that he had.

And so the merchant said to the dog, "Will you accept a fish that I have that can speak twelve languages?"

"No," said the dog, "I will not."

"Or a goose that lays golden eggs?"

"No," said the dog, "I will not."

"Or a mirror in which you can see what anybody is thinking about?"

"No," said the dog, "I will not."

"Then what will you have?" said the merchant.

"I will have none of such presents," said the dog, "but let me fetch your daughter and take her to my house."

When the merchant heard this he was grieved, but what he had promised had to be done, so he said to the dog, "You can come and fetch my daughter after I have been at home for a week."

So at the end of the week the dog came to the merchant's house to fetch his daughter, but when he got there he stayed outside the door, and would not go in.

But the merchant's daughter did as her father told her, and came out of the house dressed for a journey and ready to go with the dog.

When the dog saw her he looked pleased, and said: "Jump on my back, and I will take you away to my house."

So she mounted on the dog's back, and away they went at a great pace until they reached the dog's house, which was many miles off.

But after she had been a month at the dog's house she began to mope and cry.

"What are you crying for?" said the dog.

"Because I want to go back to my father," she said.

The dog said, "If you will promise me that you will not stay at home more than three days I will take you there. But, first of all," said he, "what do you call me?"

"A great, foul, small-tooth dog," said she.

"Then," said he, "I will not let you go."

But she cried so pitifully that he promised again to take her home. "But before we start," said he, "tell me what you call me."

"Oh," she said, "your name is Sweet-as-a-honeycomb."

"Jump on my back," said he, "and I'll take you home."

So he trotted away with her on his back for forty miles, when they came to a stile.

"And what do you call me?" said he, before they got over the stile.

Thinking that she was safe on her way, the girl said, "A great, foul, small-tooth dog."

But when she said this he did not jump over the stile, but turned right round about at once, and galloped back to his own house with the girl on his back.

Another week went by, and again the girl wept so bitterly that the dog promised her again to take her to her father's house.

So the girl got on the dog's back again, and they reached the first stile as before, and then the dog stopped and said, "And what do you call me?"

"Sweet-as-a-honeycomb," she replied.

So the dog leaped over the stile, and they went on for twenty miles until they came to another stile.

"And what do you call me?" said the dog, with a wag of his tail.

She was thinking more of her father and her own home than of the dog, so she answered, "A great, foul, small-tooth dog."

Then the dog was in a great rage, and he turned right round about and galloped back to his own house as before.

After she had cried for another week the dog promised again to take her back to her father's house. So she mounted upon his back once more, and when they got to the first stile the dog said, "And what do you call me?"

"Sweet-as-a-honeycomb," she said.

So the dog jumped over the stile, and away they went for now the girl made up her mind to say the most loving things she could think of until they reached her father's house.

When they got to the door of the merchant's house the dog said, "And what do you call me?"

Just at that moment the girl forgot the loving things that she meant to say, and began, "A great—" but the dog began to turn, and she got fast hold of the door latch, and was going to say "foul" when she saw how grieved the dog looked and remembered how good and patient he had been with her, so she said, "Sweeter-than-a-honeycomb."

When she had said this she thought the dog would have been content and have galloped away, but instead of that he suddenly stood up on his hind legs, and with his fore legs he pulled off his dog's head and tossed it high in the air. His hairy coat dropped off, and there stood the handsomest young man in the world, with the finest and smallest teeth you ever saw.

Of course they were married, and lived together happily.

470: Friends in Life and Death

Friends in Life and Death

Friends In Life and Death
(*Norway*)

Once on a time there were two young men who were such great friends that they swore to one another they would never part, either in life or death. One of them died before he was at all old, and a little while after the other wooed a farmer's daughter, and was to be married to her. So when they were bidding guests to the wedding, the bridegroom went himself to the churchyard where his friend lay, and knocked at his grave and called him by name. No! he neither answered nor came. He knocked again, and he called again, but no one came. A third time he knocked louder and called louder to him, to come that he might talk to him. So, after a long, long time, he heard a rustling, and at last the dead man came up out of the grave.

"It was well you came at last," said the bridegroom, "for I have been standing here ever so long, knocking and calling for you."

"I was a long way off," said the dead man, "so that I did not quite hear you till the last time you called."

"All right!" said the bridegroom; "but I am going to stand bridegroom to-day, and you mind well, I dare say, what we used to talk about, and how we were to stand by each other at our weddings as best man."

"I mind it well," said the dead man, "but you must wait a bit till I have made myself a little smart; and, after all, no one can say I have on a wedding garment."

The lad was hard put to it for time, for he was overdue at home to meet the guests, and it was all but time to go to church; but still he had to wait awhile and let the dead man go into a room by himself, as he begged, so that he might brush himself up a bit, and come smart to church like the rest; for, of course, he was to go with the bridal train to church.

Yes! the dead man went with him both to church and from church, but when they had got so far on with the wedding that they had taken off the bride's crown, he said he must go. So, for old friendship's sake, the bridegroom said he would go with him to the grave again. And as they walked to the churchyard the bridegroom asked his friend if he had seen much that was wonderful, or heard anything that was pleasant to know.

"Yes! that I have," said the dead man. "I have seen much, and heard many strange things."

"That must be fine to see," said the bridegroom. "Do you know, I have a mind to go along with you, and see all that with my own eyes."

"You are quite welcome," said the dead man; "but it may chance that you may be away some time."

"So it might," said the bridegroom; but for all that he would go down into the grave.

But before they went down the dead man took and cut a turf out of the graveyard and put it on the young man's head. Down and down they went, far and far away, through dark, silent wastes, across wood, and moor, and bog, till they came to a great, heavy gate, which opened to them as soon as the dead man touched it. Inside it began to grow lighter, first as though it were moonshine, and the farther they went the lighter it got. At last they got to a spot where there were such green hills, knee-deep in grass, and on them fed a large herd of kine, who grazed as they went; but for all they ate those kine looked poor, and thin, and wretched.

"What's all this?" said the lad who had been bridegroom; "why are they so thin and in such bad case, though they eat, every one of them, as though they were well paid to eat?"

"This is a likeness of those who never can have enough, though they rake and scrape it together ever so much," said the dead man.

So they journeyed on far and farther than far, till they came to some hill pastures, where there was naught but bare rocks and stones, with here and there a blade of grass. Here was grazing another herd of kine, which were so sleek, and fat, and smooth that their coats shone again.

"What are these," asked the bridegroom, "who have so little to live on, and yet are in such good plight? I wonder what they can be."

"This," said the dead man, "is a likeness of those who are content with the little they have, however poor it be."

So they went farther and farther on till they came to a great lake, and it and all about it was so bright and shining that the bridegroom could scarce bear to look at it—it was so dazzling.

"Now, you must sit down here," said the dead man, "till I come back. I shall be away a little while."

With that he set off, and the bridegroom sat down, and as he sat sleep fell on him, and he forgot everything in sweet deep slumber. After a while the dead man came back.

"It was good of you to sit still here, so that I could find you again."

But when the bridegroom tried to get up, he was all overgrown with moss and bushes, so that he found himself sitting in a thicket of thorns and brambles.

So when he had made his way out of it, they journeyed back again, and the dead man led him by the same way to the brink of the grave. There they parted and said farewell, and as soon as the bridegroom got out of the grave he went straight home to the house where the wedding was.

But when he got where he thought the house stood, he could not find his way. Then he looked about on all sides, and asked everyone he met, but he could neither hear nor learn anything of the bride, or the wedding, or his kindred, or his father and mother; nay, he could not so much as find anyone whom he knew. And all he met wondered at the strange shape, who went about and looked for all the world like a scarecrow.

Well! as he could find no one he knew, he made his way to the priest, and told him of his kinsmen and all that had happened up to the time he stood bridegroom, and how he had gone away in the midst of his wedding. But the priest knew nothing at all about it at first; but when he had hunted in his old registers, he found out that the marriage he spoke of had happened a long, long time ago, and that all the folk he talked of had lived four hundred years before.

In that time there had grown up a great stout oak in the priest's yard, and when he saw it he clambered up into it, that he might look about him. But the greybeard who had sat in heaven and slumbered for four hundred years, and had now at last come back, did not come down from the oak as well as he went up. He was stiff and gouty, as was likely enough; and so when he was coming down he made a false step, fell down, broke his neck, and that was the end of him.

Oisin in Tir Na N-Og
(*Ireland*)

There was a king in Tir na n-Og (the land of Youth) who held the throne and crown for many a year against all comers; and the law of the kingdom was that every seventh year the champions and best men of the country should run for the office of king.

Once in seven years they all met at the front of the palace and ran to the top of a hill two miles distant. On the top of that hill was a chair and the man that sat first in the chair was king of Tir na n-Og for the next seven years. After he had ruled for ages, the king became anxious; he was afraid that someone might sit in the chair before him, and take the crown off his head. So he called up his Druid one day and asked: "How long shall I keep the chair to rule this land, and will any man sit in it before me and take the crown off my head?"

"You will keep the chair and the crown forever," said the Druid, unless your own son-in-law takes them from you."

The king had no sons and but one daughter, the finest woman in Tir na n-Og; and the like of her could not be found in Erin or any kingdom in the world. When the king heard the words of the Druid, he said, "I'll have no son-in-law, for I'll put the daughter in a way no man will marry her."

Then he took a rod of Druidic spells, and calling the daughter up before him, he struck her with the rod, and put a pig's head on her in place of her own.

Then he sent the daughter away to her own place in the castle, and turning to the Druid said:

"There is no man that will marry her now."

When the Druid saw the face that was on the princess with the pig's head that the father gave her, he grew very sorry that he had given such information to the king; and some time after he went to see the princess.

"Must I be in this way forever?" asked she of the Druid.

"You must," said he, "till you marry one of the sons of Fin Mac-Cumhail in Erin. If you marry one of Fin's sons, you'll be freed from the blot that is on you now, and get back your own head and countenance."

When she heard this she was impatient in her mind, and could never rest till she left Tir na n-Og and came to Erin. When she had inquired she heard that Fin and the Fenians of Erin were at that time living on Knock an Ar, and she made her way to the place without delay and lived there a while; and when she saw Oisin, he pleased her; and when she found out that he was a son of Fin MacCumhail, she was always making up to him and coming towards him. And it was usual for the Fenians in those days to go out hunting on the hills and mountains and in the woods of Erin, and when one of them went he always took five or six men with him to bring home the game.

On a day Oisin set out with his men and dogs to the woods; and he went so far and killed so much game that when it was brought together, the men were so tired, weak, and hungry that they couldn't carry it, but went away home and left him with the three dogs, Bran, Sciolán, and Bu-glén[1] to shift for himself.

Now the daughter of the king of Tir na n-Og, who was herself the queen of Youth, followed closely in the hunt all that day, and when the men left Oisin she came up to him; and as he stood looking at the great pile of game and said, "I am very sorry to leave behind anything that I've had the trouble of killing," she looked at him and said, "Tie up a bundle for me, and I'll carry it to lighten the load off you."

Oisin gave her a bundle of the game to carry, and took the remainder himself. The evening was very warm and the game heavy, and after they had gone some distance, Oisin said, "Let us rest a while." Both threw down their burdens, and put their backs against a great stone that was by the roadside. The woman was heated and out of breath, and opened her dress to cool herself. Then Oisin looked at her and saw her beautiful form and her white bosom.

---

1 Famous dogs of Fin MacCumhail.

"Oh, then," said he, "it's a pity you have the pig's head on you; for I have never seen such an appearance on a woman in all my life before."

"Well," said she, "my father is the king of Tir na n-Og, and I was the finest woman in his kingdom and the most beautiful of all, till he put me under a Druidic spell and gave me the pig's head that's on me now in place of my own. And the Druid of Tir na n-Og came to me afterwards, and told me that if one of the sons of Fin MacCumhail would marry me, the pig's head would vanish, and I should get back my face in the same form as it was before my father struck me with the Druid's wand. When I heard this I never stopped till I came to Erin, where I found your father and picked you out among the sons of Fin MacCumhail, and followed you to see would you marry me and set me free."

"If that is the state you are in, and if marriage with me will free you from the spell, I'll not leave the pig's head on you long."

So they got married without delay, not waiting to take home the game or to lift it from the ground. That moment the pig's head was gone, and the king's daughter had the same face and beauty that she had before her father struck her with the Druidic wand.

"Now," said the queen of Youth to Oisin, "I cannot stay here long, and unless you come with me to Tir na n-Og we must part."

"Oh," said Oisin," wherever you go I'll go, and wherever you turn I'll follow."

Then she turned and Oisin went with her, not going back to Knock an Ar to see his father or his son. That very day they set out for Tir na n-Og and never stopped till they came to her father's castle; and when they came, there was a welcome before them, for the king thought his daughter was lost. That same year there was to be a choice of a king, and when the appointed day came at the end of the seventh year all the great men and the champions, and the king himself, met together at the front of the castle to run and see who should be first in the chair on the hill; but before a man of them was half way to the hill, Oisin was sitting above in the chair before them. After that time no one stood up to run for the office against Oisin, and he spent many a happy year as king in Tir na n-Og. At last he said to his wife: "I wish I could be in Erin to-day to see my father and his men."

"If you go," said his wife, "and set foot on the land of Erin, you'll never come back here to me, and you'll become a blind old man. How long do you think it is since you came here?"

"About three years," said Oisin.

"It is three hundred years," said she, "since you came to this kingdom with me. If you must go to Erin, I'll give you this white steed to carry you; but if you come down from the steed or touch the soil of Erin with your foot, the steed will come back that minute, and you'll be where he left you, a poor old man."

"I'll come back, never fear," said Oisin. "Have I not good reason to come back? But I must see my father and my son and my friends in Erin once more; I must have even one look at them."

She prepared the steed for Oisin and said, "This steed will carry you wherever you wish to go."

Oisin never stopped till the steed touched the soil of Erin; and he went on till he came to Knock Patrick in Munster, where he saw a man herding cows. In the field, where the cows were grazing there was a broad flat stone.

"Will you come here," said Oisin to the herdsman, "and turn over this stone?"

"Indeed, then, I will not," said the herdsman; "for I could not lift it, nor twenty men more like me."

Oisin rode up to the stone, and, reaching down, caught it with his hand and turned it over. Underneath the stone was the great horn of the Fenians *(borabu),* which circled round like a seashell, and it was the rule that when any of the Fenians of Erin blew the borabu, the others would assemble at once from whatever part of the country they might be in at the time.

"Will you bring this horn to me! "asked Oisin of the herdsman.

"I will not," said the herdsman; "for neither I nor many more like me could raise it from the ground."

With that Oisin moved near the horn, and reaching down took it in his hand; but so eager was he to blow it, that he forgot everything, and slipped in reaching till one foot touched the earth. In an instant the steed was gone, and Oisin lay on the ground a blind old man.

The Gentleman who Kicked a Skull
(*Italy*)

There was once a youth who did nothing but eat, drink, and amuse himself, because he was immensely wealthy and had nothing to think about. He scoffed at everyone; he dishonored all the young girls; he played all sorts of tricks, and was tired of everything. One day he took it into his head to give a grand banquet; and thereupon he invited all his friends and many women and all his acquaintances.

While they were preparing the banquet he took a walk, and passed through a street where there was a cemetery. While walking he noticed on the ground a skull. He gave it a kick, and then he went up to it and said to it in jest: "You, too, will come, will you not, to my banquet to-night?"

Then he went his way, and returned home. At the house the banquet was ready and the guests had all arrived. They sat down to the table, and ate and drank to the sound of music, and diverted themselves joyfully.

Meanwhile midnight drew near, and when the clock was on the stroke a ringing of bells was heard. The servants went to see who it was, and beheld a great ghost, who said to them: "Tell Count Robert that I am the one he invited this morning to his banquet." They went to their master and told him what the ghost had said. The master said: "I? All those whom I invited are here, and I have invited no one else." They said: "If you should see him! It is a ghost that is terrifying." Then it came into the young man's mind that it might be that dead man; and he said to the servants: "Quick! quick! close the doors and balconies, so that he cannot enter!" The servants went to close everything; but hardly had they done so when the doors and balconies were thrown wide open and the ghost entered. He went up where they were feasting, and said: "Robert! Robert! was it not enough for you to profane everything? Have you wished to disturb the dead, also? The end has come!" All were terrified, and fled here and there, some concealing themselves, and some falling on their knees. Then the ghost seized Robert by the throat and strangled him and carried him away with him; and thus he has left this example, that it is not permitted to mock the poor dead.

500: The Name of the Helper

Rumpelstiltskin
(*Germany*)

Once there was a miller who was poor, but who had a beautiful daughter. Now it happened that he had to go and speak to the King, and in order to make himself appear important he said to him, "I have a daughter who can spin straw into gold." The King said to the miller, "That is an art which pleases me well; if your daughter is as clever as you say, bring her to-morrow to my palace, and I will try what she can do."

And when the girl was brought to him he took her into a room which was quite full of straw, gave her a spinning-wheel and a reel, and said, "Now set to work, and if by to-morrow morning early you have not spun this straw into gold during the night, you must die." Thereupon he himself locked up the room, and left her in it alone. So there sat the poor miller's daughter, and for the life of her could not tell what to do; she had no idea how straw could be spun into gold, and she grew more and more miserable, until at last she began to weep.

But all at once the door opened, and in came a little man, and said, "Good evening, Mistress Miller; why are you crying so?" "Alas!" answered the girl, "I have to spin straw into gold, and I do not know how to do it." "What will you give me," said the manikin,[1] "if I do it for you?" "My necklace," said the girl. The little man took the necklace, seated himself in front of the wheel, and "whirr, whirr, whirr," three turns, and the reel was full; then he put another on, and whirr, whirr, whirr, three times round, and the second was full too. And so it went on until the morning, when all the straw was spun, and all the reels were full of gold. By daybreak the King was already there, and when he saw the gold he was astonished and delighted, but his heart became only more greedy. He had the miller's daughter taken into another room full of straw, which was much larger, and commanded her to spin that also in one night if she valued her life. The girl knew not how to help herself, and was crying, when the door again opened, and the little man appeared, and said, "What will you give me if I spin that straw into gold for you?" "The ring on my finger," answered the girl. The little man took the ring, again began to turn the wheel, and by morning had spun all the straw into glittering gold.

The King rejoiced beyond measure at the sight, but still he had not gold enough; and he had the miller's daughter taken into a still larger room full

---

1 Very small man.

of straw, and said, "You must spin this, too, in the course of this night; but if you succeed, you shall be my wife." "Even if she be a miller's daughter," thought he, "I could not find a richer wife in the whole world."

When the girl was alone the manikin came again for the third time, and said, "What will you give me if I spin the straw for you this time also?" "I have nothing left that I could give," answered the girl. "Then promise me, if you should become Queen, your first child." "Who knows whether that will ever happen?" thought the miller's daughter; and, not knowing how else to help herself in this strait, she promised the manikin what he wanted, and for that he once more span the straw into gold.

And when the King came in the morning, and found all as he had wished, he took her in marriage, and the pretty miller's daughter became a Queen.

A year after, she had a beautiful child, and she never gave a thought to the manikin. But suddenly he came into her room, and said, "Now give me what you promised." The Queen was horror-struck, and offered the manikin all the riches of the kingdom if he would leave her the child. But the manikin said, "No, something that is living is dearer to me than all the treasures in the world." Then the Queen began to weep and cry, so that the manikin pitied her. "I will give you three days' time," said he, "if by that time you find out my name, then shall you keep your child."

So the Queen thought the whole night of all the names that she had ever heard, and she sent a messenger over the country to inquire, far and wide, for any other names that there might be. When the manikin came the next day, she began with Caspar, Melchior, Balthazar, and said all the names she knew, one after another; but to everyone the little man said, "That is not my name." On the second day she had inquiries made in the neighborhood as to the names of the people there, and she repeated to the manikin the most uncommon and curious. "Perhaps your name is Shortribs, or Sheepshanks, or Laceleg?" but he always answered, "That is not my name."

On the third day the messenger came back again, and said, "I have not been able to find a single new name, but as I came to a high mountain at the end of the forest, where the fox and the hare bid each other good night, there I saw a little house, and before the house a fire was burning, and round about the fire quite a ridiculous little man was jumping: he hopped upon one leg, and shouted—

> *To-day I bake, to-morrow brew,*
> *The next I'll have the young Queen's child.*
> *Ha! glad am I that no one knew*
> *That Rumpelstiltskin I am styled.*

You may think how glad the Queen was when she heard the name! And when soon afterwards the little man came in, and asked, "Now, Mistress Queen, what is my name?" at first she said, "Is your name Conrad?" "No." "Is your name Harry?" "No."

"Perhaps your name is Rumpelstiltskin?"

"The devil has told you that! the devil has told you that!" cried the little man, and in his anger he plunged his right foot so deep into the earth that his whole leg went in; and then in rage he pulled at his left leg so hard with both hands that he tore himself in two.

Tom Tit Tot
(*England*)

Once upon a time there was a woman, and she baked five pies. And when they came out of the oven, they were that overbaked the crusts were too hard to eat. So she says to her daughter:

"Darter," says she, "put you them there pies on the shelf, and leave 'em there a little, and they'll come again."—She meant, you know, the crust would get soft.

But the girl, she says to herself: "Well, if they'll come again, I'll eat 'em now." And she set to work and ate 'em all, first and last.

Well, come supper-time the woman said: "Go you, and get one o' them there pies. I dare say they've come again now."

The girl went and she looked, and there was nothing but the dishes. So back she came and says she: "Noo, they ain't come again."

"Not one of 'em?" says the mother.

"Not one of 'em," says she.

"Well, come again, or not come again," said the woman "I'll have one for supper."

"But you can't, if they ain't come," said the girl.

"But I can," says she. "Go you, and bring the best of 'em."

"Best or worst," says the girl, "I've ate 'em all, and you can't have one till that's come again."

Well, the woman she was done, and she took her spinning to the door to spin, and as she span she sang:

"My darter ha' ate five, five pies to-day.

My darter ha' ate five, five pies to-day."

The king was coming down the street, and he heard her sing, but what she sang he couldn't hear, so he stopped and said:

"What was that you were singing, my good woman?"

The woman was ashamed to let him hear what her daughter had been doing, so she sang, instead of that:

"My darter ha' spun five, five skeins to-day.

My darter ha' spun five, five skeins to-day."

"Stars o' mine!" said the king, "I never heard tell of anyone that could do that."

Then he said: "Look you here, I want a wife, and I'll marry your daughter. But look you here," says he, "eleven months out of the year she shall have all she likes to eat, and all the gowns she likes to get, and all the company she likes to keep; but the last month of the year she'll have to spin five skeins every day, and if she don't I shall kill her."

"All right," says the woman; for she thought what a grand marriage that was. And as for the five skeins, when the time came, there'd be plenty of ways of getting out of it, and likeliest, he'd have forgotten all about it.

Well, so they were married. And for eleven months the girl had all she liked to eat, and all the gowns she liked to get, and all the company she liked to keep.

But when the time was getting over, she began to think about the skeins and to wonder if he had 'em in mind. But not one word did he say about 'em, and she thought he'd wholly forgotten 'em.

However, the last day of the last month he takes her to a room she'd never set eyes on before. There was nothing in it but a spinning-wheel and a stool. And says he: "Now, my dear, here you'll be shut in to-morrow with some victuals and some flax, and if you haven't spun five skeins by the night, your head'll go off."

And away he went about his business.

Well, she was that frightened, she'd always been such a gatless[1] girl, that she didn't so much as know how to spin, and what was she to do to-morrow with no one to come nigh her to help her? She sat down on a stool in the kitchen, and law! how she did cry!

However, all of a sudden she heard a sort of a knocking low down on the door. She upped and oped it, and what should she see but a small little black thing with a long tail. That looked up at her right curious, and that said:

"What are you a-crying for?"

"What's that to you?" says she.

"Never you mind," that said, "but tell me what you're a-crying for."

"That won't do me no good if I do," says she.

"You don't know that," that said, and twirled that's tail round.

"Well," says she, "that won't do no harm, if that don't do no good," and she upped and told about the pies, and the skeins, and everything.

"This is what I'll do," says the little black thing, "I'll come to your win-

---

1 Senseless.

dow every morning and take the flax and bring it spun at night."

"What's your pay?" says she.

That looked out of the corner of that's eyes, and that said: "I'll give you three guesses every night to guess my name, and if you haven't guessed it before the month's up you shall be mine."

Well, she thought she'd be sure to guess that's name before the month was up. "All right," says she, "I agree."

"All right," that says, and law! how that twirled that's tail.

Well, the next day, her husband took her into the room, and there was the flax and the day's food.

"Now there's the flax," says he, "and if that ain't spun up this night, off goes your head." And then he went out and locked the door.

He'd hardly gone, when there was a knocking against the window.

She upped and she oped it, and there sure enough was the little old thing sitting on the ledge.

"Where's the flax?" says he.

"Here it be," says she. And she gave it to him.

Well, come the evening a knocking came again to the window. She upped and she oped it, and there was the little old thing with five skeins of flax on his arm.

"Here it be," says he, and he gave it to her.

"Now, what's my name?" says he.

"What, is that Bill?" says she.

"Noo, that ain't," says he, and he twirled his tail.

"Is that Ned?" says she.

"Noo, that ain't," says he, and he twirled his tail.

"Well, is that Mark?" says she.

"Noo, that ain't," says he, and he twirled his tail harder, and away he flew.

Well, when her husband came in, there were the five skeins ready for him. "I see I shan't have to kill you to-night, my dear," says he; "you'll have your food and your flax in the morning," says he, and away he goes.

Well, every day the flax and the food were brought, and every day that there little black impet used to come mornings and evenings. And all the day the girl sat trying to think of names to say to it when it came at night. But she never hit on the right one. And as it got towards the end of the month, the impet began to look so maliceful, and that twirled that's tail faster and faster each time she gave a guess.

At last it came to the last day but one. The impet came at night along with the five skeins, and that said,

"What, ain't you got my name yet?"

"Is that Nicodemus?" says she.

"Noo, t'ain't," that says.

"Is that Sammle?" says she.

"Noo, t'ain't," that says.

"A-well, is that Methusalem?" says she.

"Noo, t'ain't that neither," that says.

Then that looks at her with that's eyes like a coal o' fire, and that says: "Woman, there's only to-morrow night, and then you'll be mine!" And away it flew.

Well, she felt that horrid. However, she heard the king coming along the passage. In he came, and when he sees the five skeins, he says, says he,

"Well, my dear," says he, "I don't see but what you'll have your skeins ready to-morrow night as well, and as I reckon I shan't have to kill you, I'll have supper in here to-night." So they brought supper, and another stool for him, and down the two sat.

Well, he hadn't eaten but a mouthful or so, when he stops and begins to laugh.

"What is it?" says she.

"A-why," says he, "I was out a-hunting to-day, and I got away to a place in the wood I'd never seen before And there was an old chalk-pit. And I heard a kind of a sort of a humming. So I got off my hobby, and I went right quiet to the pit, and I looked down. Well, what should there be but the funniest little black thing you ever set eyes on. And what was that doing, but that had a little spinning-wheel, and that was spinning wonderful fast, and twirling that's tail. And as that span that sang:

"Nimmy nimmy not
My name's Tom Tit Tot."

Well, when the girl heard this, she felt as if she could have jumped out of her skin for joy, but she didn't say a word.

Next day that there little thing looked so maliceful when he came for the flax. And when night came, she heard that knocking against the window panes. She oped the window, and that come right in on the ledge. That was grinning from ear to ear, and Oo! that's tail was twirling round so fast.

"What's my name?" that says, as that gave her the skeins.

"Is that Solomon?" she says, pretending to be afeard.

"Noo, t'ain't," that says, and that came further into the room.

"Well, is that Zebedee?" says she again.

"Noo, t'ain't," says the impet. And then that laughed and twirled that's tail till you couldn't hardly see it.

"Take time, woman," that says; "next guess, and you're mine." And that stretched out that's black hands at her.

Well, she backed a step or two, and she looked at it, and then she laughed out, and says she, pointing her finger at it:

"NIMMY NIMMY NOT, YOUR NAME'S TOM TIT TOT!"

Well, when that heard her, that gave an awful shriek and away that flew into the dark, and she never saw it any more.

The Girl Who Could Spin Gold from Clay and Long Straw
(*Sweden*)

There was once an old woman who had an only daughter. The lass was good and amiable, and also extremely beautiful, but at the same time so indolent that she would hardly turn her hand to any work. This was a cause of great grief to the mother, who tried all sorts of ways to cure her daughter of so lamentable a failing; but there was no help. The old woman then thought no better plan could be devised than to set her daughter to spin on the roof of their cot, in order that all the world might be witness of her sloth. But her plan brought her no nearer the mark; the girl continued as useless as before.

One day, as the king's son was going to the chase, he rode by the cot where the old woman dwelt with her daughter. On seeing the fair spinner on the roof, he stopped and inquired why she sat spinning in such an unusual place. The old woman answered, "Aye, she sits there to let all the world see how clever she is. She is so clever that she can spin gold out of clay and long straw." At these words the prince was struck with wonder: for it never occurred to him that the old woman was ironically alluding to her daughter's sloth. He therefore said, "If what you say is true, that the young maiden can spin gold from clay and long straw, she shall no longer sit there, but shall accompany me to my palace and be my consort." The daughter thereupon descended from the roof and accompanied the prince to the royal residence, where, seated in her maiden-bower, she received a pail full of clay and a bundle of straw, by way of trial, whether she were so skillful as her mother had said.

The poor girl now found herself in a very uncomfortable state, knowing but too well that she could not spin flax, much less gold. So, sitting in her chamber, with her head resting on her hand, she wept bitterly. While she was thus sitting, the door was opened, and in walked a very little old man, who was both ugly and deformed. The old man greeted her in a friendly tone, and asked why she sat so lonely and afflicted. "I may well be sorrowful," answered the girl. "The king's son has commanded me to spin gold from clay and long straw, and if it be not done before tomorrow's dawn, my life is at stake."

The old man then said, "Fair maiden, weep not, I will help thee. Here is a pair of gloves. When thou hast them on thou wilt be able to spin gold. Tomorrow night I will return, when, if thou hast not found out my name, thou shalt accompany me home and be my wife." In her despair she agreed to the old man's condition, who then went his way. The maiden now sat and span, and by dawn she had already spun up all the clay and straw, which had become the finest gold it was possible to see.

Great was the joy throughout the whole palace, that the king's son had got a bride who was so skillful and, at the same time, so fair. But the young maiden did nothing but weep, and the more the time advanced the more she wept; for she thought of the frightful dwarf who was to come and fetch her. When evening drew nigh, the king's son returned from the chase, and went to converse with his bride. Observing that she appeared sorrowful, he strove to divert her in all sorts of ways, and said he would tell her of a curious adventure, provided only she would be cheerful. The girl entreated him to let her hear it. Then said the prince, "While rambling about in the forest to-day I witnessed an odd sort of thing. I saw a very, very little old man dancing round a juniper bush and singing a singular song." "What did he sing?" asked the maiden inquisitively; for she felt sure that the prince had met with the dwarf. "He sang these words, answered the prince:

> *I dag skall jag maltet mala,*
> *I morgon skall mitt bröllopp vara.*
> *Och jungfrun sitter i buren och gråter;*
> *Hon ver inte havad jag heter.*
> *Jag heter Titteli Ture.*
> *Jag heter Titteli Ture.*
>
> *Today I the malt shall grind,*
> *Tomorrow my wedding shall be.*
> *And the maiden sits in her bower and weeps;*
> *She knows not what I am called.*
> *I am called Titteli Ture.*
> *I am called Titteli Ture.*

Was not the maiden now glad? She begged the prince to tell her over and over again what the dwarf had sung. He then repeated the wonderful song, until she had imprinted the old man's name firmly in her memory. She then conversed lovingly with her betrothed, and the prince could not sufficiently praise his young bride's beauty and understanding. But he wondered why she was so overjoyed, being like everyone else, ignorant of the cause of her past sorrow.

When it was night, and the maiden was sitting alone in her chamber, the door was opened, and the hideous dwarf again entered. On beholding him the girl sprang up, and said, "Titteli Ture! Titteli Ture! Here are thy gloves." When the dwarf heard his name pronounced, he was furiously angry, and hastened away through the air, taking with him the whole roof of the house.

The fair maiden now laughed to herself and was joyful beyond measure. She then lay down to sleep, and slept till the sun shone. The following day her marriage with the young prince was solemnized, and nothing more was ever heard of Titteli Ture.

505: The Grateful Dead

Sila Tsarevich and Ivashka with the White Smock (*Russia*)

There was once a Tsar, named Chotei, who had three sons—the first, Aspar Tsarevich; the second, Adam Tsarevich; and the third and youngest son, Sila Tsarevich. The two eldest brothers entreated their father's permission to travel in foreign countries and see the world. Then the youngest brother, Sila Tsarevich, also begged the Tsar's permission to travel with his brothers. But Chotei said: "My dear son, you are still young, and not used to the difficulties of travelling; remain at home, and think no more of this fancy you have taken." But Sila Tsarevich had a great longing to see foreign lands, and entreated his father so much that at length the Tsar consented, and gave him a ship likewise. As soon as the three brothers embarked, each on board his ship, they all gave orders to set sail. And when they were out on the open sea, the eldest brother's ship sailed first, the second brother's next, and Sila Tsarevich sailed last.

On the third day of the voyage they saw a coffin with iron bands floating on the waves. The two eldest brothers sailed past without heeding it, but as soon as Sila Tsarevich saw the coffin, he ordered the sailors to pick it up, lay it on board his ship, and carry it to land. The next day a violent storm arose, by which Sila's ship was driven out of its course, and cast upon a steep shore in an unknown country. Then Sila ordered his sailors to take the coffin and to carry it on shore, whither he himself followed, and buried it in the earth.

Thereupon Sila Tsarevich ordered the captain to remain upon the spot where the ship was stranded, and await his return for three years; but adding that, should he not come back in that time, he should be free to set sail and return home. So saying, Sila took leave of his captain and his crew, and went forthwith, journeying on and on. He wandered about for a long while, without seeing anyone; at length he heard a man running after him, dressed all in white. Then Sila Tsarevich turned round and saw the man following him; whereupon he instantly drew his sword to be upon his guard. But no sooner did the man come up to him than he fell on his knees and thanked Sila for having saved him. And Sila asked the man what he had done to deserve his thanks. Then the stranger stood up and answered: "Ah, Sila Tsarevich, how can I thank you enough? There I lay in the coffin, which you picked up at sea and buried; and had it not been for you I might have remained floating about for a hundred years." "But how did you get into the coffin?" asked Sila. "Listen, and I will tell you the whole story," replied Ivashka. "I was a great magician; my mother was told that I did great mischief to mankind by my arts, and therefore ordered me to be put into this coffin and set adrift on the open sea: for more than a hundred years I have been floating about, and no one has ever picked me up; but to you I owe my rescue, and I will therefore serve you, and render you all the help in my power. Let me ask you whether you have not a wish to marry: I know the beautiful Queen Truda, who is worthy of being your wife." Sila replied that if this Queen were indeed beautiful, he was willing to marry her; and Ivashka told him she was the most beautiful woman in the world. When Sila heard this, he begged Ivashka to accompany him to her kingdom; so they set out and travelled on and on till they reached that country. Now, Queen Truda's kingdom was surrounded by a palisade; and upon every stake was stuck a man's head, except one, which had no head. When Sila saw this, he was terrified, and asked Ivashka what it meant; and Ivashka told him that these were the heads of heroes who had been suitors to Queen Truda. Sila shuddered on hearing this, and wished to return home without showing himself to the father of Truda; but Ivashka told him to fear nothing and go with him boldly; so Sila went on.

When they entered the kingdom, Ivashka said: "Hearken, Sila Tsarevich, I will be your servant, and when you enter the royal halls, salute King Salom humbly: then he will ask you whence you came, and whose son you are, what is your name and business. Tell him everything and conceal nothing; but say that you are come to sue for his daughter's hand; he will give her to you with great joy." So Sila Tsarevich went into the palace, and, as soon as Prince Salom saw him, he went himself to meet him, took him by his white hands, led him into the marble halls, and asked him: "Fair youth, from what country do you come, whose son are you, what is your name, and what is your business?" "I am from the kingdom of my father the Tsar Chotei," replied Sila; "my name is Sila Tsarevich, and I am come to sue for your daughter, the beautiful Queen Truda."

King Salom was overjoyed that the son of such a renowned Tsar should be his son-in-law, and immediately ordered his daughter to prepare for the wedding. And when the day for the marriage came, the King commanded all his princes and boyars to assemble in the palace; and they all went in procession to the church, and Sila Tsarevich was married to the fair Queen Truda. Then they returned to the palace, seated themselves at table, and feasted and made merry. When the time came to retire to rest, Ivashka took Sila aside and whispered to him: "Hark, ye, Sila Tsarevich, when you go to rest, beware lest you speak a word to your bride or you will not remain alive, and your head will be stuck on the last stake. She will in every way try to make you embrace her, but attend to what I say."

Then Sila Tsarevich enquired why he warned him thus, and Ivashka replied: "She is in league with an evil Spirit, who comes to her every night in the shape of a man, but flies through the air in the shape of a six-headed dragon; now, if she lays her hand upon your breast and presses it, jump up and beat her with a stick until all her strength is gone. I will meanwhile remain on watch at the door of your apartment."

When Sila Tsarevich heard this, he went with his wife to rest, and Queen Truda tried in every way to get him to kiss her, but Sila lay quite still and spoke not a word. Then Truda laid her hand upon his breast and pressed him so hard that he could scarcely breathe. But up jumped Sila Tsarevich and seized the stick which Ivashka had laid there ready for him, and fell to beating her as hard as he could. On a sudden there arose a storm, and a six-headed dragon came flying into the room and was going to devour Sila Tsarevich, but Ivashka seized a sharp sword and attacked the dragon, and they fought three hours, and Ivashka struck off two of the dragon's heads, whereupon the monster flew away. Then Ivashka desired Sila Tsarevich to go to sleep and fear nothing. Sila obeyed him, laid himself down, and fell asleep.

Early in the morning King Salom went to be informed whether his dear son still lived, and when he heard that Sila was alive and well, the King rejoiced, since he was the first who had been saved from his daughter; and he instantly ordered Sila to be called, and the whole day was spent in merrymaking.

The following night Ivashka gave Sila Tsarevich the same caution as before, not to speak a word to his wife, and he placed himself on watch at the door. Then it fell out as before, and when Sila Tsarevich began to beat the Queen, on a sudden the dragon came flying in, and was going to devour Sila Tsarevich. But Ivashka rushed from behind the door, sword in hand, and fought with the dragon and struck off two more of his heads. Then the dragon flew away, and Sila Tsarevich lay down to sleep. Early in the morning the King commanded Sila to be invited, and they spent this day in the same pleasures as before. The third night the same happened again, and Ivashka cut off the last two heads of the dragon, and he burnt all the heads and strewed the ashes in the fields.

Thus time passed on, and Sila Tsarevich lived with his father-in-law a whole year, without speaking to his wife or gaining her love. Then Ivashka told him one day to go to King Salom and ask permission to return to his native country. So Sila went to the King, who dismissed him, and gave him two squadrons of his army to accompany him as an escort. Then Sila took leave of his father-in-law, and set out with his wife on their journey to his own country.

When they had gone half-way, Ivashka told Sila Tsarevich to halt and pitch his tent. So Sila obeyed, and ordered the tent to be put up. The next day Ivashka laid pieces of wood in front of Sila's tent and set fire to them.

Then he led Queen Truda out of the tent, unsheathed his sword, and cut her in twain. Sila Tsarevich shuddered with terror and began to weep; but Ivashka said: "Weep not, she will come to life again." And presently all sorts of evil things came forth from the body, and Ivashka threw them all into the fire. Then he said to Sila Tsarevich: "See you not the evil spirits which troubled your wife? She is now relieved from them." And, so saying, he laid the parts of Truda's body together, sprinkled them with the water of life, and the Queen was instantly sound and whole as before. Then said Ivashka: "Now, farewell, Sila Tsarevich, you will find that your wife loves you truly, but you will never see me more." And so saying he vanished.

Sila Tsarevich ordered the tent to be struck, and journeyed on to his native country. And when he came to the place where his ship was waiting for him, he went on board with the fair Queen Truda, dismissed the escort which accompanied him, and set sail. And on arriving at his own kingdom, he was welcomed with salvos of cannon, and Tsar Chotei came out of his palace and took him and the beautiful Queen Truda by their lily-white hands, led them into the marble halls, placed them at table, and they feasted and made merry. Sila Tsarevich lived with his father two years; then he returned to the kingdom of King Salom, received from him the crown, and ruled over the country with his Queen Truda in great love and happiness.

The Three Pennies
(Denmark)

Many years ago an old soldier was discharged from the army. He received in consideration of his excellent and faithful service a small loaf of rye-bread and three pennies, whereupon he was at liberty to go whither he pleased. As he was walking along the high-road, he met three men; the one carried a shovel, the second a pickaxe, and the third a spade. The soldier stopped, looked at them, and said, "Where are you going?" "I will tell you," answered one of them. "To-day there was buried a man who owed each of us one penny, and now we will dig him up, since we are determined upon getting our dues." "What an idea!" returned the soldier; "you had better leave the dead man alone. At any rate, he is at present unable to pay you even one penny, so don't disturb his peace!" "It is all very fine for you to talk," answered the man; "but we must have the money, and up he must come."

When the soldier felt that his fair words could not settle the matter, he said, "Here, I have two pennies; will you take them and promise to leave the dead man undisturbed?" "Two pennies are not to be refused," said the man again, "but they will pay only two of us. What can you give the third one, since he is bent upon having his share?"

As the soldier saw that there was no dealing with these three wretches, he resumed: "Since you are so desperately determined, here is my third and last penny. Take it, and be content." Now all three were well satisfied, so they pursued their way with the three pennies in their pockets.

When the soldier had advanced a distance, a stranger came walking along. He looked rather pale, but saluted the soldier in a very civil manner, and followed him along the road without uttering a single sound. At last they reached a church, and here the stranger turned to his companion, saying, "Let us walk in!" The soldier looked wistfully at him, and answered: "That would not do. What business have we in the church at midnight?" "I tell you," replied the stranger, "we must walk in!" Upon this they entered the church and walked straight up to the altar. There was an old woman sitting with a burning light in her hand. "Take a hair from her head, and smell at it!" commanded the stranger. The soldier complied, but nothing remarkable happened. The stranger asked him to repeat the action, which he did; but there was no effect. The third time, however, when he tore a whole tuft of hair from the woman's head, she became so furious that she darted off, out above the church, carrying the whole leaden vault with her.

The two men went out of the church and down to the beach, where they found the whole leaden vault. Turning to the soldier, the stranger said, "Sit up; we will put to sea!" "Is that so?" remarked the soldier, who understood nothing of all this. "I see no ship, however." "Let me manage it all," says the stranger; "just seat yourself by me on the vault! Beyond the sea there is a princess of whom it was predicted that she would be married only to a man who should come across the sea in a leaden ship. Here you will be able to make your fortune." The leaden vault now floated out upon the open sea, and landed them safely on the other side. Great was the joy and happiness throughout the country, and the marriage between the soldier and the princess was celebrated with such pomp and splendor as was never seen, before or after.

When the ceremony had been performed, and the carriage was standing in front of the church door, bride and groom entered, with the stranger who had followed the soldier all along. The coachman asked to what place he might drive them. "Drive away, as fast as you can, towards the side where the sun will rise," said the stranger, and in a little while they were carried along at a furious rate. Somewhere they saw a large herd of cattle. They stopped, and the soldier called the herdsman to the carriage door, asking who he was. "I am the Count of Ravensburg," answered the shepherd, "and yonder is my castle." The stranger again bid the coachman drive as fast as possible. In a little while they rushed up to Ravensburg Castle. As they were ready to alight from the carriage, there was someone who knocked hard at the gate. It was the herdsman, who was anxious to come in. The stranger walked to the gate, inquiring what he could do for him. He wished to come into the castle, he said, for it belonged to him, and he had a right to demand admittance. The stranger meditated a little, whereupon he told the herdsman—who was a conjurer—that he might be allowed to come in, but first he must suffer the whole fate of the rye. "The fate of the rye!" repeated the conjurer; "what do you mean by that?" "I mean," answered the stranger, "that next fall you must be sown deep in the ground, and towards spring, when you come up, you must ripen in the sunshine and grow in the rain until you are ready for the harvest. Then you will be mowed and dried, and kept in the barn, until at length you will be threshed." "How is that!" cried the conjurer; "am I to be threshed?" "Of course you are," replied the stranger. "First you will be threshed, and then taken to the mill and ground." "Ground, too!" shouted the conjurer; "will I be ground also?" "Yes, both ground and sifted," answered the stranger. But the conjurer, hearing this, became so furious that he burst all into flint-stones.

The stranger now bid good-bye to the princess and the soldier, shook hands with them, and said: "Now I have seen you married to the princess; the troll of Ravensburg is dead and gone, and his castle, with all its treasures, is yours. I was as good to you as you were to me when you gave away your three pennies for my sake!" "What do you say?" exclaimed the soldier; "I never thought of those three pennies again!" "I know that," answered the stranger, "and otherwise I would not have been able to help you. However, I bid farewell to you and your wife, for I must return to the place where I belong."

Fair Brow
(*Italy*)

There was once a father who had a son. After this son had passed through school, his father said to him: "Son, now that you have finished your studies, you are of an age to travel. I will give you a vessel, in order that you may load it and unload it, buy and sell. Be careful what you do; take care to make gains!" He gave him six thousand scudi to buy merchandise, and the son started on his voyage. On his journey, without having yet purchased anything, he arrived at a town, and on the seashore he saw a bier, and noticed that those who passed by left there some a penny, some two; they bestowed alms on the corpse. The traveller went there and asked: "Why do you keep this dead man here? *for the dead desires the grave.*" They replied: "Because he owed a world of debts, and it is the custom here *to bury no one until his debts are paid.* Until this man's debts are paid by charity we cannot bury him." "What is the use of keeping him here?" he said. "Proclaim that all those whom he owed shall come to me and be paid." Then they issued the proclamation and he paid the debts; and, poor fellow! he did not have a farthing left—not a penny of his capital. So he returned to his father's house. "What news, son? What means your return so soon?" He replied: "On crossing the sea, we encountered pirates; they have robbed me of all my capital!" His father said: "No matter, son; it is enough that they have left you your life. Behold, I will give you more money; but you must not go again in that direction." He gave him another six thousand *scudi.* The son replied: "Yes, father, don't worry; I will change my course." He departed and began his journey. When he was well out at sea he saw a Turkish vessel. He said to himself: "Now it is better for me to summon them on board than for them to summon us." They came on board. He said to them: "Whence do you come?" They answered: "We come from the Levant." "What is your cargo?" "Nothing but a beautiful girl." "How do you come to have this girl?" "For her beauty; to sell her again. We have stolen her from the Sultan, she is so beautiful!" "Let me see this girl." When he saw her he said: "How much do you want for her?" "We want six thousand *scudi!*" The money which his father gave him he gave to those corsairs, and took the girl and carried her away to his ship. But he at once had her become a Christian and married her.

He returned to his father's house; he went up, and his father said to him:

"Welcome! O my handsome son. What merchandise of women have you made?" "My father, I bring you a handsome ring, I bring it for your reward; It cost me neither city nor castle, But the most beautiful woman you have ever seen: The daughter of the Sultan, who is in Turkey, Her I bring for my first cargo!"

"Ah, you miserable knave!" cried his father. "Is this the cargo you have brought?" He ill-treated them both, and drove them from the house. Those poor unfortunate ones did not know where to find shelter. They went away, and at a short distance from their town there were some rooms at a villa. They went to live in one of those. He said: "What shall we do here? I do not know how to do anything; I have no profession or business!" She said: "Now I can paint beautiful pictures; I will paint them, and you shall go and sell them!" He said: "Very well!" "But, remember, you must tell no one that I paint them!" "No, no!" he said.

Now let us go to Turkey. The Sultan, meanwhile, had sent out many vessels in search of his daughter. These ships went here and there in quest of her. Now it happened that one of these vessels arrived in the town near where she lived, and many of the sailors went on land. Now one day the husband said to his wife: "Make many pictures, for to-day we shall sell them!" She made them, and said to him that he should not sell them for less than twenty *scudi* apiece. She made a great many, and he carried them to the public square. Some of the Turks came there; they gave a glance at the paintings, and said to themselves: "Surely, it must be the Sultan's daughter who has painted these." They came nearer, and asked the young man how he sold them. He said they were dear; that he could not let them go for less than twenty *scudi*. They said: "Very well! we will buy them; but we want some more." He answered: "Come to the house of my wife who makes them!" They went there, and when they saw the Sultan's daughter, they seized her, bound her, and carried her far away to Turkey. This husband, then, unhappy, without wife, without a trade, alone in that house, what could he do?

Every day he walked along the beach, to see if he could find a ship that would take him on board; but he never saw any. One day he saw an old man fishing in a little boat; he cried: "Good old man, how much better off you are than I!" The old man asked: "Why, my dear son?" He said: "Good old man, will you take me to fish with you?" "Yes, my son," said he; "if you wish to come with me in this boat, I will take you!" "Thank heaven!" said he. "Good!" said the old man: "You with the rod, and I with the boat, Perhaps we shall catch some fish. I will go and sell the fish, for I am not ashamed, and we will live together!"

They ate, and afterward went to sleep; without knowing it, there arose in the night a severe storm, and the wind carried them to Turkey. The Turks, seeing this boat arrive, went on board, seized them, made slaves of them, and took them before the Sultan. He said: "Let one of them make bouquets; let the other plant flowers; put them in the garden!" They placed the old man there as gardener, and the young man to carry flowers to the Sultan's daughter, who with her maids was shut up in a very high tower for punishment. They were very comfortable there. Every day they went into the garden and made friends with the other gardeners. As time went on, the old man made some fine guitars, violins, flutes, clarionets, piccolos—all sorts of instruments he made. The young man played them beautifully when he had time. One day his wife, who was in the tower, hearing his fine songs—Fair Brow had a voice which surpassed all instruments—said: "Who is playing, who is singing so beautifully?" They went out on the balcony, and when she saw Fair Brow, she thought at once of having him come up. The Sultan's daughter said to one of those who filled the basket with flowers: "Put that young man in the basket and cover him with flowers!" He put him in, and the maids drew him up. When he was up, he came out of the basket, and beheld his wife. He embraced and kissed her and thought about escaping from there. Then she told her damsels that she wished to depart without anyone knowing it. So they loaded a large ship with pearls and precious stones, with rods of gold and jewels; then they let down Fair Brow first, then his wife; finally the damsels. They embarked and departed. When they were out at sea the husband remembered that he had forgotten the old man and left him on shore. Fair Brow said: "My sister, even if I thought I should lose my life, I would turn back, for *the word which I have given him is the mother of faith*!" So they turned back, and saw the old man, who was still awaiting them in a cave; they took him with them, and put to sea again. When they were near home, the old man said: "Now, my son, it is fitting for us to settle our accounts and divide things!" "Know, good old man," said Fair Brow to him, "that all the wealth that I have belongs half to you and half to me!" "Your wife, too, belongs half to me!" He said: "Good old man, I will leave you three quarters, and I will take one only, but leave me my wife. Do you want me to divide her in two?" Then the old man said: "You must know that I am the soul of him whom you had buried; and you have had all this good fortune because you did that good action, and converted and baptized your wife!" Then he gave him his blessing and disappeared. Fair Brow, when he heard this, as you can imagine, came near dying of joy. When they reached his city, they fired a salute, for Fair Brow had arrived with his wife, the wealthiest gentleman in the world. He sent for his father and told him all that had happened to him. He went to live with them, and as he was old, he died soon, and all his riches went to Fair Brow.

531: Faithful Ferdinand

Ferdinand the Faithful
(*Germany*)

Once on a time lived a man and a woman who so long as they were rich had no children, but when they were poor they had a little boy. They could, however, find no godfather for him, so the man said he would just go to another place to see if he could get one there. As he went, a poor man met him, who asked him where he was going. He said he was going to see if he could get a godfather, that he was poor, so no one would stand as godfather for him. "Oh," said the poor man, "you are poor, and I am poor; I will be godfather for you, but I am so ill off I can give the child nothing. Go home and tell the nurse that she is to come to the church with the child."

When they all got to the church together, the beggar was already there, and he gave the child the name of Ferdinand the Faithful.

When he was going out of the church, the beggar said, "Now go home, I can give you nothing, and you likewise ought to give me nothing." But he gave a key to the nurse, and told her when she got home she was to give it to the father, who was to take care of it until the child was fourteen years old, and then he was to go on the heath where there was a castle which the key would fit, and that all which was therein should belong to him. Now when the child was seven years old and had grown very big, he once went to play with some other boys, and each of them boasted that he had got more from his godfather than the other; but the child could say nothing, and was vexed, and went home and said to his father, "Did I get nothing at all, then, from my godfather?" "Oh, yes," said the father, "thou hadst a key if there is a castle standing on the heath, just go to it and open it." Then the boy went thither, but no castle was to be seen, or heard of.

After seven years more, when he was fourteen years old, he again went thither, and there stood the castle. When he had opened it, there was nothing within but a horse, a white one. Then the boy was so full of joy because he had a horse, that he mounted on it and galloped back to his father. "Now I have a white horse, and I will travel," said he. So he set out, and as he was on his way, a pen was lying on the road. At first he thought he would pick it up, but then again he thought to himself, "Thou shouldst leave it lying there; thou wilt easily find a pen where thou art going, if thou hast need of one." As he was thus riding away, a voice called after him, "Ferdinand the Faithful, take it with thee." He looked around, but saw no one, then he went back again and picked it up. When he had ridden a little way farther, he passed by a lake, and a fish was lying on the bank, gasping and panting for breath, so he said, "Wait, my dear fish, I will help thee get into the water," and he took hold of it by the tail, and threw it into the lake. Then the fish put its head out of the water and said, "As thou hast helped me out of the mud I will give thee a flute; when thou art in any need, play on it, and then I will help thee, and if ever thou lettest anything fall in the water, just play and I will reach it out to thee." Then he rode away, and there came to him a man who asked him where he was going. "Oh, to the next place." Then what his name was? "Ferdinand the Faithful." "So! then we have got almost the same name, I am called Ferdinand the Unfaithful." And they both set out to the inn in the nearest place.

Now it was unfortunate that Ferdinand the Unfaithful knew everything that the other had ever thought and everything he was about to do; he knew it by means of all kinds of wicked arts. There was, however, in the inn an honest girl, who had a bright face and behaved very prettily. She fell in love with Ferdinand the Faithful because he was a handsome man, and she asked him whither he was going. "Oh, I am just travelling round about," said he. Then she said he ought to stay there, for the King of that country wanted an attendant or an outrider, and he ought to enter his service. He answered he could not very well go to anyone like that and offer himself. Then said the maiden, "Oh, but I will soon do that for you." And so she went straight to the King, and told him that she knew of an excellent servant for him. He was well pleased with that, and had Ferdinand the Faithful brought to him, and wanted to make him his servant. He, however, liked better to be an outrider, for where his horse was, there he also wanted to be, so the King made him an outrider. When Ferdinand the Unfaithful learnt that, he said to the girl, "What! Dost thou help him and not me?" "Oh," said the girl, "I will help thee too." She thought, "I must keep friends with that man, for he is not to be trusted." She went to the King, and offered him as a servant, and the King was willing.

Now when the King met his lords in the morning, he always lamented and said, "Oh, if I had but my love with me." Ferdinand the Unfaithful was, however, always hostile to Ferdinand the Faithful. So once, when the King was complaining thus, he said, "You have the outrider, send him away to get her, and if he does not do it, his head must be struck off." Then the King sent for Ferdinand the Faithful, and told him that there was, in this place or in that place, a girl he loved, and that he was to bring her to him, and if he did not do it he should die.

Ferdinand the Faithful went into the stable to his white horse, and complained and lamented, "Oh, what an unhappy man I am!" Then someone behind him cried, "Ferdinand the Faithful, why weepest thou?"

He looked round but saw no one, and went on lamenting; "Oh, my dear little white horse, now must I leave thee; now must I die." Then someone cried once more, "Ferdinand the Faithful, why weepest thou?" Then for the first time he was aware that it was his little white horse who was putting that question. "Dost thou speak, my little white horse; canst thou do that?" And again, he said, "I am to go to this place and to that, and am to bring the bride; canst thou tell me how I am to set about it?" Then answered the little white horse, "Go thou to the King, and say if he will give thou what thou must have, thou wilt get her for him. If he will give thee a ship full of meat, and a ship full of bread, it will succeed. Great giants dwell on the lake, and if thou takest no meat with thee for them, they will tear thee to pieces, and there are the large birds which would pick the eyes out of thy head if thou hadst no bread for them." Then the King made all the butchers in the land kill, and all the bakers bake, that the ships might be filled. When they were full, the little white horse said to Ferdinand the Faithful, "Now mount me, and go with me into the ship, and then when the giants come, say,

> *Peace, peace, my dear little giants,*
> *I have had thought of ye,*
> *Something I have brought for ye;*

and when the birds come, thou shalt again say,

> *Peace, peace, my dear little birds,*
> *I have had thought of ye,*
> *Something I have brought for ye;*

then they will do nothing to thee, and when thou comest to the castle, the giants will help thee. Then go up to the castle, and take a couple of giants with thee. There the princess lies sleeping; thou must, however, not awaken her, but the giants must lift her up, and carry her in her bed to the ship." And now everything took place as the little white horse had said, and Ferdinand the Faithful gave the giants and the birds what he had brought with him for them, and that made the giants willing, and they carried the princess in her bed to the King. And when she came to the King, she said she could not live, she must have her writings, they had been left in her castle. Then by the instigation of Ferdinand the Unfaithful, Ferdinand the Faithful was called, and the King told him he must fetch the writings from the castle, or he should die. Then he went once more into the stable, and bemoaned himself and said, "Oh, my dear little white horse, now I am to go away again, how am I to do it?" Then the little white horse said he was just to load the ships full again. So it happened again as it had happened before, and the giants and the birds were satisfied, and made gentle by the meat. When they came to the castle, the white horse told Ferdinand the Faithful that he must go in, and that on the table in the princess's bedroom lay the writings. And Ferdinand the Faithful went in, and fetched them. When they were on the lake, he let his pen fall into the water; then said the white horse, "Now I cannot help thee at all." But he remembered his flute, and began to play on it, and the fish came with the pen in its mouth, and gave it to him. So he took the writings to the castle, where the wedding was celebrated.

The Queen, however, did not love the King because he had no nose, but she would have much liked to love Ferdinand the Faithful. Once, therefore, when all the lords of the court were together, the Queen said she could do feats of magic, that she could cut off anyone's head and put it on again, and that one of them ought just to try it. But none of them would be the first, so Ferdinand the Faithful, again at the instigation of Ferdinand the Unfaithful, undertook it and she hewed off his head, and put it on again for him, and it healed together directly, so that it looked as if he had a red thread round his throat. Then the King said to her, "My child, and where hast thou learnt that?" "Yes," she said, "I understand the art; shall I just try it on thee also?" "Oh, yes," said he. But she cut off his head, and did not put it on again; but pretended that she could not get it on, and that it would not keep fixed. Then the King was buried, but she married Ferdinand the Faithful.

He, however, always rode on his white horse, and once when he was seated on it, it told him that he was to go on to the heath which he knew, and gallop three times round it. And when he had done that, the white horse stood up on its hind legs, and was changed into a King's son.

Corvetto
(*Italy*)

There was once upon a time in the service of the King of Wide-River an excellent youth named Corvetto, who for his good conduct was beloved by his master, and for this very cause was disliked and hated by all the courtiers; in fact they were such bats of ignorance that they could not see the lustre of the virtue of Corvetto, who purchased his master's favour with the ready money of good behaviour. But the zephyrs of the kindness which the king showed Corvette were sciroccos[1] to the spite and malice of these courtiers, who were bursting with envy; so that all the day long, in every corner of the palace, they did nothing but tattle and whisper,

---

1 Hot winds from the south.

murmur and grumble at the poor lad, saying, "What sorcery has this fellow practised on the king, that he takes such a fancy to him? how comes he by this luck, that not a day passes but he receives some new favours, whilst we are forever going backwards like the rope-maker, and getting from bad to worse, though we slave like dogs, sweat like field-labourers, and race about like deer, to hit the king's pleasure to a hair? Truly one must be born to good fortune in this world, and he who has not luck may as well throw himself into the sea. What is to be done? we can only look on and burst."

These and other words flew from the bow of their mouth, like poisoned arrows aimed at the butt of Corvetto's ruin. Alas for him who is condemned to that infernal den the court, where flattery is sold by kilderkins,[1] malignity and ill offices are measured out in bushels, deceit and treachery are weighed by the ton! But who can count all the bits of orange-peel these courtiers put under his feet to make him slip, or tell the soap of falseness with which they besmeared the ladder to the king's ears, to make Corvette fall and break his neck? who can tell the pitfalls of deceit dug in the king's brain, and covered over with the sticks and straws of pretended zeal, to make him tumble? But Corvetto, who was enchanted, and perceived the traps and discovered the tricks, was aware of all the nets, and was up to all the intrigues, the ambuscades,[2] the plots and conspiracies of his enemies, kept his ears always on the alert and his eyes open, in order not to set a false step, well knowing that the fortune of courtiers is glass. But the higher the lad continued to rise, the lower the others fell; and at last being puzzled to know how to take him off his feet, as their slander was not believed, they thought of leading him to a precipice by the path of flattery (an art invented in a certain hot house, and perfected in the court), which they attempted in the following manner.

Ten miles distant from Scotland, where the seat of this king was, there dwelt an ogre, the most inhuman and savage that had ever been in ogreland, who, being persecuted by the king, had fortified himself in a lonesome wood on the top of a mountain, where no bird ever flew, and which was so thick and tangled that it could never get a sight of the sun. This ogre had a most beautiful horse, which looked as if it were formed with a pencil; and amongst other wonderful things was that it could speak like any man. Now the courtiers, who knew how wicked the ogre was, how thick the wood, how high the mountain, and how difficult it was to get at the horse, went to the king, and telling him minutely the perfections of the animal, which was a thing worthy of a king, added that he ought to endeavour by all means to get it out of the ogre's claws, and that Corvet-

1 Casks holding usually 16–18 gallons.
2 Ambushes.

to was just the lad to do this, as he was expert and clever at escaping out of the fire. The king, who knew not that under the flowers of these words a serpent was concealed, instantly called Corvetto, and said to him, "If you love me, see that in some way or another you obtain for me the horse of my enemy the ogre, and you shall have no cause to regret having done me this service."

Corvetto knew well that this drum was sounded by those who wished him ill; nevertheless, to obey the king, he set out and took the road to the mountain; then going very quietly to the ogre's stable, he saddled and mounted the horse, and fixing his feet firmly in the stirrup took his way back. But as soon as the horse saw himself spurred out of the palace, he cried aloud, "Hello! be on your guard! Corvetto is riding off with me." At this alarm the ogre instantly set out, with all the animals that served him, to cut Corvetto in pieces: from this side jumped an ape, from that was seen a large bear, here sprang forth a lion, there came running a wolf. But the youth, by the aid of bridle and spur, distanced the mountain, and galloping without stop to the city, arrived at the court, where he present-ed the horse to the king.

Then the king embraced him more than a son, and pulling out his purse filled his hands with crown-pieces. At this the rage of the courtiers knew no bounds; and whereas at first they were pulled up with a little pipe, they were now bursting with the blasts of a smith's bellows; seeing that the crowbars with which they thought to lay Corvetto's good fortune in ruins only served to smooth the road to his prosperity. Knowing howev-er that walls are not levelled by the first attack of the battering-ram, they resolved to try their luck a second time, and said to the king, "We wish you joy of the beautiful horse! it will indeed be an ornament to the royal stable; but what a pity you have not the ogre's tapestry, which is a thing more beautiful than words can tell, and would spread your fame far and wide! there is no one however able to procure this treasure but Corvetto, who is just the lad to do such a kind of service."

Then the king, who danced to every tune, and ate only the peel of this bitter but sugared fruit, called Corvetto, and begged him to procure for him the ogre's tapestry. Off went Corvetto, and in four seconds was on the top of the mountain where the ogre lived: then passing unseen into the chamber in which he slept, he hid himself under the bed, and wait-ed as still as a mouse, until Night, to make the Stars laugh, puts a carni-val-mask on the face of the Sky. And as soon as the ogre and his wife were gone to bed, Corvetto stripped the walls of the chamber very quietly, and wishing to steal the counterpane of the bed likewise, he began to pull it gently. Thereupon the ogre, suddenly starting up, told his wife not to pull so, for she was dragging all the clothes off him, and would give him his death of cold.

"Why you are uncovering *me*!" answered the ogress; "there's not a thing left upon me!"

"Where the deuce is the counterpane?" replied the ogre; and stretching out his hand to the floor, he touched Corvetto's face; whereupon he set up a loud cry, "The monaciello![1] the monaciello! hello, here, lights! run quickly!" till the whole house was turned topsy-turvy with the noise. But Corvetto, after throwing the clothes out of the window, let himself drop down upon them. Then making up a good bundle, he set out on the road to the city, where the reception he met with from the king, and the vexation of the courtiers, who were bursting with spite, are not to be told. Nevertheless they laid a plan to fall upon Corvetto with the rear-guard of their roguery, and went again to the king, who was almost beside himself with delight at the tapestry, which was not only of silk embroidered with gold, but had besides more than a thousand devices and thoughts worked on it; and amongst the rest, if I remember right, there was a cock in the act of crowing at daybreak, and out of its mouth was seen coming a motto in Tuscan—*If I only see you*; and in another part a drooping heliotrope[2] with a Tuscan motto, *At sunset*; with so many other pretty things that it would require a better memory and more time than I have to relate them.

When the courtiers came to the king, who was thus transported with joy, they said to him, "As Corvetto has done so much to serve you, it would be no great matter for him, in order to give you a signal pleasure, to get the ogre's palace, which is fit for an emperor to live in; for it has so many rooms and chambers, inside and out, that it can hold an army; and you would never believe all the courtyards, porticos, colonnades, balconies, and spiral chimneys which there are, built with such marvellous architecture, that art prides herself upon them, nature is abashed, and stupor is in delight."

The king, who had a fruitful brain which conceived quickly, called Corvetto again, and telling him the great longing that had seized him for the ogre's palace, begged him to add this service to all the others he had done him, promising to score it up with the chalk of gratitude at the tavern of memory. So Corvetto, who was a brimstone match and made a hundred miles an hour, instantly set out heels over head; and arriving at the ogre's palace, he found that the ogress had just given birth to a fine little ogreling; and whilst her husband was gone to invite the kinsfolk, she had got out of bed, and was busying herself with preparing the feast. Then Corvetto entering, with a look of compassion, said, "Good-day, my good woman! truly you are a brave housewife! but why do you torment the very life out of you in this way? only yesterday you were put to bed,

---

1   "Little Monk", a traditional Neapolitan fairy.
2   A fragrant purple flower.

and now you are slaving thus, and have no pity on your own flesh."

"What would you have me do?" replied the ogress, "I have no one to help me."

"I am here," answered Corvetto, "ready to help you tooth and nail."

"Welcome then!" said the ogress; "and as you proffer me so much kindness, just help me to split four logs of wood."

"With all my heart," answered Corvetto; "but if four logs are not enow,[1] let me split five." And taking up a newly-ground axe, instead of striking the wood, he struck the ogress on the neck, and made her fall to the ground like a pear. Then running quickly to the gate, he dug a deep hole before the entrance, and covering it over with bushes and earth, he hid himself behind the gate.

As soon as Corvetto saw the ogre coming with his kinsfolk, he set up a loud cry in the courtyard, "Stop, stop! I've caught him!" and "Long live the king of Wide-River!" When the ogre heard this challenge, he ran like mad at Corvetto, to make a hash of him; but rushing furiously towards the gate, down he tumbled with all his companions, head over heels to the bottom of the pit, where Corvetto speedily stoned them to death. Then he shut the door, and took the keys to the king, who seeing the valour and cleverness of the lad, in spite of ill-fortune and the envy and annoyance of the courtiers, gave him his daughter to wife; so that the crosses of envy had proved rollers to launch Corvetto's bark of life on the sea of greatness; whilst his enemies remained confounded and bursting with rage, and went to bed without a candle; for

> *The punishment of ill deeds past,*
> *Though long delay'd, yet comes at last.*

The Golden Palace That Hung in the Air (*Norway*)

Once on a time there was a poor man who had three sons. When he died the two eldest were to go out into the world to try their luck; but as for the youngest they would not have him at any price.

'As for you,' they said, 'you are fit for nothing but to sit and hold fir tapers, and grub in the ashes and blow up the embers. That's what you are fit for.'

'Well, well,' said Boots, 'then I must e'en go alone by myself: at any rate I shan't fall out with my company.'

---

1 Enough.

So the two went their way, and when they had travelled some days they came to a great wood. There they sat down to rest, and were just going to take out a meal from their knapsack, for they were both tired and hungry. So as they sat there up came an old hag out of a hillock, and begged for a morsel of meat. She was so old and feeble that her nose and mouth met, and she nodded with her head, and could only walk with a stick. As for meat she had not had, she said, a morsel in her mouth these hundred years. But the lads only laughed at her, and ate on and told her as she had lived so long on nothing, she might very well hold out the rest of her life, even though she did not eat up their scanty fare, for they had little to eat and nothing to spare.

So when they had eaten their fill and could eat no more, and were quite rested, they went on their way again, and, sooner or later, they came to the King's Grange, and there they each of them got a place.

A while after they had started from home, Boots gathered together the crumbs which his brothers had thrown on one side, and put them into his little scrip,[1] and he took with him the old gun which had no lock, for he thought it might be some good on the way; and so he set off. So when he had wandered some days, he too came into the big wood through which his brothers had passed, and as he got tired and hungry, he sat down under a tree that he might rest and eat; but he had his eyes about him for all that, and as he opened his scrip he saw a picture hanging on a tree, and on it was painted the likeness of a young girl or princess, whom he thought so lovely he couldn't keep his eyes off her. So he forgot both food and scrip, and took down the painting and lay and stared at it. Just then came up the old hag out of the hillock, who hobbled along with her stick, whose nose and mouth met, and whose head nodded. Then she begged for a little food, for she hadn't had a morsel of bread in her mouth for a hundred years. That was what she said.

'Then it's high time you had a little to live on, granny,' said the lad; and with that he gave her some of the crumbs he had. The old hag said no one had ever called her 'granny' these hundred years, and she would be as a mother to him in her turn. Then she gave him a grey ball of wool, which he had only to roll on before him and he would come to whatever place he wished; but as for the painting she said he mustn't bother himself about that, he would only fall into ill luck if he did. As for Boots, he thought it was very kind of her to say that, but he could not bear to be without the painting, so he took it under his arm and rolled the ball of wool before him, and it was not long before he came to the King's Grange, where his brothers served. There he too begged for a place, but all the answer he got was they had nothing to put him to, for they had just got two new

---

1 Pouch or wallet.

serving men. But as he begged so prettily, at last he got leave to be with the coachman, and learn how to groom and handle horses. That he was right glad to do, for he was fond of horses, and he was both quick and ready, so that he soon learnt how to bed and rub them down, and it was not long before everyone in the King's Grange was fond of him; but every hour he had to himself he was up in the loft looking at the picture, for he had hung it up in a corner of the hay-loft.

As for his brothers, they were dull and lazy, and so they often got scolding and stripes, and when they saw that Boots fared better than they, they got jealous of him, and told the coachman he was a worshipper of false gods, for he prayed to a picture and not to Our Lord. Now, even though the coachman thought well of the lad, still he wasn't long before he told the king what he had heard. But the king only swore and snapped at him, for he had grown very sad and sorrowful since his daughters had been carried off by trolls. But they so dinned it into the king's ears, that at last he must and would know what it was that the lad did. But when he went up into the hay-loft and set his eyes on the picture, he saw it was his youngest daughter who was painted on it. But when the brothers of Boots heard that, they were ready with an answer, and said to the coachman,

'If our brother only would, he has said he was good to get the king's daughter back.'

You may fancy it was not long before the coachman went to the king with this story, and when the king heard it, he called for Boots, and said,

'Your brothers say you can bring back my daughter again, and now you must do it.'

Boots answered, he had never known it was the king's daughter till the king said so himself, and if he could free her and fetch her he would be sure to do his best; but two days he must have to think over it and fit himself out. Yes, he might have two days.

So Boots took the grey ball of wool and threw it down on the road, and it rolled and rolled before him, and he followed it till he came to the old hag, from whom he had got it. Her he asked what he must do, and she said he must take with him that old gun of his and three hundred chests of nails and horseshoe brads,[1] and three hundred barrels of barley, and three hundred barrels of grits, and three hundred carcases of pigs, and three hundred beeves,[2] and then he was to roll the ball of wool before him till he met a raven and a baby troll, and then he would be all right, for they were both of her stock. Yes, the lad did as she bade him; he went right on to the King's Grange, and took his old gun with him, and he asked the king for the nails and the brads, and meat and flesh, and grain, and

1   Thin, small nails.
2   Cattle.

for horses and men, and carts to carry them in. The king thought it was a good deal to ask, but if he could only get his daughter back, he might have whatever he chose, even to the half of his kingdom.

So when the lad had fitted himself out, he rolled the ball of wool before him again, and he hadn't gone many days before he came to a high hill, and there sat a raven, up in a fir tree. So Boots went on till he came close under the tree, and then he began to aim and point at the raven with his gun.

'No, no,' cried the raven, 'don't shoot me, don't shoot me, and I'll help you.'

'Well,' said Boots, 'I never heard of anyone who boasted he had eaten roast raven, and since you are so eager to save your life, I may just as well spare it.'

So he threw down his gun, and the raven came flying down to him, and said,

'Here, up on this fell there is a baby troll walking up and down, for he has lost his way and can't get down again. I will help you up, and then you can lead him home, and ask a boon which will stand you in good stead. When you get to the troll's house he will offer you all the grandest things he has, but you should not heed them a pin. Mind you take nothing else but the little grey ass which stands behind the stable door.'

Then the raven took Boots on his back and flew up on the hill with him, and put him off there. When he had gone about on it a bit, he heard the baby troll howling and whining because it couldn't get down again. So the lad talked kindly to it, and they got the best friends in the world, and he said he would help it down and guide it to the old troll's house, that it mightn't lose itself on the way back. Then they went to the raven, and he took them both on his back, and carried them off the hill troll's house.

And when the old troll saw his baby, he was so glad he was beside himself, and told Boots he might come indoors and take whatever he chose, because he had freed his child. Then they offered him both gold and silver, and all that was rare and costly; but the lad said he would rather have a horse than anything else. Yes, he should have a horse, the troll said, and off they went to the stable. It was full of the grandest horses, whose coats shone like the sun and moon; but Boots thought they were all too big for him. So he peeped behind the stable door, and when he set eyes on the little grey ass that stood there, he said,

'I'll take this one. It will suit me to a T, and if I fall off I shall be no farther from the ground than that ——high.'

The old troll did not at all like to part with his ass, but as he had given his word he had to stand by it. So Boots got the ass, and saddle, and bridle, and all that belonged to it, and then he set off. They travelled through wood and field, and over fells and wide wastes. So when they had gone farther than far, the ass asked Boots if he saw anything.

'No, I see naught else than a hill, which looks blue in the distance,' said Boots.

'Oh,' said the ass, 'that hill we have to pass through.'

'All very fine, I daresay,' said Boots, for he didn't believe a word of it.

So when they got close to the hill, an unicorn came tearing along at them, just as if he were going to eat them up all alive.

'I almost think now I'm afraid,' said Boots.

'Oh,' said the ass, 'don't say so; just throw it a score or so of beeves, and beg it to bore a hole, and break a way for us through the hill.'

So Boots did as he was told, and when the unicorn had eaten his fill, they said they would give him a score or two of pigs' carcasses, if he would go before them and bore a hole in the hill, so that they might get through it. So when he heard that he set to work and bored the hole, and broke a way so fast that they had hard work to keep up with him, and when he had done his work they threw him two score of pigs.

So when they had got well out of that they travelled far away, until they passed again through woods and fields and across fells and wide wastes.

'Do you see anything now?' asked the ass.

'Now I see naught but the bare sky and wild fells,' said Boots.

So they travelled on far and farther than far, and the higher up they came the fell got smoother and flatter, so that they could see farther about them.

'Do you see anything now?' said the ass.

'Yes, I see something far, far away,' said Boots, 'and it gleams and twinkles like a little star.'

'It's not so very little for all that,' said the ass.

So when they had gone on farther and farther than far again, the ass asked again,

'Do you see anything now?'

'Yes,' said Boots, 'I see something a long way off, that shines like a moon.'

'It is no moon,' said the ass, 'but the silver castle we are bound for. Now, when we get there you will see three dragons lying on the watch before the gate. They have not been awakened for hundreds of years, and so the moss has grown over their eyes.'

'I almost think I shall be afraid of them,' said Boots.

'Oh, don't say that,' said the ass, 'you've only got to wake up the youngest, and throw it a score or so of beeves and swine, and then it will talk to the others, and so you'll come into the castle.'

So on they travelled far and farther than far again before they came up to the castle, but when they reached it it was both grand and great, and everything they saw was cast in silver, and outside the gate lay the dragons, and blocked up the way so that no one could get in; but they had a nice easy time of it, and had not been much troubled in their watch; for they were so overgrown with moss that no one could tell what they were made of, and at their sides underwood was springing up between the tufts of moss. So Boots woke up the youngest of them, and it began to rub its eyes and clear the moss out of them. But when the dragon saw there was folk there, he came at them with his maw wide a-gape; but then the lad stood ready, and tossed into it the carcasses of beeves, and swung after them salted swine, till the dragon had got his fill, and grew a little more sensible to talk to. Then the lad begged he would wake up his fellows, and ask them to be so good as to get out of the way, so that he might get into the castle; but the dragon neither would nor dared to do that at first, for he said, as they had not been awake or tasted anything for hundreds of years, he was afraid lest they should get raving mad, and swallow up everything alive or dead.

But Boots thought there was no need to fear that, for they could leave behind them a hundred carcasses of beeves, and a hundred salt swine, and go a little way off and then the dragons would have time to eat their fill, and to come to themselves before the others came back to the castle.

Yes, the dragon was ready to do that, and so they did it; but before the dragons were well awake, and got the moss rubbed off their eyes; they went about roaring and raving, and riving and rending at everything alive or dead, so that the youngest dragon had enough to do to shield himself from them till they had snuffed up the smell of flesh. Then they swallowed down whole oxen and swine, and ate and ate till they were full. And after that they were just as tame and buxom as the youngest, and let Boots pass between them into the castle.

When he got inside it was all so grand he never could have thought anything could be so good anywhere; but there was not a soul in it, for he went from room to room, and opened all the doors, but he could see no one. Well, at last he peeped through a door that led to a bedroom, which he had not seen before, and in there sat a princess, spinning, and she was so glad and happy when she saw him.

'No, no,' she cried, 'can it be that Christian folk dare to come hither? but it will be best for you to be off again, else the troll might kill you, for you must know a troll lives with three heads.'

But Boots said he would not fly even if he had seven heads. When the princess heard that, she said she wished him to try if he could brandish the great rusty sword that hung behind the door. No, he could not brandish it, he could not so much as even lift it.

'Ah,' said the princess, 'if you can't do that you must take a drink of that flask yonder, that hangs by the side of the sword, for that's what the troll does when he goes out to use it.'

So Boots took two or three drinks, and then he could brandish the sword as though it were a rolling pin.

Just then came the troll, so that the wind sung after him.

'Hu!' he screeched out, 'what a smell of Christian blood there is in here.'

'I know there is,' said Boots, 'but you needn't blow and snort so at it; you shan't suffer long from that smell,' and in a trice he cut off all his heads.

The princess was so glad, just as if she had got something so good; but in a little while she got heavy-hearted, for she pined for her sister, who had been stolen by a troll with six heads, and lived in a golden castle three hundred miles on this side of the world's end. Boots thought that was not so very bad, for he could go and fetch both the princess and the castle; and so he took the sword and the flask, and got on the ass, and bade the dragons follow him, and carry the meat, and grain, and nails which he had.

So when they had been a while on the way, and had travelled far, far away over land and strand, the ass said one day,

'Do you see anything?'

'I see naught,' said Boots, 'but land and water and bare sky and high crags.'

So they went on far and farther than far, and then the ass said again,

'Do you see anything now?'

'Yes,' when he had looked well before him, he saw something a long, long way off, that shone like a little star.

'It will be big enough by-and-by,' said the ass.

When they had gone a good bit still, the ass asked,

'Do you see anything now?'

'Now I see it shining like a moon,' said the lad.

'Ay, ay,' said the ass, and on they went.

So when they had gone far, and farther than far away, over land and strand, and hill and heath, the ass asked,

'Do you see anything now?'

'Now, methinks,' said Boots, 'it shines most like the sun.'

'Ay,' said the ass, 'that's the golden castle for which we are bound; but outside it lives a worm, which stops the way and keeps watch and ward.'

'I think I shall be afraid of it,' said Boots.

'Oh, don't say so,' said the ass, 'we must spread over it heaps of boughs, and lay between them layers of horseshoe brads and nails, and set fire to them all, and so we shall be rid of it.'

So after a long, long time they came up to where the castle hung in the air, but the worm lay underneath it and stopped the way. So the lad gave the dragons a good meal of beeves and salted swine, that they might help him, and they spread over the worm heaps of boughs and wood, and laid between them layers of nails and brads, till they had used up the three hundred chests, and when it was all done they set fire to the pile and burned up the worm alive, in a fire at white heat.

So when they had done with him one dragon flew under the castle and lifted it up, and the two others went up high, high into the air, and unloosed the links and hooks by which it hung, and so they lowered it down and set it on the ground. When that was done Boots went inside, and there it was grander far than in the silvern castle, but he could see no folk till he came to the innermost room, and there lay a princess on a bed of gold. She slept so sound, as though she were dead, but she was not, though he was not able to wake her up, for her face was as red and white as milk and blood. And just as Boots stood there gazing at her, back came the troll tearing along. As soon as he put his first head through the door he screamed out,

'Hu! what a smell of Christian blood there is in here.'

'Maybe,' said Boots, 'but you've no need to smell and snort about that; you shan't suffer long from it.'

And with that he cut off all his heads, as though they stood on a kail stalk.

So the dragons took the golden castle on their backs and went home with it—I fancy they were not long on the way—and set it down side by side with the silvern castle, so that it shone both far and wide.

Now when the princess of the silvern castle came to her window in the morning, and caught sight of it, she was so glad that she sprang over to the golden castle at once; but when she saw her sister lying there and sleeping as though she were dead, she said to Boots that they would never get life into her before they found the water of life and death, and that stood in two wells on either side of a golden castle which hung in the air, nine hundred miles beyond the world's end, and where the third sister dwelt.

Well, Boots thought there was no help for it; he must go and fetch it, and it was not long before he was on his way. So he travelled far and farther than far, through many realms, across wood and field, over fell and firth, along hill and heath, and at last he got to the world's end, and after that he travelled far, far over crags and wastes and high rocks.

'Do you see anything?' asked the ass one day.

'I see naught but heaven and earth,' said the lad.

'Do you see anything now?' asked the ass again, when some days were past.

'Yes,' said Boots, 'now I see something that glimmers very high up, far,

far away, like a little star.'

'It's not so little for all that,' said the ass.

So when they had travelled on a while, the ass asked,

'Do you see anything now?'

'Yes,' said Boots, 'now it shines like the sun.'

'That's whither we are bound,' said the ass; 'it's the golden castle that hangs in the air, and there lives a princess who has been stolen by a troll with nine heads; but all the wild beasts there are in the world lie on watch, and stop the way thither.'

'Uf,' said Boots, 'I almost think I'm afraid of them.'

'Don't say so,' said the ass; and then he told him there was no danger, if he would only make up his mind not to linger there, but to set off on his way back as soon as ever he had filled his flasks with the water, for there was no going thither but during one hour in the day, and that began at high noon; but if he were not man enough to be ready in time and to get away, the beasts would tear him into a thousand pieces.

Well, Boots said he would be sure to do that, he would not think of staying too long.

At the stroke of twelve they reached the castle, and there lay all the wild and savage beasts that ever were, as it were a fence before the gate, and on either side of the way. But they all slumbered like stocks and stones, and there wasn't one of them that so much as lifted a paw. So Boots passed between them, and took good heed not to tread on their toes or the tips of their tails, and he filled his flasks with the waters of life and death, and while he did that he looked up at the castle, which was as though it were cast in pure gold. It was the grandest he had ever seen, and he thought it would be grander still inside than out.

'Stuff,' thought Boots, 'I have time enough, I can always look about me in half an hour,' and so he opened the door and went in. Well, inside it was grander than grand itself, and as he went out of one gorgeous room into another, it was as if it was all made of gold and pearls, and everything that was costliest in the world. Folk there were none; but at last he came into a bedroom where there lay another princess on a bed of gold, just as though she were dead too, but she was as grand as the grandest queen, and as red and white as blood on snow, and so lovely he had never seen anything so lovely but her picture; for she it was that was painted on it.

Then Boots forgot both the water he was to fetch, and the wild beasts, and the castle and everything, and could only gaze at the princess; and he thought he could never have his fill of looking at her; but all the while she slept as though she were dead, and he was not able to wake her up.

So when it drew towards evening, the troll came tearing along so that the wind sung after him, and he rattled and slammed the gates and doors till the whole castle rang again.

'Huf,' he cried; 'what a strong smell of Christian blood there is in here;' and then he stuck his first head inside the door and snuffed up the air.

'I daresay there is,' said Boots, 'but you've no need to puff and blow as though you were about to burst, for it shan't vex you long;' and as he said that he cut off all his nine heads. But when he had done that he got so weary he couldn't keep his eyes open. So he laid him down on the bed by the side of the princess, and all the while she slept both night and day, as though she would never wake again; only at midnight she just woke up for the twinkling of an eye, and then she told him that he had set her free, but she must bide there three years still, and if she didn't come home to him then he must just come and fetch her.

When the clock began to go towards one next day, Boots woke for the first time, and the first thing he heard was the ass braying and screaming and making a stir, and so he thought he would get up and set off home, but before he went he cut a breadth out of the princess's skirt, and took it away with him. And however it was, he had loitered so long there that the beasts began to wake and stir, and by the time he had mounted his ass they stood in a ring round him, so that he thought it had rather a ghastly look. But the ass said he must sprinkle on them a few drops of the water of death, and he did so, and in a trice they all fell headlong on the spot, and never stirred a limb more.

As they were on their way home, the ass said to Boots—

'Now when you come to honour and glory, see if you don't forget me and all I have done for you, so that I shall be broken-kneed for hunger.'

'Nay, nay! that should never be,' said the lad.

So when he got home to the princess with the water of life, she sprinkled a few drops over her sister, and woke her up, and then there was such great joy and they were so happy. Then they travelled home to the king, and he too was glad and joyful, because he had got those two back; but still he went about longing and longing that the three years might pass away, and his youngest daughter come home.

As for Boots, who had brought them back, the king made him a mighty man, so that he was the first in the land after the king himself. But there were many who were jealous that he should have grown to be such a man of mark, and one of them was Ritter Red, who they did say wished to have the eldest princess, and he got her to sprinkle over Boots a little of the water of death, so that he swooned off and lay as dead.

So when the three years were over, and a bit of the fourth was gone, there came sailing up a strange ship of war, and on board was the third sister, and with her she had a boy three years old. She sent word up to the King's Grange, and said she would not set her foot on land till they had sent him who had been in the golden castle and set her free. So they sent down to her one of the highest men about the court, the master of the ceremonies himself; and when he came on board the princess' ship, he took off his hat and bowed and scraped, and bent himself before her.

'Can that be your father? my son,' said the princess to her boy, who was playing with a golden apple.

'No,' said the child, 'my father doesn't crawl about like a cheesemite.'[1]

So they sent another of the same stamp, and this time it was Ritter Red. But it fared no better with him than with the first one, and the princess sent word by him, if they didn't make haste and send the right one, it should go ill with them. When they heard that they were forced to wake up Boots with the water of life; and so he went down to the ship to the princess, but he didn't make too low a bow, I should think; he only nodded his head and brought out the breadth he had cut out of the skirt of the princess in the golden castle.

'That's my father! that's my father!' bawled out the boy, and gave him the golden apple he was playing with.

Then there was great joy and mirth all over the realm, and the old king was the gladdest of all of them, because he had got his darling back again. But when what Ritter Red and the eldest princess had done to Boots came out, the king asked to have them both rolled down a hill, each in a cask full of spikes and nails; but Boots and the youngest princess begged hard for them, and so they got off with life.

Now it happened one day, as they were about to begin the bridal feast, that they stood looking out of window—it was towards spring, just when they were turning out the horses and cows after the winter—and the last that came out of the stable was the ass; but it was so starved that it came out of the stable-door on its knees.

Then Boots was cut to the heart because he had forgotten it, and he went down and did not know how to make it up to the poor beast. But the ass said the best thing he could do was to cut his head off. That he was very loath to do, but the ass begged so prettily that he had to yield, and did it at last; and as soon as ever his head fell in the yard, it was all over with the shape which had been thrown over him by witchcraft, and there stood the handsomest prince anyone cared to see. He got the second princess to wife, and they fell to keeping the bridal feast, so that it was heard and talked of over seven kingdoms.

> *Then they built themselves houses,*
> *And stitched themselves shoon,*
> *And had so many bairns*
> *They reached up to the moon.*

---

1 A small, whitish mite.

592: The Dance Among Thorns

The Gifts of the Magician
(*Finland*)

Once upon a time there was an old man who lived in a little hut in the middle of a forest. His wife was dead, and he had only one son, whom he loved dearly. Near their hut was a group of birch trees, in which some black-game had made their nests, and the youth had often begged his father's permission to shoot the birds, but the old man always strictly forbade him to do anything of the kind.

One day, however, when the father had gone to a little distance to collect some sticks for the fire, the boy fetched his bow, and shot at a bird that was just flying towards its nest. But he had not taken proper aim, and the bird was only wounded, and fluttered along the ground. The boy ran to catch it, but though he ran very fast, and the bird seemed to flutter along very slowly, he never could quite come up with it; it was always just a little in advance. But so absorbed was he in the chase that he did not notice for some time that he was now deep in the forest, in a place where he had never been before. Then he felt it would be foolish to go any further, and he turned to find his way home.

He thought it would be easy enough to follow the path along which he had come, but somehow it was always branching off in unexpected directions. He looked about for a house where he might stop and ask his way, but there was not a sign of one anywhere, and he was afraid to stand still, for it was cold, and there were many stories of wolves being seen in that part of the forest. Night fell, and he was beginning to start at every sound, when suddenly a magician came running towards him, with a pack of wolves snapping at his heels. Then all the boy's courage returned to him. He took his bow, and aiming an arrow at the largest wolf, shot him through the heart, and a few more arrows soon put the rest to flight. The magician was full of gratitude to his deliverer, and promised him a reward for his help if the youth would go back with him to his house.

'Indeed there is nothing that would be more welcome to me than a night's lodging,' answered the boy; 'I have been wandering all day in the forest, and did not know how to get home again.'

'Come with me, you must be hungry as well as tired,' said the magician, and led the way to his house, where the guest flung himself on a bed, and went fast asleep. But his host returned to the forest to get some food, for the larder was empty.

While he was absent the housekeeper went to the boy's room and tried to wake him. She stamped on the floor and shook him and called to him, telling him that he was in great danger, and must take flight at once. But nothing would rouse him, and if he did ever open his eyes he shut them again directly.

Soon after, the magician came back from the forest, and told the housekeeper to bring them something to eat. The meal was quickly ready, and the magician called to the boy to come down and eat it, but he could not be wakened, and they had to sit down to supper without him. By-and-by the magician went out into the wood again for some more hunting, and on his return he tried afresh to waken the youth. But finding it quite impossible, he went back for the third time to the forest.

While he was absent the boy woke up and dressed himself. Then he came downstairs and began to talk to the housekeeper. The girl had heard how he had saved her master's life, so she said nothing more about his running away, but instead told him that if the magician offered him the choice of a reward, he was to ask for the horse which stood in the third stall of the stable.

By-and-by the old man came back and they all sat down to dinner. When they had finished the magician said: 'Now, my son, tell me what you will have as the reward of your courage?'

'Give me the horse that stands in the third stall of your stable,' answered the youth. 'For I have a long way to go before I get home, and my feet will not carry me so far.'

'Ah! my son,' replied the magician, 'it is the best horse in my stable that you want! Will not anything else please you as well?'

But the youth declared that it was the horse, and the horse only, that he desired, and in the end the old man gave way. And besides the horse, the magician gave him a zither, a fiddle, and a flute, saying: 'If you are in danger, touch the zither; and if no one comes to your aid, then play on the fiddle; but if that brings no help, blow on the flute.'

The youth thanked the magician, and fastening his treasures about him mounted the horse and rode off. He had already gone some miles when, to his great surprise, the horse spoke, and said: 'It is no use your returning home just now, your father will only beat you. Let us visit a few towns first, and something lucky will be sure to happen to us.'

This advice pleased the boy, for he felt himself almost a man by this time, and thought it was high time he saw the world. When they entered the capital of the country everyone stopped to admire the beauty of the horse. Even the king heard of it, and came to see the splendid creature with his own eyes. Indeed, he wanted directly to buy it, and told the youth he would give any price he liked. The young man hesitated for a moment, but before he could speak, the horse contrived to whisper to him:

'Do not sell me, but ask the king to take me to his stable, and feed me there; then his other horses will become just as beautiful as I.'

The king was delighted when he was told what the horse had said, and took the animal at once to the stables, and placed it in his own particular stall. Sure enough, the horse had scarcely eaten a mouthful of corn out of the manger, when the rest of the horses seemed to have undergone a transformation. Some of them were old favourites which the king had ridden in many wars, and they bore the signs of age and of service. But now they arched their heads, and pawed the ground with their slender legs as they had been wont to do in days long gone by. The king's heart beat with delight, but the old groom who had had the care of them stood crossly by, and eyed the owner of this wonderful creature with hate and envy. Not a day passed without his bringing some story against the youth to his master, but the king understood all about the matter and paid no attention. At last the groom declared that the young man had boasted that he could find the king's war horse which had strayed into the forest several years ago, and had not been heard of since. Now the king had never ceased to mourn for his horse, so this time he listened to the tale which the groom had invented, and sent for the youth. 'Find me my horse in three days,' said he, 'or it will be the worse for you.'

The youth was thunderstruck at this command, but he only bowed, and went off at once to the stable.

'Do not worry yourself,' answered his own horse. 'Ask the king to give you a hundred oxen, and to let them be killed and cut into small pieces. Then we will start on our journey, and ride till we reach a certain river. There a horse will come up to you, but take no notice of him. Soon another will appear, and this also you must leave alone, but when the third horse shows itself, throw my bridle over it.'

Everything happened just as the horse had said, and the third horse was safely bridled. Then the other horse spoke again: 'The magician's raven will try to eat us as we ride away, but throw it some of the oxen's flesh, and then I will gallop like the wind, and carry you safe out of the dragon's clutches.'

So the young man did as he was told, and brought the horse back to the king.

The old stableman was very jealous when he heard of it, and wondered what he could do to injure the youth in the eyes of his royal master. At last he hit upon a plan, and told the king that the young man had boasted that he could bring home the king's wife, who had vanished many months before, without leaving a trace behind her. Then the king bade the young man come into his presence, and desired him to fetch the queen home again, as he had boasted he could do. And if he failed, his head would pay the penalty.

The poor youth's heart stood still as he listened. Find the queen? But how was he to do that, when nobody in the palace had been able to do so! Slowly he walked to the stable, and laying his head on his horse's shoulder, he said: 'The king has ordered me to bring his wife home again, and how can I do that when she disappeared so long ago, and no one can tell me anything about her?'

'Cheer up!' answered the horse, 'we will manage to find her. You have only got to ride me back to the same river that we went to yesterday, and I will plunge into it and take my proper shape again. For I am the king's wife, who was turned into a horse by the magician from whom you saved me.'

Joyfully the young man sprang into the saddle and rode away to the banks of the river. Then he threw himself off, and waited while the horse plunged in. The moment it dipped its head into the water its black skin vanished, and the most beautiful woman in the world was floating on the water. She came smiling towards the youth, and held out her hand, and he took it and led her back to the palace. Great was the king's surprise and happiness when he beheld his lost wife stand before him, and in gratitude to her rescuer he loaded him with gifts.

You would have thought that after this the poor youth would have been left in peace; but no, his enemy the stableman hated him as much as ever, and laid a new plot for his undoing. This time he presented himself before the king and told him that the youth was so puffed up with what he had done that he had declared he would seize the king's throne for himself.

At this news the king waxed so furious that he ordered a gallows to be erected at once, and the young man to be hanged without a trial. He was not even allowed to speak in his own defence, but on the very steps of the gallows he sent a message to the king and begged, as a last favour, that he might play a tune on his zither. Leave was given him, and taking the instrument from under his cloak he touched the strings. Scarcely had the first notes sounded than the hangman and his helper began to dance, and the louder grew the music the higher they capered, till at last they cried for mercy. But the youth paid no heed, and the tunes rang out more merrily than before, and by the time the sun set they both sank on the ground exhausted, and declared that the hanging must be put off till to-morrow.

The story of the zither soon spread through the town, and on the following morning the king and his whole court and a large crowd of people were gathered at the foot of the gallows to see the youth hanged. Once more he asked a favour—permission to play on his fiddle, and this the king was graciously pleased to grant. But with the first notes, the leg of every man in the crowd was lifted high, and they danced to the sound of the music the whole day till darkness fell, and there was no light to hang the musician by.

The third day came, and the youth asked leave to play on his flute. 'No, no,' said the king, 'you made me dance all day yesterday, and if I do it again it will certainly be my death. You shall play no more tunes. Quick! the rope round his neck.'

At these words the young man looked so sorrowful that the courtiers said to the king: 'He is very young to die. Let him play a tune if it will make him happy.' So, very unwillingly, the king gave him leave; but first he had himself bound to a big fir tree, for fear that he should be made to dance.

When he was made fast, the young man began to blow softly on his flute, and bound though he was, the king's body moved to the sound, up and down the fir tree till his clothes were in tatters, and the skin nearly rubbed off his back. But the youth had no pity, and went on blowing, till suddenly the old magician appeared and asked: 'What danger are you in, my son, that you have sent for me?'

'They want to hang me,' answered the young man; 'the gallows are all ready and the hangman is only waiting for me to stop playing.'

'Oh, I will put that right,' said the magician; and taking the gallows, he tore it up and flung it into the air, and no one knows where it came down. 'Who has ordered you to be hanged?' asked he.

The young man pointed to the king, who was still bound to the fir; and without wasting words the magician took hold of the tree also, and with a mighty heave both fir and man went spinning through the air, and vanished in the clouds after the gallows.

Then the youth was declared to be free, and the people elected him for their king; and the stable helper drowned himself from envy, for, after all, if it had not been for him the young man would have remained poor all the days of his life.

Little Freddy With His Fiddle
(*Norway*)

Once on a time there was a cottager who had an only son, and this lad was weakly, and hadn't much health to speak of; so he couldn't go out to work in the field.

His name was Freddy, and undersized he was too; and so they called him Little Freddy. At home there was little either to bite or sup, and so his father went about the country trying to bind him over as a cowherd or an errand-boy; but there was no one who would take his son till he came to the sheriff, and he was ready to take him, for he had just packed off his errand-boy, and there was no one who would fill his place, for the story went that he was a skinflint.

But the cottager thought it was better there than nowhere; he would get his food, for all the pay he was to get was his board—there was nothing said about wages or clothes. So when the lad had served three years he wanted to leave, and then the sheriff gave him all his wages at one time. He was to have a penny a year. "It couldn't well be less," said the sheriff. And so he got threepence in all.

As for little Freddy, he thought it was a great sum, for he had never owned so much; but for all that, he asked if he wasn't to have something more.

"You have already had more than you ought to have," said the sheriff.

"Shan't I have anything, then, for clothes?" asked little Freddy; "for those I had on when I came here are worn to rags, and I have had no new ones."

And, to tell the truth, he was so ragged that the tatters hung and flapped about him.

"When you have got what we agreed on," said the sheriff, "and three whole pennies beside, I have nothing more to do with you. Be off!"

But for all that, he got leave just to go into the kitchen and get a little food to put in his scrip;[1] and after that he set off on the road to buy himself more clothes. He was both merry and glad, for he had never seen a penny before; and every now and then he felt in his pockets as he went along to see if he had them all three. So when he had gone far and farther than far, he got into a narrow dale, with high fells on all sides, so that he couldn't tell if there were any way to pass out; and he began to wonder what there could be on the other side of those fells, and how he ever should get over them.

But up and up he had to go, and on he strode; he was not strong on his legs, and had to rest every now and then—and then he counted and counted how many pennies he had got. So when he had got quite up to the very top, there was nothing but a great plain overgrown with moss. There he sat him down, and began to see if his money was all right; and before he was aware of him a beggar-man came up to him, and he was so tall and big that the lad began to scream and screech when he got a good look of him, and saw his height and length.

"Don't you be afraid," said the beggar-man; "I'll do you no harm. I only beg for a penny, in God's name."

"Heaven help me!" said the lad. "I have only three pennies, and with them I was going to the town to buy clothes."

"It is worse for me than for you," said the beggar-man. "I have got no penny, and I am still more ragged than you."

1 Small pouch or wallet.

"Well, then, you shall have it," said the lad.

So when he had walked on awhile he got weary, and sat down to rest again. But when he looked up there he saw another beggar-man, and he was still taller and uglier than the first; and so when the lad saw how very tall and ugly and long he was, he fell a-screeching.

"Now, don't you be afraid of me," said the beggar; "I'll not do you any harm. I only beg for a penny, in God's name."

"Now, may Heaven help me!" said the lad. "I've only got two pence, and with them I was going to the town to buy clothes. If I had only met you sooner, then——"

"It's worse for me than for you," said the beggar-man. "I have no penny, and a bigger body and less clothing."

"Well, you may have it," said the lad.

So he went awhile farther, till he got weary, and then he sat down to rest; but he had scarce sat down than a third beggar-man came to him. He was so tall and ugly and long, that the lad had to look up and up, right up to the sky. And when he took him all in with his eyes, and saw how very, very tall and ugly and ragged he was, he fell a-screeching and screaming again.

"Now, don't you be afraid of me, my lad," said the beggar-man; "I'll do you no harm; for I am only a beggar-man, who begs for a penny in God's name."

"May Heaven help me!" said the lad. "I have only one penny left, and with it I was going to the town to buy clothes. If I had only met you sooner, then——"

"As for that," said the beggar-man, "I have no penny at all, that I haven't, and a bigger body and less clothes, so it is worse for me than for you."

"Yes," said little Freddy, he must have the penny then there was no help for it; for so each would have what belonged to him, and he would have nothing.

"Well," said the beggar-man, "since you have such a good heart that you gave away all that you had in the world, I will give you a wish for each penny." For you must know it was the same beggar-man who had got them all three; he had only changed his shape each time, that the lad might not know him again.

"I have always had such a longing to hear a fiddle go, and see folk so glad and merry that they couldn't help dancing," said the lad; "and so, if I may wish what I choose, I will wish myself such a fiddle, that everything that has life must dance to its tune."

"That he might have," said the beggar-man; but it was a sorry wish. "You must wish something better for the other two pennies."

"I have always had such a love for hunting and shooting," said little

Freddy; "so if I may wish what I choose, I will wish myself such a gun that I shall hit everything I aim at, were it ever so far off."

"That he might have," said the beggar-man; but it was a sorry wish. "You must wish better for the last penny."

"I have always had a longing to be in company with folk who were kind and good," said little Freddy; "and so, if I could get what I wish, I would wish it to be so that no one can say 'Nay' to the first thing I ask."

"That wish was not so sorry," said the beggar-man; and off he strode between the hills, and he saw him no more. And so the lad lay down to sleep, and the next day he came down from the fell with his fiddle and his gun.

First he went to the storekeeper and asked for clothes, and at one farm he asked for a horse, and at another for a sledge; and at this place he asked for a fur coat, and no one said him "Nay"—even the stingiest folk, they were all forced to give him what he asked for. At last he went through the country as a fine gentleman, and had his horse and his sledge; and so when he had gone a bit he met the sheriff with whom he had served.

"Good day, master," said little Freddy, as he pulled up and took off his hat.

"Good day," said the sheriff. And then he went on, "When was I ever your master?"

"Oh, yes," said little Freddy. "Don't you remember how I served you three years for three pence?"

"Heaven help us!" said the sheriff. "How you have got on all of a hurry! And pray, how was it that you got to be such a fine gentleman?"

"Oh, that's tellings," said little Freddy.

"And are you full of fun, that you carry a fiddle about with you?" asked the sheriff.

"Yes, yes," said Freddy. "I have always had such a longing to get folk to dance; but the funniest thing of all is this gun, for it brings down almost anything that I aim at, however far it may be off. Do you see that magpie yonder, sitting in the spruce fir? What'll you bet I don't bag it as we stand here?"

On that the sheriff was ready to stake horse and groom, and a hundred dollars beside, that he couldn't do it; but as it was, he would bet all the money he had about him; and he would go to fetch it when it fell—for he never thought it possible for any gun to carry so far.

But as the gun went off down fell the magpie, and into a great bramble thicket; and away went the sheriff up into the brambles after it, and he picked it up and showed it to the lad. But in a trice little Freddy began to scrape his fiddle, and the sheriff began to dance, and the thorns to tear him; but still the lad played on, and the sheriff danced, and cried, and begged till his clothes flew to tatters, and he scarce had a thread to his back.

"Yes," said little Freddy, "now I think you're about as ragged as I was when I left your service; so now you may get off with what you have got."

But first of all, the sheriff had to pay him what he had wagered that he could not hit the magpie.

So when the lad came to the town he turned aside into an inn, and he began to play, and all who came danced, and he lived merrily and well. He had no care, for no one would say him "Nay" to anything he asked.

But just as they were all in the midst of their fun, up came the watchmen to drag the lad off to the town-hall; for the sheriff had laid a charge against him, and said he had waylaid him and robbed him, and nearly taken his life. And now he was to be hanged—they would not hear of anything else. But little Freddy had a cure for all trouble, and that was his fiddle. He began to play on it, and the watchmen fell a-dancing, till they lay down and gasped for breath.

So they sent soldiers and the guard on their way; but it was no better with them than with the watchmen. As soon as ever little Freddy scraped his fiddle, they were all bound to dance, so long as he could lift a finger to play a tune; but they were half dead long before he was tired. At last they stole a march on him, and took him while he lay asleep by night; and when they had caught him, he was doomed to be hanged on the spot, and away they hurried him to the gallows-tree.

There a great crowd of people flocked together to see this wonder, and the sheriff, he too was there; and he was so glad at last at getting amends for the money and the skin he had lost, and that he might see him hanged with his own eyes. But they did not get him to the gallows very fast, for little Freddy was always weak on his legs, and now he made himself weaker still. His fiddle and his gun he had with him also—it was hard to part him from them; and so, when he came to the gallows, and had to mount the steps, he halted on each step; and when he got to the top he sat down, and asked if they could deny him a wish, and if he might have leave to do one thing? He had such a longing, he said, to scrape a tune and play a bar on his fiddle before they hanged him.

"No, no," they said; "it were sin and shame to deny him that." For, you know, no one could gainsay what he asked.

But the sheriff he begged them, for God's sake, not to let him have leave to touch a string, else it was all over with them altogether; and if the lad got leave, he begged them to bind him to the birch that stood there.

So little Freddy was not slow in getting his fiddle to speak, and all that were there fell a-dancing at once, those who went on two legs, and those who went on four; both the dean and the parson, and the lawyer, and the bailiff, and the sheriff, masters and men, dogs and swine—they all danced and laughed and screeched at one another. Some danced till they lay for dead; some danced till they fell into a swoon. It went badly with all of them, but worst of all with the sheriff; for there he stood bound to the birch, and he danced and scraped great bits off his back against the trunk. There was not one of them who thought of doing anything to little Freddy, and away he went with his fiddle and his gun, just as he chose; and he lived merrily and happily all his days, for there was no one who could say him "Nay" to the first thing he asked for.

The Friar and the Boy
(*England*)

'You good-for-nothing boy, you! It's always meal-times when you come home: that's all you care about here. Look at the knees of your trousers; why, playing marbles in the street with all the other filthy little brats is about all you're fit for. How d'you think I'm going to spend all my time patching up your holes and tatters? Drat you! Get out of it and wipe your boots before you come into a clean kitchen. I've been all the afternoon tidying up for the good Friar's visit this evening, and now you—'

'Hang the good Friar!' said Jack under his breath, for he was sick and tired of his stepmother's sour tongue, and more than sick and tired of the good Friar, who, he knew, was only 'good' when he was not feeling well. Taking a fairy-tale book from the shelf he went and sat in the inglenook,[1] thus sheltering himself from a further storm of abuse from his stepmother.

The fact of the matter was that thrice upon a time his father had married. Jack, a merry-hearted boy, and lovable for all his mischief, was his son by his first wife. The other two had no children, and the stepmother now living seemed to resent the fact of Jack's existence. His father loved him dearly, but, when the father was away, Jack had a sore time with his sour-tempered stepmother. No wonder he only came home to meals; no wonder he preferred his fairy-tale book to her venomous tongue.

When supper-time came, Jack was always summoned to his food well in time for it to be cleared away before his father came in; and the reason for this was that his father should not see how he was stinted.

But one day the father got to know about these things, and taxed his wife on her treatment of the boy.

'Look here, sir,' said she, 'I wish to goodness you would take your wretched son away and put him in a school for saints, since you think he is so good. As for me, he plagues my life out, and, if you keep him here

---

1 A space adjoining a fireplace.

with his ne'er-do-well ways, you'll come home some evening to find me gone.'

Instead of beating his wife for these words—as some men do when their wives so beseech them—the goodman put his hand on her shoulder and said, 'Nay, nay, my dear; the boy is only a boy; let him stay with us another year until he can fend for himself. Now, I'll tell you what: let the man who looks after the sheep come in here and do the work about the house, and Jack will take his place in the field. The man can have Jack's bed, and Jack will be delighted to sleep in the outhouse. What say you?'

The wife could not object to this, for, at least, the man would be more useful and less troublesome about the house than Jack could ever be. So she agreed to her husband's proposal.

The next day the plan was put into operation.

The man was set to work about the house, and Jack was sent out into the fields to mind the sheep. As he went he sang merrily, for he loved the green fields and the animals. He doubted the dinner his stepmother had put up for him, wrapped in a kitchen clout; yet he sang merrily as he went in search of the sheep:

> *Green gravel! Green gravel!*
> *Thy grass is so green.*
> *'Tis the fairies' green gravel*
> *With the daisies between.*

Then, when he had found them:

> *Snowy sheepie-woolsides,*
> *Save your wool for me;*
> *Then in snowy yuletides*
> *Snug and warm I'll be.*

Then, later, when he began to get hungry, it was:

> *Sheepie, wander, wander*
> *All the fields about;*
> *Grass is growing under,*
> *Clover budding out.*
> *My mother does not squander*
> *Cakes on me, I doubt;*
> *What is here, I wonder,*
> *In this kitchen clout?*

And, sitting down on a mossy bank, he opened the clout in which his stepmother had wrapped his dinner. Lo and behold, it was dry bread, with a very thick layer of dripping scraped off from it back into the pot.

He ate very little, thinking that surely his father would give him some-thing nicer to eat when he got home.

In the afternoon he sat on the hillside watching the sheep and singing merrily, when he saw an aged man with a staff making his way towards him.

'God bless you, son,' said the aged one.

'Good-morrow, father,' replied the boy. 'You are weary. Rest a while on this mossy bank.'

'Ay, I will,' said the old man, sitting down beside the boy. 'You speak truly: I am weary, and hungry, and thirsty too. Have you any food? And would your young legs take you to the stream to bring me back a draught of water?'

'I have food, such as it is,' replied Jack readily; and he offered him the dry bread and scrape that his stepmother had given him. 'As for water, I have a pannikin,[1] and I'll soon fill it at the stream.' And with that he hur-ried off to fetch the water.

When he returned, and the old man had eaten and drank, he thanked the boy. 'God love you, child,' he said; 'you have been kind to me. And now, in return, I am minded to grant you three wishes of your heart. Think well, and then name them; and it shall be as I say.'

Jack thought and thought; but all he could decide on to begin with was a bow and arrow. So he asked for that.

'Certainly!' said the old man; and, rising, he went behind the bank, and presently returned with the bow and arrow, which he gave to the boy.

'This will last you all your life,' he said; 'and it will never break. All you have to do is to draw it with the arrow on the string, and whatever you aim at will fall, pierced by the arrow.'

Jack was delighted, and, in order to test it, he fixed an arrow and let it fly at a hawk passing overhead. The arrow sped and pierced the body of the hawk, which came down plump at their feet.

At this Jack considered his second wish, for he said to himself, 'An old man who can give me a bow and arrow that can never miss, can give me almost anything.' Then he made up his mind and asked for a pipe on which to play tunes.

'I have always wanted a pipe,' he said; 'I would like one so much, no matter how small it is.'

Then the old man got up and went behind the bank, and came back presently with a beautiful pipe, which he gave to the boy.

'It is a strange pipe,' he said. 'When you play upon it anyone besides yourself who hears the music must dance, and keep on dancing till the music stops.'

---

1 Small metal drinking cup.

Jack thought this was fine, and would have played a tune there and then, but he looked at the aged man and saw that it would hurt him to dance; so he waited: there was always the 'good Friar' to pipe to.

'Now, child,' said the old man at last, 'what is your third and last wish?'

Jack pondered a long time, and at last he chuckled and clapped his hands with glee. When the old man asked him what tickled him so, he could not reply at once, as he was so busy enjoying some joke beforehand. At last, when he was able to speak, he said, 'Father, it has just crossed my mind that my stepmother is always looking at me sourly and always scolding me. I wish that when she does this she will laugh, and go on laughing till I give her the word to stop. Can you grant that wish, father?'

'I can,' said the old man; 'and it will be so. When she looks at you sourly or speaks to you crossly, she will laugh until she falls to the ground, and then go on laughing until you tell her to stop.'

When Jack had thanked him, the old man said good-bye and tottered away, leaning heavily on his staff. Meanwhile Jack sat and nursed his three wishes, feeling as gay-hearted about his good luck as a lambkin with three tails.

When the sun set at last and his day's work was done, he rose and trudged homewards in great glee. As he went he played his pipe, and all the sheep and cattle and horses and dogs danced, till he left off for laughing at the sight of them kicking up their heels. Even the birds and the bees waltzed in the air, and, as he crossed a bridge, he saw the little fishes pirouetting in the stream below.

As soon as he reached home he put the pipe away, and, going into the house, found his father at supper.

'Father,' said he, 'I am terribly hungry after looking to the sheep all day; and, besides, my dinner was very dry.'

'Here you are, my son,' replied his father; and, cutting a wing from the roast capon[1] on the table before him, he set it on a plate and pushed it over to the boy.

At this the stepmother, grudging to see such a nice portion given to the boy, turned upon him with a look that would have made a cow give sour milk. Then, on the instant, she burst out laughing. Her husband stared at her in amazement, but still she laughed, her sides shaking with her shrill peals; and louder and louder she laughed, until the rafters shook and she fell to the ground, still laughing as if she would die of it.

At last Jack, with his capon's wing in both hands before him, stopped eating to cry, 'Enough, I say!' And immediately the stepmother ceased her

---

1 A neutered and fattened rooster.

laughter and struggled to her feet, looking more dead than alive.

Now, the next day, when Jack was minding the sheep, the good Friar called at the house, and the stepmother told him what a naughty boy Jack was, and how he had made her laugh till she had nearly died, and then mocked her.

'Go you, now,' she said; 'go and find him in the fields and give him a sound beating for my sake. It will do him good—and me too.'

So the Friar went out into the fields and at last found the boy, with his bow and arrow in his hands.

'Young man,' said the Friar, 'tell me at once what you have done to your stepmother that she is so angered with you. Tell me at once, I say, or I will give you a sound beating.'

'What's the matter with you?' replied Jack. 'If my stepmother wants me beaten, let her do it herself. See that bird?' He pointed to a very plump bird flying overhead. 'If you fetch it when it drops, you can have it.'

With this he let fly an arrow and pierced the bird, which fell to earth a little way off in a bramble patch. As the Friar darted forward to get it— for it was indeed a plump bird—Jack drew forth his pipe and began to play.

It is said that he who hops among thorns is either chasing a snake or being chased by one; and it looked as if either the one or the other was the Friar's case, for he hopped high in the bramble bushes and danced as if he had gone mad in both heels at once.

To see the good Friar dancing willy-nilly among the bramble bushes, kicking up his heels to the tune of the pipe, higher still and higher—oh, it was a sight for Jack's eyes, for he loved the Friar to distraction in less ways than one. So long as Jack piped, the Friar danced. His dress was torn to shreds, but that seemed a small matter. The thorns did admirable work, but the Friar did not care. On with the dance! *Tara-tara-tara-ra-ra*—the Friar seemed to be enjoying himself, though more for Jack's benefit than his own. Faster and faster shrilled the pipe, and faster danced the Friar, until at last he fell down among the brambles, a sorry spectacle, still kicking his feet in the air to the merry rhythm. Then Jack ceased piping, but only to laugh; for he had small pity for the Friar.

'Friend Jack!' cried the Friar, gathering himself up, 'forbear, I pray you. I am nigh to death. Permit me to depart and I will be your friend forever.'

'Get up and go, then,' cried Jack, 'before I begin to play again.'

The good Friar needed no further permission. What remnant of a robe was left him he gathered up, and fled to his own home. There he clothed himself decently and made all haste to Jack's parents.

When they saw his woebegone countenance they questioned him close- ly.

'I have been with your son,' he replied. 'Grammercy! By these scratches on my face, and by others you cannot see, he is in league with the Evil One, or I am no holy Friar. He played a tune on his pipe and I danced—danced!—think of it! And all in the bramble bushes! Your son is plainly lost; I hesitate to think what it will cost you to save his soul from the devil's clutch.'

'Here is a fine thing,' exclaimed the wife, turning to her husband. 'This your son has nearly killed the holy Father!'

'Benedicite!' said the good man fervently, and the Friar wondered for a moment what he meant exactly.

When Jack returned home his father at once asked him what he had been doing. He replied that he had been having a merry time with the good Friar, who was so fond of music that he could dance to it anywhere—among bramble bushes for preference. These saints, of course——

'But what music is this you play?' broke in his father, who was growing vastly interested. 'I should like to hear it.'

'Heaven forfend!' cried the Friar, getting uneasy.

'Yes, yes; I should like to hear it,' persisted his father.

'Then, if that is so, and you must hear his accursed tune, I beg that you will bind me to the door-post so that I cannot move. I have had more than enough of it.'

They took him at his word and bound him securely to the door-post; so that he was, so to speak, out of the dance when Jack took his pipe and began to play.

Then had you seen a merry spectacle! At the first notes the good man and his wife began to tread a sprightly measure, while the Friar, bound fast to the post, squirmed and wriggled, showing plainly that he would foot it if he could, and dispense with the brambles for once.

As the piping went on, the merry measure became a tarantelle.[1] The staid old folks threw off their age, and kicked their heels high in the air. Faster and faster went the music; wilder and wilder grew the dance. The Friar burst his bonds and joined in. Nothing was safe: chairs were hustled into the fire; the table was pushed this way and that, and the lighted lamp upon it was rocking.

Seeing the fury of the thing, Jack got up and led the way out into the street, still piping. They followed; the neighbours flocked out and joined in the dance; even those who had gone to bed rushed down, and all followed at Jack's heels down the village street, dancing madly to his wild piping. People jostled and fell and went on dancing on all fours, but the Friar kept his feet, if not his head, and whirled many a maid into the thick of it.

At length, when they had reached the village green, and the scene had

---

1 An upbeat folk dance from Southern Italy.

become one of indescribable confusion and abandon, Jack's father drew near him and said, as he whirled by: 'Jack! if you have any consideration for your poor old father, for heaven's sake, stop!'

Now the boy loved his father; so, on hearing these words, he ceased his piping. Suddenly all came to a standstill. There was a rapid melting away as if people had awakened from a dream in which they had been making themselves ridiculous. And, in the midst of this, came forward the Friar with Jack's stepmother in close attendance.

'That cursed boy!' cried he, shaking his fist at Jack. 'See here, my fine fellow, you cannot do this kind of thing with impunity. I hereby summon you before the Judge next Friday, and see to it that you appear in person to answer the charges I shall bring against you.'

At this the boy raised his pipe again to his lips; but, before he could blow a single note, they had all taken to their heels in dismay, leaving him standing there alone in the empty square.

It was Friday, and the Judge, be-wigged and severe, sat on the bench, with all the appearance of a great case before him. The Friar was there as prosecutor; the King's Proctor was watching the case—in case; the Public Persuader was there with his suave and well-paid manner, admonishing all sides; Jack's parents and all his relations and friends were there, wondering greatly whether Jack, who stood in the dock, would live to tell the tale of what death was meted out to him.

'M'lud!' said the Friar when there was silence in court; 'I have brought before you a wicked boy who, by associating with the Evil One, has corrupted the manners of this community, and brought sorrow and trouble to all. Though young he is none the less a wizard, having infernal skill.'

'Ay, that he is,' put in the stepmother. 'He is in league—in league——' But she got no further, for, in a trice, she was laughing as none had ever been known to laugh.

The Judge was scandalised.

'Woman!' he said. 'This Court itself has been known to laugh, but this behaviour on your part is unseemly.'

'Stop it!' said Jack from the dock, and he spoke short and sharp.

She ceased immediately, and then the Judge requested her to tell her tale; but she was so exhausted that the Friar had to tell it for her.

'M'lud,' he said, 'it is simply this: the prisoner here has a pipe, and, when he plays upon it, all who hear must dance themselves to death, whether they like it or not.'

'Ah!' said the Judge, 'I should like to hear this Dance of Death. You have heard it, good father, and you still live. Maybe, when I have heard it, I shall be charmed, like the serpent, and come out to be killed at once.

Let him play his music.'

And, with this remark, the Judge sat back, while Jack took up his pipe to play.

'Stop! stop!' cried the Friar in dismay. But Jack heeded not. At the nod of the Judge he started up a merry tune, and immediately the whole Court began to imagine itself a ballroom. Set to partners—cross—ladies' chain—chassé! It was a regular whirl as the boy piped faster and faster. The Judge himself leapt down from the bench and joined in, holding up his robes and footing it merrily. But, when he bruised his shins severely against the clerk's desk, he yelled for the boy to cease piping.

'Yes, I will,' cried Jack, and as he paused with his pipe raised to his lips they all waited on his words: 'I will, if they will all promise to treat me properly from this time forward.'

'I think,' said the Judge, 'if you will put your pipe away, they will consent to an amicable arrangement.'

Then he climbed back to the bench and sat himself down, and put on his considering cap to pass sentence.

There was silence in court for some minutes. Then came in solemn tones:

'Judgment for the defendant—with costs!'

And so, all parties being satisfied, the Court adjourned, and everyone went home to supper quite happy.

650A: The Sharp Hans

The Young Giant
(*Germany*)

Once on a time a countryman had a son who was as big as a thumb, and did not become any bigger, and during several years did not grow one hair's breadth. Once when the father was going out to plough, the little one said, "Father, I will go out with you." "Thou wouldst go out with me?" said the father. "Stay here, thou wilt be of no use out there, besides thou mightest get lost!" Then Thumbling began to cry, and for the sake of peace his father put him in his pocket, and took him with him. When he was outside in the field, he took him out again, and set him in a freshly-cut furrow. Whilst he was there, a great giant came over the hill. "Do thou see that great bogie?" said the father, for he wanted to frighten the little fellow to make him good; "he is coming to fetch thee." The giant, however, had scarcely taken two steps with his long legs before he was in the furrow. He took up little Thumbling carefully with two fingers, examined him, and without saying one word went away with him. His father stood by, but could not utter a sound for terror, and he thought nothing else but that his child was lost, and that as long as he lived he should never set eyes on him again.

The giant, however, carried him home, suckled him, and Thumbling grew and became tall and strong after the manner of giants. When two years had passed, the old giant took him into the forest, wanted to try him, and said, "Pull up a stick for thyself." Then the boy was already so strong that he tore up a young tree out of the earth by the roots. But the giant thought, "We must do better than that," took him back again, and suckled him two years longer. When he tried him, his strength had increased so much that he could tear an old tree out of the ground. That was still not enough for the giant; he again suckled him for two years, and when he then went with him into the forest and said, "Now just tear up a proper stick for me," the boy tore up the strongest oak-tree from the earth, so that it split, and that was a mere trifle to him. "Now that will do," said the giant, "thou art perfect," and took him back to the field from whence he had brought him. His father was there following the plough. The young giant went up to him, and said, "Does my father see what a fine man his son has grown into?"

The farmer was alarmed, and said, "No, thou art not my son; I don't want thee leave me!" "Truly I am your son; allow me to do your work, I can plough as well as you, nay better." "No, no, thou art not my son; and thou canst not plough, go away!" However, as he was afraid of this great man, he left go of the plough, stepped back and stood at one side of the piece of land. Then the youth took the plough, and just pressed it with one hand, but his grasp was so strong that the plough went deep into the earth. The farmer could not bear to see that, and called to him, "If thou art determined to plough, thou must not press so hard on it, that makes bad work." The youth, however, unharnessed the horses, and drew the plough himself, saying, "Just go home, father, and bid my mother make ready a large dish of food, and in the meantime I will go over the field." Then the farmer went home, and ordered his wife to prepare the food; but the youth ploughed the field which was two acres large, quite alone, and then he harnessed himself to the harrow, and harrowed the whole of the land, using two harrows at once. When he had done it, he went into the forest, and pulled up two oak-trees, laid them across his shoulders, and hung on them one harrow behind and one before, and also one horse behind and one before, and carried all as if it had been a bundle of straw, to his parents' house. When he entered the yard, his mother did not recognize him, and asked, "Who is that horrible tall man?" The farmer said, "That is our son." She said, "No that cannot be our son, we never had such a tall one, ours was a little thing." She called to him, "Go away, we do not want thee!" The youth was silent, but led his horses to the stable, gave them some oats and hay, and all that they wanted. When he had done this, he went into the parlour, sat down on the bench and said, "Mother, now I should like something to eat, will it soon be ready?" Then she said, "Yes," and brought in two immense dishes full of food, which would have been enough to satisfy herself and her husband for a week. The youth, however, ate the whole of it himself, and asked if she had nothing more to set before him. "No," she replied, "that is all we have." "But that was only a taste, I must have more." She did not dare to oppose him, and went and put a huge caldron full of food on the fire, and when it was ready, carried it in. "At length come a few crumbs," said he, and ate all there was, but it was still not sufficient to appease his hunger. Then said he, "Father, I see well that with you I shall never have food enough; if you will get me an iron staff which is strong, and which I cannot break against my knees, I will go out into the world." The farmer was glad, put his two horses in his cart, and fetched from the smith a staff so large and thick, that the two horses could only just bring it away. The youth laid it across his knees, and snap! he broke it in two in the middle like a bean-stalk, and threw it away. The father then harnessed four horses, and brought a bar which was so long and thick, that the four horses could only just drag it. The son snapped this also in twain against his knees, threw it away, and said, "Father, this can be of no use to me, you must harness more horses, and bring a stronger staff." So the father harnessed eight horses, and brought one which was so long and thick, that the eight horses could only just carry it. When the son took it in his hand, he broke off a bit from the top of it also, and said, "Father, I see that you will not be able to procure me any such staff as I want, I will remain no longer with you."

So he went away, and gave out that he was a smith's apprentice. He arrived at a village, wherein lived a smith who was a greedy fellow, who never did a kindness to anyone, but wanted everything for himself. The youth went into the smithy and asked if he needed a journeyman. "Yes," said the smith, and looked at him, and thought, "That is a strong fellow who will strike out well, and earn his bread." So he asked, "How much wages dost thou want?" "I don't want any at all," he replied, "only every fortnight, when the other journeymen are paid, I will give thee two blows, and thou must bear them." The miser was heartily satisfied, and thought he would thus save much money. Next morning, the strange journeyman was to begin to work, but when the master brought the glowing bar, and the youth struck his first blow, the iron flew asunder, and the anvil sank so deep into the earth, that there was no bringing it out again. Then the miser grew angry, and said, "Oh, but I can't make any use of you, you strike far too powerfully; what will you have for the one blow?"

Then said he, "I will only give you quite a small blow, that's all." And he raised his foot, and gave him such a kick that he flew away over four loads of hay. Then he sought out the thickest iron bar in the smithy for himself, took it as a stick in his hand and went onwards.

When he had walked for some time, he came to a small farm, and asked the bailiff if he did not require a head-servant. "Yes," said the bailiff, "I can make use of one; you look a strong fellow who can do something, how much a year do you want as wages?" He again replied that he wanted no wages at all, but that every year he would give him three blows, which he must bear. Then the bailiff was satisfied, for he, too, was a covetous fellow. Next morning all the servants were to go into the wood, and the others were already up, but the head-servant was still in bed. Then one of them called to him, "Get up, it is time; we are going into the wood, and thou must go with us." "Ah," said he quite roughly and surlily, "you may just go, then; I shall be back again before any of you." Then the others went to the bailiff, and told him that the head-man was still lying in bed, and would not go into the wood with them. The bailiff said they were to awaken him again, and tell him to harness the horses. The head-man, however, said as before, "Just go there, I shall be back again before any of you." And then he stayed in bed two hours longer. At length he arose from the feathers, but first he got himself two bushels of peas from the loft, made himself some broth with them, ate it at his leisure, and when that was done, went and harnessed the horses, and drove into the wood. Not far from the wood was a ravine through which he had to pass, so he first drove the horses on, and then stopped them, and went behind the cart, took trees and brushwood, and made a great barricade, so that no horse could get through. When he was entering the wood, the others were just driving out of it with their loaded carts to go home; then said he to them, "Drive on, I will still get home before you do." He did not drive far into the wood, but at once tore two of the very largest trees of all out of the earth, threw them on his cart, and turned round. When he came to the barricade, the others were still standing there, not able to get through. "Don't you see," said he, "that if you had stayed with me, you would have got home just as quickly, and would have had another hour's sleep?" He now wanted to drive on, but his horses could not work their way through, so he unharnessed them, laid them on the top of the cart, took the shafts in his own hands, and pulled it all through, and he did this just as easily as if it had been laden with feathers. When he was over, he said to the others, "There, you see, I have got over quicker than you," and drove on, and the others had to stay where they were. In the yard, however, he took a tree in his hand, showed it to the bailiff, and said, "Isn't that a fine bundle of wood?" Then said the bailiff to his wife, "The servant is a good one, if he does sleep long, he is still home before the others." So he served the bailiff for a year, and when that was over, and the other servants were getting their wages, he said it was time for him to take his too. The bailiff, however, was afraid of the blows which he was to receive, and earnestly entreated him to excuse him from having them; for rather than that, he himself would be head-servant, and the youth should be bailiff. "No," said he, "I will not be a bailiff, I am head-servant, and will remain so, but I will administer that which we agreed on." The bailiff was willing to give him whatsoever he demanded, but it was of no use, the head-servant said no to everything. Then the bailiff did not know what to do, and begged for a fortnight's delay, for he wanted to find some way of escape. The head-servant consented to this delay. The bailiff summoned all his clerks together, and they were to think the matter over, and give him advice. The clerks pondered for a long time, but at last they said that no one was sure of his life with the head-servant, for he could kill a man as easily as a midge, and that the bailiff ought to make him get into the well and clean it, and when he was down below, they would roll up one of the mill-stones which was lying there, and throw it on his head; and then he would never return to daylight. The advice pleased the bailiff, and the head-servant was quite willing to go down the well. When he was standing down below at the bottom, they rolled down the largest mill-stone and thought they had broken his skull, but he cried, "Chase away those hens from the well, they are scratching in the sand up there, and throwing the grains into my eyes, so that I can't see."

So the bailiff cried, "Sh–sh," and pretended to frighten the hens away. When the head-servant had finished his work, he climbed up and said, "Just look what a beautiful neck-tie I have on," and behold it was the mill-stone which he was wearing round his neck. The head-servant now wanted to take his reward, but the bailiff again begged for a fortnight's delay. The clerks met together and advised him to send the head-servant to the haunted mill to grind corn by night, for from thence as yet no man had ever returned in the morning alive. The proposal pleased the bailiff, he called the head-servant that very evening, and ordered him to take eight bushels of corn to the mill, and grind it that night, for it was wanted. So the head-servant went to the loft, and put two bushels in his right pocket, and two in his left, and took four in a wallet, half on his back, and half on his breast, and thus laden went to the haunted mill. The miller told him that he could grind there very well by day, but not by night, for the mill was haunted, and that up to the present time whosoever had gone into it at night had been found in the morning lying dead inside. He said, "I will manage it, just you go away to bed." Then he went into the mill, and poured out the corn. About eleven o'clock he went into the miller's room, and sat down on the bench. When he had sat there a while, a door suddenly opened, and a large table came in, and on the table, wine and roasted meats placed themselves, and much good food besides, but everything came of itself, for no one was there to carry it. After this the chairs pushed themselves up, but no people came, until all at once he beheld fingers, which handled knives and forks, and laid food on the plates, but with this exception he saw nothing. As he was hungry, and saw the food, he, too, placed himself at the table, ate with those who were eating and enjoyed it. When he had had enough, and the others also had quite emptied their dishes, he distinctly heard all the candles being suddenly snuffed out, and as it was now pitch dark, he felt something like a box on the ear. Then he said, "If anything of that kind comes again, I shall strike out in return." And when he had received a second box on the ear, he, too struck out. And so it continued the whole night. He took nothing without returning it, but repaid everything with interest, and did not lay about him in vain. At daybreak, however, everything ceased. When the miller had got up, he wanted to look after him, and wondered if he were still alive. Then the youth said, "I have eaten my fill, have received some boxes on the ears, but I have given some in return." The miller rejoiced, and said that the mill was now released from the spell, and wanted to give him much money as a reward. But he said, "Money, I will not have, I have enough of it." So he took his meal on his back, went home, and told the bailiff that he had done what he had been told to do, and would now have the reward agreed on. When the bailiff heard that, he was seriously alarmed and quite beside himself; he walked backwards and forwards in the room, and drops of perspiration ran down from his forehead. Then he opened the window to get some fresh air, but before he was aware, the head-servant had given him such a kick that he flew through the window out into the air, and so far away that no one ever saw him again. Then said the head-servant to the bailiff's wife, "If he does not come back, you must take the other blow." She cried, "No, no I cannot bear it," and opened the other window, because drops of perspiration were running down her forehead. Then he gave her such a kick that she, too, flew out, and as she was lighter she went much higher than her husband. Her husband cried, "Do come to me," but she replied, "Come thou to me, I cannot come to thee." And they hovered about there in the air, and could not get to each other, and whether they are still hovering about, or not, I do not know, but the young giant took up his iron bar, and went on his way.

Rumble-Mumble Goose-Egg
(*Norway*)

Once five women were reaping in a field. Each of them was childless and wanted a child of her own. Suddenly they came upon a giant goose-egg. It was as big as a man's head.

"I saw it first," one said.

"I saw it just as soon," yelled another.

"What? I mean to have it. I was the one that first set eyes on it!" snarled a third.

They went on quarrelling over the egg and were quite ready to tear each other's hair, but at long last they agreed to keep it all five of them and sit on it like the goose does, to hatch out the gosling. The first of them sat for a week like a broody goose and had an easy time of it. She didn't have to work while the others toiled to feed themselves and her. Then one of them cursed her for being lazy in a goose's way.

"You couldn't twitter till you'd been in the egg a while yourself," said the one who was brooding. "But in this egg there's something human, I tell you. It seems to be mumbling 'Herring and gruel and porridge and milk' over and over again. Now you can sit on it for a week, and the rest of us can feed you in turns."

After the fifth woman had been sitting there brooding for a week, she could hear beyond doubt that there was a curious creature inside the egg. It went on shouting for "Herring and gruel and porridge and milk," So she picked a hole in the eggshell. There burst forth a human child with a big head and a little body. The infant was as ugly as could be, not anything like a gosling.

His first cry was: "Herring and gruel and porridge and milk!" They agreed to call him Rumble-Mumble Goose-egg.

He was such an ugly fellow from the start; they all became fond of him. But in a very short time he became so hungry that he ate all their food. Again and again when they made porridge and gruel enough for the six of them, the newcomer gulped down all of it. That's why they didn't want to keep him any longer. They said,

"That blasted imp!"

Rumble-Mumble Goose-egg overheard their complaints and at once got ready to leave. If they could do without him, he could do without them, he said. Off he went.

He walked far and asked for service on a farm in the pretty country. It so happened they were in need of a labourer. The old man who owned the farm told him to clear stones from the fields. Rumble-Mumble picked up the stones well. He gathered big ones that made up several cart-loads each, and put the whole lot, both big and small, into his pockets. Soon he had finished his job and went back to the farm to find out what to do next.

"Clear away the stones from the field," said the farmer. "You've hardly begun, young man."

The tall Rumble-Mumble Goose-egg now emptied his pockets and threw all the stones in a heap, so the farmer could see he had done the work very well. But from this moment on the farmer felt he ought to watch his step with such a strong man. He told him he had better come in and have something to eat. This suited Rumble-Mumble. He cleaned up the meal at once. There was nothing left for anybody else. And still he wasn't more than halfway satisfied.

Nobody could match him as a worker, but none matched him as an eater either. Feeding him was like pouring water through a sieve.

"A worker like that could eat a poor farmer out of house and home in three shakes of a lamb's tail," muttered the farmer to himself, and then he found no more work for him at all. It was best that Rumble-Mumble went to the king's farm at once.

He did and was taken on. He found there was food and work enough. He was to do errands and do odd jobs. First he could split up a bit of firewood, they said. Rumble-Mumble set to work and sent the splinters flying from his chopping and splitting. He chopped up all the wood there was, timber and wood set aside for planks and tools, and when he had finished he came along and asked what they wanted him to do next.

"Finish chopping wood," they said.

"There isn't any more," said Rumble-Mumble.

The bailiff came along with him and took a look at the woodshed. Rumble-Mumble had chopped up even the timber logs. The bailiff said this was a disgrace, and that Rumble-Mumble wouldn't get a bite to eat till he had been to the woods and felled as much timber as he had split up into firewood.

Rumble-Mumble at once ran down to the forge and had the smith help him make an axe of 250 kilos or so. Off to the forest. He cut down mast-timber and everything else to be found in the woods of the king and those of his neighbours. He left the branches on, and the forests looked as though they had been swept down by a whirlwind. He piled a solid load on the sledge and harnessed all the horses in front. He tugged at their bridles to get the load moving, and then he pulled all their heads off by accident. So in the end he was forced to pull the load to the king's farm himself.

The king and forester were standing in the porch when he arrived. They wanted to have a word with him about the way he treated the woods, for the forester had been along there and seen it all. But when the king saw Rumble-Mumble dragging half the forest behind him, he lost his nerve. He got vexed, alarmed and all at once saw no reason to fall out with such a man.

"You're a fit worker," said the king. "You're hungry now, I bet."

They set about preparing food. In the meantime Rumble-Mumble was to bring in a load of wood for the cook. He stacked the whole wood-pile on a sledge, and wanted to pull it though the door. But he was a bit rough again, so that wall timbers were pushed askew, corners slipped out of joint and the whole building nearly fell down.

All the same, while this happened, they could manage to make twelve hubs of meal to a portion of porridge for Rumble-Mumble, and much less for the other men around. When the dinner was just about ready, they sent him to call in the men. He shouted so loud that the hills echoed all around as they often do in a thunderstorm, and yet Rumble-Mumble thought the men were too slow in coming. He had a quarrel with them and in so doing knocked the life out of twelve.

Food was served. And then there was no need to feed him for a while.

"He knocked the life out of twelve," said the king, "and he eats much more than one hundred and forty-eight men, that is twelve times twelve, I reckon. How much work do you do, my lad?"

"Much more than twelve times twelve do," said Rumble-Mumble.

After dinner he was sent to the barn to thresh corn. He lifted the ridge-pole off the roof to use as a flail, and when the roof started collapsing, he took a giant spruce with all its branches on and put it along the ridge of the roof instead. And then he threshed grain and straw and hay all together. It didn't turn out well. Both corn and chaff were whirled through the air and spread like a cloud over all the farm.

When he had almost got the threshing done, an enemy invaded the country. So now the king was at war. He asked Rumble-Mumble to take some men with him, march against the enemy and meet him in battle, for the king was sure the enemy would kill him.

But Rumble-Mumble would fight alone. He didn't want to have men with him.

All the better, thought the king, the sooner I get rid of him.

But Rumble-Mumble had to have a good, solid club. The smith forged a club that weighed 100 kilos, and Rumble-Mumble said it was good enough to crack nuts with. Then the smith forged a club of 250 kilos. Rumble-Mumble said it was good enough to sole shoes with. Anyhow, the smith said it was the biggest job his men could do. And so Rumble-Mumble made a club of 2000 kilos, that is two tons. It took a hundred men to turn it on the anvil. He could make do with this new club. He also had to have a knapsack. They made it out of fifteen oxhides and packed it with food. Off he tramped with his club on his shoulder.

He came to the enemy's camp. They wanted to know if he was ready for battle.

"Just wait till I've had a bite to eat," said Rumble-Mumble, sat down behind his big knapsack and began his meal.

But the enemy wouldn't wait, started firing at once, and bullets showered down on him. But both lead and steel bounced off him, and besides his knapsack gave plenty of cover.

"I can do without all this firing and shooting," said Rumble-Mumble.

And yet they went on. They even started throwing grenades and shooting cannonballs.

"There's no need to tickle me," he said each time one touched him. Then he got a grenade stuck in his throat.

"Ugh," he said and spat it out. Next there came a chain-shot that cut through his butter-box, and then another chain-shot carried off a sandwich he was holding in his hand.

"That does it," he muttered. Angrily he jumped up, seized his big club and drummed it on the ground. He asked them if they meant to keep on blowing the bread out of his mouth with their pea-shooters. He beat on the ground so that hills and mountains trembled and the enemy were scattered. That was the end of that war, for all we know.

He returned to the king and asked for more work. The king grew pale, for he had hoped to get rid of him this time. The only thing he could think of was to send him to hell.

"Go off to Old Nick[1] and collect the rent at once," he said. Off went lonely Rumble-Mumble with his sack on his back and his dear club on his shoulder. He made a quick journey out of it, but when he got there,

---

1 The devil.

Old Nick was busy hearing the catechism for confirmation. None was at home but his mother, and she had never heard of any rent owing. He had better come back some time later, she suggested.

"No matter what, I'll wait till I've got the rent I was sent for," he insisted.

Time began to drag after he had had his meal. That's why he called to Old Nick's mother once again. She had to pay up straight away. She refused. She wouldn't pay the rent. Then he darted up to the top of a great pine outside the gate of hell, and bent and twisted it like a willow wand and asked her whether she would pay anyhow.

She dared not do otherwise. In a thrice she found as many coins as he could carry in his sack. He set off towards the king's farm. No sooner had he left than Old Nick came back home. He was soon told what Rumble had done, and that he had made off with a big sack of his money, and set out in a big hurry to catch up. But first he took the time to wallop his own dear mother quite a bit for letting go of all that money.

Old Nick soon drew near to Rumble-Mumble. The devil carried no sack, and could fly through the air when he so chose. Rumble-Mumble on the other hand had to keep to the ground with his heavy sack. But when Old Nick came hurrying at his heels, he put a spurt on and racked along as fast as he could, brandishing his club to keep him off.

They ran on and on, Rumble-Mumble holding the handle tight and Old Nick grabbing at the head of the club, till they came to a very deep valley. There Rumble showed himself capable of leaping from one mountain top to the other. Old Nick flew after him over the valley in such a rush that he dashed foolishly against the club and tumbled down into the valley and broke off his foot. There he lay.

"Here's your rent," said Rumble-Mumble when he reached the royal farm, and tossed the sack at the king's feet. Crash, boom, bang, the whole porch shook.

The king at once made a fine speech to thank him, and promised him a rich reward and safe journey home if he so wished. But Rumble-Mumble only wanted more work. He was an honest worker.

"So what do you want me to do next?" he asked.

The king scratched his neck and then came up with the idea:

"Go to the big troll that once stole my grandfather's sword, the one who lives in a castle by the sea where none has ever dared come near."

Rumble-Mumble packed some bundles of food in his knapsack and off he went once more. He travelled a long, long way over wild hills this time, till he came to some tall, wild-looking rocks. They were the castle of the troll he was after. But the troll was nowhere to be seen, the rocks were shut, and Rumble-Mumble couldn't find a way in.

He fell in with some quarrymen who were quarrying stone in this district. He set about to help, and they had never had such help before. He broke up the mountain-face and split the rocks and sent boulders as big as houses toppling down.

When it was time for him to rest and have his dinner, he went to open one of his bundles and found it had all been eaten up by someone.

"That could only be the troll," Rumble-Mumble considered, "I have a good appetite myself, but this fellow has eaten all the bones also."

The first day was soon passed, and on the second the same thing happened; someone stole his food. But on the third day Rumble-Mumble set out to break stones, he took the third bundle with him. And he was careful to lay down behind it and pretend to be sleeping.

The mountain opened while he lay in ambush like that. Suddenly a troll with seven heads came out and started to gobble the food in Rumble-Mumble's bundle. Rumble-Mumble rose rather quickly and struck all the eating heads off with one blow of his club. That was the end of it. He went inside the mountain through the wide open portals the troll had left. While inside he found a horse eating from a tub of red-hot embers, and behind it was a tub of oats.

"Why not eat the oats?" he asked the horse.

"I can't turn around. I'm bound. That's why," said the horse.

"I can turn you around," said Rumble-Mumble.

"I'd rather you tore off my head," said the horse. "That's what a comrade would do. Deeds like these are what a lot comrades are for, you know."

"Is that really so?" said Rumble-Mumble, halfway doubting. Yet he did as he was instructed. All once the horse became a fair young man. He told Rumble-Mumble he had been bewitched and changed into a horse by that ugly monster. He also helped Rumble-Mumble to find the sword the troll had hidden at the bottom of the bed. In that bed the troll's own mother lay snoring away.

They set off towards the king's farm across the sea. The troll's mama awoke a little after that, and found out what had taken place. She hurried down to the water, but could not catch them. They were too far away as they sailed off in the only boat around. In a rage she began drinking the water. She drank so much that the level of the water sank. She didn't manage to drink up all the ocean, so in the end she burst.

"What else was to be expected?" Rumble-Mumble wondered as he sailed on, "I know a bit of that."

Rumble-Mumble sent word to the king as soon as they had landed near his place. The king could come and get his sword. He sent four horses, but they could not move it. He sent eight and then he sent twelve, and still the sword stayed where it was. They couldn't make it stir and move. Rumble-Mumble picked it up and carried it along to the king's farm himself. The king couldn't believe his eyes when he saw that one again. But he made a fine speech.

After it, Rumble-Mumble asked for more work. He was told to go to an enchanted castle where none dared stay. He was to make his home there till he had built a bridge over the sound nearby, so that people could get across. The king would reward him well, he said. He would even give Rumble-Mumble his own daughter for it.

That looked promising, so Rumble-Mumble agreed to the bargain, although none had ever come back from the enchanted castle alive. The king was quite certain that this time he had got rid of him. Rumble-Mumble set off. Along with his food he took with him a good hard stump of pine, a small axe, a wedge, and some kindling wood and little else from the king's farm.

He reached the sound. The river was full of ice, but the feet of Rumble-Mumble were firm enough for wading there anyway, so he crossed safely to the other side. He got into the castle at once. Rumble-Mumble warmed himself by the fire and had his supper. He felt ready for a night's sleep, but all of a sudden he heard a terrible din. The whole castle was being turned upside down. All he could see was a gaping jaw as big as the doorway. It was the Devil in one of his guises.

He and Rumble-Mumble started to play cards, because it mattered to the Devil. He needed to win back some money Rumble-Mumble had got out of his mother. Yet can you guess who was the winning one?

It so happened that Rumble had much luck. He kept winning for it. He won all the ready cash at first, and all gold and silver in the spellbound castle later. It was then that the fire went out.

"We must cut some wood," said Rumble-Mumble, who was in luck and needed to see to play. He didn't want to stop, so he struck the stump of pine with his axe so as to cleave it, but the old log was gnarled and tough. It wouldn't split.

"You're supposed to be strong," he said to the Devil. "Dig in your claws. Wrench this log apart!"

The Devil got to work as hard as he could. While he did his best Rumble-Mumble happened to drive out the wedge so that the Devil got caught in a pucker.

Rumble-Mumble understood at once he had an excellent opportunity to try out the head of his axe on the back of the devil and have the time of his life. The Devil begged to get freed, but Rumble-Mumble refused to listen till the devil had promised he would never come and harry anyone there again ever after. He also took an oath that he would build the bridge over the sound so that people could cross it safely in summer as winter. The Devil's great project was to be ready as soon as the ice in the river melted.

"Those are hard terms," said the Devil. Anyhow, he had no choice if he wanted to be free. In the end he wanted no other bargain, no more deals. And Rumble-Mumble agreed at last.

The Devil was set free and sped off and away towards hell—it happened to be his only home. Rumble-Mumble went to bed to sleep and was still asleep rather late next day, as the king came along to see if he lay torn to pieces. Instead he saw gold and silver enough to wade in it. Sacks of the stuff lay heaped along walls, and in the bed Rumble-Mumble lay snoring.

"Heaven help me and my daughter," said the king, readily seeing his mistake: Rumble-Mumble was alive and kicking. A wonderful job had he done. Yet the king insisted that there could scarcely be a wedding till after the bridge stood complete.

Then one day it happened. The bridge stood all finished, just as the Devil had promised on his life. Rumble-Mumble wanted to take the king with him to try out the bridge, but the king didn't like that new idea.

"Oh no, thanks! I won't do that!" the king said. And to himself he whistled,

"This bridge check could easily bring on hateful revenge for my han-ky-panky tricks!"

At that very moment he woke up to hear ten little birds start to sing a little way off:

> *Let Rumble-Mumble be, let him be. Then you'll see.*
> *Look at your nose.*
> *Build a cloister in those*
> *Far-away regions*
> *As soon as you can*
> *Or bear all the burden...*

None else could understand them, so he grabbed his staff at once and hurried away to one of his very distant cottages in the far-away mountains, where he wanted to settle as a hermit to make amends by building a good cloister.

He also allowed the big Rumble-Mumble to take over and run the farm and country from that blissful moment, for as the king later said in his cottage, "I had the good fortune to wed my daughter to a man with an enormous appetite. It will bring many blessings."

Snip snap snout, that wedding came about.

The Bear's Son
(*Serbia*)

Once upon a time a bear married a woman, and they had one son. When the boy was yet a little fellow he begged very hard to be allowed to leave the bear's cave, and to go out into the world to see what was in it.

His father, however, the bear, would not consent to this, saying, "You are too young yet, and not strong enough. In the world there are multitudes of wicked beasts, called men, who will kill you."

So the boy was quieted for a while, and remained in the cave.

But, after some time, the boy prayed so earnestly that the bear, his father, would let him go into the world, that the bear brought him into the wood, and showed him a beech tree, saying, "If you can pull up that beech by the roots, I will let you go; but if you cannot, then this is a proof that you are still too weak, and must remain with me."

The boy tried to pull up the tree, but, after long trying, had to give it up, and go home again to the cave.

Again some time passed, and he then begged again to be allowed to go into the world, and his father told him, as before, if he could pull up the beech tree he might go out into the world. This time the boy pulled up the tree, so the bear consented to let him go, first, however, making him cut away the branches from the beech, so that he might use the trunk for a club. The boy now started on his journey, carrying the trunk of the beech over his shoulder.

One day as the bear's son was journeying, he came to a field where he found hundreds of plowmen working for their master. He asked them to give him something to eat, and they told him to wait a bit till their dinner was brought them, when he should have some—for, they said, "Where so many are dining one mouth more or less matters but little."

Whilst they were speaking there came carts, horses, mules, and asses, all carrying the dinner. But when the meats were spread out the bear's son declared he could eat all that up himself. The workmen wondered greatly at his words, not believing it possible that one man could consume as great a quantity of victuals as would satisfy several hundred men. This, however, the bear's son persisted in affirming he could do, and offered to bet with them that he would do this. He proposed that the stakes should be all the iron of their plowshares and other agricultural implements. To this they assented. No sooner had they made the wager than he fell upon the provisions, and in a short time consumed the whole. Not a fragment was left. Hereupon the laborers, in accordance with their wager, gave him all the iron which they possessed.

When the bear's son had collected all the iron, he tore up a young birch tree, twisted it into a band and tied up the iron into a bundle, which he hung at the end of his staff, and throwing it across his shoulder, trudged off from the astonished and affrighted laborers.

Going on a short distance, he arrived at a forge in which a smith was employed making a plowshare. This man he requested to make him a mace with the iron which he was carrying. This the smith undertook to do; but putting aside half the iron, he made of the rest a small, coarsely finished mace.

Bear's son saw at a glance that he had been cheated by the smith. Moreover, he was disgusted at the roughness of the workmanship. He however took it, and declared his intention of testing it. Then fastening it to the end of his club and throwing it into the air high above the clouds he stood still and allowed it to fall on his shoulder. It had no sooner struck him than the mace shivered into fragments, some of which fell on and destroyed the forge. Taking up his staff, bear's son reproached the smith for his dishonesty, and killed him on the spot.

Having collected the whole of the iron, the bear's son went to another smithy, and desired the smith whom he found there to make him a mace, saying to him, "Please play no tricks on me. I bring you these fragments of iron for you to use in making a mace. Beware that you do not attempt to cheat me as I was cheated before!"

As the smith had heard what had happened to the other one, he collected his work-people, threw all the iron on his fire, and welded the whole together and made a large mace of perfect workmanship.

When it was fastened on the head of his club the bear's son, to prove it, threw it up high, and caught it on his back. This time the mace did not break, but rebounded.

Then the bear's son got up and said, "This work is well done!" and, putting it on his shoulder, walked away. A little farther on he came to a field wherein a man was plowing with two oxen, and he went up to him and asked for something to eat.

The man said, "I expect any moment my daughter to come with my dinner, then we shall see what God has given us!"

The bear's son told him how he had eaten up all the dinner prepared for many hundreds of plowmen, and asked, "From a dinner prepared for one person how much can come to me or to you?"

Meanwhile the girl brought the dinner. The moment she put it down, bear's son stretched out his hand to begin to eat, but the man stopped him. "No!" said he, "you must first say grace, as I do!"

The bear's son, hungry as he was, obeyed, and, having said grace, they both began to eat. The bear's son, looking at the girl who brought the dinner (she was a tall, strong, beautiful girl), became very fond of her, and said to the father, "Will you give me your daughter for a wife?"

The man answered, "I would give her to you very gladly but I have promised her already to the Moustached."

The bear's son exclaimed, "What do I care for Moustachio? I have my mace for him!"

But the man answered, "Hush! hush! Moustachio is also somebody! You will see him here soon."

Shortly after a noise was heard afar off, and lo! behind a hill a moustache showed itself, and in it were three hundred and sixty-five bird's nests. Shortly after appeared the other moustache, and then came Moustachio himself. Having reached them, he lay down on the ground immediately, to rest. He put his head on the girl's knee and told her to scratch his head a little.

The girl obeyed him, and the bear's son, getting up, struck him with his club over the head. Whereupon Moustachio, pointing to the place with his finger, said," Something bit me here!"

The bear's son struck with his mace on another spot, and Moustachio again pointed to the place, saying to the girl, "Something has bitten me here!"

When he was struck a third time, he said to the girl angrily, "Look you! Something bites me here!"

Then the girl said, "Nothing has bitten you; a man struck you!"

When Moustachio heard that he jumped up, but bear's son had thrown away his mace and ran away. Moustachio pursued him, and though the bear's son was lighter than he, and had gotten the start of him a considerable distance, he would not give up pursuing him.

At length the bear's son, in the course of his flight, came to a wide river, and found, near it, some men threshing corn. "Help me, my brothers, help—for God's sake!" he cried; "Help! Moustachio is pursuing me! What shall I do? How can I get across the river?"

One of the men stretched out his shovel, saying, "Here! Sit down on it, and I will throw you over the river!"

The bear's son sat on the shovel, and the man threw him over the water to the other shore. Soon after Moustachio came up, and asked, "Has anyone passed here?"

The threshers replied that a man had passed.

Moustachio demanded, "How did he cross the river?"

They answered, "He sprang over."

Then Moustachio went back a little to take a start, and with a hop he sprang to the other side, and continued to pursue the bear's son. Meanwhile this last, running hastily up a hill, got very tired. At the top of the hill he found a man sowing, and the sack with seeds was hanging on his neck. After every handful of seed sown in the ground, the man put a handful in his mouth and ate them.

The bear's son shouted to him, "Help, brother, help!—for God's sake! Moustachio is following me, and will soon catch me! Hide me somewhere!"

Then the man said, "Indeed, it is no joke to have Moustachio pursuing you. But I have nowhere to hide you, unless in this sack among the seeds."

So he put him in the sack. When Moustachio came up to the sower he asked him if he had seen the bear's son anywhere?

The man replied, "Yes, he passed by long ago, and God knows where he has got before this!"

Then Moustachio went back again. By-and-by the sower forgot that bear's son was in his sack, and he took him out with a handful of seeds, and put him in his mouth. Then bear's son was afraid of being swallowed, so he looked round the mouth quickly, and, seeing a hollow tooth, hid himself in it.

When the sower returned home in the evening, he called to his sisters-in-law, "Children, give me my toothpick! There is something in my broken tooth."

The sisters-in-law brought him two iron picks, and, standing one on each side, they poked about with the two picks in his tooth till the bear's son jumped out.

Then the man remembered him, and said, "What bad luck you have! I had very nearly swallowed you."

After they had taken supper they talked about many different things, till at last the bear's son asked what had happened to break that one tooth, whilst the others were all strong and healthy. Then the man told me in these words: *[note: paragraph break for story within a story]*

Once on a time ten of us started with thirty horses to the sea-shore to buy some salt. We found a girl in a field watching sheep, and she asked us where we were going. We said we were going to the sea-shore to buy salt.

She said, "Why go so far? I have in the bag in my hand here some salt which remained over after feeding the sheep. I think it will be enough for you."

So we settled about the price, and then she took the salt from her bag, whilst we took the sacks from the thirty horses, and we weighed the salt and filled the sacks with it till all the thirty sacks were full. We then paid the girl, and returned home. It was a very fine autumn day; but as we were crossing a high mountain, the sky became very cloudy and it began to snow, and there was a cold north wind, so we could not see our path and wandered about here and there.

At last, by good luck, one of us shouted, "Here, brothers! Here is a dry place!"

So we went in one after the other till we were all, with the thirty horses, under shelter. Then we took the sacks from the horses, made a good fire, and passed the night there as if it were a house. Next morning, just think what we saw! We were all in one man's head, which lay in the midst of some vineyards; and whilst we were yet wondering and loading our horses, the keeper of the vineyards came and picked the head up. He put it in a sling and slinging it about several times, threw it over his head, and cast it far away over the vines to frighten the starlings away from his grapes. So we rolled down a hill, and it was then that I broke my tooth.

675: The Wish-Fish

Hans Dumb
(*Germany*)

There was a king who lived happily with his daughter, who was his only child, but one day the princess gave birth to a child, and no one knew who the father was. For a long time the king did not know what to do, but in the end he ordered the princess to go to church with the child, where he was to be given a lemon, and whomever he gave it to was to be the father of the child and the husband of the princess. This was done, but the order was given that none but beautiful people should be admitted to the church. But there was a small, crooked, and hunchbacked lad in town who was not very clever, and so was called Hans Dumb, who pushed his way into the church unseen among the others, and the child handed the lemon to Hans Dumb. The princess was horrified, and the king was so outraged that he had her and the child put into a cask with Hans Dumb and put out to sea. The cask soon floated away, and when they were alone at sea, the princess complained and said, "You nasty, hunchbacked, nosey boy, you are to blame for my misfortune, why did you force yourself into the church? You have no business with the child." — "Oh, yes," said Hans Dumb, "it was my business, for I once wished you to have a child, and what I wished came true." — "If that is so, then wish us to have something to eat here." — "I can do that," said Hans Dumb, but he wished for a bowl full of potatoes. The princess would have liked something better, but because she was so hungry, she ate the potatoes with him. After they had eaten their fill, Hans Dumb said, "Now I should like to wish us a fine ship," and no sooner had he said that than they were sitting in a splendid ship with everything you could possibly want. The helmsman drove straight ashore, and when they got out, Hans Dumb said, "Now there shall be a castle there!" There stood a splendid castle, and servants dressed in gold came and led the princess and the child into it, and when they were in the middle of the hall, Hans Dumb said, "now I wish that I may become a young and clever prince!" Then his hump was lost and he was handsome and straight and friendly, and he pleased the princess well and became her husband.

They lived thus happily for a long time. Then one day the old king was out riding, lost his way, and came to the castle. He was astonished because he had never seen it before, and he went inside. The princess recognized her father at once, but he did not recognize her, for he thought she had drowned in the sea long ago. She entertained him splendidly, and when he wished again to go home, she secretly put a golden cup in his pocket. After he had left, she sent some horses after him to stop him and check whether he had not stolen the golden cup, and when they found it in his pocket, they brought him back with them. He swore to the princess that he had not stolen it, and that he did not know how it came to be in his pocket. "You see," she said, "one must be careful not to assume that someone is guilty," and she revealed herself as his daughter. The king rejoiced and they lived happily together, and after his death, Hans became king.

Emelyan the Fool
(*Russia*)

In a certain village lived at one time a peasant, who had three sons, two of whom were clever, but the third was a fool, and his name was Emelyan. And when the peasant had lived a long time, and was grown very old, he called his three sons to him, and said to them: "My dear children, I feel that I have not much longer to live; so I give you the house and cattle, which you will divide among you, share and share alike. I have also given you each a hundred roubles." Soon after, the old man died, and the sons, when they had buried him, lived on happy and contented.

Some time afterwards Emelyan's brothers took a fancy to go to the city and trade with the hundred roubles their father had left them. So they said to Emelyan: "Hark ye, fool! we are going to the city, and will take your hundred roubles with us; and, if we prosper in trade, we will buy you a red coat, red boots, and a red cap. But do you stay here at home; and when our wives, your sisters-in-law, desire you to do anything, do as they bid you." The fool, who had a great longing for a red coat and cap, and red boots, answered that he would do whatever his sisters-in-law bade him. So his brothers went off to the city, and the fool stayed at home with his two sisters.

One day, when the winter was come, and the cold was great, his sisters-in-law told him to go out and fetch water; but the fool remained lying on the stove, and said: "Ay, indeed, and who then are you?" The sisters began to scold him, and said: "How now, fool! we are what you see. You know how cold it is, and that it is a man's business to go." But he said: "I am lazy." "How!" they exclaimed, "you are lazy? Surely you will want to eat, and if we have no water we cannot cook. But never mind," they added, "we will only tell our husbands not to give him anything when they have bought the fine red coat and all for him!"

The fool heard what they said; and, as he longed greatly to have the red coat and cap, he saw that he must go; so he got down from the stove and began to put on his shoes and stockings and to dress himself to go out. When he was dressed, he took the buckets and the axe and went down to the river hard by. And when he came to the river he began to cut a large hole in the ice. Then he drew water in the buckets, and setting them on the ice, he stood by the hole, looking into the water. And as the fool was looking, he saw a large pike swimming about. However stupid Emelyan was, he felt a wish to catch this pike; so he stole cautiously and softly to the edge of the hole, and making a sudden grasp at the pike he caught him, and pulled him out of the water. Then, putting him in his bosom, he was hastening home with him, when the pike cried out: "Ho, fool! why have you caught me?" He answered: "To take you home and get my sisters-in-law to cook you." "Nay, fool! do not take me home, but throw me back into the water and I will make a rich man of you." But the fool would not consent, and jogged on his way home. When the pike saw that the fool was not for letting him go, he said to him: "Hark ye, fool! put me back in the water and I will do for you everything you do not like to do yourself; you will only have to wish and it shall be done."

On hearing this the fool rejoiced beyond measure for, as he was uncommonly lazy, he thought to himself: "If the pike does everything I have no mind to do, all will be done without my being troubled to work." So he said to the pike: "I will throw you back into the water if you do all you promise." The pike said: "Let me go first and then I will keep my promise." But the fool answered: "Nay, nay, you must first perform your promise, and then I will let you go." When the pike saw that Emelyan would not put him into the water he said: "If you wish me to do all you desire, you must first tell me what your desire is." "I wish," said the fool, "that my buckets should go of themselves from the river up the hill to the village without spilling any of the water." Then said the pike: "Listen now, and remember the words I say to you: At the pike's command, and at my desire, go, buckets, of yourselves up the hill!" Then the fool repeated after him these words, and instantly, with the speed of thought, the buckets ran up the hill. When Emelyan saw this he was amazed beyond measure, and he said to the pike: "But will it always be so?" "Everything you desire will be done," replied the pike; "but I warn you not to forget the words I have taught you." Then Emelyan put the pike into the water and followed his buckets home.

The neighbours were all amazed and said to one another: "This fool makes the buckets come up of themselves from the river, and he follows them home at his leisure." But Emelyan took no notice of them, and went his way home. The buckets were by this time in the house, and standing in their place on the foot-bench; so the fool got up and stretched himself on the stove.

After some time his sisters-in-law said to him again: "Emelyan, why are you lazying there? Get up and go cut wood." But the fool replied: "Yes! and you—who are you?" "Don't you see it is now winter, and if you don't cut wood you will be frozen?" "I am lazy," said the fool. "What! you are lazy?" cried the sisters. "If you do not go instantly and cut wood, we will tell our husbands not to give you the red coat, or the red cap, or the fine red boots!" The fool, who longed for the red cap, coat, and boots, saw that he must go and cut the wood; but as it was bitterly cold, and he did not like to come down from off the stove, he repeated in an undertone, as he lay, the words: "At the pike's command, and at my desire, up, axe, and hew the wood! and do you, logs, come of yourselves in the stove!" Instantly the axe jumped up, ran out into the yard, and began to cut up the wood; and the logs came of themselves into the house, and laid themselves in the stove. When the sisters saw this, they wondered exceedingly at the cleverness of the fool; and, as the axe did of its own accord the work whenever Emelyan was wanted to cut wood, he lived for some time in peace and harmony with them. At length the wood was all finished, and they said to him: "Emelyan, we have no more wood, so you must go to the forest and cut some." "Ay," said the fool, "and you, who are you, then?" The sisters replied: "The wood is far off, and it is winter, and too cold for us to go." But the fool only said: "I am lazy." "How! you are lazy," cried they; "you will be frozen then; and moreover, we will take care, when our husbands come home, that they shall not give you the red coat, cap, and boots." As the fool longed for the clothes, he saw that he must go and cut the wood; so he got off the stove, put on his shoes and stockings, and dressed himself; and, when he was dressed, he went into the yard, dragged the sledge out of the shed, took a rope and the axe with him, and called out to his sisters-in-law: "Open the gate."

When the sisters saw that he was riding off without any horses, they cried: "Why, Emelyan, you have got on the sledge without yoking the horses!" But he answered that he wanted no horses, and bade them only open the gate. So the sisters threw open the gate, and the fool repeated the words: "At the pike's command, and at my desire, away, sledge, off to the wood!" Instantly the sledge galloped out of the yard at such a rate that the people of the village, when they saw it, were filled with amazement at Emelyan's riding the sledge without horses, and with such speed that a pair of horses could never have drawn it at such a rate. The fool had to pass through the town on his way to the wood, and away he dashed at full speed. But the fool did not know that he should cry out: "Make way!" so that he should not run over anyone; but away he went, and rode over quite a lot of people; and, though they ran after him, no one was able to overtake and bring him back. At last Emelyan, having got clear of the town, came to the wood and stopped his sledge. Then he got down and said: "At the pike's command, and at my desire, up, axe, hew wood; and you, logs! lay yourselves on the sledge, and tie yourselves together." Scarcely had the fool uttered these words when the axe began to cut wood, the logs to lay themselves on the sledge, and the rope to tie them down. When the axe had cut wood enough, Emelyan desired it to cut him a good cudgel; and when the axe had done this, he mounted the sledge and cried: "Up, and away! At the pike's command, and at my desire, go home, sledge!" Away then went the sledge at the top of its speed, and when he came to the town, where he had hurt so many people, he found a crowd waiting to catch him; and, as soon as he got into the gates, they laid hold of him, dragged him off his sledge, and fell to beating him. When the fool saw how they were treating him, he said in an under voice: "At the pike's command, and at my desire, up, cudgel, and thrash them!" Instantly the cudgel began to lay about it on all sides; and, when the people were all driven away, he made his escape, and came to his own village. The cudgel, having thrashed all soundly, rolled home after him; and Emelyan, as usual, when he got home, climbed up and lay upon the stove.

After he had left the town, all the people fell to talking, not so much of the number of persons he had injured, as of their amazement at his riding in a sledge without horses; and the news spread from one to another, till it reached the Court and came to the ears of the King. And when the King heard it, he felt an extreme desire to see him: so he sent an officer with some soldiers to look for him. The officer instantly started, and took the road that the fool had taken; and when he came to the village where Emelyan lived, he summoned the Starosta, or head-man of the village, and said to him: "I am sent by the King to take a certain fool, and bring him before his Majesty." The Starosta at once showed him the house where Emelyan lived, and the officer went into it and asked where the fool was. He was lying on the stove, and answered: "What is it you want with me?" "How!" said the officer, "what do I want with you? Get up this instant and dress yourself; I must take you to the King." But Emelyan said: "What to do?" Whereat the officer became so enraged at the rudeness of his replies that he hit him on the cheek. "At the pike's command, and at my desire," said the fool, "up, cudgel, and thrash them!" Instantly up sprang the cudgel and began to lay about it on all sides. So the officer was obliged to go back to the town as fast as he could; and when he came before the King, and told him how the fool had cudgelled him, the King marvelled greatly, and would not believe the story.

Then the King called to him a wise man and ordered him to bring the fool by craft, if nothing else would do; so the wise man went to the village where Emelyan lived, called the Starosta before him and said: "I am ordered by the King to take your fool; and therefore ask for the persons with whom he lived." Then the Starosta ran and fetched Emelyan's sisters-in-law. The King's messenger asked them what it was the fool liked, and they answered: "Noble sir, if anyone entreats our fool earnestly to do anything, he flatly refuses the first and second time; the third time he consents, and does what he is required, for he dislikes to be roughly treated."

The King's messenger thereupon dismissed them and forbade them to tell Emelyan that he had summoned them before him. Then he brought raisins, baked plums, and grapes, and went to the fool. When he came into the room, he went up to the stove and said: "Emelyan, why are you lying there?" and with that he gave him the raisins, the baked plums, and the grapes, and said: "Emelyan, we will go together to the King: I will take you with me." But the fool replied: "I am very warm here"; for there was nothing he liked so much as being warm. Then the messenger began to entreat him: "Be so good, Emelyan, do let us go! You will like the Court vastly." "No," said the fool, "I am lazy." But the messenger entreated him once more: "Do come with me, there's a good fellow, and the King will give you a fine red coat and cap, and a pair of red boots." When the fool heard of the red coat he said: "Go on before, I will follow you." The messenger pressed him no further, but went out and asked the sisters-in-law if there was any danger of the fool's deceiving him. They assured him there was not, and he went away.

Emelyan, who remained lying on the stove, then said to himself: "How I dislike this going to the King!" And after a minute's thought, he said: "At the pike's command, and at my desire, up, stove, and away to the town!" And instantly the wall of the room opened, and the stove moved out; and when it got clear of the yard, it went at such a rate that there was no overtaking it; soon it came up with the King's messenger, and went along with him into the palace. When the King saw the fool coming, he went forth with all his Court to meet him; and he was amazed beyond measure at seeing Emelyan come riding on the stove. But the fool lay still and said nothing. Then the King asked him why he had upset so many people on his way to the wood. "It was their own fault," said the fool; "why did they not get out of the way?"

Just at that moment the King's daughter came to the window, and Emelyan happening suddenly to look up, and seeing how handsome she was, said in a whisper: "At the pike's command, and at my desire, let this lovely maiden fall in love with me!" And scarcely had he spoken the words when the King's daughter fell desperately in love with him. Then said the fool: "At the pike's command, and at my desire, up, stove, and away home!" Immediately the stove left the palace, went through the town, returned home, and set itself in its old place. And Emelyan lived there for some time comfortably and happy.

But it was very different in the town; for, at the word of Emelyan, the King's daughter had fallen in love, and she began to implore her father to give her the fool for her husband. The King was in a great rage, both with her and the fool, but he knew not how to catch him; then his minister proposed that the same officer, as a punishment for not succeeding the first time, should be sent again to take Emelyan. This advice pleased the King, and he summoned the officer to his presence, and said: "Hark ye, friend! I sent you before for the fool, and you came back without him; to punish you I now send you for him a second time. If you bring him, you shall be rewarded; if you return without him, you shall be punished."

When the officer heard this, he left the King and lost no time in going in quest of the fool; and on coming to the village he called for the Starosta and said to him: "Here is money for you; buy everything necessary for a good dinner to-morrow. Invite Emelyan, and when he comes, make him drink until he falls asleep." The Starosta, knowing that the officer came from the King, was obliged to obey him; so he bought all that was required and invited the fool. And Emelyan said he would come, whereat the officer was greatly rejoiced. So next day the fool came to dinner, and the Starosta plied him so well with drink that he fell fast asleep. When the officer saw this, he ordered the kibitka[1] to be brought; and putting the fool into it, they drove off to the town, and went straight to the palace. As soon as the King heard that they were come, he ordered a large cask to be provided without delay, and to be bound with strong iron hoops. When the cask was brought to the King, and he saw that everything was ready as he desired, he commanded his daughter and the fool to be put in it, and the cask to be well pitched; and, when this was all done, the cask was thrown into the sea, and left to the mercy of the waves. Then the King returned to his palace, and the cask floated along upon the sea. All this time the fool was fast asleep; when he awoke, and saw that it was quite dark, he said to himself: "Where am I?" for he thought he was alone. But the Princess said: "You are in a cask, Emelyan! and I am shut up with you in it." "But who are you?" said the fool. "I am the King's daughter," replied she. And she told him why she had been shut up there with him. Then she besought him to free himself and her out of the cask; but the fool said: "Nay, I am warm enough here." "But grant me at least the favour," said the Princess; "have pity on my tears, and deliver me out of this cask." "Why so?" said Emelyan; "I am lazy." Then the Princess began to entreat him still more urgently, until the fool was at last moved by her tears and entreaties, and said: "Well, I will do this for you." Then he said softly: "At the pike's command, and at my desire, cast us, O sea! upon the shore, where we may dwell on dry land; but let it be near our own country; and, cask! fall to pieces on the shore."

Scarcely had the fool uttered these words when the waves began to roll,

____

1 Carriage.

and the cask was thrown on a dry place, and fell to pieces of itself. So Emelyan got up and went with the Princess round about the spot where they were cast; and the fool saw that they were on a fine island, where there was an abundance of trees, with all kinds of fruit upon them. When the Princess saw this, she was greatly rejoiced and said: "But, Emelyan, where shall we live? there is not even a nook here." "You want too much," said the fool. "Grant me one favour," replied the Princess: "let there be at least a little cottage in which we may shelter ourselves from the rain"; for the Princess knew that he could do everything that he wished. But the fool said: "I am lazy." Nevertheless, she went on entreating him, until at last Emelyan was obliged to do as she desired. Then he stepped aside and said: "At the pike's command, and at my desire, let me have in the middle of this island a finer castle than the King's, and let a crystal bridge lead from my castle to the royal palace; and let there be attendants of all conditions in the court!" Hardly were the words spoken, when there appeared a splendid castle, with a crystal bridge. The fool went with the Princess into the castle and beheld the apartments all magnificently furnished, and a number of persons, footmen and all kinds of officers, who waited for the fool's commands. When he saw that all these men were like men, and that he alone was ugly and stupid, he wished to be better, so he said: "At the pike's command, and at my desire, away! let me become a youth without an equal, and extremely wise!" And hardly had he spoken, when he became so handsome and so wise that all were amazed.

Emelyan now sent one of his servants to the King to invite him and all his Court. So the servant went along the crystal bridge which the fool had made, and when he came to the Court, the ministers brought him before the King, and Emelyan's messenger said: "Please, your Majesty, I am sent by my master to invite you to dinner." The King asked him who his master was, but he answered: "Please, your Majesty, I can tell you nothing about my master (for the fool had ordered him not to tell who he was), but if you come to dine with him, he will inform you himself." The King, being curious to know who had sent to invite him, told the messenger that he would go without fail. The servant went away, and when he got home the King and his Court set out along the crystal bridge to go and visit the fool; and, when they arrived at the castle, Emelyan came forth to meet the King, took him by his white hands, kissed him on his sugared lips, led him into his castle, and seated him at the oaken tables covered with fine diaper tablecloths, and spread with sugar-meats and honey-drinks. The King and his ministers ate and drank and made merry. When they rose from the table and retired, the fool said to the King: "Does your Majesty know who I am?" As Emelyan was now dressed in fine clothes, and was very handsome, it was not possible to recognize him; so the King replied that he did not know him. Then the fool said: "Does not your Majesty recollect how a fool came riding on a stove to your Court, and how you fastened him up in a pitched cask with your daughter, and cast them into the sea? Know me now—I am that Emelyan."

When the King saw him thus in his presence he was greatly terrified and knew not what to do. But the fool went to the Princess and led her out to him; and the King, on seeing his daughter, was greatly rejoiced, and said: "I have been very unjust to you, and so I gladly give you my daughter, to wife." The fool humbly thanked the King; and when Emelyan had prepared everything for the wedding, it was celebrated with great magnificence, and the following day the fool gave a feast to the ministers and all the people. When the festivities were at an end, the King wanted to give up his kingdom to his son-in-law, but Emelyan did not wish to have the crown. So the King went back to his kingdom, and the fool remained in the castle and lived happily.

Peruonto
(*Italy*)

Once upon a time a woman who lived in a village, and was called Ceccarella, had a son named Peruonto, who was one of the most stupid lads that ever was born. This made his mother very unhappy, and all day long she would grieve because of this great misfortune. For whether she asked him kindly, or stormed at him till her throat was dry, the foolish fellow would not stir to do the slightest hand's turn for her. At last, after a thousand dinnings at his brain, and a thousand splittings of his head, and saying "I tell you" and "I told you" day after day, she got him to go to the wood for a faggot, saying, "Come now, it is time for us to get a morsel to eat, so run off for some sticks, and don't forget yourself on the way, but come back as quick as you can, and we will boil ourselves some cabbage, to keep the life in us."

Away went the stupid Peruonto, hanging down his head as if he was going to gaol. Away he went, walking as if he were a jackdaw, or treading on eggs, counting his steps, at the pace of a snail's gallop, and making all sorts of zigzags and excursions on his way to the wood, to come there after the fashion of a raven. And when he reached the middle of a plain, through which ran a river growling and murmuring at the bad manners of the stones that were stopping its way, he saw three youths who had made themselves a bed of grass and a pillow of a great flint stone, and were lying sound asleep under the blaze of the Sun, who was shooting his rays down on them point blank. When Peruonto saw these poor creatures, looking as if they were in the midst of a fountain of fire, he felt pity for them, and cutting some branches of oak, he made a handsome arbour over them. Meanwhile, the youths, who were the sons of a fairy, awoke, and, seeing the kindness and courtesy of Peruonto, they gave him a charm, that every thing he asked for should be done.

Peruonto, having performed this good action, went his ways towards the wood, where he made up such an enormous faggot that it would have needed an engine to draw it; and, seeing that he could not in any way get in on his back, he set himself astride of it and cried, "Oh, what a lucky fellow I should be if this faggot would carry me riding a-horseback!" And the word was hardly out of his mouth when the faggot began to trot and gallop like a great horse, and when it came in front of the King's palace it pranced and capered and curvetted in a way that would amaze you. The ladies who were standing at one of the windows, on seeing such a wonderful sight, ran to call Vastolla, the daughter of the King, who, going to the window and observing the caracoles of a faggot and the bounds of a bundle of wood, burst out a-laughing—a thing which, owing to a natural melancholy, she never remembered to have done before. Peruonto raised his head, and, seeing that it was at him that they were laughing, exclaimed, "Oh, Vastolla, I wish that I could be your husband and I would soon cure you of laughing at me!" And so saying, he struck his heels into the faggot, and in a dashing gallop he was quickly at home, with such a train of little boys at his heels that if his mother had not been quick to shut the door they would soon have killed him with the stones and sticks with which they pelted him.

Now came the question of marrying Vastolla to some great prince, and her father invited all he knew to come and visit him and pay their respects to the Princess. But she refused to have anything to say to either of them, and only answered, "I will marry none but the young man who rode on the faggot." So that the King got more and more angry with every refusal, and at last he was quite unable to contain himself any longer, and called his Council together and said, "You know by this time how my honour has been shamed, and that my daughter has acted in such a manner that all the chronicles will tell the story against me, so now speak and advise me. I say that she is unworthy to live, seeing that she has brought me into such discredit, and I wish to put her altogether out of the world before she does more mischief." The Councillors, who had in their time learned much wisdom, said, "Of a truth she deserves to be severely punished. But, after all, it is this audacious scoundrel who has give you the annoyance, and it is not right that he should escape through the meshes of the net. Let us wait, then, till he comes to light, and we discover the root of this disgrace, and then we will think it over and resolve what were best to be done." This counsel pleased the King, for he saw that they spoke like sensible, prudent men, so he held his hand and said, "Let us wait and see the end of this business."

So then the King made a great banquet, and invited every one of his nobles and all the gentlemen in his kingdom to come to it, and set Vastolla at the high table at the top of the hall, for, he said, "No common man can have done this, and when she recognises the fellow we shall see her eyes turn to him, and we will instantly lay hold on him and put him out of the way." But when the feasting was done, and all the guests passed out in a line, Vastolla took no more notice of them than Alexander's bull-dog did of the rabbits; and the King grew more angry than ever, and vowed that he would kill her without more delay. Again, however, the Councillors pacified him and said, "Softly, softly, your Majesty! quiet your wrath. Let us make another banquet to-morrow, not for people of condition but for the lower sort. Some women always attach themselves to the worst, and we shall find among the cutlers, and bead-makers, and comb-sellers, the root of your anger, which we have not discovered among the cavaliers."

This reasoning took the fancy of the King, and he ordered a second banquet to be prepared, to which, on proclamation being made, came all the riff-raff and rag-tag and bob-tail of the city, such as rogues, scavengers, tinkers, pedlars, sweeps, beggars, and such like rabble, who were all in high glee; and, taking their seats like noblemen at a great long table, they began to feast and gobble away.

Now, when Ceccarella heard this proclamation, she began to urge Peruonto to go there too, until at last she got him to set out for the feast. And scarcely had he arrived there when Vastolla cried out without thinking, "That is my Knight of the Faggot." When the King heard this he tore his beard, seeing that the bean of the cake, the prize in the lottery, had fallen to an ugly lout, the very sight of whom he could not endure, with a shaggy head, owl's eyes, a parrot's nose, a deer's mouth, and legs bare and bandy. Then, heaving a deep sigh, he said, "What can that jade of a daughter of mine have seen to make her take a fancy to this ogre, or strike up a dance with this hairy-foot? Ah, vile, false creature, who has cast so base a spell on her? But why do we wait? Let her suffer the punishment she deserves; let her undergo the penalty that shall be decreed by you, and take her from my presence, for I cannot bear to look longer upon her."

Then the Councillors consulted together and they resolved that she, as well as the evil-doer, should be shut up in a cask and thrown into the sea; so that without staining the King's hands with the blood of one of his family, they should carry out the sentence. No sooner was the judgment pronounced, than the cask was brought and both were put into it; but before they coopered it up, some of Vastolla's ladies, crying and sobbing as if their hearts would break, put into it a basket of raisins and dried figs that she might have wherewithal to live on for a little while. And when the cask was closed up, it was flung into the sea, on which it went floating as the wind drove it.

Meanwhile Vastolla, weeping till her eyes ran like two rivers, said to Peruonto, "What a sad misfortune is this of ours! Oh, if I but knew who has played me this trick, to have me caged in this dungeon! Alas, alas, to find myself in this plight without knowing how. Tell me, tell me, O cruel man, what incantation was it you made, and what spell did you employ, to bring me within the circle of this cask?" Peruonto, who had been for some time paying little attention to her, at last said, "If you want me to tell you, you must give me some figs and raisins." So Vastolla, to draw the secret out of him, gave him a handful of both; and as soon as he had eaten them he told her truly all that had befallen him, with the three youths, and with the faggot, and with herself at the window: which, when the poor lady heard, she took heart and said to Peruonto, "My friend, shall we then let our lives run out in a cask? Why don't you cause this tub to be changed into a fine ship and run into some good harbour to escape this danger?" And Peruonto replied—

> *If you would have me say the spell,*
> *With figs and raisins feed me well!*

So Vastolla, to make him open his mouth, filled it with fruit; and so she fished the words out of him. And lo! as soon as Peruonto had said what she desired, the cask was turned into a beautiful ship; with sails and sailors and everything that could be wished for; and guns and trumpets and a splendid cabin in which Vastolla sat filled with delight.

It being now the hour when the Moon begins to play at see-saw with the Sun, Vastolla said to Peruonto, "My fine lad, now make this ship to be changed into a palace, for then we shall be more secure; you know the saying, "Praise the Sea, but keep to the Land." And Peruonto replied—

> *If you would have me say the spell,*
> *With figs and raisins feed me well!*

So Vastolla, at once, fed him again, and Peruonto, swallowing down the raisins and figs, did her pleasure; and immediately the ship came to land and was changed into a beautiful palace, fitted up in a most sumptuous manner, and so full of furniture and curtains and hangings that there was nothing more to ask for. So that Vastolla, who a little before would not have set the price of a farthing on her life, did not now wish to change places with the greatest lady in the world, seeing herself served and treated like a queen. Then to put the seal on all her good fortune, she besought Peruonto to obtain grace to become handsome and polished in his manner, that they might live happy together; for though the proverb says, "Better to have a pig for a husband, than a smile from an emperor," still, if his appearance were changed, she should think herself the happiest woman in the universe. And Peruonto replied as before—

> *If you would have me say the spell,*
> *With figs and raisins feed me well!*

Then Vastolla quickly opened his lips, and scarcely had he spoken the words when he was changed, as it were from an owl to a nightingale, from an ogre to a beautiful youth, from a scarecrow to a fine gentleman. Vastolla, seeing such a transformation, clasped him in her arms and was almost beside herself with joy. Then they were married and lived happily for years.

Meanwhile the King grew old and very sad, so that, one day, the courtiers persuaded him to go a-hunting to cheer him up. Night overtook him, and, seeing a light in a palace, he sent a servant to know if he could be entertained there; and he was answered that everything was at his disposal. So the King went to the palace and passing into a great guest-chamber he saw no living soul, but two little boys, who skipped around him crying, "Welcome, welcome!" The King, surprised and astonished, stood like one that was enchanted, and sitting down to rest himself at a table, to his amazement he saw invisibly spread on it a Flanders tablecloth, with dishes full of roast meats and all sorts of viands; so that, in truth, he feasted like a King, waited on by those beautiful children, and all the while he sat at table a concert of lutes and tambourines never ceased—such delicious music that it went to the tips of his fingers and toes. When he had done eating, a bed suddenly appeared all made of gold, and having his boots taken off, he went to rest and all his courtiers did the same, after having fed heartily at a hundred tables, which were laid out in the other rooms.

When morning came, the King wished to thank the two little children, but with them appeared Vastolla and her husband; and casting herself at his feet she asked his pardon and related the whole story. The King, seeing that he had found two grandsons who were two jewels and a son-in-law who was a fairy, embraced first one and then the other; and taking up the children in his arms, they all returned to the city where there was a great festival that lasted many days.

PROTO-GERMANIC-ITALO-CELTIC

365: Specter Bridegrooms

The Specter Bridegroom

The Specter Bridegroom
(*England*)

Long, long ago a farmer named Lenine lived in Boscean. He had but one son, Frank Lenine, who was indulged into waywardness by both his parents. In addition to the farm servants, there was one, a young girl, Nancy Trenoweth, who especially assisted Mrs. Lenine in all the various duties of a small farmhouse.

Nancy Trenoweth was very pretty, and although perfectly uneducated, in the sense in which we now employ the term education, she possessed many native graces, and she had acquired much knowledge really useful to one whose aspirations would probably never rise higher than to be mistress of a farm of a few acres. Educated by parents who had certainly never seen the world beyond Penzance, her ideas of the world were limited to a few miles around the Land's-End. But although her book of nature was a small one, it had deeply impressed her mind with its influences. The wild waste, the small but fertile valley, the rugged hills, with their crowns of cairns, the moors rich in the golden furze and the purple heath, the sea-beaten cliffs and the silver sands, were the pages she had studied, under the guidance of a mother who conceived, in the sublimity of her ignorance, that everything in nature was the home of some spirit form. The soul of the girl was imbued with the deeply religious dye of her mother's mind, whose religion was only a sense of an unknown world immediately beyond our own. The elder Nancy Trenoweth exerted over the villagers around her considerable power. They did not exactly fear her. She was too free from evil for that; but they were conscious of a mental superiority, and yielded without complaining to her sway.

The result of this was that the younger Nancy, although compelled to service, always exhibited some pride, from a feeling that her mother was a superior woman to any around her.

She never felt herself inferior to her master and mistress, yet she complained not of being in subjection to them. There were so many interesting features in the character of this young servant girl that she became in many respects like a daughter to her mistress. There was no broad line of division in those days, in even the manorial hall, between the lord and his domestics, and still less defined was the position of the employer and the employed in a small farmhouse. Consequent on this condition of things, Frank Lenine and Nancy were thrown as much together as if they had been brother and sister. Frank was rarely checked in anything by his over-fond parents, who were especially proud of their son, since he was regarded as the handsomest young man in the parish. Frank conceived a very warm attachment for Nancy, and she was not a little proud of her lover. Although it was evident to all the parish that Frank and Nancy were seriously devoted to each other, the young man's parents were blind to it, and were taken by surprise when one day Frank asked his father and mother to consent to his marrying Nancy.

The Lenines had allowed their son to have his own way from his youth up; and now, in a matter which brought into play the strongest of human feelings, they were angry because he refused to bend to their wills.

The old man felt it would be a degradation for a Lenine to marry a Trenoweth, and, in the most unreasoning manner, he resolved it should never be.

The first act was to send Nancy home to Alsia Mill, where her parents resided; the next was an imperious command to his son never again to see the girl.

The commands of the old are generally powerless upon the young where the affairs of the heart are concerned. So were they upon Frank. He who was rarely seen of an evening beyond the garden of his father's cottage, was now as constantly absent from his home. The house, which was wont to be a pleasant one, was strangely altered. A gloom had fallen over all things; the father and son rarely met as friends—the mother and her boy had now a feeling of reserve. Often there were angry altercations between the father and son, and the mother felt she could not become the defender of her boy, in his open acts of disobedience, his bold defiance of his parents' commands.

Rarely an evening passed that did not find Nancy and Frank together in some retired nook. The Holy Well was a favourite meeting-place, and here the most solemn vows were made. Locks of hair were exchanged; a wedding-ring, taken from the finger of a corpse, was broken, when they vowed that they would be united either dead or alive; and they even climbed at night the granite-pile at Treryn, and swore by the Logan Rock the same strong vow.

Time passed onward unhappily, and as the result of the endeavours to quench out the passion by force, it grew stronger under the repressing power, and, like imprisoned steam, eventually burst through all restraint.

Nancy's parents discovered at length that moonlight meetings between two untrained, impulsive youths had a natural result, and they were now doubly earnest in their endeavours to compel Frank to marry their daughter.

The elder Lenine could not be brought to consent to this, and he firmly resolved to remove his son entirely from what he considered the hateful influences of the Trenoweths. He resolved to go to Plymouth, to take his son with him, and, if possible, to send him away to sea, hoping thus to wean him from his folly, as he considered this love-madness. Frank, poor fellow, with the best intentions, was not capable of any sustained effort, and consequently he at length succumbed to his father; and, to escape his persecution, he entered a ship bound for India, and bade adieu to his native land.

Frank could not write, and this happened in days when letters could be forwarded only with extreme difficulty, consequently Nancy never heard from her lover.

A babe had been born into a troublesome world, and the infant became a real solace to the young mother. As the child grew, it became an especial favourite with its grandmother; the elder Nancy rejoiced over the little prattler, and forgot her cause of sorrow. Young Nancy lived for her child, and on the memory of its father. Subdued in spirit she was, but her affliction had given force to her character, and she had been heard to declare that wherever Frank might be, she was ever present with him, whatever might be the temptations of the hour, that her influence was all powerful over him for good. She felt that no distance could separate their souls, that no time could be long enough to destroy the bond between them.

A period of distress fell upon the Trenoweths, and it was necessary that Nancy should leave her home once more, and go again into service. Her mother took charge of the babe, and she found a situation in the village of Kimyall, in the parish of Paul. Nancy, like her mother, contrived by force of character to maintain an ascendancy amongst her companions. She had formed an acquaintance, which certainly never grew into friendship, with some of the daughters of the small farmers around. These girls were all full of the superstitions of the time and place.

The winter was coming on, and nearly three years had passed away since Frank Lenine left his country. As yet there was no sign. Nor father, nor mother, nor maiden had heard of him, and they all sorrowed over his absence. The Lenines desired to have Nancy's child, but the Trenoweths would not part with it. They went so far even as to endeavour to persuade Nancy to live again with them, but Nancy was not at all disposed to submit to their wishes.

It was All-Hallows' eve, and two of Nancy's companions persuaded her—no very difficult task—to go with them and sow hemp-seed.

At midnight the three maidens stole out unperceived into Kimyall town-place to perform their incantation. Nancy was the first to sow, the others being less bold than she.

Boldly she advanced, saying, as she scattered the seed—

> *Hemp-seed I sow thee.*
> *Hemp-seed grow thee;*

> *And he who will my true love be.*
> *Come after me*
> *And shaw thee.*

This was repeated three times, when, looking back over her left shoulder, she saw Lenine; but he looked so angry that she shrieked with fear, and broke the spell. One of the other girls, however, resolved now to make trial of the spell, and the result of her labours was the vision of a white coffin. Fear now fell on all, and they went home sorrowful, to spend, each one, a sleepless night.

November came with its storms, and during one terrific night a large vessel was thrown upon the rocks in Bernowhall Cliff, and, beaten by the impetuous waves, she was soon in pieces. Amongst the bodies of the crew washed ashore, nearly all of whom had perished, was Frank Lenine. He was not dead when found, but the only words he lived to speak were begging the people to send for Nancy Trenoweth, that he might make her his wife before he died.

Rapidly sinking, Frank was borne by his friends on a litter to Boscean, but he died as he reached the townplace. His parents, overwhelmed in their own sorrows, thought nothing of Nancy, and without her knowing that Lenine had returned, the poor fellow was laid in his last bed, in Burian Churchyard.

On the night of the funeral, Nancy went, as was her custom, to lock the door of the house, and as was her custom too, she looked out into the night. At this instant a horseman rode up in hot haste, called her by name, and hailed her in a voice that chilled her blood.

The voice was the voice of Lenine. She could never forget that; and the horse she now saw was her sweetheart's favourite colt, on which he had often ridden at night to Alsia.

The rider was imperfectly seen; but he looked very sorrowful, and deathly pale, still Nancy knew him to be Frank Lenine.

He told her that he had just arrived home, and that the first moment he was at liberty he had taken horse to fetch his loved one, and to make her his bride.

Nancy's excitement was so great, that she was easily persuaded to spring on the horse behind him, that they might reach his home before the morning.

When she took Lenine's hand a cold shiver passed through her, and as she grasped his waist to secure herself in her seat, her arm became as stiff as ice. She lost all power of speech, and suffered deep fear, yet she knew not why. The moon had arisen, and now burst out in a full flood of light, through the heavy clouds which had obscured it. The horse pursued its journey with great rapidity, and whenever in weariness it slackened its speed, the peculiar voice of the rider aroused its drooping energies. Beyond this no word was spoken since Nancy had mounted behind her lover. They now came to Trove Bottom, where there was no bridge at that time; they dashed into the river. The moon shone full in their faces. Nancy looked into the stream, and saw that the rider was in a shroud and other grave-clothes. She now knew that she was being carried away by a spirit, yet she had no power to save herself; indeed, the inclination to do so did not exist.

On went the horse at a furious pace, until they came to the blacksmith's shop, near Burian Church-town, when she knew by the light from the forge fire thrown across the road that the smith was still at his labours. She now recovered speech. "Save me! save me! save me!" she cried with all her might. The smith sprang from the door of the smithy, with a red-hot iron in his hand, and as the horse rushed by, caught the woman's dress, and pulled her to the ground. The spirit, however, also seized Nancy's dress in one hand, and his grasp was like that of a vice. The horse passed like the wind, and Nancy and the smith were pulled down as far as the old Alms-houses, near the churchyard. Here the horse for a moment stopped. The smith seized that moment, and with his hot iron burned off the dress from the rider's hand, thus saving Nancy, more dead than alive; while the rider passed over the wall of the churchyard, and vanished on the grave in which Lenine had been laid but a few hours before.

The smith took Nancy into his shop, and he soon aroused some of his neighbours, who took the poor girl back to Alsia. Her parents laid her on her bed. She spoke no word but to ask for her child, to request her mother to give up her child to Lenine's parents, and her desire to be buried in his grave. Before the morning light fell on the world Nancy had breathed her last breath.

A horse was seen that night to pass through the Church-town like a ball from a musket, and in the morning Lenine's colt was found dead in Bernowhall Cliff, covered with foam, its eyes forced from its head, and its swollen tongue hanging out of its mouth. On Lenine's grave was found the piece of Nancy's dress which was left in the spirit's hand when the smith burnt her from his grasp.

It is said that one or two of the sailors who survived the wreck related after the funeral, how, on the 30th of October, at night, Lenine was like one mad; they could scarcely keep him in the ship. He seemed more asleep than awake, and, after great excitement, he fell as if dead upon the deck, and lay so for hours. When he came to himself, he told them that he had been taken to the village of Kimyall, and that if he ever married the woman who had cast the spell, he would make her suffer the longest day she had to live for drawing his soul out of his body.

Poor Nancy was buried in Lenine's grave, and her companion in sowing hemp-seed, who saw the white coffin, slept beside her within the year.

The Deacon of Myrká
(*Iceland*)

A long time ago a deacon lived at Myrká, in Egafjördur. He was in love with a girl named Gudrún, who dwelt in a farm on the opposite side of the valley, separated from his house by a river.

The deacon had a horse with a gray mane, which he was always in the habit of riding, and which he called Faxi.

A short time before Christmas, the deacon rode to the farm at which his betrothed lived and invited her to join in the Christmas festivities at Myrká, promising to fetch her on Christmas Eve. Some time before he had started out on this ride there had been heavy snow and frost, but this very day there came so rapid a thaw that the river over which the deacon had safely ridden, trusting to the firmness of the ice, became impassable during the short time he spent with his betrothed. The floods rose, and huge masses of drift ice were whirled down the stream.

When the deacon had left the farm, he rode on to the river, and being deep in thought did not perceive at first the change that had taken place. As soon, however, as he saw in what state the stream was, he rode up the banks until he came to a bridge of ice, on to which he spurred his horse. But when he arrived at the middle of the bridge, it broke beneath him, and he was drowned in the flood.

Next morning, a neighboring farmer saw the deacon's horse grazing in a field, but could discover nothing of its owner, whom he had seen the day before cross the river, but not return. He at once suspected what had occurred, and going down to the river, found the corpse of the deacon, which had drifted to the bank, with all the flesh torn off the back of his head, and the bare white skull visible. So he brought the body back to Myrká, where it was buried a week before Christmas.

Up to Christmas Eve the river continued so swollen that no communication could take place between the dwellers on the opposite banks, but that morning it subsided, and Gudrún, utterly ignorant of the deacon's death, looked forward with joy to the festivities to which she had been invited by him.

In the afternoon Gudrún began to dress in her best clothes, but before she had quite finished, she heard a knock at the door of the farm. One of the maidservants opened the door, but seeing nobody there, thought it was because the night was not sufficiently light, for the moon was hidden for the time by clouds. So saying, "Wait there till I bring a light," went back into the house. But she had no sooner shut the outer door behind her, than the knock was repeated, and Gudrún cried out from her room, "It is someone waiting for me."

As she had by this time finished dressing, she slipped only one sleeve of her winter cloak on, and threw the rest over her shoulders hurriedly. When she opened the door, she saw the well known Faxi standing outside, and by him a man whom she knew to be the deacon. Without a word he placed Gudrún on the horse, and mounted in front of her himself, and off they rode.

When they came to the river it was frozen over, all except the current in the middle, which the frost had not yet hardened. The horse walked onto the ice, and leaped over the black and rapid stream which flowed in the middle. At the same moment the head of the deacon nodded forward, so that his hat fell over his eyes, and Gudrún saw the large patch of bare skull gleam white in the midst of his hair. Directly afterwards, a cloud moved from before the moon, and the deacon said,

> *The moon glides,*
> *Death rides,*
> *Seest thou not the white place*
> *In the back of my head*
> *Garún, Garún?*

Not a word more was spoken till they came to Myrká, where they dismounted. Then the man said,

> *Wait here for me, Garún, Garún,*
> *While I am taking Faxi, Faxi,*
> *Outside the hedges, the hedges!*

When he had gone, Gudrún saw near her in the churchyard, where she was standing, an open grave, and half sick with horror, ran to the church porch, and seizing the rope, tolled the bells with all her strength. But as she began to ring them, she felt someone grasp her and pull so fiercely at her cloak that it was torn off her, leaving only the one sleeve into which she had thrust her arm before starting from home. Then turning round, she saw the deacon jump headlong into the yawning grave, with the tattered cloak in his hand, and the heaps of earth on both sides fall in over him, and close the grave up to the brink.

Gudrún knew now that it was the deacon's ghost with whom she had had to do, and continued ringing the bells till she roused all the farm servants at Myrká.

That same night, after Gudrún had got shelter at Myrká and was in bed, the deacon came again from his grave and endeavored to drag her away, so that no one could sleep for the noise of their struggle.

This was repeated every night for a fortnight, and Gudrún could never be left alone for a single instant, lest the goblin deacon should get the better of her. From time to time, also, a neighboring priest came and sat on the edge of the bed, reading the Psalms of David to protect her against this ghostly persecution.

But nothing availed, till they sent for a man from the north country, skilled in witchcraft, who dug up a large stone from the field, and placed it in the middle of the guest room at Myrká. When the deacon rose that night from his grave and came into the house to torment Gudrún, this man seized him, and by uttering potent spells over him, forced him beneath the stone, and exorcised the passionate demon that possessed him, so that there he lies in peace to this day.

The Lover's Ghost
(*Hungary*)

Somewhere, I don't know where, even beyond the Operencian Seas, there was once a maid. She had lost her father and mother, but she loved the handsomest lad in the village where she lived. They were as happy together as a pair of turtle-doves in the wood. They fixed the day of the wedding at a not very distant date, and invited their most intimate friends to it; the girl, her godmother—the lad, a dear old friend of his.

Time went on, and the wedding would have taken place in another week, but in the meantime war broke out in the country. The king called out all his fighting-men to march against the enemy. The sabres were sharpened, and gallant fellows, on fine, gaily-caparisoned horses, swarmed to the banners of the king, like bees. John, our hero, too, took leave of his pretty *fiancée*; he led out his grey charger, mounted, and said to his young bride: "I shall be back in three years, my dove; wait until then, and don't be afraid; I promise to bring you back my love and remain faithful to you, even were I tempted by the beauty of a thousand other girls." The lass accompanied him as far as the frontier, and before parting solemnly promised to him, amidst a shower of tears, that all the treasures of the whole world should not tempt her to marry another, even if she had to wait ten years for her John.

The war lasted two years, and then peace was concluded between the belligerents. The girl was highly pleased with the news, because she expected to see her lover return with the others. She grew impatient, and would sally forth on the road by which he was expected to return, to meet him. She would go out often ten times a day, but as yet she had no tidings of her John. Three years elapsed; four years had gone by, and the bride-groom had not yet returned. The girl could not wait any longer, but went to see her godmother, and asked for her advice, who (I must tell you, between ourselves) was a witch. The old hag received her well, and gave her the following direction: "As it will be full moon to-morrow night, go into the cemetery, my dear girl, and ask the gravedigger to give you a human skull. If he should refuse, tell him that it is I who sent you. Then bring the skull home to me, and we shall place it in a huge earthenware pot, and boil it with some millet, for, say, two hours. You may be sure it will let you know whether your lover is alive yet or dead, and perchance it will entice him here." The girl thanked her for her good advice, and went to the cemetery next night. She found the gravedigger enjoying his pipe in front of the gate.

"Good evening to you, dear old father."

"Good evening, my lass! What are you doing here at this hour of the night?"

"I have come to you to ask you to grant me a favour."

"Let me hear what it is; and, if I can, I will comply with your request."

"Well, then, give me a human skull!"

"With pleasure; but what do you intend to do with it?"

"I don't know exactly, myself; my godmother has sent me for it."

"Well and good; here is one, take it."

The girl carefully wrapped up the skull, and ran home with it. Having arrived at home, she put it in a huge earthenware pot with some millet, and at once placed it on the fire. The millet soon began to boil and throw up bubbles as big as two fists. The girl was eagerly watching it and wondering what would happen. When, all of a sudden, a huge bubble formed on the surface of the boiling mass, and went off with a loud report like a musket. The next moment the girl saw the skull balanced on the rim of the pot. "He has started," it said, in a vicious tone. The girl waited a little longer, when two more loud reports came from the pot, and the skull said, "He has got halfway." Another few moments elapsed, when the pot gave three very loud reports, and the skull was heard to say, "He has arrived outside in the yard." The maid thereupon rushed out, and found her lover standing close to the threshold. His charger was snow-white, and he himself was clad entirely in white, including his helmet and boots. As soon as he caught sight of the girl, he asked: "Will you come to the country where I dwell?" "To be sure, my dear Jack; to the very end of the world." "Then come up into my saddle."

The girl mounted into the saddle, and they embraced and kissed one another ever so many times.

"And is the country where you live very far from here?"

"Yes, my love, it is very far; but in spite of the distance it will not take us long to get there."

Then they started on their journey. When they got outside the village, they saw ten mounted men rush past, all clad in spotless white, like to the finest wheat flour. As soon as they vanished, another ten appeared, and could be very well seen in the moonlight, when suddenly John said:

> *How beautifully shines the moon, the moon;*
> *How beautifully march past the dead.*
> *Are you afraid, my love, my little Judith?*

"I am not afraid while I can see you, my dear Jack."
As they proceeded, the girl saw a hundred mounted men; they rode past in beautiful military order, like soldiers. So soon as the hundred vanished another hundred appeared and followed the others. Again her lover said:

> *How beautifully shines the moon, the moon;*
> *How beautifully march past the dead.*
> *Are you afraid, my love, my little Judith?*

"I am not afraid while I can see you, my darling Jack."

And as they proceeded the mounted men appeared in fast increasing numbers, so that she could not count them; some rode past so close that they nearly brushed against her. Again her lover said:

> *How beautifully shines the moon, the moon;*
> *How beautifully march past the dead.*
> *Are you afraid, my love, my little Judith?*

"I am not afraid while I see you, Jack, my darling."

"You are a brave and good girl, my dove; I see that you would do anything for me. As a reward, you shall have everything that your heart can wish when we get to my new country."

They went along till they came to an old burial-ground, which was inclosed by a black wall. John stopped here and said to his sweetheart: "This is our country, my little Judith, we shall soon come to our house." The house to which John alluded was an open grave, at the bottom of which an empty coffin could be seen with the lid off. "Go in, my darling," said the lad. "You had better go first, my love Jack," replied the girl, "you know the way." Thereupon the lad descended into the grave and laid down in the coffin; but the lass, instead of following him, ran away as fast as her feet would carry her, and took refuge in a mansion that was situated a couple of miles from the cemetery. When she had reached the mansion she shook every door, but none of them would open to her entreaties, except one that led to a long corridor, at the end of which there was a dead body laid out in state in a coffin. The lass secreted herself in a dark corner of the fire-place.

As soon as John discovered that his bride had run away he jumped out of the grave and pursued the lass, but in spite of all his exertions could not overtake her. When he reached the door at the end of the corridor he knocked and exclaimed: "Dead man, open the door to a fellow dead man." The corpse inside began to tremble at the sound of these words. Again said Jack, "Dead man, open the door to a fellow dead man." Now the corpse sat up in the coffin, and as Jack repeated a third time the words "Dead man, open the door to a fellow dead man," the corpse walked to the door and opened it.

"Is my bride here?"

"Yes, there she is, hiding in the corner of the fire-place."

"Come and let us tear her in pieces." And with this intention they both approached the girl, but just as they were about to lay hands upon her the cock in the loft began to crow, and announced daybreak, and the two dead men disappeared.

The next moment a most richly attired gentleman entered from one of the neighbouring rooms. Judging by his appearance one would have believed it was the king himself, who at once approached the girl and overwhelmed her with his embraces and kisses.

"Thank you so much. The corpse that you saw here laid out in state was my brother. I have already had him buried three hundred and sixty-five times with the greatest pomp, but he has returned each time. As you have relieved me of him, my sweet, pretty darling, you shall become mine and I yours; not even the hoe and the spade shall separate us from one another!"

The girl consented to the proposal of the rich gentleman, and they got married and celebrated their wedding-feast during the same winter.

This is how far the tale goes. This is the end of it.

471A: The Monk and the Bird

The Monk and the Bird of Paradise
(*Sweden*)

The banks of the Rhine stood a large Monastery, where dwelt a company of monks. These holy men were not only distinguished for sanctity, but also for their wisdom and learning, and one of the foremost was Brother Bernard, whom all reverenced for his piety. From far and near students came to consult him, and his words were quoted as if he were an oracle.

In spite of his holiness, however, Brother Bernard had serious misgivings as to the state of his own soul. He could not imagine himself living in Paradise forever without becoming weary of it.

"Alas!" he cried, "we tire of everything upon this earth, and I fear that even an eternity of bliss would at last become monotonous. The vesper hymn is very sweet, but I should not care for it unceasingly."

He was so tormented by this thought that he could neither read nor pray. At the foot of the mountain on which the Monastery was built stood a great forest, and here he wandered for hours in the shade of the giant trees, so absorbed in his reflections that he paid no heed to where he trod. At last he prayed that God would work some miracle that he might know that life in Heaven would neither be dull nor dreary.

After a while he grew fatigued by his long ramble and looked around to see whence he had come. To his surprise he found himself in an unknown part of the forest, and on reaching a clearing where the sunlight streamed on the fallen needles of the pines, he threw himself into the midst of their fragrance to rest awhile. Just then a little bird, with plumage the colour of the sky itself, alighted on the branch above him, and began to sing. So pure and exquisite were its notes that Brother Bernard listened in ecstasy until the sweet song ceased. As the bird vanished, the monk rose from his seat. "Dear me," he cried, "how stiff I am! I must have walked much further than I thought."

In stooping to brush the pine-needles from his robe he noticed that his beard was snowy white, and that his hands were wrinkled, like those of an old man. Even the forest itself looked changed to him, for the trees were larger, and the bushes had disappeared. He wondered if he could be dreaming, for otherwise, he thought, his senses must be deceiving him. With great difficulty he found his way back to the village, where he was surprised to meet unfamiliar faces. He rubbed his eyes again and again, feeling greatly disturbed.

"I thought that I knew everyone," he muttered to himself, "but here are people whom I never met before. Who are they, and why do they stare at me as if I were some wild man of the woods, instead of hastening to kiss my hand and receive my benediction?" He was too weary to question them, however, and made his way to the Monastery. His astonishment increased when he found a stranger in charge of the gate instead of good Brother Antoine, who had held the office for more than fifty years.

"Where is the porter?" he asked him falteringly, "and what has happened to cause the changes which I see around me?"

The Brother looked at him curiously.

"I do not know what you mean," he said, "for I have been porter here for thirty years, and I can assure you that there have been no changes in *my* time."

"Then what can have happened to me?" exclaimed the bewildered monk. "I went out this morning to walk in the forest, and on my return I find no trace of my old comrades."

Just then two aged monks came slowly by, and Brother Bernard stepped in front of them.

"Do you not recognise me?" he asked. "Is there no one here who knows Brother Bernard?"

"'Brother Bernard'?" said the oldest, reflectively. "We have no Brother of that name in the Monastery now, but I remember having read of him in our chronicles. He was a most holy man, with the simple faith of a little child. One morning, they say, he quitted the Monastery and went to the forest that he might meditate and pray with nothing between him and the floor of Heaven. He never returned, and though a diligent search was made, no trace of him could be found. It was thought that he had been carried up to the skies, like the prophet Elijah, in a chariot of fire: a fitting end to his life of sanctity."

"How long ago was this?" asked Brother Bernard tremblingly.

"A THOUSAND years," said the old monk. "You may see by our books that this is so."

On hearing this Brother Bernard fell on his knees.

"God heard my prayer, and worked a miracle," he cried, "that I might have faith. He sent His Bird of Paradise to sing to me, and, while I listened, a thousand years passed by. Now indeed I believe, and would feign enter His Holy Kingdom."

He bowed his head in silence, and when they spoke to him again they found that his spirit had passed away. The smile on his lips was so full of sweetness that the monks marvelled greatly, and they noted with awe that his wrinkled face had grown smooth again.

"God is good to His Saints," murmured one monk. "Amen," returned the others solemnly.

The Monk and the Bird
(*Germany*)

Many years ago the young monk Urban lived in a cloister. He stood out as more earnest and devout than his fellows and was therefore entrusted with the key of the convent library. He took very good care of the books and scrolls and other things there, besides reading in the books himself. One day he read, "A day is like a thousand years, and a thousand years are like a day." The thought seemed impossible to him.

One morning the monk went out of the library into the cloister-garden and saw a little bird perched on the bough of a tree there, singing sweetly. The bird was a nightingale, and did not move when the monk came nearer until he was quite close. Then she flew to another bough and again another as the monk followed her. Still singing the same sweet song, the nightingale flew on. The monk, eager to hear her song, followed her on out of the garden into the world outside for three minutes. Then he stopped and turned back to the cloister.

But everything about it seemed changed to him. Everything had become larger, more beautiful and older—both the buildings and the garden. And in the place of the low, humble cloister-church there was a large cathedral with three towers toward the sky. This seemed very strange to the monk, but he walked on to the cloister-gate and timidly rang the bell.

A porter that was wholly unknown to him answered his summons and drew back in amazement when he saw the monk.

The monk went in and wandered through the church, gazing with astonishment on memorial-stones that he never remembered to have seen before. Then the brethren of the cloister entered the church, but all stepped back when they saw the monk.

The abbot only—but not his abbot —stooped and stretched a crucifix before him, exclaiming, "Who are you? And what do you seek here among the living?"

The monk suddenly trembled and tottered like an old man. When he looked down, he noticed for the first time a long silvery beard was flowing from his chin and down over his girdle, where the key of the library was still hanging.

The monks now led him to the chair of the abbot with a mixture of awe and admiration. There the long-bearded monk gave the key of the library to a young man, who opened it and read a chronicle about the monk Urban who had disappeared three hundred years ago. No one knew what had become of him.

"Forest bird, is this due to your song?" said the monk Urban with a heavy sigh. "I followed you for three minutes it seemed, listening to your notes, and yet three hundred years passed away! You must be an awfully old bird! Now I know."

With these words he sank to the ground while his spirit swooshed into heaven.

Rhys at the Fairy-Dance
(*Wales*)

Rhys and Llewellyn, two farmer's servants, who had been all day carrying lime for their master, were driving in the twilight their mountain ponies before them, returning home from their work. On reaching a little plain, Rhys called to his companion to stop and listen to the music, saying it was a tune to which he had danced a hundred times, and must go and have a dance now. He bade him go on with the horses, and he would soon overtake him. Llewellyn could hear nothing, and began to remonstrate; but away sprang Rhys, and he called after him in vain. He went home, put up the ponies, ate his supper, and went to bed, thinking that Rhys had only made a pretext for going to the ale-house. But when morning came, and still no sign of Rhys, he told his master what had occurred. Search was then made everywhere, but no Rhys could be found. Suspicion now fell upon Llewellyn of having murdered him, and he was thrown into prison, though there was no evidence against him. A farmer, however, skilled in fairy-matters, having an idea of how things might have been, proposed that himself and some others should accompany Llewellyn to the place where he parted with Rhys. On coming to it, they found it green as the mountain ash. "Hush!" cried Llewellyn, "I hear music, I hear sweet harps." We all listened, says the narrator, for I was one of them, but could hear nothing. "Put your foot on mine, David," said he to me (his own foot was at the time on the outward edge of the fairy-ring). I did so, and so did we all, one after another, and then we heard the sound of many harps, and saw within a circle, about twenty feet across, great numbers of little people, of the size of children of three or four years old, dancing round and round. Among them we saw Rhys, and Llewellyn catching him by the smock-frock, as he came by him, pulled him out of the circle. "Where are the horses? where are the horses?" cried he. "Horses, indeed!" said Llewellyn. Rhys urged him to go home, and let him finish his dance, in which he averred he had not been engaged more than five minutes. It was by main force they took him from the place. He still asserted he had been only five minutes away, and could give no account of the people he had been with. He became melancholy, took to his bed, and soon after died. "The morning after," says the narrator, "we went to look at the place, and we found the edge of the ring quite red, as if trodden down, and I could see the marks of little heels, about the size of my thumb-nail."

PROTO-BALTO-SLAVIC

307: The Princess in the Shroud

The Princess in the Chest

The Princess in the Chest
(*Denmark*)

There were once a king and a queen who lived in a beautiful castle, and had a large, and fair, and rich, and happy land to rule over. From the very first they loved each other greatly, and lived very happily together, but they had no heir.

They had been married for seven years, but had neither son nor daughter, and that was a great grief to both of them. More than once it happened that when the king was in a bad temper, he let it out on the poor queen, and said that here they were now, getting old, and neither they nor the kingdom had an heir, and it was all her fault. This was hard to listen to, and she went and cried and vexed herself.

Finally, the king said to her one day, 'This can't be borne any longer. I go about childless, and it's your fault. I am going on a journey and shall be away for a year. If you have a child when I come back again, all will be well, and I shall love you beyond all measure, and never more say an angry word to you. But if the nest is just as empty when I come home, then I must part with you.'

After the king had set out on his journey, the queen went about in her loneliness, and sorrowed and vexed herself more than ever. At last her maid said to her one day, 'I think that some help could be found, if your majesty would seek it.' Then she told about a wise old woman in that country, who had helped many in troubles of the same kind, and could no doubt help the queen as well, if she would send for her. The queen did so, and the wise woman came, and to her she confided her sorrow, that she was childless, and the king and his kingdom had no heir.

The wise woman knew help for this. 'Out in the king's garden,' said she, 'under the great oak that stands on the left hand, just as one goes out from the castle, is a little bush, rather brown than green, with hairy leaves and long spikes. On that bush there are just at this moment three buds. If your majesty goes out there alone, fasting, before sunrise, and takes the middle one of the three buds and eats it, then in six months you will bring a princess into the world. As soon as she is born, she must have a nurse, whom I shall provide, and this nurse must live with the child in a secluded part of the palace; no other person must visit the child; neither the king nor the queen must see it until it is fourteen years old, for that would cause great sorrow and misfortune.'

The queen rewarded the old woman richly, and next morning before the sun rose, she was down in the garden and found at once the little bush with the three buds, plucked the middle one and ate it. It was sweet to taste, but afterwards was as bitter as gall. Six months after this, she brought into the world a little girl. There was a nurse in readiness, whom the wise woman had provided, and preparations were made for her living with the child, quite alone, in a secluded wing of the castle, looking out on the pleasure-park. The queen did as the wise woman had told her; she gave up the child immediately, and the nurse took it and lived with it there.

When the king came home and heard that a daughter had been born to him, he was of course very pleased and happy, and wanted to see her at once.

The queen had then to tell him this much of the story, that it had been foretold that it would cause great sorrow and misfortune if either he or she got a sight of the child until it had completed its fourteenth year.

This was a long time to wait. The king longed so much to get a sight of his daughter, and the queen no less than he, but she knew that it was not like other children, for it could speak immediately after it was born, and was as wise as older folk. This the nurse had told her, for with her the queen had a talk now and again, but there was no one who had ever seen the princess. The queen had also seen what the wise woman could do, so she insisted strongly that her warning should be obeyed. The king often lost his patience, and was determined to see his daughter, but the queen always put him off the idea, and so things went on, until the very day before the princess completed her fourteenth year.

The king and the queen were out in the garden then, and the king said, 'Now I can't and I won't wait any longer. I must see my daughter at once. A few hours, more or less, can't make any difference.'

The queen begged him to have patience till the morning. When they had waited so long, they could surely wait a single day more. But the king was quite unreasonable. 'No nonsense,' said he; 'she is just as much mine as yours, and I will see her,' and with that he went straight up to her room.

He burst the door open, and pushed aside the nurse, who tried to stop him, and there he saw his daughter. She was the loveliest young princess, red and white, like milk and blood, with clear blue eyes and golden hair, but right in the middle of her forehead there was a little tuft of brown hair.

The princess went to meet her father, fell on his neck and kissed him, but with that she said, 'O father, father! what have you done now? to-morrow I must die, and you must choose one of three things: either the land must be smitten with the black pestilence, or you must have a long and bloody war, or you must as soon as I am dead, lay me in a plain wooden chest, and set it in the church, and for a whole year place a sentinel beside it every night.'

The king was frightened indeed, and thought she was raving, but in order to please her, he said, 'Well, of these three things I shall choose the last; if you die, I shall lay you at once in a plain wooden chest, and have it set in the church, and every night I shall place a sentinel beside it. But you shall not die, even if you are ill now.'

He immediately summoned all the best doctors in the country, and they came with all their prescriptions and their medicine bottles, but next day the princess was stiff and cold in death. All the doctors could certify to that and they all put their names to this and appended their seals, and then they had done all they could.

The king kept his promise. The princess's body was lain the same day in a plain wooden chest, and set in the chapel of the castle, and on that night and every night after it, a sentinel was posted in the church, to keep watch over the chest.

The first morning when they came to let the sentinel out, there was no sentinel there. They thought he had just got frightened and run away, and next evening a new one was posted in the church. In the morning he was also gone. So it went every night. When they came in the morning to let the sentinel out, there was no one there, and it was impossible to discover which way he had gone if he had run away. And what should they run away for, every one of them, so that nothing more was overheard or seen of them, from the hour that they were set on guard beside the princess's chest?

It became now a general belief that the princess's ghost walked, and ate up all those who were to guard her chest, and very soon there was no one left who would be placed on this duty, and the king's soldiers deserted the service before their turn came to be her bodyguard. The king then promised a large reward to the soldier who would volunteer for the post. This did for some time, as there were found a few reckless fellows who wished to earn this good payment. But they never got it, for in the morning, they too had disappeared like the rest.

So it had gone on for something like a whole year; every night a sentinel had been placed beside the chest, either by compulsion or of his own free will, but not a single one of the sentinels was to be seen, either on the following day or any time thereafter. And so it had also gone with one, on the night before a certain day, when a merry young smith came wandering to the town where the king's castle stood. It was the capital of the country, and people of every king came to it to get work. This smith, whose name was Christian, had come for that same purpose. There was no work for him in the place he belonged to, and he wanted now to seek a place in the capital.

There he entered an inn where he sat down in the public room, and got something to eat. Some under-officers were sitting there, who were out to try to get someone enlisted to stand sentry. They had to go in this way, day after day, and hitherto they had always succeeded in finding one or other reckless fellow. But on this day they had, as yet, found no one. It was too well known how all the sentinels disappeared who were set on that post, and all that they had got hold of had refused with thanks. These sat down beside Christian, and ordered drinks, and drank along with him. Now Christian was a merry fellow who liked good company; he could both drink and sing, and talk and boast as well, when he got a little drop in his head. He told these under-officers that he was one of that kind of folk who never are afraid of anything. Then he was just the kind of man they liked, said they, and he might easily earn a good penny before he was a day older, for the king paid a hundred dollars to anyone who would stand as sentinel in the church all night, beside his daughter's chest.

Christian was not afraid of that; he wasn't afraid of anything, so they drank another bottle of wine on this, and Christian went with them up to the colonel, where he was put into uniform with musket, and all the rest, and was then shut up in the church, to stand as sentinel that night.

It was eight o'clock when he took up his post, and for the first hour he was quite proud of his courage; during the second hour he was well pleased with the large reward that he would get, but in the third hour, when it was getting near eleven, the effects of the wine passed off, and he began to get uncomfortable, for he had heard about this post; that no one had ever escaped alive from it, so far as was known. But neither did any-one know what had become of all the sentinels. The thought of this ran in his head so much, after the wine was out of it, that he searched about everywhere for a way of escape, and finally, at eleven o'clock, he found a little postern in the steeple which was not locked, and out at this he crept, intending to run away.

At the same moment as he put his foot outside the church door, he saw standing before him a little man, who said, 'Good evening, Christian, where are you going?'

With that he felt as if he were rooted to the spot and could not move.

'Nowhere,' said he.

'Oh, yes,' said the little man, 'You were just about to run away, but you have taken upon you to stand sentinel in the church to-night, and there you must stay.'

Christian said, very humbly, that he dared not, and therefore wanted to get away, and begged to be let go.

'No,' said the little one, 'you must remain at your post, but I shall give you a piece of good advice; you shall go up into the pulpit, and remain standing there. You need never mind what you see or hear, it will not be able to do you any harm, if you remain in your place until you hear the lid of the chest slam down again behind the dead; then all danger is past, and you can go about the church, wherever you please.'

The little man then pushed him in at the door again, and locked it after him. Christian made haste to get up into the pulpit, and stood there, without noticing anything, until the clock struck twelve. Then the lid of the princess's chest sprang up, and out of it there came something like the princess, dressed as you see in the picture. It shrieked and howled, 'Sentry, where are you? Sentry, where are you? If you don't come, you shall get the most cruel death anyone had ever got.'

It went all round the church, and when it finally caught sight of the smith, up in the pulpit, it came rushing thither and mounted the steps. But it could not get up the whole way, and for all that it stretched and strained, it could not touch Christian, who meanwhile stood and trembled up in the pulpit. When the clock struck one, the appearance had to go back into the chest again, and Christian heard the lid slam after it. After this there was dead silence in the church. He lay down where he was and fell asleep, and did not awake before it was bright daylight, and he heard steps outside, and the noise of the key being put into the lock. Then he came down from the pulpit, and stood with his musket in front of the princess's chest.

It was the colonel himself who came with the patrol, and he was not a little surprised when he found the recruit safe and sound. He wanted to have a report, but Christian would give him none, so he took him straight up to the king, and announced for the first time that here was the sentinel who had stood guard in the church overnight. The king immediately got out of bed, and laid the hundred dollars for him on the table, and then wanted to question him. 'Have you seen anything?' said he. 'Have you seen my daughter?' 'I have stood at my post,' said the young smith, 'and that is quite enough; I undertook nothing more.' He was not sure whether he dared tell what he had seen and heard, and besides he was also a little conceited because he had done what no other man had been able to do, or had had courage for. The king professed to be quite satisfied, and asked him whether he would engage himself to stand on guard again the following night. 'No, thank you,' said Christian, 'I will have no more of that!'

'As you please,' said the king, 'you have behaved like a brave fellow, and now you shall have your breakfast. You must be needing something to strengthen you after that turn.'

The king had breakfast laid for him, and sat down at the table with him in person; he kept constantly filling his glass for him and praising him, and drinking his health. Christian needed no pressing, but did full justice both to the food and drink, and not least to the latter. Finally he grew bold, and said that if the king would give him two hundred dollars for it, he was his man to stand sentry next night as well.

When this was arranged, Christian bade him 'Good-day,' and went down among the guards, and then out into the town along with other soldiers and under-officers. He had his pocket full of money, and treated them, and drank with them and boasted and made game of the good-for-nothings who were afraid to stand on guard because they were frightened that the dead princess would eat them. See whether she had eaten him! So the day passed in mirth and glee, but when eight o'clock came, Christian was again shut up in the church, all alone.

Before he had been there two hours, he got tired of it, and thought only of getting away. He found a little door behind the altar which was not locked, and at ten o'clock he slipped out at it, and took to his heels and made for the beach. He had got half-way thither, when all at once the same little man stood in front of him and said, 'Good evening, Christian, where are you going?' 'I've leave to go where I please,' said the smith, but at the same time he noticed that he could not move a foot. 'No, you have undertaken to keep guard to-night as well,' said the little man, 'and you must attend to that.' He then took hold of him, and however unwilling he was, Christian had to go with him right back to the same little door that he had crept out at. When they got there, the little man said to him, 'Go in front of the altar now, and take in your hand the book that is lying there. There you shall stay till you hear the lid of the chest slam down over the dead. In that way you will come to no harm.'

With that the little man shoved him in at the door, and locked it. Christian then immediately went in front of the altar, and took the book in his hand, and stood thus until the clock struck twelve, and the appearance sprang out of the chest. 'Sentry, where are you? Sentry, where are you?' it shrieked, and then rushed to the pulpit, and right up into it. But there was no one there that night. Then it howled and shrieked again,

> *My father has set no sentry in,*
> *War and Pest this night begin.*

At the same moment, it noticed the smith standing in front of the altar, and came rushing towards him. 'Are you there?' it screamed; 'now I'll catch you.' But it could not come up over the step in front of the altar, and there it continued to howl, and scream, and threaten, until the clock struck one, when it had to go into the chest again, and Christian heard the lid slam above it. That night, however, it had not the same appearance as on the previous one; it was less ugly.

When all was quiet in the church, the smith lay down before the altar and slept calmly till the following morning, when the colonel came to fetch him. He was taken up to the king again, and things went on as the day before. He got his money, but would give no explanation whether he had seen the king's daughter, and he would not take the post again, he said. But after he had got a good breakfast, and tasted well of the king's wines, he undertook to go on guard again the third night, but he would not do it for less than the half of the kingdom, he said, for it was a dangerous post, and the king had to agree, and promise him this.

The remainder of the day went like the previous one. He played the boastful soldier, and the merry smith, and he had comrades and boon-companions in plenty. At eight o'clock he had to put on his uniform again, and was shut up in the church. He had not been there for an hour before he had come to his senses, and thought, 'It's best to stop now, while the game is going well.' The third night, he was sure, would be the worst; he had been drunk when he promised it, and the half of the kingdom, the king could never have been in earnest about that! So he decided to leave, without waiting so long as on the previous nights. In that way he would escape the little man who had watched him before. All the doors and posterns were locked, but he finally thought of creeping up to a window, and opening that, and as the clock struck nine, he crept out there. It was fairly high in the wall, but he got to the ground with no bones broken, and started to run. He got down to the shore without meeting anyone, and there he got into a boat, and pushed off from land. He laughed immensely to himself at the thought of how cleverly he had managed and how he had cheated the little man. Just then he heard a voice from the shore, 'Good evening, Christian, where are you going?' He gave no answer. 'To-night your legs will be too short,' he thought, and pulled at the oars. But he then felt something lay hold of the boat, and drag it straight in to shore, for all that he sat and struggled with the oars.

The man then laid hold of him, and said, 'You must remain at your post, as you have promised,' and whether he liked it or not, Christian had just to go back with him the whole way to the church.

He could never get in at that window again, Christian said; it was far too high up.

'You must go in there, and you shall go in there,' said the little man, and with that he lifted him up on to the window-sill. Then he said to him: 'Notice well now what you have to do. This evening you must stretch yourself out on the left-hand side of her chest. The lid opens to the right, and she comes out to the left. When she has got out of the chest and passed over you, you must get into it and lie there, and that in a hurry, without her seeing you. There you must remain lying until day dawns, and whether she threatens you or entreats you, you must not come out of it, or give her any answer. Then she has no power over you, and both you and she are freed.'

The smith then had to go in at the window, just as he came out, and went and laid himself all his length on the left side of the princess's chest, close up to it, and there he lay stiff as a rock until the clock struck twelve. Then the lid sprang up to the right, and the princess came out, straight over him, and rushed round the church, howling and shrieking 'Sentry, where are you? Sentry, where are you?' She went towards the altar, and right up to it, but there was no one there; then she screamed again,

> *My father has set no sentry in,*
> *War and Pest will now begin.*

Then she went round the whole church, both up and down, sighing and weeping,

> *My father has set no sentry in,*
> *War and Pest will now begin.*

Then she went away again, and at the same moment the clock in the tower struck one.

Then the smith heard in the church a soft music, which grew louder and louder, and soon filled the whole building. He heard also a multitude of footsteps, as if the church was being filled with people. He heard the priest go through the service in front of the altar, and there was singing more beautiful than he had ever heard before. Then he also heard the priest offer up a prayer of thanksgiving because the land had been freed from war and pestilence, and from all misfortune, and the king's daughter delivered from the evil one. Many voices joined in, and a hymn of praise was sung; then he heard the priest again, and heard his own name and that of the princess, and thought that he was being wedded to her. The church was packed full, but he could see nothing. Then he heard again the many footsteps as ol' folk leaving the church, while the music sounded fainter and fainter, until it altogether died away. When it was silent, the light of day began to break in through the windows.

The smith sprang up out of the chest and fell on his knees and thanked God. The church was empty, but up in front of the altar lay the princess, white and red, like a human being, but sobbing and crying, and shaking with cold in her white shroud. The smith took his sentry coat and wrapped it round her; then she dried her tears, and took his hand and thanked him, and said that he had now freed her from all the sorcery that had been in her from her birth, and which had come over her again when her father broke the command against seeing her until she had completed her fourteenth year.

She said further that if he who had delivered her would take her in marriage, she would be his. If not, she would go into a nunnery, and he could marry no other as long as she lived, for he was wedded to her with the service of the dead, which he had heard.

She was now the most beautiful young princess that anyone could wish to see, and he was now lord of half the kingdom, which had been promised him for standing on guard the third night. So they agreed that they would have each other, and love each other all their days.

With the first sunbeam the watch came and opened the church, and not only was the colonel there, but the king in person, come to see what had happened to the sentinel. He found them both sitting hand in hand on the step in front of the altar, and immediately knew his daughter again, and took her in his arms, thanking God and her deliverer. He made no objections to what they had arranged, and so Christian the smith held his wedding with the princess, and got half the kingdom at once, and the whole of it when the king died.

As for the other sentries, with so many doors and windows open, no doubt they had run away, and gone into the Prussian service. And as for what Christian said he saw, he had been drinking more wine than was good for him.

The Three Girls
(*Slovak, Moravian, and Bohemian*)

Somewhere there was a king who had three daughters, princesses. Those three sisters used to go to meet the devils, and the father knew not where they went to. But there was one called Jankos; Halenka[1] aided him.

The king asks Jankos, "Don't you know where my daughters go? Not one single night are they at home, and they are always wearing out new shoes."

Then Jankos lay down in front of the door, and kept watch to see where they went to. But Halenka told him everything; she aided him. "They will, when they come, fling fire on you, and prick you with needles." Halenka told him he must not stir, but be like a corpse.

They came, those devils, for the girls, and straightway the girls set out with them to hell. On, on, they walked, but he stuck close to them. As the girls went to hell he followed close behind, but so that they knew it not. He went through the diamond forest; when he came there he cut himself a diamond twig from the forest. He follows; straightway they, those girls, cried, "Jankos is coming behind us." For when he broke it, he made a great noise. The girls heard it. "Jankos is coming behind us."

But the devils said, "What does it matter if he is?"

---

1 A fairy.

Next they went through the forest of glass, and once more he cut off a twig; now he had two tokens. Then they went through the golden forest, and once more he cut off a twig; so now he had three.

Then Halenka tells him, "I shall change you into a fly, and when you come into hell, creep under the bed, hide yourself there, and see what will happen."

Then the devils danced with the girls, who tore their shoes all to pieces, for they danced upon blades of knives, and so they must tear them. Then they flung the shoes under the bed, where Jankos took them, so that he might show them at home. When the devils had danced with the girls, each of them threw his girl upon the bed and lay with her; thus did they with two of them, but the third would not yield herself.

Then Jankos, having got all he wanted, returned home and lay down again in front of the door, "that the girls may know I am lying here."

The girls returned after midnight, and went to bed in their room as if nothing had happened. But Jankos knew well what had happened, and straightway he went to their father, the king, and showed him the tokens. "I know where your daughters go: to hell. The three girls must own they were there, in the fire. Isn't it true? weren't you there? And if you believe me not, I will show you the tokens. See, here is one token from the diamond forest; then here is one from the forest of glass; a third from the golden forest; and the fourth is the shoes which you tore dancing with the devils. And two of you lay with the devils, but that third one not, she would not yield herself."

Straightway the king seized his rifle, and straightway he shot them dead. Then he seized a knife, and slit up their bellies, and straightway the devils were scattered out from their bellies. Then he buried them in the church, and laid each coffin in front of the altar, and every night a soldier stood guard over them. But every night those two used to rend the soldier in pieces; more than a hundred were rent thus. At last it fell to a new soldier, a recruit, to stand guard; when he went upon guard he was weeping.

But a little old man came to him—it was my God; and Jankos was there with the soldier. And the old man tells him, "When the twelfth hour strikes and they come out of their coffins, straightway jump in and lie down in the coffin, and don't leave the coffin, for if you do they will rend you. So don't you go out, even if they beg you and fling fire on you, for they will beg you hard to come out."

Thus then till morning he lay in the coffin. In the morning those two were alive again, and both kneeling in front of the altar. They were lovelier than ever. Then the soldier took one to wife, and Jankos took the other. Then when they came home with them their father was very glad. Then Jankos and the soldier got married, and if they are not dead they are still alive.

The Princess' Curse
(*Hungary*)

Once lived a great king with a famously beautiful daughter; in the neighboring kingdom ruled another king, who had two equally handsome sons. The younger son went to ask for the princess' hand in marriage and they fell in love, but her father said the prince wasn't worthy of his daughter yet—he ordered him to go and travel for three years, see the world, learn, and then come back ready for marriage. The princess was sad that they had to part for three years, but promised to patiently wait.

While the younger prince was away, his older brother tried to seduce the princess for himself, telling her lies about his little brother—but she couldn't be swayed. When three years passed and the young prince returned home, his older brother managed to persuade him that the princess forgot all about him, and was now engaged to someone else.

The princess waited and waited, and grew more desperate; she stopped eating and drinking, and one day she told her father she would die in 3 days' time if her lover didn't return. She asked her father to bury her in the cathedral's crypt, and have her guarded by armed soldiers.

Three days later the princess died. The kingdom dressed in mourning, and she was laid to rest in the crypt. Just as this was happening, the older prince arrived and was shocked to find out that the princess he hoped to marry was dead. Feeling remorse, he volunteered to stand guard in the cathedral that night.

As the bells tolled ten at night, the crypt opened, and the princess walked out, pale as death and with a terrible look in her eyes.

"You have lied to your brother about me! You broke my heart, and for that you'll die."

She ripped the prince apart, piled his bones in a corner, and went back to her grave.

The next day the younger prince finally showed up, and was shocked to find out that his lover and his brother were both dead. He volunteered to stand guard that night.

At ten, the crypt opened, and out came the princess:

"You believed the lies you were told, and didn't have faith in me. For that you will die!"

She ripped him apart, piled his bones up, and returned to her grave.

Every night from that point on, someone stood guard at the crypt—and every night, they were murdered by the dead princess. The pile of bones grew and grew.

Eventually a former solder called János came into town, and he offered to guard the princess' crypt as long as the king was willing to pay him a bushel of gold for every night. The king was desperate and he agreed, but as János walked over to the cathedral he realized he might have taken on more than he could handle, and decided to run away instead. He got as far as the city walls when he was stopped by an old man. The old man didn't only know why János was running, but also knew how he could survive a night; they agreed to split the gold, and János returned to the cathedral, armed with new knowledge.

When the bells tolled ten, he climbed the tower and hid himself inside the middle bell. The princess came out of the crypt and started looking for him; she almost got to the bell in the middle when the bells started tolling midnight, and she had no power in the world of the living anymore. She returned to her crypt.

The king was overjoyed to see János alive in the morning, and paid him the bushel of gold. János returned to the old man, they split the gold, and the old man told him where to hide on the next night.

When the bells tolled ten that night, János hid himself under the pile of bones. The princess emerged from her grave, ran to the bells; when she saw they were empty she started turning the entire cathedral upside down, rummaging in every corner, looking for the guard. She was just about to get to the pile of bones when the bells tolled midnight, and she had to return to her grave.

For the third night, the old man gave János the riskiest task yet: He had to stand in plain sight on the pulpit, with a book. The pulpit had stairs on both sides—the princess would go up on one side, he would run down the other. He had to reach her coffin before her, and hide himself in it.

Everything happened as planned. János locked himself inside the coffin, and held on while the princess screamed, and yelled, and threatened, and begged to get him to come out. The bells tolled midnight, and she screamed even more... but once the tolling ended, the curse broke, and she was her own living self once again.

The king arrived in the morning, and almost died out of sheer joy at seeing his daughter alive. János and the princess were married. On their wedding day the old man showed up, and he drew a sword on the newlyweds—it was a reminder that no one should ever break his given word. János ordered the entire payment of gold to be given to the old man, as a sign of his gratitude.

They all lived happily ever after.

312 D: Rescue by the Brother

Childe Rowland
(*England*)

Childe Rowland and his brothers twain
Were playing at the ball,
And there was their sister Burd Ellen
In the midst, among them all.

Childe Rowland kicked it with his foot
And caught it with his knee;
At last as he plunged among them all
O'er the church he made it flee.

Burd Ellen round about the aisle
To seek the ball is gone,
But long they waited, and longer still,
And she came not back again.

They sought her east, they sought her west,
They sought her up and down,
And woe were the hearts of those brethren,
For she was not to be found.

So at last her eldest brother went to the Warlock Merlin and told him all the case, and asked him if he knew where Burd Ellen was. "The fair Burd Ellen," said the Warlock Merlin, "must have been carried off by the fairies, because she went round the church 'widershins'—the opposite way to the sun. She is now in the Dark Tower of the King of Elfland; it would take the boldest knight in Christendom to bring her back."

"If it is possible to bring her back," said her brother, "I'll do it, or perish in the attempt."

"Possible it is," said the Warlock Merlin, "but woe to the man or mother's son that attempts it, if he is not well taught beforehand what he is to do."

The eldest brother of Burd Ellen was not to be put off, by any fear of danger, from attempting to get her back, so he begged the Warlock Merlin to tell him what he should do, and what he should not do, in going to seek his sister. And after he had been taught, and had repeated his lesson, he set out for Elfland.

But long they waited, and longer still,

With doubt and muckle pain,
But woe were the hearts of his brethren,
For he came not back again.

Then the second brother got tired and sick of waiting, and he went to the Warlock Merlin and asked him the same as his brother. So he set out to find Burd Ellen.

But long they waited, and longer still,
With muckle doubt and pain,
And woe were his mother's and brother's heart,
For he came not back again.

And when they had waited and waited a good long time, Childe Rowland, the youngest of Burd Ellen's brothers, wished to go, and went to his mother, the good queen, to ask her to let him go. But she would not at first, for he was the last of her children she now had, and if he was lost, all would be lost. But he begged, and he begged, till at last the good queen let him go, and gave him his father's good brand that never struck in vain. And as she girt it round his waist, she said the spell that would give it victory.

So Childe Rowland said good-bye to the good queen, his mother, and went to the cave of the Warlock Merlin. "Once more, and but once more," he said to the Warlock, "tell how man or mother's son may rescue Burd Ellen and her brothers twain."

"Well, my son," said the Warlock Merlin, "there are but two things, simple they may seem, but hard they are to do. One thing to do, and one thing not to do. And the thing to do is this: after you have entered the land of Fairy, whoever speaks to you, till you meet the Burd Ellen, you must out with your father's brand and off with their head. And what you've not to do is this: bite no bit, and drink no drop, however hungry or thirsty you be; drink a drop, or bite a bit, while in Elfland you be and never will you see Middle Earth again."

So Childe Rowland said the two things over and over again, till he knew them by heart, and he thanked the Warlock Merlin and went on his way. And he went along, and along, and along, and still further along, till he came to the horse-herd of the King of Elfland feeding his horses. These he knew by their fiery eyes, and knew that he was at last in the land of Fairy. "Canst thou tell me," said Childe Rowland to the horse-herd, "where the King of Elfland's Dark Tower is?" "I cannot tell thee," said the horse-herd, "but go on a little further and thou wilt come to the cow-herd, and he, maybe, can tell thee."

Then, without a word more, Childe Rowland drew the good brand that never struck in vain, and off went the horse-herd's head, and Childe

Rowland went on further, till he came to the cow-herd, and asked him the same question. "I can't tell thee," said he, "but go on a little farther, and thou wilt come to the hen-wife, and she is sure to know." Then Childe Rowland out with his good brand, that never struck in vain, and off went the cow-herd's head. And he went on a little further, till he came to an old woman in a grey cloak, and he asked her if she knew where the Dark Tower of the King of Elfland was. "Go on a little further," said the hen-wife, "till you come to a round green hill, surrounded with terrace-rings, from the bottom to the top; go round it three times, widershins, and each time say:

> *Open, door! open, door!*
> *And let me come in.*

and the third time the door will open, and you may go in." And Childe Rowland was just going on, when he remembered what he had to do; so he out with the good brand, that never struck in vain, and off went the hen-wife's head.

Then he went on, and on, and on, till he came to the round green hill with the terrace-rings from top to bottom, and he went round it three times, widershins, saying each time:

> *Open, door! open, door!*
> *And let me come in.*

And the third time the door did open, and he went in, and it closed with a click, and Childe Rowland was left in the dark.

It was not exactly dark, but a kind of twilight or gloaming. There were neither windows nor candles, and he could not make out where the twilight came from, if not through the walls and roof. These were rough arches made of a transparent rock, incrusted with sheepsilver and rock spar, and other bright stones. But though it was rock, the air was quite warm, as it always is in Elfland. So he went through this passage till at last he came to two wide and high folding-doors which stood ajar. And when he opened them, there he saw a most wonderful and glorious sight. A large and spacious hall, so large that it seemed to be as long, and as broad, as the green hill itself. The roof was supported by fine pillars, so large and lofty, that the pillars of a cathedral were as nothing to them. They were all of gold and silver, with fretted work, and between them and around them, wreaths of flowers, composed of what do you think? Why, of diamonds and emeralds, and all manner of precious stones. And the very key-stones of the arches had for ornaments clusters of diamonds and rubies, and pearls, and other precious stones. And all these arches met in the middle of the roof, and just there, hung by a gold chain, an immense lamp made out of one big pearl hollowed out and quite transparent. And in the middle of this was a big, huge carbuncle, which kept spinning round and round, and this was what gave light by its rays to the whole hall, which seemed as if the setting sun was shining on it.

The hall was furnished in a manner equally grand, and at one end of it was a glorious couch of velvet, silk and gold, and there sate Burd Ellen, combing her golden hair with a silver comb. And when she saw Childe Rowland she stood up and said:

> *God pity ye, poor luckless fool,*
> *What have ye here to do?*
>
> *Hear ye this, my youngest brother,*
> *Why didn't ye bide at home?*
> *Had you a hundred thousand lives*
> *Ye couldn't spare any a one.*
>
> *But sit ye down; but woe, O, woe,*
> *That ever ye were born,*
> *For come the King of Elfland in,*
> *Your fortune is forlorn.*

Then they sate down together, and Childe Rowland told her all that he had done, and she told him how their two brothers had reached the Dark Tower, but had been enchanted by the King of Elfland, and lay there entombed as if dead. And then after they had talked a little longer Childe Rowland began to feel hungry from his long travels, and told his sister Burd Ellen how hungry he was and asked for some food, forgetting all about the Warlock Merlin's warning.

Burd Ellen looked at Childe Rowland sadly, and shook her head, but she was under a spell, and could not warn him. So she rose up, and went out, and soon brought back a golden basin full of bread and milk. Childe Rowland was just going to raise it to his lips, when he looked at his sister and remembered why he had come all that way. So he dashed the bowl to the ground, and said: "Not a sup will I swallow, nor a bit will I bite, till Burd Ellen is set free."

Just at that moment they heard the noise of someone approaching, and a loud voice was heard saying:

> *Fee, fi, fo, fum,*
> *I smell the blood of a Christian man,*
> *Be he dead, be he living, with my brand,*
> *I'll dash his brains from his brain-pan.*

And then the folding-doors of the hall were burst open, and the King of

Elfland rushed in.

"Strike then, Bogle, if thou darest," shouted out Childe Rowland, and rushed to meet him with his good brand that never yet did fail. They fought, and they fought, and they fought, till Childe Rowland beat the King of Elfland down on to his knees, and caused him to yield and beg for mercy. "I grant thee mercy," said Childe Rowland, "release my sister from thy spells and raise my brothers to life, and let us all go free, and thou shalt be spared." "I agree," said the Elfin King, and rising up he went to a chest from which he took a phial filled with a blood-red liquor. With this he anointed the ears, eyelids, nostrils, lips, and finger-tips, of the two brothers, and they sprang at once into life, and declared that their souls had been away, but had now returned. The Elfin king then said some words to Burd Ellen, and she was disenchanted, and they all four passed out of the hall, through the long passage, and turned their back on the Dark Tower, never to return again. And they reached home, and the good queen, their mother, and Burd Ellen never went round a church widershins again.

Don Firriulieddu
(*Italy*)

Once upon a time there was a farmer who had a daughter who used to take his dinner to him in the fields. One day he said to her: "So that you may find me I will sprinkle bran along the way; you follow the bran, and you will come to me."

By chance the old ogre passed that way, and seeing the bran, said: "This means something." So he took the bran and scattered it so that it led to his own house.

When the daughter set out to take her father his dinner, she followed the bran until she came to the ogre's house. When the ogre saw the young girl, he said: "You must be my wife." Then she began to weep. When the father saw that his daughter did not appear, he went home in the evening, and began to search for her; and not finding her, he asked God to give him a son or a daughter.

A year after, he had a son whom they called "*Don Firriulieddu.*" When the child was three days old it spoke, and said: "Have you made me a cloak? Now give me a little dog and the cloak, for I must look for my sister." So he set out and went to seek his sister.

After a while he came to a plain where he saw a number of men, and asked: "Whose cattle are these?" The herdsman replied: "They belong to the ogre, who fears neither God nor the saints, who fears *Don Firriulied-*

du, who is three days old and is on the way, and gives his dog bread and says: 'Eat, my dog, and do not bark, for we have fine things to do.'"

Afterwards he saw a flock of sheep, and asked: "Whose are these sheep?" and received the same answer as from the herdsman. Then he arrived at the ogre's house and knocked, and his sister opened the door and saw the child. "Who are you looking for?" she said. "I am looking for you, for I am your brother, and you must return to mamma."

When the ogre heard that *Don Firriulieddu* was there, he went and hid himself up-stairs. *Don Firriulieddu* asked his sister: "Where is the ogre?" "Up-stairs." *Don Firriulieddu* said to his dog: "Go up-stairs and bark, and I will follow you." The dog went up and barked, and *Firriulieddu* followed him, and killed the ogre. Then he took his sister and a quantity of money, and they went home to their mother, and are all contented.

The Three Kingdoms
(*Russia*)

In that ancient time when God's world was full of wood-demons, witches, and river-maidens, when rivers of milk were flowing between banks of jelly, when over the fields roast partridges were flying, there lived a Tsar, Goroh by name, with his Tsaritsa, Anastasia the Beautiful; and they had three sons. A misfortune not small happened—an unclean spirit carried away the Tsaritsa.

Said the eldest son to the Tsar: "Father, give me thy blessing; I will go in search of my mother."

He went away and vanished; for three years there were neither tidings nor report of him.

The second son began to ask: "Father, give me thy blessing for the road, for the journey. Perhaps I may have the luck to find my brother and my mother."

The Tsar gave his blessing. The Tsarevich rode off and also disappeared as if he had sunk in water.

Ivan, the youngest son, came to the Tsar. "My dear father, give me thy blessing for the road, for the journey; perhaps I shall find my brothers and mother."

"Go thy way, my dear son."

Ivan Tsarevich set out for a strange, distant region. He travelled and travelled, and reached the blue sea. He stopped on the shore and thought: "Whither can I hold my way now?" All at once there flew to sea three and thirty spoonbills, struck the earth, and became fair maidens—all beautiful, but one was better than all the rest. They undressed and rushed into the water. Whether they were bathing a long or short time, Ivan Tsarevich stole up and took the girdle of that maiden who was better than all the rest and hid it in his bosom. When they had finished bathing they came out on shore and began to dress. One girdle was gone.

"Ah! Ivan Tsarevich," said the beauty, "give me my girdle."

"Tell me first where my mother is."

"Thy mother is at the house of my father, Raven son of Raven.[1] Go up along the sea, thou wilt meet a silver bird with a golden crest; wherever it flies do thou follow."

Ivan Tsarevich gave her the girdle and went along the sea; there he met his brothers, exchanged greetings, and took them with him. They went together along the shore, saw the golden-tufted silver bird, and ran after it. The bird flew and flew till it rushed under an iron plate into an opening.

"Well, brothers," said Ivan Tsarevich, "give me your blessing in the place of father and mother. I will let myself down into this opening and discover what a land of strange faith is like—perhaps our mother is there."

His brothers gave him their blessing. He sat on a rope swing, crawled into that deep opening, and went down no short distance. Just three years was he letting himself down, and then went on his road and way. He went and went, went and went. He saw the Copper Kingdom. In the castle were sitting three and thirty spoonbill maidens. They were embroidering towels with cunning designs, with towns and suburbs.

"Hail, Ivan Tsarevich!" said the Tsaritsa of the Copper Kingdom. "Whither dost thou hold thy way?"

"I am going in search of my mother."

"Thy mother is with my father, Raven son of Raven. He is cunning and wise; over mountains and valleys, over caves and clouds, has he flown. He will slay thee, good youth. Here is a ball for thee. Go to my second sister; hear what she will tell thee. If thou comest back, forget me not."

Ivan rolled the ball and followed; he came to the Silver Kingdom. The Tsaritsa of the Silver Kingdom said: "Till now the Russian odor was not to be seen with sight nor heard with hearing; but now the Russian odor appears visibly. Well, Ivan Tsarevich, art fleeing from work, or seekest work?"

"Ah, fair maiden! I am in search of my mother."

"Thy mother is with my father, Raven son of Raven. Cunning is he and wise; over mountains, over valleys has he flown, over caves, over clouds has he swept. Oh, Tsarevich, he will slay thee! Here is a ball. Go to my youngest sister; hear what she will say to thee, whether to go on or come back."

1 Voron Voronovich.

Ivan Tsarevich came to the Golden Kingdom; there three and thirty spoonbill maidens were sitting embroidering towels. Taller than all, fairer than all, was the Tsaritsa of the Golden Kingdom—a beauty that could not be told of in a tale or described with a pen.

"Hail, Ivan Tsarevich!" said she. "Whither dost thou hold thy way?"

"I am going to seek my mother."

"Thy mother is with my father, Raven son of Raven. Cunning is he and wise. Oh, Tsarevich, he will slay thee surely! Here is a ball for thee. Go now to the Pearl Kingdom; there thy mother lives. When she sees thee she will be rejoiced, and that moment will say, 'Nurses, and maidens, bring my son green wine,' but take it not. Ask her to give thee wine three years old that is in the cupboard, and a burnt crust for lunch, and do not forget that my father has in the yard two jars of water—one water of strength, the other of weakness; put each in the place of the other, and drink of the water of strength."

The Tsarevich talked a long time with the Tsaritsa, and they fell in love with each other to such a degree that they hated to part; but there was no help for them. Ivan Tsarevich took farewell of her and went on his journey. He travelled and travelled till he came to the Pearl Kingdom. His mother saw him, was delighted, and cried out, "Nurses and maidens, bring my son green wine."

"I drink no common wine; give me wine three years old, and for a bite a burnt crust." He drank wine three years old, ate the burnt crust, went out in the broad court, put each jar in the place of the other, and fell to drinking the water of strength.

All at once Raven son of Raven flew home, bright as the clear day; but when he saw Ivan Tsarevich he grew gloomier than the dark night. He stooped down to the jar, and began to drink the water of weakness. Then Ivan Tsarevich fell upon his wings, and Raven son of Raven soared high, high; he bore Ivan over mountains, over valleys, over caves, over clouds. "What dost thou need, Ivan Tsarevich? If thou wishest, I will give thee treasure."

"I want nothing but the feather staff."

"No, Ivan Tsarevich, thou wishest to sit in a very wide sleigh." And again Raven son of Raven bore him over mountains, over valleys, over caves, over clouds.

Ivan held firmly, bore down with all his weight, and nearly broke the wings of Raven son of Raven, who screamed, "Break not my wings; take the feather staff!" He gave Ivan the feather staff, became a common raven himself, and flew away to the steep mountains.

Ivan Tsarevich went back, came to the Pearl Kingdom, took his mother, and set out for home. He looked; the Pearl Kingdom had turned into a ball, and was rolling after him. He came to the Golden Kingdom, then to the Silver, and then to the Copper Kingdom. He took and brought with him the three beautiful Tsaritsas, and those kingdoms were wound into balls and rolled after him. He came to the rope swing and sounded a golden trumpet: "My own brothers, if ye are alive, do not betray me."

The brothers heard the call, and drew out into the white world the beautiful soul maiden, the Tsaritsa of the Copper Kingdom. They saw her, and began to fight among themselves; one would not yield to the other.

"Why fight, good youths?" said the maiden. "Down there are better than I."

They let down the rope swing and drew up the Tsaritsa of the Silver Kingdom. Again they began to dispute and fight; one said, "Let her be mine, and come to me;" the other said, "I won't let her be thine."

"Do not fight, good youths; down there is a maiden more beautiful than I."

They stopped fighting, put down the rope swing, and drew up the Tsaritsa of the Golden Kingdom. Again they began to fight; but the Tsaritsa, the beauty, immediately stopped them, saying: "Your mother is waiting for you." They drew out their mother, and let down the rope swing for Ivan Tsarevich; they raised him half way, and cut the rope. Ivan Tsarevich fell into the depth and was terribly shocked; he lay half a year without senses, came to himself, and looked around, remembered everything that had happened to him, took out the feather staff, and struck the earth with it. That moment twelve youths appeared. "What is thy command, Ivan Tsarevich?"

"Take me out into the free world."

The youths seized him under the arms and bore him into the free world. Ivan Tsarevich inquired about his brothers, and heard that they had married long before. The Tsaritsa of the Copper Kingdom married the second brother; the Tsaritsa of the Silver Kingdom, his eldest brother; but his own bride would not marry any man: his old father wanted to marry her. He summoned a council, accused his wife of intimacy with evil spirits, and gave command to cut her head off. After the execution he said to the Tsaritsa of the Golden Kingdom: "Wilt thou marry me?"

"I will when thou makest shoes for me without measure."

The Tsar gave command to issue a call and ask all and each, would any man make shoes for the Tsaritsa without taking her measure. At this time Ivan Tsarevich had come to his own kingdom, and hired as a workman with a certain old man; and he sent him to the Tsar: "Go, grandfather, take this affair on thyself, and I will make the shoes for thee; but do not tell about me."

The old man went to the Tsar. "I," said he, "am ready to undertake the work."

The Tsar gave him leather for a pair of shoes, and asked: "But canst thou do it, old man?"

"Never fear, Gosudár. I have a son who is a shoemaker."

When he came home the old man gave the leather to Ivan Tsarevich, who cut it into bits and threw it out of the window; then he opened the Golden Kingdom and took out shoes already made. "Here, grandfather, take these and carry them to the Tsar."

The Tsar was delighted, and urged the bride: "Shall we go to the crown soon?"

She answered: "I will marry thee if thou wilt make for me robes to fit without measure."

The Tsar again was in trouble; he assembled all the dressmakers, and offered them much money if they would only make robes to fit without measuring the Tsaritsa.

Ivan Tsarevich said to the old man: "Grandfather, go to the Tsar, get cloth; I will sew robes for thee, but do not tell of me."

The old man dragged himself off to the palace, took satin and velvet, came home, and gave it to the Tsarevich. Ivan Tsarevich took scissors straightway, and cut all the satin and velvet to pieces and threw them out of the window. Then he opened the Golden Kingdom and took out the most beautiful robes and gave them to the old man, saying, "Take these to the palace."

The Tsar was delighted. "Well, my beloved bride, is it not time for us to go to the crown?"

The Tsaritsa answered: "I will marry thee when thou wilt take the son of that old man and command that he be boiled in milk."

The Tsar thought awhile, then gave the command; and that day they collected three gallons of milk from each house, filled a great caldron, and boiled it on a hot fire. They brought Ivan Tsarevich. He took farewell of all, bowed to the earth, then threw himself into the caldron, dived once, dived twice, sprang out such a beauty that it could neither be told of in a tale nor described with a pen.

Said the Tsaritsa: "Look, Tsar! Whom shall I marry—thee, old man, or that gallant youth?"

The Tsar thought awhile. "If I bathe in the milk, I shall become just such a beauty as he." He sprang into the caldron, and was cooked in a minute. But Ivan Tsarevich went to be crowned with the Tsaritsa of the Golden Kingdom; they were crowned, and began to live and live on, gaining wealth.

314A*: Animal Helper in the Flight

Baba Yaga

Baba Yaga
(*Russia*)

Once upon a time there was an old couple. The husband lost his wife and married again. But he had a daughter by the first marriage, a young girl, and she found no favor in the eyes of her evil stepmother, who used to beat her, and consider how she could get her killed outright. One day the father went away somewhere or other, so the stepmother said to the girl, "Go to your aunt, my sister, and ask her for a needle and thread to make you a shift."

Now that aunt was a Baba Yaga. Well, the girl was no fool, so she went to a real aunt of hers first, and says she:

"Good morning, auntie!"

"Good morning, my dear! what have you come for?"

"Mother has sent me to her sister, to ask for a needle and thread to make me a shift."

Then her aunt instructed her what to do. "There is a birch-tree there, niece, which would hit you in the eye—you must tie a ribbon round it; there are doors which would creak and bang—you must pour oil on their hinges; there are dogs which would tear you in pieces—you must throw them these rolls; there is a cat which would scratch your eyes out—you must give it a piece of bacon."

So the girl went away, and walked and walked, till she came to the place. There stood a hut, and in it sat weaving the Baba Yaga, the Bony-shanks.

"Good morning, auntie," says the girl.

"Good morning, my dear," replies the Baba Yaga.

"Mother has sent me to ask you for a needle and thread to make me a shift."

"Very well; sit down and weave a little in the meantime."

So the girl sat down behind the loom, and the Baba Yaga went outside, and said to her servant-maid:

"Go and heat the bath, and get my niece washed; and mind you look sharp after her. I want to breakfast off her."

Well, the girl sat there in such a fright that she was as much dead as alive. Presently she spoke imploringly to the servant-maid, saying:

"Kinswoman dear, do please wet the firewood instead of making it burn; and fetch the water for the bath in a sieve." And she made her a present of a handkerchief.

The Baba Yaga waited awhile; then she came to the window and asked:

"Are you weaving, niece? are you weaving, my dear?"

"Oh yes, dear aunt, I'm weaving." So the Baba Yaga went away again, and the girl gave the Cat a piece of bacon, and asked:

"Is there no way of escaping from here?"

"Here's a comb for you and a towel," said the Cat; "take them, and be off. The Baba Yaga will pursue you, but you must lay your ear on the ground, and when you hear that she is close at hand, first of all throw down the towel. It will become a wide, wide river. And if the Baba Yaga gets across the river, and tries to catch you, then you must lay your ear on the ground again, and when you hear that she is close at hand, throw down the comb. It will become a dense, dense forest; through that she won't be able to force her way anyhow."

The girl took the towel and the comb and fled. The dogs would have rent her, but she threw them the rolls, and they let her go by; the doors would have begun to bang, but she poured oil on their hinges, and they let her pass through; the birch-tree would have poked her eyes out, but she tied the ribbon around it, and it let her pass on. And the Cat sat down to the loom, and worked away; muddled everything about, if it didn't do much weaving. Up came the Baba Yaga to the window, and asked:

"Are you weaving, niece? are you weaving, my dear?"

"I'm weaving, dear aunt, I'm weaving," gruffly replied the Cat.

The Baba Yaga rushed into the hut, saw that the girl was gone, and took to beating the Cat, and abusing it for not having scratched the girl's eyes out. "Long as I've served you," said the Cat, "you've never given me so much as a bone; but she gave me bacon." Then the Baba Yaga pounced upon the dogs, on the doors, on the birch-tree, and on the servant-maid, and set to work to abuse them all, and to knock them about. Then the dogs said to her, "Long as we've served you, you've never so much as pitched us a burnt crust; but she gave us rolls to eat." And the doors said, "Long as we've served you, you've never poured even a drop of water on our hinges; but she poured oil on us." The birch-tree said, "Long as I've served you, you've never tied a single thread round me; but she fastened a ribbon around me." And the servant-maid said, "Long as I've served you, you've never given me so much as a rag; but she gave me a handkerchief."

The Baba Yaga, bony of limb, quickly jumped into her mortar, sent it flying along with the pestle, sweeping away the while all traces of its flight with a broom, and set off in pursuit of the girl. Then the girl put her ear to the ground, and when she heard that the Baba Yaga was chasing her, and was now close at hand, she flung down the towel. And it became a wide, such a wide river! Up came the Baba Yaga to the river, and gnashed her teeth with spite; then she went home for her oxen, and drove them to the river. The oxen drank up every drop of the river, and then the Baba

Yaga began the pursuit anew. But the girl put her ear to the ground again, and when she heard that the Baba Yaga was near, she flung down the comb, and instantly a forest sprang up, such an awfully thick one! The Baba Yaga began gnawing away at it, but however hard she worked, she couldn't gnaw her way through it, so she had to go back again.

But by this time the girl's father had returned home, and he asked:

"Where's my daughter?"

"She's gone to her aunt's," replied her stepmother.

Soon afterwards the girl herself came running home.

"Where have you been?" asked her father.

"Ah, father!" she said, "mother sent me to aunt's to ask for a needle and thread to make me a shift. But aunt's a Baba Yaga, and she wanted to eat me!"

"And how did you get away, daughter?"

"Why like this," said the girl, and explained the whole matter. As soon as her father had heard all about it, he became wroth with his wife, and shot her. But he and his daughter lived on and flourished, and everything went well with them.

The Girl and the Evil Spirit
(*Siberia*)

There lived a girl who knew no man. Nor could she tell who were her parents. She was rich in reindeer and other property. So she walked about, singing lustily. She never went to watch over her reindeer. When the reindeer strayed away too far, she would merely sing one of her songs, and they would come back of their own will. She sang and sang; and when she came back to her home, she would find the fire burning, the food cooked, and everything ready. Thus she lived on without work, care, or trouble.

One day she saw that half the sky was darkened. This darkness approached nearer and nearer. It was the evil spirit. One of his lips touched the sky, the other dragged along the ground. Between was an open mouth, ready to swallow up whatever came in its way. "Ah!" said the girl, "my death is coming. What shall I do?" She took her iron-tipped staff and fled.

The evil spirit gave chase, and was gaining on her. She drew from her pocket a small comb of ivory and threw it back over her shoulder. The comb turned into a dense forest. The girl ran onward. When the evil spirit reached the forest he swallowed it, chewed it, and gulped it down. He digested it and then defecated. The dense forest turned again into a small ivory comb. After that he continued his pursuit and was gaining on her, as before. She loosened from her waist a red handkerchief, which became a fire extending from heaven to earth. The evil spirit reached the fire. He went to a river and drank it completely dry. Then he came back to the fire, and poured the water upon it. The fire was extinguished. Only a red handkerchief lay on the ground, quite small, and dripping wet.

After that he gave chase again, and gained steadily on the girl. She struck the ground with her iron-tipped staff, and all at once she turned into an arctic fox. In this form she sped on, swifter than ever. The big mouth, however, followed after, wide open, and ready to swallow her. She struck the ground with her iron-tipped staff, turned into a wolverine and fled swifter than ever, but the evil mouth followed after. She struck the ground with her iron-tipped staff and turned into a wolf and sped away swifter than ever. She struck the ground with her iron-pointed staff and turned into a bear, with a copper bell in each ear. She ran off swifter than ever, but the big mouth followed and gained on her steadily. Finally, it came very near, and was going to swallow her.

Then she saw a Lamut tent covered with white skins. She summoned all her strength, and rushed on toward that tent. She stumbled at the entrance and fell down, exhausted and senseless. After a while, she came to herself and looked about. On each side of her stood a young man, their caps adorned with large silver plates. She looked backward, and saw the evil spirit who had turned into a handsome youth, fairer than the sun. He was combing and parting his hair, making it smooth and fine. The girl rose to her feet.

The three young men came to her and asked her to enter the tent. The one who had appeared in the form of the evil spirit said, "We are three brothers, and I am the eldest one. I wanted to bring you to my tent. Now you must tell us which of us you will choose for your husband." She chose the eldest, and married him, and they lived together.

The Story of Little Tsar Novishny, the False Sister, and the Faithful Beasts
(*Russia*)

Once upon a time, in a certain kingdom, in a certain empire, there dwelt a certain Tsar who had never had a child. One day this Tsar went to the bazaar (such a bazaar as we have at Kherson) to buy food for his needs. For though he was a Tsar, he had a mean and churlish soul, and used always to do his own marketing, and so now, too, he bought a little salt fish and went home with it. On his way homeward, a great thirst suddenly fell upon him, so he turned aside into a lonely mountain where he knew, as his father had known before him, there was a spring of crystal-clear water. He was so very thirsty that he flung himself down headlong by this spring without first crossing himself, wherefore that Accursed One, Satan, immediately had power over him, and caught him by the beard. The Tsar sprang back in terror, and cried, "Let me go!" But the Accursed One held him all the tighter. "Nay, I will not let thee go!" cried he. Then the Tsar began to entreat him piteously. "Ask what thou wilt of me," said he, "only let me go." — "Give me, then," said the Accursed One, "something that thou hast in the house, and then I'll let thee go!" — "Let me see, what have I got?" said the Tsar. "Oh, I know. I've got eight horses at home, the like of which I have seen nowhere else, and I'll immediately bid my equerry[1] bring them to thee to this spring — take them." — "I *won't* have them!" cried the Accursed One, and he held him still more tightly by the beard. "Well, then, hearken now!" cried the Tsar. "I have eight oxen. They have never yet gone a-ploughing for me, or done a day's work. I'll have them brought hither. I'll feast my eyes on them once more, and then I'll have them driven into thy steppes — take them." — "No, that won't do either!" said the Accursed One. The Tsar went over, one by one, all the most precious things he had at home, but the Accursed One said "No!" all along, and pulled him more and more tightly by the beard. When the Tsar saw that the Accursed One would take none of all these things, he said to him at last, "Look now! I have a wife so lovely that the like of her is not to be found in the whole world, take her and let me go!" — "No!" replied the Accursed One, "I will not have her." The Tsar was in great straits. "What am I to do now?" thought he. "I have offered him my lovely wife, who is the very choicest of my chattels, and he won't have her!" — "Then," said the Accursed One, "Promise me what thou shalt find awaiting thee at home, and I'll let thee go."

The Tsar gladly promised this, for he could think of naught else that he had, and then the Accursed One let him go.

But while he had been away from home, there had been born to him a Tsarevko and a Tsarivna; and they grew up not by the day, or even by the hour, but by the minute: never were known such fine children. And his wife saw him coming from afar, and went out to meet him, with her two children, with great joy. But he, the moment he saw them, burst into tears. "Nay, my dear love," cried she, "wherefore dost thou burst into tears? Or art thou so delighted that such children have been born unto thee that thou canst not find thy voice for tears of joy?" — And he answered her, "My darling wife, on my way back from the bazaar I was athirst, and turned toward a mountain known of old to my father and

---

1 Officer in charge of the stables.

me, and it seemed to me as though there were a spring of water there, though the water was very near dried up. But looking closer, I saw that it was quite full; so I bethought me that I would drink thereof, and I leaned over, when lo! that Evil-wanton (I mean the Devil) caught me by the beard and would not let me go. I begged and prayed, but still he held me tight. 'Give me,' said he, 'what thou hast at home, or I'll never let thee go!' — And I said to him, 'Lo! now, I have horses.' — 'I don't want thy horses!' said he. — 'I have oxen,' I said. — 'I don't want thine oxen!' said he. — 'I have,' said I, 'a wife so fair that the like of her is not to be found in God's fair world; take her, but let me go.' — 'I don't want thy fair wife!' said he. — Then I promised him what I should find at home when I got there, for I never thought that God had blessed me so. Come now, my darling wife! and let us bury them both lest he take them!" — "Nay, nay! my dear husband, we had better hide them somewhere. Let us dig a ditch by our hut—just under the gables!" (For there were no lordly mansions in those days, and the Tsars dwelt in peasants' huts.) So they dug a ditch right under the gables, and put their children inside it, and gave them provision of bread and water. Then they covered it up and smoothed it down, and turned into their own little hut.

Presently the serpent (for the Accursed One had changed himself into a serpent) came flying up in search of the children. He raged up and down outside the hut—but there was nothing to be seen. At last he cried out to the stove, "Stove, stove, where has the Tsar hidden his children?" — The stove replied, "The Tsar has been a good master to me; he has put lots of warm fuel inside me; I hold to him." — So, finding he could get nothing out of the stove, he cried to the hearth-broom, "Hearth-broom, hearth-broom, where has the Tsar hidden his children?" — But the hearth-broom answered, "The Tsar has always been a good master to me, for he always cleans the warm grate with me; I hold to him." So the Accursed One could get nothing out of the hearth-broom. — Then he cried to the hatchet, "Hatchet, hatchet, where has the Tsar hidden his children?" — The hatchet replied, "The Tsar has always been a good master to me. He chops his wood with me, and gives me a place to lie down in; so I'll not have him disturbed." — Then the Devil cried to the gimlet, "Gimlet, gimlet, where has the Tsar hidden his children?" — But the gimlet replied, "The Tsar has always been a good master to me. He drills little holes with me, and then lets me rest; so I'll let him rest too." — Then the serpent said to the gimlet, "So the Tsar's a good master to thee, eh! Well, I can only say that if he's the good master thou sayest he is, I am rather surprised that he knocks thee on the head so much with a hammer." — "Well, that's true," said the gimlet, "I never thought of that. Thou mayst take hold of me if thou wilt, and draw me out of the top of the hut, near the front gable; and wherever I fall into the marshy ground, there set to work and dig with me!"

The Devil did so, and began digging at the spot where the gimlet fell out on the marshy ground till he had dug out the children. Now, as they had been growing all along, they were children no more, but a stately youth and a fair damsel; and the serpent took them up and carried them off. But they were big and heavy, so he soon got tired and lay down to rest, and presently fell asleep. Then the Tsarivna sat down on his head, and the Tsarevko sat down beside her, till a horse came running up. The horse ran right up to them and said, "Hail! little Tsar Novishny; art thou here by thy leave or against thy leave?" — And the little Tsar Novishny replied, "Nay, little nag! we are here against our leave, not by our leave." — "Then sit on my back!" said the horse, "and I'll carry you off!" So they got on his back, for the serpent was asleep all the time. Then the horse galloped off with them; and he galloped far, far away. Presently the serpent awoke, looked all round him, and could see nothing till he had got up out of the reeds in which he lay, when he saw them in the far distance, and gave chase. He soon caught them up; and little Tsar Novishny said to the horse, "Oh! little nag, how hot it is. It is all up with thee and us!" And, in truth, the horse's tail was already singed to a coal, for the serpent was hard behind them, blazing like fire. The horse perceived that he could do no more, so he gave one last wriggle and died; but they, poor things, were left alive. "Whom have you been listening to?" said the serpent as he flew up to them. "Don't you know that I only am your father and tsar, and have the right to carry you away?" — "Oh, dear daddy! we'll never listen to anybody else again!" — "Well, I'll forgive you this time," said the serpent; "but mind you never do it again."

Again the serpent took them up and carried them off. Presently he grew tired and again lay down to rest, and nodded off. Then the Tsarivna sat down on his head, and the Tsarevko sat down beside her, till a humble-bee came flying up. "Hail, little Tsar Novishny!" cried the humble-bee. — "Hail, little humble-bee!" said the little Tsar. — "Say, friends, are you here by your leave or against your leave?" — "Alas! little humble-bum-ble-bee, 'tis not with my leave I have been brought hither, but against my leave, as thou mayst see for thyself." — "Then sit on my back," said the bee, "and I'll carry you away." — "But, dear little humble-humble-bee, if a horse couldn't save us, how will you?" — "I cannot tell till I try," said the humble-bee. "But if I cannot save you, I'll let you fall." — "Well, then," said the little Tsar, "we'll try. For we two must perish in any case, but thou perhaps mayst get off scot-free." So they embraced each other, sat on the humble-bee, and off they went. When the serpent awoke he missed them, and raising his head above the reeds and rushes, saw them flying far away, and set off after them at full speed. "Alas! little hum-ble-bumble-bee," cried little Tsar Novishny, "how burning hot 'tis getting. We shall all three perish!" Then the humble-bee turned his wing and shook them off. They fell to the earth, and he flew away. Then the serpent came flying up and fell upon them with open jaws. "Ah-ha!" cried he, with a snort, "you've come to grief again, eh? Didn't I tell you to listen to nobody but me!" Then they fell to weeping and entreating, "We'll listen to you alone and to nobody else!" and they wept and entreated so much that at last he forgave them.

So he took them up and carried them off once more. Again he sat down to rest and fell asleep, and again the Tsarivna sat upon his head and the Tsarevko sat down by her side, till a bullock came up, full tilt, and said to them, "Hail, little Tsar Novishny! art thou here with thy leave or art thou here against thy leave?" — "Alas! dear little bullock, I came not hither by my leave; but maybe I was brought here against my leave!" — "Sit on my back, then," said the bullock, "and I'll carry you away." — But they said, "Nay, if a horse and a bee could not manage it, how wilt thou?" — "Nonsense!" said the bullock. "Sit down, and I'll carry you off!" So he persuaded them. — "Well, we can only perish once!" they cried; and the bullock carried them off. And every little while they went a little mile, and jolted so that they very nearly tumbled off. Presently the serpent awoke and was very very wrath. He rose high above the woods and flew after them—oh! how fast he did fly! Then cried the little Tsar, "Alas! bullock, how hot it turns. Thou wilt perish, and we shall perish also!" — Then said the bullock, "Little Tsar! look into my left ear and thou wilt see a horse-comb. Pull it out and throw it behind thee!" — The little Tsar took out the comb and threw it behind him, and it became a huge wood, as thick and jagged as the teeth of a horse-comb. But the bullock went on at his old pace: every little while they went a little mile, and jolted so that they nearly tumbled off. The serpent, however, managed to gnaw his way through the wood, and then flew after them again. Then cried the little Tsar, "Alas! bullock, it begins to burn again. Thou wilt perish, and we shall perish also!" — Then said the bullock, "Look into my right ear, and pull out the brush thou dost find there, and fling it behind thee!" — So he threw it behind him, and it became a forest as thick as a brush. Then the serpent came up to the forest and began to gnaw at it; and at last he gnawed his way right through it. But the bullock went on at his old pace: every little while they went a little mile, and they jolted so that they nearly tumbled off. But when the serpent had gnawed his way through the forest, he again pursued them; and again they felt a burning. And the little Tsar said, "Alas! bullock, look! look! how it burns. Look! look! how we perish." Now the bullock was already nearing the sea. "Look into my right ear," said the bullock, "draw out the little handkerchief thou findest there, and throw it in front of me." He drew it out and flung it, and before them stood a bridge. Over this bridge they galloped, and by the time they had done so, the serpent reached the sea. Then said the bullock to the little Tsar, "Take up the handkerchief again and wave it behind me." Then he took and waved it till the bridge doubled up behind them, and went and spread out again right in front of them. The serpent came up to the edge of the sea; but there he had to stop, for he had nothing to run upon.

So they crossed over that sea right to the other side, and the serpent remained on his own side. Then the bullock said to them, "I'll lead you to a hut close to the sea, and in that hut you must live, and you must take and slay me." But they fell a-weeping sore. "How shall we slay thee!" they cried; "thou art our own little dad, and hast saved us from death!" — "Nay!" said the bullock; "but you must slay me, and one quarter of me you must hang up on the stove, and the second quarter you must place on the ground in a corner, and the third quarter you must put in the corner at the entrance of the hut, and the fourth quarter you must put round the threshold, so that there will be a quarter in all four corners." So they took and slew him in front of the threshold, and they hung his four quarters in the four corners as he had bidden them, and then they laid them down to sleep. Now the Tsarevko awoke at midnight, and saw in the right-hand corner a horse so gorgeously caparisoned that he could not resist rising at once and mounting it; and in the threshold corner there was a self-slicing sword, and in the third corner stood the dog *Protius* and in the stove corner stood the dog *Nedviga*. The little Tsar longed to be off. "Rise, little sister!" cried he. "God has been good to us! Rise, dear little sister, and let us pray to God!" So they arose and prayed to God, and while they prayed the day dawned. Then he mounted his horse and took the dogs with him, that he might live by what they caught.

So they lived in their hut by the sea, and one day the sister went down to the sea to wash her bed-linen and her body-linen in the blue waters. And the serpent came and said to her, "How didst thou manage to jump over the sea?" — "Look, now!" said she, "we crossed over in this way. My brother has a handkerchief which becomes a bridge when he waves it behind him." — And the serpent said to her, "I tell thee what, ask him for this handkerchief; say thou dost want to wash it, and take and wave it, and I'll then be able to cross over to thee and live with thee, and we'll poison thy brother." — Then she went home and said to her brother, "Give me that handkerchief, dear little brother; it is dirty, so I'll wash and give it back to thee." And he believed her and gave it to her, for she was dear to him, and he thought her good and true. Then she took the handkerchief, went down to the sea, and waved it—and behold there was a bridge. Then the serpent crossed over to her side, and they walked to the hut together and consulted as to the best way of destroying her brother and removing him from God's fair world. Now it was his custom to rise at dawn, mount his horse, and go a-hunting, for hunting he dearly loved. So the serpent said to her, "Take to thy bed and pretend to be ill, and say to him, 'I dreamed a dream, dear brother, and lo, I saw thee go and fetch me wolf's milk to make me well.' Then he'll go and fetch it, and the wolves will tear his dogs to pieces, and then we can take and do to him as we list, for his strength is in his dogs."

So when the brother came home from hunting the serpent hid himself, but the sister said, "I have dreamed a dream, dear brother. Methought thou didst go and fetch me wolf's milk, and I drank of it, and my health came back to me, for I am so weak that God grant I die not." — "I'll fetch it," said her brother. So he mounted his horse and set off. Presently he came to a little thicket, and immediately a she-wolf came out. Then Protius ran her down and Nedviga held her fast, and the little Tsar milked her and let her go. And the she-wolf looked round and said, "Well for thee, little Tsar Novishny, that thou hast let me go. Methought thou wouldst not let me go alive. For that thou hast let me go, I'll give thee, little Tsar Novishny, a wolf-whelp." — Then she said to the little wolf, "Thou shalt serve this dear little Tsar as though he were thine own dear father." Then the little Tsar went back, and now there were with him two dogs and a little wolf-whelp that trotted behind them.

Now the serpent and the false sister saw him coming from afar, and three dogs trotting behind him. And the serpent said to her, "What a sly, wily one it is! He has added another watch-dog to his train! Lie down, and make thyself out worse than ever, and ask bear's milk of him, for the bears will tear him to pieces without doubt." Then the serpent turned himself into a needle, and she took him up and stuck him in the wall. Meanwhile the brother dismounted from his horse and came with his dogs and the wolf to the hut, and the dogs began snuffing at the needle in the wall. And his sister said to him, "Tell me, why dost thou keep these big dogs? They let me have no rest." Then he called to the dogs, and they sat down. And his sister said to him, "I dreamed a dream, my brother. I saw thee go and search and fetch me from somewhere bear's milk, and I drank of it, and my health came back to me." — "I will fetch it," said her brother.

But first of all he laid him down to sleep. Nedviga lay at his head, and Protius at his feet, and *Vovchok* by his side. So he slept through the night, and at dawn he arose and mounted his good steed and hied him thence. Again they came to a little thicket, and this time a she-bear came out. Protius ran her down, Nedviga held her fast, and the little Tsar milked her and let her go. Then the she-bear said, "Hail to thee, little Tsar Novishny; because thou hast let me go, I'll give thee a bear-cub." But to the little bear she said, "Obey him as though he were thine own father." So he set off home, and the serpent and his sister saw that four were now trotting behind him. "Look!" said the serpent, "if there are not four running behind him! Shall we never be able to destroy him? I tell thee what. Ask him to get thee hare's milk; perhaps his beasts will gobble up the hare before he can milk it." So he turned himself into a needle again, and she fastened him in the wall, only a little higher up, so that the dogs should not get at him. Then, when the little Tsar dismounted from his horse, he and his dogs came into the hut, and the dogs began snuffing at the needle in the wall and barked at it, but the brother knew not the cause thereof. But his sister burst into tears and said, "Why dost thou keep such monstrous dogs? Such a kennel of them makes me ill with anguish!" Then he shouted to the dogs, and they sat down quite still. Then she said to him, "I am so ill, brother, that nothing will make me well but hare's milk. Go and get it for me." — "I'll get it," said he.

But first he laid him down to sleep. Nedviga lay at his head, Protius at his feet, and Vovchok and *Medvedik* each on one side. He slept through the night, but at dawn he mounted his steed, took his pack with him, and departed. Again he came to a little thicket, and a she-hare popped out. Protius ran her down, Nedviga held her fast, then he milked her and let her go. Then the hare said, "Hail to thee, little Tsar Novishny; because thou hast let me go—I thought thou wouldst have torn me to pieces with thy dogs—I'll give thee a leveret." But to the leveret she said, "Obey him, as though he were thine own father." Then he went home, and again they saw him from afar. "What a wily rogue it is!" said they. "All five are following him, and he is as well as ever!" — "Ask him to get thee fox's milk!" said the serpent; "perhaps when he goes for it his beasts will leave him in the lurch!" Then he changed himself into a needle, and she stuck him still higher in the wall, so that the dogs could not get at him. The Tsar again dismounted from his horse, and his dogs rushed up to the hut and began snuffing at the needle. But his sister fell a-weeping, and said, "Why dost thou keep such monstrous dogs?" He shouted to them, and they sat down quietly on their haunches. Then his sister said again, "I am ailing, my brother; go and get me fox's milk, and I shall be well." — "I'll fetch it for thee," said her brother.

But first he lay down to sleep. Nedviga lay at his head, Protius at his feet, and Vovchok, Medvedik, and the leveret by his side. The little Tsar slept through the night, and at dawn he arose, mounted his horse, took his pack with him, and went off. They came to a little thicket, and a vixen popped out. Protius ran her down, Nedviga held her fast, and the little Tsar milked her and let her go. Then said the vixen to him, "Thanks to thee, little Tsar Novishny, that thou hast let me go. Methought thou wouldst tear me in pieces with thy dogs. For thy kindness I'll give thee a little fox." But to the little fox she said, "Obey him as though he were thine own father." So he went home, and they saw him coming from afar, and lo! now he had six guardians, and yet had come by no harm. "'Tis no good; we shall never do for him," said the serpent. "Look, now! Make thyself worse than ever, and say to him, 'I am very ill, my brother, because in another realm, far, far away, there is a wild boar who ploughs with his nose, and sows with his ears, and harrows with his tail—and in that same empire there is a mill with twelve furnaces that grinds its own grain and casts forth its own meal, and if thou wilt bring me of the meal that is beneath these twelve furnaces, so that I may make me a cake of it and eat, my soul shall live.'" — Then her brother said to her, "Methinks thou art not my sister, but my foe!" — But she replied, "How can I be thy foe when we two live all alone together in a strange land?" — "Well, I will get it for thee," said he. For again he believed in his sister.

So he mounted his steed, took his pack with him, and departed, and he came to the land where were that boar and that mill she had told him of. He came up to the mill, tied his horse to it, and entered into it. And there were twelve furnaces there and twelve doors, and these twelve doors needed no man to open or shut them, for they opened and shut themselves. He took meal from beneath the first furnace and went through the second door, but the dogs were shut in by the doors. Through all twelve doors he went, and came out again at the first door, and looked about him, and—there were no dogs to be seen. He whistled, and he heard his dogs whining where they could not get out. Then he wept sore, mounted his horse, and went home. He got home, and there was his sister making merry with the serpent. And no sooner did the brother enter the hut than the serpent said, "Well, we wanted flesh, and now flesh has come to us!" For they had just slain a bullock, and on the ground where they had slain it there sprang up a whitethorn-tree, so lovely that it may be told of in tales, but neither imagined nor divined. When the little Tsar saw it, he said, "Oh, my dear brother-in-law!" (for without his dogs he must needs be courteous to the serpent) "pray let me climb up that whitethorn-tree, and have a good look about me!" But the sister said to the serpent, "Dear friend, make him get ready boiling water for himself, and we will boil him, for it does not become thee to dirty thy hands." — "Very well," said the serpent; "he shall make the boiling water ready!" So they ordered the little Tsar to go and chop wood and get the hot water ready. Then he went and chopped wood, but as he was doing so, a starling flew out and said to him, "Not so fast, not so fast, little Tsar Novishny. Be as slow as thou canst, for thy dogs have gnawed their way through two doors."

Then the little Tsar poured water into the cauldron, and put fire under it. But the wood that he had cut was rotten and very very dry, so that it burned most fiercely, and he took and sprinkled it with water, and sprinkled it again and again, so that it might not burn too much. And when he went out into the courtyard for more water, the starling said to him, "Not so fast, not so fast, little Tsar Novishny, for thy dogs have gnawed their way through four doors!" As he was returning to the hut his sister said to him, "That water does not boil up quickly enough! Take the fire-shovel and poke the fire!" So he did so, and the faggots blazed up, but when she had gone away he sprinkled them with water again, so that they might burn more slowly. Then he went into the courtyard again, and the starling met him and said, "Not so fast, not so fast, little Tsar; be as slow as thou canst, for thy dogs have gnawed their way through six doors." Then he returned to the hut, and his sister again took up the shovel and made him poke up the fire, and when she went away he again flung water on the burning coals. So he kept going in and out of the courtyard. "'Tis weary work!" cried he; but the starling said to him, "Not so fast, not so fast, little Tsar Novishny, for thy dogs have already gnawed their way through ten doors!" The little Tsar picked up the rottenest wood he could find and flung it on the fire, to make believe he was making haste, but sprinkled it at the same time with water, so that it might not burn up too quickly, and yet the kettle soon began to boil. Again he went to the forest for more wood, and the starling said to him, "Not so fast, not so fast, little Tsar, for thy dogs have already gnawed their way through all the doors, and are now resting!" But now the water was boiling, and his sister ran up and said to him, "Come, boil thyself, be quick; how much longer art thou going to keep us waiting?" Then he, poor thing, began ladling the boiling water over himself, while she got the table ready and spread the cloth, that the serpent might eat her brother on that very table.

But he, poor thing, kept ladling himself, and cried, "Oh, my dear brother-in-law, pray let me climb up to the top of that whitethorn-tree; let me have a look out from the top of it, for thence one can see afar!" — "Don't let him, dear!" said the sister to the serpent; "he will stay there too long and lose our precious time." — But the serpent replied, "It doesn't matter, it doesn't matter; let him climb up if he likes." So the little Tsar went up to the tree, and began to climb it; he did not miss a single branch, and stopped a little at each one to gain time, and so he climbed up to the very top, and then he took out his flute and began to play upon it. But the starling flew up to him and said, "Not so fast, little Tsar Novishny, for lo! thy dogs are running to thee with all their might." But his sister ran out and said, "What art thou playing up there for? Thou dost forget perhaps that we are waiting for thee down here!" Then he began to descend the tree, but he stopped at every branch on his way down, while his sister kept on calling to him to come down quicker. At last he came to the last branch, and as he stood upon it and leaped down to the ground, he thought to himself, "Now I perish!" At that same instant his dogs and his beasts, growling loudly, came running up, and stood in a circle around him. Then he crossed himself and said, "Glory to Thee, O Lord! I have still, perchance, a little time to live in Thy fair world!" Then he called aloud to the serpent and said, "And now, dear brother-in-law, come out, for I am ready for thee!" Out came the serpent to eat him, but he said to his dogs and his beasts, "Vovchok! Medvedik! Protius! Nedviga! Seize him!" Then the dogs and the beasts rushed upon him and tore him to bits.

Then the little Tsar collected the pieces and burnt them to ashes, and the little fox rolled his brush in the ashes till it was covered with them, and then went out into the open field and scattered them to the four winds. But while they were tearing the serpent to pieces the wicked sister knocked out his tooth and hid it. After it was all over the little Tsar said to her, "As thou hast been such a false friend to me, sister, thou must remain here while I go into another kingdom." Then he made two buckets and hung them up on the whitethorn-tree, and said to his sister, "Look now, sister! if thou weepest for me, this bucket will fill with tears, but if thou weepest for the serpent that bucket will fill with blood!" Then she fell a-weeping and praying, and said to him, "Don't leave me, brother, but take me with thee." — "I won't," said he; "such a false friend as thou art I'll not have with me. Stay where thou art." So he mounted his horse, called to him his dogs and his beasts, and went his way into another kingdom and into another empire.

He went on and on till he came to a certain city, and in this city there was only one spring, and in this spring sat a dragon with twelve heads. And it was so that when any went to draw water from this well the dragon rose up and ate them, and there was no other place whence that city could draw its water. So the little Tsar came to that town and put up at the stranger's inn, and he asked his host, "What is the meaning of all this running and crying of the people in the streets?" — "Why, dost thou not know?" said he; "it is the turn of the Tsar to send his daughter to the dragon!" — Then he went out and listened, and heard the people say, "The Tsar proclaims that whoever is able to slay the dragon, to him will he give his daughter and one-half of his tsardom!" Then little Tsar Novishny stepped forth and said, "I am able to slay this evil dragon!" So all the people immediately sent and told the Tsar, "A stranger has come hither who says he is ready to meet and slay the dragon." Then the Tsar bade them take him to the watch-house and put him among the guards.

Then they led out the Tsarivna, and behind her they led him, and behind him came his beasts and his horse. And the Tsarivna was so lovely and so richly attired that all who beheld her burst into tears. But the moment the dragon appeared and opened his mouth to devour the Tsarivna, the little Tsar cried to his self-slicing sword, "Fall upon him!" and to his beasts he cried, "Protius! Medvedik! Vovchok! Nedviga! Seize him!" Then the self-slicing sword and the beasts fell upon him, and tore him into little bits. When they had finished tearing him, the little Tsar took the remains of the body and burnt them to ashes, and the little fox took up all the ashes on her tail, and scattered them to the four winds. Then he took the Tsarivna by the hand, and led her to the Tsar, and the people rejoiced because their water was free again. And the Tsarivna gave him the nuptial ring.

Then they set off home again. They went on and on, for it was a long way from the tsardom of that Tsar, and at last he grew weary and lay down in the grass, and she sat at his head. Then his lackey crept up to him, unfastened the self-slicing sword from his side, went up to the little Tsar, and said, "Self-slicing sword! slay him!" Then the self-slicing sword cut him into little bits, and his beasts knew nothing about it, for they were sleeping after their labours. After that the lackey said to the Tsarivna, "Thou must say now to all men that I saved thee from death, or if not, I will do to thee what I have done to him. Swear that thou wilt say this thing!" Then she said, "I will swear that thou didst save me from death," for she was sore afraid of the lackey. Then they returned to the city, and the Tsar was very glad to see them, and clothed the lackey in goodly apparel, and they all made merry together.

Now when Nedviga awoke he perceived that his master was no longer there, and immediately awoke all the rest, and they all began to think and consider which of them was the swiftest. And when they had thought it well over they judged that the hare was the swiftest, and they resolved that the hare should run and get living and healing water and the apple of youth also. So the hare ran to fetch this water and this apple, and he ran and ran till he came to a certain land, and in this land the hare saw a spring, and close to the spring grew an apple-tree with the apples of youth, and this spring and this apple-tree were guarded by a Muscovite, oh! so strong, so strong, and he waved his sabre again and again so that not even a mouse could make its way up to that well. What was to be done? Then the little hare had resort to subtlety, and made herself crooked, and limped toward the spring as if she were lame. When the Muscovite saw her he said, "What sort of a little beast is this? I never saw the like of it before!" So the hare passed him by, and went farther and farther on till she came right up to the well. The Muscovite stood there and opened his eyes wide, but the hare had now got up to the spring, and took a little flask of the water and nipped off a little apple, and was off in a trice.

She ran back to the little Tsar Novishny, and Nedviga immediately took the water and sprinkled therewith the fragments of the little Tsar, and the fragments came together again. Then he poured some of the living water into his mouth and he became alive, and gave him a bite of the apple of youth, and he instantly grew young again and stronger than ever. Then the little Tsar rose upon his feet, stretched himself, and yawned. "What a long time I've been asleep!" cried he. — "'Tis a good thing for thee that we got the living and healing water!" said Protius. — "But what shall we do next?" said they all. Then they all took council together, and agreed that the little Tsar should disguise himself as an old man, and so go to the Tsar's palace.

So the little Tsar Novishny disguised himself as an old man, and went to the palace of the Tsar. And when he got there he begged them to let him in that he might see the young married people. But the lackeys would not let him in. Then the Tsarivna herself heard the sound of his begging and praying, and commanded them to admit him. Now when he entered the room and took off his cap and cloak, the ring which the Tsarivna had given him when he slew the serpent sparkled so that she knew him, but, not believing her own eyes, she said to him, "Come hither, thou godly old pilgrim, that I may show thee hospitality!" Then the little Tsar drew near to the table, and the Tsarivna poured him out a glass of wine and gave it to him, and he took it with his left hand. She marked that he did not take it with the hand on which was the ring, so she drank off that glass herself. Then she filled another glass and gave it him, and he took it with his right hand. Then she immediately recognized her ring, and said to her father, "This man is my husband who delivered me from death, but that fellow"—pointing to the lackey—"that rascally slavish soul killed my husband and made me say that he was my husband." When the Tsar heard this he boiled over with rage. "So *that* is what thou art!" said he to the lackey, and immediately he bade them bind him and tie him to the tail of a horse so savage that no man could ride it, and then turn it loose into the endless steppe. But the little Tsar Novishny sat down behind the table and made merry.

So the Tsarevko and the Tsarivna lived a long time together in happiness, but one day she asked him, "What of thy kindred and thy father's house?" Then he told her all about his sister. She immediately bade him saddle his horse, and taking his beasts with him, go in search of her. They came to the place where he had left her, and saw that the bucket which was put up for the serpent was full of blood, but that the little Tsar's bucket was all dry and falling to pieces. Then he perceived that she was still lamenting for the serpent, and said to her, "God be with thee, but I will know thee no more. Stay here, and never will I look upon thy face again!" But she began to entreat and caress and implore him that he would take her with him. Then the brother had compassion on his sister and took her away with him.

Now when they got home she took out the serpent's tooth which she had hidden about her, and put it beneath his pillow on the bed whereon he slept. And at night-time the little Tsar went to lie down and the tooth killed him. His wife thought that he was sulky, and therefore did not speak to her, so she begged him not to be angry; and, getting no answer, took him by the hand, and lo! his hand was cold, as cold as lead, and she screamed out. But Protius came bounding through the door and kissed his master. Then the little Tsar became alive again, but Protius died. Then Nedviga kissed Protius and Protius became alive, but Nedviga died. Then the Tsarevko said to Medvedik, "Kiss Nedviga!" He did so, and Nedviga became alive again, but Medvedik died. And so they went on kissing each other from the greatest to the smallest, till the turn came to the hare. She kissed Vovchok and died, but Vovchok remained alive. What was to be done? Now that the little hare had died there was none to kiss her back into life again. "Kiss her," said the little Tsar to the little fox. But the little fox was artful, and taking the little hare on his shoulder, he trotted off to the forest. He carried her to a place where lay a felled oak, with two branches one on the top of the other, and put the hare on the lower branch; then he ran under the branch and kissed the hare, but took good care that the branch should be between them. Thereupon the serpent's tooth flew out of the hare and fastened itself in the upper branch, and both fox and hare scampered back out of the forest alive and well. When the others saw them both alive they rejoiced greatly that no harm had come to any of them from the tooth. But they seized the sister and tied her to the tail of a savage horse and let her loose upon the endless steppe.

So they all lived the merry lives of Tsars who feast continually. And I was there too, and drank wine and mead till my mouth ran over and it trickled all down my beard. So there's the whole *kazka* for you.

318: The Faithless Wife

The Three Snake-Leaves
(*Germany*)

There was once on a time a poor man, who could no longer support his only son. Then said the son, "Dear father, things go so badly with us that I am a burden to you. I would rather go away and see how I can earn my bread." So the father gave him his blessing, and with great sorrow took leave of him. At this time the King of a mighty empire was at war, and the youth took service with him, and with him went out to fight. And when he came before the enemy, there was a battle, and great danger, and it rained shot until his comrades fell on all sides, and when the leader also was killed, those left were about to take flight, but the youth stepped forth, spoke boldly to them, and cried, "We will not let our fatherland be ruined!" Then the others followed him, and he pressed on and conquered the enemy. When the King heard that he owed the victory to him alone, he raised him above all the others, gave him great treasures, and made him the first in the kingdom.

The King had a daughter who was very beautiful, but she was also very strange. She had made a vow to take no one as her lord and husband who did not promise to let himself be buried alive with her if she died first. "If he loves me with all his heart," said she, "of what use will life be to him afterwards?" On her side she would do the same, and if he died first, would go down to the grave with him. This strange oath had up to this time frightened away all wooers, but the youth became so charmed with her beauty that he cared for nothing, but asked her father for her. "But dost thou know what thou must promise?" said the King. "I must be buried with her," he replied, "if I outlive her, but my love is so great that I do not mind the danger." Then the King consented, and the wedding was solemnized with great splendour.

They lived now for a while happy and contented with each other, and then it befell that the young Queen was attacked by a severe illness, and no physician could save her. And as she lay there dead, the young King remembered what he had been obliged to promise, and was horrified at having to lie down alive in the grave, but there was no escape. The King had placed sentries at all the gates, and it was not possible to avoid his fate. When the day came when the corpse was to be buried, he was taken down into the royal vault with it and then the door was shut and bolted.

Near the coffin stood a table on which were four candles, four loaves of bread, and four bottles of wine, and when this provision came to an end, he would have to die of hunger. And now he sat there full of pain and grief, ate every day only a little piece of bread, drank only a mouthful of wine, and nevertheless saw death daily drawing nearer. Whilst he thus gazed before him, he saw a snake creep out of a corner of the vault and approach the dead body. And as he thought it came to gnaw at it, he drew his sword and said, "As long as I live, thou shalt not touch her," and hewed the snake in three pieces. After a time a second snake crept out of the hole, and when it saw the other lying dead and cut in pieces, it went back, but soon came again with three green leaves in its mouth. Then it took the three pieces of the snake, laid them together, as they ought to go, and placed one of the leaves on each wound. Immediately the severed parts joined themselves together, the snake moved, and became alive again, and both of them hastened away together. The leaves were left lying on the ground, and a desire came into the mind of the unhappy man who had been watching all this, to know if the wondrous power of the leaves which had brought the snake to life again, could not likewise be of service to a human being. So he picked up the leaves and laid one of them on the mouth of his dead wife, and the two others on her eyes. And hardly had he done this than the blood stirred in her veins, rose into her pale face, and coloured it again. Then she drew breath, opened her eyes, and said, "Ah, God, where am I?" "Thou art with me, dear wife," he answered, and told her how everything had happened, and how he had brought her back again to life. Then he gave her some wine and bread, and when she had regained her strength, he raised her up and they went to the door and knocked, and called so loudly that the sentries heard it, and told the King. The King came down himself and opened the door, and there he found both strong and well, and rejoiced with them that now all sorrow was over. The young King, however, took the three snake-leaves with him, gave them to a servant and said, "Keep them for me carefully, and carry them constantly about thee; who knows in what trouble they may yet be of service to us!"

A change had, however, taken place in his wife; after she had been restored to life, it seemed as if all love for her husband had gone out of her heart. After some time, when he wanted to make a voyage over the sea, to visit his old father, and they had gone on board a ship, she forgot the great love and fidelity which he had shown her, and which had been the means of rescuing her from death, and conceived a wicked inclination for the skipper. And once when the young King lay there asleep, she called in the skipper and seized the sleeper by the head, and the skipper took him by the feet, and thus they threw him down into the sea. When the shameful deed was done, she said, "Now let us return home, and say that he died on the way. I will extol and praise thee so to my father that he will marry me to thee, and make thee the heir to his crown." But the faithful servant who had seen all that they did, unseen by them, unfastened a little boat from the ship, got into it, sailed after his master, and let the traitors go on their way. He fished up the dead body, and by the help of the three snake-leaves which he carried about with him, and laid on the eyes and mouth, he fortunately brought the young King back to life.

They both rowed with all their strength day and night, and their little boat flew so swiftly that they reached the old King before the others did. He was astonished when he saw them come alone, and asked what had happened to them. When he learnt the wickedness of his daughter he said, "I cannot believe that she has behaved so ill, but the truth will soon come to light," and bade both go into a secret chamber and keep themselves hidden from everyone. Soon afterwards the great ship came sailing in, and the godless woman appeared before her father with a troubled countenance. He said, "Why dost thou come back alone? Where is thy husband?" "Ah, dear father," she replied, "I come home again in great grief; during the voyage, my husband became suddenly ill and died, and if the good skipper had not given me his help, it would have gone ill with me. He was present at his death, and can tell you all." The King said, "I will make the dead alive again," and opened the chamber, and bade the two come out. When the woman saw her husband, she was thunderstruck, and fell on her knees and begged for mercy. The King said, "There is no mercy. He was ready to die with thee and restored thee to life again, but thou hast murdered him in his sleep, and shalt receive the reward that thou deservest." Then she was placed with her accomplice in a ship which had been pierced with holes, and sent out to sea, where they soon sank amid the waves.

Lay of the Werewolf
(*France*)

In Brittany there dwelt a baron who was marvellously esteemed of all his fellows. He was a stout knight, and a comely, and a man of office and repute. Right private was he to the mind of his lord, and dear to the counsel of his neighbours. This baron was wedded to a very worthy dame, right fair to see, and sweet of semblance. All his love was set on her, and all her love was given again to him. One only grief had this lady. For three whole days in every week her lord was absent from her side. She knew not where he went, nor on what errand. Neither did any of his house know the business which called him forth.

On a day when this lord was come again to his house, altogether joyous and content, the lady took him to task, right sweetly, in this fashion,

"Husband," said she, "and fair, sweet friend, I have a certain thing to pray of you. Right willingly would I receive this gift, but I fear to anger you in the asking. It is better for me to have an empty hand, than to gain hard words."

When the lord heard this matter, he took the lady in his arms, very tenderly, and kissed her.

"Wife," he answered, "ask what you will. What would you have, for it is yours already?"

"By my faith," said the lady, "soon shall I be whole. Husband, right long and wearisome are the days that you spend away from your home. I rise from my bed in the morning, sick at heart, I know not why. So fearful am I, lest you do aught to your loss, that I may not find any comfort. Very quickly shall I die for reason of my dread. Tell me now, where you go, and on what business! How may the knowledge of one who loves so closely, bring you to harm?"

"Wife," made answer the lord, "nothing but evil can come if I tell you this secret. For the mercy of God do not require it of me. If you but knew, you would withdraw yourself from my love, and I should be lost indeed."

When the lady heard this, she was persuaded that her baron sought to put her by with jesting words. Therefore she prayed and required him the more urgently, with tender looks and speech, till he was overborne, and told her all the story, hiding naught.

"Wife, I become Bisclavaret.[1] I enter in the forest, and live on prey and roots, within the thickest of the wood."

After she had learned his secret, she prayed and entreated the more as to whether he ran in his raiment, or went spoiled of vesture.

"Wife," said he, "I go naked as a beast."

"Tell me, for hope of grace, what you do with your clothing?"

"Fair wife, that will I never. If I should lose my raiment, or even be marked as I quit my vesture, then a Were-Wolf I must go for all the days of my life. Never again should I become man, save in that hour my clothing were given back to me. For this reason never will I show my lair."

"Husband," replied the lady to him, "I love you better than all the world. The less cause have you for doubting my faith, or hiding any tittle from me. What savour is here of friendship? How have I made forfeit of your love; for what sin do you mistrust my honour? Open now your heart, and tell what is good to be known."

So at the end, outwearied and overborne by her importunity, he could no longer refrain, but told her all.

"Wife," said he, "within this wood, a little from the path, there is a hidden way, and at the end thereof an ancient chapel, where oftentimes

---

1 "The Werewolf".

I have bewailed my lot. Near by is a great hollow stone, concealed by a bush, and there is the secret place where I hide my raiment, till I would return to my own home."

On hearing this marvel the lady became sanguine of visage, because of her exceeding fear. She dared no longer to lie at his side, and turned over in her mind, this way and that, how best she could get her from him. Now there was a certain knight of those parts, who, for a great while, had sought and required this lady for her love. This knight had spent long years in her service, but little enough had he got thereby, not even fair words, or a promise. To him the dame wrote a letter, and meeting, made her purpose plain.

"Fair friend," said she, "be happy. That which you have coveted so long a time, I will grant without delay. Never again will I deny your suit. My heart, and all I have to give, are yours, so take me now as love and dame."

Right sweetly the knight thanked her for her grace, and pledged her faith and fealty. When she had confirmed him by an oath, then she told him all this business of her lord—why he went, and what he became, and of his ravening within the wood. So she showed him of the chapel, and of the hollow stone, and of how to spoil the Were-Wolf of his vesture. Thus, by the kiss of his wife, was Bisclavaret betrayed. Often enough had he ravished his prey in desolate places, but from this journey he never returned. His kinsfolk and acquaintance came together to ask of his tidings, when this absence was noised abroad. Many a man, on many a day, searched the woodland, but none might find him, nor learn where Bisclavaret was gone.

The lady was wedded to the knight who had cherished her for so long a space. More than a year had passed since Bisclavaret disappeared. Then it chanced that the King would hunt in that self-same wood where the Were-Wolf lurked. When the hounds were unleashed they ran this way and that, and swiftly came upon his scent. At the view the huntsman winded on his horn, and the whole pack were at his heels. They followed him from morn to eve, till he was torn and bleeding, and was all adread lest they should pull him down. Now the King was very close to the quarry, and when Bisclavaret looked upon his master, he ran to him for pity and for grace. He took the stirrup within his paws, and fawned upon the prince's foot. The King was very fearful at this sight, but presently he called his courtiers to his aid.

"Lords," cried he, "hasten hither, and see this marvellous thing. Here is a beast who has the sense of man. He abases himself before his foe, and cries for mercy, although he cannot speak. Beat off the hounds, and let no man do him harm. We will hunt no more to-day, but return to our own place, with the wonderful quarry we have taken."

The King turned him about, and rode to his hall, Bisclavaret following at his side. Very near to his master the Were-Wolf went, like any dog,
and had no care to seek again the wood. When the King had brought him
safely to his own castle, he rejoiced greatly, for the beast was fair and
strong, no mightier had any man seen. Much pride had the King in his
marvellous beast. He held him so dear that he bade all those who wished
for his love to cross the Wolf in naught, neither to strike him with a rod,
but ever to see that he was richly fed and kennelled warm. This com-
mandment the Court observed willingly. So all the day the Wolf sported
with the lords, and at night he lay within the chamber of the King. There
was not a man who did not make much of the beast, so frank was he and
debonair. None had reason to do him wrong, forever was he about his
master, and for his part did evil to none. Every day were these two companions together, and all perceived that the King loved him as his friend.

Hearken now to that which chanced.

The King held a high Court, and bade his great vassals and barons, and
all the lords of his venery to the feast. Never was there a goodlier feast,
nor one set forth with sweeter show and pomp. Amongst those who were
bidden, came that same knight who had the wife of Bisclavaret for dame.
He came to the castle, richly gowned, with a fair company, but little he
deemed whom he would find so near. Bisclavaret marked his foe the moment he stood within the hall. He ran towards him, and seized him with
his fangs, in the King's very presence, and to the view of all. Doubtless he
would have done him much mischief, had not the King called and chid-
den him, and threatened him with a rod. Once, and twice, again, the Wolf
set upon the knight in the very light of day. All men marvelled at his malice, for sweet and serviceable was the beast, and to that hour had shown
hatred of none. With one consent the household deemed that this deed
was done with full reason, and that the Wolf had suffered at the knight's
hand some bitter wrong. Right wary of his foe was the knight until the
feast had ended, and all the barons had taken farewell of their lord, and
departed, each to his own house. With these, amongst the very first, went
that lord whom Bisclavaret so fiercely had assailed. Small was the wonder
that he was glad to go.

No long while after this adventure it came to pass that the courteous
King would hunt in that forest where Bisclavaret was found. With the
prince came his wolf, and a fair company. Now at nightfall the King
abode within a certain lodge of that country, and this was known of that
dame who before was the wife of Bisclavaret. In the morning the lady
clothed her in her most dainty apparel, and hastened to the lodge, since
she desired to speak with the King, and to offer him a rich present. When
the lady entered in the chamber, neither man nor leash might restrain
the fury of the Wolf. He became as a mad dog in his hatred and malice.

Breaking from his bonds he sprang at the lady's face, and bit the nose from her visage. From every side men ran to the succour of the dame. They beat off the wolf from his prey, and for a little would have cut him in pieces with their swords. But a certain wise counsellor said to the King,

"Sire, hearken now to me. This beast is always with you, and there is not one of us all who has not known him for long. He goes in and out amongst us, nor has molested any man, neither done wrong or felony to any, save only to this dame, one only time as we have seen. He has done evil to this lady, and to that knight, who is now the husband of the dame. Sire, she was once the wife of that lord who was so close and private to your heart, but who went, and none might find where he had gone. Now, therefore, put the dame in a sure place, and question her straitly, so that she may tell—if perchance she knows thereof—for what reason this Beast holds her in such mortal hate. For many a strange deed has chanced, as well we know, in this marvellous land of Brittany."

The King listened to these words, and deemed the counsel good. He laid hands upon the knight, and put the dame in surety in another place. He caused them to be questioned right straitly, so that their torment was very grievous. At the end, partly because of her distress, and partly by reason of her exceeding fear, the lady's lips were loosed, and she told her tale. She showed them of the betrayal of her lord, and how his raiment was stolen from the hollow stone. Since then she knew not where he went, nor what had befallen him, for he had never come again to his own land. Only, in her heart, well she deemed and was persuaded, that Bisclavaret was he.

Straightway the King demanded the vesture of his baron, whether this were to the wish of the lady, or whether it were against her wish. When the raiment was brought him, he caused it to be spread before Bisclavaret, but the Wolf made as though he had not seen. Then that cunning and crafty counsellor took the King apart, that he might give him a fresh rede.[1]

"Sire," said he, "you do not wisely, nor well, to set this raiment before Bisclavaret, in the sight of all. In shame and much tribulation must he lay aside the beast, and again become man. Carry your wolf within your most secret chamber, and put his vestment therein. Then close the door upon him, and leave him alone for a space. So we shall see presently whether the ravening beast may indeed return to human shape."

The King carried the Wolf to his chamber, and shut the doors upon him fast. He delayed for a brief while, and taking two lords of his fellowship with him, came again to the room. Entering therein, all three, softly together, they found the knight sleeping in the King's bed, like a little

1 Fresh advice.

child. The King ran swiftly to the bed and taking his friend in his arms, embraced and kissed him fondly, above a hundred times. When man's speech returned once more, he told him of his adventure. Then the King restored to his friend the fief that was stolen from him, and gave such rich gifts, moreover, as I cannot tell. As for the wife who had betrayed Bisclavaret, he bade her avoid his country, and chased her from the realm. So she went forth, she and her second lord together, to seek a more abiding city, and were no more seen.

The adventure that you have heard is no vain fable. Verily and indeed it chanced as I have said. The Lay of the Were-Wolf, truly, was written that it should ever be borne in mind.

The Enchanted Ring
(*Russia*)

In a certain kingdom in a certain empire, there lived, once upon a time, an old man and an old woman, and they had a son called little Martin. Time went on, the old man fell ill and died, and though he had worked hard all his days, the only inheritance he left behind him was two hundred rubles. The old woman did not want to waste this money, but what was to be done? There was nothing to eat, so she had to have recourse to the pot containing the patrimony. The old woman counted out a hundred rubles, and sent her son to town to buy provision of bread for a whole year. So Martin the widow's son went to town. He went past the meat market, and saw crowds of people gathered together, and his ears were deafened by the din and noise and racket. Little Martin went into the midst of the throng and saw that the butchers had caught a terrier, and had fastened it to a post, and were beating it unmercifully. Little Martin was sorry for the poor dog, and said to the butchers, "My brothers! why do you beat the poor dog so unmercifully?" – "Why should we not beat him, when he has spoiled a whole quarter of beef?" – "Yet, beat him not, my brothers! 'Twere better to sell him to me!" – "Buy him if you like then!" said the butchers, mockingly, "but for such a treasure as that we could not take less than a hundred rubles." – "Well, one hundred rubles is only one hundred rubles after all!" replied little Martin, and he drew out the money and gave it for the dog. But the dog's name was Jurka. Martin then went home, and his mother asked him, "What hast thou bought?" – "Why look, I have bought Jurka!" replied her son. His mother fell a-scolding him, and reproached him bitterly: "Art thou not ashamed? Soon we shall not have a morsel to eat, and thou hast gone and thrown away so much money on a pagan dog." The next day the old woman sent her son into the town again, and said to him, "Now there is our last one hundred rubles, buy with it provision of bread. To-day I will collect together the scrapings of the meal-tub and bake us fritters, but to-morrow there will not even be that!" Little Martin got to town and walked along the streets and looked about him, and he saw a boy who had fastened a cord round a cat's neck and was dragging it off to drown it. "Stop!" shrieked Martin, "whither art thou dragging Vaska?" – "I am dragging him off to be drowned!" – "Why, what has he done?" – "He is a great rascal. He has stolen a whole goose." – "Don't drown him, far better sell him to me!" – "I'll take nothing less than one hundred rubles!" – "Well, one hundred rubles is only one hundred rubles after all; here! take the money!" And he took Vaska from the boy. "What hast thou bought, my son?" asked his mother when he got home. – "Why the cat Vaska!" – "And what besides?" – "Well, perhaps there's some money still left, and then we can buy something else." – "Oh, oh, oh! what a fool thou art!" screeched the old woman. "Go out of the house this instant and beg thy bread from the stranger!"

Martin dared not gainsay his mother, so he took Jurka and Vaska with him and went into the neighbouring village to seek work. And there met him a rich farmer. "Whither art thou going?" said he. "I want to hire myself out as a day-labourer." – "Come to me then. I take labourers without any contract, but if thou serve me well for a year thou shalt not lose by it." Martin agreed, and for a whole year he worked for this farmer without ceasing. The time of payment came round. The farmer led Martin into the barn, showed him two full sacks, and said, "Take which thou wilt." Martin looked; in one of the sacks was riches, in the other sand, and he thought to himself, "That's not done without a reason; there's some trickery here. I'll take the sand; something will come of it no doubt." So Martin put the sack of sand on his back, and went to seek another place. He went on and on, and strayed into a dark and dreary wood. In the midst of the wood was a field, and on the field a fire was burning, and in the fire a maiden was sitting; and it was such a lovely maiden that it was a delight to look at her. And the Beauty said to him, "Martin the widow's son, if thou wishest to find happiness, save me. Extinguish this flame with the sand which thou hast gotten for thy faithful service." – "Well, really," thought Martin, "why should I go on dragging this load about on my shoulders? Far better to help a body with it." So he undid his sack and emptied all the sand on the fire. The fire immediately went out, but the lovely damsel turned into a serpent, bounded on to the bosom of the good youth, wound itself round his neck, and said, "Fear me not, Martin the widow's son. Go boldly into the land of Thrice-ten, into the underground realm where my dear father rules. Only mark this; he will offer thee lots of gold and silver and precious stones; thou, however, must take none of them, but beg him for the little ring off his little finger. That ring is no common ring; if thou move it from one hand to the other twelve young heroes will immediately appear, and whatever thou dost bid them do they will do it in a single night."

Then the young man set out on his long, long journey, whether 'twere a long time or a short I know not, but at last he drew nigh to the kingdom of Thrice-ten, and came to a place where a huge stone lay across the way. Here the snake leaped from his neck, lit on the damp ground, and turned into the former lovely damsel. "Follow me," said she to Martin, and showed him a little hole beneath the stone. For a long time they went through this underground way, and came into a wide plain beneath the open sky; and in this plain a castle was built entirely of porphyry, with a roof of golden fish-scales, with sharp-pointed golden pinnacles. "That's where my father lives, the Tsar of this underground region," said the lovely damsel to Martin.

The wanderers entered the castle, and the Tsar met them kindly and made them welcome. "My dear daughter," said he to the lovely damsel, "I did not expect to see thee here. Where hast thou been knocking about all these years?" – "Dear father, and light of my eyes, I should have been lost altogether but for this good youth, who saved me from an unavoidable death!" The Tsar turned, looked with a friendly eye at Martin, and said to him, "I thank thee, good youth. I am ready to reward thee for thy good deeds with whatever thou desirest. Take of my gold and silver and precious stones as much as thy soul longs for." – "I thank thee, Sovereign Tsar, for thy good words. But I want no precious stones, nor silver, nor gold; but if thou of thy royal grace and favour wouldst indeed reward me, then give me, I pray, the ring from the little finger of thy royal hand. Whenever I look upon that ring I'll think of thee; but if ever I meet with a bride after mine own heart I will give it to her." The Tsar immediately took off the ring, gave it to Martin, and said, "By all means, good youth, take the ring, and may it be to thy health! But mark this one thing: tell no one that this ring of thine is no common ring, or it will be to thy hurt and harm!"

Martin the widow's son thanked the Tsar and took the ring, and returned by the same way through which he had reached the underground realm. He returned to his native place, sought out his old widowed mother, and lived and dwelt with her without either want or care. Yet for all the good life he led, Martin seemed sorrowful; and why should he not? for Martin wanted to marry, and the bride of his choice was not his like in birth, for she was a king's daughter. So he consulted his mother, and sent her away as his matchmaker, and said to her, "Go to the King himself, and woo for me the thrice-lovely Princess." – "Alas! my dear son," said his old mother, "'twould be far better for thee if thou wert to chop thine own wood. But what art thou thinking of? How can I go to the King and ask him for his daughter for thee? 'Twould be as much as thy head and my head were worth." – "Fear not, dear mother! If I send thee, thou mayest go boldly. And mind thou dost not come back from the King without an answer."

So the old woman dragged herself to the royal palace. She went into the royal courtyard, and without being announced she went right up to the very staircase of the King. The guards shook their arms at her as a sign that nobody was allowed to go there, but she didn't trouble her head about that one bit, but kept on creeping up. Then all the royal lacqueys came running up, and took the old woman under the arms and would have quite gently led her down again; but the old woman made such a to-do and fell a-shrieking so loudly that it pierced through everything, and the King himself in his lofty carved palace heard the noise, and looked out of his little window into the courtyard, and saw his servants dragging an old woman down the staircase, and preventing her from entering the royal apartments, while the old woman was resisting and shrieking with all her might. "I won't go out! I have come to the King on a good errand!" The King commanded them to admit the old woman. The old woman entered the carved palace, and saw sitting in the front corner, on the high carved throne, on cushions of purple velvet, the King in state, holding a council in the midst of his grandees and his councillors. The old woman invoked the aid of the holy ikons, and bowed very low before the King. "What hast thou to say, old woman?" asked the King. – "Now, lo! I have come to your Majesty – be not wroth at my words – I have come to your Majesty as a matchmaker!" – "Art thou in thy senses, old woman?" cried the King, and his brow was wrinkled with a frown. – "Nay, O father-king! pray do not be angry; pray give me an answer. You have the wares – a little daughter, a beauty; I have the purchaser – a young man, so wise, so cunning, a master of every trade, so that you could not find a better son-in-law. Tell me, therefore, straight out, won't you give your daughter to my son?" The King listened and listened to the old woman, and at first his frown was blacker than night, but he thought to himself, "Does it become me, a king, to be wroth with a silly old woman?" And the royal councillors were amazed, for they saw the wrinkles on the King's forehead smoothing out, and the King looked at the old woman with a smile. "If thy son is so cunning, and a master of every trade, let him build me within twenty-four hours a palace more gorgeous than my own, and let him hang a crystal bridge between this palace and my palace, and let luxuriant apple trees grow up all along this bridge, and let them bear silver and golden pippins, and let birds of paradise sing within these apple trees. And on the right-hand side of this crystal bridge let him build a cathedral five storeys high, with golden pinnacles, where he may receive the

wedding crown with my daughter, and where the marriage may be celebrated. But if thy son fulfil not all this, then for thy and his presumption
I will have you both smeared with tar and rolled in feathers and down,
and hanged up in cages in the market-place as a laughing-stock to all
good people." And the King condescended to smile still more pleasantly,
and his grandees and his councillors held their sides, and rolled about the
floor for laughter, and they began with one voice to praise his wisdom and
thought amongst themselves, "What fun it will be to see the old woman and her son hung up in cages! 'Tis as plain as daylight; a beard will
sooner grow out of the palm of his hand than he be able to accomplish
so shrewd a task." The poor old woman was near to swooning. "What!"
said she to the King, "is this thy final sovereign word? Is this what I must
say to my son?" – "Yes, thus must thou say: if he accomplish this task,
I will give him my daughter; if he does not accomplish it, I will put you
both into cages."

The poor old woman went home more dead than alive. She staggered
from side to side, and shed floods of scalding tears. When she saw Martin, she began screeching at him from afar. "Did not I tell thee, my son, to
go and chop thine own wood? Now thou seest that our poor little heads
are lost." And she told her son all about it. "Cheer up, mother," said little
Martin, "pray to God and lie down to sleep, the morning is always wiser
than the evening." But he himself went out of the hut, took his little ring
from one hand and put it on the other, and the twelve youths immediately
appeared before him and said, "What dost thou require?" He told them
of the royal task, and the twelve youths answered, "To-morrow, everything will be ready."

The King awoke next morning, and lo! right in front of his palace tow-
ered another palace, and a crystal bridge led from one to the other. Along
the sides of the bridge stood luxuriant apple trees, and upon them hung
golden pippins, and birds of paradise were singing in the trees; and on the
right hand of the bridge, blazing like fire in the sun, stood the cathedral
with its golden pinnacles; and the bells of the cathedral were ringing and
pealing in all directions. The King had to keep his word. He raised his
son-in-law high in rank, gave him a rich inheritance with his daughter,
and he took her to wife. Great was the wedding-feast. The wine flowed in
streams, and they drank of mead and beer till they could drink no more.

So Martin lived in his palace, and he ate of the best and drank of the
best, and his life went as smoothly as cheese with butter. But the Princess
did not love him at heart, and when she reflected that they had not married her to the son of a tsar, or the son of a king, or even to a prince from
across the sea, but to simple Martin the widow's son, her wrath waxed
hot within her. And she fell a-thinking by what means she might best rid
herself of a husband she hated. So she took care to caress him, and flat-

ter him, and waited upon him herself, and made him comfortable, and when they were quite alone she would ask him what it was that made him so wise and clever. And it happened one day that when he had been the King's guest, and had drunk and made merry with all his lords one after another, and had returned home and laid him down to rest, that the Princess came to him and caressed him, and coaxed him with wheedling words, and made him drunk with strong mead, and in that way found out what she wanted to know, for Martin told her all about his enchanted ring, and showed her how to turn it. And no sooner was little Martin asleep and snoring than the Princess took off the enchanted ring from his little finger, went forth into the broad courtyard, moved the ring from one finger to the other, and the twelve youths immediately appeared before her. "What is thy pleasure, and what is thy desire?" – "That to-morrow morning there may be neither palace, nor bridge, nor cathedral on this spot, but only a wretched little hut as heretofore, and cast this drunkard into it, but remove me far from him into the Empire of Thrice-ten." – "It shall be done," replied the twelve youths with one voice.

In the morning, when the King awoke, he felt inclined to go and pay a visit to his son-in-law and his daughter, so he went out upon the balcony, and lo! there was neither palace, nor bridge, nor cathedral, nor garden. In place of them stood a wretched old hut, leaning on one side, and scarce able to stand at all. The King sent for his son-in-law, and began asking him what it all meant; but little Martin could only stare blankly at him without uttering a word. And the King bade them sit in judgment on his son-in-law for deceiving him by magic, and destroying his daughter, the thrice-lovely Princess, and they condemned Martin to be put on the top of a lofty stone column with nothing to eat or drink; there he was to be left to die of hunger.

Then it was that Jurka and Vaska remembered how little Martin had saved them from an evil death, and they came and laid their heads together about it. Jurka growled and snarled, and was ready to tear everyone to bits, for his master's sake; but Vaska purred and hummed and scratched himself behind the ear with his velvet paw, and began to think the matter over. And the artful cat hit upon a plan, and said to Jurka, "Let us go for a walk about the town, and as soon as we meet a roll-baker with a tin on his head, you run between his legs and knock the tin off his head, and I'll be close behind and immediately seize the rolls, and take them to master." No sooner said than done. Jurka and the cat took a run into the town, and they met a roll-baker. He was carrying a tin on his head, and he looked about him on all sides and cried with a loud voice, "Hot rolls, hot rolls, fresh from the oven!" Jurka ran between his legs, the baker stumbled, the tin fell, and all the rolls were scattered about. But while the angry baker was chasing Jurka, Vaska hid all the rolls in the hedges. Then the cat and

Jurka ran to the tower where Martin was placed, dragged with them the stores of bread, and Vaska scrambled up to the top, looked in at the little window, called to his master, and said, "Alive, eh?" – "Scarcely alive!" replied little Martin; "I am quite exhausted from want of food, and it will not be long before I die of hunger." – "Don't grieve; wait a bit, and we'll feed you," said Vaska, and he began to drag the food up from below – rolls and cakes, and all kinds of bread, till he had dragged up for his master a large store. Then he said, "Master, Jurka and I will go to the kingdom of Thrice-ten, and get you back your enchanted ring. Take care to make the bread last till we return." Then they both took leave of their master, and departed on their long journey.

They ran on and on, and they smelt out the scent everywhere and followed it; paid great attention to what people told them; carefully made friends with all the other dogs and cats they met; asked about the Princess, and found out at last that they were not far from the kingdom of Thrice-ten, whither she had told the twelve youths to carry her. They ran into the kingdom, went to the palace, and made friends with all the dogs and cats there, asked them all about the Princess's ways, and turned the conversation to the subject of the enchanted ring; but no one could give them certain information about it. But one day it happened that Vaska went a-hunting in the royal cellars. There he waylaid a big fat mouse, threw himself upon it, dug his cruel claws into it, and was going to begin with its head, when the big mouse spoke to him: "Dear little Vaska, don't hurt me, don't kill me. Perhaps I may be of service to you. I'll do all I can for you. But if you kill me, the Mouse-Tsar, all my mousey tsardom will fall to pieces." – "Very well," said Vaska; "I'll spare you; but this is the service you must do me. In this palace dwells the Princess, the wicked wife of our master; she has stolen from him his wonder-working ring; till you have got me that ring, I will not let you out of my claws under any pretence whatever." – "Agreed," said the Mouse-Tsar, "I'll try"; and he piped and whistled all his people together. A countless multitude of mice assembled, both small and great, and they sat all round the cat Vaska, and waited to hear what the Mouse-Tsar would say to them from beneath Vaska's claws. And the Mouse-Tsar said to them: "Whichever of you shall get the wonder-working ring from the Princess, he will save me from a cruel death, and I will raise him to the highest place about my person." Then a little mouse rose up and said: "I have often been in the Princess's bed-chamber, and I've noticed that the Princess's eye rests more often on a certain little ring than on anything else. In the daytime she wears it on her little finger, but at night she stuffs it into her mouth behind her cheeks. If you wait a bit, I'll get you that ring." And the little mouse ran into the Princess's bed-chamber and waited till night, and as soon as ever the Princess was asleep, it wriggled into her bed, picked the down out of her swan-feathered bolster, and strewed it all about under her nose. The fine down went up the Princess's nose and into her mouth, she sprang up and began to sneeze and cough, and spat out the enchanted ring on to the counterpane. The little mouse immediately snatched it up, and ran off with it to save the life of the Mouse-Tsar.

Vaska and Jurka set off to bring their master the wonder-working ring. Whether they took a long time or a short time matters not, but they arrived at last, and ran to the tower in which Martin was put to die from starvation. The cat immediately climbed up to the window, and called to its master, "Art thou alive, Martin the widow's son?" – "I am scarce able to keep body and soul together. This is the third day I have been sitting here without bread." – "Well, thy woes are over now. There will be a feast in our street now; we have brought you your ring." Martin was overjoyed, and began to stroke the cat, and the cat rubbed itself against him, and began purring its own little songs through its nose; but at the bottom of the tower Jurka was leaping and whining and barking for joy, and leaping high in the air. Martin took the ring and turned it from one hand to the other. The twelve youths immediately appeared: "What is thy pleasure, and what thy command?" – "Give me to eat and drink till I can eat and drink no more, and let cunning music be played on the top of this tower to me all day." When the music began to play, the good folks hastened to the King, and told him that little Martin was up to no good in the tower there. "He ought to have ceased to be among the living long ago," they said, "and yet he is having such a merry time of it on the top of the tower. They are stamping with their feet, and knocking their plates, and clashing their glasses, and such splendid music is playing, that you can't help listening to it." The King sent an express messenger to the tower, and there he stood and listened to the music; the King sent his highest officer, and there they all remained standing, and opened wide their ears. The King himself went to the tower, and the music seemed to turn him into a statue. But little Martin again called his twelve youths, and said to them, "Restore my old palace, as it was before; throw a crystal bridge across from it to the royal palace; let the former five-storeyed cathedral stand by the side of the palace; and let my faithless wife also be found in the palace." And while he was yet expressing the wish, the whole thing was done. And he went out of the tower, took his father-in-law the King by the hand, led him into the palace, led him up to the sleeping-chamber, where the Princess, in fear and trembling, awaited an evil death, and said to the King, "My dear little father-in-law, a great deal of trouble and anguish has befallen me from living with thy daughter; what shall we sentence her to?" – "My dear son-in-law, let mercy prevail over justice; exhort her with good words, and live with her as heretofore." And Martin listened to his father-in-law, upbraided his wife for her treachery, and to the end of his life he never parted with the ring, nor with Jurka and Vaska, and saw no more misery.

321: Eyes Recovered from Witch

Grandfather's Eyes
(*Czech Republic*)

Once upon a time there was a poor boy whom everybody called Yanechek. His father and mother were dead and he was forced to start out alone in the world to make a living. For a long time he could find nothing to do. He wandered on and on and at last he came to a little house that stood by itself near the edge of the woods. An old man sat on the doorstep and Yanechek could see that he was blind, for there were empty holes where his eyes used to be.

Some goats that were penned in a shed near the house began bleating and the old man said:

"You poor things, you want to go to pasture, don't you? But I can't see to drive you and I have no one else to send."

"Send me, grandfather," Yanechek said. "Take me as your goatherd and let me work for you."

"Who are you?" the old man asked.

Yanechek told him who he was and the old man agreed to take him.

"And now," he said, "drive the goats to pasture. But one thing, Yanechek: don't take them to the hill over there in the woods or the Yezinkas may get you! That's where they caught me!"

Now Yanechek knew that the Yezinkas were wicked witches who lived in a cave in the woods and went about in the guise of beautiful young women. If they met you they would greet you modestly and say something like "God bless you!" to make you think they were good and kind and then, once they had you in their power, they would put you to sleep and gouge out your eyes! Oh, yes, Yanechek knew about the Yezinkas.

"Never fear, grandfather, the Yezinkas won't get me!"

The first day and the second day Yanechek kept the goats near home. But the third day he said to himself: "I think I'll try the hill in the woods. There's better grass there and I'm not afraid of the Yezinkas."

Before he started out he cut three long slender switches from a blackberry bramble, wound them into small coils, and hid them in the crown of his hat. Then he drove the goats through the woods where they nibbled at leaves and branches, beside a deep river where they paused to drink, and up the grassy slopes of the hill.

There the goats scattered this way and that and Yanechek sat down on a stone in the shade. He was hardly seated when he looked up and there before him, dressed all in white, stood the most beautiful maiden in the world. Her skin was red as roses and white as milk, her eyes were black as sloe berries, and her hair, dark as the raven's wing, fell about her shoulders in long waving tresses. She smiled and offered Yanechek a big red apple.

"God bless you, shepherd boy," she said. "Here's something for you that grew in my own garden."

But Yanechek knew that she must be a Yezinka and that, if he ate the apple, he would fall asleep and then she would gouge out his eyes. So he said, politely: "No, thank you, beautiful maiden. My master has a tree in his garden with apples that are bigger than yours and I have eaten as many as I want."

When the maiden saw that Yanechek was not to be coaxed, she disappeared.

Presently a second maiden came, more beautiful, if possible, than the first. In her hand she carried a lovely red rose.

"God bless you, shepherd boy," she said. "Isn't this a lovely rose? I picked it myself from the hedge. How fragrant it is! Will you smell it?"

She offered him the rose but Yanechek refused it.

"No, thank you, beautiful maiden. My master's garden is full of roses much sweeter than yours and I smell roses all the time."

At that the second maiden shrugged her shoulders and disappeared.

Presently a third one came, the youngest and most beautiful of them all. In her hand she carried a golden comb.

"God bless you, shepherd boy."

"Good day to you, beautiful maiden."

She smiled at Yanechek and said: "Truly you are a handsome lad, but you would be handsomer still if your hair were nicely combed. Come, let me comb it for you."

Yanechek said nothing but he took off his hat without letting the maiden see what was hidden in its crown. She came up close to him and then, just as she was about to comb his hair, he whipped out one of the long blackberry switches and struck her over the hands. She screamed and tried to escape but she could not because it is the fate of a Yezinka not to be able to move if ever a human being strikes her over the hands with a switch of bramble.

So Yanechek took her two hands and bound them together with the long thorny switch while she wept and struggled.

"Help, sisters! Help!" she cried.

At that the two other Yezinkas came running and when they saw what had happened they, too, began to weep and to beg Yanechek to unbind their sister's hands and let her go.

But Yanechek only laughed and said: "No. You unbind them."

"But, Yanechek, how can we? Our hands are soft and the thorns will prick us."

However, when they saw that Yanechek was not to be moved, they went to their sister and tried to help her. Whereupon Yanechek whipped out the other two blackberry switches and struck them also on their soft pretty hands, first one and then the other. After that they, too, could not move and it was easy enough to bind them and make them prisoners.

"Now I've got the three of you, you wicked Yezinkas!" Yanechek said. "It was you who gouged out my poor old master's eyes, you know it was! And you shall not escape until you do as I ask."

He left them there and ran home to his master to whom he said: "Come, grandfather, for I have found a means of restoring your eyes!"

He took the old man by the hand and led him through the woods, along the bank of the river, and up the grassy hillside where the three Yezinkas were still struggling and weeping.

Then he said to the first of them: "Tell me now where my master's eyes are. If you don't tell me, I'll throw you into the river."

The first Yezinka pretended she didn't know. So Yanechek lifted her up and started down the hill toward the river.

That frightened the maiden and she cried out: "Don't throw me into the river, Yanechek, and I'll find you your master's eyes, I promise you I will!"

So Yanechek put her down and she led him to a cave in the hillside where she and her wicked sisters had piled up a great heap of eyes—all kinds of eyes they were: big eyes, little eyes, black eyes, red eyes, blue eyes, green eyes—every kind of eye in the world that you can think of.

She went to the heap and picked out two eyes which she said were the right ones. But when the poor old man tried to look through them, he cried out in fright:

"I see nothing but dark treetops with sleeping birds and flying bats! These are not my eyes! They are owls' eyes! Take them out! Take them out!"

When Yanechek saw how the first Yezinka had deceived him, without another word he picked her up, threw her into the river, and that was the end of her.

Then he said to the second sister: "Now you tell me where my master's eyes are."

At first she, too, pretended she didn't know, but when Yanechek threatened to throw her likewise into the river, she was glad enough to lead him back to the cave and pick out two eyes that she said were the right ones.

But when the poor old man tried to look through them, again he cried out in fright: "I see nothing but tangled underbrush and snapping teeth and hot red tongues! These are not my eyes! They are wolves' eyes! Take them out! Take them out!"

When Yanechek saw how the second Yezinka had deceived him, without another word he picked her up, and threw her also into the river, and that was the end of her.

Then Yanechek said to the third sister: "Now you tell me where my master's eyes are."

At first she, too, pretended she didn't know, but when Yanechek threatened to throw her likewise into the river, she was glad enough to lead him to the cave and pick out two eyes that she said were the right ones.

But when the poor old man tried to look through them, again he cried out in fright: "I see nothing but swirling waters and flashing fins! These are not my eyes! They are fishes' eyes! Take them out! Take them out!"

When Yanechek saw how the third Yezinka had deceived him, without another word he was ready to serve her as he had served her sisters. But she begged him not to drown her and she said:

"Let me try again, Yanechek, and I'll find you the right eyes, I promise you I will!"

So Yanechek let her try again and from the very bottom of the heap she picked out two more eyes that she swore were the right ones.

When the old man looked through them, he clapped his hands and said: "These are my own eyes, praise God! Now I can see as well as ever!"

After that the old man and Yanechek lived on happily together. Yanechek pastured the goats and the old man made cheeses at home and they ate them together. And you may be sure that the third Yezinka never showed herself again on that hill!

True and Untrue
(*Norway*)

Once on a time there were two brothers; one was called True, and the other Untrue. True was always upright and good towards all, but Untrue was bad and full of lies, so that no one could believe what he said. Their mother was a widow, and hadn't much to live on; so when her sons had grown up, she was forced to send them away, that they might earn their bread in the world. Each got a little scrip[1] with some food in it, and then they went their way.

Now, when they had walked till evening, they sat down on a windfall in the wood, and took out their scraps, for they were hungry after walking the whole day, and thought a morsel of food would be sweet enough.

"If you're of my mind", said Untrue, "I think we had better eat out of

---

1 Pouch or wallet.

your scrip, so long as there is anything in it, and after that we can take to mine."

Yes! True was well pleased with this, so they fell to eating, but Untrue got all the best bits, and stuffed himself with them, while True got only the burnt crusts and scraps.

Next morning they broke their fast off True's food, and they dined off it too, and then there was nothing left in his scrip. So when they had walked till late at night, and were ready to eat again, True wanted to eat out of his brother's scrip, but Untrue said "No", the food was his, and he had only enough for himself.

"Nay! but you know you ate out of my scrip so long as there was anything in it", said True.

"All very fine, I daresay", answered Untrue; "but if you are such a fool as to let others eat up your food before your face, you must make the best of it; for now all you have to do is to sit here and starve."

"Very well!" said True, "you're Untrue by name and untrue by nature; so you have been, and so you will be all your life long."

Now when Untrue heard this, he flew into a rage, and rushed at his brother, and plucked out both his eyes. "Now, try if you can see whether folk are untrue or not, you blind buzzard!" and so saying, he ran away and left him.

Poor True! there he went walking along and feeling his way through the thick wood. Blind and alone, he scarce knew which way to turn, when all at once he caught hold of the trunk of a great bushy lime-tree, so he thought he would climb up into it, and sit there till the night was over for fear of the wild beasts.

"When the birds begin to sing", he said to himself, "then I shall know it is day, and I can try to grope my way farther on." So he climbed up into the lime-tree. After he had sat there a little time, he heard how someone came and began to make a stir and clatter under the tree, and soon after others came; and when they began to greet one another, he found out it was Bruin the bear, and Greylegs the wolf, and Slyboots the fox, and Longears the hare who had come to keep St. John's eve under the tree. So they began to eat and drink, and be merry; and when they had done eating, they fell to gossiping together. At last the Fox said:

"Shan't we, each of us, tell a little story while we sit here?" Well! the others had nothing against that. It would be good fun, they said, and the Bear began; for you may fancy he was king of the company.

"The king of England", said Bruin, "has such bad eyesight, he can scarce see a yard before him; but if he only came to this lime-tree in the morning, while the dew is still on the leaves, and took and rubbed his eyes with the dew, he would get back his sight as good as ever."

"Very true!" said Greylegs. "The king of England has a deaf and dumb daughter too; but if he only knew what I know, he would soon cure her. Last year she went to the communion. She let a crumb of the bread fall out of her mouth, and a great toad came and swallowed it down; but if they only dug up the chancel floor, they would find the toad sitting right under the altar rails, with the bread still sticking in his throat. If they were to cut the toad open and take and give the bread to the princess, she would be like other folk again as to her speech and hearing."

"That's all very well", said the Fox; "but if the king of England knew what I know, he would not be so badly off for water in his palace; for under the great stone, in his palace-yard, is a spring of the clearest water one could wish for, if he only knew to dig for it there."

"Ah!" said the Hare in a small voice; "the king of England has the finest orchard in the whole land, but it does not bear so much as a crab, for there lies a heavy gold chain in three turns round the orchard. If he got that dug up, there would not be a garden like it for bearing in all his kingdom."

"Very true, I dare say", said the Fox; "but now it's getting very late, and we may as well go home."

So they all went away together.

After they were gone, True fell asleep as he sat up in the tree; but when the birds began to sing at dawn, he woke up, and took the dew from the leaves, and rubbed his eyes with it, and so got his sight back as good as it was before Untrue plucked his eyes out.

Then he went straight to the king of England's palace, and begged for work, and got it on the spot. So one day the king came out into the palace-yard, and when he had walked about a bit, he wanted to drink out of his pump; for you must know the day was hot, and the king very thirsty; but when they poured him out a glass, it was so muddy, and nasty, and foul, that the king got quite vexed.

"I don't think there's ever a man in my whole kingdom who has such bad water in his yard as I, and yet I bring it in pipes from far over hill and dale", cried out the king. "Like enough, your Majesty", said True; "but if you would let me have some men to help me to dig up this great stone which lies here in the middle of your yard, you would soon see good water, and plenty of it."

Well! the king was willing enough; and they had scarcely got the stone well out, and dug under it a while, before a jet of water sprang out high up into the air, as clear and full as if it came out of a conduit, and clearer water was not to be found in all England.

A little while after the king was out in his palace-yard again, and there came a great hawk flying after his chicken, and all the king's men began to clap their hands and bawl out, "There he flies!" "There he flies!" The king caught up his gun and tried to shoot the hawk, but he couldn't see so far, so he fell into great grief.

"Would to Heaven", he said, "there was anyone who could tell me a cure for my eyes; for I think I shall soon go quite blind!"

"I can tell you one soon enough", said True; and then he told the king what he had done to cure his own eyes, and the king set off that very afternoon to the lime-tree, as you may fancy, and his eyes were quite cured as soon as he rubbed them with the dew which was on the leaves in the morning. From that time forth there was no one whom the king held so dear as True, and he had to be with him wherever he went, both at home and abroad.

So one day, as they were walking together in the orchard, the king said, "I can't tell how it is *that* I can't! there isn't a man in England who spends so much on his orchard as I, and yet I can't get one of the trees to bear so much as a crab."

"Well! well!" said True; "if I may have what lies three times twisted round your orchard, and men to dig it up, your orchard will bear well enough."

Yes! the king was quite willing, so True got men and began to dig, and at last he dug up the whole gold chain. Now True was a rich man; far richer indeed than the king himself, but still the king was well pleased, for his orchard bore so that the boughs of the trees hung down to the ground, and such sweet apples and pears nobody had ever tasted.

Another day too the king and True were walking about, and talking together, when the princess passed them, and the king was quite downcast when he saw her.

"Isn't it a pity, now, that so lovely a princess as mine should want speech and hearing", he said to True.

"Ay, but there is a cure for that", said True.

When the king heard that, he was so glad that he promised him the princess to wife, and half his kingdom into the bargain, if he could get her right again. So True took a few men, and went into the church, and dug up the toad which sat under the altar-rails. Then he cut open the toad, and took out the bread and gave it to the king's daughter; and from that hour she got back her speech, and could talk like other people.

Now True was to have the princess, and they got ready for the bridal feast, and such a feast had never been seen before; it was the talk of the whole land. Just as they were in the midst of dancing the bridal-dance in came a beggar lad, and begged for a morsel of food, and he was so ragged and wretched that everyone crossed themselves when they looked at him; but True knew him at once, and saw that it was Untrue, his brother.

"Do you know me again?" said True.

"Oh! where should such a one as I ever have seen so great a lord", said Untrue.

"Still you *have* seen me before", said True. "It was I whose eyes you plucked out a year ago this very day. Untrue by name, and untrue by nature; so I said before, and so I say now; but you are still my brother, and so you shall have some food. After that, you may go to the lime-tree where I sat last year; if you hear anything that can do you good, you will be lucky."

So Untrue did not wait to be told twice. "If True has got so much good by sitting in the lime-tree, that in one year he has come to be king over half England, what good may not I get", he thought. So he set off and climbed up into the lime-tree. He had not sat there long, before all the beasts came as before, and ate and drank, and kept St. John's eve under the tree. When they had left off eating, the Fox wished that they should begin to tell stories, and Untrue got ready to listen with all his might, till his ears were almost fit to fall off. But Bruin the bear was surly, and growled and said:

"Someone has been chattering about what we said last year, and so now we will hold our tongues about what we know"; and with that the beasts bade one another "Good-night", and parted, and Untrue was just as wise as he was before, and the reason was that his name was Untrue, and his nature untrue too.

Mogarzea and His Son
(*Romania*)

There was once a little boy, whose father and mother, when they were dying, left him to the care of a guardian. But the guardian whom they chose turned out to be a wicked man, and spent all the money, so the boy determined to go away and strike out a path for himself.

So one day he set off, and walked and walked through woods and meadows till when evening came he was very tired, and did not know where to sleep. He climbed a hill and looked about him to see if there was no light shining from a window. At first all seemed dark, but at length he noticed a tiny spark far, far off, and, plucking up his spirits, he at once went in search of it.

The night was nearly half over before he reached the spark, which turned out to be a big fire, and by the fire a man was sleeping who was so tall he might have been a giant. The boy hesitated for a moment what he should do; then he crept close up to the man, and lay down by his legs.

When the man awoke in the morning he was much surprised to find the boy nestling up close to him.

'Dear me! where do you come from?' said he.

'I am your son, born in the night,' replied the boy.

'If that is true,' said the man, 'you shall take care of my sheep, and I will give you food. But take care you never cross the border of my land, or you will repent it.' Then he pointed out where the border of his land lay, and bade the boy begin his work at once.

The young shepherd led his flock out to the richest meadows and stayed with them till evening, when he brought them back, and helped the man to milk them. When this was done, they both sat down to supper, and while they were eating the boy asked the big man: 'What is your name, father?'

'Mogarzea,' answered he.

'I wonder you are not tired of living by yourself in this lonely place.'

'There is no reason you should wonder! Don't you know that there was never a bear yet who danced of his own free will?'

'Yes, that is true,' replied the boy. 'But why is it you are always so sad? Tell me your history, father.'

'What is the use of my telling you things that would only make you sad too?'

'Oh, never mind that! I should like to hear. Are you not my father, and am I not your son?'

'Well, if you really want to know my story, this is it: As I told you, my name is Mogarzea, and my father is an emperor. I was on my way to the Sweet Milk Lake, which lies not far from here, to marry one of the three fairies who have made the lake their home. But on the road three wicked elves fell on me, and robbed me of my soul, so that ever since I have stayed in this spot watching my sheep without wishing for anything different, without having felt one moment's joy, or ever once being able to laugh. And the horrible elves are so ill-natured that if anyone sets one foot on their land he is instantly punished. That is why I warn you to be careful, lest you should share my fate.'

'All right, I will take great care. Do let me go, father,' said the boy, as they stretched themselves out to sleep.

At sunrise the boy got up and led his sheep out to feed, and for some reason he did not feel tempted to cross into the grassy meadows belonging to the elves, but let his flock pick up what pasture they could on Mogarzea's dry ground.

On the third day he was sitting under the shadow of a tree, playing on his flute—and there was nobody in the world who could play a flute better—when one of his sheep strayed across the fence into the flowery fields of the elves, and another and another followed it. But the boy was so absorbed in his flute that he noticed nothing till half the flock were on the other side.

He jumped up, still playing on his flute, and went after the sheep, meaning to drive them back to their own side of the border, when suddenly he saw before him three beautiful maidens who stopped in front of him, and began to dance. The boy understood what he must do, and played with all his might, but the maidens danced on till evening.

'Now let me go,' he cried at last, 'for poor Mogarzea must be dying of hunger. I will come and play for you to-morrow.'

'Well, you may go!' they said, 'but remember that even if you break your promise you will not escape us.'

So they both agreed that the next day he should come straight there with the sheep, and play to them till the sun went down. This being settled, they each returned home.

Mogarzea was surprised to find that his sheep gave so much more milk than usual, but as the boy declared he had never crossed the border the big man did not trouble his head further, and ate his supper heartily.

With the earliest gleams of light, the boy was off with his sheep to the elfin meadow, and at the first notes of his flute the maidens appeared before him and danced and danced and danced till evening came. Then the boy let the flute slip through his fingers, and trod on it, as if by accident.

If you had heard the noise he made, and how he wrung his hands and wept and cried that he had lost his only companion, you would have been sorry for him. The hearts of the elves were quite melted, and they did all they could to comfort him.

'I shall never find another flute like that, moaned he. 'I have never heard one whose tone was as sweet as mine! It was cut from the centre of a seven-year-old cherry tree!'

'There is a cherry tree in our garden that is exactly seven years old,' said they. 'Come with us, and you shall make yourself another flute.'

So they all went to the cherry tree, and when they were standing round it the youth explained that if he tried to cut it down with an axe he might very likely split open the heart of the tree, which was needed for the flute. In order to prevent this, he would make a little cut in the bark, just large enough for them to put their fingers in, and with this help he could manage to tear the tree in two, so that the heart should run no risk of damage. The elves did as he told them without a thought; then he quickly drew out the axe, which had been sticking into the cleft, and behold! all their fingers were imprisoned tight in the tree.

It was in vain that they shrieked with pain and tried to free themselves. They could do nothing, and the young man remained cold as marble to all their entreaties.

Then he demanded of them Mogarzea's soul.

'Oh, well, if you must have it, it is in a bottle on the window sill,' said they, hoping that they might obtain their freedom at once. But they were mistaken.

'You have made so many men suffer,' answered he sternly, 'that it is but just you should suffer yourselves, but to-morrow I will let you go.' And he turned towards home, taking his sheep and the soul of Mogarzea with him.

Mogarzea was waiting at the door, and as the boy drew near he began scolding him for being so late. But at the first word of explanation the man became beside himself with joy, and he sprang so high into the air that the false soul which the elves had given him flew out of his mouth, and his own, which had been shut tightly into the flask of water, took its place.

When his excitement had somewhat calmed down, he cried to the boy, 'Whether you are really my son matters nothing to me; tell me, how can I repay you for what you have done for me?'

'By showing me where the Milk Lake is, and how I can get one of the three fairies who lives there to wife, and by letting me remain your son forever.'

The night was passed by Mogarzea and his son in songs and feasting, for both were too happy to sleep, and when day dawned they set out together to free the elves from the tree. When they reached the place of their imprisonment, Mogarzea took the cherry tree and all the elves with it on his back, and carried them off to his father's kingdom, where everyone rejoiced to see him home again. But all he did was to point to the boy who had saved him, and had followed him with his flock.

For three days the boy stayed in the palace, receiving the thanks and praises of the whole court. Then he said to Mogarzea:

'The time has come for me to go hence, but tell me, I pray you, how to find the Sweet Milk Lake, and I will return, and will bring my wife back with me.'

Mogarzea tried in vain to make him stay, but, finding it was useless, he told him all he knew, for he himself had never seen the lake.

For three summer days the boy and his flute journeyed on, till one evening he reached the lake, which lay in the kingdom of a powerful fairy. The next morning had scarcely dawned when the youth went down to the shore, and began to play on his flute, and the first notes had hardly sounded when he saw a beautiful fairy standing before him, with hair and robes that shone like gold. He gazed at her in wonder, when suddenly she began to dance. Her movements were so graceful that he forgot to play, and as soon as the notes of his flute ceased she vanished from his sight. The next day the same thing happened, but on the third he took courage, and drew a little nearer, playing on his flute all the while. Suddenly he sprang forward, seized her in his arms and kissed her, and plucked a rose from her hair.

The fairy gave a cry, and begged him to give her back her rose, but he would not. He only stuck the rose in his hat, and turned a deaf ear to all her prayers.

At last she saw that her entreaties were vain, and agreed to marry him, as he wished. And they went together to the palace, where Mogarzea was still waiting for him, and the marriage was celebrated by the emperor himself. But every May they returned to the Milk Lake, they and their children, and bathed in its waters.

334: Household of the Witch

Frau Trude
(*Germany*)

There was once a little girl who was obstinate and inquisitive, and when her parents told her to do anything, she did not obey them, so how could she fare well? One day she said to her parents, "I have heard so much of Frau Trude, I will go to her some day. People say that everything about her does look so strange, and that there are such odd things in her house, that I have become quite curious!" Her parents absolutely forbade her, and said, "Frau Trude is a bad woman, who does wicked things, and if thou goest to her; thou art no longer our child." But the maiden did not let herself be turned aside by her parent's prohibition, and still went to Frau Trude. And when she got to her, Frau Trude said, "Why art thou so pale?" "Ah," she replied, and her whole body trembled, "I have been so terrified at what I have seen." "What hast thou seen?" "I saw a black man on your steps." "That was a collier." "Then I saw a green man." "That was a huntsman." "After that I saw a blood-red man." "That was a butcher." "Ah, Frau Trude, I was terrified; I looked through the window and saw not you, but, as I verily believe, the devil himself with a head of fire." "Oho!" said she, "then thou hast seen the witch in her proper costume. I have been waiting for thee, and wanting thee a long time already; thou shalt give me some light." Then she changed the girl into a block of wood, and threw it into the fire. And when it was in full blaze she sat down close to it, and warmed herself by it, and said, "That shines bright for once in a way."

Little Red Riding Hood
(*France*)

Once upon a time there lived in a certain village a little country girl, the prettiest creature was ever seen. Her mother was excessively fond of her; and her grandmother doted on her still more. This good woman had made for her a little red riding-hood; which became the girl so extremely well that everybody called her Little Red Riding-Hood.

One day her mother, having made some custards, said to her:

"Go, my dear, and see how thy grandmamma does, for I hear she has been very ill; carry her a custard, and this little pot of butter."

Little Red Riding-Hood set out immediately to go to her grandmother, who lived in another village.

As she was going through the wood, she met with Gaffer Wolf, who had a very great mind to eat her up, but he dared not, because of some faggot-makers hard by in the forest. He asked her whither she was going. The poor child, who did not know that it was dangerous to stay and hear a wolf talk, said to him:

"I am going to see my grandmamma and carry her a custard and a little pot of butter from my mamma."

"Does she live far off?" said the Wolf.

"Oh! ay," answered Little Red Riding-Hood; "it is beyond that mill you see there, at the first house in the village."

"Well," said the Wolf, "and I'll go and see her too. I'll go this way and you go that, and we shall see who will be there soonest."

The Wolf began to run as fast as he could, taking the nearest way, and the little girl went by that farthest about, diverting herself in gathering nuts, running after butterflies, and making nosegays of such little flowers as she met with. The Wolf was not long before he got to the old woman's house. He knocked at the door—tap, tap.

"Who's there?"

"Your grandchild, Little Red Riding-Hood," replied the Wolf, counterfeiting her voice; "who has brought you a custard and a little pot of butter sent you by mamma."

The good grandmother, who was in bed, because she was somewhat ill, cried out:

"Pull the bobbin, and the latch will go up."

The Wolf pulled the bobbin, and the door opened, and then presently he fell upon the good woman and ate her up in a moment, for it was above three days that he had not touched a bit. He then shut the door and went into the grandmother's bed, expecting Little Red Riding-Hood, who came some time afterward and knocked at the door—tap, tap.

"Who's there?"

Little Red Riding-Hood, hearing the big voice of the Wolf, was at first afraid; but believing her grandmother had got a cold and was hoarse, answered:

"'Tis your grandchild, Little Red Riding-Hood, who has brought you a custard and a little pot of butter mamma sends you."

The Wolf cried out to her, softening his voice as much as he could:

"Pull the bobbin, and the latch will go up."

Little Red Riding-Hood pulled the bobbin, and the door opened.

The Wolf, seeing her come in, said to her, hiding himself under the bedclothes:

"Put the custard and the little pot of butter upon the stool, and come and lie down with me."

Little Red Riding-Hood undressed herself and went into bed, where, being greatly amazed to see how her grandmother looked in her night-clothes, she said to her:

"Grandmamma, what great arms you have got!"

"That is the better to hug thee, my dear."

"Grandmamma, what great legs you have got!"

"That is to run the better, my child."

"Grandmamma, what great ears you have got!"

"That is to hear the better, my child."

"Grandmamma, what great eyes you have got!"

"It is to see the better, my child."

"Grandmamma, what great teeth you have got!"

"That is to eat thee up."

And, saying these words, this wicked wolf fell upon Little Red Riding-Hood, and ate her all up.

Vasilissa the Beautiful
(*Russia*)

In a certain Tsardom, across three times nine kingdoms, beyond high mountain chains, there once lived a merchant. He had been married for twelve years, but in that time there had been born to him only one child, a daughter, who from her cradle was called Vasilissa the Beautiful. When the little girl was eight years old the mother fell ill, and before many days it was plain to be seen that she must die. So she called her little daughter to her, and taking a tiny wooden doll from under the blanket of the bed, put it into her hands and said:

"My little Vasilissa, my dear daughter, listen to what I say, remember well my last words and fail not to carry out my wishes. I am dying, and with my blessing, I leave to thee this little doll. It is very precious for there is no other like it in the whole world. Carry it always about with thee in thy pocket and never show it to anyone. When evil threatens thee or sorrow befalls thee, go into a corner, take it from thy pocket and give it something to eat and drink. It will eat and drink a little, and then thou mayest tell it thy trouble and ask its advice, and it will tell thee how to act in thy time of need." So saying, she kissed her little daughter on the forehead, blessed her, and shortly after died.

Little Vasilissa grieved greatly for her mother, and her sorrow was so deep that when the dark night came, she lay in her bed and wept and did not sleep. At length she bethought herself of the tiny doll, so she rose and took it from the pocket of her gown and finding a piece of wheat bread and a cup of kvass,[1] she set them before it, and said: "There, my little doll, take it. Eat a little, and drink a little, and listen to my grief. My dear mother is dead and I am lonely for her."

Then the doll's eyes began to shine like fireflies, and suddenly it became alive. It ate a morsel of the bread and took a sip of the kvass, and when it had eaten and drunk, it said:

"Don't weep, little Vasilissa. Grief is worst at night. Lie down, shut thine eyes, comfort thyself and go to sleep. The morning is wiser than the evening." So Vasilissa the Beautiful lay down, comforted herself and went to sleep, and the next day her grieving was not so deep and her tears were less bitter.

Now after the death of his wife, the merchant sorrowed for many days as was right, but at the end of that time he began to desire to marry again and to look about him for a suitable wife. This was not difficult to find, for he had a fine house, with a stable of swift horses, besides being a good man who gave much to the poor. Of all the women he saw, however, the one who, to his mind, suited him best of all, was a widow of about his own age with two daughters of her own, and she, he thought, besides being a good housekeeper, would be a kind foster mother to his little Vasilissa.

So the merchant married the widow and brought her home as his wife, but the little girl soon found that her foster mother was very far from being what her father had thought. She was a cold, cruel woman, who had desired the merchant for the sake of his wealth, and had no love for his daughter. Vasilissa was the greatest beauty in the whole village, while her own daughters were as spare and homely as two crows, and because of this all three envied and hated her. They gave her all sorts of errands to run and difficult tasks to perform, in order that the toil might make her thin and worn and that her face might grow brown from sun and wind, and they treated her so cruelly as to leave few joys in life for her. But all this the little Vasilissa endured without complaint, and while the stepmother's two daughters grew always thinner and uglier, in spite of the fact that they had no hard tasks to do, never went out in cold or rain, and sat always with their arms folded like ladies of a Court, she herself had cheeks like blood and milk and grew every day more and more beautiful.

Now the reason for this was the tiny doll, without whose help little Vasilissa could never have managed to do all the work that was laid upon her. Each night, when everyone else was sound asleep, she would get up from her bed, take the doll into a closet, and locking the door, give it

1 An alcoholic drink made from rye bread.

something to eat and drink, and say: "There, my little doll, take it. Eat a little, drink a little, and listen to my grief. I live in my father's house, but my spiteful stepmother wishes to drive me out of the white world. Tell me! How shall I act, and what shall I do?"

Then the little doll's eyes would begin to shine like glow-worms, and it would become alive. It would eat a little food, and sip a little drink, and then it would comfort her and tell her how to act. While Vasilissa slept, it would get ready all her work for the next day, so that she had only to rest in the shade and gather flowers, for the doll would have the kitchen garden weeded, and the beds of cabbage watered, and plenty of fresh water brought from the well, and the stoves heated exactly right. And, besides this, the little doll told her how to make, from a certain herb, an ointment which prevented her from ever being sunburnt. So all the joy in life that came to Vasilissa came to her through the tiny doll that she always carried in her pocket.

Years passed, till Vasilissa grew up and became of an age when it is good to marry. All the young men in the village, high and low, rich and poor, asked for her hand, while not one of them stopped even to look at the stepmother's two daughters, so ill-favored were they. This angered their mother still more against Vasilissa; she answered every gallant who came with the same words: "Never shall the younger be wed before the older ones!" and each time, when she had let a suitor out of the door, she would soothe her anger and hatred by beating her stepdaughter. So while Vasilissa grew each day more lovely and graceful, she was often miserable, and but for the little doll in her pocket, would have longed to leave the white world.

Now there came a time when it became necessary for the merchant to leave his home and to travel to a distant Tsardom. He bade farewell to his wife and her two daughters, kissed Vasilissa and gave her his blessing and departed, bidding them say a prayer each day for his safe return. Scarce was he out of sight of the village, however, when his wife sold his house, packed all his goods and moved with them to another dwelling far from the town, in a gloomy neighborhood on the edge of a wild forest. Here every day, while her two daughters were working indoors, the merchant's wife would send Vasilissa on one errand or other into the forest, either to find a branch of a certain rare bush or to bring her flowers or berries.

Now deep in this forest, as the stepmother well knew, there was a green lawn and on the lawn stood a miserable little hut on hens' legs, where lived a certain Baba Yaga, an old witch grandmother. She lived alone and none dared go near the hut, for she ate people as one eats chickens. The merchant's wife sent Vasilissa into the forest each day, hoping she might meet the old witch and be devoured; but always the girl came home safe and sound, because the little doll showed her where the bush, the flowers and the berries grew, and did not let her go near the hut that stood on hens' legs. And each time the stepmother hated her more and more because she came to no harm.

One autumn evening the merchant's wife called the three girls to her and gave them each a task. One of her daughters she bade make a piece of lace, the other to knit a pair of hose, and to Vasilissa she gave a basket of flax to be spun. She bade each finish a certain amount. Then she put out all the fires in the house, leaving only a single candle lighted in the room where the three girls worked, and she herself went to sleep.

They worked an hour, they worked two hours, they worked three hours, when one of the elder daughters took up the tongs to straighten the wick of the candle. She pretended to do this awkwardly (as her mother had bidden her) and put the candle out, as if by accident.

"What are we to do now?" asked her sister. "The fires are all out, there is no other light in all the house, and our tasks are not done."

"We must go and fetch fire," said the first. "The only house near is a hut in the forest, where a Baba Yaga lives. One of us must go and borrow fire from her."

"I have enough light from my steel pins," said the one who was making the lace, "and I will not go."

"And I have plenty of light from my silver needles," said the other, who was knitting the hose, "and I will not go."

"Thou, Vasilissa," they both said, "shalt go and fetch the fire, for thou hast neither steel pins nor silver needles and cannot see to spin thy flax!" They both rose up, pushed Vasilissa out of the house and locked the door, crying:

"Thou shalt not come in till thou hast fetched the fire."

Vasilissa sat down on the doorstep, took the tiny doll from one pocket and from another the supper she had ready for it, put the food before it and said: "There, my little doll, take it. Eat a little and listen to my sorrow. I must go to the hut of the old Baba Yaga in the dark forest to borrow some fire and I fear she will eat me. Tell me! What shall I do?"

Then the doll's eyes began to shine like two stars and it became alive. It ate a little and said: "Do not fear, little Vasilissa. Go where thou hast been sent. While I am with thee no harm shall come to thee from the old witch." So Vasilissa put the doll back into her pocket, crossed herself and started out into the dark, wild forest.

Whether she walked a short way or a long way the telling is easy, but the journey was hard. The wood was very dark, and she could not help trembling from fear. Suddenly she heard the sound of a horse's hoofs and a man on horseback galloped past her. He was dressed all in white, the horse under him was milk-white and the harness was white, and just as he passed her it became twilight.

She went a little further and again she heard the sound of a horse's hoofs and there came another man on horseback galloping past her. He was dressed all in red, and the horse under him was blood-red and its harness was red, and just as he passed her the sun rose.

That whole day Vasilissa walked, for she had lost her way. She could find no path at all in the dark wood and she had no food to set before the little doll to make it alive.

But at evening she came all at once to the green lawn where the wretched little hut stood on its hens' legs. The wall around the hut was made of human bones and on its top were skulls. There was a gate in the wall, whose hinges were the bones of human feet and whose locks were jawbones set with sharp teeth. The sight filled Vasilissa with horror and she stopped as still as a post buried in the ground.

As she stood there a third man on horseback came galloping up. His face was black, he was dressed all in black, and the horse he rode was coal-black. He galloped up to the gate of the hut and disappeared there as if he had sunk through the ground and at that moment the night came and the forest grew dark.

But it was not dark on the green lawn, for instantly the eyes of all the skulls on the wall were lighted up and shone till the place was as bright as day. When she saw this Vasilissa trembled so with fear that she could not run away.

Then suddenly the wood became full of a terrible noise; the trees began to groan, the branches to creak and the dry leaves to rustle, and the Baba Yaga came flying from the forest. She was riding in a great iron mortar and driving it with the pestle, and as she came she swept away her trail behind her with a kitchen broom.

She rode up to the gate and stopping, said:

> *Little House, little House,*
> *Stand the way thy mother placed thee,*
> *Turn thy back to the forest and thy face to me!*

And the little hut turned facing her and stood still. Then smelling all around her, she cried: "Foo! Foo! I smell a smell that is Russian. Who is here?"

Vasilissa, in great fright, came nearer to the old woman and bowing very low, said: "It is only Vasilissa, grandmother. My stepmother's daughters sent me to thee to borrow some fire."

"Well," said the old witch, "I know them. But if I give thee the fire thou shalt stay with me some time and do some work to pay for it. If not, thou shalt be eaten for my supper." Then she turned to the gate and shouted: "Ho! Ye, my solid locks, unlock! Thou, my stout gate, open!" Instantly the locks unlocked, the gate opened of itself, and the Baba Yaga rode in whistling. Vasilissa entered behind her and immediately the gate shut again and the locks snapped tight.

When they had entered the hut the old witch threw herself down on the stove, stretched out her bony legs and said:

"Come, fetch and put on the table at once everything that is in the oven. I am hungry." So Vasilissa ran and lighted a splinter of wood from one of the skulls on the wall and took the food from the oven and set it before her. There was enough cooked meat for three strong men. She brought also from the cellar kvass, honey, and red wine, and the Baba Yaga ate and drank the whole, leaving the girl only a little cabbage soup, a crust of bread and a morsel of suckling pig.

When her hunger was satisfied, the old witch, growing drowsy, lay down on the stove and said: "Listen to me well, and do what I bid thee. Tomorrow when I drive away, do thou clean the yard, sweep the floors and cook my supper. Then take a quarter of a measure of wheat from my store house and pick out of it all the black grains and the wild peas. Mind thou dost all that I have bade; if not, thou shalt be eaten for my supper."

Presently the Baba Yaga turned toward the wall and began to snore and Vasilissa knew that she was fast asleep. Then she went into the corner, took the tiny doll from her pocket, put before it a bit of bread and a little cabbage soup that she had saved, burst into tears and said: "There, my little doll, take it. Eat a little, drink a little, and listen to my grief. Here I am in the house of the old witch and the gate in the wall is locked and I am afraid. She has given me a difficult task and if I do not do all she has bade, she will eat me tomorrow. Tell me: What shall I do?"

Then the eyes of the little doll began to shine like two candles. It ate a little of the bread and drank a little of the soup and said: "Do not be afraid, Vasilissa the Beautiful. Be comforted. Say thy prayers, and go to sleep. The morning is wiser than the evening." So Vasilissa trusted the little doll and was comforted. She said her prayers, lay down on the floor and went fast asleep.

When she woke next morning, very early, it was still dark. She rose and looked out of the window, and she saw that the eyes of the skulls on the wall were growing dim. As she looked, the man dressed all in white, riding the milk-white horse, galloped swiftly around the corner of the hut, leaped the wall and disappeared, and as he went, it became quite light and the eyes of the skulls flickered and went out. The old witch was in the yard; now she began to whistle and the great iron mortar and pestle and the kitchen broom flew out of the hut to her. As she got into the mortar the man dressed all in red, mounted on the blood-red horse, galloped like the wind around the corner of the hut, leaped the wall and was gone, and at that moment the sun rose. Then the Baba Yaga shouted: "Ho! Ye, my solid locks, unlock! Thou, my stout gate, open!" And the locks unlocked and the gate opened and she rode away in the mortar, driving with the pestle and sweeping away her path behind her with the broom.

When Vasilissa found herself left alone, she examined the hut, wondering to find it filled with such an abundance of everything. Then she stood still, remembering all the work that she had been bidden to do and wondering what to begin first. But as she looked she rubbed her eyes, for the yard was already neatly cleaned and the floors were nicely swept, and the little doll was sitting in the storehouse picking the last black grains and wild peas out of the quarter-measure of wheat.

Vasilissa ran and took the little doll in her arms. "My dearest little doll!" she cried. "Thou hast saved me from my trouble! Now I have only to cook the Baba Yaga's supper, since all the rest of the tasks are done!"

"Cook it, with God's help," said the doll, "and then rest, and may the cooking of it make thee healthy!" And so saying it crept into her pocket and became again only a little wooden doll.

So Vasilissa rested all day and was refreshed; and when it grew toward evening she laid the table for the old witch's supper, and sat looking out of the window, waiting for her coming. After awhile she heard the sound of a horse's hoofs and the man in black, on the coal-black horse, galloped up to the wall gate and disappeared like a great dark shadow, and instantly it became quite dark and the eyes of all the skulls began to glitter and shine.

Then all at once the trees of the forest began to creak and groan and the leaves and the bushes to moan and sigh, and the Baba Yaga came riding out of the dark wood in the huge iron mortar, driving with the pestle and sweeping out the trail behind her with the kitchen broom. Vasilissa let her in; and the witch, smelling all around her, asked:

"Well, hast thou done perfectly all the tasks I gave thee to do, or am I to eat thee for my supper?"

"Be so good as to look for thyself, grandmother," answered Vasilissa.

The Baba Yaga went all about the place, tapping with her iron pestle, and carefully examining everything. But so well had the little doll done its work that, try as hard as she might, she could not find anything to complain of. There was not a weed left in the yard, nor a speck of dust on the floors, nor a single black grain or wild pea in the wheat.

The old witch was greatly angered, but was obliged to pretend to be pleased. "Well," she said, "thou hast done all well." Then, clapping her hands, she shouted: "Ho! my faithful servants! Friends of my heart! Haste and grind my wheat!" Immediately three pairs of hands appeared, seized the measure of wheat and carried it away.

The Baba Yaga sat down to supper, and Vasilissa put before her all the food from the oven, with kvass, honey, and red wine. The old witch ate it, bones and all, almost to the last morsel, enough for four strong men, and then, growing drowsy, stretched her bony legs on the stove and said: "To-morrow do as thou hast done today, and besides these tasks take from my storehouse a half-measure of poppy seeds and clean them one by one. Someone has mixed earth with them to do me a mischief and to anger me, and I will have them made perfectly clean." So saying she turned to the wall and soon began to snore.

When she was fast asleep Vasilissa went into the corner, took the little doll from her pocket, set before it a part of the food that was left and asked its advice. And the doll, when it had become alive, and eaten a little food and sipped a little drink, said: "Don't worry, beautiful Vasilissa! Be comforted. Do as thou didst last night: say thy prayers and go to sleep." So Vasilissa was comforted. She said her prayers and went to sleep and did not wake till next morning when she heard the old witch in the yard whistling. She ran to the window just in time to see her take her place in the big iron mortar, and as she did so the man dressed all in red, riding on the blood red horse, leaped over the wall and was gone, just as the sun rose over the wild forest.

As it had happened on the first morning, so it happened now. When Vasilissa looked she found that the little doll had finished all the tasks excepting the cooking of the supper. The yard was swept and in order, the floors were as clean as new wood, and there was not a grain of earth left in the half-measure of poppy seeds. She rested and refreshed herself till the afternoon, when she cooked the supper, and when evening came she laid the table and sat down to wait for the old witch's coming.

Soon the man in black, on the coal-black horse, galloped up to the gate, and the dark fell and the eyes of the skulls began to shine like day; then the ground began to quake, and the trees of the forest began to creak and the dry leaves to rustle, and the Baba Yaga came riding in her iron mortar, driving with her pestle and sweeping away her path with her broom.

When she came in she smelled around her and went all about the hut, tapping with the pestle; but pry and examine as she might, again she could see no reason to find fault and was angrier than ever. She clapped her hands and shouted:

"Ho! my trusty servants! Friends of my soul! Haste and press the oil out of my poppy seeds!" And instantly the three pairs of hands appeared, seized the measure of poppy seeds and carried it away.

Presently the old witch sat down to supper and Vasilissa brought all she had cooked, enough for five grown men, and set it before her, and brought beer and honey, and then she herself stood silently waiting. The Baba Yaga ate and drank it all, every morsel, leaving not so much as a crumb of bread; then she said snappishly: "Well, why dost thou say nothing, but stand there as if thou wast dumb?"

"I spoke not," Vasilissa answered, "because I dared not. But if thou wilt allow me, grandmother, I wish to ask thee some questions."

"Well," said the old witch, "only remember that every question does not lead to good. If thou knowest overmuch, thou wilt grow old too soon. What wilt thou ask?"

"I would ask thee," said Vasilissa, "of the men on horseback. When I came to thy hut, a rider passed me. He was dressed all in white and he rode a milk-white horse. Who was he?"

"That was my white, bright day," answered the Baba Yaga angrily. "He is a servant of mine, but he cannot hurt thee. Ask me more."

"Afterwards," said Vasilissa, "a second rider overtook me. He was dressed in red and the horse he rode was blood-red. Who was he?"

"That was my servant, the round, red sun," answered the Baba Yaga, "and he, too, cannot injure thee," and she ground her teeth. "Ask me more."

"A third rider," said Vasilissa, "came galloping up to the gate. He was black, his clothes were black and the horse was coal-black. Who was he?"

"That was my servant, the black, dark night," answered the old witch furiously; "but he also cannot harm thee. Ask me more."

But Vasilissa, remembering what the Baba Yaga had said, that not every question led to good, was silent.

"Ask me more!" cried the old witch. "Why dost thou not ask me more? Ask me of the three pairs of hands that serve me!"

But Vasilissa saw how she snarled at her and she answered: "The three questions are enough for me. As thou hast said, grandmother, I would not, through knowing over much, become too soon old."

"It is well for thee," said the Baba Yaga, "that thou didst not ask of them, but only of what thou didst see outside of this hut. Hadst thou asked of them, my servants, the three pairs of hands would have seized thee also, as they did the wheat and poppy seeds, to be my food. Now I would ask a question in my turn: How is it that thou hast been able, in a little time, to do perfectly all the tasks I gave thee? Tell me!"

Vasilissa was so frightened to see how the old witch ground her teeth that she almost told her of the little doll; but she bethought herself just in time, and answered: "The blessing of my dead mother helps me."

Then the Baba Yaga sprang up in a fury. "Get thee out of my house this moment!" she shrieked. "I want no one who bears a blessing to cross my threshold! Get thee gone!"

Vasilissa ran to the yard, and behind her she heard the old witch shouting to the locks and the gate. The locks opened, the gate swung wide, and she ran out on to the lawn. The Baba Yaga seized from the wall one of the skulls with burning eyes and flung it after her. "There," she howled, "is the fire for thy stepmother's daughters. Take it. That is what they sent thee here for, and may they have joy of it!"

Vasilissa put the skull on the end of a stick and darted away through the forest, running as fast as she could, finding her path by the skull's glowing eyes which went out only when morning came.

Whether she ran a long way or a short way, and whether the road was smooth or rough, towards evening of the next day, when the eyes in the skull were beginning to glimmer, she came out of the dark, wild forest to her stepmother's house.

When she came near to the gate, she thought, "Surely, by this time they will have found some fire," and threw the skull into the hedge; but it spoke to her, and said: "Do not throw me away, beautiful Vasilissa; bring me to thy stepmother." So, looking at the house and seeing no spark of light in any of the windows, she took up the skull again and carried it with her.

Now since Vasilissa had gone, the stepmother and her two daughters had had neither fire nor light in all the house. When they struck flint and steel the tinder would not catch, and the fire they brought from the neighbors would go out immediately as soon as they carried it over the threshold, so that they had been unable to light or warm themselves or to cook food to eat. Therefore now, for the first time in her life, Vasilissa found herself welcomed. They opened the door to her and the merchant's wife was greatly rejoiced to find that the light in the skull did not go out as soon as it was brought in. "Maybe the witch's fire will stay," she said, and took the skull into the best room, set it on a candlestick and called her two daughters to admire it.

But the eyes of the skull suddenly began to glimmer and to glow like red coals, and wherever the three turned or ran the eyes followed them, growing larger and brighter till they flamed like two furnaces, and hotter and hotter till the merchant's wife and her two wicked daughters took fire and were burned to ashes. Only Vasilissa the Beautiful was not touched.

In the morning Vasilissa dug a deep hole in the ground and buried the skull. Then she locked the house and set out to the village, where she went to live with an old woman who was poor and childless, and so she remained for many days, waiting for her father's return from the far-distant Tsardom.

But, sitting lonely, time soon began to hang heavy on her hands. One day she said to the old woman: "It is dull for me, grandmother, to sit idly hour by hour. My hands want work to do. Go, therefore, and buy me some flax, the best and finest to be found anywhere, and at least I can spin."

The old woman hastened and bought some flax of the best sort and Vasilissa sat down to work. So well did she spin that the thread came out as even and fine as a hair, and presently there was enough to begin to weave. But so fine was the thread that no frame could be found to weave it upon, nor would any weaver undertake to make one.

Then Vasilissa went into her closet, took the little doll from her pocket, set food and drink before it and asked its help. And after it had eaten a little and drunk a little, the doll became alive and said: "Bring me an old frame and an old basket and some hairs from a horse's mane, and I will arrange everything for thee." Vasilissa hastened to fetch all the doll had asked for and when evening came, said her prayers, went to sleep, and in the morning she found ready a frame, perfectly made, to weave her fine thread upon.

She wove one month, she wove two months—all the winter Vasilissa sat weaving, weaving her fine thread, till the whole piece of linen was done, of a texture so fine that it could be passed, like thread, through the eye of a needle. When the spring came she bleached it, so white that no snow could be compared with it. Then she said to the old woman: "Take thou the linen to the market, grandmothers and sell it, and the money shall suffice to pay for my food and lodging." When the old woman examined the linen, however, she said:

"Never will I sell such cloth in the market place; no one should wear it except it be the Tsar himself, and tomorrow I shall carry it to the Palace."

Next day, accordingly, the old woman went to the Tsar's splendid Palace and fell to walking up and down before the windows. The servants came to ask her her errand but she answered them nothing, and kept walking up and down. At length the Tsar opened his window, and asked: "What dost thou want, old woman, that thou walkest here?"

"O Tsar's Majesty" the old woman answered, "I have with me a marvelous piece of linen stuff, so wondrously woven that I will show it to none but thee."

The Tsar bade them bring her before him and when he saw the linen he was struck with astonishment at its fineness and beauty. "What wilt thou take for it, old woman?" he asked.

"There is no price that can buy it, Little Father Tsar," she answered; "but I have brought it to thee as a gift." The Tsar could not thank the old woman enough. He took the linen and sent her to her house with many rich presents.

Seamstresses were called to make shirts for him out of the cloth; but when it had been cut up, so fine was it that no one of them was deft and skillful enough to sew it. The best seamstresses in all the Tsardom were summoned but none dared undertake it. So at last the Tsar sent for the old woman and said: "If thou didst know how to spin such thread and weave such linen, thou must also know how to sew me shirts from it."

And the old woman answered: "O Tsar's Majesty, it was not I who wove the linen; it is the work of my adopted daughter."

"Take it, then," the Tsar said, "and bid her do it for me." The old woman brought the linen home and told Vasilissa the Tsar's command: "Well I knew that the work would needs be done by my own hands," said Vasilissa, and, locking herself in her own room, began to make the shirts. So fast and well did she work that soon a dozen were ready. Then the old woman carried them to the Tsar, while Vasilissa washed her face, dressed her hair, put on her best gown and sat down at the window to see what would happen. And presently a servant in the livery of the Palace came to the house and entering, said: "The Tsar, our lord, desires himself to see the clever needlewoman who has made his shirts and to reward her with his own hands."

Vasilissa rose and went at once to the Palace, and as soon as the Tsar saw her, he fell in love with her with all his soul. He took her by her white hand and made her sit beside him. "Beautiful maiden," he said, "never will I part from thee and thou shalt be my wife."

So the Tsar and Vasilissa the Beautiful were married, and her father returned from the far-distant Tsardom, and he and the old woman lived always with her in the splendid Palace, in all joy and contentment. And as for the little wooden doll, she carried it about with her in her pocket all her life long.

363: The Corpse-Eater

The Brown Man

The Brown Man
(*Ireland*)

In a lonely cabin, in a lonely glen, on the shores of a lonely lough, in one of the most lonesome districts of west Munster, lived a lone woman named Guare. She had a beautiful girl, a daughter named Nora. Their cabin was the only one within three miles round them every way. As to their mode of living, it was simple enough, for all they had was one little garden of white cabbage, and they had eaten that down to a few heads between them, a sorry prospect in a place where even a handful of *prishoc* weed was not to be had without sowing it.

It was a fine morning in those parts, for it was only snowing and hailing, when Nora and her mother were sitting at the door of their little cottage, and laying out plans for the next day's dinner. On a sudden, a strange horseman rode up to the door. He was strange in more ways than one. He was dressed in brown, his hair was brown, his eyes were brown, his boots were brown, he rode a brown horse, and he was followed by a brown dog.

"I'm come to marry you, Nora Guare," said the Brown Man.

"Ax my mother fusht, if you plaise, sir," said Nora, dropping him a curtsy.

"You'll not refuse, ma'am;" said the Brown Man to the old mother, "I have money enough, and I'll make your daughter a lady, with servants at her call, and all manner of fine doings about her." And so saying, he flung a purse of gold into the widow's lap.

"Why then the heavens speed you and her together, take her away with you, and make much of her," said the old mother, quite bewildered with all the money.

"Agh, agh," said the Brown Man, as he placed her on his horse behind him without more ado. "Are you all ready now?"

"I am!" said the bride. The horse snorted, and the dog barked, and almost before the word was out of her mouth, they were all whisked away out of sight. After travelling a day and a night, faster than the wind itself, the Brown Man pulled up his horse in the middle of the Mangerton mountain, in one of the most lonesome places that eye ever looked on.

"Here is my estate," said the Brown Man.

"A'then, is it this wild bog you call an estate?" said the bride.

"Come in, wife; this is my palace," said the bridegroom.

"What! A clay-hovel, worse than my mother's!"

They dismounted, and the horse and the dog disappeared in an instant, with a horrible noise, which the girl did not know whether to call snorting, barking, or laughing.

"Are you hungry?" said the Brown Man. "If so, there is your dinner."

"A handful of raw white-eyes,[1] and a grain of salt!"

"And when you are sleepy, here is your bed," he continued, pointing to a little straw in a corner, at sight of which Nora's limbs shivered and trembled again. It may be easily supposed that she did not make a very hearty dinner that evening, nor did her husband either.

In the dead of the night, when the clock of Mucruss Abbey had just tolled one, a low nighing[2] at the door, and a soft barking at the window were heard. Nora feigned sleep. The Brown Man passed his hand over her eyes and face. She snored. "I'm coming," said he, and he arose gently from her side. In half an hour after she felt him by her side again. He was cold as ice.

The next night the same summons came. The bell tolled at Mucruss, and was heard across the lakes. The Brown Man rose again, and passed a light before the eyes of the feigning sleeper. None slumber so sound as they who *will* not wake. Her heart trembled, but her frame was quiet and firm. A voice at the door summoned the husband.

"You are very long in coming. The earth is tossed up, and I am hungry. Hurry! Hurry! Hurry! if you would not lose all."

"I'm coming!" said the Brown Man. Nora rose and followed instantly. She beheld him at a distance winding through a lane of frost-nipt sallow trees. He often paused and looked back, and once or twice retraced his steps to within a few yards of the tree, behind which she had shrunk. The moon-light, cutting the shadow close and dark about her, afforded the best concealment. He again proceeded, and she followed. In a few minutes they reached the old Abbey of Mucruss. With a sickening heart she saw him enter the church-yard. The wind rushed through the huge yew-tree and startled her. She mustered courage enough, however, to reach the gate of the church-yard and look in. The Brown Man, the horse, and the dog were there seated by an open grave, eating something; and glancing their brown, fiery eyes about in every direction. The moon-light shone full on them and her. Looking down towards her shadow on the earth, she started with horror to observe it move, although she was herself perfectly still. It waved its black arms, and motioned her back. What the feasters said, she understood not, but she seemed still fixed in the spot. She looked once more on her shadow; it raised one hand, and pointed the way to the lane; then slowly rising from the ground, and confronting her, it walked

1 Potatoes.
2 Approaching.

rapidly off in that direction. She walked off as quickly as might be.

She was scarcely in her straw, when the door creaked behind, and her husband entered. He lay down by her side, and started.

"Uf! Uf!" said she, pretending to be just awakened, "how cold you are, my love!"

"Cold inagh? Indeed you're not very warm yourself, my dear, I'm thinking."

"Little admiration I shouldn't be warm, and you leaving me alone this way at night, till my blood is snow broth, no less."

"Umph!" said the Brown Man, as he passed his arm round her waist. "Ha! your heart is beating fast?"

"Little admiration it should. I am not well, indeed. Them praties and salt don't agree with me at all."

"Umph!" said the Brown Man.

The next morning as they were sitting at the breakfast table together, Nora plucked up a heart, and asked leave to go to see her mother. The Brown Man, who ate nothing, looked at her in a way that made her think he knew all. She felt her spirit die away within her.

"If you only want to see your mother," said he, "there is no occasion for your going home. I will bring her to you here. I didn't marry you to be keeping you gadding."

The Brown Man then went out and whistled for his dog and his horse. They both came; and in a very few minutes they pulled up at the old widow's cabin-door.

The poor woman was very glad to see her son-in-law, though she did not know what could bring him so soon.

"Your daughter sends her love to you, mother," says the Brown Man, the villain, "and she'd be obliged to you for a *loan* of a *shoot* of your best clothes, as she's going to give a grand party, and the dress-maker has disappointed her."

"To be sure and welcome," said the mother; and making up a bundle of the clothes, she put them into his hands.

"Whogh! whogh!" said the horse as they drove off, "that was well done. Are we to have a mail of her?"

"Easy, ma-coppuleen, and you'll get your 'nough before night," said the Brown Man, "and you likewise my little dog."

"Boh!" cried the dog, "I'm in no hurry—I hunted down a doe this morning that was fed with milk from the horns of the moon."

Often in the course of that day did Nora Guare go to the door, and cast her eye over the weary flat before it, to discern, if possible, the distant figures of her bridegroom and mother. The dusk of the second evening found her alone in the desolate cot. She listened to every sound. At length the door opened, and an old woman, dressed in a new *jock*,[1] and leaning on a staff, entered the hut. "O mother, are you come?" said Nora, and was about to rush into her arms, when the old woman stopped her.

"Whisht! whisht! my child!—I only stepped in before the man to know how you like him? Speak softly, in dread he'd hear you—he's turning the horse loose, in the swamp, abroad, over."

"O mother, mother! such a story!"

"Whisht! easy again—how does he use you?"

"Sarrow[2] worse. That straw my bed, and them white-eyes—and bad ones they are—all my diet. And 'tisn't that same, only—"

"Whisht! easy agin! He'll hear you, maybe—Well?"

"I'd be easy enough only for his own doings. Listen, mother. The fusht night, I came about twelve o'clock—"

"Easy, speak easy, eroo!"

"He got up at the call of the horse and the dog, and stayed out a good hour. He ate nothing next day. The second night, and the second day, it was the same story. The third—"

"Husht! husht! Well, the third night?"

"The third night I said I'd watch him. Mother, don't hold my hand so hard… He got up, and I got up after him… Oh, don't laugh, mother, for 'tis frightful… I followed him to Mucruss church-yard… Mother, mother, you hurt my hand… I looked in at the gate—there was great moonlight there, and I could see everything plain as day."

"Well, darling—husht! softly! What did you see?"

"My husband by the grave, and the horse… Turn your head aside, mother, for your breath is very hot… and the dog and they eating—Ah, you are not my mother!" shrieked the miserable girl, as the Brown Man flung off his disguise, and stood before her, grinning worse than a black-smith's face through a horse-collar. He just looked at her one moment, and then darted his long fingers into her bosom, from which the red blood spouted in so many streams. She was very soon out of all pain, and a mer-ry supper the horse, the dog, and the Brown Man had that night, by all accounts.

1 Outfit.
2 Sorrow.

The Fiend
(*Russia*)

In a certain country there lived an old couple who had a daughter called Marusia (Mary). In their village it was customary to celebrate the feast of St. Andrew the First-Called.[1] The girls used to assemble in some cottage, bake *pampushki*,[2] and enjoy themselves for a whole week, or even longer. Well, the girls met together once when this festival arrived, and brewed and baked what was wanted. In the evening came the lads with the music, bringing liquor with them, and dancing and revelry commenced. All the girls danced well, but Marusia the best of all. After a while there came into the cottage such a fine fellow! Marry, come up! regular blood and milk, and smartly and richly dressed.

"Hail, fair maidens!" says he.

"Hail, good youth!" say they.

"You're merry-making?"

"Be so good as to join us."

Thereupon he pulled out of his pocket a purse full of gold, ordered liquor, nuts and gingerbread. All was ready in a trice, and he began treating the lads and lasses, giving each a share. Then he took to dancing. Why, it was a treat to look at him! Marusia struck his fancy more than anyone else; so he stuck close to her. The time came for going home.

"Marusia," says he, "come and see me off."

She went to see him off.

"Marusia, sweetheart!" says he, "would you like me to marry you?"

"If you like to marry me, I will gladly marry you. But where do you come from?"

"From such and such a place. I'm clerk at a merchant's."

Then they bade each other farewell and separated. When Marusia got home, her mother asked her:

"Well, daughter! have you enjoyed yourself?"

"Yes, mother. But I've something pleasant to tell you besides. There was a lad there from the neighborhood, good-looking and with lots of money, and he promised to marry me."

"Hark ye Marusia! When you go to where the girls are to-morrow, take a ball of thread with you, make a noose in it, and, when you are going to see him off, throw it over one of his buttons, and quietly unroll the ball; then, by means of the thread, you will be able to find out where he lives."

Next day Marusia went to the gathering, and took a ball of thread with

1 November 30.
2 A small, savoury bun.

her. The youth came again.

"Good evening, Marusia!" said he.

"Good evening!" said she.

Games began and dances. Even more than before did he stick to Marusia, not a step would he budge from her. The time came for going home.

"Come and see me off, Marusia!" says the stranger.

She went out into the street, and while she was taking leave of him she quietly dropped the noose over one of his buttons. He went his way, but she remained where she was, unrolling the ball. When she had unrolled the whole of it, she ran after the thread to find out where her betrothed lived. At first the thread followed the road, then it stretched across hedges and ditches, and led Marusia towards the church and right up to the porch. Marusia tried the door; it was locked. She went round the church, found a ladder, set it against a window, and climbed up it to see what was going on inside. Having got into the church, she looked—and saw her betrothed standing beside a grave and devouring a dead body—for a corpse had been left for that night in the church.

She wanted to get down the ladder quietly, but her fright prevented her from taking proper heed, and she made a little noise. Then she ran home—almost beside herself, fancying all the time she was being pursued. She was all but dead before she got in. Next morning her mother asked her:

"Well, Marusia! did you see the youth?"

"I saw him, mother," she replied. But what else she had seen she did not tell.

In the morning Marusia was sitting, considering whether she would go to the gathering or not.

"Go," said her mother. "Amuse yourself while you're young!"

So she went to the gathering; the Fiend was there already. Games, fun, dancing, began anew; the girls knew nothing of what had happened. When they began to separate and go homewards:

"Come, Marusia!" says the Evil One, "see me off."

She was afraid, and didn't stir. Then all the other girls opened out upon her.

"What are you thinking about? Have you grown so bashful, forsooth? Go and see the good lad off."

There was no help for it. Out she went, not knowing what would come of it. As soon as they got into the streets he began questioning her:

"You were in the church last night?"

"No."

"And saw what I was doing there?"

"No."

"Very well! To-morrow your father will die!"

Having said this, he disappeared.

Marusia returned home grave and sad. When she woke up in the morning, her father lay dead!

They wept and wailed over him, and laid him in the coffin. In the evening her mother went off to the priest's, but Marusia remained at home. At last she became afraid of being alone in the house. "Suppose I go to my friends," she thought. So she went, and found the Evil One there.

"Good evening, Marusia! why aren't you merry?"

"How can I be merry? My father is dead!"

"Oh! poor thing!"

They all grieved for her. Even the Accursed One himself grieved; just as if it hadn't all been his own doing. By and by they began saying farewell and going home.

"Marusia," says he, "see me off."

She didn't want to.

"What are you thinking of, child?" insist the girls. "What are you afraid of? Go and see him off."

So she went to see him off. They passed out into the street.

"Tell me, Marusia," says he, "were you in the church?"

"No."

"Did you see what I was doing?"

"No."

"Very well! To-morrow your mother will die."

He spoke and disappeared. Marusia returned home sadder than ever. The night went by; next morning, when she awoke, her mother lay dead! She cried all day long; but when the sun set, and it grew dark around, Marusia became afraid of being left alone; so she went to her companions.

"Why, whatever's the matter with you? you're clean out of countenance!" say the girls.

"How am I likely to be cheerful? Yesterday my father died, and to-day my mother."

"Poor thing! Poor unhappy girl!" they all exclaim sympathizingly.

Well, the time came to say good-bye. "See me off, Marusia," says the Fiend. So she went out to see him off.

"Tell me; were you in the church?"

"No."

"And saw what I was doing?"

"No."

"Very well! To-morrow evening you will die yourself!"

Marusia spent the night with her friends; in the morning she got up and considered what she should do. She bethought herself that she had a grandmother—an old, very old woman, who had become blind from length of years. "Suppose I go and ask her advice," she said, and then went off to her grandmother's.

"Good-day, granny!" says she.

"Good-day, granddaughter! What news is there with you? How are your father and mother?"

"They are dead, granny," replied the girl, and then told her all that had happened.

The old woman listened, and said:—

"Oh dear me! my poor unhappy child! Go quickly to the priest, and ask him this favor—that if you die, your body shall not be taken out of the house through the doorway, but that the ground shall be dug away from under the threshold, and that you shall be dragged out through that opening. And also beg that you may be buried at a crossway, at a spot where four roads meet."

Marusia went to the priest, wept bitterly, and made him promise to do everything according to her grandmother's instructions. Then she returned home, bought a coffin, lay down in it, and straightway expired.

Well, they told the priest, and he buried, first her father and mother, and then Marusia herself. Her body was passed underneath the threshold and buried at a crossway.

Soon afterwards a seigneur's son happened to drive past Marusia's grave. On that grave he saw growing a wondrous flower, such a one as he had never seen before. Said the young seigneur to his servant:—

"Go and pluck up that flower by the roots. We'll take it home and put it in a flower-pot. Perhaps it will blossom there."

Well, they dug up the flower, took it home, put it in a glazed flower-pot, and set it in a window. The flower began to grow larger and more beautiful. One night the servant hadn't gone to sleep somehow, and he happened to be looking at the window, when he saw a wondrous thing take place. All of a sudden the flower began to tremble, then it fell from its stem to the ground, and turned into a lovely maiden. The flower was beautiful, but the maiden was more beautiful still. She wandered from room to room, got herself various things to eat and drink, ate and drank, then stamped upon the ground and became a flower as before, mounted to the window, and resumed her place upon the stem. Next day the servant told the young seigneur of the wonders which he had seen during the night.

"Ah, brother!" said the youth, "why didn't you wake me? To-night we'll both keep watch together."

The night came; they slept not, but watched. Exactly at twelve o'clock the blossom began to shake, flew from place to place, and then fell to the ground, and the beautiful maiden appeared, got herself things to eat and drink, and sat down to supper. The young seigneur rushed forward and seized her by her white hands. Impossible was it for him sufficiently to look at her, to gaze on her beauty!

Next morning he said to his father and mother, "Please allow me to get married. I've found myself a bride."

His parents gave their consent. As for Marusia, she said:

"Only on this condition will I marry you—that for four years I need not go to church."

"Very good," said he.

Well, they were married, and they lived together one year, two years, and had a son. But one day they had visitors at their house, who enjoyed themselves, and drank, and began bragging about their wives. This one's wife was handsome; that one's was handsomer still.

"You may say what you like," says the host, "but a handsomer wife than mine does not exist in the whole world!"

"Handsome, yes!" reply the guests, "but a heathen."

"How so?"

"Why, she never goes to church."

Her husband found these observations distasteful. He waited till Sunday, and then told his wife to get dressed for church.

"I don't care what you may say," says he. "Go and get ready directly."

Well, they got ready, and went to church. The husband went in—didn't see anything particular. But when she looked round—there was the Fiend sitting at a window.

"Ha! here you are, at last!" he cried. "Remember old times. Were you in the church that night?"

"No."

"And did you see what I was doing there?"

"No."

"Very well! To-morrow both your husband and your son will die."

Marusia rushed straight out of the church and away to her grandmother. The old woman gave her two phials, the one full of holy water, the other of the water of life, and told her what she was to do. Next day both Marusia's husband and her son died. Then the Fiend came flying to her and asked:—

"Tell me; were you in the church?"

"I was."

"And did you see what I was doing?"

"You were eating a corpse."

She spoke, and splashed the holy water over him; in a moment he turned into mere dust and ashes, which blew to the winds. Afterwards she sprinkled her husband and her boy with the water of life: straightway they revived. And from that time forward they knew neither sorrow nor separation, but they all lived together long and happily.

The Vampire
(*Romania*)

There was an old woman in a village. And grown-up maidens met and span, and made a 'bee.' And the young sparks came and laid hold of the girls, and pulled them about and kissed them. But one girl had no sweetheart to lay hold of her and kiss her. And she was a strapping lass, the daughter of wealthy peasants; but three whole days no one came near her. And she looked at the big girls, her comrades. And no one troubled himself with her. Yet she was a pretty girl, a prettier was not to be found. Then came a fine young spark, and took her in his arms and kissed her, and stayed with her until cock-crow. And when the cock crowed at dawn he departed. The old woman saw he had cock's feet. And she kept looking at the lad's feet, and she said, 'Nita, my lass, did you see anything?'

'I didn't notice.'

'Then didn't I see he had cock's feet?'

'Let be, mother, I didn't see it.'

And the girl went home and slept; and she arose and went off to the spinning, where many more girls were holding a 'bee.' And the young sparks came, and took each one his sweetheart. And they kissed them, and stayed a while, and went home. And the girl's handsome young spark came and took her in his arms and kissed her and pulled her about, and stayed with her till midnight. And the cock began to crow. The young spark heard the cock crowing, and departed. What said the old woman who was in the hut, 'Nita, did you notice that he had horse's hoofs?'

'And if he had, I didn't see.'

Then the girl departed to her home. And she slept and arose in the morning, and did her work that she had to do. And night came, and she took her spindle and went to the old woman in the hut. And the other girls came, and the young sparks came, and each laid hold of his sweetheart. But the pretty girl looks at them. Then the young sparks gave over and departed home. And only the girl remained neither a long time nor a short time. Then came the girl's young spark. Then what will the girl do? She took heed, and stuck a needle and thread in his back. And he departed when the cock crew, and she knew not where he had gone to. Then the girl arose in the morning and took the thread, and followed up the thread, and saw him in a grave where he was sitting. Then the girl trembled and went back home. At night the young spark that was in the grave came to the old woman's house and saw that the girl was not there. He asked the old woman, 'Where's Nita?'

'She has not come.'

Then he went to Nita's house, where she lived, and called, 'Nita, are you at home?'

Nita answered, 'I am'.

'Tell me what you saw when you came to the church. For if you don't tell me I will kill your father.'

'I didn't see anything.'

Then he looked, and he killed her father, and departed to his grave.

Next night he came back. 'Nita, tell me what you saw.' I didn't see anything.'

'Tell me, or I will kill your mother, as I killed your father. Tell me what you saw.'

'I didn't see anything.'

Then he killed her mother, and departed to his grave. Then the girl arose in the morning. And she had twelve servants. And she said to them, 'See, I have much money and many oxen and many sheep; and they shall come to the twelve of you as a gift, for I shall die to-night. And it will fare ill with you if you bury me not in the forest at the foot of an apple-tree.'

At night came the young spark from the grave and asked, Nita, are you at home?'

'I am.'

'Tell me, Nita, what you saw three days ago, or I will kill you, as I killed your parents.'

'I have nothing to tell you.'

Then he took and killed her. Then, casting a look, he departed to his grave.

So the servants, when they arose in the morning, found Nita dead. The servants took her and laid her out decently. They sat and made a hole in the wall and passed her through the hole, and carried her, as she had bidden, and buried her in the forest by the apple-tree.

And half a year passed by, and a prince went to go and course hares with greyhounds and other dogs. And he went to hunt, and the hounds ranged the forest and came to the maiden's grave. And a flower grew out of it, the like of which for beauty there was not in the whole kingdom. So the hounds came on her monument, where she was buried, and they began to bark and scratched at the maiden's grave. Then the prince took and called the dogs with his horn, and the dogs came not. The prince said, 'Go quickly thither.'

Four huntsmen arose and came and saw the flower burning like a candle. They returned to the prince, and he asked them, 'What is it?'

'It is a flower, the like was never seen.'

Then the lad heard, and came to the maiden's grave, and saw the flower and plucked it. And he came home and showed it to his father and mother. Then he took and put it in a vase at his bed-head where he slept. Then the flower arose from the vase and turned a somersault, and became a full-grown maiden. And she took the lad and kissed him, and bit him and pulled him about, and slept with him in her arms, and put her hand under his head. And he knew it not. When the dawn came she became a flower again.

In the morning the lad rose up sick, and complained to his father and mother, 'Mammy, my shoulders hurt me, and my head hurts me.'

His mother went and brought a wise woman and tended him. He asked for something to eat and drink. And he waited a bit, and then went to his business that he had to do. And he went home again at night. And he ate and drank and lay down on his couch, and sleep seized him. Then the flower arose and again became a full-grown maiden. And she took him again in her arms, and slept with him, and sat with him in her arms. And he slept. And she went back to the vase. And he arose, and his bones hurt him, and he told his mother and his father. Then his father said to his wife, 'It began with the coming of the flower. Something must be the matter, for the boy is quite ill. Let us watch to-night, and post ourselves on one side, and see who comes to our son.'

Night came, and the prince laid himself in his bed to sleep. Then the maiden arose from the vase, and became there was never anything more fair—as burns the flame of a candle. And his mother and his father, the king, saw the maiden, and laid hands on her. Then the prince arose out of his sleep, and saw the maiden that she was fair. Then he took her in his arms and kissed her, and lay down in his bed, slept till day.

And they made a marriage and ate and drank. The folk marvelled, for a being so fair as that maiden was not to be found in all the realm. And he dwelt with her half a year, and she bore a golden boy, two apples in his hand. And it pleased the prince well.

Then her old sweetheart heard it, the vampire who had made love to her, and had killed her. He arose and came to her and asked her, 'Nita, tell me, what did you see me doing?'

'I didn't see anything.'

'Tell me truly, or I will kill your child, your little boy, as I killed your father and mother. Tell me truly.'

'I have nothing to tell you.'

And he killed her boy. And she arose and carried him to the church and buried him.

At night the vampire came again and asked her, 'Tell me, Nita, what you saw.'

'I didn't see anything.'

'Tell me, or I will kill the lord whom you have wedded.'

Then Nita arose and said, 'It shall not happen that you kill my lord. God send you burst.'

The vampire heard what Nita said, and burst. Ay, he died, and burst for very rage. In the morning Nita arose and saw the floor swimming two hand's-breadth deep in blood. Then Nita bade her father-in-law take out the vampire's heart with all speed. Her father-in-law, the king, hearkened, and opened him and took out his heart, and gave it into Nita's hand. And she went to the grave of her boy and dug the boy up, applied the heart, and the boy arose. And Nita went to her father and to her mother, and anointed them with the blood, and they arose. Then, looking on them, Nita told all the troubles she had borne, and what she had suffered at the hands of the vampire.

409: The Girl as Wolf

The Wolf's Daughter
(*Estonia*)

There was once a mother with two daughters. One of them was her own daughter, she was ugly, and the other was her stepdaughter, she was beautiful. On Thursday evening, a suitor arrived with his entourage. The mother placed her own daughter on top of the oven and gave her bread and butter to eat, and told the stepdaughter to go and stir the mash for the pigs. She asked the suitor which daughter he wanted. The suitor answered he wanted the one who was stirring pig mash. But the mother wanted to get her own daughter married and therefore told the suitor's entourage to come back another Thursday. Then, she put the stepdaughter on top of the oven and told her own daughter to stir the mash for pigs. But this time, the suitors chose the one eating bread and butter on top of the oven. The mother apologised and asked them to come a third time. Now again, she told her own daughter to sit on top of the oven eating bread and butter, and the stepdaughter to stir the mash for the pigs. Once again, the suitor chose the stepdaughter. Therefore, the suit was agreed and the stepdaughter was to get married.

When the wedding party arrived back from the church, the mother took the stepdaughter's clothes and put them on her own daughter, and shut in the stepdaughter under a vat. The wedding party started off towards the groom's home. Under way, they heard a voice calling:

> *Bridegroom, stop your sledge,*
> *You took a stranger, left your wife!*

But the bride reassured the groom that this was nothing:

> *Those're my beads jingling,*
> *My pins rattling,*
> *My brooches banging,*
> *My silver singing.*

The wedding party continued for a long time, and again there was a voice calling:

> *Bridegroom, stop your sledge,*
> *You took a stranger, left your wife!*

On a bridge, they stopped and the groom saw his wife, naked, running after them. The rooster had jumped up to crow on the edge of the vat, the vat had tipped over and the wife had escaped. Now the wedding garments were taken from the false wife and put on the wedded wife. The false wife was left behind under the bridge.

In a year's time, the mother was on her way to see the daughter's new baby, and had a pot of porridge hanging from a spurtle[1] on her shoulder to take some porridge to her granddaughter. On her way, she reached the bridge and went underneath to pluck some (chervil)[2] straws, saying:

> *Picking straws, plucking straws,*
> *For my granddaughter to play with!*

The chervil answered:

> *Don't you pluck, mother dear,*
> *Your own daughter's navel string!*

So the mother took her daughter along and they went together to where the stepdaughter was living with her husband. The nanny was outdoors and the child was already playing. Knowing the child's mother to be indoors, the mother entered the house, tore off the young wife's clothes and put them on her own daughter, then she cast a wolf's hide on the young wife, so that she ran into the forest and became a werewolf; her own daughter stayed behind as the child's mother. Every time she started nursing the baby, she turned her face towards the wall; the baby couldn't suckle and was screaming all the time. There was no other way, the husband went to the wise man and told him about his trouble: every time his wife nurses the baby, she turns herself towards the wall, and the baby is screaming. The wise man understood and said:

Let the nanny take the baby and go to the big boulder in the field on Thursday night, and sing:

> *Come home, baby's mother,*
> *Come suckle the child,*
> *Give the little one some milk,*
> *From her we get just birch bark*
> *And copper wires to gnaw on!*

The husband thanked the wise man and went home. On Thursday night, the nanny took the baby to the big boulder in the field, and sang as the wise man had told him. After that, the wolf came out of the forest, threw

---

1   A wooden tool used for stirring.
2   A mild, parsley-like herb.

her wolf skin on the boulder and suckled the baby. When she was done, she put on the skin and went back to the forest again. On another Thursday night, the nanny went to the field again and sang:

> *Come home, baby's mother,*
> *Come suckle the child,*
> *Give the little one some milk,*
> *From her we get just birch bark*
> *And copper wires to gnaw on!*

And again the werewolf came out of the forest and suckled the baby. When leaving, she said:

"I will come once more, but after that I will not be able to come, I have to run with the big pack."

On the third Thursday night, the nanny sang the same song. The wolf suckled the baby and said:

"This is the last time, I cannot come any more, but what is it that smells burnt here?"

"They are singeing pigs in the village," the nanny answered.

The wolf turned to go, and took the wolf skin from the stone, but it was quite burnt and didn't fit her any longer. The woman had to stay naked and wanted to run into the forest, but the husband caught her and took her home. Now, the man had two wives. What to do about it? He heated the sauna oven very hot. He dug a big hole in front of the ladder and put a pot of boiling water there, which he covered with a white sheet.

He told the women that the one who got to the sweating bench first would remain his wife. Then he told his real wife quietly:

"Don't you run too fast!"

The unwedded wife wanted to be first on the sweating bench and rushed to the ladder. There she tumbled into the cauldron of boiling water. After a while, a magpie flew out of the cauldron. The woman had turned into a magpie. This is how magpie came into being.

The Goat-Girl
(*Greece*)

There was once a husbandman with his wife who had no children. His wife besought God to give her a child, though it were no better than a kid. In course of time she accordingly gave birth to a kid. It grew up and became a fine she-goat. Her mother said to her, once on a time, "Who will take water for your father to the field?" Said she, "Fasten it to my horn, and I will take it." So she fastened it, and she took it to her father. On her return, she found a sunny pot, where she took off her hide to clean it.

As a Prince passed by to go to the chase, he saw her, and his eyes were dazzled with her beauty, which shone like the sun. When she saw the Prince, she straightway went into her hide, and set off home. The Prince sent people to follow her, and watch where she went in. Then the Prince returned to his mother, and said, "Send to say I am suitor for the hand of the she-goat." When his mother heard that she began to wail, and beat her breast, and said, "My son, if you want to marry, take a princess."

"Nay," said he, "but I will take her."

His mother saw his distress and affliction, and sent two women to get the goat. The mother of the she-goat took a cudgel to them. "Why have you come to mock me?" said she, "me, who have no daughter, only this goat that God has given me to console me!"

So the women went back and told the treatment they had met with.

The Prince said to his mother, "Go yourself."

So, willy-nilly, she went, and said to the she-goat's mother, "There's no help for it!"

"The latter was so frightened when she saw the Queen, that she let her have the goat. So the Queen took her and brought her to her son. Then her son was glad, for he had eaten no bread for five days for grief.

One day the Queen made ready to knead a cake: the she-goat came with her horn and tore the dough to bits; so the Queen hit her a whack with the rolling-pin.

The next day the maid took the bread and put it into the oven. The she-goat went frisking by her side, and when she reached the oven, the goat went and spoiled the loaf with her horn. The cook seized the shovel and hit her a bang with it.

At that time a cousin of the King was to be married, and her father invited his kinsfolk to the wedding. So they made ready and went to the wedding, and tied the goat to a bench. When they were all gone, and the goat was left by herself, she, too, laid aside her hide, and dressed herself in golden embroidery, and went to the wedding, and sat by her mother-in-law. When her mother-in-law saw her beauty, she said to herself, "Would that such an one were my son's wife!" So she asked her, "Whence do you come, my child?"

"From the rolling-pin!" said she.

She went down to the dance, and danced. When her betrothed saw her he knew her, and when the dance slackened, she flung down a golden apple, and put on her hide, and fled. In the evening, the Queen came home with her son, and said, "Did you see a fair woman at the dance?"

Said her son, "I did; but did not you ask her whence she came?"

And she said, "Yes: but I don't know what she said; I did not hear aright."

"If she come to-morrow, mind you ask her, mother!" said her son.

On the morrow, they all went again to the marriage festivities, and the goat also went, and sat by her future mother-in-law. So she asked her, "Whence come you, my child?"

Said she, "From the fire-shovel."

Then she went down to the dance, and danced. When the dance slackened, again she flung down a golden apple, so as to astonish the people, that she might get away. Again she put on her hide, and sat down, tied by the bench. The Prince did not know how to get the hide off her. In the evening, he came home again with his mother, and asked her, "Mother, did you ask where that fair one came from?"

"She told me, my son, but I have forgotten," said his mother.

In the morning, the Prince arose and went to the cook, and said to him. "Make the oven very hot, and don't bake bread for anyone, because you give me no cake." Then he said to his mother, "Go you to the marriage feast—I will come later on."

So they all went out, and he shut himself up in a neighbouring house. The goat puts off her hide, and goes to the feast. The Prince seizes the skin and flings it in the oven. The smell of the singeing hide came to her nostrils, and she left the dance and rushed to cast herself into the oven. The Prince burst forth and seized her—and said to her, "I don't mean you for the oven, my lady!" And he took her in his arms and shut her in the glasschamber. And he went no more to the feast, but stayed with her. His mother sent the nurse to see why her son did not come, and the nurse said to him, "Why did not you come to the feast?"

He said, "I have a head-ache. Let my mother enjoy herself, and I will come in later on."

So his mother waited, but he did not come. So she set off and went home alone.

Then the Prince said to her, "See, mother; take the key and bring me a mug from the glass-chamber."

As his mother went to open the door, the chamber shone. Then his mother uttered a loud cry, and told him there was a fairy in the chamber. And the Prince laughed, and said, "You have good eyes, mother!"

Then he took his mother by the hand, and they went in together. And the bride came and kissed her hand. And the Prince said to her, "See, mother, that's the goat!"

Then the Queen embraced her, and said to her, "My child, why have you not shown yourself all this long time?"

And straightway, on the morrow, the Queen went and called all her royal kinsfolk to the wedding; and she went and called the mother and father of the bride as well. But they were afraid lest they should behead them; and they told the King they were afraid, and would not come. Then the King had clothes made for the mother and father, and went himself and brought them; and the daughter came to meet them, and kissed her hand to them from the foot of the staircase, and welcomed her mother and father, and they celebrated the wedding, and lived happily.

The Dun Cow
(*Russia*)

In a certain kingdom, in a certain land, there once lived a Tsar and Tsarítsa, who had one only daughter, Márya Tsarévna. But the old Tsarítsa died and the Tsar took to him a second wife, who was a witch. And the witch had three daughters, one of whom had one eye, the next two eyes, and the third had three. The stepmother could not abide Márya Tsarévna, and sent the girl with a dun cow on to the heath, and gave her a dry crust as her only food.

Márya Tsarévna went on to the heath, bowed down to the right foot of the cow, and all at once was splendidly dressed, and had as much to eat and drink as she liked. So she guarded the dun cow the whole day, and looked as gay as any lady in the land. And at night she bowed down again in front of the right foot, and again became shabby and went home. And the bit of bread she took with her and offered it to her stepmother.

"Whatever is she living on?" the witch thought, and she gave her the same piece of bread next day, and told her eldest daughter to watch what Márya Tsarévna did.

When they reached the heath Márya Tsarévna said: "Come, little sister, I will find a cushion for your head." So she went to look, but whispered to herself:

> *Sleep, my sister, sleep,*
> *Sleep, O sister mine;*
> *One eye go to sleep,*
> *Close that eye of thine.*

The sister went to sleep, and Márya Tsarévna stood up, went to her dear dun cow, bowed down to the right foot, and ate, and drank, and went about all day long like a princess.

In the evening she woke up her sister and said: "Get up, sister; get up, dearest; and we will go home."

"Oh! oh! oh!" her sister whimpered, "I have been asleep all day long and have not seen anything, and mother will be so angry!"

When they got home, the stepmother asked: "What was it Márya Tsarévna ate and drank?"

"I did not see anything."

So the witch scolded her, and next day sent the two-eyed sister with Márya. "Go," she said, "and see what she eats and drinks."

And the girls came to the heath, and Márya Tsarévna said, "Come, little sister, I will find a cushion for your head." So she went to search, and whispered to herself:

> *Sleep, my sister, sleep,*
> *Sleep, O sister mine;*
> *Two-eyes go to sleep,*
> *Close both eyes of thine.*

Two-eyes went to sleep, and Márya Tsarévna bowed down as before, to the right foot of the cow, and looked like a princess all day long. In the evening she roused Two-eyes; and if the stepmother was angry before, she was much angrier this time.

So next day she sent Three-eyes, and Márya Tsarévna sent her to sleep in the same way; only she forgot the third eye, and that went on looking and looking at what Márya Tsarévna did. For she ran to her dun cow's right foot, bowed down, and ate, and drank, and went about all day long splendidly attired.

And when she got home she laid the dry crust on the table. And the mother asked the daughter what Márya Tsarévna had eaten and drunk. Three-eyes told her everything; and the witch ordered the dun cow to be slain.

"You must be mad, woman," said the Tsar, "it's quite a young heifer and so beautiful!"

"I tell you," said the stepmother, "it must be done"; and the old Tsar consented.

But Márya Tsarévna asked him: "Father, do at least give me a little tiny bit out of the cow!"

The old man gave her the piece, and she planted it; and a bush with sweet berries grew up, with little birds singing on it, singing songs fit for kings and peasants.

Now Iván Tsarévich had heard of Márya Tsarévna, went to her stepmother, laid a bowl on the table, and said: "Whichever of the maidens brings me the bowl full of berries, I will marry."

So the mother sent One-eye to get the berries. But the birds drove her away from the bush and almost pecked out her one eye; and so with Two-eyes and Three-eyes. At last Márya Tsarévna had to go. Márya Tsarévna took the bowl and gathered the berries, and the little birds helped her in the task. When she got home she put the bowl on the table and bowed down to Iván Tsarévich. So Iván Tsarévich took Márya Tsarévna to be his wife, and they celebrated a merry wedding and lived a happy life.

But, after a while, Márya Tsarévna bore a son. She wanted to show him to her father, and, together with her husband, went to visit him. Then the stepmother turned her into a goose, and decked her eldest daughter as though she were the wife of Iván Tsarévich. And Iván Tsarévich returned home.

The old man, who tended the children, got up early in the morning, washed himself clean, took the child on his arm and went out to the field, to the bush in the field. Grey geese were flying over it.

"Geese, ye grey ones, where is the baby's mother?"

"In the next flock!"

Then the next flock came by.

"Geese, ye grey ones, where is the baby's mother?"

Then the baby's mother came to them, threw off her feathers, and gave her little child the breast, and began weeping:

"For this one day I may come, and to-morrow, but the next day I must fly away over the woods and over the hills."

The old man went back home, and the boy slept all day long, until next morning, and did not wake up. The false wife was angry with him for taking the child into the fields where it must be much too cold.

But next morning the old man again got up very early, washed himself clean, and took the child into the field. Iván Tsarévich followed him secretly and hid in the bush. Then the grey geese began soaring by.

"Geese, ye grey ones, where is the baby's mother?"

"In the next flock!"

Then the next flock came by.

"Geese, ye grey ones, where is the baby's mother?"

Then the baby's mother came to them, threw off her feathers, and gave her little child the breast, and began weeping: "For this one day I may come, but to-morrow I must fly away over the woods and over the hills."

Then she asked: "What do I smell there?" and wanted to put on her feathers again, but could not find them anywhere.

Iván Tsarévich had burnt them. He seized hold of Márya Tsarévna, but she turned first into a frog, then into a lizard, and into all sorts of insects, and last of all into a spindle. Iván Tsarévich took the spindle and broke it in halves, threw the dull end behind him and the sharp one in front; and his beautiful young wife stood in front of him, and they went home.

Then the daughter of the witch cried out: "The destroyer and the wicked woman have come."

But Iván Tsarévich assembled all the Princes and the *boyárs*, and he asked them: "With which wife shall I live?"

They said: "With the first."

But he answered, "My lords, whichever wife leaps quickest to the door shall remain with me."

So the witch's daughter climbed up at once, but Márya Tsarévna clung on. Then Iván Tsarévich took his gun and shot the substitute wife, and lived happy ever after with Márya Tsarévna.

425M: The Snake Bridegroom

The Snake-Prince
(*Greece*)

Once upon a time there was a merchant, and he traded "all the way to Bagdad," as the saying is. He had twelve ships which sailed to foreign countries, and he had besides three pretty daughters.

Well, as time went on, luck turned against the merchant. His wife died; one by one he lost his ships; and every year he became poorer and poorer. At last he had lost all his property with the exception of one farm, and he went to live there with his daughters. As they had now no money to hire laborers, the merchant told the girls that they must set to and work on the farm in order that they might gain a living.

"We cannot do farm work," replied the two eldest, tossing their heads. "We are not accustomed to it."

But the youngest, whose name was Rosa, loved her father very dearly; and she at once prepared to do as he wished. So she set to with a will, and digged in the garden, and raked, and planted; and when the fruits and vegetables were grown, she rose early in the morning to gather them for her father to carry to market.

Time passed, and after many months tidings came to the merchant that three of his belated ships had come into port laden with costly goods, when he immediately prepared to go to the city. But before mounting his horse, he asked his daughters what each desired as a present.

The two eldest begged for fine silken gowns; but when he asked the youngest, she said, "I want nothing, papa mine, now that I see you released from your poverty." And when her father pressed her, she said, "Well, then, papa mine, bring me a rose, a beautiful, sweet-smelling damask rose."

So the merchant set off for the port, and landed his goods. In twelve days' time he had sold them all save the two silken gowns which he had kept for his daughters; but he had found no rose for the youngest.

As he was riding home to his farm, it began to rain so heavily that when they came to the open gateway of a house by the wayside, his horse trotted through it into the courtyard. There was no one about, so he put the horse in the stable, and went up to the house. The door stood wide open, so he walked in and sat himself down on a seat in the hall. At once he found by his side coffee and sweetmeats, and a long pipe filled with fragrant tobacco, without his seeing who had brought them.

Presently the rain ceased, and the merchant arose and went from chamber to chamber to seek the host and thank him for the shelter and entertainment. Finding no one, however, he was going forth to take his beast from the stable and continue his journey, when, as he crossed the courtyard, he caught sight of a bush of damask roses which had three blossoms on one stem.

No sooner, however, had he stretched out his hand and plucked them than there appeared at his feet a snake, who said, "Ah, thankless man! After I have opened my doors to save thee from the storm, canst not see a rose or two without desiring and plucking them?"

"I sought through the chambers to find the host and say a 'Thank you' to him, but found him not," the merchant replied.

"Listen to me," then said the snake. "Thou hast three daughters, and thou must bring me the youngest. Think not to thyself that I am only a snake, and cannot come and find thee if thou dost not my bidding."

The poor man asked how many days' grace he would give him; and he granted him forty days.

At last he got home to his house; his daughters gathered round him; and when the two eldest had got their gowns he gave the roses to the youngest, and then sat down weeping.

"What is the matter, papa mine, that you weep?" she asked, anxiously.

Then, as the merchant related his adventure, Rosa's sisters began to reproach her, and point their fingers at her, saying, "Wretched girl that thou art! A gown was not good enough for thee, but thou must have a damask rose, forsooth, that the snake might come and destroy us!"

When her father had also told them of the forty days' grace, Rosa went to her chamber and wrote down the date; and she did not seem at all troubled, though her sisters were continually reproaching her.

On the thirty-eighth day she went to her father and said, "Papa mine, saddle now the horse so that we may go where I am invited."

"Can I take thee, my darling child, to the snake who will destroy thee?" cried the unhappy man.

"The snake will not destroy me, if I do his bidding," replied Rosa. "What ill-will can he have against me? Arise, and let us be gone."

She bade farewell to her sisters; she and her father set out on their journey, and on the fortieth day they arrived at the snake's abode. The gate was open, as before, and when the merchant had stabled his horse he led his daughter into the house, and they sate them down.

Soon came coffee and sweets, as before, without anyone being seen; and in a little while the snake appeared and said to the merchant, "So thou hast done my bidding and brought thy daughter?"

"Yea, I have brought her, as I promised," he replied; and when he had kissed and embraced his daughter, he mounted his horse and rode home again. But in a few days he fell ill with grief and took to his bed. So the poor girl was left alone with the snake.

And it became the snake's custom, every day when she was taking her coffee after dinner, to climb into her lap and ask her, "Wilt thou take me for thy husband?"

And she would reply, "But I am afraid of thee."

And she was very sad and lonely because her father did not come to see her as he had promised. Well, one day, as she was sitting at the table, it suddenly opened before her and disclosed a mirror in which all the world was reflected; and, when she saw in it her father lying ill in bed, she began to weep and tear her hair.

The snake, who was in the garden, hearing her cries and her breast-beatings, hurried to her and asked, "What ails thee, my Rose?"

"See in the mirror," she cried, "how my father lies nigh unto death!"

Then said the snake, "Open the table drawer and thou wilt find a ring. Put it on thy finger, and tell me how many days thou wilt be absent?"

"I will come back," she replied, "as soon as my father recovers."

"Well, I will give thee thirty-one days' leave. If thou come one day later, thou wilt find me dead on some mound in the garden."

"Do thyself no harm," said the girl. "When my leave has expired I will return to thee."

The snake ordered supper to be served, and when she had eaten, he said, "Put the ring on thy tongue, and thou wilt find thyself at home in thy chamber."

Rosa lay down, put the ring on her tongue, and closed her eyes. Her father's servants, passing the door of her chamber, heard her breathing, and ran to tell their young mistresses, who hastened in and found her asleep on her bed. The maiden awoke, and when she found that she was indeed at home again she praised God.

Her father was rejoiced to see his Rosa again, and asked her many questions about her life with the snake. When she told him what the snake had said to her every day at dinner time, and that she had replied, "But I am afraid of thee," he said to her, "My daughter dear, the next time he asks thee that question, do thou answer, 'Yea, I will take thee!' and we shall see what will hap."

And she promised to say this. Her sisters, however, tried to persuade her not to go back, so that the snake might die and they would be rid of him.

But Rosa was indignant, and replied, "How could I leave my beast to die, who have received such help from him?"

So she remained with her father, whose joy she was, for as many days as she had leave. Then, bidding him and her sisters farewell, she lay down on her bed, put the ring in her mouth, and went back to the snake.

When he saw her, he said, "Ah, thou hast come back to me, my Rose!"

And after dinner, when coffee was served, and he lay in her lap as before and asked, "Wilt thou take me for thy husband?" she replied, "Yea, I will take thee!"

When she had said these words the snake's skin fell off him, and he became a handsome prince. And the table again opened and all the world was seen therein. Then Rosa asked him what manner of man he was, and how he had become a snake. And he told her how that he had fallen under the spell of an enchantress who had changed him into a snake, and had doomed him to retain that shape until he should find a maiden who would consent to marry him.

"But now," he said, "I will return to my kingdom. Thy father and sisters shall be conveyed thither, and then we will hold our wedding."

So they were married, and the prince made his father-in-law his grand vizier. And we will leave them well, and return and find them better—God be praised!

The Snake Who Became the King's Son-in-law (*Romania*)

There were an old man and an old woman. From their youth up to their old age they had never had any children.[1] So the old woman was always scolding with the old man—what can they do, for there they are old, old people? The old woman said, 'Who will look after us when we grow older still?'

'Well, what am I to do, old woman?'

'Go you, old man, and find a son for us.'

So the old man arose in the morning, and took his axe in his hand, and departed and journeyed till mid-day, and came into a forest, and sought three days and found nothing. Then the old man could do no more for hunger. He set out to return home. So as he was coming back, he found a little snake and put it in a handkerchief, and carried it home. And he brought up the snake on sweet milk. The snake grew a week and two days, and he put it in a jar. The time came when the snake grew as big as the jar. The snake talked with his father, 'My time has come to marry me. Go, father, to the king, and ask his daughter for me.'

When the old man heard that the snake wants the king's daughter, he smote himself with his hands. 'Woe is me, darling! How can I go to the king? For the king will kill me.'

What said he? 'Go, father, and fear not. For what he wants of you, that

---

1 Lit. 'made any children of their bones'.

will I give him.'

The old man went to the king. 'All hail, O king!'

'Thank you, old man.'

'King, I am come to form an alliance by marriage.'

'An alliance by marriage!' said the king. 'You are a peasant, and I am a king.'

'That matters not, O king. If you will give me your daughter, I will give you whatever you want.'

What said the king? 'Old man, if that be so, see this great forest. Fell it all, and make it a level field; and plough it for me, and break up all the earth; and sow it with millet by to-morrow. And mark well what I tell you: you must bring me a cake made with sweet milk. Then will I give you the maiden.'

Said the old man, 'All right, O king.'

The old man went weeping to the snake. When the snake saw his father weeping he said, 'Why weepest thou, father?'

'How should I not weep, darling? For see what the king said, that I must fell this great forest, and sow millet; and it must grow up by to-morrow, and be ripe. And I must make a cake with sweet milk and give it him. Then he will give me his daughter.'

What said the snake? 'Father, don't fear for that, for I will do what you have told me.'

The old man: 'All right, darling, if you can manage it.' The old man went off to bed.

What did the snake? He arose and made the forest a level plain, and sowed millet, and thought and thought, and it was grown up by daybreak. When the old man got up, he finds a sack of millet, and he made a cake with sweet milk. The old man took the cake and went to the king.

'Here, O king, I have done your bidding.'

When the king saw that, he marvelled. 'My old fellow, hearken to me. I have one thing more for you to do. Make me a golden bridge from my palace to your house, and let golden apple-trees and pear-trees grow on the side of this bridge. Then will I give you my daughter.'

When the old man heard that, he began to weep, and went home.

What said the snake? 'Why weepest thou, father?'

The old man said, 'I am weeping, darling, for the miseries which God sends me. The king wants a golden bridge from his palace to our house, and apple and pear-trees on the side of this bridge.'

The snake said, 'Fear not, father, for I will do as the king said.' Then the snake thought and thought, and the golden bridge was made as the king had said. The snake did that in the night-time. The king arose at midnight; he thought the sun was at meat.[1] He scolded the servants for not having called him in the morning.

The servants said, 'King, it is night, not day'; and, seeing that, the king marvelled.

In the morning the old man came. 'Good-day, father-in-law.'

'Thank you, father-in-law. Go, father-in-law, and bring your son, that we may hold the wedding.'

He, when he went, said, 'Hearken, what says the king? You are to go there for the king to see you.'

What said the snake? 'My father, if that be so, fetch the cart, and put in the horses, and I will get into it to go to the king.'

No sooner said, no sooner done. He got into the cart and drove to the king. When the king saw him, he trembled with all his lords. One lord older than the rest, said, 'Fly not, O king, it were not well of you. For he did what you told him; and shall not you do what you promised? He will kill us all. Give him your daughter, and hold the marriage as you promised.'

What said the king? 'My old man, here is the maiden whom you demand. Take her to you.'

And he gave him also a house by itself for her to live in with her husband. She, the bride, trembled at him.

The snake said, 'Fear not, my wife, for I am no snake as you see me. Behold me as I am.'

He turned a somersault, and became a golden youth, in armour clad; he had but to wish to get anything. The maiden, when she saw that, took him in her arms and kissed him, and said, 'Live, my king, many years. I thought you would eat me.'

The king sent a man to see how it fares with his daughter. When the king's servant came, what does he see? The maiden fairer, lovelier than before. He went back to the king. 'O king, your daughter is safe and sound.'

'As God wills with her,' said the king. Then he called many people and held the marriage; and they kept it up three days and three nights, and the marriage was consummated. And I came away and told the story.

The Serpent
(*Italy*)

There was once on a time a gardener's wife, who longed to have a son more than the suitor longs for a sentence in his favour, a sick man for

---

1   i.e. it was noon.

cold water, or the innkeeper for the arrival of the mail-coach.

It chanced one day that the poor man went to the mountain to get a faggot; and when he came home and opened it, he found a pretty little serpent among the twigs. At the sight of this, Sapatella (for that was the name of the gardener's wife) heaved a deep sigh and said, "Alas! even the serpents have their little serpents; but I brought ill-luck with me into this world." At these words the little serpent spoke, and said, "Well then, since you cannot have children, take me for a child, and you will make a good bargain, for I shall love you better than my own mother." Sapatella, hearing a serpent speak thus, had like to have fainted; but plucking up courage she said, "If it were for nothing else than for the affection which you offer, I am content to take you, and treat you as if you were really my own child." So saying, she assigned him a hole in a corner of the house for a cradle, and gave him for food a share of what she had, with the greatest affection in the world.

The serpent increased in size from day to day; and when he was grown pretty big, he said to Cola Matteo, the gardener, whom he looked upon as his father, "Daddy, I want to get married." – "With all my heart," said Cola Matteo; "we must look out for another serpent like yourself, and try to make up a match between you." – "What serpent are you talking of?" said the little serpent: "I suppose, forsooth, we are all the same with the vipers and adders! It is easy to see you are nothing but an Antony, and make a nosegay[1] of every plant. I want the king's daughter; so go this very instant and ask the king for her, and tell him it is a serpent that demands her."

Cola Matteo, who was a plain, straightforward sort of man, and knew nothing about matters of this kind, went innocently to the king and delivered his message, saying, "The messenger should not be beaten more than the sands upon the shore. Know then that a serpent wants your daughter for his wife, and I am come therefore to try if we can make a match between a serpent and a dove." The king, who saw at a glance that he was a blockhead, to get rid of him said, "Go and tell the serpent that I will give him my daughter if he turns all the fruit of this orchard into gold." And so saying, he burst out a-laughing and dismissed him.

When Cola Matteo went home, and delivered the answer to the serpent, he said, "Go tomorrow morning and gather up all the fruit-stones you can find in the city, and sow them in the orchard, and you will see pearls strung on rushes." Cola Matteo, who was no conjuror, neither knew how to comply or refuse; so next morning, as soon as the Sun with his golden broom had swept away the dirt of the Night from the fields watered by the Dawn, he took a basket on his arm, and went from street

---

1 A small bouquet of scented flowers.

to street picking up all the stones of peaches, plums, nectarines, apricots and cherries that he could find: then he went to the orchard of the palace, and sowed them as the serpent had desired. In an instant the trees shot up, and stems and branches, leaves, flowers and fruit, were all of glistening gold; at the sight of which the king was in an ecstasy of amazement, and cried aloud with joy.

But when Cola Matteo was sent by the serpent to the king to demand the performance of his promise, the king said, "Fair and easy, I must first have something else, if he would have my daughter; and it is that he make all the walls and the ground in the orchard to be of precious stones."

When the gardener told this to the serpent, he made answer, "Go to-morrow morning and gather up all the bits of broken crockery-ware you can find, and throw them on the walks, and on the wall of the orchard, for we will not let this difficulty stand in our way." As soon therefore as the Night, having stood by and backed the robbers, is banished from the sky, and goes about collecting the faggots of twilight. Cola Matteo took a basket under his arm, and went about collecting bits of tiles, lids and bottoms of pipkins, pieces of plates and dishes, handles of jugs, spouts of pitchers; picking up all the spoilt, broken, flawed, cracked lamps, and all the fragments of pottery of every sort he could find in his way. And when he had done all that the serpent had told him, there was to be seen the whole orchard mantled with emeralds and chalcedonies,[1] and coated with rubies and carbuncles, in such sort that the lustre sequestered the sight in the warehouses of the eyes, and planted admiration in the fields of the heart. The king was struck all of a heap at the sight, and knew not what had befallen him. But when the serpent sent again to let him know that he was expecting the performance of his promise, the king answered, "Oh! all that has been done is nothing, if he does not turn this palace into gold."

When Cola Matteo told the serpent this new fancy of the king's, the serpent said, "Go and get a bundle of herbs of different kinds, and rub the bottom of the palace walls with them: we shall see if we cannot sat-isfy this whim." Away went Cola Matteo that very moment, and made a great broom of cabbages, radishes, rockets, purslain, turnips and carrots; and when he had rubbed the lower part of the palace with it, instant-ly you might see it shining like a gilded pill to purge melancholy from a hundred houses that were ill-treated by fortune. And when the gardener came again to demand the princess to wife in the name of the serpent, the king, seeing all retreat cut off, called his daughter, and said to her, "My dear Grannonia, I have endeavoured to get rid of a suitor who asked you for his wife by making such conditions as seemed to me impossible; but

---

1 Multi-coloured gemstones.

seeing myself foiled, and obliged to consent I know not how, I pray you, as you are a dutiful daughter, to enable me to keep my word, and to be content with what Heaven wills and I am obliged to do."

"Do as you please, papa," said Grannonia; "I shall not oppose a single jot of your will." The king hearing this bade Cola Matteo tell the serpent to come.

The serpent, on receiving the invitation, set out for the palace mounted on a car all of gold, and drawn by four golden elephants. But wherever he came the people fled away in terror, at seeing such a large and frightful serpent making his progress through the city: and when he arrived at the palace, the courtiers all trembled like rushes, and ran away, and even the very scullions[1] did not dare to stay in the place. The king and queen also, shivering with fear, crept into a chamber, and Grannonia alone stood her ground; for though her father and her mother kept crying out, "Fly, fly, Grannonia! save yourself, Rienzo!" she would not stir from the spot, saying, "Why should I fly from the husband whom you have given me?" And when the serpent came into the room, he took Grannonia by the waist in his tail, and gave her such a shower of kisses that the king writhed like a worm; and I warrant, if he had been bled, not a single drop of blood would have come. Then the serpent carried her into another room, and fastened the door; and shaking off his skin on the ground, he became a most beautiful youth, with a head all covered with ringlets of gold, and with eyes that would enchant you.

When the king saw the serpent going into the room with his daughter, and shutting the door after him, he said to his wife, "Heaven have mercy on that good soul my daughter! for she is dead to a certainty, and that accursed serpent has doubtless swallowed her down like the yolk of an egg!" Then he put his eye to the keyhole, to see what had become of her; but when he saw the exceeding beauty of the youth, and the skin of the serpent that he had left lying on the ground, he gave the door a kick; then in they rushed, and taking the skin, flung it into the fire and burned it.

When the youth saw this, he cried out, "Ah you renegade dogs, you have done for me!" and instantly he turned himself into a dove, and was going to fly away through the window; but he struck his head against the panes until he broke them, and cut himself in such a manner that there did not remain a whole spot on his pate.[2]

Grannonia, who thus saw herself at the same moment happy and un-happy, joyful and miserable, rich and poor, tore her face and bewailed her fate, reproaching her father and mother for this interruption of plea-sure, this poisoning of sweets, this overthrow of good-fortune; but they

1 Kitchen servants.
2 Head.

excused themselves, declaring that they had not meant to do harm. But Grannonia went on weeping and wailing, until Night came forth to illuminate the catafalque[1] of the sky for the funeral pomp of the Sun; and when she saw that all were in bed, she took her jewels, which were in a writing-desk, and went out by a back-door, intending to search everywhere till she found the treasure she had lost.

So she went out of the city, guided by the light of the moon, and on her way she met a fox, who asked her if she wished for company. "Of all things, my friend," answered Grannonia, "I should be delighted, for I am not over-well acquainted with the country." So they travelled along together till they came to a wood, where the trees, at play like children, were making baby-houses for the shadows to lie in; and being now wearied with their journey, and wishing to repose, they retired to the covert of the leaves, where a fountain was playing carnival pranks with the green grass, flinging the water on it by dishfuls; and stretching themselves on a mattress of tender soft grass, they paid the duty of repose which they owed to Nature for the merchandize of life.

They did not awake till the Sun, with his usual fire, gave the signal to sailors and couriers to set out on their road; and after they awoke, they still stayed for some time listening to the singing of the various birds, for Grannonia showed great pleasure in hearing the warbling and twittering they made; and the fox seeing this, said to her, "You would feel twice as much pleasure if you understood, like me, what they are saying." At these words Grannonia—for women are by nature as curious as they are talkative—begged the fox to tell her what he had heard the birds saying in their own language. So after having let her entreat him for a long time, in order to raise her curiosity about what he was going to relate, he told her that the birds were talking to one another of what had lately befallen the king's son, who was as beautiful as a fay, and because he would not comply with the wishes of a wicked ogress, had been laid under a spell by her magic power to pass seven years in the form of a serpent; that he had nearly ended the seven years, when he fell in love with the daughter of a king; and being one day in a room with the maiden, and having cast his skin on the ground, her father and mother, out of curiosity, rushed in and burned his skin; whereupon as the prince was flying away in the shape of a dove, he broke a pane in the window to escape, and had hurt his head in such a manner that he was given over by the doctors.

Grannonia, who thus heard her own onions spoken of, first of all asked whose son this prince was, and then if there was any hope of cure for his accident. And the fox replied that the birds had said his father was the king of Big Valley, and that there was no other secret for stopping the

1 A raised bier supporting a coffin, usually of a distinguished person.

holes in his skull, to prevent his soul getting out at them, than to anoint his wounds with the blood of those very birds who had been telling the story. When Grannonia heard these words, she fell down on her knees to the fox, entreating of him to oblige her by catching those birds for her, that she might get their blood, adding that then, like honest comrades, they would share the gain. "Fair and softly," said the fox, "let us wait till night, and when the birds are gone to bed, let your mammy alone, for I will climb up the tree and weasen[1] them one after another."

So they passed the whole day, talking one time of the beauty of the young prince, then of the mistake made by the maiden's father, then of the mishap that had befallen the prince, chatting and chatting away till Day was gone, and Earth had spread out her large black piece of pasteboard, to collect the wax that might drop from the tapers of Night. Then the fox, as soon as he saw all the birds fast asleep on the branches, stole up quite softly, and, one after another, throttled all the linnets, larks, tomtits, blackbirds, woodpeckers, thrushes, jays, flycatchers, little owls, goldfinches, bullfinches, chaffinches and redbreasts that were on the trees. And when he had killed them all, they put the blood into a little bottle which the fox carried with him to refresh himself on the road.

Grannonia was so overjoyed that she hardly touched the ground; but the fox said to her, "What fine joy in a dream is this, my daughter! you have done nothing unless you have my blood also to mix with that of the birds;" and so saying he set off running away. Grannonia, who saw all her hopes destroyed, had recourse to women's art, cunning and flattery; and she said to him, "Gossip fox, there would be some reason for your saving your hide if I were not under so many obligations to you, and if there were no other foxes in the world; but as you know how much I owe you, and know also that there is no scarcity of the like of you in these plains, you may rely on my good faith. So don't act like the cow that kicks down the pad when she has just filled it with milk. You have done the chief part, and now you fail at the best. Do stop; believe me, and come with me to the city of this king, where you may sell me for a slave if you will."

The fox, who never dreamed that the quintessence of foxery was to be met with, found himself out-foxed by a woman. So he agreed to travel on with Grannonia; but they had hardly gone fifty paces when she lifted up the stick she carried, and gave him with it such a neat rap that he forthwith stretched his legs. Then cutting his throat, she quickly took the blood and poured it into the little bottle; and setting off again, she stopped not until she came to Big Valley, where she went straightway to the royal palace, and sent word to the king that she was come to cure the prince.

Then the king ordered her to come into his presence, and he was aston-

1 Throttle.

ished at seeing a girl undertake a thing which the best doctors in his kingdom had failed to do: however, as a trial could do no harm, he said that he wished greatly to see the experiment made. But Grannonia answered, "If I show you the effect that you desire, you must promise to give him to me for a husband." The king, who looked upon his son to be all one as dead, answered her, "If you give him to me safe and sound, I will give him to you sound and safe; for it is no great matter to give a husband to her who gives me a son."

So they went to the chamber of the prince, and hardly had she anointed him with the blood when he found himself just as if nothing had ever ailed him. And Grannonia, when she saw the prince stout and hearty, bade the king keep his word; whereupon the king turning round to his son said, "My son, a moment ago you were all but dead, and now I see you alive, and can hardly believe it. Therefore, as I have promised this maiden that if she cured you she should have you for a husband, now that Heaven has shown you favour, enable me to perform my promise, by all the love you bear me, since gratitude obliges me to pay this debt."

When the prince heard these words he replied, "Sir, I would that I had such freedom of my will as to prove to you the love I bear you; but as I have already pledged my faith to another woman, you would not consent that I should break my word, nor would this maiden wish me to do such a wrong to her whom I love; nor can I indeed alter my mind."

Grannonia, hearing this, felt a secret pleasure not to be described at finding herself still alive in the memory of the prince; her whole face became crimson, and she said, "If I should induce this maiden whom you love to resign her claims to me, would you then consent to my wish?" – "Never," replied the prince, "never will I banish from this breast the fair image of her I love; and whether she makes for me a conserve of her love, or gives me a dose of cassia, I shall ever remain of the same mind and will; and I would sooner see myself in danger of losing my place at the table of life than play such a trick or make this exchange."

Grannonia could no longer remain in the trammels of disguise, and discovered to the prince who she was; for the chamber being darkened on account of the wounds in his head, and she being disguised, he had not known her. But the prince, now that he recognized her, embraced her with a joy that would amaze you, telling his father who she was, and what he had done and suffered for her. Then they sent to invite her parents, the king and queen of Long-Field, and they celebrated the wedding with wonderful festivity, making great sport of the ninny of a fox, and concluding at the last of the last, that

> *Pain doth indeed a seasoning prove*
> *Unto the joys of constant love.*

460B: The
Journey

The Journey to the Sun and the Moon
(*Russia*)

There were once two young people who loved each other dearly. The young man was called Jean, the girl, Annette. In her sweetness she was like unto a dove, in her strength and bravery she resembled an eagle.

Her father was a rich farmer, and owned a large estate, but Jean's father was only a poor mountain shepherd. Annette did not in the least mind her lover being poor, for he was rich in goodness: nor did she think her father would object to their marrying.

One day Jean put on his best clothes, and went to ask the farmer for his daughter's hand. The farmer listened without interrupting him, and then replied, "If you would marry Annette, go and ask of the Sun why he does not warm the night as well as the day. Then inquire of the Moon why she does not shine by day as well as by night. When you return with these answers you shall not only have my daughter but all my wealth."

These conditions in no way daunted Jean, who placed his hat on the side of his head, and taking a loving farewell of Annette, set out in search of the Sun. On reaching a small town at the close of day, he looked about for a place wherein to pass the night. Some kind people offered him shelter and invited him to sup with them, inquiring as to the object of his journey. When they heard that he was on his way to visit the Sun and Moon, the master of the house begged him to ask the Sun why the finest pear-tree they had in the town had, for several years, ceased to bear fruit, for it used to produce the most delicious pears in the world.

Jean willingly promised to make this inquiry, and the next day continued his journey.

He walked on and on, over mountain and moor, through valley and dense forest, until he came to a land where there was no drinking water. The inhabitants, when they heard the object of Jean's journey, begged him to ask the Sun and Moon why a well, that was the chief water supply of the district, no longer gave good water. Jean promised to do so, and resumed his journey.

After long and weary wanderings he reached the Sun's abode, and found him about to start on his travels.

"O Sun," said he, "stop one moment, do not depart without first answering a few questions."

"Be quick then and speak, for I have to go all round the world to-day."

"Pray tell me why you do not warm or light the earth by night as well as day?"

"For this simple reason, that if I did, the world and everything upon it would be very soon burnt up."

Jean then put his questions concerning the pear-tree and the well. But the Sun replied that his sister, the Moon, would be able to answer him on those points.

Hardly had the Sun finished speaking before he was obliged to hurry off, and Jean travelled far and fast to meet the Moon. On coming up to her he said, "Would you kindly stop one moment? there are a few questions I should like to ask you."

"Very well, be quick, for the earth is waiting for me," answered she, and stood still at once.

"Tell me, dear Moon, why you do not light the world by day as well as by night? And why you never warm it?"

"Because if I lit up the world by day as well as by night the plants would produce neither fruit nor flower. And though I do not warm the earth, I supply it with dew, which makes it fertile and fruitful."

She was then about to continue her course, but Jean, begging her to stop one moment longer, questioned her about the pear-tree which had ceased to bear fruit.

And she answered him thus: "While the king's eldest daughter remained unmarried the tree bore fruit every year. After her wedding she had a little child who died and was buried under this tree. Since then there has been neither fruit nor flower on its branches: if the child be given Christian burial the tree will produce blossom and fruit as in the past."

The Moon was just moving off when Jean begged her to stop and answer one more question, which was, why the inhabitants of a certain land were unable to obtain from their well the clear and wholesome water it had formerly poured forth.

She replied: "Under the mouth of the well, just where the water should flow, lies an enormous toad which poisons it continually: the brim of the well must be broken and the toad killed, then the water will be as pure and wholesome as formerly."

The Moon then resumed her journey, for Jean had no more questions to ask her.

He joyfully went back to claim his Annette, but forgot not to stop on coming to the land where they were short of water. The inhabitants ran out to meet him, anxious to know what he had found out.

Jean led them to the well and there explained the instructions he had received from the Moon, at the same time showing them what to do. Sure enough, right underneath the brim of the well they found a horrible toad which poisoned everything. When they had killed it, the water immediately became pure and transparent, and sweet to the taste as before.

All the people brought Jean presents, and thus laden with riches he again set out. On arriving at the town where grew the unfruitful pear-tree, he was warmly welcomed by the prince, who at once asked if he had forgotten to question the stars about the tree.

"I never forget a promise once made," replied Jean, "but I doubt whether it will be agreeable to your majesty to know the cause of the evil."

He then related all the Moon had said, and when his directions had been carried out they were rewarded by seeing the tree blossom immediately. Jean was loaded with rich gifts, and the king presented him with a most valuable horse, by means of which he reached home very quickly.

Little Annette was wild with joy on hearing of her lover's safe return, for she had wept and suffered much during his absence. But her father's feelings were very different; he wished never to see Jean again, and had, indeed, sent him in search of the Sun with the hope that he might be burnt up by the heat. True it is that "Man proposes and God disposes." Our young shepherd returned, not only safe and sound, but with more knowledge than any of his evil-wishers. For he had learnt why the Sun neither lights nor warms the earth by night as in the day; also why the Moon does not give warmth, and only lights up during the night. Besides all this he had brought with him riches which far exceeded those of his father-in-law, and a steed full of fire and vigour.

So Annette's father could find no fault, and the wedding was celebrated with joy and feasting. Large quantities of roasted crane were eaten, and glasses overflowing with mead were emptied. So beautiful, too, was the music, that for long, long after it was heard to echo among the mountains, and even now its sweet sounds are heard at times by travellers among those regions.

The Story of Marko the Rich and Vasily the Luckless
(*Russia*)

Not in our time, but a long time ago, in a certain realm, lived a very rich merchant, Marko by name, and surnamed the Rich. Cruel and hard was he by nature, greedy of lucre and unmerciful to the poor. Whenever the lowly and the needy came begging beneath his window he sent his servants to drive them away, and let loose his dogs upon them. There was only one thing in the world he loved, and that was his daughter, the thrice-fair Anastasia. To her only he was not hard, and though she was only five years old, he never gainsaid her one of her wishes, and gave her all her heart's desire.

And once on a cold frosty day, three gray-haired men came under the window and asked an alms. Marko saw them, and ordered the dogs to be let loose. The thrice-fair Anastasia heard of it, and implored her father and said: "My own dear father, for my sake don't drive them away, but let them pass the night in the cattle-stall." The father consented, and bade them let the poor old beggar-men into the cattle-stall for the night. As soon as everyone was asleep Anastasia rose up, made her way on tiptoe to the stall, climbed up into the loft, and looked at the beggars. The old beggar-men were crouching together in the middle of the stall, leaning on their crutch-staves with their wrinkled hands, and over their hands flowed their gray beards, and they were talking softly among themselves. One of the old men, the oldest of them all, looked at the others and said: "What news from the wide world?" The second one immediately replied: "In the village Pogoryeloe, in the house of Ivan the Luckless, a seventh son is born; what shall we call him, and with what inheritance shall we bless him?" And the third old man, after meditating a little, said: "We'll call him Vasily, and we'll enrich him with the riches of Marko the Rich, under whose roof we are now passing the night." When they had thus said they prepared to depart, bowed low to the holy ikons, and with soft footsteps prepared to depart from the stall. Anastasia heard all this, went straight to her father, and told him the words of the old men.

Marko the Rich thought deeply over it. He thought and thought, and he went to the village Pogoryeloe. "I'll find out for certain," thought he, "whether such a babe really has been born there." He went straight to the priest and told him all about it. "Yes," replied the priest, "yesterday we had a babe born here, the son of our poorest serf; I christened him Vasily, and luckless he certainly is; he is the seventh son in the family, and the eldest son of the family is only seven years old; the sons of this poor peasant are wee, wee little things; there is next to nothing to eat and drink there; and such hunger and want is in the house that there's none in the village who will even stand sponsor." At this news the heart of Marko the Rich began to ache. Marko thought of the unhappy youngster, declared he would be godfather, asked the priest's wife to be godmother, and bade them make ready a rich table; and they brought the little fellow, christened him, and sat down and feasted.

At the banquet Marko the Rich spoke friendly words to Ivan the Luckless, and said to him: "Gossip, thou art a poor man, and cannot afford to bring up thy son; give him to me; I will bring him up among well-to-do people, and I will give into thy hand at once for thine own maintenance one thousand rubles." The poor man thought the matter over, and then shook hands upon it. Marko gave gifts to his fellow-sponsor, took the child, wrapped him in fox furs, put him in his carriage, and drove homewards. They had got some ten versts[1] from the village when Marko stopped the horses, took up the child, went to the brink of a great precipice, whirled the child over his head, and pitched it down the precipice, exclaiming: "There you go, and now take possession of my goods if you can!"

Shortly after that some merchants from beyond the sea chanced to be travelling by the self-same road; these merchants brought with them twelve thousand rubles which they owed to Marko the Rich. They passed along by the side of the precipice, and they heard within the precipice the crying of a child. They stopped their horses, went to the precipice, and looked amongst the snowdrifts of the green meadows, and on a meadow a little child was sitting and playing with flowers. The merchants took up the child, wrapped him round with furs, and went on their way. They came to the house of Marko the Rich, and told him of their strange discovery. Marko immediately guessed that the matter concerned his own little serf boy, and he said to the merchants: "I should very much like to look at your foundling; if you will give him to me out and out I'll forgive you your debt to me." The merchants agreed, gave the child to Marko, and departed. But Marko that same night took the child, put it in a little cask, tarred it all over, and threw it into the sea.

The cask sailed and sailed along, and at last it came to a monastery. The monks happened to be on the shore just then; they were spreading out their fishing-nets to dry, and all at once they heard the crying of a child. They guessed that the crying came from the cask, and they immediately seized the cask, broke it open, and there was the child. They took the child to the abbot, and as soon as the abbot heard that the child had been cast upon the shore in a cask, he decided that the youngster's name should be Vasily, and that he should be surnamed the Luckless. And henceforth Vasily lived in the monastery till he was sixteen years old, and he grew up fair of face, soft of heart, and strong in mind. The abbot loved him because he learned his letters so quickly that he was able to read and sing in the church better than all the others, and because he was deft and skilful in affairs. And the abbot made him sacristan.[2]

And it happened that once Marko the Rich was travelling on business, and came to this very monastery. The monks treated him with honour as a rich guest. The abbot commanded the sacristan to run and open the church; the sacristan ran at once, lit the candles, and remained in the choir, and read and sang. And Marko the Rich asked the abbot if the young man had dwelt there long, and the abbot told him all about it. Marko began to think, and it struck him that this could be no other than

1   A measure of length, about 1.1 km.
2   Sexton, the officer of the church in charge of the sacristy and its contents.

his serf-boy. And he said to the abbot: "Would that I could lay my hands upon such a smart young fellow as your sacristan, I would place all my treasures beneath his care; I would make him the chief overseer of all my goods, and you know yourselves what goods are mine." The abbot began to make excuses, but Marko promised the monastery a donation of ten thousand rubles. The abbot wavered; he began to consult the brothers, and the brothers said to him: "Why should we stand in Vasily's way? let Marko the Rich take him and make him his overseer." So they deliberated, and agreed to send away Vasily the Luckless with Marko the Rich.

But Marko sent Vasily home in a ship, and wrote to his wife this letter: "When the bearer of this letter reaches thee, go with him at once to our soap-works, and when thou dost pass the great boiling cauldron, shove him in. If thou dost not do this I will punish thee severely, for this youth is my prime enemy and evil-doer." Vasily duly arrived in port and went on his way, and there met him in the road three poor old men, and they asked him: "Whither art thou going, Vasily the Luckless?" – "Why, to the house of Marko the Rich, I have a letter for his wife." – "Show us the letter," said the old men. Vasily took out the letter and gave it them. The old men breathed on the letter and said: "Go now, and give the letter to the wife of Marko the Rich—God will not forsake thee."

Vasily came to the house of Marko the Rich and gave the letter to his wife. The wife read Marko's letter, and called her daughter, for she could not believe her own eyes, but in the letter was written as plain as plain could be: "Wife, the next day after thou dost receive this my letter, marry my daughter, Anastasia, to the bearer, and do so without delay. If thou doest it not thou shalt answer to me for it." Anastasia looked at Vasily, and Vasily stared at her. And they dressed Vasily in rich attire, and the next day they wedded him to Anastasia.

Marko the Rich came home from the sea, and his wife with his daughter and son-in-law met him on the quay. Marko looked at Vasily, fell into a furious passion with his wife, and said to her: "How darest thou wed our daughter away without my consent?" But the wife replied: "I dared not disobey thy strict command!" and she gave the threatening letter to her husband. Marko read the letter, and saw that the handwriting was his own if the intention was not, and he thought to himself: "Good! thrice hast thou escaped ruin at my hands, but now I will send thee where not even the ravens shall pick thy bones."

Marko lived for a month with his son-in-law and treated him and his daughter most kindly; from his face nobody could have thought that he nourished evil thoughts against him in his heart. One day Marko called Vasily to him and said to him: "Go to the land of Thrice-nine, in the Empire of Thrice-ten, to Tsar Zmy; twelve years ago he built a palace on my land. Thou therefore take rent from him for all the twelve years, and get news from him concerning my twelve ships, which have been wrecked about his kingdom for the last three years, and have left no trace behind them." Vasily dared not gainsay his father-in-law, but prepared for his journey, took leave of his young wife, took a sack of sweetmeats as provision by the way, and set out.

He went on and on, and whether it was long or short, far or near, matters not, but anyhow at last he heard a voice which said: "Vasily the Luckless, whither art thou going? is thy journey far?" – Vasily looked around him on all sides and answered: "Who called me? speak!" – "'Tis I, the old leafless oak, and I ask thee whither art thou going, and is thy journey far?" – "I am going to Tsar Zmy to collect arrears of rent for the last twelve years." And again the oak said to him: "If thou arrivest in time, think of me and ask him: here the old leafless oak has been standing all these three hundred years, and is withered and rotten to the very root— how much longer must he be tormented in this wide world?" Vasily listened attentively, and then went further. He came to a river and sat in the ferry-boat, but the old ferryman looked at him and said: "Is thy journey before thee a long one, Vasily the Luckless?" – Vasily told him. "Well," said the ferryman, "if thou art in time, remember me, and say to him I have been ferrying here all these thirty years; how much longer, I should like to know, shall I have to go backwards and forwards?" – "Good!" said Vasily, "I will say so."

He went on to the straits of the sea, and across the straits a whale-fish was lying stretched out, and a road marked out by posts went across its back, and people passed to and fro there. When Vasily stepped on to the whale, the whale-fish spoke to him with a man's voice and said: "Whither art thou going, Vasily the Luckless, and is thy journey far?" Vasily told it everything, and the whale-fish said again: "If thou art in time, remember me; the poor whale-fish has been lying across this sea these three years, and a road marked out by posts goes across its back, and horse and foot trample into its very ribs, and it has no rest night or day; how much longer, pray, is it to lie here?" – "Good!" said Vasily, "I will say so," and went on further.

Vasily went on and on, and he came to a broad green meadow. In the meadow stood a gigantic palace; the white marble walls glistened, the roof shone like a rainbow, and was covered with mother-of-pearl, and the crystal windows burned like fire in the sun. Vasily entered the palace; he went from room to room, and marvelled at the indescribable wealth of them. He went into the last room of all, and saw a lovely damsel sitting on a bed. When she saw Vasily, she cried: "Is it Vasily the Luckless that has fallen into this accursed place?" Vasily told her everything, and why he had come, and what had befallen him in the way. And the damsel said to Vasily: "Not to take tribute wast thou sent here, but as food for the serpent, and to thine own destruction." Scarcely had she spoken these words than the whole palace trembled, and there was clanging and a banging in the courtyard. The damsel shoved Vasily into a coffer beneath the floor, locked him in, and whispered: "Listen to what I say to the Serpent." And with that she went to meet Tsar Serpent.

A monstrous serpent rolled into the room, and straightway got on to the bed and said: "I have been flying over the Russian land; I'm frightfully tired, and I want to go to sleep." The lovely damsel flattered him and said: "Everything is known to thee, O Tsar, and without thee I cannot interpret a very hard dream I have dreamed: wilt thou interpret it for me?" – "Well, out with it, quick!" – "I dreamt I was going along a road, and an oak tree cried to me, 'Ask the Tsar how long I am to stand here'!" – "It will stand till someone comes and kicks it with his foot, and then it will be rooted out and fall, and beneath it is a great quantity of gold and silver: Marko the Rich himself has not got as much." – "But then I dreamed that I came to a river, and the ferryman on the ferry-boat said to me: 'Shall I ferry here long'?" – "'Tis his own fault. Let him put the first who comes to him on the ferry-boat, and push him with the ferry-boat away from the shore, and he will change places with him, and ferry forevermore." – "And after that I came in my dreams to the sea, and crossed over it on a whale-fish, and it said to me: 'Ask the Tsar how long I am to be here!'" – "He must lie there till he has cast up the twelve ships of Marko the Rich, then he may go into the water, and his body will grow again."

All this the serpent said, and then turned over on its other side and fell a-snoring so loudly that all the crystal windows in the palace rattled. Then the damsel let Vasily out of the coffer, opened the garden-gate for him, and showed him the way. Vasily thanked her, and began his return journey.

He came to the straits of the sea where the whale-fish lay, and the whale-fish asked: "Did he say anything about me?" – "Take me over to the other side, and I'll tell thee." When he had crossed over, he said to the whale-fish: "Thou must bring up again the twelve ships of Marko the Rich, which thou swallowed three years ago." The whale-fish cleared its throat and brought up again all the ships quite whole and not a bit hurt, and in its joy leaped about so in the water that Vasily the Luckless, who was standing on the bank, suddenly found himself up to his knees in the sea. He went on further and came to the ferry. "Hast thou spoken about me to Tsar Serpent?" asked the ferryman. "I have; ferry me over first, and I'll tell thee." And as soon as he had crossed over, he said to the ferryman: "Whoever comes to thee after me, seat him in the ferry-boat and shove him from the bank, and he will have to ferry in thy place forever and ever, but thou wilt be as free as the air." After that, Vasily came to the old leafless oak, kicked it with his foot, and the oak rolled over and the roots sprang out of the ground, and beneath the roots and beneath the stump there was gold and silver and precious stones without number. Vasily looked about him, and lo! up to the very place were sailing the twelve ships of Marko the Rich, the self-same which the whale-fish had brought up; and in the foremost ship, in the very stern, stood the self-same old men who had met Vasily when he had the letter to Marko the Rich, and saved him from destruction. And the old men said to Vasily: "Dost thou not see, Vasily, how the Lord has blessed thee?" And they got off the ship and went their way. And the sailors put all the gold and silver in the ships, and went home by sea.

Marko the Rich was more furious than ever. He bade them saddle his horse, and hastened off to Tsar Serpent to the land of Thrice-ten; he wanted to arrange matters with Tsar Serpent himself. When he came to the river, he got on to the ferry-boat, but the ferryman pushed him away from the shore, and there Marko remained as ferryman ever after, and there he is ferrying still. But Vasily the Luckless lived with his wife and mother-in-law, and was happy and prosperous and kind to the poor, and gave them meat and drink and clothed them, and disposed of all the wealth of Marko the Rich.

Lucky Luck
(*Hungary*)

Once upon a time there was a king who had an only son. When the lad was about eighteen years old his father had to go to fight in a war against a neighbouring country, and the king led his troops in person. He bade his son act as Regent in his absence, but ordered him on no account to marry till his return.

Time went by. The prince ruled the country and never even thought of marrying. But when he reached his twenty-fifth birthday he began to think that it might be rather nice to have a wife, and he thought so much that at last he got quite eager about it. He remembered, however, what his father had said, and waited some time longer, till at last it was ten years since the king went out to war. Then the prince called his courtiers about him and set off with a great retinue to seek a bride. He hardly knew which way to go, so he wandered about for twenty days, when, suddenly, he found himself in his father's camp.

The king was delighted to see his son, and had a great many questions to ask and answer; but when he heard that instead of quietly waiting for him at home the prince was starting off to seek a wife he was very angry, and said: 'You may go where you please but I will not leave any of my people with you.'

Only one faithful servant stayed with the prince and refused to part from him. They journeyed over hill and dale till they came to a place called Goldtown. The King of Goldtown had a lovely daughter, and the prince, who soon heard about her beauty, could not rest till he saw her.

He was very kindly received, for he was extremely good-looking and had charming manners, so he lost no time in asking for her hand and her parents gave her to him with joy. The wedding took place at once, and the feasting and rejoicings went on for a whole month. At the end of the month they set off for home, but as the journey was a long one they spent the first evening at an inn. Everyone in the house slept, and only the faithful servant kept watch. About midnight he heard three crows, who had flown to the roof, talking together.

'That's a handsome couple which arrived here tonight. It seems quite a pity they should lose their lives so soon.'

'Truly,' said the second crow; 'for to-morrow, when midday strikes, the bridge over the Gold Stream will break just as they are driving over it. But, listen! whoever overhears and tells what we have said will be turned to stone up to his knees.'

The crows had hardly done speaking when away they flew. And close upon them followed three pigeons.

'Even if the prince and princess get safe over the bridge they will perish,' said they; 'for the king is going to send a carriage to meet them which looks as new as paint. But when they are seated in it a raging wind will rise and whirl the carriage away into the clouds. Then it will fall suddenly to earth, and they will be killed. But anyone who hears and betrays what we have said will be turned to stone up to his waist.'

With that the pigeons flew off and three eagles took their places, and this is what they said:

'If the young couple does manage to escape the dangers of the bridge and the carriage, the king means to send them each a splendid gold embroidered robe. When they put these on they will be burnt up at once. But whoever hears and repeats this will turn to stone from head to foot.'

Early next morning the travellers got up and breakfasted. They began to tell each other their dreams. At last the servant said:

'Gracious prince, I dreamt that if your Royal Highness would grant all I asked we should get home safe and sound; but if you did not we should certainly be lost. My dreams never deceive me, so I entreat you to follow my advice during the rest of the journey.'

'Don't make such a fuss about a dream,' said the prince; 'dreams are but clouds. Still, to prevent your being anxious I will promise to do as you wish.'

With that they set out on their journey.

At midday they reached the Gold Stream. When they got to the bridge the servant said: 'Let us leave the carriage here, my prince, and walk a little way. The town is not far off and we can easily get another carriage there, for the wheels of this one are bad and will not hold out much longer.'

The prince looked well at the carriage. He did not think it looked so unsafe as his servant said; but he had given his word and he held to it.

They got down and loaded the horses with the luggage. The prince and his bride walked over the bridge, but the servant said he would ride the horses through the stream so as to water and bathe them.

They reached the other side without harm, and bought a new carriage in the town, which was quite near, and set off once more on their travels; but they had not gone far when they met a messenger from the king who said to the prince: 'His Majesty has sent your Royal Highness this beautiful carriage so that you may make a fitting entry into your own country and amongst your own people.'

The prince was so delighted that he could not speak. But the servant said: 'My lord, let me examine this carriage first and then you can get in if I find it is all right; otherwise we had better stay in our own.'

The prince made no objections, and after looking the carriage well over the servant said: 'It is as bad as it is smart'; and with that he knocked it all to pieces, and they went on in the one that they had bought.

At last they reached the frontier; there another messenger was waiting for them, who said that the king had sent two splendid robes for the prince and his bride, and begged that they would wear them for their state entry. But the servant implored the prince to have nothing to do with them, and never gave him any peace till he had obtained leave to destroy the robes.

The old king was furious when he found that all his arts had failed; that his son still lived and that he would have to give up the crown to him now he was married, for that was the law of the land. He longed to know how the prince had escaped, and said: 'My dear son, I do indeed rejoice to have you safely back, but I cannot imagine why the beautiful carriage and the splendid robes I sent did not please you; why you had them destroyed.'

'Indeed, sire,' said the prince, 'I was myself much annoyed at their destruction; but my servant had begged to direct everything on the journey and I had promised him that he should do so. He declared that we could not possibly get home safely unless I did as he told me.'

The old king fell into a tremendous rage. He called his Council together and condemned the servant to death.

The gallows was put up in the square in front of the palace. The servant was led out and his sentence read to him.

The rope was being placed round his neck, when he begged to be allowed a few last words. 'On our journey home,' he said, 'we spent the first night at an inn. I did not sleep but kept watch all night.' And then he went on to tell what the crows had said, and as he spoke he turned to stone up to his knees. The prince called to him to say no more as he had proved his innocence. But the servant paid no heed to him, and by the time his story was done he had turned to stone from head to foot.

Oh! how grieved the prince was to lose his faithful servant! And what pained him most was the thought that he was lost through his very faithfulness, and he determined to travel all over the world and never rest till he found some means of restoring him to life.

Now there lived at Court an old woman who had been the prince's nurse. To her he confided all his plans, and left his wife, the princess, in her care. 'You have a long way before you, my son,' said the old woman; 'you must never return till you have met with Lucky Luck. If he cannot help you no one on earth can.'

So the prince set off to try to find Lucky Luck. He walked and walked till he got beyond his own country, and he wandered through a wood for three days but did not meet a living being in it. At the end of the third day he came to a river near which stood a large mill. Here he spent the night. When he was leaving next morning the miller asked him: 'My gracious lord, where are you going all alone?'

And the prince told him.

'Then I beg your Highness to ask Lucky Luck this question: Why is it that though I have an excellent mill, with all its machinery complete, and get plenty of grain to grind, I am so poor that I hardly know how to live from one day to another?'

The prince promised to inquire, and went on his way. He wandered about for three days more, and at the end of the third day saw a little town. It was quite late when he reached it, but he could discover no light anywhere, and walked almost right through it without finding a house where he could turn in. But far away at the end of the town he saw a light in a window. He went straight to it and in the house were three girls playing a game together. The prince asked for a night's lodging and they took him in, gave him some supper and got a room ready for him, where he slept.

Next morning when he was leaving they asked where he was going and he told them his story. 'Gracious prince,' said the maidens, 'do ask Lucky Luck how it happens that here we are over thirty years old and no lover has come to woo us, though we are good, pretty, and very industrious.'

The prince promised to inquire, and went on his way.

Then he came to a great forest and wandered about in it from morning to night and from night to morning before he got near the other end.

Here he found a pretty stream which was different from other streams as, instead of flowing, it stood still and began to talk: 'Sir prince, tell me what brings you into these wilds? I must have been flowing here a hundred years and more and no one has ever yet come by.'

'I will tell you,' answered the prince, 'if you will divide yourself so that I may walk through.'

The stream parted at once, and the prince walked through without wetting his feet; and directly he got to the other side he told his story as he had promised.

'Oh, do ask Lucky Luck,' cried the brook, 'why, though I am such a clear, bright, rapid stream I never have a fish or any other living creature in my waters.'

The prince said he would do so, and continued his journey.

When he got quite clear of the forest he walked on through a lovely valley till he reached a little house thatched with rushes, and he went in to rest for he was very tired.

Everything in the house was beautifully clean and tidy, and a cheerful honest-looking old woman was sitting by the fire.

'Good-morning, mother,' said the prince.

'May Luck be with you, my son. What brings you into these parts?'

'I am looking for Lucky Luck,' replied the prince.

'Then you have come to the right place, my son, for I am his mother. He is not at home just now, he is out digging in the vineyard. Do you go too. Here are two spades. When you find him begin to dig, but don't speak a word to him. It is now eleven o'clock. When he sits down to eat his dinner sit beside him and eat with him. After dinner he will question you, and then tell him all your troubles freely. He will answer whatever you may ask.'

With that she showed him the way, and the prince went and did just as she had told him. After dinner they lay down to rest.

All of a sudden Lucky Luck began to speak and said: 'Tell me, what sort of man are you, for since you came here you have not spoken a word?'

'I am not dumb,' replied the young man, 'but I am that unhappy prince whose faithful servant has been turned to stone, and I want to know how to help him.'

'And you do well, for he deserves everything. Go back, and when you get home your wife will just have had a little boy. Take three drops of blood from the child's little finger, rub them on your servant's wrists with a blade of grass and he will return to life.'

'I have another thing to ask,' said the prince, when he had thanked him. 'In the forest near here is a fine stream but not a fish or other living creature in it. Why is this?'

'Because no one has ever been drowned in the stream. But take care, in crossing, to get as near the other side as you can before you say so, or you may be the first victim yourself.'

'Another question, please, before I go. On my way here I lodged one night in the house of three maidens. All were well-mannered, hard-working, and pretty, and yet none has had a wooer. Why was this?'

'Because they always throw out their sweepings in the face of the sun.'

'And why is it that a miller, who has a large mill with all the best machinery and gets plenty of corn to grind is so poor that he can hardly live from day to day?'

'Because the miller keeps everything for himself, and does not give to those who need it.'

The prince wrote down the answers to his questions, took a friendly leave of Lucky Luck, and set off for home.

When he reached the stream it asked if he brought it any good news. 'When I get across I will tell you,' said he. So the stream parted; he walked through and on to the highest part of the bank. He stopped and shouted out:

'Listen, oh stream! Lucky Luck says you will never have any living creature in your waters until someone is drowned in you.'

The words were hardly out of his mouth when the stream swelled and overflowed till it reached the rock up which he had climbed, and dashed so far up it that the spray flew over him. But he clung on tight, and after failing to reach him three times the stream returned to its proper course. Then the prince climbed down, dried himself in the sun, and set out on his march home.

He spent the night once more at the mill and gave the miller his answer, and by-and-by he told the three sisters not to throw out all their sweepings in the face of the sun.

The prince had hardly arrived at home when some thieves tried to ford the stream with a fine horse they had stolen. When they were half-way across, the stream rose so suddenly that it swept them all away. From that time it became the best fishing stream in the country-side.

The miller, too, began to give alms and became a very good man, and in time grew so rich that he hardly knew how much he had.

And the three sisters, now that they no longer insulted the sun, had each a wooer within a week.

When the prince got home he found that his wife had just got a fine little boy. He did not lose a moment in pricking the baby's finger till the blood ran, and he brushed it on the wrists of the stone figure, which shuddered all over and split with a loud noise in seven parts and there was the faithful servant alive and well.

When the old king saw this he foamed with rage, stared wildly about, flung himself on the ground and died.

The servant stayed on with his royal master and served him faithfully all the rest of his life; and, if neither of them is dead, he is serving him still.

475: The Man as Heater

The Devil's Sooty Brother
(*Germany*)

A disbanded soldier had nothing to live on, and did not know how to get on. So he went out into the forest and when he had walked for a short time, he met a little man who was, however, the Devil. The little man said to him, "What ails you, you seem so very sorrowful?" Then the soldier said, "I am hungry, but have no money." The Devil said, "If you will hire yourself to me, and be my serving-man, you shall have enough for all your life. You shall serve me for seven years, and after that you shall again be free. But one thing I must tell you, and that is, you must not wash, comb, or trim yourself, or cut your hair or nails, or wipe the water from your eyes." The soldier said, "All right, if there is no help for it," and went off with the little man, who straightway led him down into hell. Then he told him what he had to do. He was to poke the fire under the kettles wherein the hell-broth was stewing, keep the house clean, drive all the sweepings behind the doors, and see that everything was in order, but if he once peeped into the kettles, it would go ill with him. The soldier said, "Good, I will take care." And then the old Devil went out again on his wanderings, and the soldier entered upon his new duties, made the fire, and swept the dirt well behind the doors, just as he had been bidden. When the old Devil came back again, he looked to see if all had been done, appeared satisfied, and went forth a second time. The soldier now took a good look on every side; the kettles were standing all round hell with a mighty fire below them, and inside they were boiling and sputtering. He would have given anything to look inside them if the Devil had not so particularly forbidden him: at last, he could no longer restrain himself, slightly raised the lid of the first kettle, and peeped in, and there he saw his former corporal shut in. "Aha, old bird!" said he, "Do I meet you here? You once had me in your power, now I have you," and he quickly let the lid fall, poked the fire, and added a fresh log. After that, he went to the second kettle, raised its lid also a little, and peeped in; his former ensign was in that. "Aha, old bird, so I find you here! you once had me in your power, now I have you." He closed the lid again, and fetched yet another log to make it really hot. Then he wanted to see who might be sitting up in the third kettle—and who should it be but his general. "Aha, old bird, do I meet you here? Once you had me in your power, now I have you." And he fetched the bellows and made hell-fire blaze right under him. So he did his work seven years in hell, did not wash, comb, or trim himself, or cut his hair or nails, or wash the water out of his eyes, and the seven years seemed so short to him that he thought he had only been half a year. Now when the time had fully gone by, the Devil came and said, "Well Hans, what have you done?" "I poked the fire under the kettles, and I have swept all the dirt well behind the doors."

"But you have peeped into the kettles as well; it is lucky for you that you added fresh logs to them, or else your life would have been forfeited; now that your time is up, will you go home again?" "Yes," said the soldier, "I should very much like to see what my father is doing at home." The Devil said, "In order that you may receive the wages you have earned, go and fill your knapsack full of the sweepings, and take it home with you. You must also go unwashed and uncombed, with long hair on your head and beard, and with uncut nails and dim eyes, and when you are asked whence you come, you must say, "From hell," and when you are asked who you are, you are to say, "The Devil's sooty brother, and my King as well." The soldier held his peace, and did as the Devil bade him, but he was not at all satisfied with his wages. Then as soon as he was up in the forest again, he took his knapsack from his back to empty it, but on opening it, the sweepings had become pure gold. "I should never have expected that," said he, and was well pleased, and entered the town. The landlord was standing in front of the inn, and when he saw the soldier approaching, he was terrified, because Hans looked so horrible, worse than a scare-crow. He called to him and asked, "Whence comest thou?" "From hell." "Who art thou?" "The Devil's sooty brother, and my King as well." Then the host would not let him enter, but when Hans showed him the gold, he came and unlatched the door himself. Hans then ordered the best room and attendance, ate, and drank his fill, but neither washed nor combed himself as the Devil had bidden him, and at last lay down to sleep. But the knapsack full of gold remained before the eyes of the landlord, and left him no peace, and during the night he crept in and stole it away. Next morning, however, when Hans got up and wanted to pay the landlord and travel further, behold his knapsack was gone! But he soon composed himself and thought, "Thou hast been unfortunate from no fault of thine own," and straightway went back again to hell, complained of his misfortune to the old Devil, and begged for his help. The Devil said, "Seat yourself, I will wash, comb, and trim you, cut your hair and nails, and wash your eyes for you," and when he had done with him, he gave him the knapsack back again full of sweepings, and said, "Go and tell the landlord that he must return you your money, or else I will come and fetch him, and he shall poke the fire in your place." Hans went up and said to the landlord, "Thou hast stolen my money; if thou dost not return it, thou shalt go down to hell in my place, and wilt look as horrible as I." Then the landlord gave him the money, and more besides, only begging him to keep it secret, and Hans was now a rich man.

He set out on his way home to his father, bought himself a shabby smock-frock to wear, and strolled about making music, for he had learned to do that while he was with the Devil in hell. There was however, an old King in that country before whom he had to play, and the King was so delighted with his playing that he promised him his eldest daughter in marriage. But when she heard that she was to be married to a common fellow in a smock-frock, she said, "Rather than do that, I would go into the deepest water." Then the King gave him the youngest, who was quite willing to do it to please her father, and thus the Devil's sooty brother got the King's daughter, and when the aged King died, the whole kingdom likewise.

The Serf as Hell's Stoker
(*Estonia*)

Back in the days of serfdom, there was a serf who ran into the woods because his master had beaten him too cruelly. While wandering in the woods, he thought to himself: "For how long will I be able to hide in this forest? One day, they'll find me anyway and then I'll get beaten even harder. Oh, how horrid is the life of a farmer! I'd rather go to work in hell!"

As he was pondering, a strange man covered in black approached him and said "What are you worrying about, man? Is your life so bad that you are complaining in the forest?"

The serf answered "Well, would you be well off getting beaten like a dog and fed like a hen?"

"Don't blame me for your misfortune, it's not my fault. If you're being treated so poorly, come with me and be my servant! You'll get a good salary there and you'll be treated well."

Being happy about the offer, the serf replied: "What kind of work will you give me? I might not be up to the task."

Don't worry, it's really not that hard! And you'll be as well off as a squire!"

"I'll come to wherever I'll be fed. Let's get going!"

The stranger led the way and the serf followed right behind. The forest got denser and more alien as they went deeper in. The serf already regretted coming along, but he was curious and followed the strange man. As the sun set, the men were still walking through the vast forest. By midnight, mysterious lights started appearing in front of them. After a short while, they were standing in front of a stunning castle with golden gates. The castle itself had thousands of lights that shined unlike anything the serf had seen before. The strange man knocked on the gates and they opened by themselves. The strange man and the serf walked into the castle. Blinded by all the splendour before him, the serf started strolling through the castle as the stranger showed him around the castle. Suddenly, the stranger stopped in front of a grandiose room and told the serf to wait there. The serf sat on a comfortable sofa and waited for the stranger's return. He returned with multiple footmen who brought an abundance of various dishes and set them on the table. The serf sat on a comfortable sofa and waited for the stranger's return. He returned with multiple footmen who brought an abundance of various dishes and set them on the table.

With the table set, the stranger and the serf sat down. The serf started eating right away, greedily shoveling these extravagant dishes. When stuffed full, he crossed his hands like he used to at home. The stranger quickly protested, saying: "Stop that right now, here it is unacceptable! Also keep in mind that you must never cross your hands after a meal, say the name of God, wash your eyes and hair or shave your beard. Obey these rules and you will be treated well, you can even leave after a year with ample salary if you so desire. Remember that you are now in hell!"

The serf was initially horrified after hearing where he was, but then thought to himself: "What problem have I got here? Hell isn't so bad as everyone says, glory and greatness everywhere! I could manage a year here." So he said: "I want to remember these rules and follow them for my time here."

"That is good," said the master, who turned out to be the Devil himself: "Tomorrow morning I shall instruct you and give you your first assignment. But now, let's go to bed."

The Devil showed the serf to his chambers and left. Lying down, the serf thought to himself: "Well damn! It sure is nice here in hell. If life here actually is this good, I'll stay here forever!"

On the second morning, the Devil visited his new servant. He was already awake and wanted to ask for water to wash his eyes, but promptly recalled his master's rules.

The Devil said: "Well! It's good you're already awake, it shows your potential as a loyal servant. Let's go to work then!"

They passed by darker and darker rooms until they arrived in a grimy lair. There, the serf saw multiple cauldrons and a fire below each. There were workers lighting the fires. The master said: "It is your job to light the fires below these cauldrons. The better you do it, the more you'll get paid. But keep in mind that the fire must never go out, or you will be in trouble! In every cauldron is a person who'll throw you in there when the fire goes out. Every day, I will bring you here and take you away."

The Devil proceeded to go away with another worker and the new servant begun his work. He didn't need to look far for wood because there were stacks of firewood all around him. Log by log, he kept the fires lit. Every once in a while, he had the time to look around and maybe even smoke a pipe. He thought to himself: "The master said that there would be a person in every cauldron, maybe I should take a look and see whether or not I'll recognize them." As he said that, he was already lifting the lid off a cauldron. "Oh!" he said. "My former master is here! You used to beat me three times a day and feed me rotten sprats or stale bread, but now I am in control of you and I will cause you suffering." He put the lid back on and lit that fire even more fiercely.

He took the lid off another cauldron and exclaimed: "Now this is jolly! My overseer who always beat me free of guilt. I wish to harm you as well." He closed the lid and continued to light the fire under the overseer's cauldron.

The serf approached the third cauldron: "I'll check out whoever is in here." He lifted the lid off and saw his squire in there. "Oh it's you, greybeard, as well! I have heard old and young people complain about your horrible actions. It is only right that you shall be incinerated here. Be quiet when I keep your fire lit!" He shut the lid and proceeded to keep the fire lit. "It is good that my former torturers are here. Oh, how great is the joy of causing them pain!"

In the evening, his master came in to check on him.

"What problem have I got with all of my former torturers under my control!" reported the serf.

The master became worried and asked "But how did you dare to look inside the cauldrons? Weren't you afraid that they would throw you in there themselves?"

"Not really," replied the serf, "I kept their fires lit so that they couldn't come out!"

"That was a good idea, otherwise you would be in the cauldron by now! Good, keep the fires lit, then you are a good servant!" He led the serf to his chamber as another servant took his place. The days went by and the serf didn't even notice that a year had passed. On the last day, the master said to the serf: "You have served here for a year and you can leave if you so desire." The serf didn't want to go yet because he wanted to burn his enemies for another year. The master was pleased by his servant's loyalty and promised to reward it well. The serf thought: "I don't know what reward I need. I am well fed, what else can I want here in hell? Besides, torturing such criminals is nice." And another year passed serenely.

The serf stayed for one more year and then wanted to leave and see what had happened on Earth. On the day he left, his master brought him a bag of sweepings and said: "For serving me well for three years, take this as a reward!"

The serf looked at the sweepings and angrily said: "So this is what I get for my service! I don't need sweepings if I can't get anything better!"

The master silenced him by saying: "Don't be angry! These sweepings will be worth a lot on Earth!"

The serf said: "We'll see." and accepted the bag.

He was thanked by the Devil once again and said: "If you ever want to return here, go to where we met." The Devil patted his back three times and the serf was amazed to find himself in the woods, where he met with the Devil for the first time three years ago. He wanted to start moving, but the bag filled with sweepings was suddenly so heavy that the man couldn't move it. He looked into the bag and saw that it was filled with pure gold. He buried most of the gold in the woods with his own fingernails, which had grown so long in hell.

He then went towards the mansion to inform the squire of his father's fate. To his surprise, everybody ran away from him because they thought that he was the devil. He did look like a devil after being in hell for three years. His hair and beard had grown very long. And so he ran into the mansion, where servants ran away from the hideous monster. The squire heard the screaming outside and went there to find out the cause for it and ran into his old serf. He was mortified because he too thought that the serf is the devil. With his frightening voice, the serf said: "Prepare yourself, because soon, you'll have to join your father in hell! He has a big cauldron there, you could fit in there nicely!"

Hearing those words, the squire was struck with such fear that he died. The former serf bought the mansion then shaved his beard and hair. He dug up the gold he had buried in the woods and stored it in the mansion's basement. He married another squire's daughter and lived a jolly life. He had enough money for a grand lifestyle, even his grandchildren were well off.

The Magic Shirt
(*Russia*)

A brave soldier was serving in his regiment when he received a hundred roubles from home. His feldwebel[1] found out about it and borrowed the money, but when it was time to pay it off, he ordered the soldier to be whipped instead. "I've never even seen your money," he said, "you shouldn't have slandered me!" The soldier got mad and ran away to the

---

1 A Russian non-commissioned officer rank.

woods. He laid down for a rest under a tree and saw a six-headed dragon flying across the sky. The dragon flew up to him, asked him about life and said, "There's no use in dragging yourself around the forest, come work for me for three years." "With pleasure!" the soldier replied. "Well, climb onto me then." The soldier started to load his belongings onto the dragon. "Why are you taking all this rubbish?" "A soldier gets beaten for a button out of place here, so why would he leave any of his belongings behind?"

The dragon brought the soldier to his chambers and told him the following, "Sit by the cauldron for three years, keep the fire up and cook the porridge!" and then took off to travel the world. It wasn't a hard job: just add wood to the fire and sit there—sip some vodka and eat some snacks, and the dragon's vodka is unlike anything he'd had, all else tastes like water by comparison. Three years passed and the dragon came back. "So, my dear serviceman, is the porridge ready?" "Has to be ready! The fire never went out the whole time." The dragon ate all of porridge at once, praised the soldier for his service and hired him for another three years.

Another three years passed; the dragon ate the porridge and kept the soldier for three more years. The soldier cooked for two years, and at the end of the third year he thought, "It's already the ninth year that I'm living here, cooking the porridge, but haven't even had it myself. I want to try it!" He lifted the lid and saw the feldwebel sitting in the cauldron. "Good," he thought, "I'll sure make you have a good time. Do you a service for your whipping." and started stacking as much wood under the cauldron as he could. Made such a fire that it boiled not only the meat, but the bones too! The dragon came back, ate the porridge, and praised the soldier: "Well, my friend! Your last porridge was good, but this one is even better! Here, choose yourself a reward for your service." The soldier looked around and chose a bogatyr's steed and a thick canvas shirt. The shirt wasn't an ordinary one: just put it on, and you'll become a bogatyr[1] yourself.

The soldier came to a king, helped him in a difficult war, and married his daughter. However, the princess didn't like that she was given to a simple soldier. She started an affair with a neighbouring prince and, to find out the source of her husband's power, she started sweet-talking him into telling her. Once she found out, she seized the moment, took the shirt off her sleeping husband and gave it to the prince. He put the magic shirt on, grabbed his sword, cut the soldier into tiny pieces, put them in a bag and told his grooms: "take this bag, attach it to some nag and run it into open field!" The grooms went to carry out the order when the bogatyr's steed turned into a nag and immediately caught their eye. They attached the

1 A knight-errant.

bag to the steed and chased it into the field. The steed took off faster than the wind, came to the dragon, stopped in front of his palace, and neighed for three days and three nights without stopping.

The dragon was asleep at the time; he had hardly woken up and heard the horse neighing and tramping when he came outside, looked in the bag, and gasped in awe! He took the chopped pieces, put them together, washed them with the water of death—the soldier's body grew together; he splashed it with water of life—and the soldier came back to life. "Oh," he said, "I slept for so long!" "You would sleep for much longer if not for your loyal steed!" the dragon replied and taught the soldier the art of taking the shape of whatever he wanted. The soldier turned into a pigeon, flew back to the prince with whom his unfaithful wife now lived, and sat in a kitchen window. A young kitchen maid saw him. "Ah," she said, "what a pretty pigeon!" She opened the window and let him into the kitchen. The pigeon struck the floor and turned back into a brave soldier: "Do me a service, fair maiden! I will make you my wife in return." "But how can I help you?" "Get me the prince's canvas shirt." "But he never takes it off! Perhaps only when he swims in the sea."

The soldier asked her when the prince swims, came out onto the road and turned into a flower. Some time later, the prince and the princess came walking to the beach, with the kitchen maid behind them carrying clean clothes. The prince saw the flower and started watching it in admiration, but the princess realized that it was a trick: "Ah, it must be that damn soldier again!" She picked the flower and crushed it and plucked all its petals. The flower turned into a tiny fly and hid in the kitchen maid's bosom. Once the prince undressed and got in the water, the fly turned into a falcon, grabbed the shirt, turned back into a man, and put it on at once. The soldier then took out his sword, put his traitor wife and her lover to death, and then married a beautiful woman—the young kitchen maid.

519: The Strong Woman as Bride

The Snow, the Crow, and the Blood
(*Ireland*)

One day in the dead of winter, when the snow lay like a linen tablecloth over the world, Jack, the King of Ireland's son, went out to shoot. He saw a crow, and he shot it, and it fell down on the snow. Jack went up to it, and he thought he never saw anything blacker than that crow, or redder than its blood, nor anything whiter than the snow round about.

He said to himself: "I'll never rest till I get a wife whose hair is as black as that crow, whose cheeks are as red as that blood, and whose skin is as white as that snow."

So he went home, and told his father and mother this. He said he was going to set off before him and look for such a girl.

The King and Queen told Jack that it would be impossible ever to get a girl that would answer that description, and tried to persuade Jack from setting out, but Jack wouldn't be persuaded.

He started off with his father's and his mother's blessing, and a hundred guineas that his father had given him in his pocket. He traveled away and away very far, and about the middle of the day on the second day out, passing a graveyard, he saw a crowd there wrangling over a corpse. He went in and inquired what was the matter, and he found there were bailiffs wanting to seize the corpse for a debt of a hundred guineas. Jack was sorry for the poor corpse, so he put his hand in his pocket, took out the hundred guineas, and paid them down; and then the friends of the corpse thanked him heartily and buried the body.

That very same evening Jack was overtaken by a little red man who asked him where he was going.

Says Jack: "I'm going in search of a wife."

"Well," says the little red man, "such a handsome young fellow as you won't have to go far."

"Far enough," says Jack, "because the girl I want must have hair as black as the blackest crow, cheeks as red as the reddest blood, and skin as white as the whitest snow."

"Then," said the little red man, "there's only one such woman in the world, and she is the Princess of the East. There's many a brave young man went there before you to court her, but none of them ever came back alive again.

"For life or for death," says Jack, "I'll never rest until I reach the Princess of the East and court her."

"Well," said the little red man, "you'll want a boy with you. Let me be your boy."

"But I have no money to pay you," says Jack. "That will be all right," says the little red man. "I'll go with you."

That night late they reached a great castle. "This castle," says the little red man, "is the castle of the Giant of the Cloak of Darkness."

"Oh," says Jack, "I've heard of that terrible giant. We'll pass on, and look for somewhere else to stop."

"No other place we'll stop than here," says the little red man, knocking at the gates.

Jack was too brave to run away, so he stood by the little red man till a great and terrible giant came to the gates and opened them, and asked them what they wanted.

"We want supper and a bed for the night," says the red fellow.

"That's good," says the giant. "I want supper and bed too. I'll make my supper off you both, and my bed on your bones." And then he let a terrible laugh out of him that made the hair stand up on poor Jack's head.

But in a flash, the wee red fellow whips out his sword and struck out at the giant, and the giant then pulled out his, and struck out at the wee red man. Both of them fell to it hard and fast, and they fought a terrible fight for a long time; but in the end the wee red man ran the giant through the heart and killed him.

Then he took Jack in, and they spread for themselves a grand supper with the best of everything eatable and drinkable, and had a good sleep, and in the morning they started off, the wee red fellow taking with him the Cloak of Darkness belonging to the giant he had killed.

They traveled on and on that day, and at night they reached another castle.

"What castle is this?" says Jack.

"This," says the wee red man, "is the castle of the Giant of the Purse of Plenty."

"Then," says Jack, "I've heard of that terrible giant. We'll push on and look for somewhere else to stop tonight."

"Nowhere else than here we'll stop," says the wee red man. "No danger ever frightened me in all my life before, and it's too late to begin to learn fright now."

And before Jack could say anything he had knocked at the gates, and a giant with two heads came out roaring, and asked them what they wanted and what brought them there.

"We don't want much," says the little red man, "only what every traveler expects—a sweet supper and a soft bed."

"I want both myself, too," says the giant, "and I'll make a sweet supper off you both, and a soft bed of your bones."

Then he laughed an awful laugh that shook the castle and made the hair stand up on poor Jack's head.

But that minute the wee red man whipped out his sword and made at him, and the giant whipped out his and made at the wee red man; and both of them fell to and had a fight long and hard, but at length the wee red man ran his sword through the giant's heart and killed him.

Then they went in, and spread for themselves a grand supper and a fine bed, in which they slept soundly till morning. And in the morning they went off, the little red man taking with him the Purse of Plenty.

All that day they traveled on before them, and when night fell they came to another great castle.

"What castle is this?" says Jack.

"This," says the little red man, "is the castle of the Giant of the Sword of Light."

"Oh," says Jack, "I've heard of that terrible giant and his awful sword, and," he says, "I want to get out of his neighborhood as fast as possible."

"Fear never made me turn my back on man or mortal yet," says the little red man, "and I don't think I'll begin this late in life. As we're here, we'll lodge here this night."

So on the gates he rattled, and out came a frightful giant, with three great heads on him, and he roared so that the hills shook; and he asked them what they were doing here and what they wanted.

"We are two poor travelers on a journey," says the little red man, "and as night fell on us we thought we would ask you to give us bed and board for the night."

"Ha! Ha!" says the giant, laughing a terrible laugh. "I'll board myself on you two this night, and I'll bed me on your bones."

And at that he drew from his scabbard the terrible Sword of Light, whose flash traveled thrice round the world every time it was drawn, and whose lightest stroke killed any being, natural or enchanted.

But that instant the little red man drew around him the Cloak of Darkness, so that he should disappear from the giant's eyes, and drawing his own sword he began whacking and hacking, hewing and cutting the giant, while the giant couldn't see him to strike him in return, and in two minutes the wee red man had run his sword through the giant's heart and killed him.

He and Jack went into the castle, and they made a hearty supper and slept soundly in the softest beds they could get, and in the morning they went off again, the wee red man taking with him the Sword of Light.

Having the Purse of Plenty, they could not know want from this forward. So they went on their journey right merrily. They traveled far and long until at length they came into the East, and pushed on for the castle of the Princess. And when they came to where the Princess lived, they took their horses (for they were now riding two beautiful steeds) to a blacksmith's forge and had them shod with gold. And when they had had them shod, they rode up to the castle. By the wee red fellow's order, they didn't wait to knock at any gates, but put their golden spurs to their horses and leaped them over the castle walls.

When the servants and soldiers saw the pair come bounding over the castle walls upon horses shod with gold, they ran out in wonder. From the Purse of Plenty the red fellow, as Jack's servant, pulled out handfuls and handfuls of silver and of gold and scattered them among the crowd.

Then the servants quickly brought word to the Princess of the East of the beautiful and rich gentleman who had come, with his servant, to court her. They told her how they had both leaped the castle walls on horses shod with gold, and that they threw away their gold in handfuls.

She sent word for Jack to be brought to her, and when Jack came into her presence, he was enchanted with the look of her; for her hair was so black, her cheeks and lips were so red, and her skin was so white, he had never seen in all his life anyone so beautiful.

"I understand you have come to court me," says she.

"That I have," says Jack.

"Well," says she, "to everyone that comes to court me, I give three tasks. If anyone performs the three tasks I give him he will win me; but if he fails in any one of the three, he will lose his head. Are you willing to try on such conditions?" says she.

"I'll try," says Jack, "upon any conditions."

She took him out then into the Garden of Heads, and showed him three hundred and sixty-five rose bushes, and for every flower there was a man's head on every one of three hundred and sixty-four of the bushes.

"There's one bush without a flower yet, Jack," says she, "but in less than three days I hope to see your head flowering on it."

Then she took him into the castle again, and treated him to a fine supper. And when they had finished supper and drunk their wine and chatted, she got up to bid him good-night.

She took out of her hair a gold comb, and showed it to him. "Now," she says, "I will wear that golden comb all night, and I'll spend this night from midnight to cockcrow neither on the earth nor under the earth. Yet you must have that comb for me in the morning, and it must be taken from my head between midnight and cockcrow." Then she stuck the comb into her hair again and went off.

Poor Jack acknowledged to himself that he had a task before him which he couldn't do. He wandered down the stairs and out of the castle, and went meandering into the garden in low spirits.

The wee red man soon came to him and asked him what was the matter.

"Oh, matter enough," says Jack, and commenced telling him all.

"Keep up your heart," says the wee red man, "and I'll see what I can do for you,"

So the little red man went and got his Cloak of Darkness, and then watched till midnight outside the Princess's door.

Just one second before the stroke of midnight, the Princess came out of her room with the golden comb in her hair, and went off to Hell. The little red man threw his Cloak of Darkness around him, and followed her.

She didn't stop till she came to Hell, where she went in, and the little red man went in after her.

The Devil was very glad to see her, and he kissed her, and the two sat down side by side and began to chat. And as they couldn't see the wee red man for his Cloak of Darkness, he came up behind and snatched the gold comb out of her hair, and went off with it; and when he came to earth, he gave the comb to Jack.

In the morning when the Princess of the East appeared at breakfast, Jack handed her her gold comb across the table. She was furious, and the eyes of her flashed fire. That night she showed him a diamond ring on her finger, and she said she would not be on earth or under the earth between midnight and cockcrow, yet he must get that ring between those two times, and have it for her in the morning.

And when she went away, Jack went down to the garden, and was wandering about there when the wee red man came up to him and asked him what was the matter, and he told the wee red man.

"Well," says the wee red man, "I'll try what I can do." And so he took his Cloak of Darkness and watched for her that night again, and just before midnight, she came out and went off. He followed her, and she didn't stop till she was in Hell, where the Devil was very glad to see her and kissed her, and they sat down side by side to chat.

The little red fellow, with his Cloak of Darkness, came up beside her and waited, and the first opportunity he got, he snatched the ring off her finger, and went off and gave it to Jack.

So when she came down to breakfast the next morning Jack handed her over the table her diamond ring; and this morning she was doubly as furious as on the morning before. "Well," she said, "you've done two of the tasks, but the third you never will do."

So that night she told him: "I will spend all the time between midnight and cockcrow neither on the earth nor under the earth; and I want you to have for me in the morning the lips I shall have kissed while I have been away. Your head I'll surely have now, for the sword was never yet made by mortal man that can cut those lips."

Then she went away.

Poor Jack, he wandered out into the garden very down-hearted at this, and sure and certain that he would lose his head in the morning.

The little red man came up to him and asked him what was the matter. Jack told him and the red fellow said: "Keep up your heart, and I'll see what can be done." And he reminded Jack that he had the Sword of Light, which was never made by mortal man.

He threw his Cloak of Darkness about him, took the Sword of Light with him, and watched by the Princess's door. Just before midnight she came out and went off, and he followed her to Hell, where the Devil welcomed her with a kiss, and as he did so the little red man raised the Sword of Light and cut the lips off of him and went off as fast as he could.

So in the morning Jack handed them across the table to the Princess, who was shaking with rage, and then he demanded her hand in marriage. And she had to consent.

As soon as they were married, the little red man said to Jack: "I have a wedding present for you." So he gave him ten blackthorns and told him to break one of these blackthorns on his wife every morning for ten mornings, and if he followed out his instructions faithfully, he would have a good wife on the tenth day.

Seeing the little red man had been such a good friend to him, Jack consented to do this. He broke a blackthorn on her every morning for ten mornings, and for every blackthorn he broke on her she was dispossessed of a devil. And on the tenth day she had lost all her rage and all her fury and all the devils, and she was the best and most perfect girl, as well as the most beautiful one, in all the world.

The little red man on the tenth day asked Jack if he remembered when he set out on his travels paying a hundred guineas to get a corpse buried. Jack said he did.

"Then," said the little red man, "it was I whom you buried, and I have tried to repay you a little. Now, good-bye, and may you and your wife prosper ever after."

The little red man disappeared, and Jack and his beautiful wife lived long and happily.

Princess on the Glass Hill
(*Germany*)

Once on a time there was a man who had a meadow which lay high up on the hill-side, and in the meadow was a barn, which he had built to keep his hay in. Now, I must tell you, there hadn't been much in the barn for the last year or two, for every St. John's night, when the grass stood greenest and deepest, the meadow was eaten down to the very ground the next morning, just as if a whole drove of sheep had been there feeding on it over night. This happened once, and it happened twice; so at last the man grew weary of losing his crop of hay, and said to his sons—for he had three of them, and the youngest was nicknamed Boots, of course—that now one of them must just go and sleep in the barn in the outlying field when St. John's night came, for it was too good a joke that his grass should be eaten, root and blade, this year, as it had been the last two years. So whichever of them went must keep a sharp look-out; that was what their father said.

Well, the eldest son was ready to go and watch the meadow; trust him for looking after the grass! It shouldn't be his fault if man or beast, or the fiend himself, got a blade of grass. So, when evening came, he set off to the barn, and lay down to sleep; but a little on in the night came such a clatter, and such an earthquake, that walls and roof shook, and groaned, and creaked; then up jumped the lad, and took to his heels as fast as ever he could; nor dared he once look round till he reached home; and as for the hay, why it was eaten up this year just as it had been twice before.

The next St. John's night, the man said again, it would never do to lose all the grass in the outlying field year after year in this way, so one of his sons must just trudge off to watch it, and watch it well too. Well, the next oldest son was ready to try his luck, so he set off, and lay down to sleep in the barn as his brother had done before him; but as the night wore on, there came on a rumbling and quaking of the earth, worse even than on the last St. John's night, and when the lad heard it, he got frightened, and took to his heels as though he were running a race.

Next year the turn came to Boots; but when he made ready to go, the other two began to laugh and to make game of him, saying,

"You're just the man to watch the hay, that you are; you, who have done nothing all your life but sit in the ashes and toast yourself by the fire."

But Boots did not care a pin for their chattering, and stumped away as evening drew on, up the hill-side to the outlying field. There he went inside the barn and lay down; but in about an hour's time the barn began to groan and creak, so that it was dreadful to hear.

"Well", said Boots to himself, "if it isn't worse than this, I can stand it well enough."

A little while after came another creak and an earthquake, so that the litter in the barn flew about the lad's ears.

"Oh!" said Boots to himself, "if it isn't worse than this, I daresay I can stand it out."

But just then came a third rumbling, and a third earthquake, so that the lad thought walls and roof were coming down on his head; but it passed off, and all was still as death about him.

"It'll come again, I'll be bound", thought Boots; but no, it didn't come again; still it was, and still it stayed; but after he had lain a little while, he heard a noise as if a horse were standing just outside the barn-door, and cropping the grass. He stole to the door, and peeped through a chink, and there stood a horse feeding away. So big, and fat, and grand a horse, Boots had never set eyes on; by his side on the grass lay a saddle and bridle, and a full set of armour for a knight, all of brass, so bright that the light gleamed from it.

"Ho, ho!" thought the lad; "it's you, is it, that eats up our hay? I'll soon put a spoke in your wheel, just see if I don't."

So he lost no time, but took the steel out of his tinder-box, and threw it over the horse; then it had no power to stir from the spot, and became so tame that the lad could do what he liked with it. So he got on its back, and rode off with it to a place which no one knew of, and there he put up the horse. When he got home, his brothers laughed and asked how he had fared?

"You didn't lie long in the barn, even if you had the heart to go so far as the field."

"Well", said Boots, "all I can say is, I lay in the barn till the sun rose, and neither saw nor heard anything; I can't think what there was in the barn to make you both so afraid."

"A pretty story", said his brothers; "but we'll soon see how you have watched the meadow"; so they set off; but when they reached it, there stood the grass as deep and thick as it had been over night.

Well, the next St. John's eve it was the same story over again; neither of the elder brothers dared to go out to the outlying field to watch the crop; but Boots, he had the heart to go, and everything happened just as it had happened the year before. First a clatter and an earthquake, then a greater clatter and another earthquake, and so on a third time; only this year the earthquakes were far worse than the year before. Then all at once everything was as still as death, and the lad heard how something was cropping the grass outside the barn-door, so he stole to the door, and peeped through a chink; and what do you think he saw? why, another horse standing right up against the wall, and chewing and champing with might and main. It was far finer and fatter than that which came the year before, and it had a saddle on its back, and a bridle on its neck, and a full suit of mail for a knight lay by its side, all of silver, and as grand as you would wish to see.

"Ho ho!" said Boots to himself; "it's you that gobbles up our hay, is it? I'll soon put a spoke in your wheel"; and with that he took the steel out of his tinder-box, and threw it over the horse's crest, which stood as still as a lamb. Well, the lad rode this horse, too, to the hiding-place where he kept the other one, and after that he went home.

"I suppose you'll tell us", said one of his brothers, "there's a fine crop this year too, up in the hayfield."

"Well, so there is", said Boots; and off ran the others to see, and there stood the grass thick and deep, as it was the year before; but they didn't give Boots softer words for all that.

Now, when the third St. John's eve came, the two elder still hadn't the heart to lie out in the barn and watch the grass, for they had got so scared at heart the night they lay there before that they couldn't get over the fright; but Boots, he dared to go; and, to make a long story short, the very same thing happened this time as had happened twice before. Three earthquakes came, one after the other, each worse than the one which went before, and when the last came, the lad danced about with the shock from one barn wall to the other; and after that, all at once, it was still as death. Now when he had lain a little while, he heard something tugging away at the grass outside the barn, so he stole again to the door-chink, and peeped out, and there stood a horse close outside—far, far bigger and fatter than the two he had taken before.

"Ho, ho!" said the lad to himself, "it's you, is it, that comes here eating up our hay? I'll soon stop that—I'll soon put a spoke in your wheel." So he caught up his steel and threw it over the horse's neck, and in a trice it stood as if it were nailed to the ground, and Boots could do as he pleased with it. Then he rode off with it to the hiding-place where he kept the other two, and then went home. When he got home, his two brothers made game of him as they had done before, saying, they could see he had watched the grass well, for he looked for all the world as if he were walking in his sleep, and many other spiteful things they said, but Boots gave no heed to them, only asking them to go and see for themselves; and when they went, there stood the grass as fine and deep this time as it had been twice before.

Now, you must know that the king of the country where Boots lived had a daughter, whom he would only give to the man who could ride up over the hill of glass, for there was a high, high hill, all of glass, as smooth and slippery as ice, close by the king's palace. Upon the tip top of the hill the king's daughter was to sit, with three golden apples in her lap, and the man who could ride up and carry off the three golden apples, was to have half the kingdom, and the Princess to wife. This the king had stuck up on all the church-doors in his realm, and had given it out in many other kingdoms besides. Now, this Princess was so lovely that all who set eyes on her fell over head and ears in love with her whether they would or no. So I needn't tell you how all the princes and knights who heard of her were eager to win her to wife, and half the kingdom beside; and how they came riding from all parts of the world on high prancing horses, and clad in the grandest clothes, for there wasn't one of them who hadn't made up his mind that he, and he alone, was to win the Princess.

So when the day of trial came, which the king had fixed, there was such a crowd of princes and knights under the glass hill that it made one's head whirl to look at them; and everyone in the country who could even crawl along was off to the hill, for they all were eager to see the man who was to win the Princess. So the two elder brothers set off with the rest; but as for Boots, they said outright he shouldn't go with them, for if they were seen with such a dirty changeling, all begrimed with smut from cleaning their shoes and sifting cinders in the dust-hole, they said folk would make game of them.

"Very well", said Boots, "it's all one to me. I can go alone, and stand or fall by myself."

Now when the two brothers came to the hill of glass, the knights and princes were all hard at it, riding their horses till they were all in a foam; but it was no good, by my troth; for as soon as ever the horses set foot on the hill, down they slipped, and there wasn't one who could get a yard or two up; and no wonder, for the hill was as smooth as a sheet of glass, and as steep as a house-wall. But all were eager to have the Princess and half the kingdom. So they rode and slipped, and slipped and rode, and still it was the same story over again. At last all their horses were so weary that they could scarce lift a leg, and in such a sweat that the lather dripped from them, and so the knights had to give up trying any more. So the king was just thinking that he would proclaim a new trial for the next day, to see if they would have better luck, when all at once a knight came riding up on so brave a steed that no one had ever seen the like of it in his born days, and the knight had mail of brass, and the horse a brass bit in his mouth, so bright that the sunbeams shone from it. Then all the others called out to him he might just as well spare himself the trouble of riding at the hill, for it would lead to no good; but he gave no heed to them, and put his horse at the hill, and went up it like nothing for a good way, about a third of the height; and when he had got so far, he turned his horse round and rode down again. So lovely a knight the Princess thought she had never yet seen; and while he was riding, she sat and thought to herself: "Would to heaven he might only come up and down the other side."

And when she saw him turning back, she threw down one of the golden apples after him, and it rolled down into his shoe. But when he got to the bottom of the hill he rode off so fast that no one could tell what had become of him. That evening all the knights and princes were to go before the king, that he who had ridden so far up the hill might show the apple which the princess had thrown, but there was no one who had anything to show. One after the other they all came, but not a man of them could show the apple.

At even the brothers of Boots came home too, and had such a long story to tell about the riding up the hill.

"First of all", they said, "there was not one of the whole lot who could get so much as a stride up; but at last came one who had a suit of brass mail, and a brass bridle and saddle, all so bright that the sun shone from them a mile off. He was a chap to ride, just! He rode a third of the way up the hill of glass, and he could easily have ridden the whole way up, if he chose; but he turned round and rode down, thinking, maybe, that was enough for once."

"Oh! I should so like to have seen him, that I should", said Boots, who sat by the fireside, and stuck his feet into the cinders, as was his wont.

"Oh!" said his brothers, "you would, would you? You; look fit to keep company with such high lords, nasty beast that you are, sitting there amongst the ashes."

Next day the brothers were all for setting off again, and Boots begged them this time, too, to let him go with them and see the riding; but no, they wouldn't have him at any price, he was too ugly and nasty, they said.

"Well, well!" said Boots;" if I go at all, I must go by myself. I'm not afraid."

So when the brothers got to the hill of glass, all the princes and knights began to ride again, and you may fancy they had taken care to shoe their horses sharp; but it was no good—they rode and slipped, and slipped and rode, just as they had done the day before, and there was not one who could get so far as a yard up the hill. And when they had worn out their horses, so that they could not stir a leg, they were all forced to give it up as a bad job. So the king thought he might as well proclaim that the riding should take place the day after for the last time, just to give them one chance more; but all at once it came across his mind that he might as well wait a little longer, to see if the knight in brass mail would come this day too. Well! they saw nothing of him; but all at once came one riding on a steed, far, far, braver and finer than that on which the knight in brass had ridden, and he had silver mail, and a silver saddle and bridle, all so bright that the sun-beams gleamed and glanced from them far away. Then the others shouted out to him again, saying he might as well hold hard, and not try to ride up the hill, for all his trouble would be thrown away; but the knight paid no heed to them, and rode straight at the hill, and right up it, till he had gone two-thirds of the way, and then he wheeled his horse round and rode down again. To tell the truth, the Princess liked him still better than the knight in brass, and she sat and wished he might only be able to come right up to the top, and down the other side; but when she saw him turning back, she threw the second apple after him, and it rolled down and fell into his shoe. But, as soon as ever he had come down from the hill of glass, he rode off so fast that no one could see what became of him.

At even, when all were to go in before the king and the Princess, that he who had the golden apple might show it, in they went, one after the other, but there was no one who had any apple to show, and the two brothers, as they had done on the former day, went home and told how things had gone, and how all had ridden at the hill, and none got up.

"But, last of all", they said, "came one in a silver suit, and his horse had a silver saddle and a silver bridle. He was just a chap to ride; and he got two-thirds up the hill, and then turned back. He was a fine fellow, and no mistake; and the Princess threw the second gold apple to him."

"Oh!" said Boots, "I should so like to have seen him too, that I should."

"A pretty story", they said. "Perhaps you think his coat of mail was as bright as the ashes you are always poking about, and sifting, you nasty dirty beast."

The third day everything happened as it had happened the two days before. Boots begged to go and see the sight, but the two wouldn't hear of his going with them. When they got to the hill there was no one who could get so much as a yard up it; and now all waited for the knight in silver mail, but they neither saw nor heard of him. At last came one riding on a steed, so brave that no one had ever seen his match; and the knight had a suit of golden mail, and a golden saddle and bridle, so wondrous bright that the sunbeams gleamed from them a mile off. The other knights and princes could not find time to call out to him not to try his luck, for they were amazed to see how grand he was. So he rode right at the hill, and tore up it like nothing, so that the Princess hadn't even time to wish that he might get up the whole way. As soon as ever he reached the top, he took the third golden apple from the Princess' lap, and then turned his horse and rode down again. As soon as he got down, he rode off at full speed, and was out of sight in no time.

Now, when the brothers got home at even, you may fancy what long stories they told, how the riding had gone off that day; and amongst other things, they had a deal to say about the knight in golden mail.

"He just was a chap to ride!" they said; "so grand a knight isn't to be found in the wide world."

"Oh!" said Boots, "I should so like to have seen him, that I should."

"Ah! "said his brothers, "his mail shone a deal brighter than the glowing coals which you are always poking and digging at; nasty dirty beast that you are."

Next day all the knights and princes were to pass before the king and the Princess—it was too late to do so the night before, I suppose—that he who had the gold apple might bring it forth; but one came after another, first the princes, and then the knights, and still no one could show the gold apple.

"Well", said the king, "someone must have it, for it was something that we all saw with our own eyes, how a man came and rode up and bore it off."

So he commanded that everyone who was in the kingdom should come up to the palace and see if they could show the apple. Well, they all came one after another, but no one had the golden apple, and after a long time the two brothers of Boots came. They were the last of all, so the king asked them if there was no one else in the kingdom who hadn't come.

"Oh, yes", said they; "we have a brother, but he never carried off the golden apple. He hasn't stirred out of the dusthole on any of the three days."

"Never mind that", said the king; "he may as well come up to the palace like the rest."

So Boots had to go up to the palace.

"How, now", said the king; "have you got the golden apple? Speak out!"

"Yes, I have", said Boots; "here is the first, and here is the second, and here is the third too"; and with that he pulled all three golden apples out of his pocket, and at the same time threw off his sooty rags, and stood before them in his gleaming golden mail.

"Yes!" said the king; "you shall have my daughter, and half my kingdom, for you well deserve both her and it."

So they got ready for the wedding, and Boots got the Princess to wife, and there was great merry-making at the bridal-feast, you may fancy, for they could all be merry though they couldn't ride up the hill of glass; and all I can say is, if they haven't left off their merry-making yet, why, they're still at it.

The Legless Knight and the Blind Knight
(*Russia*)

In a certain kingdom in a certain land a Tsar and his Tsarítsa lived. They had a son called Iván Tsarévich, and the son had an attendant who was called Katomá Dyádka of the oaken-cap. When the Tsar and the Tsarítsa had reached a great age both of them became ill, and they felt that they would never become hale again. So they called Iván Tsarévich, and said to him: "If we die, always follow Katomá's advice, and do well by him, then you will live happily; but if you do not, you will falter and fail like a fly."

Next day the Tsar and the Tsarítsa died. Iván Tsarévich buried his parents, heeded their advice, and always took counsel with Katomá before undertaking any enterprise.

Very soon, maybe a long time, maybe short, he grew up, and he wanted to marry. He said to Katomá: "Katomá Oaken-cap, it is so melancholy living by oneself; I want to marry."

"Tsarévich," Katomá replied, "you are of the age at which you ought to look for a bride: go into the great hall, where you will see pictures of all the Korolévny and Tsarévny in the world. Gaze on them carefully, and select for yourself a bride, one who pleases you, and you shall marry her."

Iván Tsarévich went into the great hall, looked at the pictures, and he was most delighted with Anna the Fair. She was so fair that she was fairer than any princess in the world. But under her portrait there was a legend: "*He who can set her a riddle she cannot solve is to marry her. Anyone whose riddle she solves dies.*"

Iván Tsarévich read the legend, and was very sad. He went up to Katomá and said: "I was in the great hall, and I selected as my bride Anna the Fair: but I do not know whether I can woo her."

"Yes, Tsarévich, it will be hard for you; if you had to go there by yourself, you would never win her. Take me. Do what I say, and all will go well."

Then Iván Tsarévich begged Katomá Oaken-cap to fare there with him, and pledged him his word of honour he would obey him in joy and sorrow.

So they set out on the way to seek Anna the Fair Tsarévna. They journeyed for one year, the second year, and the third year, and they traversed many lands. Iván Tsarévich said, "We have been so long on the journey and are at last approaching the realms of Anna the Fair, and still we have not thought out any riddles for her!"

"Time enough yet," Katomá replied.

So they rode on, and Katomá saw a purse lying on the road and said: "Iván Tsarévich, there is your riddle for the Tsarévna; give her this riddle to solve: 'Good lies on the road: we took the good with good, and set it down to our good.' That she will never solve all her life long, for every riddle she has solved at once, for she had only to look in her magical book; and she would then have your head cut off."

At last the Tsarévich and Katomá came to a lofty castle, where the fair Tsarévna lived. She was just standing at her balcony, and sent her messengers to meet them, to know whence they came and what was their will.

Iván Tsarévich answered: "I have come from my distant realm in order to woo Anna Tsarévna the Fair."

This she was told, and she bade the Tsarévich be introduced into her castle: he was to set her a riddle in front of all her councillors and her princes and *boyárs*.[1] "For I have sworn," she said, "to marry him who

1 Nobles.

sets me a riddle I cannot solve: but if I guess it, then he must die." The fair
Tsarévna listened to the riddle: "Good lies on the road; we took the good
with good, and set it down to our good."

Anna the Fair took her conjuring book and searched it through for the
riddle—looked the whole book through in vain. So the princes and *boyárs*
decided that she must marry the Tsarévich. But she was very gloomy over
it, yet still had to make ready. But in her heart of hearts she kept thinking: "How could I postpone the date and get rid of my bridegroom?" So
she decided to tire him out through severe tasks. One day she called Iván
Tsarévich to her and said: "Dear Iván Tsarévich, my chosen mate, we
must get ready for the marriage. Do me a small service. In my realm there
stands in a certain village a great iron column: bring it to the great kitchen
and split it up into little logs as firewood for the cook."

"What do you want, Tsarévna? Have I come to cut down fuel for you?
Is that my duty? Oh, my servant can see to that!" So he called Katomá,
and he told him to bring the iron column into the kitchen and to hew it
into small logs as fuel for the cook.

Katomá at once went, took the pillar in his two hands, brought it into
the kitchen and split it up. But he kept back four iron shafts and put them
into his pocket, for he thought: "Later I may make use of them!"

Next day the Tsarévna said, "Dear Tsarévich, my chosen husband,
to-morrow we shall marry. I shall go in a carriage to church, and you will
have a fine prancing steed given you. You must get him ready yourself."

"I must get the horse ready! Oh, my servant can do that!"

So Iván Tsarévich called Katomá, and said: "Come into the stable and
command the grooms to bring the horse out; ride it, and to-morrow I will
go to church on it."

But Katomá could see the guile in the Tsarévna's heart, and instantly went into the stable and ordered them to bring the horse out. Twelve
grooms opened the twelve locks, undid twelve doors, and led the magical
horse out by twelve chains. Katomá went up to him, and as soon as ever
he had swung himself on to the horse's back the steed rose high into the
air, higher than the tree-tops in the forest, lower than the clouds in heav-
en. But Katomá had a firm seat, and with one hand he held the mane, and
with the other he fetched an iron sheet out of his pocket and struck the
palfrey[1] between the ears.

One sheet broke, then he took a second and a third; and after the third
broke he was taking the fourth. The horse was so tired that it could not
resist him anymore, but spoke in a human voice: "Father Katomá, leave
me some life, and I will come down to earth and whatever you will I will
do."

---

1 A particular variety of riding horse.

"Listen then, wretched animal!" Katomá answered. "To-morrow Iván Tsarévich will ride you to his wedding. Listen! When the servants take you into the broad courtyard, and he comes up to you and lays his hand on you, stand still: do not prick your ear. When he mounts, kneel down with your hoofs on the ground, and step under him with a heavy tread as if you were bearing a burdensome load." So the horse sank half-dead on to the earth. Katomá, seated by the tail, hailed the grooms and said, "Ho, you there! grooms and coachmen, take this carrion into the stable."

Next day came, and the hour for going to church. The Tsarévna had a carriage ready, and the Tsarévich was given the magical horse. And from all parts of the country the people had assembled in multitudes, countless multitudes, to see the bride and bridegroom leave the white stone palace. And the Tsarévna went into the carriage and was waiting to see what would happen to Iván Tsarévich. She thought to herself that the horse would prance him up against the winds, and that she could already see his bones scattered in the open fields.

Iván Tsarévich went up to the horse, laid his hand on its back, put his foot into the stirrup, and the magical horse stood there as though he were made of stone, and never pricked an ear. The Tsarévich mounted it, and the horse bowed deep to the earth. Then his twelve chains were taken off. And he stood with a heavy even tread, whilst the sweat ran down his back in streams.

"What a hero he is! What enormous strength!" all the people said as Iván Tsarévich paced by.

So the bride and the bridegroom were betrothed, and went hand-in-hand out of the church.

The Tsarévna still wanted to test her husband's strength, and squeezed his hand, but she squeezed so hard that he could not stand it, and his blood mounted to his head, and his eyes almost fell out of their sockets. "That's the manner of hero *you* are!" she thought. "Your man, Katomá Oaken-cap, has deceived me finely. But I shall soon be even with him."

Anna Tsarévna the Fair lived with her God-sent husband as a good wife should, and always listened to his words. But she was ever thinking how she might destroy Katomá. If she knew that, she could very easily dispose of the Tsarévich. But, however many slanders she might think of to tell him, Iván Tsarévich never believed her, but held Katomá fast.

One year later he said to his wife: "Dear wife, beautiful Tsarévna, I should like to go home with you."

"Yes, we will go together. I have long wished to see your kingdom."

So they set out, and Katomá sat behind the coachman. As they drove out Iván Tsarévich dozed off.

Then Anna the Fair suddenly roused him from his sleep and complained. "Listen, Iván Tsarévich: you are always asleep and notice nothing. Katomá will not obey me, but is purposely taking the horses over all the cobbles and into all the ditches, as if he wanted to destroy us. I spoke to him very gently, but he only laughs at me. I will not go on living if you do not punish him!"

Iván Tsarévich was drowsy, and very angry with Katomá, and said to the king's daughter: "Do with him as you will."

So the king's daughter at once made her servants cut off Katomá's legs. He submitted to his torturers and thought: "If I must suffer, still the Tsarévich will soon learn something of what trouble is."

His two legs were cut off: the Tsarévna looked round and noticed a lofty stump at the edge of the road. She bade her servants set Katomá on it. And as to the Tsarévich, she tied him to a rope behind the carriage, and so returned to her own kingdom. Katomá sat on his tree stem and wept bitter tears.

"Farewell, Iván Tsarévich: forget me not!"

Iván Tsarévich had to leap behind the carriage, and knew very well that he had made a mistake, but it could not be cured.

When Anna the Fair had again reached her kingdom the Tsarévich had to mind the cows. Every morning he drove them into the open field, and every evening drove them back into the royal courtyard; and the Tsarévna sat on the balcony and saw that none of the cows was missing. Iván Tsarévich had to count the cows and to stable them all, and to give the last one a kiss under its tail. The cow knew what was expected of her, and remained standing at the door and lifted her tail up.

Katomá all day long sat on his tree-stump without meat or drink, but could not descend, and he thought: "I must die of hunger." But nearby there was a thick forest, and there a knight lived who was blind but very strong. This knight used to scent the animals which ran by, run after them and catch them, not minding whether it were a rabbit, or fox, or a bear. He could roast them for lunch. And he could run so fast, faster than any animal that leaps. One day a fox came by, and the knight heard him and ran after him. The fox ran up to the tree on which Katomá sat, and turned round there. In his haste the blind man struck the tree so hard with his forehead that it fell out with its roots. Katomá tumbled down and asked: "Who are you?"

"I am the blind knight, and for three years I have lived in the wood, feeding myself on the animals I can catch and bake on my fire; otherwise I should have died of hunger."

"Were you blind from birth?"

"No; Anna the Fair put my eyes out."

"Brother!" said Katomá, "she also cut off my legs, both of them."

So the two knights decided they would live together and aid each other.

The blind man said to Katomá, "Sit on my back and show me the way:

I will serve you with my feet and you me with your eyes." The blind man lifted Katomá up, and the legless man cried out, "Left; right; straight on!" So for a long while they lived in the wood and used to catch rabbits, foxes and bears for their food.

One day Katomá said: "Why should we live alone here? I am told that there is in the town a rich merchant and his daughter. She, they say, is indescribably kind towards the poor men and cripples, and gives them alms with her own hands. Brother, we must carry her off. She shall live with us as the mistress of the house."

So the blind man took a barrow, put the legless knight into it, and ran him into the town, up to the merchant's house. When the daughter looked out of the window she instantly rushed out in order to give them alms. She came to Katomá and said, "Take this as God's blessing!"

He accepted her gift and laid hold of her hand, dragged her into the barrow, and cried out to the blind man, who ran away so fast, faster than any horses could overtake him. It was all in vain for the merchant to try to overtake the two knights. The knights brought the merchant's daughter to their *izbá*[1] in the wood and said: "Stay with us as our sister, and become the mistress of the house. We poor folk have no one to cook our food or to do the washing. God will not desert you therefor."

So the merchant's daughter remained with them, and the two knights honoured and loved her as though she were their own sister. Sometimes they went a-hunting, and then the sister remained alone in the house looking after the domestic service, cooking the food and doing the washing. But one day Bába Yagá with the bony legs came into the hut and sucked the blood out of the fair maiden's breast. And whenever the two knights went away on the chase, Bába Yagá came back, so that very soon the merchant's fair daughter became thin and feeble. But the blind man did not notice: only Katomá noticed that something had gone wrong, so he told his companion, and both asked their sister what was the cause.

Bába Yagá had forbidden her to tell them anything about it; she was therefore much too frightened for a long time to tell them what was her trouble. But at last they persuaded her, and she told them: "Every time when you go out on the chase an ancient hag comes into the hut. She has an evil face and long grey hairs. She hangs her head down over me and sucks my white breast."

"Oh," said the blind man, "that is the Bába Yagá! Wait a little bit. We must deal with her in her own fashion. To-morrow we must not go hunting: we will try to catch her in the house and to capture her."

Next morning both of them went out. "Creep under the bench," said the blind man to Katomá, and sit still. "I will go into the courtyard, and

---

1 A traditional Slavic rural log house.

wait under the window. And you, Sister, sit down. If Bába Yagá comes, whilst you are combing her hair weave a part of her hair and hang the knot on to the window. I will then seize her by her grey tresses," It was said and done. The blind man seized Bába Yagá by her grey tresses, and cried out, "Ho, Katomá! come out and hold the evil hag till I get into the hut."

Bába Yagá heard it, and she wanted to lift her head and leap away, but she was unable. She tore and grumbled, but it was no good. Katomá crept out from the bank and turned round on her, threw himself on her like a mountain of iron. He strangled her until the heavens appeared to her as small as a sheepskin.

The blind man sprang out of the hut and said: "We must build a big faggot-heap and burn the old hag and scatter her ashes to the four winds."

Bába Yagá besought them: "Father, doveling, forgive me. Whatever you will I will do!"

"Very well, ancient witch," said the knights, "show us the well with the waters of Life and Death."

"If you will only not lay me low, I will show it you."

Then Katomá mounted the blind man's back and he took Bába Yagá by her hair. So they fared into the deepest part of the slumberous forest, and she there showed them a well and said: "This is the healing water that renders life."

"Take care, Katomá, do not make a mistake. If she deceives us this time we may not be able to repair it all our life long."

So Katomá broke off a twig. It had hardly fallen into the water before it flamed up.

"Ah! that was a further deceit of yours!"

So the two knights made ready to throw Bába Yagá into the fiery brook. But she still prayed for mercy as before, and swore a great oath she would not deceive any more.

"Really and truly I will show you the right water!"

So the two knights were ready once more to adventure it, and Bába Yagá took them to another well. Katomá broke off a dry twig from the tree and threw it into the well. The twig had hardly fallen into the water before it sprouted up and became green and blue. "This water is right," said Katomá, so the blind man washed his eyes and could at once see. And he put the cripple into the water, and his legs grew on to him.

Then they were both very glad, and said, "Now we are healthy, we will again talk of our own rights; but we must first settle our account with Bába Yagá. If we now forgive her, we shall get no good thereby, for she will strive ever against us all her life." So they took her back to the fiery brook and threw her into it, and she was burned to death.

Katomá then married the merchant's daughter, and all three went back into the kingdom of Anna Tsarévna the Fair to free Iván Tsarévich. They went into the capital, and there he met them with his herd of cows.

"Stay, herd," said Katomá, "whither are you driving the cattle?"

"Into the Queen's courtyard; the Tsarévna counts them every day to see whether all the cows have come home."

"Herd, put on my clothes; I will put on yours and will drive the cows home."

"No, brother, that will never do. Should the Tsarévna notice it, I should suffer."

"Fear nothing; nothing will happen, you will come by no harm; Katomá is your surety."

Iván sighed: "O good man! if only he were here I should not be herding cows."

Then Katomá showed himself who he was, and the Tsarévich embraced him tenderly and wept bitterly. "I never expected I should see you any more!"

So they changed clothes, and Katomá drove the cows into the royal courtyard. Anna Tsarévna came out on to her balcony and counted the cattle. Then she commanded to take them all into the stable. All the cows went into the stable: only the last stayed behind and raised her tail. Katomá sprang up at her and cried out, "Wretched animal! why are you stopping here?" So he gripped and snatched the tail so mightily that the entire skin remained in his hand.

When Anna Tsarévna saw this she cried out aloud, "What is that wretched herdsman doing? Lay hold of him and bring him to me."

So the attendants laid hold on Katomá and dragged him into the castle. Katomá suffered it without resistance and relied on his strength.

He was taken up to the Tsarévna, who looked at him and said, "Who are you?"

"I am Katomá, whose legs you once cut off and then set on a tree trunk."

Then the Tsarévna thought, "If he can get his legs back, I can do no more against him." And she asked for forgiveness from him and the Tsarévich. She repented of her sins and swore an oath that she would ever love Iván Tsarévich and obey him in all things.

Iván Tsarévich forgave her, and forthwith they lived in peace and unison. The knight who was once blind stayed by them. But Katomá went away with his wife to the rich merchant and abode in his house.

575: The Prince's Wings

The Flying Trunk
(*Denmark*)

There was once a merchant who was so rich that he could have paved the whole street, and perhaps even a little side-street besides, with silver. But he did not do that; he knew another way of spending his money. If he spent a shilling he got back a florin—such an excellent merchant he was till he died.

Now his son inherited all this money. He lived very merrily; he went every night to the theatre, made paper kites out of five-pound notes, and played ducks and drakes with sovereigns instead of stones. In this way the money was likely to come soon to an end, and so it did.

At last he had nothing left but four shillings, and he had no clothes except a pair of slippers and an old dressing-gown.

His friends did not trouble themselves any more about him; they would not even walk down the street with him.

But one of them who was rather good-natured sent him an old trunk with the message, 'Pack up!" That was all very well, but he had nothing to pack up, so he got into the trunk himself.

It was an enchanted trunk, for as soon as the lock was pressed it could fly. He pressed it, and away he flew in it up the chimney, high into the clouds, further and further away. But whenever the bottom gave a little creak he was in terror lest the trunk should go to pieces, for then he would have turned a dreadful somersault—just think of it!

In this way he arrived at the land of the Turks. He hid the trunk in a wood under some dry leaves, and then walked into the town. He could do that quite well, for all the Turks were dressed just as he was—in a dressing-gown and slippers.

He met a nurse with a little child.

'Hello! you Turkish nurse,' said he, 'what is that great castle there close to the town? The one with the windows so high up?'

'The sultan's daughter lives there,' she replied. 'It is prophesied that she will be very unlucky in her husband, and so no one is allowed to see her except when the sultan and sultana are by.'

'Thank you,' said the merchant's son, and he went into the wood, sat himself in his trunk, flew on to the roof, and crept through the window into the princess's room.

She was lying on the sofa asleep, and was so beautiful that the young merchant had to kiss her. Then she woke up and was very much frightened, but he said he was a Turkish god who had come through the air to see her, and that pleased her very much.

They sat close to each other, and he told her a story about her eyes. They were beautiful dark lakes in which her thoughts swam about like mermaids. And her forehead was a snowy mountain, grand and shining. These were lovely stories.

Then he asked the princess to marry him, and she said yes at once.

'But you must come here on Saturday,' she said, 'for then the sultan and the sultana are coming to tea with me. They will be indeed proud that I receive the god of the Turks. But mind you have a really good story ready, for my parents like them immensely. My mother likes something rather moral and high-flown, and my father likes something merry to make him laugh.'

'Yes, I shall only bring a fairy story for my dowry,' said he, and so they parted. But the princess gave him a sabre set with gold pieces which he could use.

Then he flew away, bought himself a new dressing-gown, and sat down in the wood and began to make up a story, for it had to be ready by Saturday, and that was no easy matter.

When he had it ready it was Saturday.

The sultan, the sultana, and the whole court were at tea with the princess.

He was most graciously received.

'Will you tell us a story?' said the sultana; 'one that is thoughtful and instructive?'

'But something that we can laugh at,' said the sultan.

'Oh, certainly,' he replied, and began: *'Now, listen attentively. There was once a box of matches which lay between a tinder-box and an old iron pot, and they told the story of their youth.'*

'"We used to be on the green fir-boughs. Every morning and evening we had diamond-tea, which was the dew, and the whole day long we had sunshine, and the little birds used to tell us stories. We were very rich, because the other trees only dressed in summer, but we had green dresses in summer and in winter. Then the woodcutter came, and our family was split up. We have now the task of making light for the lowest people. That is why we grand people are in the kitchen."

'"My fate was quite different," said the iron pot, near which the matches lay.

'"Since I came into the world I have been many times scoured, and have cooked much. My only pleasure is to have a good chat with my companions when I am lying nice and clean in my place after dinner."

'"Now you are talking too fast," spluttered the fire.

'"Yes, let us decide who is the grandest!" said the matches.

'"No, I don't like talking about myself," said the pot.

'"Let us arrange an evening's entertainment. I will tell the story of my life.

'"On the Baltic by the Danish shore—"

'"What a beautiful beginning!" said all the plates. "That's a story that will please us all."

'And the end was just as good as the beginning. All the plates clattered for joy.

'"Now I will dance," said the tongs, and she danced. Oh! how high she could kick!

'The old chair-cover in the corner split when he saw her.

'The urn would have sung but she said she had a cold; she could not sing unless she boiled.

'In the window was an old quill pen. There was nothing remarkable about her except that she had been dipped too deeply into the ink. But she was very proud of that.

'"If the urn will not sing," said she, "outside the door hangs a nightingale in a cage who will sing."

'"I don't think it's proper," said the kettle, "that such a foreign bird should be heard."

'"Oh, let us have some acting," said everyone. "Do let us!"

'Suddenly the door opened and the maid came in. Everyone was quite quiet. There was not a sound. But each pot knew what he might have done, and how grand he was.

'The maid took the matches and lit the fire with them. How they spluttered and flamed, to be sure! "Now everyone can see," they thought, "that we are the grandest! How we sparkle! What a light—"

'But here they were burnt out.'

'That was a delightful story!' said the sultana. 'I quite feel myself in the kitchen with the matches. Yes, now you shall marry our daughter.'

'Yes, indeed,' said the sultan, 'you shall marry our daughter on Monday.' And they treated the young man as one of the family.

The wedding was arranged, and the night before the whole town was illuminated.

Biscuits and gingerbreads were thrown among the people, the street boys stood on tiptoe crying hurrahs and whistling through their fingers. It was all splendid.

'Now I must also give them a treat,' thought the merchant's son. And so he bought rockets, crackers, and all the kinds of fireworks you can think of, put them in his trunk, and flew up with them into the air.

Whirr-r-r, how they fizzed and blazed!

All the Turks jumped so high that their slippers flew above their heads; such a splendid glitter they had never seen before.

Now they could quite well understand that it was the god of the Turks himself who was to marry the princess.

As soon as the young merchant came down again into the wood with his trunk he thought, 'Now I will just go into the town to see how the show has taken.'

And it was quite natural that he should want to do this.

Oh! what stories the people had to tell!

Each one whom he asked had seen it differently, but they had all found it beautiful.

'I saw the Turkish god himself,' said one. 'He had eyes like glittering stars, and a beard like foaming water.'

'He flew away in a cloak of fire,' said another. They were splendid things that he heard, and the next day was to be his wedding day.

Then he went back into the wood to sit in his trunk; but what had become of it? The trunk had been burnt. A spark of the fireworks had set it alight, and the trunk was in ashes. He could no longer fly, and could never reach his bride.

She stood the whole day long on the roof and waited; perhaps she is waiting there still.

But he wandered through the world and told stories; though they are not so merry as the one he told about the matches.

The Winged Hero
(Romania)

There was a certain great craftsman, and he was rich. He took to drinking and gambling, and drank away all his wealth, and grew poor, so that he had nothing to eat. He saw a dream, that he should make himself wings; and he made himself wings, and screwed them on, and flew to the Ninth Region, to the emperor's castle, and lighted down. And the emperor's son went forth to meet him, and asked him, 'Where do you come from, my man?'

'I come from afar.'

'Sell me your wings.'

'I will.'

'What do you want for them?'

'A thousand gold pieces.'

And he gave him them, and said to him, 'Go home with the wings, and come back in a month's time.'

He flew home, and came back in a month; and the prince said to him, 'Screw the wings on to me.'

And he screwed them on, and wrote down for the prince which peg he was to turn to fly, and which peg he was to turn to alight. The prince flew a little, and let himself down on the ground, and gave him another thousand florins more, and gave him also a horse, that he might ride home. The prince screwed on the wings, and flew to the south. A wind arose from the south, and tossed the trees, and drove him to the north. In the north dwelt the wind, drove him to the Ninth Region. And a fire was shining in the city. And he lighted down on the earth, and unscrewed his wings, and folded them by his side, and came into the house. There was an old woman, and he asked for food. She gave him a dry crust, and he ate it not. He lay down and slept. And in the morning he wrote a letter for her, and gave her money, and sent her to a cookshop with a letter to the cookshop to give him good food. And the old woman came home, and gave him to eat, and he also gave to the old woman. He went outside, and saw the emperor's palace with three stories of stone and the fourth of glass. And he asked the old woman, 'Who lives in the palace? and who lives in the fourth story?'

'The emperor's daughter lives there. He won't let her go out. He gives her her food there by a rope.'

And the maid-servant lowered the rope, and they fastened the victuals to it, and she drew them up by the rope. And the maid-servant had a bed-chamber apart, where she slept only of a night, and the day she passed with the princess.

And that emperor's son screwed on his wings and flew up, flew to the glass house, and he looked to see how the bars opened, and opened them, and let himself in. And she was lying lifeless on the bed. And he shakes her, and she never speaks. And he took the candle from her head; and she arose, and embraced him, and said to him, 'Since you are come to me, you are mine, and I am yours.' They loved one another till daybreak; then he went out, placed the candle at her head, and she was dead. And he closed the bars again, and flew back to the old woman.

Half a year he visited the princess. She fell with child. The maid-servant noticed that she was growing big, and her clothes did not fit her. She wrote a letter to the emperor: 'What will this be, that your daughter is big?' The emperor wrote back a letter to her: 'Smear the floor at night with dough, and whoever comes will leave his mark on the floor.' She placed the candle at her head, and the girl lay dead. And she smeared the floor with dough, and went to her chamber. The emperor's son came again to her, and let himself in to her, and never noticed they had smeared the floor, and made footprints with his shoes, and the dough stuck to his shoes, but he never noticed it, and went home to the old woman, and lay down and slept. The servant-maid went to the emperor's daughter, and saw the footprints, and wrote a letter to the emperor, and took the measure of the footprints, and sent it to the emperor. The emperor summoned two servants, and gave them a letter, and gave them the measure of the footprints. 'Whose shoes the measure shall fit, bring him to me.' They traversed the whole city, and found nothing.

And one said, 'Let's try the old woman's.'

And another said, 'No, there's nobody there.'

'Stay here. I'll go.'

And he saw him sleeping, and applied the measure to his shoes. They summoned him. 'Come to the emperor.'

'All right.'

He bought himself a great cloak, and put it on, so that his wings might not be noticed, and went to the emperor. The emperor asked him, 'Have you been going to my daughter?'

'I have.'

'With what purpose have you done so?'

'I want to marry her.'

The emperor said, 'Bah! you'll not marry her, for I'll burn you both with thorns.'

The emperor commanded his servants, and they gathered three loads of thorns, and set them on fire, and lowered her down, to put them both on the fire. The emperor's son asked, 'Allow us to say a *pater noster*.' He said to the girl, 'When I fall on my knees, do you creep under the cloak and clasp me round the neck, for I'll fly upwards with you.'

She clasped him round the neck, and quickly he screwed the wings, and flew upwards. The cloak flew off, the soldiers fired their guns at it; on he flew. She cried, 'Let yourself down, for I shall bear a child.'

He said, 'Hold out.'

He flew further, and alighted on a rock on a mountain, and she brought forth a child there. She said, 'Make a fire.' He saw a fire in a field afar off. He screwed his wings, and flew to the fire, and took a brand of it, and returned. And a spark fell on one wing, and the wing caught fire. Just as he was under the mountain the wing fell off, and he flung away the other one as well. And he walked round the mountain, and could not ascend it.

And God came to him and said, 'Why weepest thou?' Ah! how should I not weep? for I cannot ascend the mountain, and my wife has brought forth a child.'

'What will you give me if I carry you up to the top?'

'I will give you whatever you want.'

'Will you give me what is dearest to you?'

'I will.'

'Let us make an agreement.'

They made one. God cast him into a deep sleep, and her as well, and God bore them home to his father's, to his own bed, and left them there, and departed. And the child cried. The warders heard a child crying in the bedchamber. They went and opened the door, and recognised him, the emperor's son. And they went to the emperor and told him, Your son has come, O emperor.'

'Call him to me.'

They came to the emperor; they bowed themselves before him; they tarried there a year. The boy grew big, and was playing one day. The emperor and the empress went to church, and his nurse too went to the church. God came, disguised like a beggar. The emperor's son said to the little lad, 'Take a handful of money, and give it to the beggar.'

The beggar said, 'I don't want this money; it's bad. Tell your father to give me what he vowed he would.'

The emperor's son was angry, and he took his sword in his hand, and went to the old man to kill him. The old man took the sword into his own hand and said, 'Give me what you swore to me—the child, you know—when you were weeping under the mountain.'

'I will give you money, I will not give you the child.'

God took the child by the head, and the father took him by the feet, and they tugged, and God cut the child in half.

'One half for you, and one half for me.'

'Now you've killed him, I don't want him. Take him and be hanged to you.'

God took him, and went outside, and put him together; and he was healed, and lived again.

'Do you take him now.'

For God cut off his sins.

Cleomades and Claremond
(*Spain*)

Ectriva, Queen of Southern Spain, held a great tournament at Seville, at which Marchabias, Prince of Sardinia, so distinguished himself as to win her heart. She bestowed her hand upon the youthful champion, and their union was a happy one, being blessed in time with three daughters and a son. To the boy they gave the name of Cleomades, while his sisters were called Melior, Soliadis, and Maxima.

Cleomades was dispatched upon his travels at an early age. But after he had visited several foreign countries he was summoned home to be present at the wedding of his sisters, who were about to be married to three great princes, all of whom were famous as practitioners of the magic art. They were Melicandus, King of Barbary; Bardagans, King of Armenia; and Croppart, King of Hungary. The last-named monarch was so unfortunate as to be a hunchback, and to his deformity he added a bitter tongue and a wicked heart.

The three monarchs had encountered one another while still some distance from Seville, and had agreed to give such presents to the King and Queen as would necessitate a gift in return. Melicandus presented the royal pair with the golden image of a man, holding in his right hand a trumpet of the same metal, which he sounded if treason came near him. Bardagans gave a hen and six chickens of gold, so skilfully made that they picked up grain and seemed to be alive. Every third day the hen laid an egg of pearl. Croppart gave a large wooden horse magnificently caparisoned, which he told his hosts could travel over land and sea at the rate of fifty leagues an hour.

The King and Queen, generous to a fault, invited the strangers to ask anything that it was in their power to bestow. Melicandus requested the hand of the Princess Melior, Bardagans that of Soliadis, while Croppart demanded that Maxima should be given him as a consort. The two elder sisters were pleased with their suitors, who were both handsome and amiable, but when Maxima beheld the hideous and deformed Croppart she ran to her brother Cleomades and begged him to deliver her from such an unsightly monster.

Cleomades represented to his father the wrong done by him in consenting to such a match. But Croppart insisted that the King's word had been passed and that he could not retire from his promise. Cleomades, casting about for an argument, told the Hungarian king that the value of the gifts of Melicandus and Bardagans had been proved, but that, so far as anyone knew, his story about the wooden horse might be a mere fable. Croppart offered to test the capacity of his wooden steed. At this the golden man blew his trumpet loudly, but all were so interested in the proposed trial that no one noticed it. The prince mounted the gaudily harnessed bobby, and at the request of Croppart turned a pin of steel in its head, and was immediately carried into the air with such velocity that in a few moments he was lost to sight.

The King and Queen, filled with indignation, had Croppart seized, but he argued that the prince should have waited until he had shown him how to manage the wooden horse. Meanwhile Cleomades sped onward for miles and miles. His strange steed continued to cleave the air at a terrific speed, and at length darkness fell without any signs of its slackening its pace. All night Cleomades continued to fly, and during the hours of gloom had plenty of time to ponder upon his awkward situation. Recollecting that there were pins upon the horse's shoulders like those upon its head, he resolved to try their effect. He found that by turning one of them to right or left the horse went in either direction, and that when the other was turned the wooden hippogriff[1] slackened speed and descended. Morning now broke, and he saw that he was over a great city. By skilful manipulation of his steed he managed to alight upon a lofty tower which stood in the garden of a great palace.

Descending through a trap-door in the roof, he entered a gorgeous sleeping apartment, and beheld a beautiful lady reclining on a sumptuous couch. At his entrance she awoke, and cried out: "Rash man, how have you presumed to enter this apartment? Are you perchance that King Liopatris to whom my father has affianced me?"

"I am that monarch," replied Cleomades. "May I not speak with you?" he continued, for on beholding the princess he had at once fallen violently in love with her.

Retire to the garden," she said, "and I will come to you there."

The prince obeyed. In a few moments the princess joined him. But they had not been long together when the lady's father, King Cornuant of Tuscany, appeared, and at once denounced Cleomades as an impostor, condemning him to death. The prince begged that he might be permitted to meet his fate mounted upon his wooden horse. To this the King assented, and the magical steed was brought. Mounting it, he immediately turned the pin, and rose high in the air, calling out to the princess, as he did so, that he would remain faithful to her.

Shortly he arrived again in Seville, to the immense relief of his parents. Croppart was requested to quit the country. But he had no mind to do so, and in the guise of an Eastern physician remained in the city. The two elder princesses were married to Melicandus and Bardagans. As for Cleomades, he could not forget the beautiful Princess Claremond, and, once more mounting his aery steed, he set off in the direction of her father's kingdom.

On this occasion he had timed his visit so as to arrive by night at the palace of his lady-love. Alighting in the garden, he made his way to the chamber of Claremond, whom he found fast asleep. He awoke her gently, and told her his name and station, avowed his love, and placed himself at her mercy.

"What!" exclaimed the princess. "Are you indeed that Cleomades whom we regard as the very mirror of knighthood?" The prince assured her that such was the case, and taking from his arm a splendid bracelet containing his mother's portrait and his own, he presented her with it as an assurance that he spoke truly. The princess confessed her love, and at his entreaty mounted behind him on the magic horse. As they rose, Cleomades beheld the King in the gardens beneath, surrounded by his courtiers. He called to him to fear nothing for his daughter, and, setting the

____

1 A mythical creature with the front of an eagle and the hindquarters of a horse.

head of his mount toward Seville, sped onward.

Alighting at a small rural palace some distance from the Court, Cleomades left the princess there to recover from her journey, while he proceeded to acquaint his royal parents with the result of his adventure. Claremond, having refreshed herself, was walking in the garden for exercise, as she felt somewhat stiff after her aerial voyage, when, as ill-luck would have it, she was observed by Croppart, who, in the guise of an Indian physician, had entered the garden, ostensibly to cull simples for medicinal purposes, but in reality to spy out the land.

Croppart, seeing his own wooden horse, and hearing the princess murmur the name of Cleomades, speedily formed a plan to carry the damsel off. Approaching her, he offered to take her to Cleomades at once on the back of the enchanted horse, and, fearing no evil, she accepted his offer, and permitted herself to be placed on its back. Croppart immediately turned the pin, and the horse ascended with terrific velocity. At first Claremond was quite unsuspicious of the designs of her abductor, but as time passed her fears were aroused, and, looking down, she beheld, instead of populous cities, only gloomy forests and deserted mountains. She begged Croppart to return with her to the palace garden, but he merely laughed at her entreaties, and at last, worn out with grief and disappointment, she swooned away.

Descending near a fountain, Croppart sprinkled the princess with its water until she revived. Then he acquainted her with his intention to make her Queen of Hungary. But the princess did not lack wit, and told him that she was merely a slave-girl whom Cleomades had purchased from her parents. This intelligence made the ferocious Croppart treat her with even less respect than before, so that to save herself from his violence she consented to wed him at the first city to which they might chance to come.

When he had wrung this promise from Claremond, Croppart, who suffered greatly from thirst, drank deeply of the fountain. So icy cold were its waters that on quaffing them he fell to the ground, almost insensible. Claremond, overcome by fatigue and anxiety, fell fast asleep. In this condition they were discovered by Mendulus, King of Salerno, who at once conceived a strong attachment to the sleeping damsel, and had her conveyed to his palace, where he lodged her in a fair apartment. As for Croppart, so severe was the disorder which he had contracted by drinking of the icy fountain that he expired shortly afterward.

Claremond told King Mendulus that she was only a foundling whose name was Trouvee, and that she had accompanied Croppart, a travelling physician, from one place to another, seeking a precarious livelihood. This did not prevent him, however, from offering her his hand and crown. To save herself from this new danger, Claremond had recourse to feigned madness, and so convincingly did she play her part that Mendulus had perforce to confine her under the charge of ten chosen women, whose duty it was to restrain her.

Meanwhile the Court of Spain was thrown into the utmost confusion. Cleomades, returning to the summer palace with his parents, could find no trace of Claremond, and, overcome with grief, was brought back to the capital in a state bordering upon frenzy. When he recovered he set out for the kingdom of Tuscany in the hope that there he might obtain tidings of his lady. Riding alone, he came to a castle, where he encountered and overthrew two knights who refused to let him pass. From them he learned that when a prince named Liopatris, who had been betrothed to Claremond, arrived at the Court of Tuscany, three of his knights had accused three of Claremond's maids of honour of being accomplices in the abduction of their mistress. The knights whom Cleomades had worsted were suitors for the hands of two of those ladies, and had challenged their detractors, but as one of them had been wounded by Cleomades, they could not now make good their challenge. Cleomades graciously offered to take the place of the wounded man, and with his unwounded comrade set out for the court of King Cornuant.

Next morning the combatants appeared in the lists. The three accusers were overthrown, and the maids of honour pronounced innocent, according to the laws of chivalry. Taking the damsels with them, Cleomades and his new brother-in-arms returned to the castle whence they had come, and when he had doffed his armour the prince-errant was recognized by the ladies whom he had helped to rescue. Great was their grief when they learned of the fate of Claremond. But one of them begged Cleomades to seek the assistance of a famous astrologer who dwelt at Salerno, "who saw most secret things right clear." Cleomades instantly resolved to go and consult this sage, and accordingly next morning he set out for the city of Salerno, after having taken an affectionate leave of the lovers.

Arrived at Salerno, Cleomades put up at an inn, and lost no time in inquiring of the landlord where the astrologer might be found.

"Alas, sir! "said the host, "it is now a year since he passed away. Never did we need him more. For had he been alive, he might have served our King by restoring to reason the most beautiful creature who ever lived." And he told Cleomades the story of how Mendulus had found the hunchback and the maid. At the mention of the wooden horse Cleomades started, but kept his presence of mind, and assured the innkeeper that he possessed an infallible cure for madness. He begged the man to lead him to the King, and, on the plea that his arms might excite suspicion, donned a false beard and the dress of a physician.

He was at once admitted to the royal presence, and on hearing of his skill the King led him to the place where Claremond was confined. Cleomades had taken with him a glove belonging to his lady-love, which he had stuffed with herbs, and on the pretence that these would cure her he placed it upon her cheek. Seeing her own glove, she regarded the seeming physician earnestly, and succeeded in penetrating his disguise. But, still feigning insanity, she begged that her wooden horse might be brought, so that it could dispute with the learned doctor. It was carried into the garden where they were, and the princess pretended to have a whim that she could only be cured if she and the physician mounted the wooden steed. To this Mendulus consented, and when they be-strode the artificial hippogriff Cleomades turned the pin, and in a moment they rose like an arrow from the bow. Next morning the happy pair arrived in Seville. Their nuptials were immediately performed, and Liopatris was consoled with Princess Maxima, so that no one was left lamenting.

665: The Man Who Flew and Swam

Boots and the Beasts
(*Norway*)

Once on a time there was a man who had an only son, but he lived in need and wretchedness, and when he lay on his death-bed, he told his son he had nothing in the world but a sword, a bit of coarse linen, and a few crusts of bread—that was all he had to leave him. Well! when the man was dead, the lad made up his mind to go out into the world to try his luck; so he girded the sword about him, and took the crusts and laid them in the bit of linen for his travelling fare; for you must know they lived far away up on a hillside in the wood, far from folk. Now the way he went took him over a fell, and when he had got up so high that he could look over the country, he set his eyes on a lion, a falcon, and an ant, who stood there quarrelling over a dead horse. The lad was sore afraid when he saw the lion, but he called out to him and said he must come and settle the strife between them and share the horse, so that each should get what he ought to have.

So the lad took his sword and shared the horse as well as he could. To the lion he gave the carcass and the greater portion; the falcon got some of the entrails and other titbits; and the ant got the head. When he had done, he said—

'Now I think it is fairly shared. The lion shall have most, because he is biggest and strongest; the falcon shall have the best, because he is nice and dainty; and the ant shall have the skull, because he loves to creep about in holes and crannies.'

Yes! they were all well pleased with his sharing; and so they asked him what he would like to have for sharing the horse so well.

'Oh,' he said, 'if I have done you a service, and you are pleased with it, I am also pleased; but I won't be paid.'

'Yes; but he must have something,' they said.

'If you won't have anything else,' said the lion, 'you shall have three wishes.'

But the lad knew not what to wish for; and so the lion asked him if he wouldn't wish that he might be able to turn himself into a lion; and the two others asked him if he wouldn't wish to be able to turn himself into a falcon and an ant. Yes! all that seemed to him good and right; and so he wished these three wishes.

Then he threw aside his sword and wallet, turned himself into a falcon, and began to fly. So he flew on and on, till he came over a great lake; but when he had almost flown across it he got so tired and sore on the wing he couldn't fly any longer; and as he saw a steep rock that rose out of the water, he perched on it and rested himself. He thought it a wondrous strong rock, and walked about it for a while; but when he had taken a good rest, he turned himself again into a little falcon, and flew away till he came to the king's grange. There he perched on a tree, just before the princess's windows. When she saw the falcon she set her heart on catching it. So she lured it to her; and as soon as the falcon came under the casement she was ready, and pop! she shut to the window, and caught the bird and put him into a cage.

In the night the lad turned himself into an ant and crept out of the cage; and then he turned himself into his own shape, and went up and sat down by the princess's bed. Then she got so afraid that she fell to screeching out and awoke the king, who came into her room and asked whatever was the matter.

'Oh!' said the princess, 'there is someone here.'

But in a trice the lad became an ant, crept into the cage, and turned himself into a falcon. The king could see nothing for her to be afraid of; so he said to the princess it must have been the nightmare riding her. But he was hardly out of the door before it was all the same story over again. The lad crept out of the cage as an ant, and then became his own self, and sat down by the bedside of the princess.

Then she screamed loud, and the king came again to see what was the matter.

'There is someone here,' screamed the princess. But the lad crept into the cage again, and sat perched up there like a falcon. The king looked and hunted high and low; and when he could see nothing he got cross that his rest was broken, and said it was all a trick of the princess.

'If you scream like that again,' he said, 'you shall soon know that your father is the king.'

But for all that, the king's back was scarcely turned before the lad was by the princess's side again. This time she did not scream, although she was so afraid she did not know which way to turn.

So the lad asked why she was so afraid.

Didn't he know? She was promised to a hill-ogre, and the very first time she came under bare sky he was to come and take her; and so when the lad came she thought it was the hill-ogre. And, besides, every Thursday morning came a messenger from the hill-ogre, and that was a dragon, to whom the king had to give nine fat pigs every time he came; and that was why he had given it out that the man who could free him from the dragon should have the princess and half the kingdom.

The lad said he would soon do that; and as soon as it was daybreak the princess went to the king and said there was a man in there who would free him from the dragon and the tax of pigs. As soon as the king heard that, he was very glad, for the dragon had eaten up so many pigs, there would soon have been no more left in the whole kingdom. It happened that day was just a Thursday morning, and so the lad strode off to the spot where the dragon used to come to eat the pigs, and the shoeblack in the king's grange showed him the way.

Yes! the dragon came; and he had nine heads, and he was so wild and wroth that fire and flame flared out of his nostrils when he did not see his feast of pigs; and he flew upon the lad as though he would gobble him up alive. But, pop! he turned himself into a lion and fought with the dragon, and tore one head off him after another. The dragon was strong, that he was; and he spat fire and venom. But as the fight went on he hadn't more than one head left, though that was the toughest. At last the lad got that torn off, too; and then it was all over with the dragon.

So he went to the king, and there was great joy all over the palace; and the lad was to have the princess. But once on a time, as they were walking in the garden, the hill-ogre came flying at them himself, and caught up the princess and bore her off through the air.

As for the lad, he was for going after her at once; but the king said he mustn't do that, for he had no one else to lean on now he had lost his daughter. But for all that, neither prayers nor preaching were any good: the lad turned himself into a falcon and flew off. But when he could not see them anywhere, he called to mind that wonderful rock in the lake, where he had rested the first time he ever flew. So he settled there, and after he had done that he turned himself into an ant, and crept down through a crack in the rock. So when he had crept about awhile, he came to a door which was locked. But he knew a way how to get in, for he crept through the key-hole, and what do you think he saw there? Why, a strange princess, combing a hill-ogre's hair that had three heads.

'I have come all right,' said the lad to himself; for he had heard how the king had lost two daughters before, whom the trolls had taken.

'Maybe, I shall find the second also,' he said to himself, as he crept through the key-hole of a second door. There sat a strange princess combing a hill-ogre's hair who had six heads. So he crept through a third key-hole still, and there sat the youngest princess, combing a hill-ogre's hair with nine heads. Then he crept up her leg and stung her, and so she knew it was the lad who wished to talk to her; and then she begged leave of the hill-ogre to go out.

When she came out the lad was himself again, and so he told her she must ask the hill-ogre whether she would never get away and go home to her father. Then he turned himself into an ant and sat on her foot, and so the princess went into the house again, and fell to combing the hill-ogre's hair.

So when she had done this awhile, she fell a-thinking.

'You're forgetting to comb me,' said the hill-ogre. 'What is it you're thinking of?'

'Oh, I am doubting whether I shall ever get away from this place, and home to my father's grange,' said the princess.

'Nay! nay! that you'll never do!' said the hill-ogre; 'not unless you can find the grain of sand which lies under the ninth tongue of the ninth head of the dragon to which your father paid tax; but that no one will ever find, for if that grain of sand came over the rock all the hill-ogres would burst, and the rock itself would become a gilded palace, and the lake green meadows.'

As soon as the lad heard that he crept out through the keyholes, and through the crack in the rock, till he got outside. Then he turned himself into a falcon, and flew whither the dragon lay. Then he hunted till he found the grain of sand under the ninth tongue of the ninth head, and flew off with it; but when he came to the lake he got so tired, so tired, that he had to sink down and perch on a stone by the strand. And just as he sat there he dozed and nodded for the twinkling of an eye; and, meantime, the grain of sand fell out of his bill down among the sand on the shore. So he searched for it three days before he found it again. But as soon as he had found it he flew straight off to the steep rock with it, and dropped it down the crack. Then all the hill-ogres burst, and the rock was rent, and there stood a gilded castle, which was the grandest castle in all the world; and the lake became the loveliest fields and the greenest meads anyone ever saw.

So they travelled back to the king's grange, and there arose, as you may fancy, joy and gladness. The lad and the youngest princess were to have one another; and they kept up the bridal feast over the whole kingdom for seven full weeks. And if they did not fare well, I only hope you may fare better still.

The Troll's Daughter
(*Denmark*)

There was once a lad who went to look for a place. As he went along he met a man, who asked him where he was going. He told him his errand, and the stranger said, 'Then you can serve me; I am just in want of a lad like you, and I will give you good wages—a bushel of money the first year, two the second year, and three the third year, for you must serve me three years, and obey me in everything, however strange it seems to you. You need not be afraid of taking service with me, for there is no danger in it if you only know how to obey.'

The bargain was made, and the lad went home with the man to whom he had engaged himself. It was a strange place indeed, for he lived in a bank in the middle of the wild forest, and the lad saw there no other person than his master. The latter was a great troll, and had marvellous power over both men and beasts.

Next day the lad had to begin his service. The first thing that the troll set him to was to feed all the wild animals from the forest. These the troll had tied up, and there were both wolves and bears, deer and hares, which the troll had gathered in the stalls and folds in his stable down beneath the ground, and that stable was a mile long. The boy, however, accomplished all this work on that day, and the troll praised him and said that it was very well done.

Next morning the troll said to him, 'To-day the animals are not to be fed; they don't get the like of that every day. You shall have leave to play about for a little, until they are to be fed again.'

Then the troll said some words to him which he did not understand, and with that the lad turned into a hare, and ran out into the wood. He got plenty to run for, too, for all the hunters aimed at him, and tried to shoot him, and the dogs barked and ran after him wherever they got wind of him. He was the only animal that was left in the wood now, for the troll had tied up all the others, and every hunter in the whole country was eager to knock him over. But in this they met with no success; there was no dog that could overtake him, and no marksman that could hit him. They shot and shot at him, and he ran and ran. It was an unquiet life, but in the long run he got used to it, when he saw that there was no danger in it, and it even amused him to befool all the hunters and dogs that were so eager after him.

Thus a whole year passed, and when it was over the troll called him home, for he was now in his power like all the other animals. The troll then said some words to him which he did not understand, and the hare immediately became a human being again. 'Well, how do you like to serve me?' said the troll, 'and how do you like being a hare?'

The lad replied that he liked it very well; he had never been able to go over the ground so quickly before. The troll then showed him the bushel of money that he had already earned, and the lad was well pleased to serve him for another year.

The first day of the second year the boy had the same work to do as on the previous one—namely, to feed all the wild animals in the troll's stable. When he had done this the troll again said some words to him, and with that he became a raven, and flew high up into the air. This was delightful, the lad thought; he could go even faster now than when he was a hare, and the dogs could not come after him here. This was a great delight to him, but he soon found out that he was not to be left quite at peace, for all the marksmen and hunters who saw him aimed at him and fired away, for they had no other birds to shoot at than himself, as the troll had tied up all the others.

This, however, he also got used to, when he saw that they could never hit him, and in this way he flew about all that year, until the troll called him home again, said some strange words to him, and gave him his human shape again. 'Well, how did you like being a raven?' said the troll.

'I liked it very well,' said the lad, 'for never in all my days have I been able to rise so high.' The troll then showed him the two bushels of money which he had earned that year, and the lad was well content to remain in his service for another year.

Next day he got his old task of feeding all the wild beasts. When this was done the troll again said some words to him, and at these he turned into a fish, and sprang into the river. He swam up and he swam down, and thought it was pleasant to let himself drive with the stream. In this way he came right out into the sea, and swam further and further out. At last he came to a glass palace, which stood at the bottom of the sea. He could see into all the rooms and halls, where everything was very grand; all the furniture was of white ivory, inlaid with gold and pearl. There were soft rugs and cushions of all the colours of the rainbow, and beautiful carpets that looked like the finest moss, and flowers and trees with curiously crooked branches, both green and yellow, white and red, and there were also little fountains which sprang up from the most beautiful snail-shells, and fell into bright mussel-shells, and at the same time made a most delightful music, which filled the whole palace.

The most beautiful thing of all, however, was a young girl who went about there, all alone. She went about from one room to another, but did not seem to be happy with all the grandeur she had about her. She walked in solitude and melancholy, and never even thought of looking at her own image in the polished glass walls that were on every side of her, although she was the prettiest creature anyone could wish to see. The lad thought so too while he swam round the palace and peeped in from every side.

'Here, indeed, it would be better to be a man than such a poor dumb fish as I am now,' said he to himself; 'if I could only remember the words that the troll says when he changes my shape, then perhaps I could help myself to become a man again.' He swam and he pondered and he thought over this until he remembered the sound of what the troll said, and then he tried to say it himself. In a moment he stood in human form at the bottom of the sea.

He made haste then to enter the glass palace, and went up to the young girl and spoke to her.

At first he nearly frightened the life out of her, but he talked to her so kindly and explained how he had come down there that she soon recovered from her alarm, and was very pleased to have some company to relieve the terrible solitude that she lived in. Time passed so quickly for both of them that the youth (for now he was quite a young man, and no more a lad) forgot altogether how long he had been there.

One day the girl said to him that now it was close on the time when he must become a fish again—the troll would soon call him home, and he would have to go, but before that he must put on the shape of the fish, otherwise he could not pass through the sea alive. Before this, while he was staying down there, she had told him that she was a daughter of the same troll whom the youth served, and he had shut her up there to keep her away from everyone. She had now devised a plan by which they could perhaps succeed in getting to see each other again, and spending the rest of their lives together. But there was much to attend to, and he must give careful heed to all that she told him.

She told him then that all the kings in the country round about were in debt to her father the troll, and the king of a certain kingdom, the name of which she told him, was the first who had to pay, and if he could not do so at the time appointed he would lose his head. 'And he cannot pay,' said she; 'I know that for certain. Now you must, first of all, give up your service with my father; the three years are past, and you are at liberty to go. You will go off with your six bushels of money, to the kingdom that I have told you of, and there enter the service of the king. When the time comes near for his debt becoming due you will be able to notice by his manner that he is ill at ease. You shall then say to him that you know well enough what it is that is weighing upon him—that it is the debt which he owes to the troll and cannot pay, but that you can lend him the money. The amount is six bushels—just what you have. You shall, however, only lend them to him on condition that you may accompany him when he goes to make the payment, and that you then have permission to run before him as a fool. When you arrive at the troll's abode, you must perform all kinds of foolish tricks, and see that you break a whole lot of his windows, and do all other damage that you can. My father will then get very angry, and as the king must answer for what his fool does he will sentence him, even although he has paid his debt, either to answer three questions or to lose his life. The first question my father will ask will be, "Where is my daughter?" Then you shall step forward and answer "She is at the bottom of the sea." He will then ask you whether you can recognise her, and to this you will answer "Yes." Then he will bring forward a whole troop of women, and cause them to pass before you, in order that you may pick out the one that you take for his daughter. You will not be able to recognise me at all, and therefore I will catch hold of you as I go past, so that you can notice it, and you must then make haste to catch me and hold me fast. You have then answered his first question. His next question will be, "Where is my heart?" You shall then step forward again and answer, "It is in a fish." "Do you know that fish?" he will say, and you will again answer "Yes." He will then cause all kinds of fish to come before you, and you shall choose between them. I shall take good care to keep by your side, and when the right fish comes I will give you a little push, and with that you will seize the fish and cut it up. Then all will be over with the troll; he will ask no more questions, and we shall be free to wed.'

When the youth had got all these directions as to what he had to do when he got ashore again the next thing was to remember the words which the troll said when he changed him from a human being to an animal; but these he had forgotten, and the girl did not know them either. He went about all day in despair, and thought and thought, but he could not remember what they sounded like. During the night he could not sleep, until towards morning he fell into a slumber, and all at once it flashed upon him what the troll used to say. He made haste to repeat the words, and at the same moment he became a fish again and slipped out into the sea. Immediately after this he was called upon, and swam through the sea up the river to where the troll stood on the bank and restored him to human shape with the same words as before.

'Well, how do you like to be a fish?' asked the troll.

It was what he had liked best of all, said the youth, and that was no lie, as everybody can guess.

The troll then showed him the three bushels of money which he had earned during the past year; they stood beside the other three, and all the six now belonged to him.

'Perhaps you will serve me for another year yet,' said the troll, 'and you will get six bushels of money for it; that makes twelve in all, and that is a pretty penny.'

'No,' said the youth; he thought he had done enough, and was anxious to go to some other place to serve, and learn other people's ways; but he would, perhaps, come back to the troll some other time.

The troll said that he would always be welcome; he had served him faithfully for the three years they had agreed upon, and he could make no objections to his leaving now.

The youth then got his six bushels of money, and with these he betook himself straight to the kingdom which his sweetheart had told him of. He got his money buried in a lonely spot close to the king's palace, and then went in there and asked to be taken into service. He obtained his request, and was taken on as stableman, to tend the king's horses.

Some time passed, and he noticed how the king always went about sorrowing and grieving, and was never glad or happy. One day the king came into the stable, where there was no one present except the youth, who said straight out to him that, with his majesty's permission, he wished to ask him why he was so sorrowful.

'It's of no use speaking about that,' said the king; 'you cannot help me, at any rate.'

'You don't know about that,' said the youth; 'I know well enough what it is that lies so heavy on your mind, and I know also of a plan to get the money paid.'

This was quite another case, and the king had more talk with the stableman, who said that he could easily lend the king the six bushels of money, but would only do it on condition that he should be allowed to accompany the king when he went to pay the debt, and that he should then be dressed like the king's court fool, and run before him. He would cause some trouble, for which the king would be severely spoken to, but he would answer for it that no harm would befall him.

The king gladly agreed to all that the youth proposed, and it was now high time for them to set out.

When they came to the troll's dwelling it was no longer in the bank, but on the top of this there stood a large castle which the youth had never seen before. The troll could, in fact, make it visible or invisible, just as he pleased, and, knowing as much as he did of the troll's magic arts, the youth was not at all surprised at this.

When they came near to this castle, which looked as if it was of pure glass, the youth ran on in front as the king's fool. He ran sometimes facing forwards, sometimes backwards, stood sometimes on his head, and sometimes on his feet, and he dashed in pieces so many of the troll's big glass windows and doors that it was something awful to see, and overturned everything he could, and made a fearful disturbance.

The troll came rushing out, and was so angry and furious, and abused the king with all his might for bringing such a wretched fool with him, as he was sure that he could not pay the least bit of all the damage that had been done when he could not even pay off his old debt.

The fool, however, spoke up, and said that he could do so quite easily, and the king then came forward with the six bushels of money which the youth had lent him. They were measured and found to be correct. This the troll had not reckoned on, but he could make no objection against it. The old debt was honestly paid, and the king got his bond back again.

But there still remained all the damage that had been done that day, and the king had nothing with which to pay for this. The troll, therefore, sentenced the king, either to answer three questions that he would put to him, or have his head taken off, as was agreed on in the old bond.

There was nothing else to be done than to try to answer the troll's riddles. The fool then stationed himself just by the king's side while the troll came forward with his questions. He first asked, 'Where is my daughter?'

The fool spoke up and said, 'She is at the bottom of the sea.'

'How do you know that?' said the troll.

'The little fish saw it,' said the fool.

'Would you know her?' said the troll.

'Yes, bring her forward,' said the fool.

The troll made a whole crowd of women go past them, one after the other, but all these were nothing but shadows and deceptions. Amongst the very last was the troll's real daughter, who pinched the fool as she went past him to make him aware of her presence. He thereupon caught her round the waist and held her fast, and the troll had to admit that his first riddle was solved.

Then the troll asked again: 'Where is my heart?'

'It is in a fish,' said the fool.

'Would you know that fish?' said the troll.

'Yes, bring it forward,' said the fool.

Then all the fishes came swimming past them, and meanwhile the troll's daughter stood just by the youth's side. When at last the right fish came swimming along she gave him a nudge, and he seized it at once, drove his knife into it, and split it up, took the heart out of it, and cut it through the middle.

At the same moment the troll fell dead and turned into pieces of flint. With that all the bonds that the troll had bound were broken; all the wild beasts and birds which he had caught and hid under the ground were free now, and dispersed themselves in the woods and in the air.

The youth and his sweetheart entered the castle, which was now theirs, and held their wedding; and all the kings roundabout, who had been in the troll's debt, and were now out of it, came to the wedding, and saluted the youth as their emperor, and he ruled over them all, and kept peace between them, and lived in his castle with his beautiful empress in great joy and magnificence. And if they have not died since they are living there to this day.

Fortunio and the Siren
(*Italy*)

Once upon a time there lived in one of the remoter districts of Lombardy a man called Bernio, who, although he was not over well endowed with the gifts of fortune, was held to be in no way wanting with respect to good qualities of head and heart. This man took to wife a worthy and amiable woman named Alchia, who, though she chanced to be of low origin, was nevertheless of good parts and exemplary conduct, and loved her husband as dearly as any woman could. This married pair greatly desired to have children, but such a gift of God was not granted to them, peradventure for the reason that man often, in his ignorance, asks for those things which would not be to his advantage. Now, forasmuch as this desire for offspring still continued to possess them, and as fortune obstinately refused to grant their prayer, they determined at last to adopt a child whom they would nurture and treat in every way as if he were their own legitimate son. So one morning early they betook themselves to a certain spot where young children who had been cast off by their parents were often left, and, having seen there one who appeared to them more seemly and attractive than the rest, they took him home with them, and brought him up with the utmost care and good governance. Now after a time it came to pass (according to the good pleasure of Him who rules the universe and tempers and modifies everything according to His will) that Alchia became with child, and when her time of delivery was come, was brought to bed with a boy who resembled his father exactly. On this account both father and mother rejoiced exceedingly, and called their son by the name of Valentino.

The infant was well nurtured, and grew up strong and healthy and well-mannered; moreover, he loved so dearly his brother—to whom the name of Fortunio had been given—that he was inclined almost to fret himself to death whenever they chanced to be separated the one from the other. But the genius of discord, the foe of everything that is good, becoming aware of their warm and loving friendship, and being able no longer to suffer their good understanding to continue, one day interposed between them, and worked her evil will so effectively that before long the two friends began to taste her bitter fruits. Wherefore as they were sporting together one day (after the manner of boys) they grew somewhat excited over their game, and Valentino, who could not bear that Fortunio should get any advantage over him in their play, became inflamed with violent anger, and more than once called his companion a bastard and the son of a vile woman. Fortunio, when he heard these words, was much astonished, and perturbed as well, and turning to Valentin he said to him, 'And why am I a bastard?' In reply, Valentino, muttering angrily between his teeth, repeated what he had already said, and even more. Whereupon Fortunio, greatly grieved and disturbed in mind, gave over playing and went forthwith to his so-called mother, and asked her whether he was in sooth the son of Bernio and herself. Alchia answered that he was, and, having learned that Fortunio had been insulted by Valentino, she rated the latter soundly, and declared that she would give him heavy chastisement if he should repeat his offence. But the words which Alchia had spoken roused fresh suspicion in Fortunio, and made him well nigh certain that he was not her legitimate son; indeed, there often came upon him the desire to put her to the test, to see whether she really was his mother or not, and thus discover the truth. In the end he questioned and importuned her so closely that she acknowledged he was not born of her, but that he had been adopted and brought up in their house for the love of God and for the alleviation of the misfortune which had been sent upon herself and her husband. These words were as so many dagger-thrusts in the young man's heart, piling up one sorrow upon another, and at last his grief grew beyond endurance; but, seeing that he could not bring himself to seek refuge from his trouble by a violent death, he determined to depart from Bernio's roof, and, in wandering up and down the world, to seek a better fortune.

Alchia, when she perceived that Fortunio's desire to quit the house grew stronger every day, was greatly incensed against him, and, as she found herself powerless to dissuade him from his purpose, she heaped all sorts of curses upon him, praying that if ever he should venture upon the sea he might be engulfed in the waves and swallowed up by the sirens, as ships are often swallowed up by storms. Fortunio, driven on by a headlong access of rage, took no heed of Alchia's malediction, and, without saying any further words of farewell, either to her or to Bernio, departed, and took his way towards the east. He journeyed on, passing by marshes, by valleys, by rocks, and all kinds of wild and desert spots, and at last, one day between sext and none, he came upon a thick and densely-tangled forest, in the midst of which, by strange chance, he found a wolf and an eagle and an ant, who were engaged in a long and sharp contention over the body of a stag which they had lately captured, without being able to agree as to how the venison should be divided amongst themselves. When Fortunio came upon the three animals they were in the midst of their stubborn dispute, and not one was disposed in any way to yield to the others; but after a while they agreed that this young man, who had thus unexpectedly come amongst them, should adjudicate the matter in question, and assign to each one of them such part of the spoil as he might deem most fitting. Then, when they had assented to these preliminaries, and had promised that they would be satisfied with and observe the terms of any award he might make, even though it might seem to be unjust, Fortunio readily undertook the task, and after he had carefully considered the case, he divided the prey amongst them in the following manner. To the wolf, as to a voracious animal and one very handy with his sharp teeth, he gave, as the guerdon of his toil in the chase, all the bones of the deer and all the lean flesh. To the eagle, a rapacious fowl, but furnished with no teeth, he gave the entrails, and all the fat lying round the lean parts and the bones. To the provident and industrious ant, which had none of that strength which nature had bestowed up on the wolf and the eagle, he gave the soft brains as her share of reward for the labour she had undergone. When the three animals understood the terms of this just and carefully-considered decision, they were fully satisfied, and thanked Fortunio as well as they could for the courtesy he had shown them.

Now these three animals held—and with justice—that, of all the vices, ingratitude was the most reprehensible; so with one accord they insisted that the young man should not depart until they have fully rewarded him for the great service he had done them. Wherefore the wolf, speaking first, said: 'My brother, I give you the power, if at any time the desire should come upon you to be a wolf instead of a man, to become one forthwith, merely by saying the words, "Would that I were a wolf!" At the same time you will be able to return to your former shape whenever you may desire.' And in like manner both the eagle and the ant endowed him with power to take upon him their form and similitude.

Then Fortunio, rejoicing greatly at the potent virtues thus given to him, and rendering to all three of the animals the warmest gratitude for their boon, took his leave and wandered far abroad, until at last he came to Polonia, a populous city of great renown, which was at that time under the rule of Odescalco, a powerful and valorous sovereign, who had but one child, a daughter called Doralice. Now the king was ambitious to find a noble mate for this princess, and it chanced that, at the time when Fortunio arrived in Polonia, he had proclaimed throughout his kingdom that a grand tournament should be held in the city, and that the Princess Doralice should be given in marriage to the man who should be the victor in the jousts. And already many dukes and marquises and other powerful nobles had come together from all parts to contend for this noble prize, and on the first day of the tournament, which had already passed, the honours of the tilting were borne off by a foul Saracen of hideous aspect and ungainly form, and with a face as black as pitch. The king's daughter, when she viewed the deformed and unseemly figure of the conqueror of the day, was overwhelmed with grief that fate should have awarded to such a one the victory in the joust, and, burying her face, which was crimson with shame, in her tender delicate hands, she wept and lamented sore, execrating her cruel and malignant destiny, and begging that death might take her rather than that she should become the wife of this misshapen barbarian. Fortunio, when he entered the city gate, noted the festal array on all sides and the great concourse of people about the streets, and when he learned the cause of all this magnificent display he was straightway possessed with an ardent desire to prove his valour by contending in the tournament, but when he came to consider that he was lacking in all the apparel needful in such honourable contests, his heart fell and heavy sorrow came over him. While he was in this doleful mood it chanced that his steps led him past the palace of the king, and raising his eyes from the ground he espied Doralice, the daughter of the king, who was leaning out of one of the windows of her apartment. She was surrounded by a group of lovely and highborn dames and maidens, but she shone out amongst them all on account of her beauty, as the radiant glorious sun shines out amidst the lesser lights of heaven.

By-and-by, when the dark night had fallen, and all the ladies of the court had retired to their apartments, Doralice, restless and sad at heart, betook herself alone to a small and exquisitely ornamented chamber and gazed once more out into the night, and there below, as luck would have it, was Fortunio. When the youth saw her standing solitary at the open window, he was so overcome by the charms of her beauty that he forthwith whispered to himself in an amorous sigh: "Ah! wherefore am I not an eagle?" Scarcely had these words issued from his lips when he found himself transformed into an eagle, whereupon he flew at once into the window of the chamber, and, having willed to become a man again, was restored to his own shape. He went forward with a light and joyful air to greet the princess, but she, as soon as she saw him, was filled with terror and began to cry out in a loud voice, just as if she were being attacked and torn by savage dogs. The king, who happened to be in an apartment not far distant from his daughter's, heard her cries of alarm and ran immediately to seek the cause thereof, and, having heard from her that there was a young man in the room, he at once ordered it to be searched in every part. But nothing of the sort was found, because Fortunio had once more changed himself into an eagle and had flown out of the window. Hardly, however, had the father gone back to his chamber when the maiden began to cry aloud just the same as before, because, forsooth, Fortunio had once more come into her presence.

But Fortunio, when he again heard the terrified cries of the maiden, began to fear for his life, and straightway changed himself into an ant, and crept into hiding beneath the blond tresses of the lovely damsel's hair. Odescalco, hearing the loud outcries of his daughter, ran to her succour, but when he found nothing more this second time than he had found before, he was greatly incensed against her, and threatened her harshly that if she should cry out again and disturb him he would play her some trick which would not please her, and thus he left her with angry words, suspecting that what had caused her trouble was some vision of one or other of the youths who for love of her had met their deaths in the tournament. Fortunio listened attentively to what the king said to his daughter, and, as soon as he had left the apartment, once more put off the shape of an ant and stood revealed in his own form. Doralice, who in the meanwhile had gone to bed, was so terror-stricken when she saw him that she tried to spring from her couch and to give the alarm, but she was not able to do this, because Fortunio placed one of his hands on her lips, and thus spake: 'Signora, fear not that I have come here to despoil you of your honour, or to steal aught that belongs to you. I am come rather to succour you to the best of my power, and to proclaim myself your most humble servant. If you cry out, one or other of two misfortunes will befall us, either your honour and fair name will be tarnished, or you will be the cause of your death and of my own. Therefore, dear lady of my heart, take care lest at the same time you cast a stain upon your reputation and imperil the lives of us both.'

While Fortunio was thus speaking, Doralice was weeping bitterly, her presence of mind being completely overthrown by this unexpected declaration on his part, and the young man, when he perceived how powerfully agitated she was, went on addressing her in words gentle and persuasive enough to have melted the heart of a stone. At last, conquered by his words and tender manner, she softened towards him, and consented to let him make his peace with her. And after a little, when she saw how handsome the youth was in face, and how strong and well knit in body and limb, she fell a-thinking about the ugliness and deformity of the Saracen, who, as the conqueror in the jousts, must before long be the master of her person. While these thoughts were passing through her mind the young man said to her: 'Dear lady, if I had the fitting equipment, how willingly would I enter the jousts to tilt on your behalf; and my heart tells me that, were I to contend, I should surely conquer.' Whereupon the damsel in reply said: 'If this, indeed, were to come to pass, if you should prove victorious in the lists, I would give myself to you alone.' And when she saw what a well-disposed youth he was, and how ardent in her cause, she brought forth a great quantity of gems and a heavy purse of gold, and bade him take them. Fortunio accepted them with his heart full of joy, and inquired of her what garb she wished him to wear in the lists to-morrow. And she bade him array himself in white satin, and in this matter he did as she commanded him.

On the following day Fortunio, encased in polished armour, over which he wore a surcoat of white satin richly embroidered with the finest gold, and studded with jewels most delicately carven, rode into the piazza unknown to anybody there present. He was mounted on a powerful and fiery charger, which was caparisoned and decked in the same colours as its rider. The crowd, which had already come together to witness the grand spectacle of the tournament, no sooner caught sight of the gallant unknown champion, with lance in hand all ready for the fray, than every person was lost in wonderment at so brave a sight, and each one, gazing fixedly at Fortunio, and astonished at his grace, began to inquire of his neighbour: 'Ah! who can this knight be who rides so gallantly and splendidly arrayed into the lists? Know you not what is his name?' In the meantime Fortunio, having entered the lists, called upon some rival to advance, and for the first course the Saracen presented himself; whereupon the two champions, keeping low the points of their trusty lances, rushed one upon the other like two lions loosened from their bonds, and so shrewd was the stroke dealt by Fortunio upon the head of the Saracen, that the latter was driven right over the crupper of his horse, and fell dead upon the bare earth, mangled and broken up as a fragile glass is broken when it is thrown against a wall. And Fortunio ran his course just as victoriously in encountering every other champion who ventured to oppose him in the lists. The damsel, when she saw how the fortune of the day was going, was greatly rejoiced, and kept her eyes steadily fixed on Fortunio in deepest admiration, and, thanking God in her heart for having thus graciously delivered her from the bondage of the Saracen, prayed to Him that this brave youth might he the final victor.

When the night had come they bade Doralice come to supper with the rest of the court; but to this bidding she made demur, and commanded them bring her certain rich viands and delicate wines to her chamber, feigning that she had not yet any desire for food, but would eat, perchance, later on if any appetite should come upon her. Then, having locked herself in her chamber and opened the window thereof, she watched with ardent desire for the coming of her lover, and when he had gained admittance to the chamber by the same means as he had used the previous day, they supped joyfully together. Then Fortunio demanded of her in what fashion she would that he should array himself for the morrow, and she made answer that he must bear a badge of green satin all embroidered with the finest thread of silver and gold, and that his horse should be caparisoned in like manner. On the following morning Fortunio appeared, attired as Doralice had directed, and, having duly presented himself in the piazza at the appointed time, he entered the lists and proved himself again as valiant a champion as he had proved to be on the day before. So great was the admiration of the people of his prowess that the shout went up with one voice that he had worthily won the gracious princess for his bride.

On the evening of that day the princess, full of merriment and happiness and joyous expectations, made the same pretext for absenting herself from supper as she had made the day before, and, having locked the door of her chamber, awaited there the coming of her lover, and supped pleasantly with him. And when he asked her once more with what vestments he should clothe himself on the following day, she answered that she wished him to wear a surcoat of crimson satin, all worked and embroidered with gold and pearls, and to see that the trappings of his horse were made in the same fashion; adding that she herself would, on the morrow, be clad in similar wise. 'Lady,' replied Fortunio, 'if by any chance I should tarry somewhat in making my entry into the lists, be not astonished, for I shall not be late without good cause.'

When the morning of the third day had come, the spectators awaited the issue of the momentous strife with the most earnest expectation, but, on account of the inexhaustible valour of the gallant unknown champion, there was no opponent found who dared to enter the lists against him, and he himself for some hidden reason did not appear. After a time the spectators began to grow impatient at his non-appearance, and injurious words were dropped. Even Doralice herself was assailed by suspicions as to his worth, although she had been warned by Fortunio himself that probably his coming would be delayed: so, overcome by this hidden trouble of hers—concerning which no one else knew anything—she well nigh swooned with grief. At last, when it was told to her that the unknown knight was advancing into the piazza, her failing senses began to revive. Fortunio was clad in a rich and sumptuous dress, and the trappings of his horse were of the finest cloth of gold, all embroidered with shining rubies and emeralds and sapphires and great pearls. When the people saw these they affirmed that the price of them would be equal to a great kingdom, and when Fortunio came into the piazza, everyone cried out in a loud voice: 'Long live the unknown knight!' and after this they all applauded vigorously and clapped their hands. Then the jousting began, and Fortunio once more carried himself so valiantly that he bore to earth all those who dared to oppose him, and in the end was hailed as the victor in the tournament. And when he had dismounted from his noble horse, the chief magnates and the wealthy citizens of the town bore him aloft on their shoulders, and to the sound of trumpets and all other kinds of musical instruments, and with loud shouts which went up to the heavens, they carried him into the presence of the king. When they had taken off his helmet and his shining armour the king perceived what a seemly graceful youth he was, and, having called his daughter into his presence, he betrothed them forthwith, and celebrated the nuptials with the greatest pomp, keeping open table at the court for the space of a month.

After Fortunio had lived for a certain space of time in loving dalliance with his fair wife, he was seized one day with the thought that he was playing the part of an unworthy sluggard in thus passing the days in indolence, merely counting the hours as they sped by, after the manner of foolish folk, and of those who consider not the duties of a man. Wherefore he made up his mind to go afield into certain regions, where there might be found due scope and recognition for his valour and enterprise; so, having got ready a galley and taken a large treasure which his father-in-law had given him, he embarked after taking leave of his wife and of King Odescalco. He sailed away, wafted on by gentle and favourable breezes, until he came into the Atlantic Ocean, but before he had gone more than ten miles thereon, there arose from the waves the most beautiful Siren that ever was seen, and singing softly, she began to swim towards the ship.

Fortunio, who was reclining by the side of the galley, bent his head low down over the water to listen to her song, and straightway fell asleep, and, while he thus slept, the Siren drew him gently from where he lay, and, bearing him in her arms, sank with him headlong into the depths of the sea. The mariners, after having vainly essayed to save him, broke out into loud lamentations over his sad fate, and, weeping and mourning, they decked the galley with black ensigns of grief, and returned to the unfortunate Odescalco to tell him of the terrible mischance which had befallen them during their voyage. The king and Doralice, when the sad news was brought to them, were overwhelmed with the deepest grief—as indeed was everyone else in the city—and all put on garments of mourning black.

Now at the time of Fortunio's departure Doralice was with child, and when the season of her delivery had come she gave birth to a beautiful boy, who was delicately and carefully nurtured until he came to be two years of age. At this time the sad and despairing Doralice, who had always brooded over her unhappy fate in losing the company of her beloved husband, began to abandon all hope of ever seeing him again; so she, like a brave and great-souled woman, resolved to put her fortune to the test and go to seek for him upon the deep, even though the king her father should not consent to let her depart. So she caused to be set in order for her voyage an armed galley, well fitted for such a purpose, and she took with her three apples, each one a masterpiece of handicraft, of which one was fashioned out of golden bronze, another of silver, and the last of the finest gold. Then, having taken leave of her father the king, she embarked with her child on board the galley, and sailed away before a prosperous wind into the open sea.

After the sad and woe-stricken lady had sailed a certain time over the calm sea, she bade the sailors steer the ship forthwith towards the spot where her husband had been carried off by the Siren, and this command they immediately obeyed. And when the vessel had been brought to the aforesaid spot, the child began to cry fretfully, and would in no wise be pacified by his mother's endearments; so she gave him the apple which was made of golden bronze to appease him. While the child was thus sporting with the apple, he was espied by the Siren, who, having come near to the galley and lifted her head a little space out of the foaming waves, thus spake to Doralice: 'Lady, give me that apple, for I desire greatly to have it.' But the princess answered her that this thing could not be done, inasmuch as the apple was her child's plaything. 'If you will consent to give it to me,' the Siren went on, 'I will show you the husband you have lost as far as his breast.' Doralice, when she heard these words, at once took the apple from the child and handed it courteously to the Siren, for she longed above all things else to get sight of her beloved husband.

The Siren was faithful to her promise, and after a little time brought Fortunio to the surface of the sea and showed him as far as the breast to Doralice, as a reward for the gift of the apple, and then plunged with him once more into the depths of the ocean, and disappeared from sight.

Doralice, who had naturally feasted her eyes upon the form of her husband what time he was above the water, only felt the desire to see him once more grow stronger after he was gone under again, and, not knowing what to do or to say, she sought comfort in the caresses of her child, and when the little one began to cry once more, the mother gave to it the silver apple to soothe its fancy. Again the Siren was on the watch and espied the silver apple in the child's hand, and having raised her head above the waves, begged Doralice to give her the apple, but the latter, shrugging her shoulders, said that the apple served to divert the child, and could not be spared. Whereupon the Siren said: 'If only you will give me this apple, which is far more beautiful than the other, I promise I will show you your husband as far as his knees.' Poor Doralice, who was now consumed with desire to see her beloved husband again, put aside the satisfaction of the child's fancy, and, having taken away from him the silver apple, handed it eagerly to the Siren, who, after she had once more brought Fortunio to the surface and exhibited him to Doralice as far as his knees (according to her promise), plunged again beneath the waves.

For a while the princess sat brooding in silent grief and suspense, trying in vain to hit upon some plan by which she might rescue her husband from his piteous fate, and at last she caught up her child in her arms and tried to comfort herself with him and to still his weeping. The child, mindful of the fair apple he had been playing with, continued to cry; so the mother, to appease him, gave him at last the apple of fine gold. When the covetous Siren, who was still watching the galley, saw this apple, and perceived that it was much fairer than either of the others, she at once demanded it as a gift from Doralice, and she begged so long and persistently, and at last made a promise to the princess that, in return for the gift of this apple, she would bring Fortunio once more into the light, and show him from head to foot; so Doralice took the apple from the boy, in spite of his chiding, and gave it to the Siren. Whereupon the latter, in order to carry out her promise, came quite close to the galley, bearing Fortunio upon her back, and having raised herself somewhat above the surface of the water, showed the person of Fortunio from head to foot. Now, as soon as Fortunio felt that he was quite clear of the water, and resting free upon the back of the Siren, he was filled with great joy in his heart, and, without hesitating for a moment, he cried out, 'Ah! would that I were an eagle,' and scarcely had he ceased speaking when he was forthwith transformed into an eagle, and, having poised himself for flight, he flew high above the sail yards of the galley, from whence—all the shipmen looking on the while in wonder—he descended into the ship and returned to his proper shape, and kissed and embraced his wife and his child and all the sailors on the galley.

Then, all of them rejoicing at the rescue of Fortunio, they sailed back to King Odescalco's kingdom, and as soon as they entered the port they began to play upon the trumpets and tabors and drums and all the other musical instruments they had with them, so that the king, when he heard the sound of these, was much astonished, and in the greatest suspense waited to learn what might be the meaning thereof. And before very long time had elapsed the herald came before him, and announced to the king how his dear daughter, having rescued her husband from the Siren, had come back. When they were disembarked from the galley, they all repaired to the royal palace, where their return was celebrated by sumptuous banquets and rejoicings. But after some days had passed, Fortunio betook himself for a while to his old home, and there, after having transformed himself into a wolf, he devoured Alchia, his adoptive mother, and Valentino her son, in revenge for the injuries they had worked him. Then, after he had returned to his rightful shape, he mounted his horse and rode back to his father-in-law's kingdom, where, with Doralice his dear wife, he lived in peace for many years to the great delight of both of them.

672: The Serpent's Crown

The Grass Snake of the House

The Grass Snake of the House
(*Austria*)

A little girl at times got a dish of milk and a hard roll as a between-meal by her mother. The girl sat down in the yard outside with her little feast. And as the child calmly and delightfully ate and drank, came a grass snake that lived in the farmstead, and sat down near her, and crept ever nearer. Probably the grass snake smelt the food and was hungry. And the animal-loving girl let the grass snake sponge unhindered.

The trust shown by the grass snake made the girl so happy that from now on, if she had something eatable, the grass snake said:

"We two love the food your mother makes."

And the grass snake was never missing and ate so much that it had to be more careful, so as not to overeat. But the grass snake also showed how grateful he was. He brought a precious jewel from his secret treasure to the girl, and beads and golden decorations of marvellous splendour. Because of the gifts the girl grew more beautiful and bright.

The girl's mother did not know anything about the friendship between her child and the grass snake. One day she was frightened to see how the animal coiled itself in the lap of her daughter. And since the mother got scared and feared the grass snake might harm her daughter, she grasped it and dashed it against the stone floor till it lay dead.

Afterwards a sad change came over the girl. She grew so ill that the night swallows called to her and the robin brought her dead leaves. Then one early morning, when the mother came to look after her child, she had passed away.

Second Tale of the Snake
(*Germany*)

An orphan child was sitting on the town walls spinning, when she saw a snake coming out of a hole low down in the wall. Swiftly she spread out beside this one of the blue silk handkerchiefs which snakes have such a strong liking for, and which are the only things they will creep on. As soon as the snake saw it, it went back, then returned, bringing with it a small golden crown, laid it on the handkerchief, and then went away again. The girl took up the crown, it glittered and was of delicate golden filagree work. It was not long before the snake came back for the second time, but when it no longer saw the crown, it crept up to the wall, and in its grief smote its little head against it as long as it had strength to do so, until at last it lay there dead. If the girl had but left the crown where it was, the snake would certainly have brought still more of its treasures out of the hole.

The Adder-Queen
(*Germany*)

There was once a young shepherd who possessed two things besides the homely clothes which he wore on his back,—his fife,[1] and his Mechthild, a plump, brown little maid with lips as red as cherries. The fife he had carved out himself; the maid he had found in the forest, where her father burned charcoal. They were both agreed that some time they would become man and wife. The old charcoal-burner had nothing against it either, and they might have been married right away if they had had anything besides their love; but love alone, be it ever so warm, will not cook the supper nor heat the children's broth. "So, let us wait," thought they, and hoped for better times. One day the beautiful Mechthild was sitting not far from the charcoal kiln, where her father was busy stirring the fire, and near her stood her lover, while the sheep were wandering about in the wood, guarded by the dog. Over the maiden's head an old mountain-ash spread its boughs, from which hung bunches of scarlet berries. She had plucked a number of them, and was now engaged in stringing the single berries on a long thread. This made a splendid coral necklace. Wendelin, as the young shepherd was called, watched the maid as she moved her little fingers busily, and then he looked on her rosy cheeks, her smooth brow and all her charms one after another, and thought to himself, "How lovely she is!"

Now the string of jewels was finished. Mechthild twined it around the tightly twisted braids of her dark-brown hair, and smiled at her lover like a happy child. But he looked suddenly sorrowful.

"Ah, Mechthild," he sighed, "why am I so poor? Why can I not place a gold ring on thy finger or put a garnet necklace around thy neck?"

"It is no worse now than it has been," said the maid, consolingly. "But are the red berries not beautiful?"

The shepherd did not seem to have heard her words. He was looking

---

1 A piccolo-like instrument.

at the smoke which arose from the charcoal kiln and floated away in blue clouds over the tops of the fir-trees. "Why will good luck never visit me? said he sadly. "There are so many treasures lying concealed and bewitched in the mountains; but fortune only laughs at stupid people; and when they are about to seize the gold exultingly, it sinks miles deep into the earth. I have been into the forest at every hour of the night, but no blue flames light up for me, no pale lady beckons to me, and no dwarf leads me to the treasure in the hollow stone."

"Wendelin," said the maiden, earnestly, "don't go about digging and searching for magic treasures! No good will come of it." And she continued playfully, "You can more easily win great riches through the golden-horned stag, on which Lady Holle rides through the forest. Every year the magic deer sheds his antlers. Seek for them, my Wendelin! Those of this year must still be lying somewhere in the wood."

The charcoal-burner had come along and heard the last words.

"Oho," he said, "so you would like to find the golden antlers? You ask for a great deal. Wouldn't a handful of golden flax-seed husks do as well? Or how would you like the little crown belonging to the Adder-Queen, who lives under the red stone by the water? If there is anything I wish for, it is the fernseed, which makes one invisible. Oh, what fun I would have! What a face the big landlord of the Bear would make up, if every evening I could make his best beer-barrel lighter and fish the biggest sausage out of the kettle without his seeing me!"

They went on talking in the same strain. Much was said about the magic pervading the forest, and the shepherd became more and more thoughtful. He usually played a tune on his fife to his sweetheart before he left her; but today he never gave it a thought when the time came for his departure. With head bent down he went after the flock, which the dog kept together by his barking.

The sun had almost finished his course, and a ruddy glow lay on the mountains when the shepherd came out of the woods with the sheep. Before him lay a green field, through the midst of which ran a broad, shallow brook, and on the further side of the water, like a gigantic gravestone, stood a single rock of a reddish color. Bramble-bushes and golden-yellow broom grew luxuriantly about it, and to the crevices clung moss and wild thyme. Here, then, was where the Adder-Princess was said to dwell.

After the sheep had satisfied their thirst, the shepherd drove them through the brook, for the town where he and the flock belonged lay on the other side of the mountain. He intended to pass by the red stone as usual, but he stood chained to the spot, for it seemed to him as if something stirred in the bushes.

"If it should be the Adder-Queen!" thought he; and as he had once heard that snakes loved to hear violin and flute playing, he drew his fife out of his shepherd's pouch, and began to play a gentle melody.

But lo and behold! There, out of the broom, arose the head of a great white snake, forking her tongue and wearing a shining crown.

The youth was so frightened that he stopped playing his fife, and in a twinkling the Adder had vanished.

What the charcoal-burner had said was true then. The shepherd timidly retreated, and drove the flock in a wide circuit around the stone to the town.

The Adder-Queen, or, rather, her golden crown, lay on his mind day and night. But how should he contrive to get possession of the ornament? The old village blacksmith was a wise man, and knew a great deal besides how to eat his bread; perhaps something might be learned about it from him. So he betook himself one evening to the blacksmith's, after the master and his apprentices had left off working; for a pretense, asked some advice in regard to a sick sheep, and after beating about the bush for some time, finally brought the conversation to the Adder-Queen. He had come to the right person. The old blacksmith knew quite enough about the ways to get possession of the little crown, and was not at all loth to show his knowledge.

"Whoever would rob the Adder-Queen of her crown," he explained, "has nothing more to do than to spread a white cloth on the ground before the hole where she lives. Immediately the snake will come out, lay the jewel on the cloth, and disappear again. Now is the time to seize it quickly, and with all possible speed to strive to reach water. For as soon as the Adder-Queen notices that she has been robbed, she will start after the fugitive, hissing frightfully; and if he cannot get across water, he is a dead man. But if he is fortunate enough to reach the farther shore, the serpent can do him no harm, and the crown is his."

This was the blacksmith's story, and the shepherd drank in every word. Some days later the beautiful daughter of the charcoal-burner was sitting in front of their cottage. All of a sudden her lover came running with all his might, threw a little sparkling coronet into her lap, and dropped lifeless on the ground. Mechthild gave a scream. Her father came to her, and a glance at the jewel told him what had happened. "He has stolen the little crown from the Adder-Queen," said he. Then he lifted the swooning youth, bore him into the hut, and tried to bring him back to consciousness. His efforts were successful, but the whole night long he lay tossing in delirium on the couch of leaves: not till morning did rest come to him.

In the course of the day he recovered entirely and was able to talk. Anxiety and care retreated from the charcoal-burner's cottage, and joy entered in. There lay the hard-won serpent's jewel before the lovers, who sat together hand in hand, making plans for the future. Of course they could not keep the little crown; it must go to the goldsmith's in the town:

but in its place the bridal wreath would soon adorn the beautiful Mechthild's head; and after the wedding festivities were over, Wendelin would take his young wife to a pleasant little house, and they would kindle a fire on their own hearth. Oh, blissful time! Oh, blissful time!

On the following morning Wendelin returned to the village. He wisely avoided the red stone.

The Adder-Queen's crown had twelve points, each tipped with a blood-red stone. As soon as her lover was gone, Mechthild took it out of the chest, where she had hidden it away, and placed it on her head. It was indeed a very different ornament from the red berries of the mountain-ash. If she could see how becoming the jewels were; but there was no looking-glass in the charcoal-burner's cottage. Whenever Mechthild wished to look at her nut-brown face, she ran to the well-spring, which bubbled up out of the mould of the forest, not far from the charcoal-kiln; and hither she turned her footsteps now. She bent over the clear water, and was charmed with her sparkling ornament. "You like me, don't you?" she said to a fat frog sitting on the edge of the spring. And the frog said, "Gloog!" jumped into the water, and dived under to tell the lady-frog at the bottom what a wonderful sight he had beheld. A gray-green lizard rustled through the leaves; she raised her head and looked curiously at the bejeweled maid. Then she slipped away into her underground chamber, and told her sisters about the beautiful damsel with the crown in her hair. And the blue titmice came fluttering inquisitively by, and the golden-crested wrens bristled their tufts with envy, when they saw the glistening jewels on the maiden's head. The squirrel peeped out curiously from behind the trunk of a pine-tree, and a weasel frisked about over the wood-plants to take a look at the crowned maiden.

Tramp, tramp, now sounded in her ears; perhaps it was a red deer, attracted by the glitter of her crown. But no; stags and does do not tread the earth with hoofs that are shod: it is the sound of horses. Bright dresses could be seen between the branches of the trees, and the merry sound of people's voices came through the air. She sprang away from the brim of the well, and was about to hasten to the house, but the riders had already drawn up in front of the charcoal-burner's cottage. There were gentlemen in rich hunting-costume and ladies in long, flowing riding-dresses, slender young falconers, and sunburned huntsmen with long beards.

The maiden dropped a low courtesy. The stately gentleman on the roan horse was the count who owned the land, and the beautiful lady by his side was his young wife.

Mechthild replied respectfully to the question concerning the nearest way to the meadow, through which the water flowed. Then the countess caught sight of the crown on the maiden's head, and cried out in the greatest surprise, "Tell me, my dear girl, how you came by such jewelry as that."

The maiden, in her embarrassment, made no reply; but the charcoal-burner, who had come along in the meantime, answered shrewdly, "It is an old heir-loom, most gracious lady; something my great-grandfather brought home from the war in Italy. If it pleases you, pray take it."

The countess had the crown brought to her, and the maids of honor, who accompanied her, looked curiously at the precious ornament. "I must have the little crown," said the lady, casting a tender glance toward the count.

He smiled and unfastened a heavy purse from his belt. "Take that for the crown," said he to the charcoal-burner; "it is gold. You foolish people have probably never known what a treasure your cottage concealed."

The maids of honor fastened the crown with two silver pins to their lady's velvet hood; then the riders spurred on their horses, waved a farewell to the charcoal-burner and his daughter, and galloped off through the woods.

The hunters had soon left the forest behind, and before them lay the broad meadow valley and the red stone.

The lazily-flowing brook formed here and there pools and little eddies, much frequented by ducks, herons, and other water-fowl.

The hawkers gave the falcons over to the ladies, and all eyes were directed towards the reeds surrounding the water.

And now up flew a silver heron, noisily flapping his wings. The countess quickly took the hood from the falcon's head, and let him loose. Screaming, the falcon flew aloft, till he hovered over the heron. Then he swooped down, cleverly avoided the threatening bill, and seized the bird with his talons. For some time there was a fierce struggle in the air; then both circled round and round, and the vanquished heron fell with flapping wings on the meadow near the red stone.

The countess was the first to reach the spot where he fell. Her cheeks glowing with excitement, she sprang out of the saddle to release the heron from the falcon's talons, and to place the silver ring, which bore her name, on his foot. Then she gave a sudden cry and fell on the ground.

Her terrified companions hastened to her side. The count took his young wife in his arms, and anxiously inquired what had happened.

She cried out with pain and pointed to her foot. The count bent down, and saw that her silk stocking was stained with a drop of blood.

"You have scratched yourself with a thorn," he said, laughing; "that is nothing." But the lady moaned slightly, her temples began to beat violently, and her face grew as pale as death.

The terror-stricken count gave orders for two huntsmen to go for doctors. He himself wrapped his wife in his mantle, took her in front of him on his saddle, and, followed by the others, galloped at full speed toward the nearest village. There he had a couch prepared for the sufferer, and anxiously waited for the doctors to come.

Her malady grew worse from hour to hour. The old smith, whose advice was asked, looked at the wound and shook his head, and said that it was no thorn-prick, but rather the bite of a poisonous serpent. The same opinion was given later by the doctors. They spoke Latin together, shrugged their shoulders, and used salves and potions as their art prescribed. But they did no good. The sufferer grew weaker and weaker, and when the evening star hung over the forest, she lay unconscious on her bed of pain. Death stood without before the door.

In the meantime Wendelin, the shepherd, was driving his flock home to the village. Mechthild had told him how the countess had purchased the serpent's crown, and then they counted the pieces of gold and took counsel about the spending of the money. Now the shepherd was cheerfully wending his way along in front of his flock and playing a little tune on his fife.

Then suddenly his breath failed him, and his hair stood on end.

Out of the bushes before him came the Adder-Queen, and raised her crownless head, forking her tongue at him.

"Stand still, or you shall die!" hissed the snake. And the poor youth stood still, and clung to his crook with trembling hands.

"Listen, young man, to what I tell you," said the serpent. "The lady who wore my crown is sick unto death; I stung her in the foot. But I guard the plant whose juice will make her well. Follow me, and I will show you the healing herb."

The snake glided through the grass, and the shepherd followed her with beating heart. The adder stopped near the red stone. She broke off an herb and handed it to the shepherd. It was a delicate little plant, and resembled the forked tongue of a serpent.

"Now hasten," said the adder, "as fast as you can to the village where the sick lady lies; and if you let one drop of the sap of the plant fall on her wound, she will be cured. But as a reward demand the crown, and bring it back to me. Swear that you will."

The trembling shepherd swore as the Adder-Queen desired, then hastened to the village, and asked to be taken to the sufferer.

The countess was still living, but her breathing was faint. On her right sat the count, with his face buried in his hands; on her left sat a priest murmuring prayers.

"Try your skill," said the count to the shepherd. "If you succeed in healing her, I will make you rich."

Then the shepherd raised his eyes to Heaven in a hasty prayer and let one drop of the sap of the herb fall on the wound. The sufferer at once opened her eyes and took a long breath. Then she lifted her beautiful head from the pillows and looked confidingly at her husband. And from that hour the fever left her, and with the dawn the countess' cheeks again took on their rosy color, and all her suffering had passed away.

She gave the crown gladly to the shepherd who had healed her, and he, true to his oath, carried it without delay to the red stone by the water, where the Adder-Queen received it.

The count kept his word too. He presented the shepherd with a stately mansion, in which Mechthild soon made her entrance as bride.

Whether the Adder-Queen still dwells under the red stone by the water, and whether she still wears her little crown, that I cannot tell. But the manor which the count gave to the shepherd, is still standing, and is called Schlangenhof, or the Serpent's Court.

673: The White Serpent's Flesh

The White Snake
(*Germany*)

A long time ago there lived a king who was famed for his wisdom through all the land. Nothing was hidden from him, and it seemed as if news of the most secret things was brought to him through the air. But he had a strange custom; every day after dinner, when the table was cleared, and no one else was present, a trusty servant had to bring him one more dish. It was covered, however, and even the servant did not know what was in it, neither did anyone know, for the King never took off the cover to eat of it until he was quite alone.

This had gone on for a long time, when one day the servant, who took away the dish, was overcome with such curiosity that he could not help carrying the dish into his room. When he had carefully locked the door, he lifted up the cover, and saw a white snake lying on the dish. But when he saw it he could not deny himself the pleasure of tasting it, so he cut off a little bit and put it into his mouth. No sooner had it touched his tongue than he heard a strange whispering of little voices outside his window. He went and listened, and then noticed that it was the sparrows who were chattering together, and telling one another of all kinds of things which they had seen in the fields and woods. Eating the snake had given him power of understanding the language of animals.

Now it so happened that on this very day the Queen lost her most beautiful ring, and suspicion of having stolen it fell upon this trusty servant, who was allowed to go everywhere. The King ordered the man to be brought before him, and threatened with angry words that unless he could before the morrow point out the thief, he himself should be looked upon as guilty and executed. In vain he declared his innocence; he was dismissed with no better answer.

In his trouble and fear he went down into the courtyard and took thought how to help himself out of his trouble. Now some ducks were sitting together quietly by a brook and taking their rest; and, whilst they were making their feathers smooth with their bills, they were having a confidential conversation together. The servant stood by and listened. They were telling one another of all the places where they had been waddling about all the morning, and what good food they had found, and one said in a pitiful tone, "Something lies heavy on my stomach; as I was eating in haste I swallowed a ring which lay under the Queen's window." The servant at once seized her by the neck, carried her to the kitchen, and said to the cook, "Here is a fine duck; pray, kill her." "Yes," said the cook, and weighed her in his hand; "she has spared no trouble to fatten herself, and has been waiting to be roasted long enough." So he cut off her head, and as she was being dressed for the spit, the Queen's ring was found inside her.

The servant could now easily prove his innocence; and the King, to make amends for the wrong, allowed him to ask a favor, and promised him the best place in the court that he could wish for. The servant refused everything, and only asked for a horse and some money for traveling, as he had a mind to see the world and go about a little.

When his request was granted he set out on his way, and one day came to a pond, where he saw three fishes caught in the reeds and gasping for water. Now, though it is said that fishes are dumb, he heard them lamenting that they must perish so miserably, and, as he had a kind heart, he got off his horse and put the three prisoners back into the water. They quivered with delight, put out their heads, and cried to him, "We will remember you and repay you for saving us!"

He rode on, and after a while it seemed to him that he heard a voice in the sand at his feet. He listened, and heard an ant-king complain, "Why cannot folks, with their clumsy beasts, keep off our bodies? That stupid horse, with his heavy hoofs, has been treading down my people without mercy!" So he turned on to a side path and the ant-king cried out to him, "We will remember you—one good turn deserves another!"

The path led him into a wood, and here he saw two old ravens standing by their nest, and throwing out their young ones. "Out with you, you idle, good-for-nothing creatures!" cried they; "we cannot find food for you any longer; you are big enough, and can provide for yourselves." But the poor young ravens lay upon the ground, flapping their wings, and crying, "Oh, what helpless chicks we are! We must shift for ourselves, and yet we cannot fly! What can we do but lie here and starve?" So the good young fellow alighted and killed his horse with his sword, and gave it to them for food. Then they came hopping up to it, satisfied their hunger, and cried, "We will remember you—one good turn deserves another!"

And now he had to use his own legs, and when he had walked a long way, he came to a large city. There was a great noise and crowd in the streets, and a man rode up on horseback, crying aloud, "The King's daughter wants a husband; but whoever sues for her hand must perform a hard task, and if he does not succeed he will forfeit his life." Many had already made the attempt, but in vain; nevertheless when the youth saw the King's daughter he was so overcome by her great beauty that he forgot all danger, went before the King, and declared himself a suitor.

So he was led out to the sea, and a gold ring was thrown into it in his sight; then the King ordered him to fetch this ring up from the bottom of the sea, and added, "If you come up again without it you will be thrown in again and again until you perish amid the waves." All the people grieved for the handsome youth; then they went away, leaving him alone by the sea.

He stood on the shore and considered what he should do, when suddenly he saw three fishes come swimming towards him, and they were the very fishes whose lives he had saved. The one in the middle held a mussel in its mouth, which it laid on the shore at the youth's feet, and when he had taken it up and opened it, there lay the gold ring in the shell. Full of joy he took it to the King, and expected that he would grant him the promised reward.

But when the proud princess perceived that he was not her equal in birth, she scorned him, and required him first to perform another task. She went down into the garden and strewed with her own hands ten sacks-full of millet-seed on the grass; then she said, "To-morrow morning before sunrise these must be picked up, and not a single grain be wanting."

The youth sat down in the garden and considered how it might be possible to perform this task, but he could think of nothing, and there he sat sorrowfully awaiting the break of day, when he should be led to death. But as soon as the first rays of the sun shone into the garden he saw all the ten sacks standing side by side, quite full, and not a single grain was missing. The ant-king had come in the night with thousands and thousands of ants, and the grateful creatures had by great industry picked up all the millet-seed and gathered them into the sacks.

Presently the King's daughter herself came down into the garden, and was amazed to see that the young man had done the task she had given him. But she could not yet conquer her proud heart, and said, "Although he has performed both the tasks, he shall not be my husband until he has brought me an apple from the Tree of Life."

The youth did not know where the Tree of Life stood, but he set out, and would have gone on forever, as long as his legs would carry him, though he had no hope of finding it. After he had wandered through three kingdoms, he came one evening to a wood, and lay down under a tree to sleep. But he heard a rustling in the branches, and a golden apple fell into his hand. At the same time three ravens flew down to him, perched themselves upon his knee, and said, "We are the three young ravens whom you saved from starving; when we had grown big, and heard that you were seeking the Golden Apple, we flew over the sea to the end of the world, where the Tree of Life stands, and have brought you the apple." The youth, full of joy, set out homewards, and took the Golden Apple to the King's beautiful daughter, who had no more excuses left to make. They cut the Apple of Life in two and ate it together; and then her heart became full of love for him, and they lived in undisturbed happiness to a great age.

The Story of Michael Scott
(*Scotland*)

Michael Scott, who lived during the thirteenth century, was known far and near as a great scholar, and it is told that he had dealings with the fairies and other spirits. When he wanted to erect a house or a bridge he called the "wee folk" to his aid, and they did the work for him in a single night. He had great skill as a healer of wounds and curer of diseases, and the people called him a magician.

When Michael was a young man he set out on a journey to Edinburgh with two companions. They travelled on foot, and one day, when they were climbing a high hill, they sat down to rest. No sooner had they done so than they heard a loud hissing sound. They looked in the direction whence the sound came, and saw with horror a great white serpent, curved in wheel shape, rolling towards them at a rapid speed. It was evident that the monster was going to attack them, and when it began to roll up the hill-side as swiftly as it had crossed the moor, Michael's two companions sprang to their feet and ran away, shouting with terror. Michael was a man who knew no fear, and he made up his mind to attack the serpent. He stood waiting for it, with his staff firmly grasped in his right hand.

When the serpent came close to Michael it uncurved its body and, throwing itself into a coil, raised its head to strike, its jaws gaping wide and its forked tongue thrust out like an arrow. Michael at once raised his staff, and struck the monster so fierce a blow that he cut its body into three parts. Then he turned away, and called upon his friends to wait for him. They heard his voice, stopped running, and gazed upon him with wonder as he walked towards them very calmly and at an easy pace. It was a great relief to them to learn from Michael that he had slain the fearsome monster.

They walked on together, and had not gone far when they came to a house in which lived a wise old woman. As the sun was beginning to set and it would soon be dark, they asked her for a night's lodging, and she invited them to enter the house. One of the men then told her of their adventure with the wheeling serpent which Michael had slain.

Said the Wise Woman: "Are you sure the white serpent is dead?"

"It must be dead," Michael answered, "because I cut its body into three parts."

Said the Wise Woman: "This white serpent is no ordinary serpent. It has power to unite the severed parts of its body again. Once before it was attacked by a brave man, who cut it in two. The head part of its body, however, crawled to a stream. After bathing in the stream it crawled back and joined itself to the tail part. The serpent then became whole again, and once more it bathed in the healing waters of the stream. All serpents do this after attacking a human being. If a man who has been stung by a serpent should hasten to the stream before the serpent can reach it, he will be cured and the serpent will die."

"You have great knowledge of the mysteries," Michael exclaimed with wonder.

Said the Wise Woman: "You have overcome the white serpent this time, but you may not be so fortunate when next it comes against you. Be assured of this: the serpent will, after it has been healed, lie in wait for you to take vengeance. When next it attacks, you will receive no warning that it is near."

"I shall never cross the high mountain again," Michael declared.

Said the Wise Woman: "The serpent will search for you and find you, no matter where you may be."

"Alas!" Michael exclaimed, "evil is my fate. What can I do to protect myself against the serpent?"

Said the Wise Woman: "Go now to the place where you smote the serpent, and carry away the middle part of its body. Make haste, lest you be too late."

Michael took her advice, and asked his companions to go with him; but they were afraid to do so, and he set out alone.

He walked quickly, and soon came to the place where he had struck down the monster. He found the middle part and the tail part of the white serpent's body, but the head part was nowhere to be seen. He knew then that the woman had spoken truly, and, as darkness was coming on, he did not care to search for the stream to which the head part had gone. Lifting up the middle part of the body, which still quivered, he hastened back towards the house of the Wise Woman. The sky darkened, and the stars began to appear. Michael grew uneasy. He felt sure that something was following him at a distance, so he quickened his steps and never looked back. At length he reached the house in safety, and he was glad to find that there were charms above the door which prevented any evil spirit from entering.

The Wise Woman welcomed Michael, and asked him to give her the part of the serpent's body which he had brought with him. He did so willingly, and she thanked him, and said: "Now I shall prepare a meal for you and your companions."

The woman at once set to work and cooked an excellent meal. Michael began to wonder why she showed him and his friends so much kindness and why she was in such high spirits. She laughed and talked as merrily as a girl, and he suspected she had been made happy because he had brought her the middle part of the white serpent's body. He resolved to watch her and find out, if possible, what she was going to do with it.

After eating his supper Michael pretended that he suffered from pain, and went into the kitchen to sit beside the fire. He told the woman that the heat took away the pain, and asked her to allow him to sleep in a chair in front of the fire. She said, "Very well," so he sat down, while his weary companions went to bed. The woman put a pot on the fire, and placed in it the middle part of the serpent's body.

Michael took note of this, but said nothing. He pretended to sleep. The part of the serpent began to frizzle in the pot, and the woman came from another room, lifted off the lid, and looked in. Then she touched the cut of the serpent with her right finger. When she did so a cock crew on the roof of the house. Michael was startled. He opened his eyes and looked round.

Said the Wise Woman: "I thought you were fast asleep."

"I cannot sleep because of the pain I suffer," Michael told her.

Said the Wise Woman: "If you cannot sleep, you may be of service to me. I am very weary and wish to sleep. I am cooking the part of the serpent. Watch the pot for me, and see that the part does not burn. Call me when it is properly cooked, but be sure not to touch it before you do so."

"I shall not sleep," Michael said, "so I may as well have something to do."

The Wise Woman smiled, and said: "After you call me, I shall cure your trouble." Then she went to her bed and lay down to sleep.

Michael sat watching the pot, and when he found that the portion of the serpent's body was fully cooked, he lifted the pot off the fire. Before calling the old woman, he thought he would first do what she had done when she lifted the lid off the pot. He dipped his finger into the juice of the serpent's body. The tip of his right finger was badly burned, so he thrust it into his mouth. The cock on the roof flapped its wings at once, and crowed so loudly that the old woman woke up in bed and screamed.

Michael felt that there must be magic in the juice of the serpent. New light and knowledge broke in upon him, and he discovered that he had the power to foretell events, to work magic cures, and to read the minds of other people.

The old woman came out of her room. "You did not call me," she said in a sad voice.

Michael knew what she meant. Had he called her, she would have been the first to taste the juice of the white serpent and receive from it the great power he now himself possessed.

"I slew the serpent," he said, "and had the first right to taste of its juice."

Said the Wise Woman: "I dare not scold you now. Nor need I tell you what powers you possess, for you have become wiser than I am. You can cure diseases, you can foretell and foresee what is to take place, you have power to make the fairies obey your commands, and you can obtain greater knowledge about the hidden mysteries than any other man alive. All that I ask of you is your friendship."

"I give you my friendship willingly," Michael said to her. Then the Wise Woman sat down beside him and asked him many questions about hidden things, and Michael found himself able to answer each one. They sat together talking until dawn. Then Michael awoke his companions, and the woman cooked a breakfast. When Michael bade her good-bye, she said: "Do not forget me, for you owe much to me."

"I shall never forget you," he promised her.

Michael and his companions resumed their journey. They walked until sunset, but did not reach a house.

"To-night," one of the men said, "we must sleep on the heather."

Michael smiled. "To-night," said he, "we shall sleep in Edinburgh."

"It is still a day's journey from here," the man reminded him.

Michael laid his staff on the ground and said: "Let us three sit on this staff and see how we fare."

His companions laughed, and sat down as he asked them to do. They thought it a great joke.

"Hold tight!" Michael advised them. The men, still amused, grasped the staff in their hands and held it tightly.

"Staff of mine!" Michael cried, "carry us to Edinburgh."

No sooner did he speak than the staff rose high in the air. The men were terror-stricken as the staff flew towards the clouds and then went forward with the speed of lightning. They shivered with fear and with cold. Snow-flakes fell on them as the staff flew across the sky, for they were higher up than the peak of Ben Nevis. When night was falling and the stars came out one by one, the staff began to descend. Happy were Michael's companions when they came down safely on the outskirts of Edinburgh.

They walked into the town in silence, and the first man they met stood and gazed with wonder upon them in the lamplight.

"Why do you stare at strangers?" Michael asked.

Said the man: "There is snow on your caps, and your shoulders."

Having spoken thus, a sudden fear overcame him, and he turned and fled, believing that the three strangers were either wizards or fairies.

Michael shook the snow off his cap and shoulders, and his companions did the same. They then sought out a lodging, and having eaten their suppers, went to bed.

Next morning Michael found that his companions had risen early and gone away. He knew that they were afraid of him, so he smiled and said to himself: "I bear them no ill-will. I prefer now to be alone."

Michael soon became famous as a builder. When he was asked to build a house, he called the fairies to his aid, and they did the work in the night-time for him.

Once he was travelling towards Inverness, and came to a river which was in flood. The ford could not be crossed, and several men stood beside it looking across the deep turbid waters. "It is a pity," one said to Michael, "there is no bridge here."

Said Michael: "I have come to build a bridge, and my workers will begin to erect it to-night."

Those who heard him laughed and turned away, but great was their surprise next morning to find that a bridge had been built. They crossed over it with their horses and cattle, and as they went on their way they spread the fame of Michael far and wide.

As time went on Michael found that his fairy workers wished to do more than he required of them. They began to visit him every evening, crying out: "Work! work! work!"

So Michael thought one day that he would set them to perform a task beyond their powers, and when next they came to him crying out: "Work! work! work!" he told them to close up the Inverness firth and cut it off from the sea. The fairies at once hastened away to obey his command.

Michael thought of the swift tides and of the great volume of water flowing down from the rivers by night and by day, and was certain that the fairies would not be able to close the firth.

Next morning, however, he found that the river Ness was rising rapidly, and threatening to flood the town of Inverness. He climbed a hill and looked seaward. Then he found that the fairies had very nearly finished the work he had set them to do. They had made two long promontories which jutted across the firth, and there remained only a narrow space through which the water surged. The incoming tide kept back the waters flowing from the river, and that was why the Ness was rising in flood. Not until after the tide turned did the waters of the river begin to fall.

Michael summoned his fairy workers that evening, and ordered them to open up the firth again. They hastened away to obey him, and after darkness came on they began to destroy the promontories. The moon rose as they went on with their work. A holy man walking along the shore saw the fairies, and prayed for protection against them. When he did so the fairies fled away, and were unable again to visit the promontories, and so these still lie jutting across the firth like crab's toes. The one has been named Chanonry Point, and on the peninsula opposite it there now stands Fort George, which was placed there to prevent enemy ships from sailing up to Inverness.

When the fairies found they were unable to complete their task they returned to Michael, crying out again: "Work! work! work!"

Michael then thought of an impossible task which would keep them busy. He said: "Go and make rope-ladders that will reach to the back of the moon. They must be made of sea sand and white foam."

The fairies hastened away to obey his command. They could not, however, make the ropes for Michael, try as they might.

Some say that Michael's workers are still attempting to carry out the work he last set them to do, and that is why wreaths of foam and ropes of twisted sand are sometimes found on the seashore till this day.

It is told that one weak-minded and clumsy old fairy man used to spend night after night trying to make ropes of sand and foam on the shore of Kirkcaldy Bay. When he grew weary he lay down to rest himself, and on cold nights he could be heard moaning: "My toes are cold, my toes are cold."

Fearachur Leigh
(*Scotland*)

Now, Farquhar was one time a drover in the Reay country, and he went from Glen Gollich to England (some say Falkirk), to sell cattle; and the staff that he had in his hand was hazel. One day a doctor met him. "What's that," said he, "that ye have got in y'r hand?" "It is a staff of hazel." "And where did ye cut that?" "In Glen Gollig: north, in Lord Reay's country." "Do ye mind the place and the tree?" "That do I." "Could ye get the tree?" "Easy." "Well, I will give ye gold more than ye can lift if ye will go back there and bring me a wand of that hazel tree; and take this bottle and bring me something more, and I will give you as much gold again. Watch at the hole at the foot, and put the bottle to it; let the six serpents go that come out first, and put the seventh one into the bottle, and tell no man, but come back straight with it here."

So Farquhar went back to the hazel glen, and when he had cut some boughs off the tree he looked about for the hole that the doctor had spoken of. And what should come out but six serpents, brown and barred like adders. These he let go, and clapped the bottle to the hole's mouth, to see would any more come out. By and by a white snake came rolling through. Farquhar had him in the bottle in a minute, tied him down, and hurried back to England with him.

The doctor gave him siller[1] enough to buy the Reay country, but asked him to stay and help him with the white snake. They lit a fire with the hazel sticks, and put the snake into a pot to boil. The doctor bid Farquhar watch it, and not let any one touch it, and not to let the steam escape, "for fear," he said, "folk might know what they were at."

He wrapped up paper round the pot lid, but he had not made all straight when the water began to boil, and the steam began to come out at one place.

Well, Farquhar saw this, and thought he would push the paper down round the thing; so he put his finger to the bit, and then his finger into his mouth, for it was wet with the bree.[2]

Lo! he knew everything, and the eyes of his mind were opened. "I will keep it quiet though," said he to himself.

Presently the doctor came back, and took the pot from the fire. He lifted the lid, and dipping his finger in the steam drops he sucked it; but the virtue had gone out of it, and it was no more than water to him.

"Who has done this!" he cried, and he saw in Farquhar's face that it was he. "Since you have taken the bree of it, take the flesh too," he said in a rage, and threw the pot at him. Now Farquhar had become allwise. He set up as a doctor, and there was no secret hid from him, and nothing that he could not cure.

He went from place to place and healed men, and so they called him Farquhar Leigheach.[3] Now he heard that the king was sick, and he went to the city of the king to know what would ail him. "It was his knee," said all the folk, "and he has many doctors, and pays them all greatly; and whiles they can give him relief, but not for long, and then it is worse than ever with him, and you may hear him roar and cry with the pain that is in his knee, in the bones of it." One day Farquhar walked up and down before the king's house. And he cried—

> *An daol dubh ris a chnamh gheal.*
> *The black beetle to the white bone.*

And the people looked at him, and said that the strange man from the Reay country was through-other.[4]

The next day Farquhar stood at the gate and cried, "The black beetle to the white bone!" and the king sent to know who it was that cried outside, and what was his business. The man, they said, was a stranger, and men called him the Physician. So the king, who was wild with pain, called

1 Silver.
2 Broth.
3 "The healer."
4 Disorderly.

him in; and Farquhar stood before the king, and aye "The black beetle to the white bone!" said he. And so it was proved. The doctors, to keep the king ill, and get their money, put at whiles a black beetle into the wound in the knee, and the beast was eating the bone and his flesh, and made him cry day and night. Then the doctors took it out again, for fear he should die; and when he was better they put it back again. This Farquhar knew by the serpent's wisdom that he had, when he laid his finger under his teeth; and the king was cured, and had all his doctors hung.

Then the king said that he would give Farquhar lands or gold, or whatever he asked. Then Farquhar asked to have the king's daughter, and all the isles that the sea runs round, from point of Storr to Stromness in the Orkneys; so the king gave him a grant of all the isles. But Farquhar the physician never came to be Farquhar the king, for he had an ill-wisher that poisoned him, and he died.

735: The Rich and Poor Man

Two Kinds of Luck
(*Russia*)

Once upon a time there lived a man who raised two sons, and died. The brothers decided to get married: the eldest got a poor wife, the youngest got a rich one. They lived together but shared nothing. So the wives started to dispute and quarrel. One said, "My husband is the eldest, I should be in charge!" And the other said "No, I'm in charge! I'm wealthier than you!" The brothers watched and watched, saw that their wives would not get along, split their father's wealth in half, and parted their ways. Every year, the eldest had new children born, but the household got worse and worse, and eventually he went broke. When he had food and money, looking at his children filled him with joy, but now that he had nothing, not even children could make him happy. He went to the youngest brother and said, "Help me in my poverty!" But the brother declined — "Live how you can! I have my own children to look after."

After a while, the poor brother came back to the rich one. "Lend me a horse," he begged, "at least for a day. I have nothing to plough with!" "Alright, go to the field and take one for a day, but don't work it too hard!" The poor brother came to the field and saw some people ploughing the land with his brother's horses. "Hold on!" he shouted, "Tell me, who are you people?" "And why do you ask?" "Because these are my brother's horses!" "But can't you see," replied one of the ploughmen, "that I am your brother's Happiness? He drinks, parties, lives with no worries, and we work for him." "Then where did my Happiness go?" "Yours is there, he sleeps under the bush. Does nothing but sleep day and night!" "All right," thought the man, "I'll get to you then."

He went ahead, cut out a stick, snuck up on his Happiness, and whipped its side as hard as he could. The Happiness woke up and asked, "Why did you hit me?" "I'll hit you even harder! Honest people plough the land while you sleep without waking!" "And you want me to plough for you? Don't even think about it!" "Then what? Are you going to lie under the bush all day? I'll starve to death this way!" "Well, if you want me to help you, give up your peasantry and take up trade. I'm not used to your work, but know a lot about the merchant business." "Take up trade! If only I had the means! I have nothing to eat, let alone sell." "Take your woman's old sarafan and sell it. Buy a new one for that money and sell it again. And I'll be helping you through it, I won't leave you for a second!" "Alright!"

The next morning the man told his wife, "Pack up, we're moving to the city." "Why?" "I want to start trading, become a freeman." "Are you mad? Our children are starving, and now you want to go to the city!" "None of your business! Pack up your belongings, take the kids and let's go!" They packed up, prayed to God, and were about to shut the door when they heard someone crying inside. The man asked, "Who's crying in there?" "It is me, Sorrow!" "Why are you crying?" "Why wouldn't I? You are moving to the city and leaving me here alone." "No dear! Of course I'm not leaving you here, I'll take you with me. Hey, wife!" he said, "throw your luggage out of the chest." The wife emptied the chest. "Here you go Sorrow, get in!" Sorrow did, and the man locked the chest with three locks, buried it in the ground and said, "Rot in there, damn you! Never wish to see you again!"

The man came to the city with his wife and children, rented a house and started trading, took his wife's old sarafan to a bazaar and sold it for a rouble. He bought a new one for that money and then sold it for two roubles. Trading this way, earning double the price of everything he bought, he got rich in no time and became a merchant. His brother heard of him, came to visit, and asked, "Tell me, please, how did you manage this—going from being poor to being rich?" "Easy," the merchant said, "I locked my Sorrow in a chest and buried it." "Where?" "In my old yard, in the village." The youngest brother nearly cried out of jealousy. Right away he went to the village, dug up the chest and let the Sorrow out. "Go," he said, "to my brother, and ruin him again!" "No!" said Sorrow, "I'd much rather stick with you, not with him. You are a kind man, you let me out! And he is a vile man—he buried me here!" It was not long until the jealous brother went from being a rich man to being a barefoot beggar.

Luck, Luck in the Red Coat!
(*Lithuania*)

There was once a man who had two sons. He led a lovely orderly life. He brought up his sons well, and gave them good teaching. At last he died. After his death, his children took over the property. They lived together, and never quarrelled.

So they lived on for some time. Then the elder wished to marry. He took a poor wife, but she pleased him. Not long after this, the younger married. He took a rich wife. She brought as her dowry three hundred cattle and many other things. Now that the two brothers were married, each received his portion of the property. Then they separated and each lived by himself.

Everything went well with the younger. He became richer and richer. But with the elder, things went downhill. At last he was a very poor man indeed. He had no more bread. His rickety hut was almost tumbled down, and his farm he had to lease. There was left him but a small garden, and he had nothing to plow it with.

With his brother, things were going better and better. His grain throve, his meadows grew green and his cattle increased. Ten yokes of oxen plowed his field.

Then thought the elder to himself, "I will go to my brother. Ten yokes of oxen are plowing his field. Perhaps he will lend me one ox, with which I may plow my garden. He is such a good man, and has given me bread more than once, and has helped me in my need!"

He went therefore to him, and said:

"Listen, dear Brother! My last miserable nag is no more, and I have nothing with which to plow my garden. Ten yokes of oxen are plowing your field. Won't you lend me just one?"

"Well, why shouldn't I? Go to the field and take what you want."

The elder went there and met a servant.

"Stop!" said he to him, "Your master has given me those oxen to plow my garden."

"I will not let you have them."

"Why not? Who are you that you dare to disobey your master?"

"I am your brother's Luck."

"And where is my Luck?" asked he.

"Oh! He lies over yonder by the bushes, and has on a red coat."

"Just you wait!" thought the elder brother to himself. "That Luck of my brother's plows his fields for him, while you loaf round, and are bringing me to ruin!"

Then he cut himself a good alder stick, went over to his Luck, and struck the red coat again and again—whack! whack! whack!

"Oh-o-o-o-o!" said the Luck. "What do you want of me?"

"Why don't you help me, Monster?"

"If you want me to help you, sell your farm and become a merchant."

Very good!

The man went home and immediately sold his garden. Then he bought a horse and wagon, set his wife and children in the wagon, took a leather bag and put in it all sorts of things—needles and little bark-shoes. Then he closed his hut, and started off. But he had gone only a little way, when he heard something cheeping, chirping inside his hut.

He thought to himself, "I certainly left nothing behind. What can be cheeping? I'll go back and see."

He went, looked about, and could see nothing.

Then he spoke up, "Who is cheeping here?"

"It is we, your Need and Misery," answered something from a corner.

"Aha! Why do you cheep?" he gave back.

"We want to go with you, and you have shut us up in the hut and left us behind."

"Crawl into my bag!" said the man.

Then Need and Misery slipped quick! slick! into the bag.

"Just you wait!" thought the man to himself. "You have tormented me till this day. Now I will repay you."

He dug a hole under the doorsill, and threw into it Need and Misery, bag and all, and filled up the hole.

Then he went back to his wagon, climbed in, and drove on. He drove and drove. By evening he reached a city. He put up for the night in a wretched hut by the roadside. Then he went into the city and bought bread. In the market he saw fish, and bought a huge, beautiful pike. He carried it home to his wife for her to dress and cook.

As she was cutting it up, she found in its stomach a diamond of indescribable magnificence. It sparkled even in the dark. She could not look at it enough, and set it in the window. Then they all sat down to eat their supper.

Just then a nobleman came driving past with six horses. He saw something shining in the window of the hut. It was not fire or a candle. He ordered the driver to stop, stepped down from the coach, and entered the hut. He talked for a few minutes then asked:

"What kind of a thing is that, lighting the window so brightly?"

"Gracious Sir, that is a costly thing, but I do not know its value."

"Will you sell it?"

"Well! Why not? I am a very poor man.

"Good! I will give you a farm with eight farmhands. Do you agree to that?"

"Thanks, gracious Sir, I do."

Then the nobleman bade him, his wife, and children take their seats in the coach, and he drove them to the farm he had promised.

There the man lived for a few years, as he was contented to do, and things went quite well with him. But he began to think that he must be a merchant. He sold the farm, drove to the city, opened a shop, and started to trade. He had such wonderful Luck that everything he bought for one ruble, he sold for two; and what he bought for twenty, he sold for forty.

So he lived on for some time, and became the very richest merchant in the city. The other merchants could do nothing without him, so they made him Chief of the Merchants.

About this time, the youngest brother came to the city with thirty loads of flax. The merchants were going to buy the flax, when they found much bad stuff mixed with it, and threw the poor man into prison. After three days they led him before the Chief of the Merchants, to pronounce judgment on him. The Chief recognized his own brother and thought of the good he had done. So he set him free, bought all his flax, and paid him well.

Then he took him home, entertained him, and gave him presents besides. When the younger brother was about to leave, he asked his elder brother:

"How have you come by such riches?"

The elder told him all that had happened.

When the younger brother reached home, he said to his wife:

"Listen! We live finely, but we cannot compare with my brother in anything. He deals in thousands. He is Chief of all the merchants. Besides he is a good man. God give him health! He freed me from my misfortune, entertained me richly, and bestowed presents on me."

"How could he become rich so quickly?" asked his wife.

"It came about in this way," he answered. "He has buried all his Need and Misery under the doorsill of his hut, and that has brought him Good Luck in everything."

This displeased his wife. Envy took hold of her.

So-o! The brother had buried his Need and Misery had he? Well! She would let them out so they might go back to him. She hurried to the hut, dug, opened the bag, and said:

"Now Need and Misery, go back to the brother of my husband!"

"We cannot find him again," replied Need and Misery. "We would rather stay with you!"

And there they stayed! They drove the younger brother to poverty.

But the elder brother lived on with Good Luck, and was a merchant, and is one today.

Fate
(*Serbia*)

There were two brothers living together in a house, one of whom did all the work, while the other did nothing but idle, and eat and drink what was ready at hand. And God gave them prosperity in everything—in cattle, in horses, in sheep, in swine, in bees, and in everything else. The one that worked one day began to think to himself: 'Why should I work for that lazybones as well? It is better that we should separate, and that I should work for myself, and he do as he likes.' So one day he said to his brother: 'Brother, it isn't right. I do all the work, and you don't help in anything, but merely eat and drink what's ready. I have made up my mind that we separate.' The other began to dissuade him: 'Don't, brother; it is good for us to be tenants in common; you have everything in your hands, both your own and mine, and I am content whatever you do.' But the first abode by his determination, so the second gave way, and said to him: 'If it is so, take your own course; make the division yourself, as you know how.' Then he divided everything in order, and took everything that was his before him. The do-nothing engaged a herdsman for his cattle, a horsekeeper for his horses, a shepherd for his sheep, a goatherd for his goats, a swineherd for his swine, a beeman for his bees, and said to them: 'I leave all my property in your hands and God's,' and began to live at home as before. The first took pains about his property himself as before, watched and overlooked, but saw no prosperity, but all loss. From day to day everything went worse, till he became so poverty-stricken that he hadn't shoes to his feet, but went barefoot. Then said he to himself: 'I will go to my brother, and see how it is with him.' He did so, and as he went came to a flock of sheep in a meadow, and with the sheep there was no shepherd, but a very beautiful damsel was sitting there spinning golden thread. He addressed her: 'God help you!' and inquired whose the sheep were. She replied: 'The sheep belong to the person to whom I belong.' He asked her further: 'To whom do you belong?' She answered: 'I am your brother's luck.' He was put out, and said to her: 'And where is my luck?' The damsel answered him: 'Your luck is far from you.' 'But can I find it?' inquired he, and she replied: 'You can; go, seek for it.' When he heard this, and saw that his brother's sheep were good—so good, that they could not be better, he didn't care about going further to see other cattle, but went off straight to his brother. When his brother saw him, he had compassion on him, and began to weep: 'Where have you been so long a time?' Then, seeing him barehead and barefoot, he gave him at once a pair of boots and some money. Afterwards, when they had enjoyed each other's company for some days, the visitor rose up to go to his own house. When he got home, he took a wallet on his back, some bread in it, and a staff in his hand, and went into the world to look for his luck. As he travelled, he came to a large wood, and as he went through it, he saw a gray-haired old maid asleep under a bush, and reached out his staff to give her a push. She barely raised herself up, and, hardly opening her eyes for the rheum,[1] addressed him: 'Thank God that I fell asleep, for, if I had been awake, you wouldn't have obtained even that pair of boots.' Then he said to her: 'Who are you, that I shouldn't even have obtained this pair of boots?' She replied: 'I am your luck.' When he heard this, he began to beat his breast: 'If you are my luck, God slay you! Who gave you to me?'

---

1 Eye-crust.

She quickly rejoined: 'Fate gave me to you.' He then inquired: 'And where is this Fate?' She answered: 'Go and look for him.' And that instant she disappeared. Then the man went on to look for Fate. As he journeyed, he came to a village, and saw in the village a large farmhouse, and in it a large fire, and said to himself: 'Here there is surely some merry-making or festival,' and went in. When he went in, on the fire was a large caldron, in which supper was cooking, and in front of the fire sat the master of the house. The traveller, on going into the house, addressed the master: 'Good-evening!' The master replied: 'God give you prosperity!' and bade him sit down with him, and then began to ask him whence he came, and whither he was going. He related to him everything: how he had been a master, how he had become impoverished, and how he was now going to Fate to ask him why he was so poor. Then he inquired of the master of the house why he was preparing so large a quantity of food, and the master said to him: 'Well, my brother, I am master here, and have enough of everything, but I cannot anyhow satisfy my people; it is quite as if a dragon were in their stomachs. You'll see, when we begin to sup, what they will do.' When they sat down to sup, everybody snatched and grabbed from everybody else, and that large caldron of food was empty in no time. After supper, a maidservant came in, put all the bones in a heap, and threw them behind the stove; and he began to wonder why the young woman threw the bones behind the stove, till all at once out came two old poverty-stricken spectres, as dry as ghosts, and began to suck the bones. Then he asked the master of the house: 'What's this, brother, behind the stove?' He replied: 'Those, brother, are my father and mother; just as if they were fettered to this world, they will not quit it.' The next day, at his departure, the master of the house said to him: 'Brother, remember me, too, if anywhere you find Fate, and ask him what manner of misfortune it is that I cannot satisfy my people, and why my father and mother do not die.' He promised to ask him the question, took leave of him, and went on to look for Fate. As on he went, he came, after a long time, to another village, and begged at a certain house that they would take him in for a night's lodging. They did so, and asked him whither he was going; and he told them all in order, what it was, and how it was. Then they began to say to him: 'In God's name, brother, when you get there, ask him with regard to us too, why our cattle are not productive, but the contrary.' He promised them to ask Fate the question, and the next day went on. As he went, he came to a stream of water, and began to shout: 'Water! water! carry me across.' The water asked him: 'Whither are you going?' He told it whither he was going. Then the water carried him across, and said to him: 'I pray you, brother, ask Fate why I have no offspring.' He promised the stream to ask the question, and then went on. He went on for a long time, and at last came to a wood, where he found a hermit whom he asked whether he could tell him anything about Fate. The hermit answered: 'Go over the hill yonder, and you will come right in front of his abode; but when you come into Fate's presence, do not say a word, but do exactly what he does, until he questions you himself.' The man thanked the hermit, and went over the hill. When he came to Fate's abode, there was something for him to see. It was just as if it were an emperor's palace; there were men-servants and maid-servants there; everything was in good order, and Fate himself was sitting at a golden dinner-table at supper. When the man saw this, he, too, sat down to table, and began to sup. After supper, Fate lay down to sleep, and he lay down too. About midnight a terrible noise arose, and out of the noise a voice was heard: 'Fate! Fate! so many souls have been born to-day; assign them what you will.' Then Fate arose, and opened a chest with money in it, and began to throw nothing but ducats behind him, saying: 'As to me to-day, so to them for life!' When on the morrow day dawned, that large palace was no more, but instead of it a moderate-sized house; but in it again there was enough of everything.

At the approach of evening Fate sat down to supper; and he, too, sat down with him, but neither spoke a single word. After supper they lay down to sleep. About midnight a terrible noise began, and out of the noise was heard a voice: 'Fate! Fate! so many souls have been born to-day; assign them what you will.' Then Fate arose, and opened the money-chest; but there were not ducats in it, but silver coins, with an occasional ducat. Fate began to scatter the coins behind him, saying: 'As to me to-day, so to them for life.' When, on the morrow, day dawned, that house was no more, but instead of it there stood a smaller one. Thus did Fate every night, and his house became smaller every morning, till, finally, nothing remained of it but a little cottage. Fate took a mattock, and began to dig; the man, too, took a mattock and began to dig, and thus they dug all day. When it was eventide, Fate took a piece of bread, broke off half of it, and gave it to him. Thus they supped, and, after supper, lay down to sleep. About midnight, again, a terrible noise began, and out of the noise was heard a voice: 'Fate! Fate! so many souls have been born to-day; assign them what you will.' Then Fate arose, opened the chest, and began to scatter behind him nothing but bits of rag, and here and there a day-labourer's wage-penny, shouting: 'As to me to-day, so to them for life.' When he arose on the morrow, the cottage was transformed into a large palace, like that which had been there the first day. Then Fate asked him: 'Why have you come?' He detailed to him all his distress, and said that he had come to ask him why he gave him evil luck. Fate then said to him: 'You saw how the first night I scattered ducats, and what took place afterwards. As it was to me the night when anyone was born, so will it be to him for life. You were born on an unlucky night, you will be poor for life; but your brother was born on a lucky night, and he will be lucky for life.

But, as you have been so resolute, and have taken so much trouble, I will tell you how you may help yourself. Your brother has a daughter, Militza, who is lucky, just as her father is; adopt her, and, whatever you acquire, say that it is all hers.' Then he thanked Fate, and said to him again: 'In such a village there is a wealthy peasant, who has enough of everything; but he is unlucky in this, that his people can never be satisfied: they eat up a caldron full of food at a single meal, and even that is too little for them. And this peasant's father and mother are, as it were, fettered to this world; they are old and discoloured, and dried up like ghosts, but cannot die. He begged me, Fate, when I lodged with him for the night, to ask you why that was the case.' Then Fate replied: 'All that is because he does not honour his father and mother, throwing their food behind the stove; but if he puts them in the best place at table, and if he gives them the first cup of brandy, and the first cup of wine, his servants would not eat half so much, and his parents' souls would be set at liberty.' After this he again questioned Fate: 'In such a village, when I spent the night in a house, the householder complained to me that his cattle were not productive, but the contrary, and he begged me to ask you why this was the case.' Fate replied: 'That is because on the festival of his name-day he slaughters the worst animals; but if he slaughtered the best he has, his cattle would all become productive.' Then he asked him the question about the stream of water: 'Why should it be that that stream of water has no offspring?' Fate replied: 'Because it has never drowned a human being; but don't have any nonsense; don't tell it till it carries you across, for if you tell it, it will immediately drown you.' Then he thanked Fate, and went home. When he came to the water, the water asked him: 'What is the news from Fate?' He replied: 'Carry me over, and then I will tell you.' When the water had carried him over, he ran on a little, and, when he had got a little way off, turned and shouted to the water: 'Water! Water! you have never drowned a human being, therefore you have no offspring.' When the water heard that, it overflowed its banks, and after him; but he ran, and barely escaped. When he came to the man whose cattle were unproductive, he was impatiently waiting for him. 'What news, brother, in God's name? Have you asked Fate the question?' He replied: 'I have; and Fate says when you celebrate the festival of your name-day, you slaughter the worst animals; but if you slaughter the best you have, all your cattle will be productive.' When he heard this, he said to him: 'Stay, brother, with us; it isn't three days to my name-day, and, if it is really true, I will give you an apple.' He stayed till the name-day. When the name-day arrived, the householder slaughtered his best ox, and from that time forth his cattle became productive. After this, the householder presented him with five head of cattle. He thanked him, and proceeded on his way. When he came to the village of the householder who had the insatiable servants, the householder was impatiently expecting him. 'How is it, brother, in God's name? What says Fate?' He replied: 'Fate says you do not honour your father and mother, but throw their food behind the stove for them to eat; if you put them in the best place at table, and give them the first cup of brandy, and the first cup of wine, your people will not eat half as much, and your father and mother will be content.' When the householder heard this, he told his wife, and she immediately washed and combed her father and mother in law, and put nice shoes on their feet; and, when evening came, the householder put them in the best place at table, and gave them the first cup of brandy and the first cup of wine. From that time forth the household could not eat half what they did before, and on the morrow both the father and the mother departed this life. Then the householder gave him two oxen; he thanked him, and went home. When he came to his place of abode, his acquaintances began to congratulate him, and ask him: 'Whose are these cattle?' He replied to everybody: 'Brother, they are my niece Militza's.' When he got home he immediately went off to his brother, and began to beg and pray him: 'Give me, brother, your daughter Militza to be my daughter. You see that I have no one.' His brother replied: 'It is good, brother; Militza is yours.' He took Militza, and conducted her home, and afterwards acquired much, but said, with regard to everything, that it was Militza's. Once he went out into the field to go round some rye; the rye was beautiful; it could not be better. Thereupon a traveller happened to come up, and asked him: 'Whose is this rye?' He forgot himself, and said: 'Mine.' The moment he said that, the rye caught fire and began to burn. When he saw this, he ran after the man: 'Stop, brother! it is not mine; it belongs to Militza, my niece.' Then the fire in the rye went out, and he remained lucky with Militza.

735A: Bad Luck Imprisoned

The Story of the Unlucky Days
(*Ukraine*)

At the end of a village on the verge of the steppe dwelt two brothers, one rich and the other poor. One day the poor brother came to the rich brother's house and sat down at his table; but the rich brother drove him away and said, "How durst thou sit at my table? Be off! Thy proper place is in the fields to scare away the crows!" So the poor brother went into the fields to scare away the crows. The crows all flew away when they saw him, but among them was a raven that flew back again and said to him, "O man! in this village thou wilt never be able to live, for here there is neither luck nor happiness for thee, but go into another village and thou shalt do well!" Then the man went home, called together his wife and children, put up the few old clothes that still remained in his wardrobe, and went on to the next village, carrying his water-skin on his shoulders. On and on they tramped along the road, but the Unlucky Days clung on to the man behind, and said, "Why dost thou not take us with thee? We will never leave thee, for thou art ours!" So they went on with him till they came to a river, and the man, who was thirsty, went down to the water's edge for a drink. He undid his water-skin, persuaded the Unlucky Days to get into it, tied it fast again and buried it on the bank close by the river. Then he and his family went on farther. They went on and on till they came to another village, and at the very end of it was an empty hut—the people who had lived there had died of hunger. There the whole family settled down. One day they were all sitting down there when they heard something in the mountain crying, "Catch hold! catch hold! catch hold!" The man went at once into his stable, took down the bit and reins that remained to him, and climbed up into the mountain. He looked all about him as he went, and at last he saw, sitting down, an old goat with two large horns—it was the Devil himself, but of course he didn't know that. So he made a lasso of the reins, threw them round the old goat, and began to drag it gently down the mountain-side. He dragged it all the way up the ladder of his barn, when the goat disappeared, but showers and showers of money came tumbling through the ceiling. He collected them all together, and they filled two large coffers. Then the poor man made the most of his money, and in no very long time he was well-to-do. Then he sent some of his people to his rich brother, and invited him to come and live with him. The rich brother pondered the matter over. "Maybe he has nothing to eat," thought he, "and that is why he sends for me." So he bade them bake him a good store of fat pancakes, and set out according-ly. On the way he heard that his brother had grown rich, and the farther he went the more he heard of his brother's wealth. Then he regretted that he had brought all the pancakes with him, so he threw them away into the ditch. At last he came to his brother's house, and his brother showed him first one of the coffers full of money and then the other. Then envy seized upon the rich brother, and he grew quite green in the face. But his brother said to him, "Look now! I have buried a lot more money in a water-skin, hard by the river; you may dig it up and keep it if you like, for I have lots of my own here!" The rich brother did not wait to be told twice. Off he went to the river, and began digging up the water-skin straightway. He unfastened it with greedy, trembling hands; but he had no sooner opened it than the Unlucky Days all popped out and clung on to him. "Thou art ours!" said they. He went home, and when he got there he found that all his wealth was consumed, and a heap of ashes stood where his house had been. So he went and lived in the place where his brother had lived, and the Unlucky Days lived with him ever afterward.

The Pale Maiden
(*Poland*)

A peasant farmer in reduced circumstances had a beautiful daughter, whom an old knight, the proprietor of the village, wanted to marry, and that even by compulsion. But the damsel disliked him, and her parents also refused to consent to the marriage. So the proprietor persecuted them in every way in his power, and so oppressed them with forced labour and ordered them to be beaten on the slightest occasion that the poor farmer could hold out no longer, but determined to remove from the village with his whole family. In the cottage in which the farmer dwelt there was something continually grating behind the stove, but though they searched several times, and turned the seat constructed at the side of the stove upside down, yet were they unable to discover aught. But when, on the day of their departure, they were removing the rest of their goods, they heard a more and more articulate grating, and whilst they were impatiently listening, as the grating and scraping went on, out of the stove sprang a thin pale form, like a buried maiden. 'What the devil is this?' cried the father. 'For heaven's sake!' screamed the mother, and all the children after her. 'I am no devil,' said the thin pale maiden, 'but I am your Poverty. You are now taking yourselves off hence, and you are bound to take me with you to your new abode.' The poor householder was no fool; he bethought himself a little, and neither seized nor throttled his Poverty, for she was so slight that he could have done nothing of any consequence to her, but he made the lowest possible reverence to her, and said: 'Well, your gracious ladyship, if you are so well satisfied amongst us, then come with us; but, as you see, we are removing everything for ourselves, so help us to carry something, and we shall get off the quicker.' Poverty agreed to this, and wanted to take a couple of small vessels out of the house, but the householder distributed the small vessels among his children to remove, and said that there was still a block of wood in the yard which must also be taken away. Going out into the yard, he made a cut in the block from above with his axe. He then called Poverty, and politely requested her to help him remove the block. Poverty did not see on which side to lift the block, till, when the farmer pointed out the cleft to her, she put her long thin fingers in the chink. The farmer, pretending to lift the block on the other side, suddenly pulled his axe out of the cleft, and Poverty's long thin fingers remained squeezed in the block, so that, being utterly unable to pull them out, she shrieked out immediately in what pain she was. But all in vain. The farmer removed all his goods as well as his children, quitted the cottage completely, and returned to the place no more.

When the farmer settled in another village, things went with him so prosperously that ere long he was the richest man in the whole village; he married his daughter to a respectable and wealthy farmer's son, twenty years old, and the whole family prospered. On the other hand, the proprietor of the first village, the oppressor of these poor people, having to assign vacant cottages to fresh tenants, came to inspect the cottage left vacant by the reduced farmer, who had refused to give him his daughter. Seeing Poverty beside the block complaining of the pain of her fingers, he took pity on the pale maiden, took her fingers out by means of a wedge, and set her completely free. From the time of her liberation the pale maiden never quitted the side of her liberator, and when, moreover, the devil lit a fire in the old stove, and the proprietor went dotty with love in his old age, he spent and spent, and ran through everything that he had.

Woe Bogotir
(*Russia*)

In a small village—do not ask me where; in Russia, anyway—there lived two brothers; one of them was rich, the other poor. The rich brother had good luck in everything he undertook, was always successful, and had profit out of every venture. The poor brother, in spite of all his trouble and all his work, had none whatever.

The rich brother became still richer, moved into a large town, bought a big house, and was a merchant among merchants. The poor brother became very poor, so poor that very often there was no crust even in the "izba," the peasant's log cabin, and the children—all forlorn, miserable little things—cried for food.

The poor man lost patience and complained bitterly of his ill luck. He had no more courage and his head dropped heavily on his breast. One day he decided to call upon his wealthy brother for aid. He went and said to him:

"Be good, help me, for I am almost without strength."

"Why not?" answered the rich man. "We can do such things as that. There is wealth enough; but look here, there is also plenty of work to be done. Stay around the house for a while and work for me."

"All right," consented the poor fellow, and at once began to work. Now he was cleaning the big yard, now grooming horses, now bringing water from the well or splitting wood. One week passed, two weeks passed. The rich brother gave him twenty and five copecks, which means only thirteen cents. He also gave him a loaf of black rye bread.

"Many thanks," said the poor brother, humbly, and was ready to leave for his miserable home. Evidently the conscience of the rich brother smote him, so he called his brother back.

"Why so prompt?" he said; "to-morrow is my birthday; stay to the banquet with us."

The poor fellow remained. But even on such a pleasant occasion the unlucky one had no luck. His rich brother was too busy receiving his numerous friends and admirers, all of whom came to tell him how they loved him and what a good man he was. The rich merchant thanked his guests for their love, and bowing low begged his dear guests to eat, drink, and enjoy themselves. There was no time left for the poor brother, and he was overlooked entirely while he sat timidly in a corner, quite forgotten and unnoticed. He had nothing to eat, nothing to drink. But when the crowd was ready to say good-by, before going away, the bright, light-hearted guests bowed to their host and told him many lovely things, and the poor brother did exactly like them. He bowed even lower than they did and expressed more thanks than they. The guests went home singing in their new "telegi," the peasants' carts. The poor brother, hungry and very sad, walked along in silence, and the idea came to his mind:

"What if I also tried to sing a cheerful song? The people would believe that I, too, have had a pleasant time at my brother's house and that I am going home happy like them."

The good fellow began his song, began—and almost fainted away, for he heard quite distinctly someone behind his back, keeping tune with him in a shrill voice. He stopped. The voice stopped, too. He sang, and the voice continued again.

"Who is there? Come out at once!" shouted the poor man, beside himself. Ha! the monster appeared, lank and yellow, almost a skeleton, covered with rags. The poor fellow was afraid, but had the courage to make the sign of the cross and ask: "Who art thou?"

"I? I am Bitter Woe. I am one of the Russian heroes, Woe Bogotir. I pity all weak people. I pity thee, too, and want to help thee along."

"All right, Bitter Woe; let us walk together arm in arm. I presume there are no other friends for me in this world."

"Let us ride, good man," laughed the monster. "I will be thy faithful companion."

"Thanks, but on what shall we ride?"

"I do not know on what thou shalt ride, but I, I shall ride on thee," and Woe jumped on the shoulders of the unlucky man. The poor fellow had no strength to throw him off, so he crawled along his way, the long, hard way, with Woe on his shoulders. He could hardly walk, yet Woe was singing, whistling, and switching him all the time.

"Why so sad, master?" Woe would ask, when the poor man sighed. "Listen to me, I want to teach thee a song, my beloved little song:

> *I am Woe, the brave,*
> *I am Woe, the bold;*
> *He who lives with me*
> *Has his griefs controlled,*
> *And when money is lacking*
> *I'll find him gold.*

"Attention, master, thou hast twenty-five copecks; let us go and buy some wine; let us have a jolly good time."

The poor man obeyed. They went and spent all in drink. After this the unlucky fellow, with the faithful Woe on his shoulders, came home. His wife was sad, his little children were hungry and in tears, but he, under the influence of Woe and wine, danced and sang.

On the next day Woe began to sigh and said:

"I have a drunken headache. Let us drink more."

"I have no money," answered the poor man.

"Hast thou forgotten my little song? Let us trade the harrow, the plow, the sledge, the telega for money, and let us have a good time."

"All right."

The poor, weak man had no courage to refuse, and Woe Bogotir became his master and ruler. They went to a kabak[1] and spent everything; drank, sang, and had a good time.

On the next day Woe sighed again and said to the peasant:

---

1 Tavern.

"Let us drink; let us have a jolly time; let us sell or trade everything left, even ourselves."

Then the fellow understood that his ruin was near and decided to deceive the sorrowful Woe, so he said:

"I once heard the old people say that behind the village, near the dark forest, there is buried a treasure, yes, a great treasure, but it is buried under a large, heavy stone, too heavy a stone for one man to move. If we could only remove that stone, thou and I, Woe Bogotir, could have a good time and plenty to drink."

"Let us hasten!" screamed Woe; "the Bitter Woe is strong enough to do harder things than to move stones."

They went a roundabout way behind the village and saw the great big stone, such a heavy stone that five or six strong peasants could never begin to move it. But our poor fellow with his faithful Woe Bogotir removed it at once. They looked inside. Under the stone there was a pit, a dark, deep pit. At the bottom of that pit something was twinkling. The peasant said to Woe:

"Thou bold Woe, jump in, throw the gold out to me and I will hold the stone."

Woe jumped in and laughed out loud.

"I declare, master," he screamed, "there is no end of gold! There are twenty and more pots filled with it," and Woe handed one pot to the poor man, who took the pot, hastily hid it under his blouse, and slipped the heavy stone into its place. So Bitter Woe remained in the deep pit and the peasant thought to himself, "Now there is the right place for my comrade, for with such a friend, even gold would taste bitter."

The crafty fellow made the sign of the cross and hurried home. He became quite a new man, courageous, sober, and industrious; bought a grove and some cattle; remodeled the izba, and even started a trade. And very successful he was, too. Within a year he earned much money, and in place of the old hut built a fine, new log cabin.

One bright day he went into town to ask his rich brother, with his wife and children, to do him the favor of coming to a feast which was to be given in the new home.

"That's a joke!" exclaimed the rich brother. "Without a ruble in thy pockets, stupid fellow! Thou evidently desirest to imitate rich people," and then the rich brother laughed and laughed at him. But at the same time he got very anxious to know how it was with his poor brother, so he went without delay to the new place. When he arrived there he could not believe his eyes. His poor brother seemed to be quite rich, perhaps richer than himself. Everything bespoke wealth and care. The host treated his brother and the brother's family most kindly and was very hospitable. They had good things to eat and plenty of honey to drink, and all became talkative. The brother who had been poor related everything about Woe, how he decided to deceive him and how, free from such a burden, he was getting to be a very happy man.

The rich man grew eager and thought:

"Is he a fool? Out of so many pots, to take only one! Fool and nothing but fool! If one has money, even the Bitter Woe is not too bad."

So at once he decided to go in search of the stone, to remove it, to take the treasure, the whole treasure, and to send Woe Bogotir back to his brother.

No sooner thought than done. The rich brother said good-by and went away, but did not go to his wealthy home. No, he hurried to the stone. He had to toil hard with the heavy stone, but finally moved it just a little, and had not time to look inside when the hidden Bogotir had jumped out and onto his shoulders.

The rich man felt a burden, oh, what a heavy burden! looked around and perceived the hideous monster. He heard this monster whisper in his ear:

"Thou art bright! Thou didst want to let me perish in that pit? Now, dearest, thou wilt not get rid of me; now we shall always be together."

"Stupid Woe," began the rich man; "it was not I who hid thee under the stone; it was my brother; go to him."

But no, Woe would not go. The monster laughed and laughed.

"All the same, all the same," he answered to the rich man. "Let us remain dear companions."

The rich man went home under the heavy burden of the misery-giving Woe. His wealth was soon lost, but his brother, who knew how to get rid of Woe, was prosperous and is prosperous to this day.

736: Luck and Wealth

The Fish and the Ring
(*England*)

Once upon a time, there was a mighty baron in the North Countrie who was a great magician that knew everything that would come to pass. So one day, when his little boy was four years old, he looked into the Book of Fate to see what would happen to him. And to his dismay, he found that his son would wed a lowly maid that had just been born in a house under the shadow of York Minster. Now the Baron knew the father of the little girl was very, very poor, and he had five children already. So he called for his horse, and rode into York; and passed by the father's house, and saw him sitting by the door, sad and doleful. So he dismounted and went up to him and said: "What is the matter, my good man?" And the man said: "Well, your honour, the fact is, I've five children already, and now a sixth's come, a little lass, and where to get the bread from to fill their mouths, that's more than I can say."

"Don't be downhearted, my man," said the Baron. "If that's your trouble, I can help you. I'll take away the last little one, and you won't have to bother about her."

"Thank you kindly, sir," said the man; and he went in and brought out the lass and gave her to the Baron, who mounted his horse and rode away with her. And when he got by the bank of the river Ouse, he threw the little, thing into the river, and rode off to his castle.

But the little lass didn't sink; her clothes kept her up for a time, and she floated, and she floated, till she was cast ashore just in front of a fisherman's hut. There the fisherman found her, and took pity on the poor little thing and took her into his house, and she lived there till she was fifteen years old, and a fine handsome girl.

One day it happened that the Baron went out hunting with some companions along the banks of the River Ouse, and stopped at the fisherman's hut to get a drink, and the girl came out to give it to them. They all noticed her beauty, and one of them said to the Baron: "You can read fates, Baron, whom will she marry, d'ye think?"

"Oh! that's easy to guess," said the Baron; "some yokel or other. But I'll cast her horoscope. Come here girl, and tell me on what day you were born?"

"I don't know, sir," said the girl, "I was picked up just here after having been brought down by the river about fifteen years ago."

Then the Baron knew who she was, and when they went away, he rode back and said to the girl: "Hark ye, girl, I will make your fortune. Take this letter to my brother in Scarborough, and you will be settled for life." And the girl took the letter and said she would go. Now this was what he had written in the letter:

Dear Brother—Take the bearer and put her to death immediately.

Yours affectionately,

Albert.

So soon after the girl set out for Scarborough, and slept for the night at a little inn. Now that very night a band of robbers broke into the inn, and searched the girl, who had no money, and only the letter. So they opened this and read it, and thought it a shame. The captain of the robbers took a pen and paper and wrote this letter:

Dear Brother—Take the bearer and marry her to my son immediately.

Yours affectionately,

Albert.

And then he gave it to the girl, bidding her begone. So she went on to the Baron's brother at Scarborough, a noble knight with whom the Baron's son was staying. When she gave the letter to his brother, he gave orders for the wedding to be prepared at once, and they were married that very day.

Soon after, the Baron himself came to his brother's castle, and what was his surprise to find that the very thing he had plotted against had come to pass. But he was not to be put off that way; and he took out the girl for a walk, as he said, along the cliffs. And when he got her all alone, he took her by the arms, and was going to throw her over. But she begged hard for her life. "I have not done anything," she said: "if you will only spare me, I will do whatever you wish. I will never see you or your son again till you desire it." Then the Baron took off his gold ring and threw it into the sea, saying: "Never let me see your face till you can show me that ring;" and he let her go.

The poor girl wandered on and on, till at last she came to a great noble's castle, and she asked to have some work given to her; and they made her the scullion girl of the castle, for she had been used to such work in the fisherman's hut.

Now one day, who should she see coming up to the noble's house but the Baron and his brother and his son, her husband. She didn't know what to do; but thought they would not see her in the castle kitchen. So she went back to her work with a sigh, and set to cleaning a huge big fish that was to be boiled for their dinner. And, as she was cleaning it, she saw something shine inside it, and what do you think she found? Why, there was the Baron's ring, the very one he had thrown over the cliff at Scarborough. She was right glad to see it, you may be sure. Then she cooked the fish as nicely as she could, and served it up.

Well, when the fish came on the table, the guests liked it so well that they asked the noble who cooked it. He said he didn't know, but called to his servants: "Ho, there, send up the cook that cooked that fine fish." So they went down to the kitchen and told the girl she was wanted in the hall. Then she washed and tidied herself and put the Baron's gold ring on her thumb and went up into the hall.

When the banqueters saw such a young and beautiful cook they were surprised. But the Baron was in a tower of a temper, and started up as if he would do her some violence. So the girl went up to him with her hand before her with the ring on it; and she put it down before him on the table. Then at last the Baron saw that no one could fight against Fate, and he handed her to a seat and announced to all the company that this was his son's true wife; and he took her and his son home to his castle; and they all lived as happy as could be ever afterwards.

When Wheat Worked Woe
(*Netherlands*)

Many a day has the story-teller wandered along the dykes which overlook the Zuyder Zee. Once there were fertile fields, and scores of towns, where water now covers all. Then fleets of ships sailed on the bosom of Lake Flevo, and in the river which ran into the sea. Bright and beautiful cities dotted the shores, and church bells chimed merrily for the bridal, or tolled in sympathy for the sorrowing. Many were the festal days, because of the wealth, which the ships brought from lands near and far.

But to-day the waters roll over the spot and "The Dead Cities of the Zuyder Zee" are a proverb. Yet all are not dead, in one and the same sense. Some lie far down under the waves, their very names forgotten, because of the ocean's flood, which in one night, centuries ago, rushed in to destroy. Others languished, because wealth came no longer in the ships, and the seaports dried up. And one, because of a foolish woman, instead of holding thousands of homes and people, is to-day only a village nestling behind the dykes. It holds a few hundred people and only a fragment of land remains of its once great area.

In the distant ages of ice and gravel, when the long and high glaciers of Norway poked their cold noses into Friesland, Stavoren held the shrine of Stavo, the storm-god. The people were very poor, but many pilgrims came to worship at Stavo's altars. After the new religion came into the land, wealth increased, because the ships traded with the warm lands in the south. A great city sprang up, to which the counts of Holland granted a charter, with privileges second to none. It was written that Stavoren should have "the same freedom which a free city enjoys from this side of the mountains1 to the sea."

Then there came an age of gold in Stavoren. People were so rich that the bolts and hinges and the keys and locks of their doors were made of this precious yellow metal. In some of the houses, the parlor floor was paved with ducats from Spain.

Now in this city lived a married couple, whose wealth came from the ships. The man, a merchant, was a simple hearted and honest fellow, who worked hard and was easily pleased.

But his wife was discontented, always peevish and never satisfied with anything. Even her neighbors grew tired of her whining and complaints. They declared that on her tombstone should be carved these words:

> *She wanted something else*

Now on every voyage, made by the many ships he owned, the merchant charged his captains to bring home something rare and fine, as a present to his wife. Some pretty carving or picture, a roll of silk for a dress, a lace collar, a bit of splendid tapestry, a shining jewel; or, it may be, a singing bird, a strange animal for a pet, a barrel of fruit, or a box of sweetmeats was sure to be brought. With such gifts, whether large or small, the husband hoped to please his wife.

But in this good purpose, he could never succeed. So he began to think that it was his own fault. Being only a man, he could not tell what a woman wanted. So he resolved to try his own wits and tastes, to see if he could meet his wife's desires.

One day, when one of his best captains was about to sail on a voyage to the northeast, to Dantzig, which is almost as far as Russia, he inquired of his bad-tempered vrouw[2] what he should bring her.

"I want the best thing in the world," said she. "Now this time, do bring it to me."

The merchant was now very happy. He told the captain to seek out and bring back what he himself might think was the best thing on earth; but

---

1 The Alps.
2 Woman.

to make sure, he must buy a cargo of wheat.

The skipper went on board, hoisted anchor and set sail. Using his man's wits, he also decided that wheat, which makes bread, was the very thing to be desired. In talking to his mates and sailors, they agreed with him. Thus, all the men, in this matter, were of one mind, and the captain dreamed only of jolly times when on shore. On other voyages, when he had hunted around for curiosities to please the wife of the boss, he had many and anxious thoughts; but now, he was care-free.

In Dantzig, all the ship's men had a good time, for the captain made "goed koop".[1] Then the vessel, richly loaded with grain, turned its prow homeward. Arriving at Stavoren, the skipper reported to the merchant to tell him of much money made, of a sound cargo obtained, of safe arrival, and, above all, plenty of what would please his wife; for what on earth could be more valuable than wheat, which makes bread, the staff of life?

At lunch time, when the merchant came home, his wife wanted to know what made him look so joyful. Had he made "goed koop" that day?

Usually, at meal time, this quiet man hardly spoke two words an hour. To tell the truth, he sometimes irritated his wife because of his silence, but to-day he was voluble.

The man of wealth answered, "I have a joyful surprise for you. I cannot tell you now. You must come with me and see."

After lunch, he took his wife on board the ship, giving a wink of his eye to the skipper, who nodded to the sailors, and then the stout fellows opened the hatches. There, loaded to the very deck, was the precious grain. The merchant looked up, expecting to see and hear his wife clap her hands with joy.

But the greedy woman turned her back on him, and flew into a rage.

"Throw it all overboard, into the water," she screamed. "You wretch, you have deceived me."

The husband tried to calm her and explain that it was his thought to get wheat, as the world's best gift, hoping thus to please her.

At that moment, some hungry beggars standing on the wharf, heard the lady's loud voice, and falling on their knees cried to her:

"Please, madame, give us some of this wheat; we are starving."

"Yes, lady, and there are many poor in Stavoren, in spite of all its gold," said the captain. "Why not divide this wheat among the needy, if you are greatly disappointed? You will win praise for yourself. In the name of God, forgive my boldness, and do as I ask. Then, on the next voyage, I shall sail as far as China and will get you anything you ask!"

But the angry woman would listen to no one. She stayed on the ship, urging on the sailors, with their shovels, until every kernel was cast over-

---

1 "A fine bargain."

board.

"Never again will I try to please you," said her husband. "The hungry will curse you, and you may yet suffer for food, because of this wilful waste, which will make woeful want. Even you will suffer."

She listened at first in silence, and then put her fingers in her ears to hear no more. Proud of her riches, with her voice in a high key, she shouted, "I ever want? What folly to say so! I am too rich." Then, to show her contempt for such words, she slipped off a ring from her finger and threw it into the waters of the harbor. Her husband almost died of grief and shame when he saw that it was her wedding ring, which she had cast overboard.

"Hear you all! When that ring comes back to me, I shall be hungry and not before," said she, loud enough to be heard on ship, wharf, and street. Gathering up her skirts, she stepped upon the gangway, tripping to the shore, and past the poor people, who looked at her in mingled hate and fear. Then haughtily, she strode to her costly mansion.

Now to celebrate the expected new triumph and to show off her wealth and luxury, with the numerous curiosities brought her from many lands, the proud lady had already invited a score of guests. When they were all seated, the first course of soup was served in silver dishes, which everyone admired. As the fish was about to be brought in, to be eaten off golden plates, the butler begged the lady's permission to bring in first, from the chief cook, something rare and wonderful, that he had found in the mouth of the fish, which was waiting, already garnished, on the big dish. Not dreaming what it might be, the hostess clapped her hands in glee, saying to those at the table:

"Perhaps now, at last, I shall get what I have long waited for—the best thing in the world."

"We shall all hope so," the guests responded in chorus.

But when the chief cook came into the banquet hall, and, bowing low, held before his mistress a golden salver, with a finger ring on it, the proud lady turned pale.

It was the very ring which, in her anger, she had tossed overboard the day before. To add to her shame, she saw from the look of horror on their faces, that the guests had recognized the fact that it was her wedding token.

This was only the beginning of troubles. That night, her husband died of grief and vexation. The next day, the warehouses, stored with valuable merchandise of all sorts, were burned to the ground.

Before her husband had been decently buried, a great tempest blew down from the north, and news came that four of his ships had been wrecked. Their sailors hardly escaped with their lives, and both they and their families in Stavoren were now clamoring for bread.

Even when she put on her weeds of grief, these did not protect the widow from her late husband's creditors. She had to sell her house and all that was in it, to satisfy them and pay her debts. She had even to pawn her ring to the Lombards, the goldsmiths of the town, to buy money for bread.

Now that she was poor, none of the former rich folks, who had come to her grand dinners, would look at her. She had even to beg her bread on the streets; for who wanted to help the woman who wasted wheat? She was glad to go to the cow stalls, and eat what the cattle left. Before the year ended, she was found dead in a stable, in rags and starvation. Thus her miserable life ended. Without a funeral, but borne on a bier, by two men, she was buried at the expense of the city, in the potter's field.

But even this was not the end of the fruits of her wickedness, for the evil she did lived after her. It was found that, from some mysterious cause, a sand bar was forming in the river. This prevented the ships from coming up to the docks. With its trade stopped, the city grew poorer every day. What was the matter?

By and by, at low tide, some fishermen saw a green field under the surface of the harbor. It was not a garden of seaweed, for instead of leaves whirling with the tide, there were stalks that stood up high. The wheat had sprouted and taken root. In another month the tops of these stalks were visible above the water. But in such soil as sand, the wheat had reverted to its wild state. It was good for nothing, but only did harm.

For, while producing no grain for food, it held together the sand, which rolled down the river and had come all the way from the Alps to the ocean. Of old, this went out to sea and kept the harbor scoured clean, so that the ships came clear up to the wharves. Then, on many a morning, a wealthy merchant, whose house was close to the docks, looked out of his window to find the prows of his richly laden ships poked almost into his bedroom, and he liked it. Venturesome boys even climbed from their cots down the bowsprits, on to the deck of their fathers' vessels. Of such sons the fathers were proud, knowing that they would make brave sailors and navigate spice ships from the Indies. It was because of her brave mariners that Stavoren had gained her glory and greatness, being famed in all the land.

But now, within so short a time, the city's renown and wealth had faded like a dream. By degrees, the population diminished, commerce became a memory, and ships a curiosity. The people that were left had to eat rye and barley bread instead of wheat. Floods ruined the farmers and washed away large parts of the town, so that dykes had to be built to save what was left.

More terrible than all, the ocean waves rolled in and wiped out cities, towns, and farms, sinking churches, convents, monasteries, warehouses, wharves, and docks, in one common ruin, hidden far down below.

To this day the worthless wheat patch that spoiled Stavoren is called "Vrouwen Zand," or the Lady's Sand. Instead of being the staff of life, as Nature intended, the wheat, because of a power of evil greater than that of a thousand wicked fairies, became the menace of death to ruin a rich city.

No wonder the Dutch have a proverb, which might be thus translated:

> *Peevishness perverts wheat into weeds*
> *But a sweet temper turns a field into gold.*

The Three Presents
(*Germany*)

Once there was a poor weaver, and there are many of them even now. But this one was born under a lucky star, for one day three rich students came by his house, saw the great poverty he lived in, and gave him a hundred dollars to help him in his business.

The poor man looked for a long time at the coins before he touched them. He could not make up his mind what to do with them, so he hid the money in a bundle of rags, where nobody would look for it. His wife was not at home at the time.

Some time later a rag-dealer came to his house while the weaver was away, and bought from his wife the bundle of rags that the weaver had hid the money in. The weaver lamented a lot when he came home and his wife showed him the good bargain she thought she had made of the rags.

A year later the three students came again. They hoped to find the weaver well off, but he was poorer than ever and told them how he had lost the money. A second time they gave him a hundred dollars, telling him to be more careful.

This time he put the money into the ash-pit without letting his wife into the secret. But while he was away one day, his wife sold the ashes to a man who came round for them, and in return got two pieces of soap. She flattered herself she had this time acted wisely, for her husband who had cautioned her never to sell any more linen to pedlars, had said nothing about anything else.

But when the husband came home and heard of the bargain, he flew into a violent rage.

When a year had passed the students came again. When they found the weaver still in rags, they said to him while they threw a piece of lead at his feet, "What use is nutmeg to a cow! We will never come back here again!"

They went away in a rage. The weaver picked up the lead they had left and laid it on the window-sill. Soon afterwards his neighbour, a fisherman, came in and asked if he had by him a piece of lead or something else that was as heavy, so that he could sink his nets with it.

The weaver gave him the piece of lead from the windowsill. The fisherman thanked him and went away, promising to bring him the first fish he could catch in exchange for the lead.

Soon afterwards the fisherman brought in a fine fish and forced the weaver to accept it. It weighed four or five pounds. But when the weaver cut up the fish, he found a great stone in it. He placed the stone on the spot where the lead had been. Then, when it grew dark, he was surprised to see that the stone glittered and shone like a lamp."

This is a valuable stone," said he to his wife. "See to it that you do not throw it away as you did my two hundred dollars."

The next evening a nobleman rode past the cottage and saw the glittering stone on the window-sill. He went into the house and offered ten dollars for it.

"The stone is not for sale," said the weaver.

"Not for twenty dollars even?" asked the nobleman.

"Even so," said the weaver.

But the nobleman kept on bidding for it till he had offered a thousand dollars, for the stone was a costly diamond and really worth two times as much.

The weaver accepted the offer and thereby became as rich as any in the village. But his wife would have her last word and said, "All this wealth comes from my giving away the two hundred dollars, so you should thank me a lot, after all!"

PROTO-CELTIC

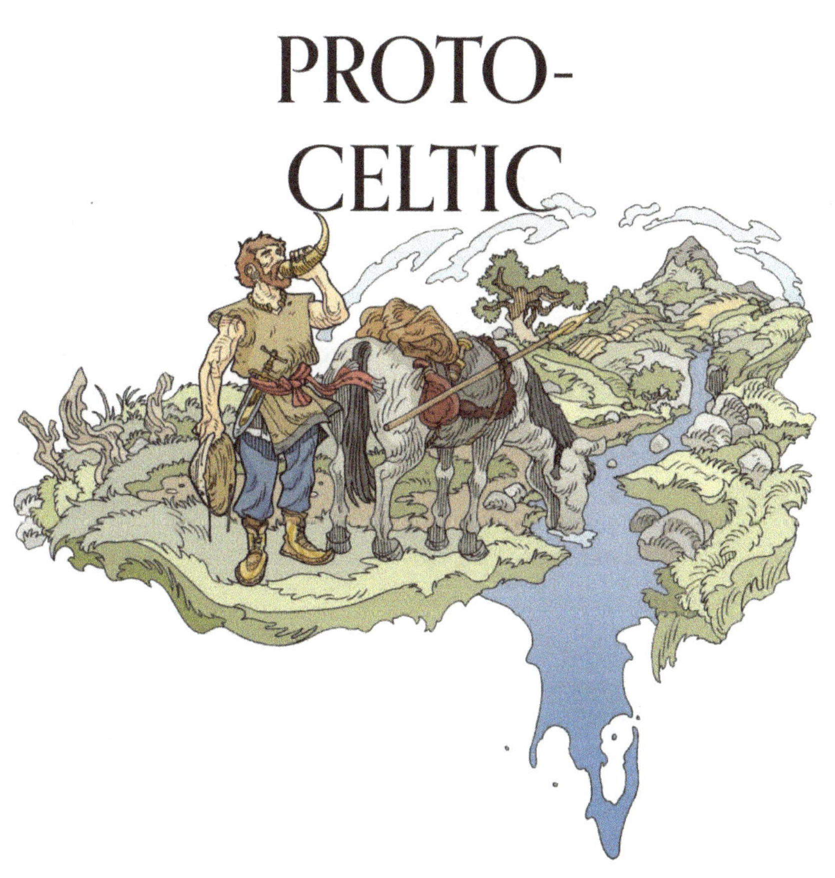

501: The Three Spinners

The Three Spinners
(*Germany*)

There was once a girl who was idle and would not spin, and let her mother say what she would, she could not bring her to it. At last the mother was once so overcome with anger and impatience, that she beat her, on which the girl began to weep loudly. Now at this very moment the Queen drove by, and when she heard the weeping she stopped her carriage, went into the house and asked the mother why she was beating her daughter so that the cries could be heard out on the road? Then the woman was ashamed to reveal the laziness of her daughter and said, "I cannot get her to leave off spinning. She insists on spinning forever and ever, and I am poor, and cannot procure the flax." Then answered the Queen, "There is nothing that I like better to hear than spinning, and I am never happier than when the wheels are humming. Let me have your daughter with me in the palace. I have flax enough, and there she shall spin as much as she likes." The mother was heartily satisfied with this, and the Queen took the girl with her. When they had arrived at the palace, she led her up into three rooms which were filled from the bottom to the top with the finest flax. "Now spin me this flax," said she, "and when thou hast done it, thou shalt have my eldest son for a husband, even if thou art poor. I care not for that, thy indefatigable industry is dowry enough." The girl was secretly terrified, for she could not have spun the flax, no, not if she had lived till she was three hundred years old, and had sat at it every day from morning till night. When therefore she was alone, she began to weep, and sat thus for three days without moving a finger. On the third day came the Queen, and when she saw that nothing had been spun yet, she was surprised; but the girl excused herself by saying that she had not been able to begin because of her great distress at leaving her mother's house. The queen was satisfied with this, but said when she was going away, "To-morrow thou must begin to work."

When the girl was alone again, she did not know what to do, and in her distress went to the window. Then she saw three women coming towards her, the first of whom had a broad flat foot, the second had such a great underlip that it hung down over her chin, and the third had a broad thumb. They remained standing before the window, looked up, and asked the girl what was amiss with her? She complained of her trouble, and then they offered her their help and said, "If thou wilt invite us to the wedding, not be ashamed of us, and wilt call us thine aunts, and likewise wilt place us at thy table, we will spin up the flax for thee, and that in a very short time." "With all my heart," she replied, "do but come in and begin the work at once." Then she let in the three strange women, and cleared a place in the first room, where they seated themselves and began their spinning. The one drew the thread and trod the wheel, the other wetted the thread, the third twisted it, and struck the table with her finger, and as often as she struck it, a skein of thread fell to the ground that was spun in the finest manner possible. The girl concealed the three spinners from the Queen, and showed her whenever she came the great quantity of spun thread, until the latter could not praise her enough. When the first room was empty she went to the second, and at last to the third, and that too was quickly cleared. Then the three women took leave and said to the girl, "Do not forget what thou hast promised us—it will make thy fortune."

When the maiden showed the Queen the empty rooms, and the great heap of yarn, she gave orders for the wedding, and the bridegroom rejoiced that he was to have such a clever and industrious wife, and praised her mightily. "I have three aunts," said the girl, "and as they have been very kind to me, I should not like to forget them in my good fortune; allow me to invite them to the wedding, and let them sit with us at table." The Queen and the bridegroom said, "Why should we not allow that?" Therefore when the feast began, the three women entered in strange apparel, and the bride said, "Welcome, dear aunts." "Ah," said the bridegroom, "how comest thou by these odious friends?" Thereupon he went to the one with the broad flat foot, and said, "How do you come by such a broad foot?" "By treading," she answered, "by treading." Then the bridegroom went to the second, and said, "How do you come by your falling lip?" "By licking," she answered, "by licking." Then he asked the third, "How do you come by your broad thumb?" "By twisting the thread," she answered, "by twisting the thread." On this the King's son was alarmed and said, "Neither now nor ever shall my beautiful bride touch a spinning-wheel." And thus she got rid of the hateful flax-spinning.

Habetrot and Scantlie Mab
(*England*)

A woman had one fair daughter, who loved play better than work, wandering in the meadows and lanes better than the spinning-wheel and distaff. The mother was heartily vexed at this, for in those days no lassie had any chance of a good husband unless she was an industrious spinster. So she coaxed, threatened, even beat her daughter, but all to no purpose; the girl remained what her mother called her, "an idle cuttie."

At last, one spring morning, the gudewife[1] gave her seven heads of lint, saying she would take no excuse; they must be returned in three days spun into yarn. The girl saw her mother was in earnest, so she plied her distaff as well as she could; but her hands were all untaught, and by the evening of the second day only a very small part of her task was done. She cried herself to sleep that night, and in the morning, throwing aside her work in despair, she strolled out into the fields, all sparkling with dew. At last she reached a knoll, at whose feet ran a little burn, shaded with woodbine and wild roses; and there she sat down, burying her face in her hands. When she looked up, she was surprised to see by the margin of the stream an old woman, quite unknown to her, drawing out the thread as she basked in the sun. There was nothing very remarkable in her appearance, except the length and thickness of her lips, only she was seated on a self-bored stone. The girl rose, went to the good dame, and gave her a friendly greeting, but could not help inquiring "What makes you so long lipped?"

"Spinning thread, my hinnie,"[2] said the old woman, pleased with her. "I wet my fingers with my lips, as I draw the thread from the distaff."

"Ah!" said the girl, "I should be spinning too, but it's all to no purpose. I shall ne'er do my task:" on which the old woman proposed to do it for her. Overjoyed, the maiden ran to fetch her lint, and placed it in her new friend's hand, asking where she should call for the yarn in the evening; but she received no reply; the old woman passed away from her among the trees and bushes. The girl, much bewildered, wandered about a little, sat down to rest, and finally fell asleep by the little knoll.

When she awoke she was surprised to find that it was evening. Causleen, the evening star, was beaming with silvery light, soon to be lost in the moon's splendour. While watching these changes, the maiden was startled by the sound of an uncouth voice, which seemed to issue from below the self-bored stone, close beside her. She laid her ear to the stone and heard the words: "Hurry up, Scantlie Mab, for I've promised the yarn and Habetrot always keeps her promise." Then looking down the hole saw her friend, the old dame, walking backwards and forwards in a deep cavern among a group of spinsters all seated on colludie stones,[3] and busy with distaff and spindle. An ugly company they were, with lips more or less disfigured, like old Habetrot's. Another of the sisterhood, who sat in a distant corner reeling the yarn, was marked, in addition, by grey eyes, which seemed starting from her head, and a long hooked nose.

While the girl was still watching, she heard Habetrot address this dame

1 "Goodwife", the mistress of the household.
2 Hinnie, a term of endearment.
3 A kind of white stone found in rivers.

by the name of Scantlie Mab, and say, "Bundle up the yarn, it is time the young lassie should give it to her mother." Delighted to hear this, the girl got up and returned homewards. Habetrot soon overtook her, and placed the yarn in her hands. "Oh, what can I do for ye in return?" exclaimed she, in delight. "Nothing—nothing," replied the dame; "but dinna tell your mother who spun the yarn."

Scarcely believing her eyes, the girl went home, where she found her mother had been busy making sausters,[1] and hanging them up in the chimney to dry, and then, tired out, had retired to rest. Finding herself very hungry after her long day on the knoll, the girl took down pudding after pudding, fried and ate them, and at last went to bed too. The mother was up first the next morning, and when she came into the kitchen and found her sausters all gone, and the seven hanks of yarn lying beautifully smooth and bright upon the table, she ran out of the house wildly, crying out—

> *My daughter's spun seven, seven, seven,*
> *My daughter's eaten seven, seven, seven,*
> *And all before daylight.*

A laird[2] who chanced to be riding by heard the exclamation, but could not understand it; so he rode up and asked the gudewife what was the matter, on which she broke out again—

> *My daughter's spun seven, seven, seven,*
> *My daughter's eaten seven, seven, seven*
> *Before daylight; and if ye dinna believe me, why come in and*
> *see it.*

The laird, he alighted and went into the cottage, where he saw the yarn, and admired it so much he begged to see the spinner.

The mother dragged in her girl. He vowed he was lonely without a wife, and had long been in search of one who was a good spinner. So their troth was plighted, and the wedding took place soon afterwards, though the bride was in great fear that she should not prove so clever at her spinning-wheel as he expected. But old Dame Habetrot came to her aid. "Bring your bonny bridegroom to my cell," said she to the young bride soon after her marriage; "he shall see what comes o' spinning, and never will he tie you to the spinning-wheel."

Accordingly the bride led her husband the next day to the flowery knoll, and bade him look through the self-bored stone. Great was his

---

1   A kind of sausage stuffed with haggis.
2   Landed proprietor, typically with a large estate.

surprise to behold Habetrot dancing and jumping over her rock, singing all the time this ditty to her sisterhood, while they kept time with their spindles:—

> *We who live in dreary den,*
> *Are both rank and foul to see?*
> *Hidden from the glorious sun,*
> *That teems the fair earth's canopie:*
> *Ever must our evenings lone*
> *Be spent on the colludie stone.*
> *Cheerless is the evening grey*
> *When Causleen hath died away,*
> *But ever bright and ever fair*
> *Are they who breathe this evening air,*
> *And lean upon the self-bored stone*
> *Unseen by all but me alone.*

The song ended, Scantlie Mab asked Habetrot what she meant by the last line, "Unseen by all but we alone."

"There is one," replied Habetrot, "whom I bid to come here at this hour, and he has heard my song through the self-bored stone." So saying she rose, opened another door, which was concealed by the roots of an old tree, and invited the pair to come in and see her family.

The laird was astonished at the weird-looking company, as he well might be, and inquired of one after another the cause of their strange lips. In a different tone of voice, and with a different twist of the mouth, each answered that it was occasioned by spinning. At least they tried to say so, but one grunted out "Nakasind," and another "Owkasaänd," while a third murmured "O-a-a-send." All, however, made the bridegroom understand what was the cause of their ugliness; while Habetrot slily hinted that if his wife were allowed to spin, her pretty lips would grow out of shape too, and her pretty face get an ugsome look. So before he left the cave he vowed that his little wife should never touch a spinning-wheel, and he kept his word. She used to wander in the meadows by his side, or ride behind him over the hills, but all the flax grown on his land was sent to old Habetrot to be converted into yarn.

The Three Aunts
(*Norway*)

Once on a time there was a poor man who lived in a hut far away in the wood, and got his living by shooting. He had an only daughter who was very pretty, and as she had lost her mother when she was a child, and was now half grown up, she said she would go out into the world and earn her bread.

"Well, lassie!" said the father, "true enough you have learnt nothing here but how to pluck birds and roast them, but still you may as well try to earn your bread."

So the girl went off to seek a place, and when she had gone a little while, she came to a palace. There she stayed and got a place, and the queen liked her so well that all the other maids got envious of her. So they made up their minds to tell the queen how the lassie said she was good to spin a pound of flax in four and twenty hours, for you must know the queen was a great housewife, and thought much of good work.

"Have you said this? then you shall do it", said the queen; "but you may have a little longer time if you choose."

Now, the poor lassie dared not say she had never spun in all her life, but she only begged for a room to herself. That she got, and the wheel and the flax were brought up to her. There she sat sad and weeping, and knew not how to help herself. She pulled the wheel this way and that, and twisted and turned it about, but she made a poor hand of it, for she had never even seen a spinning-wheel in her life.

But all at once, as she sat there, in came an old woman to her.

"What ails you, child?" she said.

"Ah!" said the lassie, with a deep sigh, "it's no good to tell you, for you'll never be able to help me."

"Who knows?" said the old wife. "Maybe I know how to help you after all."

Well, thought the lassie to herself, I may as well tell her, and so she told her how her fellow-servants had given out that she was good to spin a pound of flax in four and twenty hours.

"And here am I, wretch that I am, shut up to spin all that heap in a day and a night, when I have never even seen a spinning-wheel in all my born days."

"Well, never mind, child", said the old woman. "If you'll call me Aunt on the happiest day of your life, I'll spin this flax for you, and so you may just go away and lie down to sleep."

Yes, the lassie was willing enough, and off she went and lay down to sleep.

Next morning when she awoke, there lay all the flax spun on the table, and that so clean and fine, no one had ever seen such even and pretty yarn. The queen was very glad to get such nice yarn, and she set greater store by the lassie than ever. But the rest were still more envious, and agreed to tell the queen how the lassie had said she was good to weave the yarn she had spun in four and twenty hours. So the queen said again, as she had said it she must do it; but if she couldn't quite finish it in four and twenty hours, she wouldn't be too hard upon her, she might have a little more time. This time, too, the lassie dared not say No, but begged for a room to herself, and then she would try. There she sat again, sobbing and crying, and not knowing which way to turn, when another old woman came in and asked:

"What ails you, child?"

At first the lassie wouldn't say, but at last she told her the whole story of her grief.

"Well, well!" said the old wife, "never mind. If you'll call me Aunt on the happiest day of your life, I'll weave this yarn for you, and so you may just be off, and lie down to sleep."

Yes, the lassie was willing enough; so she went away and lay down to sleep. When she awoke, there lay the piece of linen on the table, woven so neat and close, no woof could be better. So the lassie took the piece and ran down to the queen, who was very glad to get such beautiful linen, and set greater store than ever by the lassie. But as for the others, they grew still more bitter against her, and thought of nothing but how to find out something to tell about her.

At last they told the queen the lassie had said she was good to make up the piece of linen into shirts in four and twenty hours. Well, all happened as before; the lassie dared not say she couldn't sew; so she was shut up again in a room by herself, and there she sat in tears and grief. But then another old wife came, who said she would sew the shirts for her if she would call her Aunt on the happiest day of her life. The lassie was only too glad to do this, and then she did as the old wife told her, and went and lay down to sleep.

Next morning when she woke she found the piece of linen made up into shirts, which lay on the table—and such beautiful work no one had ever set eyes on; and more than that, the shirts were all marked and ready for wear. So, when the queen saw the work, she was so glad at the way in which it was sewn that she clapped her hands, and said:

"Such sewing I never had, nor even saw in all my born days"; and after that she was as fond of the lassie as of her own children; and she said to her:

"Now, if you like to have the Prince for your husband, you shall have him; for you will never need to hire work-women. You can sew, and spin, and weave all yourself."

So as the lassie was pretty, and the Prince was glad to have her, the wedding soon came on. But just as the Prince was going to sit down with the bride to the bridal feast, in came an ugly old hag with a long nose—I'm sure it was three ells long.

So up got the bride and made a curtsey, and said: "Good-day, Auntie."

"*That* Auntie to my bride?" said the Prince.

"Yes, she was!"

"Well, then, she'd better sit down with us to the feast", said the Prince; but, to tell you the truth, both he and the rest thought she was a loathsome woman to have next to you.

But just then in came another ugly old hag. She had a back so humped and broad, she had hard work to get through the door. Up jumped the bride in a trice, and greeted her with "Good-day, Auntie!"

And the Prince asked again if that were his bride's aunt. They both said Yes; so the Prince said, if that were so, she too had better sit down with them to the feast.

But they had scarce taken their seats before another ugly old hag came in, with eyes as large as saucers, and so red and bleared, 'twas gruesome to look at her. But up jumped the bride again, with her "Good-day, Auntie", and her, too, the Prince asked to sit down; but I can't say he was very glad, for he thought to himself: "Heaven shield me from such Aunties as my bride has!" So when he had sat awhile, he could not keep his thoughts to himself any longer, but asked,

"But how, in all the world, can my bride, who is such a lovely lassie, have such loathsome, misshapen Aunts?"

"I'll soon tell you how it is", said the first. "I was just as good-looking when I was her age; but the reason why I've got this long nose is, because I was always kept sitting, and poking, and nodding over my spinning, and so my nose got stretched and stretched, until it got as long as you now see it."

"And I", said the second, "ever since I was young, I have sat and scuttled backwards and forwards over my loom, and that's how my back has got so broad and humped as you now see it."

"And I", said the third, "ever since I was little, I have sat, and stared, and sewn, and sewn and stared, night and day; and that's why my eyes have got so ugly and red, and now there's no help for them."

"So! so! "said the Prince, "'twas lucky I came to know this; for if folk can get so ugly and loathsome by all this, then my bride shall neither spin, nor weave, nor sew all her life long."

570: The Rabbit Herd

Osborn's Pipe
(*Norway*)

Once on a time there was a poor tenant-farmer who had to give up his farm to his landlord; but, if he had lost his farm, he had three sons left, and their names were Peter, Paul, and Osborn Boots. They stayed at home and sauntered about, and wouldn't do a stroke of work; *that* they thought was the right thing to do. They thought, too, they were too good for everything, and that nothing was good enough for them.

At last Peter had got to hear how the king would have a keeper to watch his hares; so he said to his father that he would be off thither: the place would just suit him, for he would serve no lower man than the king; that was what he said. The old father thought there might be work for which he was better fitted than that; for he that would keep the king's hares must be light and lissom, and no lazy-bones, and when the hares began to skip and frisk there would be quite another dance than loitering about from house to house. Well, it was all no good: Peter would go, and must go, so he took his scrip[1] on his back, and toddled away down the hill; and when he had gone far, and farther than far, he came to an old wife, who stood there with her nose stuck fast in a log of wood, and pulled and pulled at it; and as soon as he saw how she stood dragging and pulling to get free he burst into a loud fit of laughter.

"Don't stand there and grin," said the old wife, "but come and help an old cripple; I was to have split asunder a little firewood, and I got my nose fast down here, and so I have stood and tugged and torn and not tasted a morsel of food for hundreds of years." That was what she said.

But for all that Peter laughed more and more. He thought it all fine fun. All he said was, as she had stood so for hundreds of years she might hold out for hundreds of years still.

When he got to the king's grange, they took him for keeper at once. It was not bad serving there, and he was to have good food and good pay, and maybe the princess into the bargain; but if one of the king's hares got lost, they were to cut three red stripes out of his back and cast him into a pit of snakes.

So long as Peter was in the byre and home-field he kept all the hares in one flock: but as the day wore on, and they got up into the wood, all the hares began to frisk, and skip, and scuttle away up and down the hill-

---

1 Pouch or wallet.

ocks. Peter ran after them this way and that, and nearly burst himself with running, so long as he could make out that he had one of them left, and when the last was gone he was almost broken-winded. And after that he saw nothing more of them.

When it drew towards evening he sauntered along on his way home, and stood and called and called to them at each fence, but no hares came; and when he got home to the king's grange, there stood the king all ready with his knife, and he took and cut three red stripes out of Peter's back, and then rubbed pepper and salt into them, and cast him into a pit of snakes.

After a time, Paul was for going to the king's grange to keep the king's hares. The old gaffer said the same thing to him, and even still more; but he must and would set off; there was no help for it, and things went neither better nor worse with him than with Peter. The old wife stood there and tugged and tore at her nose to get it out of the log; he laughed, and thought it fine fun, and left her standing and hacking there. He got the place at once; no one said him nay; but the hares hopped and skipped away from him down all the hillocks, while he rushed about till he blew and panted like a collie-dog in the dog-days; and when he got home at night to the king's grange without a hare, the king stood ready with his knife in the porch, and took and cut three broad red stripes out of his back, and rubbed pepper and salt into them, and so down he went into the pit of snakes.

Now, when a little while had passed, Osborn Boots was all for setting off to keep the king's hares, and he told his mind to the gaffer. He thought it would be just the right work for him to go into the woods and fields, and along the wild strawberry brakes, and to drag a flock of hares with him, and between whiles to lie and sleep and warm himself on the sunny hillsides.

The gaffer thought there might be work which suited him better; if it didn't go worse, it was sure not to go better with him than with his two brothers. The man to keep the king's hares must not dawdle about like a lazy-bones with leaden soles to his stockings, or like a fly in a tar-pot; for when they fell to frisking and skipping on the sunny slopes, it would be quite another dance to catching fleas with gloves on. No; he that would get rid of that work with a whole back had need to be more than lithe and lissom, and he must fly about faster than a bladder or a bird's wing.

"Well, well, it was all no good, however bad it might be," said Osborn Boots. He would go to the king's grange and serve the king, for no lesser man would he serve, and he would soon keep the hares. They couldn't well be worse than the goat and calf at home. So Boots threw his scrip on his shoulder, and down the hill he toddled.

So when he had gone far, and farther than far, and had begun to get right down hungry, he too came to the old wife, who stood with her nose fast in the log, who tugged, and tore, and tried to get loose.

"Good-day, grandmother," said Boots. "Are you standing there whetting your nose, poor old cripple that you are?"

"Now, not a soul has called me 'mother' for hundreds of years," said the old wife. "Do come and help me to get free, and give me something to live on; for I haven't had meat in my mouth all that time. See if I don't do you a motherly turn afterwards."

Yes; he thought she might well ask for a bit of food and a drop of drink.

So he cleft the log for her, that she might get her nose out of the split, and sat down to eat and drink with her; and as the old wife had a good appetite, you may fancy she got the lion's share of the meal.

When they were done, she gave Boots a pipe, which was in this wise: when he blew into one end of it, anything that he wished away was scattered to the four winds, and when he blew into the other, all things gathered themselves together again; and if the pipe were lost or taken from him, he had only to wish for it, and it came back to him.

"Something like a pipe, this," said Osborn Boots.

When he got to the king's grange, they chose him for keeper on the spot. It was no bad service there, and food and wages he should have, and, if he were man enough to keep the king's hares, he might, perhaps, get the princess too; but if one of them got away, if it were only a leveret,[1] they were to cut three red stripes out of his back. And the king was so sure of this that he went off at once and ground his knife.

It would be a small thing to keep these hares, thought Osborn Boots; for when they set out they were almost as tame as a flock of sheep, and so long as he was in the lane and in the home-field, he had them all easily in a flock and following; but when they got upon the hill by the wood, and it looked towards midday, and the sun began to burn and shine on the slopes and hillsides, all the hares fell to frisking and skipping about, and away over the hills.

"Ho, ho! stop! will you all go? Go, then!" said Boots; and he blew into one end of the pipe, so that they ran off on all sides, and there was not one of them left. But as he went on, and came to an old charcoal pit, he blew into the other end of the pipe; and before he knew where he was, the hares were all there, and stood in lines and rows, so that he could take them all in at a glance, just like a troop of soldiers on parade. "Something like a pipe, this," said Osborn Boots; and with that he laid him down to sleep away under a sunny slope, and the hares frisked and frolicked about till eventide. Then he piped them all together again, and came down to the king's grange with them, like a flock of sheep.

---

1 A young hare.

The king and the queen, and the princess, too, all stood in the porch, and wondered what sort of fellow this was who so kept the hares that he brought them home again; and the king told and reckoned them on his fingers, and counted them over and over again; but there was not one of them missing—no! not so much as a leveret.

"Something like a lad, this," said the princess.

Next day he went off to the wood, and was to keep the hares again; but as he lay and rested himself on a strawberry brake, they sent the maid after him from the grange that she might find out how it was that he was man enough to keep the king's hares so well.

So he took out the pipe and showed it her, and then he blew into one end and made them fly like the wind over all the hills and dales; and then he blew into the other end, and they all came scampering back to the brake, and all stood in row and rank again.

"What a pretty pipe," said the maid. She would willingly give a hundred dollars for it, if he would sell it, she said.

"Yes! it is something like a pipe," said Osborn Boots; "and it was not to be had for money alone; but if she would give him the hundred dollars, and a kiss for each dollar, she should have it," he said.

Well! why not? of course she would; she would willingly give him two for each dollar, and thanks besides.

So she got the pipe; but when she had got as far as the king's grange, the pipe was gone, for Osborn Boots had wished for it back, and so, when it drew towards eventide, home he came with his hares just like any other flock of sheep; and for all the king's counting or telling, there was no help—not a hair of the hares was missing.

The third day that he kept the hares, they sent the princess on her way to try and get the pipe from him. She made herself as blithe as a lark, and she bade him two hundred dollars if he would sell her the pipe and tell her how she was to behave to bring it safe home with her.

"Yes! yes! it is something like a pipe," said Osborn Boots; "and it was not for sale," he said, "but all the same, he would do it for her sake, if she would give him two hundred dollars, and a kiss into the bargain for each dollar; then she might have the pipe. If she wished to keep it, she must look sharp after it. That was her look-out."

"This is a very high price for a hare-pipe," thought the princess; and she made mouths at giving him the kisses; "but, after all," she said, "it's far away in the wood, no one can see it or hear it—it can't be helped; for I must and will have the pipe."

So when Osborn Boots had got all he was to have, she got the pipe, and off she went, and held it fast with her fingers the whole way; but when she came to the grange, and was going to take it out, it slipped through her fingers and was gone!

Next day the queen would go herself and fetch the pipe from him. She made sure she would bring the pipe back with her.

Now she was more stingy about the money, and bade no more than fifty dollars; but she had to raise her price till it came to three hundred. Boots said it was something like a pipe, and it was no price at all; still for her sake it might go, if she would give him three hundred dollars, and a smacking kiss for each dollar into the bargain; then she might have it. And he got the kisses well paid, for on that part of the bargain she was not so squeamish.

So when she had got the pipe, she both bound it fast, and looked after it well; but she was not a hair better off than the others, for when she was going to pull it out at home, the pipe was gone; and at even down came Osborn Boots, driving the king's hares home for all the world like a flock of tame sheep.

"It is all stuff," said the king; "I see I must set off myself, if we are to get this wretched pipe from him; there's no other help for it, I can see." And when Osborn Boots had got well into the woods next day with the hares, the king stole after him, and found him lying on the same sunny hillside, where the women had tried their hands on him.

Well! they were good friends and very happy; and Osborn Boots showed him the pipe, and blew first on one end and then on the other, and the king thought it a pretty pipe, and wanted at last to buy it, even though he gave a thousand dollars for it.

"Yes! it is something like a pipe," said Boots, "and it's not to be had for money; but do you see that white horse yonder down there?" and he pointed away into the wood.

"See it! of course I see it; it's my own horse Whitey," said the king. No one had need to tell him that.

"Well! if you will give me a thousand dollars, and then go and kiss yon white horse down in the marsh there, behind the big fir-tree, you shall have my pipe."

"Isn't it to be had for any other price?" asked the king.

"No, it is not," said Osborn.

"Well! but I may put my silken pocket-handkerchief between us?" said the king.

"Very good; he might have leave to do that." And so he got the pipe, and put it into his purse. And the purse he put into his pocket, and buttoned it up tight; and so off he strode to his home. But when he reached the grange, and was going to pull out his pipe, he fared no better than the women folk; he hadn't the pipe any more than they, and there came Osborn Boots driving home the flock of hares, and not a hair was missing.

The king was both spiteful and wroth, to think that he had fooled them all round, and cheated him out of the pipe as well; and now he said Boots must lose his life, there was no question of it, and the queen said the same: it was best to put such a rogue out of the way red-handed.

Osborn thought it neither fair nor right, for he had done nothing but what they told him to do; and so he had guarded his back and life as best he might.

So the king said there was no help for it; but if he could lie the great brewing-vat so full of lies that it ran over, then he might keep his life.

That was neither a long nor perilous piece of work: he was quite game to do that, said Osborn Boots. So he began to tell how it had all happened from the very first. He told about the old wife and her nose in the log, and then he went on to say, "Well, but I must lie faster if the vat is to be full." So he went on to tell of the pipe and how he got it; and of the maid, how she came to him and wanted to buy it for a hundred dollars, and of all the kisses she had to give besides, away there in the wood. Then he told of the princess how she came and kissed him so sweetly for the pipe when no one could see or hear it all away there in the wood. Then he stopped and said, "I must lie faster if the vat is ever to be full." So he told of the queen, how close she was about the money and how overflowing she was with her smacks. "You know I must lie hard to get the vat full," said Osborn.

"For my part," said the queen, "I think it's pretty full already."

"No! no! it isn't," said the king.

So he fell to telling how the king came to him, and about the white horse down on the marsh, and how, if the king was to have the pipe, he must—"Yes, your majesty, if the vat is ever to be full I must go on and lie hard," said Osborn Boots.

"Hold! hold, lad! It's full to the brim," roared out the king; "don't you see how it is foaming over?"

So both the king and the queen thought it best he should have the princess to wife and half the kingdom. There was no help for it.

"That was something like a pipe," said Osborn Boots.

The Hare-Keeper
(*Germany*)

A certain rich king had a very pretty daughter. When she got old enough to be married, she was promised to be the bride of him who could first catch a golden apple that the princess threw up in the air, and then perform three tasks that the king set.

Many a youth had caught the apple but failed to perform the tasks. At last a shepherd-boy came to try. His first task was this:

The king had a hundred hares in his stables. Whoever led them out to pasture in the morning and brought them all safely home at night had performed the first task.

The shepherd took a day to consider whether he could do what was required. During that time he walked about the hills around. There he met and old man who asked him why he looked so thoughtful.

"Mmph, nobody can help me," the shepherd groaned.

"Tell me what is on your mind, and then maybe I can help you," said the man.

The shepherd told him all. The man gave him a small reed pipe, saying, "Keep this with care. It will be of great use to you." And without waiting to be thanked he disappeared.

The shepherd then went back to the king and said, "I will tend your hares!"

The hares were led out of the stable, but before the last came out, the first ones had disappeared over the mountains. The shepherd went into the fields and sat down on a little hillock, wondering what to do. Then he remembered his pipe and took it from his pocket. When he played a few notes on it, all the hares came to him and began to feed around him.

But the princess and her father did not like the idea that a low-born shepherd boy should win her, so they had planned to hinder him from bringing all the hares home. The princess went to him in common clothing with her face dyed so that he might not recognise her, but he did anyway. When she saw that all the hares were grazing around him, she asked if she could buy one from him.

"No," answered the shepherd, "but you can earn one."

"How?" she asked.

"If you give me a kiss and keep company with me for half an hour," he answered.

At first she would not, but when she found that she could not get a hare in any other way, she let him have his way.

After a while he caught a hare for her and placed it in her basket. But about fifteen minutes after she went away with it the shepherd blew on his pipe. The hare jumped out of her basket at once and ran back to him.

Soon the old king came. He was riding on a donkey with a basked hanging on each side of his saddle, and had dressed up to disguise himself. The boy saw who he was anyway.

"Do you have any hares to sell?" asked the king.

"No, but you may earn one, if you please," answered the shepherd.

"How?" asked the king.

"If you kiss your donkey's backside," the shepherd answered, "you will get one."

Unwilling to do such a thing, the king offered the shepherd a heavy purse of gold for the hare instead. But the shepherd said there was no other way to get a hare from him, so at last the king the king gave his donkey a big kiss on its backside.

At once the shepherd caught a hare and placed it in one of the king's baskets. The king then rode away; but he had not gone very far when the shepherd took out his pipe and whistled a few notes. The hare made way at once and came back to the others at the sound of the music.

Before long the king reached home. "He is a cunning fellow that shepherd," he said; "I could not get any hare from him!" He did not say anything about what he had done to get one.

"Yes," said the princess, "I too found him cunning!" She said nothing of what she had done to get a hare either.

And as soon as evening came, the shepherd returned and counted the hares into the stables while the king stood beside him and counted. Yes, there were exactly one hundred hares.

"Your first task is done," said the king. "Now comes the second one. In my granary lie a hundred measures of turnip-seed and a hundred measures of lentil-seed. These are all mixed together. If you separate the one from the other and make two heaps of them during the night and without a candle, you will have accomplished the second task."

The shepherd was locked up in the granary where the seed was. When everything was quiet in the castle, he blew on his pipe. At once several thousand ants came crawling and carried the seeds here and there till the turnip and lentil-seeds were divided into two heaps. The ants left as soon as they had finished the task.

Early in the morning the king came down and found the task was done. He wondered how the shepherd could have done it, but set him the third task without making any remarks about the heaps.

The third task was in one night to eat up all the bread that was placed in a certain room. When the shepherd had done it, he would get the princess, promised the king.

As soon as night came the shepherd was placed in the bread-chamber. It was packed full of bread. First he ate out a space to stand upright in. Then, when everyone else had gone to bed, he played on his pipe. At once came a vast flock of mice and started to eat bread. At daybreak they had eaten every loaf and crumb that the shepherd had left and had disappeared from the room.

When the shepherd saw this, he began to kick merrily at the door, crying out, "Open the door, hurry, open the door! I am hungry!"

Now the third task was carried out. But the king still wanted to put aside the agreement, and said to the peasant, "You will have my daughter, if you tell us a sack full of silly stories first."

The shepherd began and went on half the day with a long string of silly stories; but the sack was still declared to be only half full. At length he said, "I have been lying in the grass at the side of my princess."

At these words the princess blushed and got crimson all over her face and neck, so much so that the king suspected that it was true and wondered when and where it had happened. "But the sack is not full yet," cried the king.

So the shepherd went on, "The king has also kissed his…"

"The sack is full, it is full!" screamed the king; for he would not let his courtiers and other people know what this was about.

So the shepherd married the princess after all. The wedding festivities lasted for fourteen days and were so splendid that I wish we too could have been there.

Jesper Who Herded the Hares
(*Sweden*)

There was once a king who ruled over a kingdom somewhere between sunrise and sunset. It was as small as kingdoms usually were in old times, and when the king went up to the roof of his palace and took a look round he could see to the ends of it in every direction. But as it was all his own, he was very proud of it, and often wondered how it would get along without him. He had only one child, and that was a daughter, so he foresaw that she must be provided with a husband who would be fit to be king after him. Where to find one rich enough and clever enough to be a suitable match for the princess was what troubled him, and often kept him awake at night.

At last he devised a plan. He made a proclamation over all his kingdom (and asked his nearest neighbours to publish it in theirs as well) that whoever could bring him a dozen of the finest pearls the king had ever seen, and could perform certain tasks that would be set him, should have his daughter in marriage and in due time succeed to the throne. The pearls, he thought, could only be brought by a very wealthy man, and the tasks would require unusual talents to accomplish them.

There were plenty who tried to fulfil the terms which the king proposed. Rich merchants and foreign princes presented themselves one after the other, so that some days the number of them was quite annoying; but, though they could all produce magnificent pearls, not one of them could perform even the simplest of the tasks set them. Some turned up, too, who were mere adventurers, and tried to deceive the old king with imitation pearls; but he was not to be taken in so easily, and they were soon sent about their business. At the end of several weeks the stream of suitors began to fall off, and still there was no prospect of a suitable son-in-law.

Now it so happened that in a little corner of the king's dominions, beside the sea, there lived a poor fisher who had three sons, and their names were Peter, Paul, and Jesper. Peter and Paul were grown men, while Jesper was just coming to manhood.

The two elder brothers were much bigger and stronger than the youngest, but Jesper was far the cleverest of the three, though neither Peter nor Paul would admit this. It was a fact, however, as we shall see in the course of our story.

One day the fisherman went out fishing, and among his catch for the day he brought home three dozen oysters. When these were opened, every shell was found to contain a large and beautiful pearl. Hereupon the three brothers, at one and the same moment, fell upon the idea of offering themselves as suitors for the princess. After some discussion, it was agreed that the pearls should be divided by lot, and that each should have his chance in the order of his age: of course, if the oldest was successful the other two would be saved the trouble of trying.

Next morning Peter put his pearls in a little basket, and set off for the king's palace. He had not gone far on his way when he came upon the King of the Ants and the King of the Beetles, who, with their armies behind them, were facing each other and preparing for battle.

'Come and help me,' said the King of the Ants; 'the beetles are too big for us. I may help you some day in return.'

'I have no time to waste on other people's affairs,' said Peter; 'just fight away as best you can;' and with that he walked off and left them.

A little further on the way he met an old woman.

'Good morning, young man,' said she; 'you are early astir. What have you got in your basket?'

'Cinders,' said Peter promptly, and walked on, adding to himself, 'Take that for being so inquisitive.'

'Very well, cinders be it,' the old woman called after him, but he pretended not to hear her.

Very soon he reached the palace, and was at once brought before the king. When he took the cover off the basket, the king and all his courtiers said with one voice that these were the finest pearls they had ever seen, and they could not take their eyes off them. But then a strange thing happened: the pearls began to lose their whiteness and grew quite dim in colour; then they grew blacker and blacker till at last they were just like so many cinders. Peter was so amazed that he could say nothing for himself, but the king said quite enough for both, and Peter was glad to get away home again as fast as his legs would carry him. To his father and brothers, however, he gave no account of his attempt, except that it had been a failure.

Next day Paul set out to try his luck. He soon came upon the King of

the Ants and the King of the Beetles, who with their armies had encamp-
ed on the field of battle all night, and were ready to begin the fight again.

'Come and help me,' said the King of the Ants; 'we got the worst of it
yesterday. I may help you some day in return.'

'I don't care though you get the worst of it to-day too,' said Paul. 'I
have more important business on hand than mixing myself up in your
quarrels.'

So he walked on, and presently the same old woman met him. 'Good
morning,' said she; 'what have YOU got in your basket?'

'Cinders,' said Paul, who was quite as insolent as his brother, and quite
as anxious to teach other people good manners.

'Very well, cinders be it,' the old woman shouted after him, but Paul
neither looked back nor answered her. He thought more of what she said,
however, after his pearls also turned to cinders before the eyes of king
and court: then he lost no time in getting home again, and was very sulky
when asked how he had succeeded.

The third day came, and with it came Jesper's turn to try his fortune.
He got up and had his breakfast, while Peter and Paul lay in bed and
made rude remarks, telling him that he would come back quicker than
he went, for if they had failed it could not be supposed that he would
succeed. Jesper made no reply, but put his pearls in the little basket and
walked off.

The King of the Ants and the King of the Beetles were again marshal-
ling their hosts, but the ants were greatly reduced in numbers, and had
little hope of holding out that day.

'Come and help us,' said their king to Jesper, 'or we shall be completely
defeated. I may help you some day in return.'

Now Jesper had always heard the ants spoken of as clever and industrious little creatures, while he never heard anyone say a good word for
the beetles, so he agreed to give the wished-for help. At the first charge
he made, the ranks of the beetles broke and fled in dismay, and those escaped best that were nearest a hole, and could get into it before Jesper's
boots came down upon them. In a few minutes the ants had the field all
to themselves; and their king made quite an eloquent speech to Jesper,
thanking him for the service he had done them, and promising to assist
him in any difficulty.

'Just call on me when you want me,' he said, 'where-ever you are. I'm
never far away from anywhere, and if I can possibly help you, I shall not
fail to do it.'

Jesper was inclined to laugh at this, but he kept a grave face, said he
would remember the offer, and walked on. At a turn of the road he suddenly came upon the old woman. 'Good morning,' said she; 'what have
YOU got in your basket?'

'Pearls,' said Jesper; 'I'm going to the palace to win the princess with them.' And in case she might not believe him, he lifted the cover and let her see them.

'Beautiful,' said the old woman; 'very beautiful indeed; but they will go a very little way towards winning the princess, unless you can also perform the tasks that are set you. However,' she said, 'I see you have brought something with you to eat. Won't you give that to me: you are sure to get a good dinner at the palace.'

'Yes, of course,' said Jesper, 'I hadn't thought of that'; and he handed over the whole of his lunch to the old woman.

He had already taken a few steps on the way again, when the old woman called him back.

'Here,' she said; 'take this whistle in return for your lunch. It isn't much to look at, but if you blow it, anything that you have lost or that has been taken from you will find its way back to you in a moment.'

Jesper thanked her for the whistle, though he did not see of what use it was to be to him just then, and held on his way to the palace.

When Jesper presented his pearls to the king there were exclamations of wonder and delight from everyone who saw them. It was not pleasant, however, to discover that Jesper was a mere fisher-lad; that wasn't the kind of son-in-law that the king had expected, and he said so to the queen.

'Never mind,' said she, 'you can easily set him such tasks as he will never be able to perform: we shall soon get rid of him.'

'Yes, of course,' said the king; 'really I forget things nowadays, with all the bustle we have had of late.'

That day Jesper dined with the king and queen and their nobles, and at night was put into a bedroom grander than anything of the kind he had ever seen. It was all so new to him that he could not sleep a wink, especially as he was always wondering what kind of tasks would be set him to do, and whether he would be able to perform them. In spite of the softness of the bed, he was very glad when morning came at last.

After breakfast was over, the king said to Jesper, 'Just come with me, and I'll show you what you must do first.' He led him out to the barn, and there in the middle of the floor was a large pile of grain. 'Here,' said the king, 'you have a mixed heap of wheat, barley, oats, and rye, a sackful of each. By an hour before sunset you must have these sorted out into four heaps, and if a single grain is found to be in a wrong heap you have no further chance of marrying my daughter. I shall lock the door, so that no one can get in to assist you, and I shall return at the appointed time to see how you have succeeded.'

The king walked off, and Jesper looked in despair at the task before him. Then he sat down and tried what he could do at it, but it was soon very clear that single-handed he could never hope to accomplish it in the time. Assistance was out of the question—unless, he suddenly thought—unless the King of the Ants could help. On him he began to call, and before many minutes had passed that royal personage made his appearance. Jesper explained the trouble he was in.

'Is that all?' said the ant; 'we shall soon put that to rights.' He gave the royal signal, and in a minute or two a stream of ants came pouring into the barn, who under the king's orders set to work to separate the grain into the proper heaps.

Jesper watched them for a while, but through the continual movement of the little creatures, and his not having slept during the previous night, he soon fell sound asleep. When he woke again, the king had just come into the barn, and was amazed to find that not only was the task accomplished, but that Jesper had found time to take a nap as well.

'Wonderful,' said he; 'I couldn't have believed it possible. However, the hardest is yet to come, as you will see to-morrow.'

Jesper thought so too when the next day's task was set before him. The king's gamekeepers had caught a hundred live hares, which were to be let loose in a large meadow, and there Jesper must herd them all day, and bring them safely home in the evening: if even one were missing, he must give up all thought of marrying the princess. Before he had quite grasped the fact that this was an impossible task, the keepers had opened the sacks in which the hares were brought to the field, and, with a whisk of the short tail and a flap of the long ears, each one of the hundred flew in a different direction.

'Now,' said the king, 'as he walked away, 'let's see what your cleverness can do here.'

Jesper stared round him in bewilderment, and having nothing better to do with his hands, thrust them into his pockets, as he was in the habit of doing. Here he found something which turned out to be the whistle given to him by the old woman. He remembered what she had said about the virtues of the whistle, but was rather doubtful whether its powers would extend to a hundred hares, each of which had gone in a different direction and might be several miles distant by this time. However, he blew the whistle, and in a few minutes the hares came bounding through the hedge on all the four sides of the field, and before long were all sitting round him in a circle. After that, Jesper allowed them to run about as they pleased, so long as they stayed in the field.

The king had told one of the keepers to hang about for a little and see what became of Jesper, not doubting, however, that as soon as he saw the coast clear he would use his legs to the best advantage, and never show face at the palace again. It was therefore with great surprise and annoyance that he now learned of the mysterious return of the hares and the likelihood of Jesper carrying out his task with success.

'One of them must be got out of his hands by hook or crook,' said he. 'I'll go and see the queen about it; she's good at devising plans.'

A little later, a girl in a shabby dress came into the field and walked up to Jesper.

'Do give me one of those hares,' she said; 'we have just got visitors who are going to stay to dinner, and there's nothing we can give them to eat.'

'I can't,' said Jesper. 'For one thing, they're not mine; for another, a great deal depends on my having them all here in the evening.'

But the girl (and she was a very pretty girl, though so shabbily dressed) begged so hard for one of them that at last he said:

'Very well; give me a kiss and you shall have one of them.'

He could see that she didn't quite care for this, but she consented to the bargain, and gave him the kiss, and went away with a hare in her apron. Scarcely had she got outside the field, however, when Jesper blew his whistle, and immediately the hare wriggled out of its prison like an eel, and went back to its master at the top of its speed.

Not long after this the hare-herd had another visit. This time it was a stout old woman in the dress of a peasant, who also was after a hare to provide a dinner for unexpected visitors. Jesper again refused, but the old lady was so pressing, and would take no refusal, that at last he said:

'Very well, you shall have a hare, and pay nothing for it either, if you will only walk round me on tiptoe, look up to the sky, and cackle like a hen.'

'Fie,' said she; 'what a ridiculous thing to ask anyone to do; just think what the neighbours would say if they saw me. They would think I had taken leave of my senses.'

'Just as you like,' said Jesper; 'you know best whether you want the hare or not.'

There was no help for it, and a pretty figure the old lady made in carrying out her task; the cackling wasn't very well done, but Jesper said it would do, and gave her the hare. As soon as she had left the field, the whistle was sounded again, and back came long-legs-and-ears at a marvellous speed.

The next to appear on the same errand was a fat old fellow in the dress of a groom: it was the royal livery he wore, and he plainly thought a good deal of himself.

'Young man,' said he, 'I want one of those hares; name your price, but I MUST have one of them.'

'All right,' said Jesper; 'you can have one at an easy rate. Just stand on your head, whack your heels together, and cry "Hurrah," and the hare is yours.'

'Eh, what!' said the old fellow; 'ME stand on my head, what an idea!'

'Oh, very well,' said Jesper, 'you needn't unless you like, you know; but then you won't get the hare.'

It went very much against the grain, one could see, but after some efforts the old fellow had his head on the grass and his heels in the air; the whacking and the 'Hurrah' were rather feeble, but Jesper was not very exacting, and the hare was handed over. Of course, it wasn't long in coming back again, like the others.

Evening came, and home came Jesper with the hundred hares behind him. Great was the wonder over all the palace, and the king and queen seemed very much put out, but it was noticed that the princess actually smiled to Jesper.

'Well, well,' said the king; 'you have done that very well indeed. If you are as successful with a little task which I shall give you to-morrow we shall consider the matter settled, and you shall marry the princess.'

Next day it was announced that the task would be performed in the great hall of the palace, and everyone was invited to come and witness it. The king and queen sat on their thrones, with the princess beside them, and the lords and ladies were all round the hall. At a sign from the king, two servants carried in a large empty tub, which they set down in the open space before the throne, and Jesper was told to stand beside it.

'Now,' said the king, 'you must tell us as many undoubted truths as will fill that tub, or you can't have the princess.'

'But how are we to know when the tub is full?' said Jesper.

'Don't you trouble about that,' said the king; 'that's my part of the business.'

This seemed to everybody present rather unfair, but no one liked to be the first to say so, and Jesper had to put the best face he could on the matter, and begin his story.

'Yesterday,' he said, 'when I was herding the hares, there came to me a girl, in a shabby dress, and begged me to give her one of them. She got the hare, but she had to give me a kiss for it; AND THAT GIRL WAS THE PRINCESS. Isn't that true?' said he, looking at her.

The princess blushed and looked very uncomfortable, but had to admit that it was true.

'That hasn't filled much of the tub,' said the king. 'Go on again.'

'After that,' said Jesper, 'a stout old woman, in a peasant's dress, came and begged for a hare. Before she got it, she had to walk round me on tip-toe, turn up her eyes, and cackle like a hen; AND THAT OLD WOMAN WAS THE QUEEN. Isn't that true, now?'

The queen turned very red and hot, but couldn't deny it.

'H-m,' said the king; 'that is something, but the tub isn't full yet.' To the queen he whispered, 'I didn't think you would be such a fool.'

'What did YOU do?' she whispered in return.

'Do you suppose I would do anything for HIM?' said the king, and then hurriedly ordered Jesper to go on.

'In the next place,' said Jesper, 'there came a fat old fellow on the same errand. He was very proud and dignified, but in order to get the hare he actually stood on his head, whacked his heels together, and cried "Hurrah"; and that old fellow was the——'

'Stop, stop,' shouted the king; 'you needn't say another word; the tub is full.' Then all the court applauded, and the king and queen accepted Jesper as their son-in-law, and the princess was very well pleased, for by this time she had quite fallen in love with him, because he was so handsome and so clever. When the old king got time to think over it, he was quite convinced that his kingdom would be safe in Jesper's hands if he looked after the people as well as he herded the hares.

PROTO-GERMANIC

314A: The Shepherd and the Giants

The Widow's Son
(*Norway*)

Once on a time there was a poor, poor widow, who had an only son. She dragged on with the boy till he had been confirmed, and then she said she couldn't feed him any longer, he must just go out and earn his own bread. So the lad wandered out into the world, and when he had walked a day or so, a strange man met him.

"Whither away?" asked the man.

"Oh, I'm going out into the world to try and get a place", said the lad.

"Will you come and serve me?" said the man.

"Oh yes; just as soon you as anyone else", said the lad.

"Well, you'll have a good place with me", said the man; "for you'll only have to keep me company, and do nothing at all else beside."

So the lad stopped with him, and lived on the fat of the land, both in meat and drink, and had little or nothing to do; but he never saw a living soul in that man's house.

So one day the man said:

"Now, I'm going off for eight days, and that time you'll have to spend here all alone; but you must not go into any one of these four rooms here. If you do, I'll take your life when I come back."

"No", said the lad, he'd be sure not to do that. But when the man had been gone three or four days, the lad couldn't bear it any longer, but went into the first room, and when he got inside he looked round, but he saw nothing but a shelf over the door where a bramble-bush rod lay.

Well, indeed! thought the lad; a pretty thing to forbid my seeing this.

So when the eight days were out, the man came home, and the first thing he said was:

"You haven't been into any of these rooms, of course."

"No, no; that I haven't", said the lad.

"I'll soon see that", said the man, and went at once into the room where the lad had been.

"Nay, but you have been in here", said he; "and now you shall lose your life."

Then the lad begged and prayed so hard that he got off with his life, but the man gave him a good thrashing. And when it was over, they were as good friends as ever.

Some time after the man set off again, and said he should be away fourteen days; but before he went he forbade the lad to go into any of the rooms he had not been in before; as for that he had been in, he might go into that, and welcome. Well, it was the same story aver again, except that the lad stood out eight days before he went in. In this room, too, he saw nothing but a shelf over the door, and a big stone, and a pitcher of water on it. Well, after all, there's not much to be afraid of my seeing here, thought the lad.

But when the man came back, he asked if he had been into any of the rooms. No, the lad hadn't done anything of the kind.

"Well, well; I'll soon see that," said the man; and when he saw that the lad had been in them after all, he said, "Ah! now I'll spare you no longer; now you must lose your life."

But the lad begged and prayed for himself again, and so this time too he got off with stripes; though he got as many as his skin could carry. But when he got sound and well again, he led just as easy a life as ever, and he and the man were just as good friends.

So a while after the man was to take another journey, and now he said he should be away three weeks, and he forbade the lad anew to go into the third room, for if he went in there he might just make up his mind at once to lose his life. Then after fourteen days the lad couldn't bear it, but crept into the room, but he saw nothing at all in there but a trap door on the floor; and when he lifted it up and looked down, there stood a great copper cauldron which bubbled and boiled away down there; but he saw no fire under it.

"Well, I should just like to know if it's hot," thought the lad, and stuck his finger down into the broth, and when he pulled it out again, lo! it was gilded all over. So the lad scraped and scrubbed it, but the gilding wouldn't go off, so he bound a piece of rag round it; and when the man came back, and asked what was the matter with his finger, the lad said he'd given it such a bad cut. But the man tore off the rag, and then he soon saw what was the matter with the finger. First he wanted to kill the lad outright, but when he wept, and begged, he only gave him such a thrashing that he had to keep his bed three days. After that the man took down a pot from the wall, and rubbed him over with some stuff out of it, and so the lad was sound and fresh as ever.

So after a while the man started off again, and this time he was to be away a month. But before he went, he said to the lad, if he went into the fourth room he might give up all hope of saving his life.

Well, the lad stood out for two or three weeks, but then he couldn't holdout any longer; he must and would go into that room, and so in he stole. There stood a great black horse tied up in a stall by himself, with a manger of red-hot coals at his head, and a truss of hay at his tail. Then the lad thought this all wrong, so he changed them about, and put the hay at his head. Then said the Horse:

"Since you are so good at heart as to let me have some food, I'll set you free, that I will. For if the Troll comes back and finds you here, he'll kill you outright. But now you must go up to the room which lies just over this, and take a coat of mail out of those that hang there; and mind, whatever you do, don't take any of the bright ones, but the most rusty of all you see, that's the one to take; and sword and saddle you must choose for yourself just in the same way."

So the lad did all that; but it was a heavy load for him to carry them all down at once.

When he came back, the Horse told him to pull off his clothes and get into the cauldron which stood and boiled in the other room, and bathe himself there. "If I do", thought the lad, "I shall look an awful fright," but for all that, he did as he was told. So when he had taken his bath, he became so handsome and sleek, and as red and white as milk and blood, and much stronger than he had been before.

"Do you feel any change?" asked the Horse.

"Yes", said the lad.

"Try to lift me, then", said the Horse.

Oh yes! he could do that, and as for the sword, he brandished it like a feather.

"Now saddle me", said the Horse, "and put on the coat of mail, and then take the bramble-bush rod, and the stone, and the pitcher of water, and the pot of ointment, and then we'll be off as fast as we can."

So when the lad had got on the horse, off they went at such a rate, he couldn't at all tell how they went. But when he had ridden awhile, the Horse said,

"I think I hear a noise; look round! can you see anything?"

"Yes; there are ever so many coming after us, at least a score", said the lad.

"Aye, aye, that's the Troll coming", said the Horse; "now he's after us with his pack."

So they rode on a while, until those who followed were close behind them.

"Now throw your bramble-bush rod behind you, over your shoulder", said the Horse; "but mind you throw it a good way off my back."

So the lad did that, and all at once a close, thick bramble-wood grew up behind them. So the lad rode on a long, long time, while the Troll and his crew had to go home to fetch something to hew their way through the wood. But at last, the Horse said again,

"Look behind you! can you see anything now?"

"Yes, ever so many", said the lad, "as many as would fill a large church."

"Aye, aye, that's the Troll and his crew", said the Horse; "now he's got more to back him; but now throw down the stone, and mind you throw it far behind me."

And as soon as the lad did what the Horse said, up rose a great black hill of rock behind him. So the Troll had to be off home to fetch something to mine his way through the rock; and while the Troll did that, the lad rode a good bit further on. But still the Horse begged him to look behind him, and then he saw a troop like a whole army behind him, and they glistened in the sunbeams.

"Aye, aye", said the Horse, "that's the Troll, and now he's got his whole band with him, so throw the pitcher of water behind you, but mind you don't spill any of it upon me."

So the lad did that; but in spite of all the pains he took, he still spilt one drop on the horse's flank. So it became a great deep lake; and because of that one drop, the horse found himself far out in it, but still he swam safe to land. But when the Trolls came to the lake, they lay down to drink it dry; and so they swilled and swilled till they burst.

"Now we're rid of them", said the Horse.

So when they had gone a long, long while, they came to a green patch in a wood.

"Now, strip off all your arms", said the Horse, "and only put on your ragged clothes, and take the saddle off me, and let me loose, and hang all my clothing and your arms up inside that great hollow lime-tree yonder. Then make yourself a wig of fir-moss, and go up to the king's palace, which lies close here, and ask for a place. Whenever you need me, only come here and shake the bridle, and I'll come to you."

Yes! the lad did all his Horse told him, and as soon as ever he put on the wig of moss he became so ugly, and pale, and miserable to look at, no one would have known him again. Then he went up to the king's palace and begged first for leave to be in the kitchen, and bring in wood and water for the cook, but then the kitchen-maid asked him:

"Why do you wear that ugly wig? Off with it. I won't have such a fright in here."

"No, I can't do that", said the lad; "for I'm not quite right in my head."

"Do you think then I'll have you in here about the food", cried the cook. "Away with you to the coachman; you're best fit to go and clean the stable."

But when the coachman begged him to take his wig off, he got the same answer, and he wouldn't have him either. "You'd best go down to the gardener", said he; "you're best fit to go about and dig in the garden."

So he got leave to be with the gardener, but none of the other servants would sleep with him, and so he had to sleep by himself under the steps of the summerhouse. It stood upon beams, and had a high staircase. Under that he got some turf for his bed, and there he lay as well as he could.

So, when he had been some time at the palace, it happened one morning, just as the sun rose, that the lad had taken off his wig, and stood and washed himself, and then he was so handsome, it was a joy to look at him.

So the Princess saw from her window the lovely gardener's boy, and thought she had never seen anyone so handsome. Then she asked the gardener why he lay out there under the steps.

"Oh", said the gardener, "none of his fellow-servants will sleep with him; that's why."

"Let him come up to-night, and lie at the door inside my bedroom, and then they'll not refuse to sleep with him any more", said the Princess.

So the gardener told that to the lad.

"Do you think I'll do any such thing?" said the lad. "Why they'd say next there was something between me and the Princess."

"Yes", said the gardener, "you've good reason to fear any such thing, you who are so handsome."

"Well, well", said the lad, "since it's her will, I suppose I must go."

So, when he was to go up the steps in the evening, he tramped and stamped so on the way, that they had to beg him to tread softly lest the King should come to know it. So he came into the Princess' bedroom, lay down, and began to snore at once. Then the Princess said to her maid:

"Go gently, and just pull his wig off"; and she went up to him.

But just as she was going to whisk it off, he caught hold of it with both hands, and said she should never have it. After that he lay down again, and began to snore. Then the Princess gave her maid a wink, and this time she whisked off the wig; and there lay the lad so lovely, and white and red, just as the Princess had seen him in the morning sun.

After that the lad slept every night in the Princess' bedroom.

But it wasn't long before the King came to hear how the gardener's lad slept every night in the Princess' bedroom; and he got so wroth he almost took the lad's life. He didn't do that, however, but threw him into the prison tower; and as for his daughter, he shut her up in her own room, whence she never got leave to stir day or night. All that she begged, and all that she prayed, for the lad and herself, was no good. The King was only more wroth than ever.

Some time after came a war and uproar in the land, and the king had to take up arms against another king who wished to take the kingdom from him. So when the lad heard that, he begged the gaoler[1] to go to the king and ask for a coat of mail and a sword, and for leave to go to the war. All the rest laughed when the gaoler told his errand, and begged the king to let him have an old worn-out suit, that they might have the fun

---

1 Jailer.

of seeing such a wretch in battle. So he got that, and an old broken-down hack[1] besides, which went upon three legs and dragged the fourth after it.

Then they went out to meet the foe; but they hadn't got far from the palace before the lad got stuck fast in a bog with his hack. There he sat and dug his spurs in, and cried, "Gee up, gee up!" to his hack. And all the rest had their fun out of this, and laughed, and made game of the lad as they rode past him. But they were scarcely gone, before he ran to the lime-tree, threw on his coat of mail, and shook the bridle, and there came the horse in a trice, and said "Do now your best, and I'll do mine."

But when the lad came up the battle had begun, and the king was in a sad pinch; but no sooner had the lad rushed into the thick of it than the foe was beaten back, and put to flight. The king and his men wondered and wondered who it could be who had come to help them, but none of them got so near him as to be able to talk to him, and as soon as the fight was over he was gone. When they went back, there sat the lad still in the bog, and dug his spurs into his three-legged hack, and they all laughed again.

"No! only just look", they said; "there the fool sits still."

The next day when they went out to battle, they saw the lad sitting there still, so they laughed again, and made game of him; but as soon as ever they had ridden by, the lad ran again to the lime-tree, and all happened as on the first day. Everyone wondered what strange champion it could be that had helped them, but no one got so near him as to say a word to him; and no one guessed it could be the lad; that's easy to understand.

So when they went home at night, and saw the lad still sitting there on his hack, they burst out laughing at him again, and one of them shot an arrow at him and hit him in the leg. So he began to shriek and to bewail; 'twas enough to break one's heart; and so the king threw his pocket-handkerchief to him to bind his wound.

When they went out to battle the third day, the lad still sat there.

"Gee up! gee up!" he said to his hack.

"Nay, nay", said the king's men; "if he won't stick there till he's starved to death."

And then they rode on, and laughed at him till they were fit to fall from their horses. When they were gone, he ran again to the lime, and came up to the battle just in the very nick of time. This day he slew the enemy's king, and then the war was over at once.

When the battle was over, the king caught sight of his handkerchief, which the strange warrior had bound round his leg, and so it wasn't hard to find him out. So they took him with great joy between them to the pal-

---

1 A breed of horse used for riding and pulling carriages.

ace, and the Princess, who saw him from her window, got so glad, no one can believe it.

"Here comes my own true love", she said.

Then he took the pot of ointment and rubbed himself on the leg, and after that he rubbed all the wounded, and so they all got well again in a moment.

So he got the Princess to wife; but when he went down into the stable where his horse was on the day the wedding was to be, there it stood so dull and heavy, and hung its ears down, and wouldn't eat its corn. So when the young king—for he was now a king, and had got half the kingdom—spoke to him, and asked what ailed him, the Horse said:

"Now I have helped you on, and now I won't live any longer. So just take the sword, and cut my head off."

"No, I'll do nothing of the kind", said the young king; "but you shall have all you want, and rest all your life."

"Well", said the Horse, "If you don't do as I tell you, see if I don't take your life somehow."

So the king had to do what he asked; but when he swung the sword and was to cut his head off, he was so sorry he turned away his face, for he would not see the stroke fall. But as soon as ever he had cut off the head, there stood the loveliest Prince on the spot where the horse had stood.

"Why, where in all the world did you come from?" asked the king.

"It was I who was a horse", said the Prince; "for I was king of that land whose king you slew yesterday. He it was who threw this Troll's shape over me, and sold me to the Troll. But now he is slain I get my own again, and you and I will be neighbour kings, but war we will never make on one another."

And they didn't either; for they were friends as long as they lived, and each paid the other very many visits.

Iron John
(*Germany*)

There was once on a time a King who had a great forest near his palace, full of all kinds of wild animals. One day he sent out a huntsman to shoot him a roe, but he did not come back. "Perhaps some accident has befallen him," said the King, and the next day he sent out two more huntsmen who were to search for him, but they too stayed away. Then on the third day, he sent for all his huntsmen, and said, "Scour the whole forest through, and do not give up until ye have found all three." But of these also, none came home again, and of the pack of hounds which they had taken with them, none were seen more. From that time forth, no one would any longer venture into the forest, and it lay there in deep stillness and solitude, and nothing was seen of it, but sometimes an eagle or a hawk flying over it. This lasted for many years, when a strange huntsman announced himself to the King as seeking a situation, and offered to go into the dangerous forest. The King, however, would not give his consent, and said, "It is not safe in there; I fear it would fare with thee no better than with the others, and thou wouldst never come out again." The huntsman replied, "Lord, I will venture it at my own risk, of fear I know nothing."

The huntsman therefore betook himself with his dog to the forest. It was not long before the dog fell in with some game on the way, and wanted to pursue it; but hardly had the dog run two steps when it stood before a deep pool, could go no farther, and a naked arm stretched itself out of the water, seized it, and drew it under. When the huntsman saw that, he went back and fetched three men to come with buckets and bale out the water. When they could see to the bottom there lay a wild man whose body was brown like rusty iron, and whose hair hung over his face down to his knees. They bound him with cords, and led him away to the castle. There was great astonishment over the wild man; the King, however, had him put in an iron cage in his court-yard, and forbade the door to be opened on pain of death, and the Queen herself was to take the key into her keeping. And from this time forth everyone could again go into the forest with safety.

The King had a son of eight years, who was once playing in the court-yard, and while he was playing, his golden ball fell into the cage. The boy ran thither and said, "Give me my ball out." "Not till thou hast opened the door for me," answered the man. "No," said the boy, "I will not do that; the King has forbidden it," and ran away. The next day he again went and asked for his ball; the wild man said, "Open my door," but the boy would not. On the third day the King had ridden out hunting, and the boy went once more and said, "I cannot open the door even if I wished, for I have not the key." Then the wild man said, "It lies under thy mother's pillow, thou canst get it there." The boy, who wanted to have his ball back, cast all thought to the winds, and brought the key. The door opened with difficulty, and the boy pinched his fingers. When it was open the wild man stepped out, gave him the golden ball, and hurried away. The boy had become afraid; he called and cried after him, "Oh, wild man, do not go away, or I shall be beaten!" The wild man turned back, took him up, set him on his shoulder, and went with hasty steps into the forest. When the King came home, he observed the empty cage, and asked the Queen how that had happened? She knew nothing about it, and sought the key, but it was gone. She called the boy, but no one answered. The King sent out people to seek for him in the fields, but they did not find him. Then he could easily guess what had happened, and much grief reigned in the royal court.

When the wild man had once more reached the dark forest, he took the boy down from his shoulder, and said to him, "Thou wilt never see thy father and mother again, but I will keep thee with me, for thou hast set me free, and I have compassion on thee. If thou dost all I bid thee, thou shalt fare well. Of treasure and gold have I enough, and more than any-one in the world." He made a bed of moss for the boy on which he slept, and the next morning the man took him to a well, and said, "Behold, the gold well is as bright and clear as crystal, thou shalt sit beside it, and take care that nothing falls into it, or it will be polluted. I will come every eve-ning to see if thou hast obeyed my order." The boy placed himself by the margin of the well, and often saw a golden fish or a golden snake show itself therein, and took care that nothing fell in. As he was thus sitting, his finger hurt him so violently that he involuntarily put it in the water. He drew it quickly out again, but saw that it was quite gilded, and whatso-ever pains he took to wash the gold off again, all was to no purpose. In the evening Iron John came back, looked at the boy, and said, "What has happened to the well?" "Nothing, nothing," he answered, and held his finger behind his back, that the man might not see it. But he said, "Thou hast dipped thy finger into the water, this time it may pass, but take care thou dost not again let anything go in." By daybreak the boy was already sitting by the well and watching it. His finger hurt him again and he passed it over his head, and then unhappily a hair fell down into the well. He took it quickly out, but it was already quite gilded. Iron John came, and already knew what had happened. "Thou hast let a hair fall into the well," said he. "I will allow thee to watch by it once more, but if this hap-pens for the third time then the well is polluted, and thou canst no longer remain with me."

On the third day, the boy sat by the well, and did not stir his finger, however much it hurt him. But the time was long to him, and he looked at the reflection of his face on the surface of the water. And as he still bent down more and more while he was doing so, and trying to look straight into the eyes, his long hair fell down from his shoulders into the water. He raised himself up quickly, but the whole of the hair of his head was already golden and shone like the sun. You may imagine how terrified the poor boy was! He took his pocket-handkerchief and tied it round his head, in order that the man might not see it. When he came he already knew everything, and said, "Take the handkerchief off." Then the golden hair streamed forth, and let the boy excuse himself as he might, it was of no use. "Thou hast not stood the trial, and canst stay here no longer. Go forth into the world, there thou wilt learn what poverty is. But as thou hast not a bad heart, and as I mean well by thee, there is one thing I will grant thee; if thou fallest into any difficulty, come to the forest and cry, 'Iron John,' and then I will come and help thee. My power is great, greater than thou thinkest, and I have gold and silver in abundance."

Then the King's son left the forest, and walked by beaten and unbeaten paths ever onwards until at length he reached a great city. There he looked for work, but could find none, and he had learnt nothing by which he could help himself. At length he went to the palace, and asked if they would take him in. The people about court did not at all know what use they could make of him, but they liked him, and told him to stay. At length the cook took him into his service, and said he might carry wood and water, and rake the cinders together. Once when it so happened that no one else was at hand, the cook ordered him to carry the food to the royal table, but as he did not like to let his golden hair be seen, he kept his little cap on. Such a thing as that had never yet come under the King's notice, and he said, "When thou comest to the royal table thou must take thy hat off." He answered, "Ah, Lord, I cannot; I have a bad sore place on my head." Then the King had the cook called before him and scolded him, and asked how he could take such a boy as that into his service; and that he was to turn him off at once. The cook, however, had pity on him, and exchanged him for the gardener's boy.

And now the boy had to plant and water the garden, hoe and dig, and bear the wind and bad weather. Once in summer when he was working alone in the garden, the day was so warm he took his little cap off that the air might cool him. As the sun shone on his hair it glittered and flashed so that the rays fell into the bed-room of the King's daughter, and up she sprang to see what that could be. Then she saw the boy, and cried to him, "Boy, bring me a wreath of flowers." He put his cap on with all haste, and gathered wild field-flowers and bound them together. When he was ascending the stairs with them, the gardener met him, and said, "How canst thou take the King's daughter a garland of such common flowers? Go quickly, and get another, and seek out the prettiest and rarest." "Oh, no," replied the boy, "the wild ones have more scent, and will please her better." When he got into the room, the King's daughter said, "Take thy cap off, it is not seemly to keep it on in my presence." He again said, "I may not, I have a sore head." She, however, caught at his cap and pulled it off, and then his golden hair rolled down on his shoulders, and it was splendid to behold. He wanted to run out, but she held him by the arm, and gave him a handful of ducats. With these he departed, but he cared nothing for the gold pieces. He took them to the gardener, and said, "I present them to thy children, they can play with them." The following day the King's daughter again called to him that he was to bring her a wreath of field-flowers, and when he went in with it, she instantly snatched at his cap, and wanted to take it away from him, but he held it fast with both hands. She again gave him a handful of ducats, but he would not keep them, and gave them to the gardener for playthings for his children. On the third day things went just the same; she could not get his cap away from him, and he would not have her money.

Not long afterwards, the country was overrun by war. The King gathered together his people, and did not know whether or not he could offer any opposition to the enemy, who was superior in strength and had a mighty army. Then said the gardener's boy, "I am grown up, and will go to the wars also, only give me a horse." The others laughed, and said, "Seek one for thyself when we are gone, we will leave one behind us in the stable for thee." When they had gone forth, he went into the stable, and got the horse out; it was lame of one foot, and limped hobblety jig, hobblety jig; nevertheless he mounted it, and rode away to the dark forest. When he came to the outskirts, he called "Iron John," three times so loudly that it echoed through the trees. Thereupon the wild man appeared immediately, and said, "What dost thou desire?" "I want a strong steed, for I am going to the wars." "That thou shalt have, and still more than thou askest for." Then the wild man went back into the forest, and it was not long before a stable-boy came out of it, who led a horse that snorted with its nostrils, and could hardly be restrained, and behind them followed a great troop of soldiers entirely equipped in iron, and their swords flashed in the sun. The youth made over his three-legged horse to the stable-boy, mounted the other, and rode at the head of the soldiers. When he got near the battle-field a great part of the King's men had already fallen, and little was wanting to make the rest give way. Then the youth galloped thither with his iron soldiers, broke like a hurricane over the enemy, and beat down all who opposed him. They began to fly, but the youth pursued, and never stopped, until there was not a single man left. Instead, however, of returning to the King, he conducted his troop by bye-ways back to the forest, and called forth Iron John. "What dost thou desire?" asked the wild man. "Take back thy horse and thy troops, and give me my three-legged horse again." All that he asked was done, and soon he was riding on his three-legged horse. When the King returned to his palace, his daughter went to meet him, and wished him joy of his victory. "I am not the one who carried away the victory," said he, "but a stranger knight who came to my assistance with his soldiers." The daughter wanted to hear who the strange knight was, but the King did not know, and said, "He followed the enemy, and I did not see him again." She inquired of the gardener where his boy was, but he smiled, and said, "He has just come home on his three-legged horse, and the others have been mocking him, and crying, "Here comes our hobblety jig back again!" They asked, too, "Under what hedge hast thou been lying sleeping all the time?" He, however, said, "I did the best of all, and it would have gone badly without me." And then he was still more ridiculed.

The King said to his daughter, "I will proclaim a great feast that shall last for three days, and thou shalt throw a golden apple. Perhaps the unknown will come to it." When the feast was announced, the youth went out to the forest, and called Iron John. "What dost thou desire?" asked he. "That I may catch the King's daughter's golden apple." "It is as safe as if thou hadst it already," said Iron John. "Thou shalt likewise have a suit of red armour for the occasion, and ride on a spirited chestnut-horse." When the day came, the youth galloped to the spot, took his place amongst the knights, and was recognized by no one. The King's daughter came forward, and threw a golden apple to the knights, but none of them caught it but he, only as soon as he had it he galloped away.

On the second day Iron John equipped him as a white knight, and gave him a white horse. Again he was the only one who caught the apple, and he did not linger an instant, but galloped off with it. The King grew angry, and said, "That is not allowed; he must appear before me and tell his name." He gave the order that if the knight who caught the apple should go away again they should pursue him, and if he would not come back willingly, they were to cut him down and stab him.

On the third day, he received from Iron John a suit of black armour and a black horse, and again he caught the apple. But when he was riding off with it, the King's attendants pursued him, and one of them got so near him that he wounded the youth's leg with the point of his sword. The youth nevertheless escaped from them, but his horse leapt so violently that the helmet fell from the youth's head, and they could see that he had golden hair. They rode back and announced this to the King.

The following day the King's daughter asked the gardener about his boy. "He is at work in the garden; the queer creature has been at the festival too, and only came home yesterday evening; he has likewise shown my children three golden apples which he has won."

The King had him summoned into his presence, and he came and again had his little cap on his head. But the King's daughter went up to him and took it off, and then his golden hair fell down over his shoulders, and he was so handsome that all were amazed. "Art thou the knight who came every day to the festival, always in different colours, and who caught the three golden apples?" asked the King. "Yes," answered he, "and here the apples are," and he took them out of his pocket, and returned them to the King. "If you desire further proof, you may see the wound which your people gave me when they followed me. But I am likewise the knight who helped you to your victory over your enemies." "If thou canst perform such deeds as that, thou art no gardener's boy; tell me, who is thy father?"

"My father is a mighty King, and gold have I in plenty as great as I require." "I well see," said the King, "that I owe thanks to thee; can I do anything to please thee?" "Yes," answered he, "that indeed you can. Give me your daughter to wife." The maiden laughed, and said, "He does not stand much on ceremony, but I have already seen by his golden hair that he was no gardener's boy," and then she went and kissed him. His father and mother came to the wedding, and were in great delight, for they had given up all hope of ever seeing their dear son again. And as they were sitting at the marriage-feast, the music suddenly stopped, the doors opened, and a stately King came in with a great retinue. He went up to the youth, embraced him and said, "I am Iron John, and was by enchantment a wild man, but thou hast set me free; all the treasures which I possess, shall be thy property."

Donotknow
(*Russia*)

Once upon a time there lived a merchant who had a son, and when the son grew up he was taken into the shop. Now, the first wife of the merchant died, and he married a second.

After some months the merchant made ready to sail to foreign lands, and he loaded his ship with goods and he bade his son look after the house well and attend to business duly.

Then the merchant's son asked, "*Bátyushka*, when you go, get me my luck!"

"My beloved son," answered the old man, "where shall I find it?"

"It is not far to seek, my luck. When you get up to-morrow morning, stand at the gates and buy the first thing that meets you and give it to me."

"Very well, my son."

So next day the father got up very early, stood outside the gates, and the first thing that met him was a peasant who was selling a sorry, scabby foal—mere dog's meat. So the merchant bargained for it and got it for a silver rouble, took the foal into the courtyard and put it into the stable.

Then the merchant's son asked him, "Well, *bátyushka*, what have you found as my luck?"

"I went out to find it, and it turned into a very poor thing."

"Well, so it really had to be: whatever luck the Lord has given us we must use."

Then the father set sail with his goods into foreign lands, and the son sat on the counter and engaged in trade. He grew into the habit, whether he were going into the shop or returning home, always to go and stand in front of his foal.

Now, his stepmother did not love her stepson, and looked out for fortune-tellers to learn how to get rid of him. At last she found an old wise woman, who gave her a poison and bade her put it under the threshold just when her stepson was coming in. As he came back from the shop, the merchant's son went into the stable and saw that his foal was standing in tears, and so he stroked him and asked, "Why, my good horse, do you weep? Why your counsel do you keep?"

Then the foal answered, "Oh, Iván the merchant's son, my beloved master, why should I not weep? Your stepmother is trying to ruin you. You have a dog: when you go home let it go in front of you, and you will see what will come to it."

So the merchant's son listened, and as soon as ever the dog crossed the threshold it was torn into small atoms.

Iván the merchant's son never let his stepmother know that he saw through her spite, and set out next day to the shop, whilst the stepmother went to see the soothsayer. So the old woman got a second poison, and bade her put it into the trough. In the evening, as he went home, the merchant's son went into the stable; and once more the foal was standing on tip-toes and in tears; and he struck him on the haunches and said, "Why, my good horse, do you weep? Why your counsel do you keep?"

Then the foal answered, "Why should I not weep, my master, Iván the merchant's son? I hear a very great misfortune—that your stepmother wishes to ruin you. Look when you go into the room and sit down at the table: your mother will bring you a draught in the glass. Do you not drink it, but pour it out of the window: you will yourself see what will happen outside."

Iván the merchant's son did as he was bidden and as soon as ever he had thrown the draught out of the window it began to rend the earth; and again he never said a single word to his stepmother; so she still thought that he was in the dark.

On the third day he went to the shop, and the stepmother again went to the soothsayer. The old woman gave her an enchanted shirt. In the evening, as he was going out of the shop, the merchant's son went up to the foal, and he saw that there stood his good horse on tip-toes and in tears. So he struck him by the bridle and said, "Why do you weep, my good horse? Why your counsel do you keep?"

Then the foal answered him, "Why should I not weep? Do I not know that your stepmother is wishing to destroy you? Listen to what I say. When you go home your stepmother will send you to the bath, and she will send the boy to you with a shirt. Do not put on the shirt yourself, but put it on the boy, and you will see yourself what will come of it."

So the merchant's son went up to his attic, and his stepmother came and said to him, "Would you not like to have a steam bath? The bath is now ready."

"Very well," said Iván, and he went into the bath, and very soon after the boy brought him a shirt. As soon as ever the merchant's son put it on the boy he that very instant closed his eyes and fell on the floor, as though he were dead. And when he took the shirt off him and cast it into the stove, the boy revived, but the stove was split into small pieces.

The stepmother saw that she was doing no good, so she again went to the old soothsayer and asked and besought her how she should destroy her stepson. The old woman answered, "As long as the horse is alive nothing can be brought about. But you pretend to be ill, and when your husband comes back tell him, 'I saw in my sleep that the throat of our foal must be cut and the liver extracted, and I must be rubbed with the liver; then my disease will pass away.'"

Some time after the merchant came back, and the son went out to meet him.

"Hail, my son!" said the father. "Is all well with you at home?"

"All is well, only mother is ill," he answered.

So the merchant unloaded his wares and went home, and he found his wife lying in the bedclothes groaning, saying, "I can only recover if you will fulfil my dream."

So the merchant agreed at once, summoned his son and said, "Now, my son, I want to cut the throat of your horse: your mother is ill, and I must cure her."

So Iván the merchant's son wept bitterly and said, "Oh, father, you wish to take away from me my last luck!" Then he went into the stable.

The foal saw him and said, "My beloved master, I have saved you from three deaths—do you now save me from one. Ask your father that you may go out on my back for the last time to fare in the open fields with your companions."

So the son asked his father for leave to go into the open field for the last time on the horse, and the father agreed. Iván the merchant's son mounted his horse, leapt into the open field, and went and diverted himself with his friends and companions. Then he sent his father a letter in this wise: "Do you cure my stepmother with a twelve-tongued whip—this is the best means of curing her illness." He sent this letter with one of his good companions, and himself went into foreign lands.

The merchant read the letter, and began curing his wife with a twelve-tongued whip: and she very soon recovered.

The merchant's son went out into the open field, into the wide plains, and he saw horned cattle grazing in front of him.

So the good horse said, "Iván the merchant's son, let me go free at will, and do you pull three little hairs out of my tail: whenever I can be of service to you burn a single hair, and I shall appear at once in front of you, like a leaf in front of the grass. But you, good youth, go to the herd, buy a bull and cut its throat; dress yourself in the bull's hide, put a bladder on your head, and wherever you go, whatever you are asked about, answer only this one word, 'Idonotknow.'"

Iván the merchant's son let his horse go free, dressed himself in the bull's hide, put a bladder on his head, and went beyond the seas. On the blue sea there was a ship a-sailing. The ship's crew saw this marvel—an animal which was not an animal, a man that was not a man, with a bladder on his head and with fur all round him. So they sailed up to the shore in a light boat and began to ask him and to inquire of him. Iván the merchant's son only returned one answer, "Idonotknow."

"If it be so, then your name must be 'Donotknow.'" Then the ship's crew took him, carried him on board the boat, and they sailed to their King.

May-be long, may-be short, they at last reached a capital city, went to the King with gifts, and informed him of Donotknow. So the King bade the portent be presented before his eyes. So they brought Donotknow into the palace, and the people came up from all parts, seen and unseen, to gaze on him.

Then the King began to ask him, "What sort of a man are you?"

"Idonotknow."

"From what lands have you come?"

"Idonotknow."

"From what race and from what place?"

"Idonotknow."

Then the King put Donotknow into the garden as a scarecrow, to frighten the birds from the apple trees, and he bade him be fed from his royal kitchen.

Now this king had three daughters: the elder ones were beautiful, but the younger fairer still. Very soon the son of the King of the Arabs began asking for the hand of the youngest daughter, and he wrote to the King with threats such as this, "If you do not give her to me of your good will, I will take her by force."

This did not suit the King at all, so he answered the Arab prince in this wise, "Do you begin the war, and it shall go as God shall will."

So the Prince assembled a countless multitude and laid siege.

Donotknow shook off his oxhide, took off his bladder, went into the open fields, burnt one of the hairs, and cried out in a grim voice with a knightly whistle. From some source or other a wondrous horse appeared in front of him, and the steed galloped up, and the earth trembled. "Hail, doughty youth, why do you want me so speedily?"

"Go and prepare for war!"

So Donotknow sat on his good horse, and the horse asked him, "Where shall I carry you—aloft, under the trees, or over the standing woods?"

"Carry me over the standing woods."

So the horse raised himself from the earth and flew over the hostile host. Then Donotknow leapt upon the enemies, seized a warlike sword from one of them, tore a golden helmet from another of them, and put them on himself; covered his face with the visor, and set to slaying the Arab host. Wherever he turned, heads flew: it was like mowing hay. The King and the Princess looked on in amazement from the city wall: "What a mighty hero it must be! Whence has he come? Is it Egóri the Brave who has come to help us?"

But they never imagined that it was Donotknow whom the King had set in the garden as a scarecrow. Donotknow slew many of that host, and even more than he slew his horse trampled down, and he left only the Arab Prince alive and ten men as a suite to see him home. After this great combat he rode back to the town wall and said, "Your kingly Majesty, has my service pleased you?" Then the King thanked him and asked him in as a guest. But Donotknow would not come. He leapt into the open field, sent away his good horse, turned back home, put on the bladder and the bull's hide, and began to walk about in the garden, as before, just like a scarecrow.

Some time went by, not too much, not too little, and the Arab Prince again wrote to the King, "If you do not give me your youngest daughter's hand I will burn up all your kingdom and will take her prisoner."

This also did not please the King, and so he wrote in answer that he would await him with his host. Once again the Arab Prince collected a countless host, larger than before, and he besieged the King from all sides, having three mighty knights standing in front.

Donotknow learned of this, shook off the bull's hide, took off the bladder, summoned his good horse, and leapt to the field. One knight came to meet him. They met in combat, greeted each other and set at each other with their lances. The knight struck Donotknow so doughtily that he could hardly hold on by one stirrup. Then he got up, flew like a youth, struck off the knight's head, seized him, and threw him over, saying, "This is how all of your heads shall fly." Then another knight came out, and it happened likewise with him; and a third came, and Donotknow fought with him for one whole hour. The knight cut his hand and drew blood, but Donotknow cut off his head and threw it with the rest. Then all of the Arab host trembled and turned back. Just then the King, with the Princesses, was standing on the town wall; and the youngest Princess saw that blood was flowing from the valiant champion's hand, took a kerchief off her neck and bound up the wound herself; and the King summoned him as a guest. "I will come one day," said Donotknow, "but not this time."

So he leapt into the open field, dismissed his horse, dressed himself in his oxhide, put the bladder on his head, and began walking up and down the garden like a scarecrow.

Some time went by, not much, not little, and the King gave his two elder daughters away to famous Tsarévichi. He was making ready for a great celebration, and the guests came to walk in the garden; and they saw Donotknow and asked, "What sort of a monster is this?"

So the King said, "This is Donotknow: I am using him as a scarecrow: he keeps the birds off my apple trees."

But the youngest daughter looked at Donotknow's hand and observed her kerchief on it, blushed and never said a word. From that time she began to walk into the garden and to gaze on Donotknow, and became thoughtful, never giving heed to the festivals and to the merriment.

"Where are you always going, my daughter?" asked her father.

"Oh, father, I have lived so many years with you, I have so often walked in the garden, and I have never seen such a delightful bird as I saw there just now!"

Then she began to ask her father to give her his blessing and to wed her to Donotknow. And for all the father might do to convince her, she insisted. "If you will not give me to him, I will remain unmarried all my life and will seek no other man." So the father agreed and he betrothed them.

Soon afterwards the Arab Prince wrote to him for the third time and asked for the hand of his youngest daughter. "If you will not consent, I will consume all of your kingdom with fire, and I will take her by main force."

Then the King answered, "My daughter is already promised: if you wish, come yourself and you will see." So the Prince came, and when he saw what a monster was betrothed to the fair Princess he thought he would slay Donotknow, and he summoned him to mortal combat.

Donotknow shook off his oxhide, took the bladder from his head, summoned his good horse and rode out, so fair a youth as no tale can tell and no pen can write.

They met in the open field, in the wide plains, and the list lasted long. Iván the merchant's son killed the Arab Prince. Then at last the King recognised that Donotknow was not a monster but a splendid and handsome knight, and he made him his heir. Iván the merchant's son lived on in his kingdom for good and lived all for happiness, took his own father to stay with him, but consigned his stepmother to punishment.

331: The Spirit in the Bottle

The Spirit in the Glass Bottle
(*Germany*)

Once upon a time there was a poor woodcutter who worked from morning till late at night. When he had finally saved up some money, he said to his boy, "You are my only child, I will use the money I have earned by the sweat of my brow to educate you; if you learn an honest trade, you can feed me in my old age, when my limbs have become stiff and I have to sit at home." So, the boy went to a university and studied hard, so that his teachers praised him, and stayed there for a while. When he had gone through a few classes, but was not yet perfect in everything, the little pittance his father had saved was gone, and he had to go home to him again. "Alas," said the father sadly, "I can give you nothing more, nor can I earn a penny more in these hard times than my daily bread." "Dear father," answered the son, "don't worry about it, if it is God's will, it will turn out for my good; I'll be fine." When the father decided to go out into the forest to earn money by cutting cordwood, the son said, "I will go with you and help you. "No, my son," said the father, "that should be burdensome to you, you are not used to hard work, you will not be able to tolerate it; moreover, I have only one axe and no money left to buy another." "Go to your neighbour," replied the son, "he will lend you his axe until I have earned one for myself."

So, the father borrowed an axe from the neighbour, and the next morning at daybreak they went out into the forest together. The son helped his father and was quite cheerful and full of energy. When the sun was directly above them, the father said, "Let us rest and have lunch, after which all will be twice as good." The son took up his bread and said, "You just rest, father, I'm not tired, I want to walk about in the forest a little and look for birds' nests." "O fool," said the father, "what do you want to run about for? Afterwards you will be tired and unable even to lift your arm; stay here and sit with me."

But the son went into the forest, ate his bread, was quite cheerful, and looked into the green branches to see if he could find a nest. So, he walked to and fro until at last he came to a great and forbidding oak, which was certainly many hundred years old, and which no five men could have spanned. He stopped and looked at it, thinking, "Some bird must have built its nest in that." Suddenly it seemed as if he heard a voice. He listened and heard it call out in a rather muffled voice, "Let me out, let me out." He looked all around but could not see anything, but it seemed to him as if the voice was coming out of the ground below. Then he called out "where are you?" The voice answered, "I'm down there by the oak roots. Let me out, let me out." The student began to clear the ground under the tree and to search among the roots, until he finally discovered a glass bottle in a small hole. He lifted it up and held it up to the light and saw something shaped like a frog jumping up and down inside. "Let me out, let me out," it cried again, and the student, thinking no evil, took the stopper off the bottle. Immediately a spirit came out and began to grow. It grew so fast that in a few moments there stood before the student a horrible fellow, half as tall as the tree. "Do you know," he cried in a fearsome voice, "what your reward is for letting me out?" "No," replied the student fearlessly, "how should I know?" "I will tell you," cried the spirit, "I must break your neck for it." "You should have told me sooner," replied the student, "and I would have left you shut up inside; but my head shall stand firm where it is; more people must be asked." "More people here, more people there," cried the spirit, "your deserved reward you shall have. Thinkest thou that I have been shut up there so long out of mercy? No, it was for my punishment; I am the mighty Mercurius, whoever lets me go, I must break his neck." "Calm down," answered the student, "not so fast; first I must know that you really have been shut up in that little bottle, and that you are the right spirit; if you can get yourself back in the bottle, I will believe it, and then you may do what you like with me." The spirit said haughtily, "That is no great feat," and shrunk itself and made itself as thin and small as it had been at first, so that it crept back in through the same opening and through the neck of the bottle. But no sooner was it in than the student pushed the stopper back in and threw the bottle under the oak roots where it has been before, and so was the spirit deceived.

Now the student wanted to go back to his father, but the spirit cried out pitifully, "Oh, let me out, let me out." "No," replied the student, "not a second time: whoever has once sought my life, I will not let him go when I have caught him again." "If you set me free," cried the spirit, "I will give you so much that you will have enough for the rest of your life." "No," replied the student, "you would cheat me as you did the first time." "You are forfeiting your good luck," said the spirit, "I will do you no harm, but will reward you abundantly." The student thought, "I will chance it, perhaps it will keep its word, and in any case it shall not harm me." Then he took out the stopper, and the spirit came out as before, stretched itself, and grew as big as a giant. "Now you shall have your reward," it said, and handed the student a small cloth, like a bandage, and said, "if you rub a wound with one end, it will heal; and if you rub steel and iron with the other end, it will be turned into silver." "I must try that first," said the student, and going to a tree, he scratched the bark with his axe, and rubbed it with one end of the cloth: immediately it closed up again, and was healed. "Well, it is all right," he said to the spirit, "now we can part." The spirit thanked him for freeing it, and the student thanked the spirit for its gift, and went back to his father.

"Where have you been wandering about?" said the father, "why have you forgotten your work? I told you that you would not get anything done. "Be content, father, I will make up for it." "Right, make up for it," said the father angrily, "don't bother." "Take heed, father, I will cut down that tree and make it crash." Then he took his cloth, rubbed the axe with it, and struck a mighty blow: but because the iron was turned into silver, the edge bent back on itself. "Father, look what a bad axe you have given me, it is all crooked." Then the father was shocked, and said, "Oh, what have you done! Now I must pay for the axe, and I know not with what; this is all the good your work has done." "Do not be angry," answered the son, "I will pay for the axe." "O fool," cried the father, "wherewith wilt thou pay for it? thou hast nothing but what I give thee; these are student's tricks that are in thy head, but of wood-chopping thou hast no understanding."

After a while the student said, "Father, I can't work anymore, we'd better call it a day." "Well," he replied, "do you think I can stand around with my hands in my pockets like you? I still have to work, but you can pack your bags and go home." "Father, this is my first time here in the forest, I don't know the way alone, why don't you go with me." When his anger had subsided, the father was at last persuaded and went home with him. Then he said to the son, "Go and sell the axe you have lost and see what you get for it; I must earn the rest to pay the neighbour." The son took the axe and carried it into the town to a goldsmith, who tested it, put it on the scales, and said, "It is worth four hundred talers, I do not have that much cash." The student said, "Give me what you have and I will lend you the rest." The goldsmith gave him three hundred talers and owed him one hundred. Then the student went home and said, "Father, I have some money; go and ask what the neighbour wants for the axe." "I know that already," answered the old man, "one taler, six pennies." "Then give him two talers, twelve groschen, that is double, and will suffice; look, I have money in abundance," and he gave the father one hundred talers, saying "you shall never want, live according to your comfort." "My God," said the old man, "how did you come by this wealth?" Then he told him how everything had happened and how, trusting in his luck, he had made such a catch. With the rest of the money, he went back to the university and continued his studies, and because he could heal all wounds with his cloth, he became the most famous doctor in the whole world.

Death in a Bottle
(*Estonia*)

In the old, grey times there used to be a farmer here in Venevere. He never paid his workers; instead, when they would move to their next farm at the end of the year, he would give them bread and a drink in a bottle for the journey.

Once, another worker had come to work for him. He had been there for seven years, but was never paid. Finally, he said that he would leave and find a different workplace where he would get paid. The farmer told his wife to boil a lamb for the worker and to give him seven days' worth of bread, then he took a bottle and filled it with beer. The worker tied the bottle into a bag, put it on his shoulders and went off to find a new job, while he had seven years' service in food and drink with him.

By nightfall, he was at the edge of a forest. He sat down on a hill and opened his bag to have dinner. As he had taken the bread and meat out, he shouted: "Whoever is hungry, come and help me eat seven years' service!"

At once, a little old greying man showed up. The worker asked "Who are you?" The little man explained that he was the Devil from the underworld. However, the worker wouldn't give him a single bite, saying "I don't know you! I've never heard of you before, so I won't give anything to someone I don't know!" The Devil disappeared, so the worker called out again to see if anyone would help him eat his wage.

Another old man appeared, much older and with a longer beard. When the worker had found out that this is supposed to be the sky god, he responded: "I'm not giving anything to you! I don't know you well, but I've heard that you are the master of the sky and the earth. Why are you not fair? To some, you give fortune and treasure, while others don't even get to eat. Here I have food! I'm inviting someone poor, perhaps they will come to share the little bit I have been given, and there you are again—trying to get your share from what others desperately need. You can go, you're not getting anything!"

The old man disappeared and the worker called out again. In a bit, a middle-aged man appeared. The worker asked who he was. The man told him that he was Death, and the worker told him to eat. Together, they ate all of the seven years' worth of food. The worker was very kind to Death. He told him: "I'll gladly share with you, because you are fair. You've never asked whether someone is rich or poor, you always take equally from everyone. Thus, let's eat and drink the share that I got for my long service!"

Now that the food was eaten and the bottle was empty, the beer had gotten both of them tipsy so they were having a great time chatting. Eventually, the worker asked Death: "Please tell me, how do you get through closed doors and windows?"

"Of course I can get in!" said Death. "That's easy! See, this bottle has a tiny mouth, but I can easily get in!"

Instantly, Death's large body was no longer beside him. The worker looked inside the bottle, and Death was indeed in there. Quickly, the worker sealed the bottle tightly, took it with him and went towards the sea to drown Death in the bottle. "I want to end you so that you, the last robber and botherer, will no longer be wandering around the world," the worker thought. He travelled to Võsu beach, where he tied some rocks to the string of the bottle and let it sink deep into the bottom of the sea. "Well, here's the end of it for you," the worker thought and went his own way.

However, Death didn't die in the bottle, but now since he was no longer in Venevere, the children and the youth grew for seven years happily, while old people in grave condition were missing Death. Death was gone, no eye had seen him and no ear had heard of him. Old people were waiting for him and were in despair, 80–90-year-old people were moaning and pleading: "Death, dear Death! Come and save us from our distress! Why have even you forsaken us? Our life is bad and we are in poor health, come finally, Death, and take us to your land to sleep forever!"

Seven years after the worker had put the bottle with Death into the sea, some fishermen at Võsu beach found a bottle that had been washed ashore. The water had rotted the string, so the bottle floated up. The men who found the bottle opened it to see what's inside. A thin, boney man jumped out of the bottle—Death itself! He thanked the men for freeing him and quickly headed off to do his work, after taking a sickle from the man cutting hay near the beach. In the bottle, he starved so much that he was no more than skin and bones, as he still is today.

Whenever an old weak person is longing for death in Venevere, they are told: "Well, maybe Death is stuck in the bottle again."

The Legend of Paracelsus
(*Austria*)

It once happened that Paracelsus was walking through a forest, when he heard a voice calling to him by name. He looked around, and at length discovered that it proceeded from a fir-tree, in the trunk of which there was a spirit enclosed by a small stopper, sealed with three crosses.

The spirit begged of Paracelsus to set him free. This he readily promised, on condition that the spirit should bestow upon him a medicine capable of healing all diseases, and a tincture which would turn everything it touched to gold. The spirit acceded to his request, whereupon Paracelsus took his penknife, and succeeded, after some trouble, in getting out the stopper. A loathsome black spider crept forth, which ran down the trunk of the tree. Scarcely had it reached the ground before it was changed, and became, as if rising from the earth, a tall haggard man, with squinting red eyes, wrapped in a scarlet mantle.

He led Paracelsus to a high, overhanging, craggy mount, and with a hazel twig, which he had broken off by the way, he smote the rock, which, splitting with a crash at the blow, divided itself in twain, and the spirit disappeared within it. He, however, soon returned with two small phials, which he handed to Paracelsus—a yellow one, containing the tincture which turned all it touched to gold, and a white one, holding the medicine which healed all diseases. He then smote the rock a second time, and thereupon it instantly closed again.

Both now set forth on their return, the spirit directing his course towards Innsprück, to seize upon the magician who had banished him from that city. Now Paracelsus trembled for the consequences which his releasing the **Evil One** would entail upon him who had conjured him into the tree, and bethought how he might rescue him. When they arrived once more at the fir-tree, he asked the spirit if he could possibly transform himself again into a spider, and let him see him creep into the hole. The spirit said that it was not only possible, but that he would be most happy to make such a display of his art for the gratification of his deliverer.

Accordingly he once more assumed the form of a spider, and crept again into the well-known crevice. When he had done so, Paracelsus, who had kept the stopper all ready in his hand for the purpose, clapped it as quick as lightning into the hole, hammered it in firmly with a stone, and with his knife made three fresh crosses upon it. The spirit, mad with rage, shook the fir-tree as though with a whirlwind, that he might drive out the stopper which Paracelsus had thrust in, but his fury was of no avail. It held fast, and left him there with little hope of escape, for, on account of the great drifts of snow from the mountains, the forest will never be cut down, and, although he should call night and day, nobody in that neighbourhood ever ventures near the spot.

Paracelsus, however, found that the phials were such as he had demanded, and it was by their means that he afterwards became such a celebrated and distinguished man.

361: Bear Skin

Bearskin
(*Germany*)

There was once a young fellow who enlisted as a soldier, conducted himself bravely, and was always the foremost when it rained bullets. So long as the war lasted, all went well, but when peace was made, he received his dismissal, and the captain said he might go where he liked. His parents were dead, and he had no longer a home, so he went to his brothers and begged them to take him in, and keep him until war broke out again. The brothers, however, were hard-hearted and said, "What can we do with thee? thou art of no use to us; go and make a living for thyself." The soldier had nothing left but his gun; he took that on his shoulder, and went forth into the world. He came to a wide heath, on which nothing was to be seen but a circle of trees; under these he sat sorrowfully down, and began to think over his fate. "I have no money," thought he, "I have learnt no trade but that of fighting, and now that they have made peace they don't want me any longer; so I see beforehand that I shall have to starve." All at once he heard a rustling, and when he looked round, a strange man stood before him, who wore a green coat and looked right stately, but had a hideous cloven foot. "I know already what thou art in need of," said the man; "gold and possessions shall thou have, as much as thou canst make away with do what thou wilt, but first I must know if thou art fearless, that I may not bestow my money in vain." "A soldier and fear—how can those two things go together?" he answered; "thou canst put me to the proof." "Very well, then," answered the man, "look behind thee." The soldier turned round, and saw a large bear, which came growling towards him. "Oho!" cried the soldier, "I will tickle thy nose for thee, so that thou shalt soon lose thy fancy for growling," and he aimed at the bear and shot it through the muzzle; it fell down and never stirred again. "I see quite well," said the stranger, "that thou art not wanting in courage, but there is still another condition which thou wilt have to fulfil." "If it does not endanger my salvation," replied the soldier, who knew very well who was standing by him. "If it does, I'll have nothing to do with it." "Thou wilt look to that for thyself," answered Greencoat; "thou shalt for the next seven years neither wash thyself, nor comb thy beard, nor thy hair, nor cut thy nails, nor say one paternoster. I will give thee a coat and a cloak, which during this time thou must wear. If thou diest during these seven years, thou art mine; if thou remainest alive, thou art free, and rich to boot, for all the rest of thy life." The soldier thought of the great extremity in which he now found himself, and as he so often had gone to meet death, he resolved to risk it now also, and agreed to the terms. The Devil took off his green coat, gave it to the soldier, and said, "If thou hast this coat on thy back and puttest thy hand into the pocket, thou wilt always find it full of money." Then he pulled the skin off the bear and said, "This shall be thy cloak, and thy bed also, for thereon shalt thou sleep, and in no other bed shalt thou lie, and because of this apparel shalt thou be called Bearskin." After this the Devil vanished.

The soldier put the coat on, felt at once in the pocket, and found that the thing was really true. Then he put on the bearskin and went forth into the world, and enjoyed himself, refraining from nothing that did him good and his money harm. During the first year his appearance was passable, but during the second he began to look like a monster. His hair covered nearly the whole of his face, his beard was like a piece of coarse felt, his fingers had claws, and his face was so covered with dirt that if cress had been sown on it, it would have come up. Whosoever saw him ran away, but as he everywhere gave the poor money to pray that he might not die during the seven years, and as he paid well for everything he still always found shelter. In the fourth year, he entered an inn where the landlord would not receive him, and would not even let him have a place in the stable, because he was afraid the horses would be scared. But as Bearskin thrust his hand into his pocket and pulled out a handful of ducats, the host let himself be persuaded and gave him a room in an outhouse. Bearskin was, however, obliged to promise not to let himself be seen, lest the inn should get a bad name.

As Bearskin was sitting alone in the evening, and wishing from the bottom of his heart that the seven years were over, he heard a loud lamenting in a neighboring room. He had a compassionate heart, so he opened the door, and saw an old man weeping bitterly, and wringing his hands. Bearskin went nearer, but the man sprang to his feet and tried to escape from him. At last when the man perceived that Bearskin's voice was human he let himself be prevailed on, and by kind words Bearskin succeeded so far that the old man revealed the cause of his grief. His property had dwindled away by degrees, he and his daughters would have to starve, and he was so poor that he could not pay the innkeeper, and was to be put in prison. "If that is your only trouble," said Bearskin, "I have plenty of money." He caused the innkeeper to be brought thither, paid him and put a purse full of gold into the poor old man's pocket besides.

When the old man saw himself set free from all his troubles he did not know how to be grateful enough. "Come with me," said he to Bearskin; "my daughters are all miracles of beauty, choose one of them for thyself as a wife. When she hears what thou hast done for me, she will not refuse thee. Thou dost in truth look a little strange, but she will soon put thee to rights again." This pleased Bearskin well, and he went. When the eldest saw him she was so terribly alarmed at his face that she screamed and ran away. The second stood still and looked at him from head to foot, but then she said, "How can I accept a husband who no longer has a human form? The shaven bear that once was here and passed itself off for a man pleased me far better, for at any rate it wore a hussar's dress and white gloves. If it were nothing but ugliness, I might get used to that." The youngest, however, said, "Dear father, that must be a good man to have helped you out of your trouble, so if you have promised him a bride for doing it, your promise must be kept." It was a pity that Bearskin's face was covered with dirt and with hair, for if not they might have seen how delighted he was when he heard these words. He took a ring from his finger, broke it in two, and gave her one half, the other he kept for himself. He wrote his name, however, on her half, and hers on his, and begged her to keep her piece carefully, and then he took his leave and said, "I must still wander about for three years, and if I do not return then, thou art free, for I shall be dead. But pray to God to preserve my life."

The poor betrothed bride dressed herself entirely in black, and when she thought of her future bridegroom, tears came into her eyes. Nothing but contempt and mockery fell to her lot from her sisters. "Take care," said the eldest, "if thou givest him thy hand, he will strike his claws into it." "Beware!" said the second. "Bears like sweet things, and if he takes a fancy to thee, he will eat thee up." "Thou must always do as he likes," began the elder again, "or else he will growl." And the second continued, "But the wedding will be a merry one, for bears dance well." The bride was silent, and did not let them vex her. Bearskin, however, travelled about the world from one place to another, did good where he was able, and gave generously to the poor that they might pray for him.

At length, as the last day of the seven years dawned, he went once more out on to the heath, and seated himself beneath the circle of trees. It was not long before the wind whistled, and the Devil stood before him and looked angrily at him; then he threw Bearskin his old coat, and asked for his own green one back. "We have not got so far as that yet," answered Bearskin, "thou must first make me clean." Whether the Devil liked it or not, he was forced to fetch water, and wash Bearskin, comb his hair, and cut his nails. After this, he looked like a brave soldier, and was much handsomer than he had ever been before.

When the Devil had gone away, Bearskin was quite lighthearted. He went into the town, put on a magnificent velvet coat, seated himself in a carriage drawn by four white horses, and drove to his bride's house. No one recognized him, the father took him for a distinguished general, and led him into the room where his daughters were sitting. He was forced to place himself between the two eldest, they helped him to wine, gave him the best pieces of meat, and thought that in all the world they had never seen a handsomer man. The bride, however, sat opposite to him in her black dress, and never raised her eyes, nor spoke a word. When at length he asked the father if he would give him one of his daughters to wife, the two eldest jumped up, ran into their bedrooms to put on splendid dresses, for each of them fancied she was the chosen one. The stranger, as soon as he was alone with his bride, brought out his half of the ring, and threw it in a glass of wine which he reached across the table to her. She took the wine, but when she had drunk it, and found the half ring lying at the bottom, her heart began to beat. She got the other half, which she wore on a ribbon round her neck, joined them, and saw that the two pieces fitted exactly together. Then said he, "I am thy betrothed bridegroom, whom thou sawest as Bearskin, but through God's grace I have again received my human form, and have once more become clean." He went up to her, embraced her, and gave her a kiss. In the meantime the two sisters came back in full dress, and when they saw that the handsome man had fallen to the share of the youngest, and heard that he was Bearskin, they ran out full of anger and rage. One of them drowned herself in the well, the other hanged herself on a tree. In the evening, someone knocked at the door, and when the bridegroom opened it, it was the Devil in his green coat, who said, "Seest thou, I have now got two souls in the place of thy one!"

Never-Wash
(*Russia*)

O nce upon a time there was a soldier who had served through three campaigns, but had never earned as much as an addled egg, and was then put on the retired list. Then, as he went on the road marching on and on, he became tired and sat down by a lake. And, as he rested, he began thinking things out: "Where shall I now betake myself, and how shall I feed myself, and how the devil shall I enter into any service?"

As soon as he had spoken these words a little devil rose up at once in front of him and said, "Hail, soldier, what do you wish? Did you just now not say that you wished to become one of our servants? Why, soldier, come up and be hired: we will pay you well."

"What is the work?"

"Oh, the work is easy enough: for fifteen years you must not shave, you must not have your hair cut, you must not blow your nose, and you must not change your garb. If you serve this service, then we will go to the king, who has three daughters. Two of them are mine, but the third shall be yours."

"Very well," said the soldier, "I will undertake the contract; but I require in return to get anything my soul hankers after."

"It shall be so; be at peace; we shall not be in default."

"Well, let it befall at once. Carry me at once into the capital and give me a pile of money; you know yourself how little of these goods a soldier ever gets."

So the little devil dashed into the lake, got out a pile of gold, and instantaneously carried the soldier into the great city, and all at once he was there!

"What a fool I have been!" said the soldier: "I have not done any service, no work, and I now have the money!" So he took a room, never cut his hair, never shaved, never wiped his nose, never changed his garb, and he lived on and grew wealthy, so wealthy he did not know what to do with his money. What was he to do with his silver and gold? "Oh, very well, I will start helping the poor: possibly they may pray for my soul." So the soldier began distributing alms to the needy, to the right and to the left, and he still had money over, however much he gave away! His fame, spread over the whole kingdom, came to the ears of all.

So the soldier lived for fourteen years, and on the fifteenth year the Tsar's exchequer gave out. So he summoned the soldier. So the soldier came to him unwashed, unshaved, uncombed, with his nose unwiped and his dress unchanged.

"Health, your Majesty!"

"Listen, soldier. You, they say, are good to all folks: will you lend me some money? I have not enough to pay my troops. If you will I will make you a general at once."

"No, your Majesty, I do not wish to be a general; but if you will do me a favour, give me one of your daughters as my wife, and you shall have as much money as you wish for the Treasury."

So the king began to think: he was very fond of his daughters, but still he could not do anything whatsoever without money. "Well," he said, "I agree. Have a portrait taken of yourself; I will show it to my daughters and ask which of them will take you."

So the soldier returned, had the portrait painted, which was feature for feature, unshaved, unwashed, uncombed, his nose unwiped, and in his old garb, and sent it to the Tsar.

Now, the Tsar had three daughters, and the father summoned them and showed them the soldier's portrait. He said to the eldest, "Will you go and marry him? He will redeem me from very great embarrassment."

The Tsarévna saw what a monstrous animal had been painted, with tangled hair, uncut nails and unwiped nose. "I certainly won't!" she said, "I would sooner go to the Devil." And from somewhere or other the Devil appeared, stood behind her with pen and paper, heard what she said, and entered her soul on his register.

Then the father asked the next daughter, "Will you go and marry the soldier?"

"What! I would rather remain a maiden; I would rather tie myself up with the Devil than go with him." So the Devil went and inscribed her soul as well.

Then the father asked his youngest daughter, and she answered, "Evidently this must be my lot: I will go and marry him and see what God shall give."

Then the Tsar was very blithe at this, and he went and told the soldier to make ready for the betrothal, and he sent him twelve carts to carry the money away.

Then the soldier made use of his devil: "There are twelve carts; pile them all high at once with gold." So the devil ran into the lake and the unholy ones set to work. Some of them brought up one sack, some two, and they soon filled the carts and sent them to the Tsar, into his palace.

Then the Tsar looked, and now summoned the soldier to him every day, sat with him at one table, and ate and drank with him. When they got ready for the marriage the term of fifteen years was over. So he called the little devil and said, "Now my service is over: turn me into a youth."

So the devil cut him up into little bits, threw them into a cauldron, and began to brew him—brewed him, washed him and collected all his bones, one by one, in the proper way, every bone with every bone, every joint with every joint, every nerve with every nerve: then he sprinkled them with the water of life, and the soldier arose, such a fine young man as no tale can tell and no pen can write. He then married the youngest Tsarévna, and they began to live a merry life of good.

I was at the wedding: I drank mead and beer. They also had wine, and I drank it to the very dregs.

⸻ ❀ ⸻

But the little devil ran back into the lake, for his elder hauled him over the coals to answer for what he had done with the soldier. "He has served out his period faithfully and honourably: he has never once shaved himself, nor cut his hair, nor wiped his nose, nor changed his clothes."

Then the elder was very angry. He said, "In fifteen years you were not able to corrupt the soldier! Was all the money given in vain? What sort of a devil will you be after this?" And he had him thrown into the burning pitch.

"Oh no, please, grandfather," said the grandson, "I have lost the soldier's soul, but I have gained two others."

"What?"

"Look: the soldier thought of marrying a Tsarévna; the two elder daughters both declined and said they would rather marry a devil than the soldier. So there they are, and they belong to us."

So the grandfather-devil approved what the grandson-imp had done, and set him free. "Yes," he said, "you know your business very well indeed."

Don Giovanni de la Fortuna
(*Sicily*)

There was once a man whose name was Don Giovanni de la Fortuna, and he lived in a beautiful house that his father had built, and spent a great deal of money. Indeed, he spent so much that very soon there was none left, and Don Giovanni, instead of being a rich man with everything he could wish for, was forced to put on the dress of a pilgrim, and to wander from place to place begging his bread.

One day he was walking down a broad road when he was stopped by a handsome man he had never seen before, who, little as Don Giovanni knew it, was the devil himself.

'Would you like to be rich,' asked the devil, 'and to lead a pleasant life?'

'Yes, of course I should,' replied the Don.

'Well, here is a purse; take it and say to it, "Dear purse, give me some money," and you will get as much as you can want. But the charm will only work if you promise to remain three years, three months, and three days without washing and without combing and without shaving your beard or changing your clothes. If you do all this faithfully, when the time is up you shall keep the purse for yourself, and I will let you off any other conditions.'

Now Don Giovanni was a man who never troubled his head about the future. He did not once think how very uncomfortable he should be all those three years, but only that he should be able, by means of the purse, to have all sorts of things he had been obliged to do without; so he joyfully put the purse in his pocket and went on his way. He soon began to ask for money for the mere pleasure of it, and there was always as much as he needed. For a little while he even forgot to notice how dirty he was getting, but this did not last long, for his hair became matted with dirt and hung over his eyes, and his pilgrim's dress was a mass of horrible rags and tatters.

He was in this state when, one morning, he happened to be passing a fine palace; and, as the sun was shining bright and warm, he sat down on the steps and tried to shake off some of the dust which he had picked up on the road. But in a few minutes a maid saw him, and said to her master,

'I pray you, sir, to drive away that beggar who is sitting on the steps, or he will fill the whole house with his dirt.'

So the master went out and called from some distance off, for he was really afraid to go near the man, 'You filthy beggar, leave my house at once!'

'You need not be so rude,' said Don Giovanni; 'I am not a beggar, and if I chose I could force you and your wife to leave your house.'

'What is that you can do?' laughed the gentleman.

'Will you sell me your house?' asked Don Giovanni. 'I will buy it from you on the spot.'

'Oh, the dirty creature is quite mad!' thought the gentleman. 'I shall just accept his offer for a joke.' And aloud he said: 'All right; follow me, and we will go to a lawyer and get him to make a contract.' And Don Giovanni followed him, and an agreement was drawn up by which the house was to be sold at once, and a large sum of money paid down in eight days. Then the Don went to an inn, where he hired two rooms, and, standing in one of them, said to his purse, 'Dear purse, fill this room with gold;' and when the eight days were up it was so full you could not have put in another sovereign.

When the owner of the house came to take away his money Don Giovanni led him into the room and said: 'There, just pocket what you want.' The gentleman stared with open mouth at the astonishing sight; but he had given his word to sell the house, so he took his money, as he was told, and went away with his wife to look for some place to live in. And Don Giovanni left the inn and dwelt in the beautiful rooms, where his rags and dirt looked sadly out of place. And every day these got worse and worse.

By-and-by the fame of his riches reached the ears of the king, and, as he himself was always in need of money, he sent for Don Giovanni, as he wished to borrow a large sum. Don Giovanni readily agreed to lend him what he wanted, and sent next day a huge waggon laden with sacks of gold.

'Who can he be?' thought the king to himself. 'Why, he is much richer than I!'

The king took as much as he had need of; then ordered the rest to be returned to Don Giovanni, who refused to receive it, saying, 'Tell his majesty I am much hurt at his proposal. I shall certainly not take back that handful of gold, and, if he declines to accept it, keep it yourself.'

The servant departed and delivered the message, and the king wondered more than ever how anyone could be so rich. At last he spoke to the queen: 'Dear wife, this man has done me a great service, and has, besides, behaved like a gentleman in not allowing me to send back the money. I wish to give him the hand of our eldest daughter.'

The queen was quite pleased at this idea, and again messenger was sent to Don Giovanni, offering him the hand of the eldest princess.

'His majesty is too good,' he replied. 'I can only humbly accept the honour.'

The messenger took back this answer, but a second time returned with the request that Don Giovanni would present them with his picture, so that they might know what sort of a person to expect. But when it came, and the princess saw the horrible figure, she screamed out, 'What! marry this dirty beggar? Never, never!'

'Ah, child,' answered the king, 'how could I ever guess that the rich Don Giovanni would ever look like that? But I have passed my royal word, and I cannot break it, so there is no help for you.'

'No, father; you may cut off my head, if you choose, but marry that horrible beggar—I never will!'

And the queen took her part, and reproached her husband bitterly for wishing his daughter to marry a creature like that.

Then the youngest daughter spoke: 'Dear father, do not look so sad. As you have given your word, I will marry Don Giovanni.' The king fell on her neck, and thanked her and kissed her, but the queen and the elder girl had nothing for her but laughs and jeers.

So it was settled, and then the king bade one of his lords go to Don Giovanni and ask him when the wedding day was to be, so that the princess might make ready.

'Let it be in two months,' answered Don Giovanni, for the time was nearly up that the devil had fixed, and he wanted a whole month to himself to wash off the dirt of the past three years.

The very minute that the compact with the devil had come to an end his beard was shaved, his hair was cut, and his rags were burned, and day and night he lay in a bath of clear warm water. At length he felt he was clean again, and he put on splendid clothes, and hired a beautiful ship, and arrived in state at the king's palace.

The whole of the royal family came down to the ship to receive him, and the whole way the queen and the elder princess teased the sister about the dirty husband she was going to have. But when they saw how handsome he really was their hearts were filled with envy and anger, so that their eyes were blinded, and they fell over into the sea and were drowned. And the youngest daughter rejoiced in the good luck that had come to her, and they had a splendid wedding when the days of mourning for her mother and sister were ended.

Soon after the old king died, and Don Giovanni became king. And he was rich and happy to the end of his days, for he loved his wife, and his purse always gave him money.

461: Three Hairs

The Devil With the Three Golden Hairs

The Devil With the Three Golden Hairs
(*Germany*)

There was once a poor woman who gave birth to a little son; and as he came into the world with a caul[1] on, it was predicted that in his fourteenth year he would have the King's daughter for his wife. It happened that soon afterwards the King came into the village, and no one knew that he was the King, and when he asked the people what news there was, they answered, "A child has just been born with a caul on; whatever anyone so born undertakes turns out well. It is prophesied, too, that in his fourteenth year he will have the King's daughter for his wife."

The King, who had a bad heart, and was angry about the prophecy, went to the parents, and, seeming quite friendly, said, "You poor people, let me have your child, and I will take care of it." At first they refused, but when the stranger offered them a large amount of gold for it, and they thought, "It is a luck-child, and everything must turn out well for it," they at last consented, and gave him the child.

The King put it in a box and rode away with it until he came to a deep piece of water; then he threw the box into it and thought, "I have freed my daughter from her unlooked-for suitor."

The box, however, did not sink, but floated like a boat, and not a drop of water made its way into it. And it floated to within two miles of the King's chief city, where there was a mill, and it came to a stand-still at the mill-dam. A miller's boy, who by good luck was standing there, noticed it and pulled it out with a hook, thinking that he had found a great treasure, but when he opened it there lay a pretty boy inside, quite fresh and lively. He took him to the miller and his wife, and as they had no children they were glad, and said, "God has given him to us." They took great care of the foundling, and he grew up in all goodness.

It happened that once in a storm, the King went into the mill, and he asked the mill-folk if the tall youth was their son. "No," answered they, "he's a foundling. Fourteen years ago he floated down to the mill-dam in a box, and the mill-boy pulled him out of the water."

Then the King knew that it was none other than the luck-child which he had thrown into the water, and he said, "My good people, could not the youth take a letter to the Queen; I will give him two gold pieces as a reward?" "Just as the King commands," answered they, and they told

---

1 Birth membrane, an amniotic sac from in utero.

the boy to hold himself in readiness. Then the King wrote a letter to the Queen, wherein he said, "As soon as the boy arrives with this letter, let him be killed and buried, and all must be done before I come home."

The boy set out with this letter; but he lost his way, and in the evening came to a large forest. In the darkness he saw a small light; he went towards it and reached a cottage. When he went in, an old woman was sitting by the fire quite alone. She started when she saw the boy, and said, "Whence do you come, and whither are you going?" "I come from the mill," he answered, "and wish to go to the Queen, to whom I am taking a letter; but as I have lost my way in the forest I should like to stay here over night." "You poor boy," said the woman, "you have come into a den of thieves, and when they come home they will kill you." "Let them come," said the boy, "I am not afraid; but I am so tired that I cannot go any farther:" and he stretched himself upon a bench and fell asleep.

Soon afterwards the robbers came, and angrily asked what strange boy was lying there? "Ah," said the old woman, "it is an innocent child who has lost himself in the forest, and out of pity I have let him come in; he has to take a letter to the Queen." The robbers opened the letter and read it, and in it was written that the boy as soon as he arrived should be put to death. Then the hard-hearted robbers felt pity, and their leader tore up the letter and wrote another, saying, that as soon as the boy came, he should be married at once to the King's daughter. Then they let him lie quietly on the bench until the next morning, and when he awoke they gave him the letter, and showed him the right way.

And the Queen, when she had received the letter and read it, did as was written in it, and had a splendid wedding-feast prepared, and the King's daughter was married to the luck-child, and as the youth was handsome and agreeable she lived with him in joy and contentment.

After some time the King returned to his palace and saw that the prophecy was fulfilled, and the luck-child married to his daughter. "How has that come to pass?" said he; "I gave quite another order in my letter."

So the Queen gave him the letter, and said that he might see for himself what was written in it. The King read the letter and saw quite well that it had been exchanged for the other. He asked the youth what had become of the letter entrusted to him, and why he had brought another instead of it. "I know nothing about it," answered he; "it must have been changed in the night, when I slept in the forest." The King said in a passion, "You shall not have everything quite so much your own way; whosoever marries my daughter must fetch me from hell three golden hairs from the head of the devil; bring me what I want, and you shall keep my daughter." In this way the King hoped to be rid of him forever. But the luck-child answered, "I will fetch the golden hairs, I am not afraid of the Devil," thereupon he took leave of them and began his journey.

The road led him to a large town, where the watchman by the gates asked him what his trade was, and what he knew. "I know everything," answered the luck-child. "Then you can do us a favour," said the watchman, "if you will tell us why our market-fountain, which once flowed with wine has become dry, and no longer gives even water?" "That you shall know," answered he; "only wait until I come back."

Then he went farther and came to another town, and there also the gatekeeper asked him what was his trade, and what he knew. "I know everything," answered he. "Then you can do us a favour and tell us why a tree in our town which once bore golden apples now does not even put forth leaves?" "You shall know that," answered he; "only wait until I come back."

Then he went on and came to a wide river over which he must go. The ferryman asked him what his trade was, and what he knew. "I know everything," answered he. "Then you can do me a favour," said the ferryman, "and tell me why I must always be rowing backwards and forwards, and am never set free?" "You shall know that," answered he; "only wait until I come back."

When he had crossed the water he found the entrance to Hell. It was black and sooty within, and the Devil was not at home, but his grandmother was sitting in a large arm-chair. "What do you want?" said she to him, but she did not look so very wicked. "I should like to have three golden hairs from the devil's head," answered he, "else I cannot keep my wife." "That is a good deal to ask for," said she; "if the devil comes home and finds you, it will cost you your life; but as I pity you, I will see if I cannot help you."

She changed him into an ant and said, "Creep into the folds of my dress, you will be safe there." "Yes," answered he, "so far, so good; but there are three things besides that I want to know: why a fountain which once flowed with wine has become dry, and no longer gives even water; why a tree which once bore golden apples does not even put forth leaves; and why a ferry-man must always be going backwards and forwards, and is never set free?"

"Those are difficult questions," answered she, "but only be silent and quiet and pay attention to what the devil says when I pull out the three golden hairs."

As the evening came on, the devil returned home. No sooner had he entered than he noticed that the air was not pure. "I smell man's flesh," said he; "all is not right here." Then he pried into every corner, and searched, but could not find anything. His grandmother scolded him. "It has just been swept," said she, "and everything put in order, and now you are upsetting it again; you have always got man's flesh in your nose. Sit down and eat your supper."

When he had eaten and drunk he was tired, and laid his head in his grandmother's lap, and before long he was fast asleep, snoring and breathing heavily. Then the old woman took hold of a golden hair, pulled it out, and laid it down near her. "Oh!" cried the devil, "what are you doing?" "I have had a bad dream," answered the grandmother, "so I seized hold of your hair." "What did you dream then?" said the devil. "I dreamed that a fountain in a market-place from which wine once flowed was dried up, and not even water would flow out of it; what is the cause of it?" "Oh, ho! if they did but know it," answered the devil; "there is a toad sitting under a stone in the well; if they killed it, the wine would flow again."

He went to sleep again and snored until the windows shook. Then she pulled the second hair out. "Ha! what are you doing?" cried the devil angrily. "Do not take it ill," said she, "I did it in a dream." "What have you dreamt this time?" asked he. "I dreamt that in a certain kingdom there stood an apple-tree which had once borne golden apples, but now would not even bear leaves. What, think you, was the reason?" "Oh! if they did but know," answered the devil. "A mouse is gnawing at the root; if they killed this they would have golden apples again, but if it gnaws much longer the tree will wither altogether. But leave me alone with your dreams: if you disturb me in my sleep again you will get a box on the ear."

The grandmother spoke gently to him until he fell asleep again and snored. Then she took hold of the third golden hair and pulled it out. The devil jumped up, roared out, and would have treated her ill if she had not quieted him once more and said, "Who can help bad dreams?" "What was the dream, then?" asked he, and was quite curious. "I dreamt of a ferry-man who complained that he must always ferry from one side to the other, and was never released. What is the cause of it?" "Ah! the fool," answered the devil; "when anyone comes and wants to go across he must put the oar in his hand, and the other man will have to ferry and he will be free." As the grandmother had plucked out the three golden hairs, and the three questions were answered, she let the old serpent alone, and he slept until daybreak.

When the devil had gone out again the old woman took the ant out of the folds of her dress, and gave the luck-child his human shape again. "There are the three golden hairs for you," said she. "What the Devil said to your three questions, I suppose you heard?" "Yes," answered he, "I heard, and will take care to remember." "You have what you want," said she, "and now you can go your way." He thanked the old woman for helping him in his need, and left Hell well content that everything had turned out so fortunately.

When he came to the ferry-man he was expected to give the promised answer. "Ferry me across first," said the luck-child, "and then I will tell you how you can be set free," and when he reached the opposite shore he gave him the devil's advice: "Next time anyone comes, who wants to be ferried over, just put the oar in his hand."

He went on and came to the town wherein stood the unfruitful tree, and there too the watchman wanted an answer. So he told him what he had heard from the devil: "Kill the mouse which is gnawing at its root, and it will again bear golden apples." Then the watchman thanked him, and gave him as a reward two asses laden with gold, which followed him.

At last he came to the town whose well was dry. He told the watchman what the devil had said: "A toad is in the well beneath a stone; you must find it and kill it, and the well will again give wine in plenty." The watchman thanked him, and also gave him two asses laden with gold.

At last the luck-child got home to his wife, who was heartily glad to see him again, and to hear how well he had prospered in everything. To the King he took what he had asked for, the devil's three golden hairs, and when the King saw the four asses laden with gold he was quite content, and said, "Now all the conditions are fulfilled, and you can keep my daughter. But tell me, dear son-in-law, where did all that gold come from? This is tremendous wealth!" "I was rowed across a river," answered he, "and got it there; it lies on the shore instead of sand." "Can I too fetch some of it?" said the King; and he was quite eager about it. "As much as you like," answered he. "There is a ferry-man on the river; let him ferry you over, and you can fill your sacks on the other side." The greedy King set out in all haste, and when he came to the river he beckoned to the ferry-man to put him across. The ferry-man came and bade him get in, and when they got to the other shore he put the oar in his hand and sprang out. But from this time forth the King had to ferry, as a punishment for his sins. Perhaps he is ferrying still? If he is, it is because no one has taken the oar from him.

The Story of the Three Wonderful Beggars
(*Serbia*)

There once lived a merchant whose name was Mark, and whom people called 'Mark the Rich.' He was a very hard-hearted man, for he could not bear poor people, and if he caught sight of a beggar anywhere near his house, he would order the servants to drive him away, or would set the dogs at him.

One day three very poor old men came begging to the door, and just as he was going to let the fierce dogs loose on them, his little daughter, Anastasia, crept close up to him and said:

'Dear daddy, let the poor old men sleep here to-night, do—to please me.'

Her father could not bear to refuse her, and the three beggars were allowed to sleep in a loft, and at night, when everyone in the house was fast asleep, little Anastasia got up, climbed up to the loft, and peeped in.

The three old men stood in the middle of the loft, leaning on their sticks, with their long grey beards flowing down over their hands, and were talking together in low voices.

'What news is there?' asked the eldest.

'In the next village the peasant Ivan has just had his seventh son. What shall we name him, and what fortune shall we give him?' said the second.

The third whispered, 'Call him Vassili, and give him all the property of the hard-hearted man in whose loft we stand, and who wanted to drive us from his door.'

After a little more talk the three made themselves ready and crept softly away.

Anastasia, who had heard every word, ran straight to her father, and told him all.

Mark was very much surprised; he thought, and thought, and in the morning he drove to the next village to try and find out if such a child really had been born. He went first to the priest, and asked him about the children in his parish.

'Yesterday,' said the priest, 'a boy was born in the poorest house in the village. I named the unlucky little thing "Vassili." He is the seventh son, and the eldest is only seven years old, and they hardly have a mouthful amongst them all. Who can be got to stand godfather to such a little beggar boy?'

The merchant's heart beat fast, and his mind was full of bad thoughts about that poor little baby. He would be godfather himself, he said, and he ordered a fine christening feast; so the child was brought and christened, and Mark was very friendly to its father. After the ceremony was over he took Ivan aside and said:

'Look here, my friend, you are a poor man. How can you afford to bring up the boy? Give him to me and I'll make something of him, and I'll give you a present of a thousand crowns. Is that a bargain?'

Ivan scratched his head, and thought, and thought, and then he agreed. Mark counted out the money, wrapped the baby up in a fox skin, laid it in the sledge beside him, and drove back towards home. When he had driven some miles he drew up, carried the child to the edge of a steep precipice and threw it over, muttering, 'There, now try to take my property!'

Very soon after this some foreign merchants travelled along that same road on the way to see Mark and to pay the twelve thousand crowns which they owed him.

As they were passing near the precipice they heard a sound of crying, and on looking over they saw a little green meadow wedged in between two great heaps of snow, and on the meadow lay a baby amongst the flowers.

The merchants picked up the child, wrapped it up carefully, and drove on. When they saw Mark they told him what a strange thing they had found. Mark guessed at once that the child must be his godson, asked to see him, and said:

'That's a nice little fellow; I should like to keep him. If you will make him over to me, I will let you off your debt.'

The merchants were very pleased to make so good a bargain, left the child with Mark, and drove off.

At night Mark took the child, put it in a barrel, fastened the lid tight down, and threw it into the sea. The barrel floated away to a great distance, and at last it floated close up to a monastery. The monks were just spreading out their nets to dry on the shore, when they heard the sound of crying. It seemed to come from the barrel which was bobbing about near the water's edge. They drew it to land and opened it, and there was a little child! When the abbot heard the news, he decided to bring up the boy, and named him 'Vassili.'

The boy lived on with the monks, and grew up to be a clever, gentle, and handsome young man. No one could read, write, or sing better than he, and he did everything so well that the abbot made him wardrobe keeper.

Now, it happened about this time that the merchant, Mark, came to the monastery in the course of a journey. The monks were very polite to him and showed him their house and church and all they had. When he went into the church the choir was singing, and one voice was so clear and beautiful that he asked who it belonged to. Then the abbot told him of the wonderful way in which Vassili had come to them, and Mark saw clearly that this must be his godson whom he had twice tried to kill.

He said to the abbot: 'I can't tell you how much I enjoy that young man's singing. If he could only come to me I would make him overseer of all my business. As you say, he is so good and clever. Do spare him to me. I will make his fortune, and will present your monastery with twenty thousand crowns.'

The abbot hesitated a good deal, but he consulted all the other monks, and at last they decided that they ought not to stand in the way of Vassili's good fortune.

Then Mark wrote a letter to his wife and gave it to Vassili to take to her, and this was what was in the letter: 'When the bearer of this arrives, take him into the soap factory, and when you pass near the great boiler, push him in. If you don't obey my orders I shall be very angry, for this young man is a bad fellow who is sure to ruin us all if he lives.'

Vassili had a good voyage, and on landing set off on foot for Mark's home. On the way he met three beggars, who asked him: 'Where are you going, Vassili?'

'I am going to the house of Mark the Merchant, and have a letter for his wife,' replied Vassili.

'Show us the letter.'

Vassili handed them the letter. They blew on it and gave it back to him, saying: 'Now go and give the letter to Mark's wife. You will not be forsaken.'

Vassili reached the house and gave the letter. When the mistress read it she could hardly believe her eyes and called for her daughter. In the letter was written, quite plainly: 'When you receive this letter, get ready for a wedding, and let the bearer be married next day to my daughter, Anastasia. If you don't obey my orders I shall be very angry.'

Anastasia saw the bearer of the letter and he pleased her very much. They dressed Vassili in fine clothes and next day he was married to Anastasia.

In due time, Mark returned from his travels. His wife, daughter, and son-in-law all went out to meet him. When Mark saw Vassili he flew into a terrible rage with his wife. 'How dared you marry my daughter without my consent?' he asked.

'I only carried out your orders,' said she. 'Here is your letter.'

Mark read it. It certainly was his handwriting, but by no means his wishes.

'Well,' thought he, 'you've escaped me three times, but I think I shall get the better of you now.' And he waited a month and was very kind and pleasant to his daughter and her husband.

At the end of that time he said to Vassili one day, 'I want you to go for me to my friend the Serpent King, in his beautiful country at the world's end. Twelve years ago he built a castle on some land of mine. I want you to ask for the rent for those twelve years and also to find out from him what has become of my twelve ships which sailed for his country three years ago.'

Vassili dared not disobey. He said good-bye to his young wife, who cried bitterly at parting, hung a bag of biscuits over his shoulders, and set out.

I really cannot tell you whether the journey was long or short. As he tramped along he suddenly heard a voice saying: 'Vassili! where are you going?'

Vassili looked about him, and, seeing no one, called out: 'Who spoke to me?'

'I did; this old wide-spreading oak. Tell me where you are going.'

'I am going to the Serpent King to receive twelve years' rent from him.'

'When the time comes, remember me and ask the king: "Rotten to the roots, half dead but still green, stands the old oak. Is it to stand much longer on the earth?"'

Vassili went on further. He came to a river and got into the ferryboat. The old ferryman asked: 'Are you going far, my friend?'

'I am going to the Serpent King.'

'Then think of me and say to the king: "For thirty years the ferryman has rowed to and fro. Will the tired old man have to row much longer?"'

'Very well,' said Vassili; 'I'll ask him.'

And he walked on. In time he came to a narrow strait of the sea and across it lay a great whale over whose back people walked and drove as if it had been a bridge or a road. As he stepped on it the whale said, 'Do tell me where you are going.'

'I am going to the Serpent King.'

And the whale begged: 'Think of me and say to the king: "The poor whale has been lying three years across the strait, and men and horses have nearly trampled his back into his ribs. Is he to lie there much longer?"'

'I will remember,' said Vassili, and he went on.

He walked, and walked, and walked, till he came to a great green meadow. In the meadow stood a large and splendid castle. Its white marble walls sparkled in the light, the roof was covered with mother o' pearl, which shone like a rainbow, and the sun glowed like fire on the crystal windows. Vassili walked in, and went from one room to another astonished at all the splendour he saw.

When he reached the last room of all, he found a beautiful girl sitting on a bed.

As soon as she saw him she said: 'Oh, Vassili, what brings you to this accursed place?'

Vassili told her why he had come, and all he had seen and heard on the way.

The girl said: 'You have not been sent here to collect rents, but for your own destruction, and that the serpent may devour you.'

She had not time to say more, when the whole castle shook, and a rustling, hissing, groaning sound was heard. The girl quickly pushed Vassili into a chest under the bed, locked it and whispered: 'Listen to what the serpent and I talk about.'

Then she rose up to receive the Serpent King.

The monster rushed into the room, and threw itself panting on the bed, crying: 'I've flown half over the world. I'm tired, VERY tired, and want to sleep—scratch my head.'

The beautiful girl sat down near him, stroking his hideous head, and said in a sweet coaxing voice: 'You know everything in the world. After you left, I had such a wonderful dream. Will you tell me what it means?'

'Out with it then, quick! What was it?'

'I dreamt I was walking on a wide road, and an oak tree said to me: "Ask the king this: Rotten at the roots, half dead, and yet green stands the old oak. Is it to stand much longer on the earth?"'

'It must stand till someone comes and pushes it down with his foot. Then it will fall, and under its roots will be found more gold and silver than even Mark the Rich has got.'

'Then I dreamt I came to a river, and the old ferryman said to me: "For thirty year's the ferryman has rowed to and fro. Will the tired old man have to row much longer?"'

'That depends on himself. If someone gets into the boat to be ferried across, the old man has only to push the boat off, and go his way without looking back. The man in the boat will then have to take his place.'

'And at last I dreamt that I was walking over a bridge made of a whale's back, and the living bridge spoke to me and said: "Here have I been stretched out these three years, and men and horses have trampled my back down into my ribs. Must I lie here much longer?"'

'He will have to lie there till he has thrown up the twelve ships of Mark the Rich which he swallowed. Then he may plunge back into the sea and heal his back.'

And the Serpent King closed his eyes, turned round on his other side, and began to snore so loud that the windows rattled.

In all haste the lovely girl helped Vassili out of the chest, and showed him part of his way back. He thanked her very politely, and hurried off.

When he reached the strait the whale asked: 'Have you thought of me?'

'Yes, as soon as I am on the other side I will tell you what you want to know.'

When he was on the other side Vassili said to the whale: 'Throw up those twelve ships of Mark's which you swallowed three years ago.'

The great fish heaved itself up and threw up all the twelve ships and their crews. Then he shook himself for joy, and plunged into the sea.

Vassili went on further till he reached the ferry, where the old man asked: 'Did you think of me?'

'Yes, and as soon as you have ferried me across I will tell you what you want to know.'

When they had crossed over, Vassili said: 'Let the next man who comes stay in the boat, but do you step on shore, push the boat off, and you will be free, and the other man must take your place.

Then Vassili went on further still, and soon came to the old oak tree, pushed it with his foot, and it fell over. There, at the roots, was more gold and silver than even Mark the Rich had.

And now the twelve ships which the whale had thrown up came sailing along and anchored close by. On the deck of the first ship stood the three beggars whom Vassili had met formerly, and they said: 'Heaven has blessed you, Vassili.' Then they vanished away and he never saw them again.

The sailors carried all the gold and silver into the ship, and then they set sail for home with Vassili on board.

Mark was more furious than ever. He had his horses harnessed and drove off himself to see the Serpent King and to complain of the way in which he had been betrayed. When he reached the river he sprang into the ferryboat. The ferryman, however, did not get in but pushed the boat off....

Vassili led a good and happy life with his dear wife, and his kind mother-in-law lived with them. He helped the poor and fed and clothed the hungry and naked and all Mark's riches became his.

For many years Mark has been ferrying people across the river. His face is wrinkled, his hair and beard are snow white, and his eyes are dim; but still he rows on.

The Three Gold Hairs of Old Vsevede
(*Czech Republic*)

It is related that there was once a King who was passionately fond of hunting the wild beasts of his forests. On one occasion he chased a stag so far and so long that he lost his way. Finding himself quite alone and night coming on, he was glad to fall in with the hut of a charcoal-burner.

"Will you be so good as to conduct me to the nearest highway? I will generously reward you for the service."

"I would do it with pleasure," replied the charcoal-burner, "but I have a wife who is about to become a mother, and I cannot leave her alone. On the other hand, why cannot you pass the night with me? Go up into our hay-loft, and rest yourself upon a truss of sweet-smelling hay which you will find there, and to-morrow I will guide you on your way."

A few minutes later the charcoal-burner's wife brought into the world an infant son.

The King was unable to sleep. At midnight he noticed lights moving in the chamber beneath, and, applying his eye to a crack in the floor, he perceived the charcoal-burner sleeping; his wife lying in a half-fainting condition; and, lastly, standing by the new-born child, three old women, dressed in white and holding each a lighted wax candle, who were conversing.

The first said:—

"To this boy I give courage to dare all dangers."

The second said:—

"I will endow him with the faculty of being able to escape all dangers and to be long-lived."

The third said:—

"As for me, I will give him the hand of the daughter just born to the King who is sleeping in the hay-loft over our heads."

With the utterance of the last words, the lights went out and all was silent again.

The King was as much stunned with sorrow and surprise as if he had received a sword's point in his breast. Until dawn, without closing an eye, he lay thinking of how he might prevent the realization of the witch's prediction.

With the first beams of morning light, the infant began to cry. The charcoal-burner rose and, going to his wife's side, found that she was dead.

"Poor little orphan!" he cried, sadly; "what will become of you, bereft of a mother's care?"

"Confide this child to me," said the King; "I will take care of it, and it will find itself well off. As to yourself, I will give you so much money that you shall have no further need to tire yourself by burning charcoal."

The charcoal-burner gave his consent with pleasure, and the King departed, promising to send somebody for the infant. The Queen and the courtiers had, meanwhile, arranged to give the King an agreeable surprise, by announcing to him the birth of a charming little Princess, who had come into the world on the night when the King, her father, saw the three witches. Knitting his brow, the King called one of his attendants to him and said:—

"Go to such and such a place in the forest, to the hut of a charcoal-burner, to whom you will give this money in exchange for a new-born child. Take the brat and, somewhere on your way, drown it. Only remember that if it be not thoroughly done away with, you yourself shall take its place."

The servant received the infant in a basket, and, having reached a foot-bridge over a wide and deep river, he threw the basket and the infant into the stream.

"A good journey to you, son-in-law!" cried the King, on hearing the servant's report of his mission.

The King believed that the child was drowned, but it was neither drowned nor dead; on the contrary, supported by the basket in which it was inclosed, the little one floated gently down the river, as in a cradle, and slept as sweetly as if its mother had sung it to rest.

After awhile the basket came near the hut of a fisherman who, while busy repairing his nets, caught sight of something floating in the water in mid-stream. Quickly jumping into his boat, he rowed out to the object and, having secured it, ran to tell his wife what he had found.

"You have always desired to have a son," he cried; "here is a handsome one brought to us by the river."

The fisherman's wife received the infant with great joy, and tended it as if it were her own. They called it Plavacete[1] because it came to them floating on the waters. Years sped, the little foundling grew up to be a man, and in none of the neighbouring villages was there a youth to compare with him.

Now, it happened one day, in the summer time, that the King rode out unattended. The heat was excessive, and he reined in his steed in front of the fisherman's hut to ask for a glass of cold water. Plavacete brought it out to him; the King looked at him intently, then, turning to the fisherman, said:—

"You have a handsome youth there: is he your son?"

"Yes and no," replied the fisherman. "Twenty years ago, I found a tiny child in a basket floating down the river; I and my wife adopted him."

The King turned pale as death, for he guessed that it was the same infant that he had condemned to be drowned. Collecting himself, he dismounted and said:—

"I want to send a message to the castle, and I have nobody with me; can this youth deliver it?"

"Certainly," replied the fisherman; "your Majesty may rely on his intelligence."

Thereupon the King sat down and wrote to the Queen these words:—

"The young man who brings you this message is the most dangerous of all my enemies. As soon as he arrives, have his head chopped off. Do not delay one moment and have no pity; let him be executed before I return to the castle."

After carefully folding the letter, he fastened it with the Royal seal.

Plavacete took the letter and set off with it through the forest, which was so wide and dense that he lost his way in it. Overtaken by night in the midst of his adventurous journey, he met an old woman.

"Where are you going, Plavacete, where are you going?" she asked.

"I am intrusted with a letter for the Royal castle, but I have lost my way; can you not, good mother, set me on my right road?"

"To-day, my child, that is impossible. Darkness has come, and you would not have time to reach the Royal castle," replied the old woman. "Rest in my dwelling-place to-night—you will not be with a stranger there, for I am your god-mother."

The young man obeyed, and they entered a charming cottage which

---

1 "The Swimmer".

seemed suddenly to rise out of the ground. Now, while Plavacete was sleeping, the old woman changed his letter for another, running thus:—

"Immediately upon receiving this letter, conduct the bearer to the Princess, our daughter. This young man is our son-in-law, and I wish them to be married before my return to the castle. Such is my will."

After reading the letter, the Queen gave orders for the preparation of all that was needed for the celebration of the wedding. Both she and her daughter were greatly pleased with the behaviour of the young man, and nothing troubled the happiness of the newly-married pair.

A few days afterwards the King returned to his castle and, having previously learned what had taken place, began to scold the Queen.

"But you expressly ordered me to have them married before your return: here is your letter—read it again," replied the Queen.

He carefully examined the epistle, and was obliged to admit that the paper, the writing, and the seal were all unquestionably authentic. He thereupon called for his son-in-law, and interrogated him as to the details of his journey.

Plavacete withheld nothing from his father-in-law, and related how he had lost his way in the forest and had passed the night there in a cottage.

"What is this old woman like?" asked the King.

On hearing the description given him by Plavacete, the King was convinced that it was the identical old woman who, twenty years previously, had predicted the marriage of the Princess with the charcoal-burner's son.

After reflecting for awhile, the King went on:—

"What is done is done: only you cannot be my son-in-law on such slight grounds. For a wedding present, you must bring me three hairs plucked from the head of Dede-Vsevede, the old man who knows all and sees all."

He thought by this means to get rid of his son-in-law, whose presence embarrassed him.

Plavecete took leave of his wife departed, saying to himself:—

"I do not know which way to turn my steps; but no matter, my god-mother will direct them."

He was not deceived. Without difficulty he found the right road, and pressed forward for a long time over hill and dale and river, until he reached the shore of the Black Sea, and observed a boat with its one boatman, to whom he said:—

"Heaven bless you, old boatman!"

"The same to you, young traveller. Where do you want to go?"

"To the castle of Dede-Vsevede, to get three hairs from his head."

"If that is so, welcome! I have long awaited the arrival of such an envoy as you. For twenty years I have been rowing passengers across, and not one of them has done anything to deliver me. If you promise me to ask

Dede-Vsevede when I am to have a substitute to free me from my troubles, I will row you over in my boat."

Plavacete promised, and the boatman rowed him to the opposite shore. He thence continued his journey, and approached a great city, which was partially in ruins. Not far from it he saw a funeral procession; the King of the country followed the coffin of his father, and tears as big as peas rolled down his cheeks.

"Heaven console you in your distress," said Plavacete.

"Thanks, good traveller. Whither are you going?"

"To the castle of Dede-Vsevede, in search of three hairs from his head."

"You are really going to the castle of Dede-Vsevede? What a pity you did not come some weeks ago! We have long been waiting such an envoy as you."

Plavacete was introduced to the Court of the King, who said to him:—

"We have learned that you are bound on a mission to the castle of Dede-Vsevede: alas! we had here an apple-tree which produced youth-giving fruit; one only of its apples, as soon as it was eaten, even by a person at the point of death, instantly cured and rejuvenated him. But for the last twenty years this tree has not borne either flower or fruit. Will you promise me to ask the cause of Dede-Vsevede?"

"I promise you."

After that, Plavacete came to a large, beautiful, but silent city. Near the gate he met an old man, who, staff in hand, was hobbling along with great difficulty.

"Heaven bless you, good old man!"

"Heaven bless *you*! Whither are you going, handsome traveller?"

"To the castle of Dede-Vsevede, in search of three hairs from his head."

"Ah! you are the very envoy I have so long been expecting. I must conduct you to my master, the King. Follow me."

As soon as they arrived, the King said to him:—

"I hear that you have come on an embassy to Dede-Vsevede. We had here a well which used to fill itself, and which was so marvellous in its effects that sick people were immediately cured on drinking of its water. A few drops sprinkled upon a corpse sufficed to resuscitate it. Well, for twenty years past, this well has been dried up. If you promise to ask Dede-Vsevede how we can re-fill our well, I will reward you royally."

Plavacete promised, and the King dismissed him graciously.

Continuing his journey, he had to pass through a wide forest, in the midst of which he perceived a broad, grassy plain, full of beautiful flowers, in the centre of which stood a castle built of gold.

It was the palace of Dede-Vsevede, radiant with splendour, looking as if it were made of fire. Plavacete entered it without encountering a single moving creature, except an old woman, half-hidden in a corner spinning.

"Welcome, Plavacete! I am glad to see you here."

It was, once more, his god-mother, the same who had offered him shelter in her forest cottage when he was carrying the King's treacherous message.

"Tell me what brings you here, from so far off?"

"The King will not have me for his son-in-law without being paid for it; so he has sent me here to fetch for him three gold hairs from the head of Dede-Vsevede."

His god-mother burst into laughter, saying:—

"*The* Dede-Vsevede? Why, I am his mother—he is the shining Sun in person! Every morning he is a child; at noon he becomes a man; at evening he withers to the likeness of a decrepit, hundred-year-old man. But I will contrive to get you three gold hairs from his head, so that you may know that I am not your god-mother for nothing. For all that, however, you cannot remain here any longer as you are. My son, the Sun, is endowed with a charitable soul; but, on returning home, he is always hungry, and it would not astonish me if, as soon as he comes back, he ordered you to be roasted for his supper. To hide you I will overturn this empty box, under which you must creep."

Before obeying, Plavacete begged his god-mother to obtain from Dede-Vsevede answers to the three questions which he had promised to get from him.

"I will put the questions to him, but you must carefully listen to the answers he returns."

Suddenly the wind was unchained without, and, through a window on the western side of the castle, arrived the Sun—an old man with a head of gold.

The old man sat down to supper. After the meal was finished, he placed his head of gold upon his mother's knees and fell asleep.

As soon as she saw that he was sleeping soundly, she plucked from his head one of his gold hairs and threw it upon the floor: in falling the hair made a metallic sound, like the string of a guitar when struck.

"What do you want of me, mother?" asked the old man.

"Nothing, my son; I was sleeping and dreaming a strange dream."

"What was it about, mother?"

"I thought I saw a place—I don't know where—where there was a well supplied with water from a spring, by which sick people were cured, and even dying persons, after drinking a single mouthful of it; and more than that, corpses even were resuscitated after having been sprinkled with a few drops of this marvellous water. But for twenty years this well has remained dry: what should be done to fill it as of old?"

"The remedy is simple enough: a frog has lodged itself in the opening, and so prevents the water of the spring entering the well. Let them kill the frog, and their well will be as full of water as it used to be."

When the old man was again soundly sleeping, the old woman plucked another gold hair from his head and threw it upon the floor.

"What do you want of me, mother?"

"Nothing, my son, nothing. While sleeping I had a strange vision. It seemed to me that the inhabitants of a city—what city I do not know—had in their garden an apple-tree, the apples of which possessed the virtue of renewing the youth of whomsoever ate of them. A single apple eaten by an old man sufficed to give back to him the strength and freshness of youth. Now, for twenty years, that tree has borne neither flower nor fruit. By what means can they bring back to it its former power?"

"The means are not difficult. A viper has hidden itself amongst the roots of their tree and feeds on its sap; let them kill the viper and transplant the tree, and they will soon see it covered with fruit as it used to be."

Thereupon the old man once more went off to sleep soundly. The old woman plucked from his head the third gold hair.

"Why do you not let me sleep in peace, mother?" cried the old man, angrily, and trying to rise.

"Lie still, my beloved son, and do not disturb yourself. I am sorry for having waked you. I was having a strange dream. Fancy! I seemed to see a boatman, on the shore of the Black Sea, complaining to a traveller that, for twenty years, nobody had come to replace him: when will that poor old man be relieved of his task?"

"He is an imbecile, that is all! He has only to put his oar into the hand of the first person who wants to be rowed and jump ashore. Whoever receives the oar will replace him as boatman. But leave me in peace, mother, and do not wake me any more; for I have to be up early, first to dry the tears of the Princess, the wife of a charcoal-burner's son. The young creature passes her nights in weeping for her husband, who has been sent by the King, her father, to fetch him three gold hairs from my head."

Next morning the winds were heard howling around the palace of Dede-Vsevede, and instead of an old man, a beautiful child, with hair of gold, awoke on the old woman's knees: it was the divine Sun, who, after taking leave of his mother, flew out of the eastern window of his palace.

The old woman hastened to turn over the box, and said to Plavacete:—

"See! here are the three gold hairs, and you already know the three answers given by Dede-Vsevede. Now hasten away, and Heaven be with you on your way. You will never see me again, for you will never again have need of me."

Plavacete gratefully thanked her and departed.

On reaching the city of the dried-up well, and questioned by the King as to what good news he was the bearer of, he replied:—

"Have your well carefully cleared out; then kill the frog which obstructs the incoming of the marvellous water from the spring, and you will see it flow as freely as ever."

The King followed the direction of Plavacete, and, delighted to see his well once more filled, made him a present of twelve horses as white as swans, to which he added as much gold and silver as they could carry.

On arriving at the second city and questioned by the King as to the news he brought, he replied:—

"The news I bring you is excellent; none could be better, in fact. You have but to dig up your apple-tree and transplant it, after killing the reptile which has been living amongst its roots; that done, your tree will produce you apples as it formerly did."

Indeed, no sooner was the tree transplanted than it became covered with flowers, as if a shower of roses had fallen upon it. The King, filled with joy, made him a present of twelve horses as black as ravens, and loaded them with as much riches as they could bear.

Continuing his journey to the shore of the Black Sea, he found the boatman, who inquired whether he had learnt for him when the time of his deliverance would come. Plavacete first made him convey him and his horses on to the opposite shore: that done, he advised the boatman to hand his oar to the first traveller who required his services, so that he might be definitely released from his duty.

The King, Plavacete's father-in-law, could not at first believe his eyes on seeing him the possessor of the three gold hairs plucked from the head of Dede-Vsevede. As to the young wife, she shed hot tears, not of sadness, but of joy, at seeing her beloved back again in safety, and she said to him:—

"How were you able, dear husband, to acquire so many magnificent horses laden with riches?"

He replied:—

"All has been purchased with heaviness of heart, with the ready money of pains and labours, and services rendered by me. For example, to one King I pointed out the means by which he was able to repossess himself of the Apples of Youth; to another, I showed the secret of re-opening the spring whence flows the water which gives health and life."

"Apples of Youth! Water of Life!" interrupted the King, addressing Plavacete. "I will go in search of those treasures myself! What happiness! After eating one of those rejuvenating apples, I shall return restored to youth! Then I will drink a few drops of the water of immortality—and I shall live forever!"

Without delaying a moment, the King set off in search of those two objects—and down to the present day has never been heard of again.

562: The Spirit in the Blue Light

The Blue Light
(*Germany*)

There was once on a time a soldier who for many years had served the King faithfully, but when the war came to an end could serve no longer because of the many wounds which he had received. The King said to him, "Thou mayst return to thy home, I need thee no longer, and thou wilt not receive any more money, for he only receives wages who renders me service for them." Then the soldier did not know how to earn a living, went away greatly troubled, and walked the whole day, until in the evening he entered a forest. When darkness came on, he saw a light, which he went up to, and came to a house wherein lived a witch. "Do give me one night's lodging, and a little to eat and drink," said he to her, "or I shall starve." "Oho!" she answered, "who gives anything to a run-away soldier? Yet will I be compassionate, and take you in, if you will do what I wish." "What do you wish?" said the soldier. "That you should dig all round my garden for me, tomorrow." The soldier consented, and next day labored with all his strength, but could not finish it by the evening. "I see well enough," said the witch, "that you can do no more to-day, but I will keep you yet another night, in payment for which you must to-morrow chop me a load of wood, and make it small." The soldier spent the whole day in doing it, and in the evening the witch proposed that he should stay one night more. "To-morrow, you shall only do me a very trifling piece of work. Behind my house, there is an old dry well, into which my light has fallen, it burns blue, and never goes out, and you shall bring it up again for me." Next day the old woman took him to the well, and let him down in a basket. He found the blue light, and made her a signal to draw him up again. She did draw him up, but when he came near the edge, she stretched down her hand and wanted to take the blue light away from him. "No," said he, perceiving her evil intention, "I will not give thee the light until I am standing with both feet upon the ground." The witch fell into a passion, let him down again into the well, and went away.

The poor soldier fell without injury on the moist ground, and the blue light went on burning, but of what use was that to him? He saw very well that he could not escape death. He sat for a while very sorrowfully, then suddenly he felt in his pocket and found his tobacco pipe, which was still half full. "This shall be my last pleasure," thought he, pulled it out, lit it at the blue light and began to smoke. When the smoke had circled about the cavern, suddenly a little black dwarf stood before him, and said, "Lord, what are thy commands?" "What commands have I to give thee?" replied the soldier, quite astonished. "I must do everything thou biddest me," said the little man. "Good," said the soldier; "then in the first place help me out of this well." The little man took him by the hand, and led him through an underground passage, but he did not forget to take the blue light with him. On the way the dwarf showed him the treasures which the witch had collected and hidden there, and the soldier took as much gold as he could carry. When he was above, he said to the little man, "Now go and bind the old witch, and carry her before the judge." In a short time she, with frightful cries, came riding by, as swift as the wind on a wild tom-cat, nor was it long after that before the little man re-appeared. "It is all done," said he, "and the witch is already hanging on the gallows. What further commands has my lord?" inquired the dwarf. "At this moment, none," answered the soldier; "Thou canst return home, only be at hand immediately, if I summon thee." "Nothing more is needed than that thou shouldst light thy pipe at the blue light, and I will appear before thee at once." Thereupon he vanished from his sight.

The soldier returned to the town from which he had come. He went to the best inn, ordered himself handsome clothes, and then bade the landlord furnish him a room as handsomely as possible. When it was ready and the soldier had taken possession of it, he summoned the little black mannikin and said, "I have served the King faithfully, but he has dismissed me, and left me to hunger, and now I want to take my revenge." "What am I to do?" asked the little man. "Late at night, when the King's daughter is in bed, bring her here in her sleep, she shall do servant's work for me." The mannikin said, "That is an easy thing for me to do, but a very dangerous thing for you, for if it is discovered, you will fare ill." When twelve o'clock had struck, the door sprang open, and the mannikin carried in the princess. "Aha! art thou there?" cried the soldier, "get to thy work at once! Fetch the broom and sweep the chamber." When she had done this, he ordered her to come to his chair, and then he stretched out his feet and said, "Pull off my boots for me," and then he threw them in her face, and made her pick them up again, and clean and brighten them. She, however, did everything he bade her, without opposition, silently and with half-shut eyes. When the first cock crowed, the mannikin carried her back to the royal palace, and laid her in her bed.

Next morning when the princess arose, she went to her father, and told him that she had had a very strange dream. "I was carried through the streets with the rapidity of lightning," said she, "and taken into a soldier's room, and I had to wait upon him like a servant, sweep his room, clean his boots, and do all kinds of menial work. It was only a dream, and yet I am just as tired as if I really had done everything." "The dream may have been true," said the King, "I will give thee a piece of advice. Fill thy pocket full of peas, and make a small hole in it, and then if thou art carried away again, they will fall out and leave a track in the streets." But unseen by the King, the mannikin was standing beside him when he said that, and heard all. At night when the sleeping princess was again carried through the streets, some peas certainly did fall out of her pocket, but they made no track, for the crafty mannikin had just before scattered peas in every street there was. And again the princess was compelled to do servant's work until cock-crow.

Next morning the King sent his people out to seek the track, but it was all in vain, for in every street poor children were sitting, picking up peas, and saying, "It must have rained peas, last night." "We must think of something else," said the King; "keep thy shoes on when thou goest to bed, and before thou comest back from the place where thou art taken, hide one of them there, I will soon contrive to find it." The black mannikin heard this plot, and at night when the soldier again ordered him to bring the princess, revealed it to him, and told him that he knew of no expedient to counteract this stratagem, and that if the shoe were found in the soldier's house it would go badly with him. "Do what I bid thee," replied the soldier, and again this third night the princess was obliged to work like a servant, but before she went away, she hid her shoe under the bed.

Next morning the King had the entire town searched for his daughter's shoe. It was found at the soldier's, and the soldier himself, who at the entreaty of the dwarf had gone outside the gate, was soon brought back, and thrown into prison. In his flight he had forgotten the most valuable things he had, the blue light and the gold, and had only one ducat in his pocket. And now loaded with chains, he was standing at the window of his dungeon, when he chanced to see one of his comrades passing by. The soldier tapped at the pane of glass, and when this man came up, said to him, "Be so kind as to fetch me the small bundle I have left lying in the inn, and I will give you a ducat for doing it." His comrade ran thither and brought him what he wanted. As soon as the soldier was alone again, he lighted his pipe and summoned the black mannikin. "Have no fear," said the latter to his master. "Go wheresoever they take you, and let them do what they will, only take the blue light with you." Next day the soldier was tried, and though he had done nothing wicked, the judge condemned him to death. When he was led forth to die, he begged a last favor of the King. "What is it?" asked the King. "That I may smoke one more pipe on my way." "Thou mayst smoke three," answered the King, "but do not imagine that I will spare thy life." Then the soldier pulled out his pipe and lighted it at the blue light, and as soon as a few wreaths of smoke had ascended, the mannikin was there with a small cudgel in his hand, and said,

"What does my lord command?" "Strike down to earth that false judge there, and his constable, and spare not the King who has treated me so ill." Then the mannikin fell on them like lightning, darting this way and that way, and whosoever was so much as touched by his cudgel fell to earth, and did not venture to stir again. The King was terrified; he threw himself on the soldier's mercy, and merely to be allowed to live at all, gave him his kingdom for his own, and the princess to wife.

The Tinder-Box
(*Denmark*)

A soldier came marching along the high road—left, right! A left, right! He had his knapsack on his back and a sword by his side, for he had been to the wars and was now returning home.

An old Witch met him on the road. She was very ugly to look at: her under-lip hung down to her breast.

'Good evening, Soldier!' she said. 'What a fine sword and knapsack you have! You are something like a soldier! You ought to have as much money as you would like to carry!'

'Thank you, old Witch,' said the Soldier.

'Do you see that great tree there?' said the Witch, pointing to a tree beside them. 'It is hollow within. You must climb up to the top, and then you will see a hole through which you can let yourself down into the tree. I will tie a rope round your waist, so that I may be able to pull you up again when you call.'

'What shall I do down there?' asked the Soldier.

'Get money!' answered the Witch. 'Listen! When you reach the bottom of the tree you will find yourself in a large hall; it is light there, for there are more than three hundred lamps burning. Then you will see three doors, which you can open—the keys are in the locks. If you go into the first room, you will see a great chest in the middle of the floor with a dog sitting upon it; he has eyes as large as saucers, but you needn't trouble about him. I will give you my blue-check apron, which you must spread out on the floor, and then go back quickly and fetch the dog and set him upon it; open the chest and take as much money as you like. It is copper there. If you would rather have silver, you must go into the next room, where there is a dog with eyes as large as mill-wheels. But don't take any notice of him; just set him upon my apron, and help yourself to the money. If you prefer gold, you can get that too, if you go into the third room, and as much as you like to carry. But the dog that guards the chest there has eyes as large as the Round Tower at Copenhagen! He is a savage dog,

I can tell you; but you needn't be afraid of him either. Only, put him on my apron and he won't touch you, and you can take out of the chest as much gold as you like!'

'Come, this is not bad!' said the Soldier. 'But what am I to give you, old Witch; for surely you are not going to do this for nothing?'

'Yes, I am!' replied the Witch. 'Not a single farthing will I take! For me you shall bring nothing but an old tinder-box which my grandmother forgot last time she was down there.'

'Well, tie the rope round my waist!' said the Soldier.

'Here it is,' said the Witch, 'and here is my blue-check apron.'

Then the Soldier climbed up the tree, let himself down through the hole, and found himself standing, as the Witch had said, underground in the large hall, where the three hundred lamps were burning.

Well, he opened the first door. Ugh! there sat the dog with eyes as big as saucers glaring at him.

'You are a fine fellow!' said the Soldier, and put him on the Witch's apron, took as much copper as his pockets could hold; then he shut the chest, put the dog on it again, and went into the second room. Sure enough there sat the dog with eyes as large as mill-wheels.

'You had better not look at me so hard!' said the Soldier. 'Your eyes will come out of their sockets!'

And then he set the dog on the apron. When he saw all the silver in the chest, he threw away the copper he had taken, and filled his pockets and knapsack with nothing but silver.

Then he went into the third room. Horrors! the dog there had two eyes, each as large as the Round Tower at Copenhagen, spinning round in his head like wheels.

'Good evening!' said the Soldier and saluted, for he had never seen a dog like this before. But when he had examined him more closely, he thought to himself: 'Now then, I've had enough of this!' and put him down on the floor, and opened the chest. Heavens! what a heap of gold there was! With all that he could buy up the whole town, and all the sugar pigs, all the tin soldiers, whips and rocking-horses in the whole world. Now he threw away all the silver with which he had filled his pockets and knapsack, and filled them with gold instead—yes, all his pockets, his knapsack, cap and boots even, so that he could hardly walk. Now he was rich indeed. He put the dog back upon the chest, shut the door, and then called up through the tree:

'Now pull me up again, old Witch!'

'Have you got the tinder-box also?' asked the Witch.

'Botheration!' said the Soldier, 'I had clean forgotten it!' And then he went back and fetched it.

The Witch pulled him up, and there he stood again on the high road, with pockets, knapsack, cap and boots filled with gold.

'What do you want to do with the tinder-box?' asked the Soldier.

'That doesn't matter to you,' replied the Witch. 'You have got your money, give me my tinder-box.'

'We'll see!' said the Soldier. 'Tell me at once what you want to do with it, or I will draw my sword, and cut off your head!'

'No!' screamed the Witch.

The Soldier immediately cut off her head. That was the end of her! But he tied up all his gold in her apron, slung it like a bundle over his shoulder, put the tinder-box in his pocket, and set out towards the town.

It was a splendid town! He turned into the finest inn, ordered the best chamber and his favourite dinner; for now that he had so much money he was really rich.

It certainly occurred to the servant who had to clean his boots that they were astonishingly old boots for such a rich lord. But that was because he had not yet bought new ones; next day he appeared in respectable boots and fine clothes. Now, instead of a common soldier he had become a noble lord, and the people told him about all the grand doings of the town and the King, and what a beautiful Princess his daughter was.

'How can one get to see her?' asked the Soldier.

'She is never to be seen at all!' they told him; 'she lives in a great copper castle, surrounded by many walls and towers! No one except the King may go in or out, for it is prophesied that she will marry a common soldier, and the King cannot submit to that.'

'I should very much like to see her,' thought the Soldier; but he could not get permission.

Now he lived very gaily, went to the theatre, drove in the King's garden, and gave the poor a great deal of money, which was very nice of him; he had experienced in former times how hard it is not to have a farthing in the world. Now he was rich, wore fine clothes, and made many friends, who all said that he was an excellent man, a real nobleman. And the Soldier liked that. But as he was always spending money, and never made any more, at last the day came when he had nothing left but two shillings, and he had to leave the beautiful rooms in which he had been living, and go into a little attic under the roof, and clean his own boots, and mend them with a darning-needle. None of his friends came to visit him there, for there were too many stairs to climb.

It was a dark evening, and he could not even buy a light. But all at once it flashed across him that there was a little end of tinder in the tinder-box, which he had taken from the hollow tree into which the Witch had helped him down. He found the box with the tinder in it; but just as he was kindling a light, and had struck a spark out of the tinder-box, the door burst open, and the dog with eyes as large as saucers, which he had seen down in the tree, stood before him and said:

'What does my lord command?'

'What's the meaning of this?' exclaimed the Soldier. 'This is a pretty kind of tinder-box, if I can get whatever I want like this. Get me money!' he cried to the dog, and hey, presto! he was off and back again, holding a great purse full of money in his mouth.

Now the Soldier knew what a capital tinder-box this was. If he rubbed once, the dog that sat on the chest of copper appeared; if he rubbed twice, there came the dog that watched over the silver chest; and if he rubbed three times, the one that guarded the gold appeared. Now, the Soldier went down again to his beautiful rooms, and appeared once more in splendid clothes. All his friends immediately recognised him again, and paid him great court.

One day he thought to himself: 'It is very strange that no one can get to see the Princess. They all say she is very pretty, but what's the use of that if she has to sit forever in the great copper castle with all the towers? Can I not manage to see her somehow? Where is my tinder-box?' and so he struck a spark, and, presto! there came the dog with eyes as large as saucers.

'It is the middle of the night, I know,' said the Soldier; 'but I should very much like to see the Princess for a moment.'

The dog was already outside the door, and before the Soldier could look round, in he came with the Princess. She was lying asleep on the dog's back, and was so beautiful that anyone could see she was a real Princess. The Soldier really could not refrain from kissing her—he was such a thorough Soldier. Then the dog ran back with the Princess. But when it was morning, and the King and Queen were drinking tea, the Princess said that the night before she had had such a strange dream about a dog and a Soldier: she had ridden on the dog's back, and the Soldier had kissed her.

'That is certainly a fine story,' said the Queen. But the next night one of the ladies-in-waiting was to watch at the Princess's bed, to see if it was only a dream, or if it had actually happened.

The Soldier had an overpowering longing to see the Princess again, and so the dog came in the middle of the night and fetched her, running as fast as he could. But the lady-in-waiting slipped on india-rubber shoes and followed them. When she saw them disappear into a large house, she thought to herself: 'Now I know where it is;' and made a great cross on the door with a piece of chalk. Then she went home and lay down, and the dog came back also, with the Princess. But when he saw that a cross had been made on the door of the house where the Soldier lived, he took a piece of chalk also, and made crosses on all the doors in the town; and that was very clever, for now the lady-in-waiting could not find the right house, as there were crosses on all the doors.

Early next morning the King, Queen, ladies-in-waiting, and officers came out to see where the Princess had been.

'There it is!' said the King, when he saw the first door with a cross on it.

'No, there it is, my dear!' said the Queen, when she likewise saw a door with a cross.

'But here is one, and there is another!' they all exclaimed; wherever they looked there was a cross on the door. Then they realised that the sign would not help them at all.

But the Queen was an extremely clever woman, who could do a great deal more than just drive in a coach. She took her great golden scissors, cut up a piece of silk, and made a pretty little bag of it. This she filled with the finest buckwheat grains, and tied it round the Princess' neck; this done, she cut a little hole in the bag, so that the grains would strew the whole road wherever the Princess went.

In the night the dog came again, took the Princess on his back and ran away with her to the Soldier, who was very much in love with her, and would have liked to have been a Prince, so that he might have had her for his wife.

The dog did not notice how the grains were strewn right from the castle to the Soldier's window, where he ran up the wall with the Princess.

In the morning the King and the Queen saw plainly where their daughter had been, and they took the Soldier and put him into prison.

There he sat. Oh, how dark and dull it was there! And they told him: 'To-morrow you are to be hanged.' Hearing that did not exactly cheer him, and he had left his tinder-box in the inn.

Next morning he could see through the iron grating in front of his little window how the people were hurrying out of the town to see him hanged. He heard the drums and saw the soldiers marching; all the people were running to and fro. Just below his window was a shoemaker's apprentice, with leather apron and shoes; he was skipping along so merrily that one of his shoes flew off and fell against the wall, just where the Soldier was sitting peeping through the iron grating.

'Oh, shoemaker's boy, you needn't be in such a hurry!' said the Soldier to him. 'There's nothing going on till I arrive. But if you will run back to the house where I lived, and fetch me my tinder-box, I will give you four shillings. But you must put your best foot foremost.'

The shoemaker's boy was very willing to earn four shillings, and fetched the tinder-box, gave it to the Soldier, and—yes—now you shall hear.

Outside the town a great scaffold had been erected, and all round were standing the soldiers, and hundreds of thousands of people. The King and Queen were sitting on a magnificent throne opposite the judges and the whole council.

The Soldier was already standing on the top of the ladder; but when they wanted to put the rope round his neck, he said that the fulfilment of one innocent request was always granted to a poor criminal before he underwent his punishment. He would so much like to smoke a small pipe of tobacco; it would be his last pipe in this world.

The King could not refuse him this, and so he took out his tinder-box, and rubbed it once, twice, three times. And lo, and behold I there stood all three dogs—the one with eyes as large as saucers, the second with eyes as large as mill-wheels, and the third with eyes each as large as the Round Tower of Copenhagen.

'Help me now, so that I may not be hanged!' cried the Soldier. And thereupon the dogs fell upon the judges and the whole council, seized some by the legs, others by the nose, and threw them so high into the air that they fell and were smashed into pieces.

'I won't stand this!' said the King; but the largest dog seized him too, and the Queen as well, and threw them up after the others. This frightened the soldiers, and all the people cried: 'Good Soldier, you shall be our King, and marry the beautiful Princess!'

Then they put the Soldier into the King's coach, and the three dogs danced in front, crying 'Hurrah!' And the boys whistled and the soldiers presented arms.

The Princess came out of the copper castle, and became Queen; and that pleased her very much.

The wedding festivities lasted for eight days, and the dogs sat at table and made eyes at everyone.

Lars, My Lad!
(*Sweden*)

There was once a prince or a duke, or something of that sort, but at any rate he belonged to a very grand family, and he would not stop at home. So he traveled all over the world, and wherever he went he was well liked, and was received in the best and gayest families, for he had no end of money. He made friends and acquaintances, as you may imagine, wherever he went, for he who has a well-filled trough is sure to fall in with pigs who want to have their fill. But he went on spending his money until he came to want, and at last his purse became so empty that he had not even a farthing left. And now there was an end to all his friends as well, for they behaved like the pigs; when the trough was empty and he had no more to give them, they began to grunt and grin, and then they ran away in all directions. There he stood alone with a long face. Everybody had been so willing to help him to get rid of his money, but nobody would help him in return; and so there was nothing for it but to trudge home and beg for crusts on the way.

So late one evening he came to a great forest. He did not know where he should find a shelter for the night, but he went on looking and searching till he caught sight of an old tumble-down hut, which stood in the middle of some bushes. It was not exactly good enough for such a fine cavalier, but when you cannot get what you want you must take what you can get. And, since there was no help for it, he went into the hut.

Not a living soul was to be seen; there was not even a stool to sit upon, but alongside the wall stood a big chest. What could there be inside that chest? If only there were some bits of moldy bread in it! How nice they would taste! For, you must know, he had not had a single bit of food the whole day, and he was so hungry and his stomach so empty that it groaned with pain. He lifted the lid, but inside the chest there was another chest, and inside that chest there was another; and so it went on, each one smaller than the other, until they became quite tiny boxes. The more there were the harder he worked away, for there must be something very fine inside, he thought, since it was so well hidden.

At last he came to a tiny, little box, and in this box lay a bit of paper—and that was all he got for his trouble! It was very annoying, of course, but then he discovered there was something written on the paper, and when he looked at it he was just able to spell it out, although at first it looked somewhat difficult.

"Lars, my lad!"

As he pronounced these words something answered right in his ear, "What are master's orders?"

He looked round, but he saw nobody. This was very funny, he thought, and so he read out the words once more, "Lars, my lad!"

And the answer came as before, "What are master's orders?"

But he did not see anybody this time either.

"If there is anybody about who hears what I say, then be kind enough to bring me something to eat," he said. And the next moment there stood a table laid out with all the best things one could think of. He set to work to eat and drink, and had a proper fill. He had never enjoyed himself so much in all his life, he thought.

When he had eaten all he could get down, he began to feel sleepy, and so he took out the paper again, "Lars, my lad!"

"What are master's orders?"

"Well, you have given me food and drink, and now you must get me a bed to sleep in as well. But I want a really fine bed," he said, for you must know he was a little more bold now that his hunger was stayed. Well, there it stood, a bed so fine and dainty that even the king himself might covet it. Now this was all very well in its way, but when once you are well off you wish for still more, and he had no sooner got into bed than he began to think that the room was altogether too wretched for such a grand bed. So he took out the paper again: "Lars, my lad!"

"What are master's orders?"

"Since you are able to get me such food and such a bed here in the midst of the wild forest, I suppose you can manage to get me a better room, for you see I am accustomed to sleep in a palace, with golden mirrors and draped walls and ornaments and comforts of all kinds," he said.

Well, he had no sooner spoken the words than he found himself lying in the grandest chamber anybody had ever seen. Now he was comfortable, he thought, and felt quite satisfied as he turned his face to the wall and closed his eyes. But that was not all the grandeur; for when he woke up in the morning and looked round, he saw it was a big palace he had been sleeping in. One room led into the other, and wherever he went the place was full of all sorts of finery and luxuries, both on the walls and on the ceilings, and they glittered so much when the sun shone on them that he had to shade his eyes with his hand, so strong was the glare of gold and silver wherever he turned. He then happened to look out of the window. Good gracious! How grand it was! There was something else than pine forests and juniper bushes to look at, for there was the finest garden anyone could wish for, with splendid trees and roses of all kinds. But he could not see a single human being, or even a cat; and that, you know, was rather lonely, for otherwise he had everything so grand and had been set up as his own master again.

So he took out the bit of paper: "Lars, my lad!"

"What are master's orders?"

"Well, now you have given me food and bed and a palace to live in, I intend to remain here, for I like the place," he said, "yet I don't like to live quite by myself. I must have both lads and lasses whom I may order about to wait on me," he said.

And there they were. There came servants and stewards and scullery maids and chambermaids of all sorts, and some came bowing and some curtseying. So now the duke thought he was really satisfied. But now it happened that there was a large palace on the other side of the forest, and there the king lived who owned the forest, and the great, big fields around it. As he was walking up and down in his room he happened to look out through the window and saw the new palace, where the golden weathercocks were swinging to and fro on the roof in the sunlight, dazzling his eyes.

"This is very strange," he thought; and so he called his courtiers. They came rushing in, and began bowing and scraping. "Do you see the palace over there?" said the king.

They opened their eyes and began to stare. Yes, of course, they saw it.

"Who is it that has dared to build such a palace on my grounds?" said the king.

They bowed, and they scraped with their feet, but they did not know anything about it. The king then called his generals and captains. They came, stood at attention and presented arms. "Be gone, soldiers and troopers," said the king, "and pull down the palace over there, and hang him who has built it; and don't lose any time about it!"

Well, they set off in great haste to arm themselves, and away they went. The drummers beat the skins of their drums, and the trumpeters blew their trumpets, and the other musicians played and blew as best they could, so that the duke heard them long before he could see them.

But he had heard this kind of noise before, and knew what it meant, so he took out his scrap of paper: "Lars, my lad!"

"What are master's orders?"

"There are soldiers coming here," he said, "and now you must provide me with soldiers and horses, that I may have double as many as those over in the wood, and with sabers and pistols, and guns and cannons with all that belongs to them; but be quick about it."

And no time was lost; for when the duke looked out, he saw an immense number of soldiers, who were drawn up around the palace. When the king's men arrived, they came to a sudden halt and dared not advance. But the duke was not afraid; he went straight up to the colonel of the king's soldiers and asked him what he wanted. The colonel told him his errand.

"It's of no use," said the duke. "You see how many men I have; and if the king will listen to me, we shall become good friends, and I will help him against his enemies, and in such a way that it will be heard of far and wide," he said.

The colonel was of the same opinion, and the duke then invited him and all his soldiers inside the palace, and the men had more than one glass to drink and plenty of everything to eat as well. But while they were eating and drinking they began talking; and the duke then got to hear that the king had a daughter who was his only child, and was so wonderfully fair and beautiful that no one had ever seen her like before. And the more the king's soldiers ate and drank the more they thought she would suit the duke for a wife. And they went on talking so long that the duke at last began to be of the same opinion.

"The worst of it," said the soldiers, "is that she is just as proud as she is beautiful, and will never look at a man."

But the duke laughed at this. "If that's all," said the duke, "there's sure to be a remedy for that complaint."

When the soldiers had eaten and drunk as much as they could find room for, they shouted "Hurrah!" so that it echoed among the hills, and then they set out homeward. But, as you may imagine, they did not walk exactly in parade order, for they were rather unsteady about the knees, and many of them did not carry their guns in regulation manner. The duke asked them to greet the king from him. He would call on him the following day, he said. When the duke was alone again, he began to think of the princess, and to wonder if she were as beautiful and fair as they had made her out to be. He would like to make sure of it; and as so many strange things had happened that day it might not be impossible to find that out as well, he thought.

"Lars, my lad!"

"What are master's orders?"

"Well, now you must bring me the king's daughter as soon as she has gone to sleep," he said; "but she must not be awakened either on the way here or back. Do you hear that?" he said.

And before long the princess was lying on the bed. She slept so soundly and looked so wonderfully beautiful as she lay there. Yes, she was as sweet as sugar, I can tell you. The duke walked round about her, but she was just as beautiful from whatever point of view he looked at her. The more he looked the more he liked her.

"Lars, my lad!"

"What are master's orders?"

"You must now carry the princess home," he said, "for now I know how she looks and tomorrow I will ask for her hand," he said.

Next morning the king looked out of the window. "I suppose I shall not be troubled with the sight of that palace anymore," he thought. But, zounds! There it stood just as on the day before, and the sun shone so brightly on the roof, and the weathercocks dazzled his eyes. He now became furious, and called all his men. They came quicker than usual. The courtiers bowed and scraped, and the soldiers stood at attention and presented arms. "Do you see the palace there?" screamed the king. They stretched their necks, and stared and gaped. Yes, of course, that they did. "Have I not ordered you to pull down the palace and hang the builder?" he said.

Yes, they could not deny that; but then the colonel himself stepped forward and reported what had happened and how many soldiers the duke had, and how wonderfully grand the palace was. And next he told him what the duke had said, and how he had asked him to give his greetings to the king, and all that sort of thing. The king felt quite confused, and had to put his crown on the table and scratch his head. He could not understand all this, although he was a king; for he could take his oath it had all been built in a single night; and if the duke were not the evil one himself, he must in any case have done it by magic.

While he sat pondering, the princess came into the room. "Good morning to you, father!" she said. "Just fancy, I had such a strange and beautiful dream last night!" she said.

"What did you dream then, my girl?" said the king.

"I dreamed I was in the new palace over yonder, and that I saw a duke there, so fine and handsome that I could never have imagined the like; and now I want to get married, father," she said.

"Do you want to get married?—you, who never cared to look at a man! That's very strange!" said the king.

"That may be." Said the princess; "but it's different now, and I want to get married, and it's the duke I want," she said.

The king was quite beside himself, so frightened did he become of the duke. But all of a sudden he heard a terrible noise of drums and trumpets and instruments of all kinds; and then came a message that the duke had just arrived with a large company, all of whom were so grandly dressed that gold and silver glistened in every fold. The king put on his crown and his coronation robes, and then went out on the steps to receive them. And the princess was not slow to follow him. The duke bowed most graciously, and the king of course did likewise, and when they had talked awhile about their affairs and their grandeur they became the best of friends. A great banquet was then prepared, and the duke was placed next to the princess at the table. What they talked about is not easy to tell, but the duke spoke so well for himself that the princess could not very well say "No" to anything he said, and then he went up to the king and asked for her hand. The king could not exactly say "No" either, for he could very well see that the duke was a person with whom it was best to be on friendly terms; but give his sanction there and then, he could not very well do that either. He wanted to see the duke's palace first, and find out about the state of affairs over there, as you may understand.

So it was arranged that he should visit the duke and take the princess with him to see his palace; and with this they parted company. When the duke returned home, Lars became busier than ever, for there was so much to attend to. But he set to work and strove hard; and when the king and his daughter arrived everything was so magnificent and splendid that no words can describe it. They went through all the rooms and looked about, and they found everything as it should be, and even still more splendid, thought the king, and so he was quite pleased. The wedding then took place, and that in grand style; and on the duke's arrival home with his bride he, too, gave a great feast, and then there was an end to the festivities.

Some time passed by, and one evening the duke heard these words: "Are you satisfied now?"

It was Lars, as you may guess, but the duke could not see him. "Well, I ought to be," said the duke. "You have provided me with everything I have," he said.

"Yes, but what have I got in return?" asked Lars.

"Nothing," said the duke; "but, bless me, what could I have given you, who are not of flesh and blood, and whom I cannot see either?" he said. "But if there is anything I can do for you, tell me what it is, and I shall do it."

"Well, I should like to ask you for that little scrap of paper which you found in the chest," said Lars. "Nothing else?" said the duke. "If such a trifle can help you, I can easily do without it, for now I begin to know the words by heart," he said.

Lars thanked the duke, and asked him to put the paper on the chair in front of the bed when he retired to rest, and he would be sure to fetch it during the night. The duke did as he was told; and so he and the princess lay down and went to sleep. But early in the morning the duke awoke and felt so cold that his teeth chattered, and when he had got his eyes quite open he found that he was quite naked and had not even as much as a thread on his back; and instead of the grand bed and the beautiful bedroom, and the magnificent palace, he lay on the big chest in the old tumble-down hut.

He began to shout, "Lars, my lad!"

But he got no answer. He shouted once more, "Lars, my lad!"

But he got no answer this time either. So he shouted all he could, "Lars, my lad!"

But it was all in vain. Now he began to understand how matters stood. When Lars had got the scrap of paper he was freed from service at the same time, and now he had taken everything with him. But there was no help for it. There stood the duke in the old hut quite naked; and as for the princess she was not much better off, although she had her clothes on, for she had got them from her father, so Lars had no power over them. The duke had now to tell the princess everything, and ask her to leave him. He would have to manage as best he could, he said. But she would not hear of it. She well remembered what the parson had said when he married them, and she would never, never leave him, she said.

In the meantime the king in his palace had also awakened, and when he looked out of the window he did not see any sign whatever of the other palace where his daughter and son-in-law lived. He became uneasy, as you may imagine, and called his courtiers. They came in, and began to bow and scrape.

"Do you see the palace over yonder behind the forest?" he asked. They stretched their necks and stared with all their might. No, they did not see it.

"Where had it gone to, then?" asked the king. Well, really they did not know. It was not long before the king set out with all his court through the forest; and when he arrived at the place where the palace with the beautiful gardens should have been, he could not see anything but heather and juniper bushes and firs. But then he discovered the old tumble-down hut, which stood there among the bushes. He entered the hut and—mercy on us!—what a sight met his eyes! There stood his son-in-law, quite naked, and his daughter, who had not very many clothes on either, and who was crying and moaning.

"Dear, dear! what does all this mean?" said the king; but he did not get any answer, for the duke would rather have died than tell him. The king did his utmost to get him to speak; but in spite of all the king's promises and threats the duke remained obstinate and would not utter a word.

The king then became angry; and no wonder, for now he could see that this grand duke was not what he pretended to be, and so he ordered the duke to be hanged, and that without any loss of time. The princess begged and prayed for mercy; but neither prayers nor tears were of any help now; for an impostor he was, and as an impostor he should die, said the king. And so it had to be. They erected a gallows, and placed the rope round the duke's neck. But while they were getting the gallows ready, the princess got hold of the hangman, and gave both him and his assistant some money, that they should so manage the hanging of the duke that he should not lose his life, and in the night they were to cut him down, so that he and the princess might then flee the country. And that's how the matter was arranged.

In the meantime they had strung up the duke, and the king and his court and all the people went their way. The duke was now in great straits. He had, however, plenty of time to reflect how foolish he had been in not saving some of the crumbs when he was living in plenty, and how unpardonably stupid he had been in letting Lars have the scrap of paper. This vexed him more than all. If only he had it again, he thought, they should see he had been gaining some sense in return for all he had lost. But it is of little use snarling if you haven't got any teeth.

"Ah, well, well!" he sighed, and so he dangled his legs, which was really all he could do. The day passed slowly and tediously for him, and he was not at all displeased when he saw the sun setting behind the forest. But just before it disappeared he heard a fearful shouting, and when he looked down the hill, he saw seven cartloads of worn-out shoes, and on the top of the hindmost cart he saw a little old man in gray clothes and with a red pointed cap on his head. His face was like that of the worst scarecrow, and the rest of him was not very handsome either.

He drove straight up to the gallows, and when he arrived right under it he stopped and looked up at the duke, and then burst out laughing, the ugly old fellow! "How stupid you were!" he said; "but what should the fool do with his stupidity if he did not make use of it?" And then he laughed again. "Yes, there you are hanging now, and here am I carting away all the shoes I have worn out for your whims. I wonder if you can read what is written on this bit of paper, and if you recognize it?" he said with an ugly laugh, holding up the paper before the duke's eyes.

But all who hang are not dead, and this time it was Lars who was befooled. The duke made a clutch, and snatched the paper from him.

"Lars, my lad!"

"What are master's orders?"

"Well, you must cut me down from the gallows and put the palace and all the rest in its place again, exactly as it was before, and when the night has set in you must bring back the princess."

All went merrily as in a dance, and before long everything was in its place, just as it was when Lars took himself off. When the king awoke the next morning he looked out of the window, as was his custom, and there stood the palace again, with the weathercocks glittering so beautifully in the sunshine. He called his courtiers, and they came and began to bow and scrape. They stretched their necks as far as they could, and stared and gaped.

"Do you see the palace over there?" said the king. Yes, of course, they did. The king then sent for the princess, but she was not to be found. He then went out to see if his son-in-law was still hanging on the gallows, but neither son-in-law nor gallows was to be seen. He had to lift off his crown and scratch his head. But that did not improve matters; he could not make head or tail of either one thing or the other. He set off at once with all his court through the forest, and when he came to the place where the palace should stand, there it stood sure enough. The gardens and the roses were exactly as they used to be, and the duke's people were to be seen everywhere among the trees. His son-in-law and his daughter received him on the steps, dressed in their finest clothes.

"Well, I never saw the like of this," said the king to himself; he could scarcely believe his own eyes, so wonderful did it all seem to him.

"God's peace be with you, father, and welcome here!" said the duke.

The king stood staring at him. "Are you my son-in-law?" he asked.

"Well, I suppose I am," said the duke. "Who else should I be?"

"Did I not order you to be hanged yesterday like any common thief?" said the king.

"I think you must have been bewitched on the way," said the duke, with a laugh. "Do you think I am the man to let myself be hanged? Or is there anyone here who dares to believe it?" he said, and looked so fiercely at the courtiers that they felt as if they were being pierced through and through. They bowed and scraped and cringed before him. Who could believe such a thing? Was it at all likely?

"Well, if there is anyone who dares to say the king could have wished me such evil, let him speak out," said the duke, and fixed his eyes upon them still more fiercely than before. They went on bowing and scraping and cringing. How could anyone dare say such a thing? No, they had more sense than that, they should hope. The king did not know what to believe, for when he looked at the duke he thought he never could have wished him such evil; but still he was not quite convinced.

"Did I not come here yesterday, and was not the whole palace gone, and was there not an old hut in its place? And did not I go into that hut, and did not you stand stark naked right before my eyes?" he asked.

"I wonder the king can talk so," said the duke. "I think the trolls must have bewitched your eyes in the forest and made you quite crazy; or what do you think?" he said, and turned round to the courtiers. They bowed and bowed till their backs were bent double, and agreed with everything he said, there could be no mistake about that. The king rubbed his eyes, and looked round about him.

"I suppose it is as you say, then," he said to the duke, "and it is well I have got back my proper sight and have come to my senses again. For it would have been a sin and a shame if I had let you be hanged," he said; and so he was happy again, and nobody thought any more about the matter.

"Once bitten, twice shy," as the proverb says; and the duke now took upon himself to manage and look after most of his affairs, so that it was seldom Lars had to wear out his shoes. The king soon gave the duke half the kingdom into the bargain; so he had now plenty to do, and people said they would have to search a long time to find his equal in wise and just ruling.

Then one day Lars came to the duke, looking very little better than the first time he had seen him; but he was, of course, more humble, and did not dare giggle and make grimaces. "You do not want my help any longer, now," he said; "for although I did wear out my shoes at first, I am now unable to wear out a single pair, and my feet will soon be covered all over with moss. So I thought I might now get my leave of absence," he said.

The duke quite agreed with him. "I have tried to spare you, and I almost think I could do without you," he said. "But the palace and all the rest I do not want to lose, for such a clever builder as you I shall never get again; nor do I ever want to adorn the gallows again, as you can well understand; so I cannot give you back the paper on any account," he said.

"Well, as long as you have got it, I need not fear," said Lars; "but if anybody else should get hold of it there will be nothing but running and trudging about again, and that's what I want to avoid; for when one has been tramping about for a thousand years, as I have done, one begins to get tired of it," he said.

But they went on talking, and at last they agreed that the duke should put the paper in the box, and then bury it seven ells under the ground, under a stone fixed in the earth. They then gave mutual thanks for the time they had spent in each other's company, and so they parted. The duke carried out his part of the agreement, for he was not likely to want to change it. He lived happy and contented with the princess, and they had both sons and daughters. When the king died, he got the whole of the kingdom, and you may guess he was none the worse off for that; and there no doubt he still lives and reigns, if he is not dead. But as for the box with the scrap of paper in it, there are many who are still running about looking for it.

565: The Magic Mill

Why the Sea Is Salt

Why the Sea Is Salt
(*Norway*)

Once on a time, but it was a long, long time ago, there were two brothers, one rich and one poor. Now, one Christmas eve, the poor one hadn't so much as a crumb in the house, either of meat or bread, so he went to his brother to ask him for something to keep Christmas with, in God's name. It was not the first time his brother had been forced to help him, and you may fancy he wasn't very glad to see his face, but he said:

"If you will do what I ask you to do, I'll give you a whole flitch of bacon."

So the poor brother said he would do anything, and was full of thanks.

"Well, here is the flitch", said the rich brother, "and now go straight to Hell."

"What I have given my word to do, I must stick to", said the other; so he took the flitch and set off. He walked the whole day, and at dusk he came to a place where he saw a very bright light.

"Maybe this is the place", said the man to himself. So he turned aside, and the first thing he saw was an old, old man, with a long white beard, who stood in an outhouse, hewing wood for the Christmas fire.

"Good even", said the man with the flitch.

"The same to you; whither are you going so late?" said the man.

"Oh! I'm going to Hell, if I only knew the right way", answered the poor man.

"Well, you're not far wrong, for this is Hell", said the old man; "when you get inside they will be all for buying your flitch, for meat is scarce in Hell; but mind, you don't sell it unless you get the hand-quern[1] which stands behind the door for it. When you come out, I'll teach you how to handle the quern, for it's good to grind almost anything."

So the man with the flitch thanked the other for his good advice, and gave a great knock at the Devil's door.

When he got in, everything went just as the old man had said. All the devils, great and small, came swarming up to him like ants round an anthill, and each tried to outbid the other for the flitch.

"Well!" said the man, "by rights my old dame and I ought to have this flitch for our Christmas dinner; but since you have all set your hearts on it, I suppose I must give it up to you; but if I sell it at all, I'll have for it

---

1 A hand-mill.

that quern behind the door yonder."

At first the Devil wouldn't hear of such a bargain, and chaffered and haggled with the man; but he stuck to what he said, and at last the Devil had to part with his quern. When the man got out into the yard, he asked the old woodcutter how he was to handle the quern; and after he had learned how to use it, he thanked the old man and went off home as fast as he could, but still the clock had struck twelve on Christmas eve before he reached his own door.

"Wherever in the world have you been?" said his old dame, "here have I sat hour after hour waiting and watching, without so much as two sticks to lay together under the Christmas brose."[1]

"Oh!" said the man, "I couldn't get back before, for I had to go a long way first for one thing, and then for another; but now you shall see what you shall see."

So he put the quern on the table, and bade it first of all grind lights, then a table-cloth, then meat, then ale, and so on till they had got everything that was nice for Christmas fare. He had only to speak the word, and the quern ground out what he wanted. The old dame stood by blessing her stars, and kept on asking where he had got this wonderful quern, but he wouldn't tell her.

"It's all one where I got it from; you see the quern is a good one, and the mill-stream never freezes, that's enough."

So he ground meat and drink and dainties enough to last out till Twelfth Day, and on the third day he asked all his friends and kin to his house, and gave a great feast. Now, when his rich brother saw all that was on the table, and all that was behind in the larder, he grew quite spiteful and wild, for he couldn't bear that his brother should have anything.

"'Twas only on Christmas eve", he said to the rest, "he was in such straits, that he came and asked for a morsel of food in God's name, and now he gives a feast as if he were count or king"; and he turned to his brother and said:

"But whence, in Hell's name, have you got all this wealth?"

"From behind the door", answered the owner of the quern, for he didn't care to let the cat out of the bag. But later on the evening, when he had got a drop too much, he could keep his secret no longer, and brought out the quern and said:

"There, you see what has gotten me all this wealth"; and so he made the quern grind all kind of things. When his brother saw it, he set his heart on having the quern, and, after a deal of coaxing, he got it; but he had to pay three hundred dollars for it, and his brother bargained to keep it till hay-harvest, for he thought, if I keep it till then, I can make it grind meat

1 Porridge.

and drink that will last for years. So you may fancy the quern didn't grow rusty for want of work, and when hay-harvest came, the rich brother got it, but the other took care not to teach him how to handle it.

It was evening when the rich brother got the quern home, and next morning he told his wife to go out into the hay-field and toss, while the mowers cut the grass, and he would stay at home and get the dinner ready. So, when dinner-time drew near, he put the quern on the kitchen table and said:

"Grind herrings and broth, and grind them good and fast."

So the quern began to grind herrings and broth; first of all, all the dishes full, then all the tubs full, and so on till the kitchen floor was quite covered. Then the man twisted and twirled at the quern to get it to stop, but for all his twisting and fingering the quern went on grinding, and in a little while the broth rose so high that the man was like to drown. So he threw open the kitchen door and ran into the parlour, but it wasn't long before the quern had ground the parlour full too, and it was only at the risk of his life that the man could get hold of the latch of the house door through the stream of broth. When he got the door open, he ran out and set off down the road, with the stream of herrings and broth at his heels, roaring like a waterfall over the whole farm. Now, his old dame, who was in the field tossing hay, thought it a long time to dinner, and at last she said:

"Well! though the master doesn't call us home, we may as well go. Maybe he finds it hard work to boil the broth, and will be glad of my help."

The men were willing enough, so they sauntered homewards; but just as they had got a little way up the hill, what should they meet but herrings, and broth, and bread, all running and dashing, and splashing together in a stream, and the master himself running before them for his life, and as he passed them he bawled out:

"Would to heaven each of you had a hundred throats! but take care you're not drowned in the broth."

Away he went, as though the Evil One were at his heels, to his brother's house, and begged him for God's sake to take back the quern that instant; for, said he:

"If it grinds only one hour more, the whole parish will be swallowed up by herrings and broth."

But his brother wouldn't hear of taking it back till the other paid him down three hundred dollars more.

So the poor brother got both the money and the quern, and it wasn't long before he set up a farm-house far finer than the one in which his brother lived, and with the quern he ground so much gold that he covered it with plates of gold; and as the farm lay by the sea-side, the golden house gleamed and glistened far away over the sea. All who sailed by put ashore to see the rich man in the golden house, and to see the wonderful quern, the fame of which spread far and wide, till there was nobody who hadn't heard tell of it.

So one day there came a skipper who wanted to see the quern; and the first thing he asked was if it could grind salt.

"Grind salt!" said the owner; "I should just think it could. It can grind anything."

When the skipper heard that, he said he must have the quern, cost what it would; for if he only had it, he thought he should be rid of his long voyages across stormy seas for a lading of salt. Well, at first the man wouldn't hear of parting with the quern; but the skipper begged and prayed so hard, that at last he let him have it, but he had to pay many, many thousand dollars for it. Now, when the skipper had got the quern on his back, he soon made off with it, for he was afraid lest the man should change his mind; so he had no time to ask how to handle the quern, but got on board his ship as fast as he could, and set sail. When he had sailed a good way off, he brought the quern on deck and said:

"Grind salt, and grind both good and fast."

Well, the quern began to grind salt so that it poured out like water; and when the skipper had got the ship full, he wished to stop the quern, but whichever way he turned it, and however much he tried, it was no good; the quern kept grinding on, and the heap of salt grew higher and higher, and at last down sank the ship.

There lies the quern at the bottom of the sea, and grinds away at this very day, and that's why the sea is salt.

The Coffee Mill Which Grinds Salt
(*Denmark*)

There was once a little boy by the name of Hans. As his parents died while he was very young, his grandmother took care of him and taught him reading and writing, and to be a good boy.

When she became very old, and thought she was about to die, she called the little boy to her and said, "I am old, Hans, and may not live long. You were always a good boy, and therefore you shall have my only treasure, a coffee mill which I have always kept at the bottom of my old chest. This coffee mill will grind all that you wish. If you say to it, 'Grind a house, little mill,' it will work away, and there the house will stand. When you say, 'Stop, little mill,' it will cease to grind."

Hans thanked his grandmother kindly, and when she died, and he was alone in the world, he opened the chest, took the coffee mill, and went out into the world.

When he had walked a long distance, and needed something to eat, he placed the mill on the grass and said, "Grind some bread and butter, little mill." Very soon Hans had all that he needed, and then he bid the mill to stop.

The next day he came to a large seaport, and when he saw the many vessels, he thought it would be pleasant to see more of the great world. He therefore boarded one of the ships and offered his service to the sailors. As it just happened that the captain needed a boy of Hans's age, he told him to stay.

As soon as the ship was out of port, the sailors commenced abusing Hans. He bore the harsh treatment as well as he could, and when he had nothing to eat the mill ground all that he wished. The bad men wondered how he could always be contented, although they gave him but little to eat. One day one of them peeped through a hole in the cabin door and discovered how the coffee mill served him.

Now the sailors offered a large sum of money to Hans if he would sell his treasure. He refused, however, saying that it was all that his good old grandmother had left him. So one day these wicked men threw Hans overboard and seized the mill. As they were in need of some salt, they bid it grind for them. The mill immediately began its work, and soon they had enough. Now they asked it to stop, but as the one who had peeped through the hole into the boy's cabin had not learned the exact command, the mill refused to obey, and before long the ship was filled with salt.

The men grew desperate, but none of them was able to find a way out of the difficulty. So at length the ship sank down with the mill, the salt, and all the wicked men. The men were drowned, but the mill is yet standing at the bottom of the sea, grinding away, and for this reason the water in the ocean has and always will have a salt taste.

Sweet Porridge
(*Germany*)

There was a poor but good little girl who lived alone with her mother, and they no longer had anything to eat. So the child went into the forest, and there an aged woman met her who was aware of her sorrow, and presented her with a little pot, which when she said, "Cook, little pot, cook," would cook good, sweet porridge, and when she said, "Stop, little pot," it ceased to cook. The girl took the pot home to her mother, and now they were freed from their poverty and hunger, and ate sweet porridge as often as they chose. Once on a time when the girl had gone out, her mother said, "Cook, little pot, cook." And it did cook and she ate till she was satisfied, and then she wanted the pot to stop cooking, but did not know the word. So it went on cooking and the porridge rose over the edge, and still it cooked on until the kitchen and whole house were full, and then the next house, and then the whole street, just as if it wanted to satisfy the hunger of the whole world, and there was the greatest distress, but no one knew how to stop it. At last when only one single house remained, the child came home and just said, "Stop, little pot," and it stopped and gave up cooking, and whosoever wished to return to the town had to eat his way back.

591: The Thieving Pot

The Three-legged Pot
(*Scotland*)

Once upon a time a man and woman lived the life of wanderers with their many children. All they had to their names was a donkey and cart, the clothes on their backs, and scarce any food save what they could get that day—barely enough to keep the children alive.

One day, in their wanderings they came upon a secluded glen. Camping for the night, the man said to his wife "let's go see if we can't beg some food from the people in those houses across the valley. It's worth a try; maybe I can get a few potatoes for supper."

So the man took the donkey up the road to visit the houses in the distance. He begged at one, then another, then another still, but couldn't get anything until he came upon a house with a thatched roof, an ancient house made of huge stones, with the smell of burning wood pouring out of the chimney.

The man knocked at the door and was answered by an old man. "Please sir," begged the man, "can you spare a bit of food? Times are so bad that my wife and I can't even keep our children fed." "Times are right bad," said the old man, "that's sure enough. So bad, in fact, that I've got no food to give."

The man looked about the inside of the house, and said "can you spare anything at all? Even something I could sell for scrap?" The old man's eyes cast about the house and lighted on a three-legged pot in the corner. "Can you make use of this?" he asked as he walked over and took up the pot, bringing it back to the man at his door. "I don't use it anymore."

"I certainly could," replied the man. The old man said, "it's yours then. I don't need it, and in fact I'm glad to be rid of it." The man thanked him, loaded the pot into a bag on his donkey and rode on his way. He went from house to house begging for food and managed to hawk some of his few wares in exchange for a handful of potatoes.

When he got back to the site where he had camped his family, his wife said, "well?" The man took the pot off the donkey and set it in front of his wife who said "great! But what good is a pot without potatoes?" "Oh," replied the man, "I managed to get some at the last house."

The wife took the pot with some water, set it to boil, and threw in the potatoes. "This'll do for tonight," she said to herself, "but there won't be enough come morning—the children will be hungry again. We'll need to go begging."

The next day the man hoisted the pot on to his donkey again, and his wife asked him, "where are you taking that pot?" "I'm bringing it with me," he replied, "in case I can sell it for scrap. What good is a pot without potatoes?"

His wife looked the pot over carefully. Then after some consideration, she said "maybe don't sell it. It's quite a good pot, after all. If I gave it a good scrub it would make a fine piece of crockery indeed. We'll need it anyway," she said, "if you get yourself some potatoes." "Suit yourself," the man said, "if you're happy to clean it. It's a bit tarnished."

So off went the man and his family with their donkey and cart plus what few wares remained to them, and finally happened upon a small, empty looking house. From what he could see at a distance, the man reckoned it to have been abandoned some time ago. "Maybe we could use it," he thought to himself, "if only for now. It'll keep us warm and dry at any rate."

As they approached, they came upon a peasant whom the man asked about the house. "Ah, that old thing?" said the peasant, "it belongs to me. I don't use it for anything anymore, the hills are slowly staking their claim on it. It's not even worth knocking down." The kind peasant looked on the man and his family, and took pity on them, saying "you can take shelter in there if you like for now, only the weeds and the odd creature makes himself at home in there these days." The man thanked the peasant and took his family up to the house.

The man and his wife took up residence in the house with their children, who were glad to get out of the cold and drizzle. In a short time, they had cleared out the weeds and cleaned it up to where it was not just livable, but maybe even cozy. The kind peasant even brought them straw to make beds out of, and the wife and children collected some firewood, so after a short time they had a hearth to gather round.

The wife took some potatoes they managed to beg from the neighbouring folk and boiled them up with some milk and some fixings the kind peasant brought them, and that day the family had a right good supper for the first time in quite a long while. Her spirits raised, the wife took the pot out and cleaned and scraped and scoured and buffed until her fingers ached, but finally she managed to bring the pot to a shine. "Now that's a handsome piece of crockery," she said to herself, as she laid it at the door.

The next morning the man got up to get water and looked about for something to carry it in. His wife said to use the three-legged pot, seeing as it was clean. But when the man came upon the pot, he found much to his surprise that it was full to overflowing with oatmeal, potatoes, vegetables, and all manner of store. "Look at what the kind peasant brought for us!" he said to his wife, who was delighted at the prospect of the children getting such a hearty meal, "he must have come by in the wee hours with all this."

The wife took the pot and made up such a breakfast as her and her family hadn't eaten in some time. After another day of hawking and begging, the man came back to yet another hearty meal with the rest of the store, and the family settled down to bed that evening with full bellies.

The next day they awoke to exactly the same thing: potatoes, meal, butterfat, onions, and a great deal more. The man and his wife were beside themselves; they couldn't believe their fortune. "The peasant wouldn't have brought all this. He couldn't have, could he? What's he got left for himself?" his wife asked. "Well," the man replied, "before we tuck in, I'd better go thank him."

Up the man went to the peasant's cottage, knocked on the door, and greeted him good morning. "Good morning!" the peasant replied, "how are you finding the house?" "It suits us just fine, thank you," said the man, "it's better than pitching a tent in the rain." "Glad to hear it," replied the peasant.

"Was it you that left those potatoes?" the man asked. "Potatoes? No, I can't even get any for myself," the peasant replied. "Strange," the man muttered under his breath. "What's strange?" the peasant asked. "Oh," the man said absently, "I mean, what I mean to say is... can I buy some potatoes off of you? I mean, I didn't realize you don't have any, that is."

"I see," said the peasant with a queer look on his face. "Well, if you send one of your children up I'm happy to give him some milk, but no, I don't have any potatoes." "Thank you kindly," replied the man, then hurried back down the road.

The man came back to his wife and told her, "It wasn't him that brought those potatoes." "Well, I'm not sure who's bringing them," his wife said, "but I'm not in a hurry to find out."

The man and his wife reckoned that it was time for them to move on, so the wife gave the pot a fresh clean, then the man packed up their wares along with the pot, loaded it on to the donkey and made his way down the road. They rambled for a good long while, until they pitched their tent at dark as the sun set over a great house in the distance. "Who owns that?" the man wondered aloud, "some well-off gentleman I suppose."

The family went down to bed for the night, and the wife put the pot safely inside their tent so no one could steal it during the night. Late in the wee hours of the night they were awakened by a stir, and the wife said "it's that pot, someone's trying to steal it. Listen!" and the man replied "it's nothing. Go back to sleep." But his wife persisted, so the man got up to check but found that the pot was still there. He went back to his wife and said, "Don't worry about your pot—nobody's touched it. Go back to sleep." Once the man and his wife lay down to sleep, the pot got up on its three feet, climbed down off the barrow, and lit off away up to the big house.

Up at this house lived an old country nobleman who mistreated the people on his estate. He had grown so rich by taxing them that he had more gold than he knew what to do with, and his bags were full to bursting with it. He noticed the pot sitting in a corner and decided to store some of his surplus in it, and so filled it level with gold sovereigns. At length the old gentleman betook himself to bed, and the pot lit off again back down to the traveller man's abode, placing itself back on top of the barrow as though nothing had ever happened.

When the man's wife got up the next morning, she was stunned to see the pot filled with its store, more money than she had ever seen in her whole life. "Look!" she shouted to him, "get up! Can you believe it!"

The man got up, and much to his surprise, found the pot full up to the brim with gold sovereigns. He could hardly believe his eyes. "It must have been some band of thieves," he said, trying to make sense of it, "that stored their quarry here and made off without it." This worried him and his wife, and he said, "We'd better not touch it in case they come back."

So they left it alone, and waited. Then they waited some more, but nobody came for the pot full of gold. After suppertime, nobody had come back to claim it, so the man decided to send his wife off with one of the sovereigns to make her way to a shop down the road. "Take the donkey and the cart with you," he said, but she insisted on going by herself.

The wife went down to the shop and bought as many groceries as she could carry, and even got a fair bit of change back. She came back loaded with food, and the man said to her, "well it doesn't look like anyone is coming back for the gold, so I'm going to put it into this barrel. We can put it under the bed of straw for safe keeping."

The next day the man was out and chanced to talk to some of the folk in the area, who complained to him about the gentleman, their landlord. "We're ruined with taxes," one woman told him, "by that man up there in the house. He taxes our calves, he taxes our hens, he taxes our horses. We can't go on like this."

When he got back, he told his wife, "it looks like that great house belongs to some sort of nobleman that owns all this land. The folk that live here, they're on his estate, and he taxes them to death." "We'd better go away from here tomorrow morning," he said to her, "in case he finds out we're here. He could just as easily kill us as ignore us."

The next morning the man and his wife got up, and she went to get the pot to boil some water, then turned to the man and said "did you move the pot?" "No," he replied. "Well it's gone," she told him. "Gone? Who would steal a three-legged pot?" he replied. "Who knows?" she said, "but it's gone." The couple searched everywhere, but couldn't find the pot.

At about suppertime the man went out with the donkey to a stream to fetch water from a stream flowing over a precipice, then looked up and saw something coming toward him in the distance, but he couldn't make out what it was. He called over to his wife to come see, and when the thing came closer, the wife exclaimed "that's the pot!" The man replied, "you're blind old lady," but the wife insisted "I'm telling you, that's the pot! And there's something else waving around inside it."

Once the thing got closer the man couldn't believe his eyes, but sure enough, there was the three-legged pot, running down the road, and what's more, it had the old nobleman inside it, stuck so that he couldn't get out, and making a good racket about it.

The man and his wife watched in disbelief as the pot ran right up to the precipice, then threw itself on to its side and toppled the old nobleman out and over the edge, casting him over the cliffs and into the waterfall. Afterward the couple watched the pot return to the mouth of their tent, setting itself up as though nothing had happened. "Oh no!" the man shouted, "we'll be banished! If anybody seen that, we'll be blamed."

So the next morning the man and his wife got up, scrubbed the three-legged pot clean, packed up their belongings, and rambled on to another region as quick as they could. But from that day forward, the pot was just like any other pot, and never brought them anything again.

The Wonderful Pot
(*Denmark*)

A man and his wife were once living in a very small cottage—the smallest and most ill-looking hut in the whole village. They were very poor, and often wanted even daily bread. Somehow or other they had managed to keep an only cow, but had been obliged to sell nearly everything else that they had. At length they decided that the cow, too, must go, and the man led her away, intending to bring her to the market. As he walked along the road a stranger approached and hailed him, asking if he intended to sell the animal, and how much he would take for it.

"I think," answered he, "that twenty dollars would be a fair price."

"Money I cannot give you," resumed the stranger, "but I have something which is worth as much as twenty dollars. Here is a pot which I am willing to give for your cow." Saying this, he pulled forth an iron pot with three legs and a handle.

"A pot!" exclaimed the cow's owner. "What use would that do me when I have nothing to put in it? My wife and children cannot eat an iron pot. No; money is what I need, and what I must have."

The two men stood still a moment looking at each other and at the cow and the pot, when suddenly the three-legged being began to speak. "Just take me," said it. When the poor man heard this he thought that if it could speak no doubt it could do more than that. So he closed the bargain, received the pot, and returned home with it.

When he reached his hut he first went to the stall where the cow had been standing, for he did not dare to appear before his wife at once. Having tied the pot to the manger, he went into the room, asking for something to eat, as he was hungry from his long walk. "Well," said his wife, "did you make a good bargain at the market? Did you get a good price for the cow?" "Yes," he said, "the price was fair enough." "That is well," returned she. "The money will help us a long time." "No," said he, again, "I received no money for the cow." "Dear me!" cried she. "What did you receive, then?" He told her to go and look in the stall.

As soon as the woman learned that the three-legged pot was all that had been paid him for the cow, she scolded and abused him. "You are a great blockhead!" cried she. "I wish I had myself taken the cow to the market! I never heard of such foolishness!" Thus she went on for a while.

"Clean me and put me on the fire," suddenly shouted the pot.

The woman opened her eyes in great wonder, and now it was her turn to think that it the pot could talk no doubt it could do more than this. She cleaned and washed it carefully and put it on the fire.

"I skip, I skip!" cried the pot.

"How far do you skip?" asked the woman.

"To the rich man's house, to the rich man's house!" it cried again, running from the fireplace to the door, across the yard, and up the road, as fast as the three short legs would carry it. The rich man lived not very far away. His wife was engaged in baking bread when the pot came running in and jumped up on the table, where it remained standing quite still. "Ah," exclaimed the woman, "isn't it wonderful! I just needed you for a pudding which must be baked at once." Thus she heaped a great many good things into the pot—flour, sugar, butter, raisins, almonds, spices, and so on. The pot received it all with a good will. At length the pudding was made, but when the rich man's wife reached for it, intending to put it on the stove, tap, tap, tap went the three short legs, and the pot stood on the threshold of the open door. "Dear me, where are you going with my pudding?" cried the woman. "To the poor man's home," replied the pot, running down the road at great speed.

When the poor people saw the pot coming back, and found the pudding, they rejoiced, and the man lost no time in asking his wife whether the bargain did not seem to be an excellent one after all. Yes, she was quite pleased and contented.

Next morning the pot again cried: "I skip, I skip!" "How far do you skip?" asked they.

"To the rich man's barn!" it shouted, running up the road. When it arrived at the barn it stopped in the door. "Look at that black pot!" cried the men, who were threshing wheat. "Let us see how much it will hold." They poured a bushel of wheat into it, but it did not seem to fill rapidly. Another bushel went in, but there was still room. Now every grain of wheat went into the pot, but still it seemed capable of holding much more. As there was no more wheat to be found, the three short legs began to move, and when the men looked around the pot had reached the gate. "Stop, stop!" called they. "Where do you go with our wheat?" "To the poor man's home," replied the pot, speeding down the road and leaving the men behind, dismayed and dumfounded.

The poor people were delighted when they received wheat enough to feed them for several years.

On the third morning the pot again skipped up the road. It was a beautiful day. The sun shone so bright and pleasant that the rich man had spread his money on a table near the open window to prevent his gold from becoming mouldy. All at once the pot stood on the table before him. He began to count his money over, as wealthy men sometimes like to do, and although he could not imagine where this black pot had come from, he thought it would be a good place to keep his money in the future. So he threw in one handful after another until it held all. At the same moment the pot made a jump from the table to the window-sill. "Wait!" shouted he. "Where do you go with all my money?" "To the poor man's home," returned the pot, skipping down the road until the money danced within it. In the middle of the floor in the poor man's hut it stopped, making its owners cry out in rapture over the unexpected treasure. "Clean and wash me," said the pot, "and put me aside."

Next morning it again announced that it was ready to skip.

"How far do you skip?" asked they.

"To the rich man's house!" So it ran up the road again, never stopping until it had reached the wealthy people's kitchen. The man happened to be there himself this time, and as soon as he saw it he cried: "There is the pot which carried away our pudding, our wheat, and all our money! I shall make it return what it stole!" He flung himself upon it, but found that he was unable to get off again. "I skip, I skip!" shouted the pot. "Skip to the north pole, if you wish!" yelled the man, furiously, trying in vain to free himself. The three short legs at once moved on, carrying him rapidly down the road. The poor people saw it pass their door; but it never thought of stopping. For all that I know, it went straight to the north pole with its burden.

The poor people became wealthy, and often thought of the wonderful pot with the three short legs which skipped so cheerfully for their good. It was gone, however, and they have never seen it since it carried the rich man towards the north pole.

The Full Jar
(*Netherlands*)

Once upon a time there was a poor, poor widow woman, so poor that her last penny had been spent. She had bought some food with it, and when that was gone, she tidied up, washed the only jug she had left, and set it outside the door to dry in the sun. Then she closed the lower door and the upper door and thought, "What is to become of me?"

But while she was thinking thus, the jug had started to roll, and on it rolled until it reached a butcher's shop. Just there was a woman who had bought soup meat and had not brought anything to put it in. She saw the empty jug and said, "Well, that's just the thing to put my meat in." But no sooner had the jug felt that it was full than it rolled away. And before it could be caught, it was out of the shop and out of sight and rolling back home. Then it banged against the door. The woman called out, "Who's there?" The jug replied, "Jug's full, just feel inside my hollow, round belly." The woman opened the door and lo and behold! there she found the delicious soup meat.

The same thing happened the next day. After the woman had eaten her soup and washed the jug, she again put it outside the door to dry, and the jug started rolling again. It rolled on and on until it reached a grocer. There was someone buying coffee and candies and the grocer mistakenly put them in the jug. The jug rolled away and quickly made its way back home, again banging on the door. "Who's there?" "Jug's full, just feel inside my hollow, round belly." And yes, there the woman found coffee and sugar.

The third day the jug went to the vegetable market, and it was not long before it felt itself full again. Then it rolled back and banged against the door. "Who's there?" cried the woman. "Jug's full, just feel inside my hollow, round belly." And then the woman found that the jug was full of delicious beans.

Of course, the poor woman liked that, so the next day she put the jug outside the door to air it out again. And yes, it started rolling again and this time it rolled towards the cow market. There was a farmer who had just sold his cow and did not know where to put the money he had received. When he saw the jug, he thought, "I can put it in there nicely," and he did. But then the jug rolled away, back towards the house, and banged against the door. "Who's there?" was the cry again. "Jug's full, just feel inside my hollow, round belly." The woman did so, and now the jug was filled with money. No wonder the woman was happy.

Then she thought, "Why should I wait until tomorrow to send the jug out; perhaps it will fetch another load." So, she put it outside again. And indeed, the jug started rolling again and went to the market. It was waiting there, and it just so happened that a cow was doing a big load of business above the jug. Only then did it feel that it was filled, and it rolled home. "Who's there?" cried the woman. "Jug's full, just feel inside my hollow, round belly." The woman thought, "What could it be this time?" and greedily stuck her hand into the jug. But when she saw what it was, she became so angry that she smashed the jug on the street.

Thus, she lost her jug, but now she had enough money to live on, and if she did not die, she is still alive.

660: The Three Doctors

The Three Army-Surgeons
(*Germany*)

Three army-surgeons who thought they knew their art perfectly were travelling about the world, and they came to an inn where they wanted to pass the night. The host asked whence they came, and whither they were going? "We are roaming about the world and practising our art." "Just show me for once in a way what you can do," said the host. Then the first said he would cut off his hand, and put it on again early next morning; the second said he would tear out his heart, and replace it next morning; the third said he would cut out his eyes and heal them again next morning. "If you can do that," said the innkeeper, "you have learnt everything." They, however, had a salve, with which they rubbed themselves, which joined parts together, and they carried the little bottle in which it was, constantly with them. Then they cut the hand, heart and eyes from their bodies as they had said they would, and laid them all together on a plate, and gave it to the innkeeper. The innkeeper gave it to a servant who was to set it in the cupboard, and take good care of it. The girl, however, had a lover in secret, who was a soldier. When therefore the innkeeper, the three army-surgeons, and everyone else in the house were asleep, the soldier came and wanted something to eat. The girl opened the cupboard and brought him some food, and in her love forgot to shut the cupboard-door again; she seated herself at the table by her lover, and they chattered away together. While she sat so contentedly there, thinking of no ill luck, the cat came creeping in, found the cupboard open, took the hand and heart and eyes of the three army-surgeons, and ran off with them. When the soldier had done eating, and the girl was taking away the things and going to shut the cupboard she saw that the plate which the innkeeper had given her to take care of, was empty. Then she said in a fright to her lover, "Ah, miserable girl, what shall I do? The hand is gone, the heart and the eyes are gone too, what will become of me in the morning?" "Be easy," said he, "I will help thee out of thy trouble. There is a thief hanging outside on the gallows, I will cut off his hand. Which hand was it?" "The right one." Then the girl gave him a sharp knife, and he went and cut the poor sinner's right hand off, and brought it to her. After this he caught the cat and cut its eyes out, and now nothing but the heart was wanting. "Have you not been killing, and are not the dead pigs in the cellar?" said he. "Yes," said the girl. "That's well," said the soldier, and he went down and fetched a pig's heart. The girl placed all together on the plate, and put it in the cupboard, and when after this her lover took leave of her, she went quietly to bed.

In the morning when the three army-surgeons got up, they told the girl she was to bring them the plate on which the hand, heart, and eyes were lying. Then she brought it out of the cupboard, and the first fixed the thief's hand on and smeared it with his salve, and it grew to his arm directly. The second took the cat's eyes and put them in his own head. The third fixed the pig's heart firm in the place where his own had been, and the innkeeper stood by, admired their skill, and said he had never yet seen such a thing as that done, and would sing their praises and recommend them to everyone. Then they paid their bill, and travelled farther.

As they were on their way, the one with the pig's heart did not stay with them at all, but wherever there was a corner he ran to it, and rooted about in it with his nose as pigs do. The others wanted to hold him back by the tail of his coat, but that did no good; he tore himself loose, and ran wherever the dirt was thickest. The second also behaved very strangely; he rubbed his eyes, and said to the others, "Comrades, what is the matter? I don't see at all. Will one of you lead me, so that I do not fall." Then with difficulty they travelled on till evening, when they reached another inn. They went into the bar together, and there at a table in the corner sat a rich man counting money. The one with the thief's hand walked round about him, made a sudden movement twice with his arm, and at last when the stranger turned away, he snatched at the pile of money, and took a handful from it. One of them saw this, and said, "Comrade, what art thou about? Thou must not steal, shame on thee!" "Eh," said he, "but how can I stop myself? My hand twitches, and I am forced to snatch things whether I will or not."

After this, they lay down to sleep, and while they were lying there it was so dark that no one could see his own hand. All at once the one with the cat's eyes awoke, aroused the others, and said. "Brothers, just look up, do you see the white mice running about there?" The two sat up, but could see nothing. Then said he, "Things are not right with us, we have not got back again what is ours. We must return to the innkeeper, he has deceived us." They went back therefore, the next morning, and told the host they had not got what was their own again; that the first had a thief's hand, the second cat's eyes, and the third a pig's heart. The innkeeper said that the girl must be to blame for that, and was going to call her, but when she had seen the three coming, she had run out by the backdoor, and not come back. Then the three said he must give them a great deal of money, or they would set his house on fire. He gave them what he had, and whatever he could get together, and the three went away with it. It was enough for the rest of their lives, but they would rather have had their own proper organs.

The Three Doctors
(*France*)

One day there were three young doctors who were in a hotel. They talked together of their art, and at the end of the meal they decided to meet at the same place in a year's time to see what progress they had made. They kept their word. After a year they gathered round the same table and inquired into each other's fate and whether their knowledge had grown.

"I," said one, "can cut off my hand tonight, sleep all night, and put it back in its place tomorrow morning."

"I can do better," said the other. "I'll pull one eye out, put it on a plate, sleep all night, and put it back in its place tomorrow morning."

"I," said the third, "can do better still; I'll tear my entrails, leave them in a dish, sleep all night, and put them in their place tomorrow morning."

"To work," cried the first. "I cut my hand!"

"And I take my eye!"

"I cleave open my belly!"

"And you," said they to the maid, "keep these with care upon our awakening."

Unfortunately, the maid was a bit tipsy. She let the dog go into the kitchen, and the dog ate the hand, the eye, and the stomach. When she realized her mistake, she lamented, "what can I do?" Then she remembered that there was a hanged man in the neighborhood and ran to cut off his hand. Then she drew a cat's eye. Then she took out the entrails of a pig that had just been killed. Finally, she placed these things near the bed of the three doctors. The three doctors awoke, and took back what they thought belonged to them, and went their separate ways happily, making a new promise to reconvene at the end of a year.

In time, they met together at the same hotel.

"And your hand?"

"It's fine, but it has a very funny tendency to grasp everything that's not mine."

"And your eye?"

"It's excellent, but I don't know why it sees better in the night than the day."

"And your bowels?"

"They work perfectly, but..."

"But what?"

"But... I'll tell you at our next meeting."

Of Concord
(*Italy*)

Two physicians once resided in a city, who were admirably skilled in medicine; insomuch, that all the sick who took their prescriptions were healed; and it thence became a question with the inhabitants, which of them was the best. After a while, a dispute arose between them upon this point.

Said one, "My friend, why should discord or envy or anger separate us; let us make the trial, and whosoever is inferior in skill shall serve the other."

"But how," replied his friend, "is this to be brought about?"

The first physician answered, "Hear me. I will pluck out your eyes, without doing you the smallest injury, and lay them before you on the table; and when you desire it, I will replace them as perfect and serviceable as they were before. If in like manner you can perform this, we will then be esteemed equal, and walk as brethren through the world. But remember, he who fails in the attempt shall become the servant of the other."

"I am well pleased," returned his fellow, "to do as you say." Whereupon he who made the proposition took out his instruments and extracted the eyes, besmearing the sockets and the outer part of the lids with a certain rich ointment.

"My dear friend," said he, "what do you perceive?"

"Of a surety," cried the other, "I see nothing. I want the use of my eyes, but I feel no pain from their loss. I pray you, however, restore them to their places as you promised."

"Willingly," said his friend. He again touched the inner and outer part of the lids with the ointment, and then, with much precision, inserted the balls into their sockets.

"How do you see now?" asked he. "Excellently," returned the other, "nor do I feel the least pain." "Well, then," continued the first, "it now remains for you to treat me in a similar manner."

"I am ready," said the latter. And accordingly taking the instruments, as the first had done, he smeared the upper and under parts of the eye with a peculiar ointment, drew out the eyes and placed them upon the table. The patient felt no pain; but added, "I wish you would hasten to restore them."

The operator cheerfully complied; but as he prepared his implements, a crow entered by an open window, and seeing the eyes upon the table, snatched one of them up, and flew away with it. The physician, vexed at what had happened, said to himself, "If I do not restore the eye to my companion, I must become his slave."

At that moment a goat, browsing at no great distance, attracted his observation. Instantly he ran to it, drew out one of its eyes, and put it into the place of the lost orb.

"My dear friend," exclaimed the operator, "how do things appear to you?"

"Neither in extracting or in replacing," he answered, "did I suffer the least pain; but bless me! one eye looks up to the trees!"

"Ah!" replied the first, "this is the very perfection of medicine. Neither of us is superior; henceforward we will be friends, as we are equals; and banish far off that spirit of contention which has destroyed our peace."

The goat-eyed man of physic acquiesced; they lived from this time in the greatest amity.

PROTO-ROMANCE

315: The Treacherous Sister

Handsome Is As Handsome Does

Handsome Is As Handsome Does
(*Romania*)

Once on a time, there lived an old man and an old woman; each had two children by previous marriages. The wife took good care of her own children, feeding them well, and giving them good clothes; while the children of the husband were neglected, and left almost without food. Not content with thus ill-treating them, and seeing that they were better looking, and better behaved, than her own, she made up her mind to get rid of them.

So one day she said to her husband, "your boy and girl are too lazy and good-for-nothing, you must send them from here, or I will not eat bread and salt out of the same platter with you again.

"Where can I take them to?" asked he.

"Where you please, so long as I am no longer troubled with them."

Finding no other way of pacifying his wife, he determined to take them next day to a wood and leave them there. The boy overheard the conversation, and repeated it to his sister; so they took their precautions, and next morning they each filled a canvas bag, one with ashes, the other with *malain*,[1] before their father called them to accompany him, and on the way, the boy scattered the ashes. On arriving at the four cross roads, the father bade them wait there for him, as he was going further into the forest to cut down some branches.

Giving them some food, he disappeared amongst the thickets, and tying a hollow gourd to a tree, he returned by another way to his cottage.

When the wind blew, it struck the gourd against the tree, and produced a sound like wood-chopping, so when the children heard this they said, "hark, to father, cutting wood!"

Waiting half the day, and seeing that their father did not come, they set off to search him from whence the sound came. On reaching the tree from whence the noise proceeded they found only the gourd; so they began to cry, but by the aid of the traces of the ashes, found their home again.

The parents, with the wife's children were sitting round the fire eating long white loaves, the outside of which being burnt, the wife said to her husband "where are your children that they may eat these spoiled pieces?" "Here we are!" cried they, entering the cottage, and beginning to eat the burnt bread.

1 Corn flour.

A few days passed, and again the wife told her husband to take away his children; the second journey had the same result as the first, for the girl scattered some *malain*, and so found their way home again.

Seeing that he could not live in peace with his wife, he determined to take them to a greater distance, and on a road quite unknown to them. The girl had still some malain left, which she scattered as before, but this time rain fell and made it into a paste, which was greedily eaten up by the little birds. So they walked all day until evening, and seeing no signs of their home they climbed into a tree, and made themselves a bed amongst the branches, and slept until daybreak. When morning came, they again began their wanderings through the forest. After a time hunger seized them, and they had nothing to eat; but at last the boy cut himself a pliant stick, and taking a mesh of his sister's hair, with it and the stick made himself a bow. Soon he shot some birds, while his sister procured a fire by rubbing two pieces of wood together and setting alight some dry branches. Thus they lived for some days, until in their wanderings they met with a fox; the boy was on the point of adjusting his bow, when the fox cried "do not shoot me, and then I will give you one of my cubs, who will be useful to you," so taking the cub the boy continued his way.

Further on he encountered a she-wolf; he was again about to draw his bow when the wolf begged him to spare her life, and she would give him one of her young ones, who would be useful to him. Taking with him the young wolf, as well as the cub-fox, he went along.

Soon on his path he encountered a bear, and the same form of words and acts was gone through as with the fox and the wolf. When evening approached, the children, followed by the young animals, came suddenly on a fine palace. Entering fearlessly, the boy found in the lodge a bundle of keys; thinking that they were the keys of the palace, he took them and began to open the various doors. At length he reached a very fine carved steel door, and opening it he found there a huge giant, bound to the wall by three iron bands. When the giant saw him he called, "youngster, bring me a jug of water, for I am dying of thirst." Instead of doing this he went in search of his sister. Giving her all the keys, he told her she might enter every room excepting the one with the steel door, but if she went into that one a misfortune would befall her.

Thus saying, he set out for the chase, followed by his three young animals.

After his departure the girl began exploring the palace, and arriving at the steel door, she said to herself, "I wonder why my brother has forbidden me this chamber! perhaps there are treasures in it which he wants for himself alone—why should he do this, seeing that I am his sister?" So trying the lock, she turned the key and entered. At sight of her, the giant cried, "maiden, bring me a jug of water, and I will be of great service to you." She went quickly, and returned with the water. After the giant had drunk it, one of his irons snapped and fell asunder.

Again the giant cried, "maiden bring me another jug of water, and you shall not have cause to repent it." Quickly she came with the water, the giant drank it eagerly, and the second band fell away.

A third time he cried, "maiden bring me but one more jug, then I shall be free, I am weary of being bound for so many years, and I will do whatsoever thou desirest." She brought him water for the third time, and after he had drunk that also, the last band snapped and fell away. The giant finding himself free, said to the maiden, "where is your brother?" "Nenna is gone shooting," said she. "I should like to kill your brother," said he, "and to keep you to live with me here in this splendid palace, will you consent to this? Tell me so, for you have grown so dear to me that I cannot live without you." "How can you kill him?" said she, "he has always his fox and his wolf and his bear with him." Said the giant, "the next time he goes out, you must manœuvre to keep his beasts at home, and then I can go and swallow him up." The maiden consented, and the giant returned to his chamber.

When Nenna arrived from the forest, his sister was very loving and caressing to him; and after eating their supper they retired to rest. Next morning by daybreak, the boy was again ready to set out for the chase, but his sister fondling him, and showing signs of great affection said, "brother you amuse yourself in the forest, while I am alone all day! leave me your beasts to play with." With reluctance he consented and set off alone.

Shortly after his departure, the giant came out and bade the maiden shut up the animals securely in the room with the steel door, and to roll a heavy stone against it. Then the giant set off in pursuit of the boy, who, when he saw the giant, like a moving cloud in the distance, knew that his sister had disobeyed him, and set the giant free.

Climbing a lofty tree, he waited the approach of the giant, who was soon at the foot of the tree, calling him to come down so that he might eat him up. The boy flung him his sheep-skin cap, and called to him to gnaw at that until he had time to sing a song.

This was what he sang.

> *Il! N'ande!*
> *N'a vede!*
> *N'a grenlu pamentului,*
> *Ilsurelulu campului,*
> *Ca ve pere stapanalu.*

The fox heard this song, and said, "Hark! our master is in danger." "Shut your woollen ears," said the other two.

The giant had got to the last morsel of the sheepskin cap, so the boy flung one of his *opinci*[1] and told him to eat that also, as he had not yet finished his song.

Beginning again his song, this time the wolf heard him, but the bear said, "Be quiet! sharp ears."

By this time the sandal was devoured, and the giant in a loud voice called him to descend, but the boy flung the other sandal, and entreated him to sing one more song.

This time the bear also heard him, and said, "In truth, our master is in great peril, but how can we get to him? For we are locked in here." Said the fox, "I will make an opening," and forced himself with all his strength against the door, without success; the same result with the wolf; but when the bear put his broad back there, the door flew open, and the stone rolled twenty paces away.

Finding themselves at liberty, the wolf said, "Shall we go like wind, or as quick as thought?"

"Like the wind!" said the bear, "for if we travel as quick as thought, we shall be breathless, and incapable of fighting when we arrive."

Like the wind they arrived to help their master. The giant, seeing their approach, transformed himself into a log of wood.

The boy cried to his beasts, "you must eat up all this wood for me, and leave for my share only its heart and its liver."

They made no difficulty about it, so the boy, seizing the heart and the liver, returned home, to the great astonishment and vexation of his sister.

The boy made a wooden spit, and thrusting the liver and the heart on it, bade his sister prepare this food. When it was cooked he seized the spit, and striking his sister with it said, "this is because you set the giant free, and consented to my death—do you see?"

"I see as if I were looking through a sieve!"

Striking her again, he said, "can you see now?"

"I see as through a mist." Placing over her head nine casks, one above the other, and covering her completely with them, he said, "you will see clear when you have filled these nine casks with your tears;" and so he went on his way and left her to die.

1 Sandals.

Prince Ivan, the Witch Baby, and the Little Sister of the Sun
(*Russia*)

Once upon a time, very long ago, there was a little Prince Ivan who was dumb. Never a word had he spoken from the day that he was born—not so much as a "Yes" or a "No," or a "Please" or a "Thank you." A great sorrow he was to his father because he could not speak. Indeed, neither his father nor his mother could bear the sight of him, for they thought, "A poor sort of Tzar will a dumb boy make!" They even prayed, and said, "If only we could have another child, whatever it is like, it could be no worse than this tongue-tied brat who cannot say a word." And for that wish they were punished, as you shall hear. And they took no sort of care of the little Prince Ivan, and he spent all his time in the stables, listening to the tales of an old groom.

He was a wise man was the old groom, and he knew the past and the future, and what was happening under the earth. Maybe he had learnt his wisdom from the horses. Anyway, he knew more than other folk, and there came a day when he said to Prince Ivan—

"Little Prince," says he, "to-day you have a sister, and a bad one at that. She has come because of your father's prayers and your mother's wishes. A witch she is, and she will grow like a seed of corn. In six weeks she'll be a grown witch, and with her iron teeth she will eat up your fa ther, and eat up your mother, and eat up you too, if she gets the chance. There's no saving the old people; but if you are quick, and do what I tell you, you may escape, and keep your soul in your body. And I love you, my little dumb Prince, and do not wish to think of your little body between her iron teeth. You must go to your father and ask him for the best horse he has, and then gallop like the wind, and away to the end of the world."

The little Prince ran off and found his father. There was his father, and there was his mother, and a little baby girl was in his mother's arms, screaming like a little fury.

"Well, she's not dumb," said his father, as if he were well pleased.

"Father," says the little Prince, "may I have the fastest horse in the stable?" And those were the first words that ever left his mouth.

"What!" says his father, "have you got a voice at last? Yes, take whatever horse you want. And see, you have a little sister; a fine little girl she is too. She has teeth already. It's a pity they are black, but time will put that right, and it's better to have black teeth than to be born dumb."

Little Prince Ivan shook in his shoes when he heard of the black teeth of his little sister, for he knew that they were iron. He thanked his father and ran off to the stable. The old groom saddled the finest horse there was. Such a horse you never saw. Black it was, and its saddle and bridle were trimmed with shining silver. And little Prince Ivan climbed up and sat on the great black horse, and waved his hand to the old groom, and galloped away, on and on over the wide world.

"It's a big place, this world," thought the little Prince. "I wonder when I shall come to the end of it." You see, he had never been outside the palace grounds. And he had only ridden a little Finnish pony. And now he sat high up, perched on the back of the great black horse, who galloped with hoofs that thundered beneath him, and leapt over rivers and streams and hillocks, and anything else that came in his way.

On and on galloped the little Prince on the great black horse. There were no houses anywhere to be seen. It was a long time since they had passed any people, and little Prince Ivan began to feel very lonely, and to wonder if indeed he had come to the end of the world, and could bring his journey to an end.

Suddenly, on a wide, sandy plain, he saw two old, old women sitting in the road.

They were bent double over their work, sewing and sewing, and now one and now the other broke a needle, and took a new one out of a box between them, and threaded the needle with thread from another box, and went on sewing and sewing. Their old noses nearly touched their knees as they bent over their work.

Little Prince Ivan pulled up the great black horse in a cloud of dust, and spoke to the old women.

"Grandmothers," said he, "is this the end of the world? Let me stay here and live with you, and be safe from my baby sister, who is a witch and has iron teeth. Please let me stay with you, and I'll be very little trouble, and thread your needles for you when you break them."

"Prince Ivan, my dear," said one of the old women, "this is not the end of the world, and little good would it be to you to stay with us. For as soon as we have broken all our needles and used up all our thread we shall die, and then where would you be? Your sister with the iron teeth would have you in a minute."

The little Prince cried bitterly, for he was very little and all alone. He rode on further over the wide world, the black horse galloping and galloping, and throwing the dust from his thundering hoofs.

He came into a forest of great oaks, the biggest oak trees in the whole world. And in that forest was a dreadful noise—the crashing of trees falling, the breaking of branches, and the whistling of things hurled through the air. The Prince rode on, and there before him was the huge giant, Tree-rooter, hauling the great oaks out of the ground and flinging them aside like weeds.

"I should be safe with him," thought little Prince Ivan, "and this, surely, must be the end of the world."

He rode close up under the giant, and stopped the black horse, and shouted up into the air.

"Please, great giant," says he, "is this the end of the world? And may I live with you and be safe from my sister, who is a witch, and grows like a seed of corn, and has iron teeth?"

"Prince Ivan, my dear," says Tree-rooter, "this is not the end of the world, and little good would it be to you to stay with me. For as soon as I have rooted up all these trees I shall die, and then where would you be? Your sister would have you in a minute. And already there are not many big trees left."

And the giant set to work again, pulling up the great trees and throwing them aside. The sky was full of flying trees.

Little Prince Ivan cried bitterly, for he was very little and was all alone. He rode on further over the wide world, the black horse galloping and galloping under the tall trees, and throwing clods of earth from his thundering hoofs.

He came among the mountains. And there was a roaring and a crashing in the mountains as if the earth was falling to pieces. One after another whole mountains were lifted up into the sky and flung down to earth, so that they broke and scattered into dust. And the big black horse galloped through the mountains, and little Prince Ivan sat bravely on his back. And there, close before him, was the huge giant Mountain-tosser, picking up the mountains like pebbles and hurling them to little pieces and dust upon the ground.

"This must be the end of the world," thought the little Prince; "and at any rate I should be safe with him."

"Please, great giant," says he, "is this the end of the world? And may I live with you and be safe from my sister, who is a witch, and has iron teeth, and grows like a seed of corn?"

"Prince Ivan, my dear," says Mountain-tosser, resting for a moment and dusting the rocks off his great hands, "this is not the end of the world, and little good would it be to you to stay with me. For as soon as I have picked up all these mountains and thrown them down again I shall die, and then where would you be? Your sister would have you in a minute. And there are not very many mountains left."

And the giant set to work again, lifting up the great mountains and hurling them away. The sky was full of flying mountains.

Little Prince Ivan wept bitterly, for he was very little and was all alone. He rode on further over the wide world, the black horse galloping and galloping along the mountain paths, and throwing the stones from his thundering hoofs.

At last he came to the end of the world, and there, hanging in the sky above him, was the castle of the little sister of the Sun. Beautiful it was, made of cloud, and hanging in the sky, as if it were built of red roses.

"I should be safe up there," thought little Prince Ivan, and just then the Sun's little sister opened the window and beckoned to him.

Prince Ivan patted the big black horse and whispered to it, and it leapt up high into the air and through the window, into the very courtyard of the castle.

"Stay here and play with me," said the little sister of the Sun; and Prince Ivan tumbled off the big black horse into her arms, and laughed because he was so happy.

Merry and pretty was the Sun's little sister, and she was very kind to little Prince Ivan. They played games together, and when she was tired she let him do whatever he liked and run about her castle. This way and that he ran about the battlements of rosy cloud, hanging in the sky over the end of the world.

But one day he climbed up and up to the topmost turret of the castle. From there he could see the whole world. And far, far away, beyond the mountains, beyond the forests, beyond the wide plains, he saw his father's palace where he had been born. The roof of the palace was gone, and the walls were broken and crumbling. And little Prince Ivan came slowly down from the turret, and his eyes were red with weeping.

"My dear," says the Sun's little sister, "why are your eyes so red?"

"It is the wind up there," says little Prince Ivan.

And the Sun's little sister put her head out of the window of the castle of cloud and whispered to the winds not to blow so hard.

But next day little Prince Ivan went up again to that topmost turret, and looked far away over the wide world to the ruined palace. "She has eaten them all with her iron teeth," he said to himself. And his eyes were red when he came down.

"My dear," says the Sun's little sister, "your eyes are red again."

"It is the wind," says little Prince Ivan.

And the Sun's little sister put her head out of the window and scolded the wind.

But the third day again little Prince Ivan climbed up the stairs of cloud to that topmost turret, and looked far away to the broken palace where his father and mother had lived. And he came down from the turret with the tears running down his face.

"Why, you are crying, my dear!" says the Sun's little sister. "Tell me what it is all about."

So little Prince Ivan told the little sister of the Sun how his sister was a witch, and how he wept to think of his father and mother, and how he had seen the ruins of his father's palace far away, and how he could not stay with hen happily until he knew how it was with his parents.

"Perhaps it is not yet too late to save them from her iron teeth, though the old groom said that she would certainly eat them, and that it was the will of God. But let me ride back on my big black horse."

"Do not leave me, my dear," says the Sun's little sister. "I am lonely here by myself."

"I will ride back on my big black horse, and then I will come to you again."

"What must be, must," says the Sun's little sister; "though she is more likely to eat you than you are to save them. You shall go. But you must take with you a magic comb, a magic brush, and two apples of youth. These apples would make young once more the oldest things on earth."

Then she kissed little Prince Ivan, and he climbed up on his big black horse, and leapt out of the window of the castle down on the end of the world, and galloped off on his way back over the wide world.

He came to Mountain-tosser, the giant. There was only one mountain left, and the giant was just picking it up. Sadly he was picking it up, for he knew that when he had thrown it away his work would be done and he would have to die.

"Well, little Prince Ivan," says Mountain-tosser, "this is the end;" and he heaves up the mountain. But before he could toss it away the little Prince threw his magic brush on the plain, and the brush swelled and burst, and there were range upon range of high mountains, touching the sky itself.

"Why," says Mountain-tosser, "I have enough mountains now to last me for another thousand years. Thank you kindly, little Prince."

And he set to work again, heaving up mountains and tossing them down, while little Prince Ivan galloped on across the wide world.

He came to Tree-rooter, the giant. There were only two of the great oaks left, and the giant had one in each hand.

"Ah me, little Prince Ivan," says Tree-rooter, "my life is come to its end; for I have only to pluck up these two trees and throw them down, and then I shall die."

"Pluck them up," says little Prince Ivan. "Here are plenty more for you." And he threw down his comb. There was a noise of spreading branches, of swishing leaves, of opening buds, all together, and there before them was a forest of great oaks stretching farther than the giant could see, tall though he was.

"Why," says Tree-rooter, "here are enough trees to last me for another thousand years. Thank you kindly, little Prince."

And he set to work again, pulling up the big trees, laughing joyfully and hurling them over his head, while little Prince Ivan galloped on across the wide world.

He came to the two old women. They were crying their eyes out.

"There is only one needle left!" says the first.

"There is only one bit of thread in the box!" sobs the second.

"And then we shall die!" they say both together, mumbling with their old mouths.

"Before you use the needle and thread, just eat these apples," says little Prince Ivan, and he gives them the two apples of youth.

The two old women took the apples in their old shaking fingers and ate them, bent double, mumbling with their old lips. They had hardly finished their last mouthfuls when they sat up straight, smiled with sweet red lips, and looked at the little Prince with shining eyes. They had become young girls again, and their gray hair was black as the raven.

"Thank you kindly, little Prince," say the two young girls. "You must take with you the handkerchief we have been sewing all these years. Throw it to the ground, and it will turn into a lake of water. Perhaps some day it will be useful to you."

"Thank you," says the little Prince, and off he gallops, on and on over the wide world.

He came at last to his father's palace. The roof was gone, and there were holes in the walls. He left his horse at the edge of the garden, and crept up to the ruined palace and peeped through a hole. Inside, in the great hall, was sitting a huge baby girl, filling the whole hall. There was no room for her to move. She had knocked off the roof with a shake of her head. And she sat there in the ruined hall, sucking her thumb.

And while Prince Ivan was watching through the hole he heard her mutter to herself—

> *Eaten the father,*
> *Eaten the mother,*
> *And now to eat the little brother*

And she began shrinking, getting smaller and smaller every minute.

Little Prince Ivan had only just time to get away from the hole in the wall when a pretty little baby girl came running out of the ruined palace.

"You must be my little brother Ivan," she called out to him, and came up to him smiling. But as she smiled the little Prince saw that her teeth were black; and as she shut her mouth he heard them clink together like pokers.

"Come in," says she, and she took little Prince Ivan with her to a room in the palace, all broken down and cobwebbed. There was a dulcimer lying in the dust on the floor.

"Well, little brother," says the witch baby, "you play on the dulcimer and amuse yourself while I get supper ready. But don't stop playing, or I shall feel lonely." And she ran off and left him.

Little Prince Ivan sat down and played tunes on the dulcimer—sad enough tunes. You would not play dance music if you thought you were going to be eaten by a witch.

But while he was playing a little gray mouse came out of a crack in the floor. Some people think that this was the wise old groom, who had turned into a little gray mouse to save Ivan from the witch baby.

"Ivan, Ivan," says the little gray mouse, "run while you may. Your father and mother were eaten long ago, and well they deserved it. But be quick, or you will be eaten too. Your pretty little sister is putting an edge on her teeth!"

Little Prince Ivan thanked the mouse, and ran out from the ruined palace, and climbed up on the back of his big black horse, with its saddle and bridle trimmed with silver. Away he galloped over the wide world. The witch baby stopped her work and listened. She heard the music of the dulcimer, so she made sure he was still there. She went on sharpening her teeth with a file, and growing bigger and bigger every minute. And all the time the music of the dulcimer sounded among the ruins.

As soon as her teeth were quite sharp she rushed off to eat little Prince Ivan. She tore aside the walls of the room. There was nobody there—only a little gray mouse running and jumping this way and that on the strings of the dulcimer.

When it saw the witch baby the little mouse ran across the floor and into the crack and away, so that she never caught it. How the witch baby gnashed her teeth! Poker and tongs, poker and tongs—what a noise they made! She swelled up, bigger and bigger, till she was a baby as high as the palace. And then she jumped up so that the palace fell to pieces about her. Then off she ran after little Prince Ivan.

Little Prince Ivan, on the big black horse, heard a noise behind him. He looked back, and there was the huge witch, towering over the trees. She was dressed like a little baby, and her eyes flashed and her teeth clanged as she shut her mouth. She was running with long strides, faster even than the black horse could gallop—and he was the best horse in all the world.

Little Prince Ivan threw down the handkerchief that had been sewn by the two old women who had eaten the apples of youth. It turned into a deep, broad lake, so that the witch baby had to swim—and swimming is slower than running. It took her a long time to get across, and all that time Prince Ivan was galloping on, never stopping for a moment.

The witch baby crossed the lake and came thundering after him. Close behind she was, and would have caught him; but the giant Tree-rooter saw the little Prince galloping on the big black horse, and the witch baby tearing after him. He pulled up the great oaks in armfuls, and threw them down just in front of the witch baby. He made a huge pile of the big trees, and the witch baby had to stop and gnaw her way through them with her iron teeth.

It took her a long time to gnaw through the trees, and the black horse galloped and galloped ahead. But presently Prince Ivan heard a noise behind him. He looked back, and there was the witch baby, thirty feet high, racing after him, clanging with her teeth. Close behind she was, and the little Prince sat firm on the big black horse, and galloped and galloped. But she would have caught him if the giant Mountain-tosser had not seen the little Prince on the big black horse, and the great witch baby running after him. The giant tore up the biggest mountain in the world and flung it down in front of her, and another on the top of that. She had to bite her way through them, while the little Prince galloped and galloped.

At last little Prince Ivan saw the cloud castle of the little sister of the Sun, hanging over the end of the world and gleaming in the sky as if it were made of roses. He shouted with hope, and the black horse shook his head proudly and galloped on. The witch baby thundered after him. Nearer she came and nearer.

"Ah, little one," screams the witch baby, "you shan't get away this time!"

The Sun's little sister was looking from a window of the castle in the sky, and she saw the witch baby stretching out to grab little Prince Ivan. She flung the window open, and just in time the big black horse leapt up, and through the window and into the courtyard, with little Prince Ivan safe on its back.

How the witch baby gnashed her iron teeth!

"Give him up!" she screams.

"I will not," says the Sun's little sister.

"See you here," says the witch baby, and she makes herself smaller and smaller and smaller, till she was just like a real little girl. "Let us be weighed in the great scales, and if I am heavier than Prince Ivan, I can take him; and if he is heavier than I am, I'll say no more about it."

The Sun's little sister laughed at the witch baby and teased her, and she hung the great scales out of the cloud castle so that they swung above the end of the world.

Little Prince Ivan got into one scale, and down it went.

"Now," says the witch baby, "we shall see."

And she made herself bigger and bigger and bigger, till she was as big as she had been when she sat and sucked her thumb in the hall of the ruined palace. "I am the heavier," she shouted, and gnashed her iron teeth. Then she jumped into the other scale.

She was so heavy that the scale with the little Prince in it shot up into the air. It shot up so fast that little Prince Ivan flew up into the sky, up and up and up, and came down on the topmost turret of the cloud castle of the little sister of the Sun.

The Sun's little sister laughed, and closed the window, and went up to the turret to meet the little Prince. But the witch baby turned back the way she had come, and went off, gnashing her iron teeth until they broke. And ever since then little Prince Ivan and the little sister of the Sun play together in the castle of cloud that hangs over the end of the world. They borrow the stars to play at ball, and put them back at night whenever they remember.

"So when there are no stars?" asked Maroosia.

"It means that Prince Ivan and the Sun's little sister have gone to sleep over their games and forgotten to put their toys away."

The Chursusissa
(*Greece*)

Once upon a time there was a king who had a son and two daughters, and the youngest of these was a chursusissa,[1] devouring all the people who came to the spring to fetch water. Then the people went to the king and complained that a person came from the gate of his castle and devoured the people who came to the spring. But the king chased them away and said, "Scat, I have no ogre in my castle." Then the prince hid by the spring to see if people were telling the truth, and when his younger sister came and grabbed a person he took his sword and cut her cheek off.

Then he went to the king and demanded the death of the child. But because the king refused to let his daughter be killed, the prince fled the country with his elder sister.

In the desolation through which they wandered, they found a marble palace inhabited by forty drakes, ogres which go out to hunt humans every day. In the palace, only the old servant of the drakes was present, and at the request of the prince she hid his sister. Now, one after the other the draken came back from the hunt. One brought back ten men and the other fifteen more, he killed thirty-nine of them, but the fortieth escaped, and began a love affair with his sister. The draco advised her to feign sickness. She then asked her brother to fetch a melon from the garden of the elves, hoping that the moor guarding this garden would devour him with his throat which was the size of a cave.

The brother knocked on the elves' door and they were surprised because no one had knocked for three years. Then they told him how he should go about getting the melon, however they forbade him to eat any-

---

1 A cannibal princess.

thing from it, lest he fall asleep and be swallowed by the moors. He ate it and fell asleep. When the moor came, his horse confronted it and fought until the prince was wakened by the noise and hewed the moor with his sword. Then he broke two melons and brought one to the elves and the other to his sister.

She then sent him for the water of life, and he went back to the elves for advice. Then they whistled, and soon all the jackdaws gathered and the elves asked who of them wanted to get the water of life. Then a limping crow offered to do so and took it from the mountain which opens and closes. The elves gave the prince half of the water and kept the other half for themselves.

His sister resolved to cut his three golden hairs which gave him his strength; losing the first one made him dizzy, losing the second one made him faint, and with the third one lost, he died.

The drake cut him up and made a saddle for the prince's horse out of the pieces, and then chased it away. But the stallion ran to the elves and these revived the prince by using the water of life. Afterward, he stayed with them for two months, then smashed the drake and hung and burned his elder sister.

Then he returned to the elves, who offered him one of their daughters, however he wanted to visit his homeland first. The elves advised him against this, but when he decided not to follow the advice the elves gave him two hairs which he should burn in case he got into trouble with his younger sister.

In his father's castle, however, he met none other than his sister, the chursusissa. She gave him a warm welcome and asked him, "how many feet does your horse have?" and he answered, "four feet." So she ate one foot, and continued to ask the same question until she finished eating the entire horse. Then she said, "now I will eat you too, brother." He replied, "I beg you, give me only two days' time, and then eat me, if you still wish to do so." She granted him his wish and ate bones in the meantime to satisfy her hunger. Then the prince went into a huge forest and hid himself in a cave that was so long you could spend two hours traversing it, but the chursusissa found him anyway. Then he climbed a tree, but she gnawed the tree until it began to shake. Finally, at this point the prince decided to burn the two hairs and immediately a lamia[1] appeared and devoured the chursusissa. From this point on, the prince lived alone.

---

1 A nocturnal spirit and child-eating monster.

425E: The Enchanted Husband

The Padlock

The Padlock
(*Italy*)

Once upon a time there lived a mother who had three daughters, and misery and want had taken hold of that house (which was the very sink of all misfortunes), and they went a-begging and gathering cast-away cabbage leaves so as to keep body and soul together. One morning the old woman had gone forth a-begging at a certain palace, and the cook had given her some greens and a few things more, therefore she returned home and bade her daughters to go to the fountain to fetch some water; but one with the other kept saying, 'Thou go,' and none went, and the cat wagged her tail; till at last the old woman, seeing their unwillingness, said, 'If thou desirest to have anything done, do it thyself,' and taking the juglet, was going to fetch the water, although through her age and infirmities she could hardly put one foot before the other, when Luciella, her youngest daughter, said, 'Give me the juglet, O my mother; although I am not very strong, yet have I strength enough to do this for thee, as I like thee not to do this work,' and taking the juglet, fared forth from the city, whereto stood a fountain, that liking not to see the flowers fade with fear, kept throwing up water in their faces; and Luciella met there a handsome slave, and he said to her, 'Wilt thou come with me, O thou beauteous damsel, and I will take thee to a grotto not very far distant, and I will give thee many pretty things.'

Luciella, who had never met with kindly words and good treatment, answered, 'Let me carry this water to my mother, who is waiting for it, and then will I return to thee;' and carrying the water home, she told her mother she was going a-begging. Returning to the fountain, where she found the slave awaiting for her, they fared on to a grotto all covered by Venus-hair creeper and ivy, and when she entered it he led her to an underground palace, most splendid and shining with gold, where at once a table was laid, covered with all dainties. After she had eaten, two beautiful slave-girls came forth, and taking off the rags she wore, arrayed her in costly raiments; and in the evening they led her to a chamber where stood a bed with coverlets all purflewed with pearls and gold; where as soon as the candles were put out, someone came and slept with her, and this continued for some days.

After this time the damsel felt a longing to see her mother, and she told the slave, and the slave entered an inner chamber and spake with someone, and came forth with a bag full of gold, saying, 'Give thou these to thy mother; and be careful not to forget thy way and come back soon, but do not say where thou comest from, or whither thou goest.' The damsel went home, and the sisters beholding her so well arrayed nearly died with envy. She stayed with them a few hours, and when she desired to go back, her mother and sisters offered to attend her; but she refused their company, and returned to the same palace by the same grotto; and abiding quietly within it for two months, at the last came upon her the same longing as hithertofore, and again she told the slave, and as before was sent home with gifts to her mother. This happened three or four times, and the sisters grew ever more envious. At the last these hideous harpies took counsel together, and decided that they would confer with a ghula[1] whom they knew, and she told them how it was with Luciella. So when the damsel came to visit them, they said to her, 'Although thou wouldst not tell us anything of thy enjoyance, thou must know that we are aware of these, and we know that every night thou sleepest with a handsome youth, whom thou hast never seen because they drug thy drinks, and thou art always fast asleep. But thou wilt always remain as thou art, if thou do not resolve to do the rede[2] that those that love thee will advise. In the end, thou art our flesh and blood, and we only desire thy weal and thy pleasure; therefore, when the evening shall come, and thou shalt go to thy bed, and the slave shall come bringing thee thy night-drink and water to wash thy mouth bid thou him go and fetch thee a towel to wipe thy mouth, and when he is gone on his errand throw the drink away, so that thou mayst remain awake in the night; and when thou perceivest thy husband fast asleep, open this padlock, and thus he will be obliged to break the spell in spite of himself, and thou wilt remain the happiest woman in all the world.' Poor Luciella knew not that under the velvet saddle the thorns were hid, and amongst the flowers the adder slept, and in the golden bowl the poison was prepared. She believed the words of her sisters, and returning to the grotto, went within the palace, and when night came, did as those wretches had told her, and when all things lay still, she struck a light, and lit the candle, and beheld by her side a flower of beauty, a youth like lilies and roses, and sighting so much beauty, said, 'By my faith, thou shalt not escape from my hands, ever,' and taking the padlock, she unlocked it, and beheld some women carrying some skeins of thread on their head. One of these let fall a skein, and Luciella, who was very kind hearted, remembering not where she was, cried out in a loud voice, 'Pick up thy thread, madam.' At the cry the youth woke up; and was so disgusted and angered in being seen by Luciella that, at once calling the slaves, he bade them dress her in the same rags that she wore before, and

---

1 A servant.
2 To take the advice.

send her home to her mother and sisters.

This they did, and when she stood before them with pale face and sorrow-stricken heart, they bade her go her ways with insolent words; and she, knowing not whither to turn her steps, wandered about the world, and after much travail the unhappy damsel, being big with child, arrived at the city of Torre-Longa, and going to the royal palace, went round to the stables, and sought a place upon the straw wherein to rest. Here one of the court maids of honour found her, and kindly entreated her. So the time for child-bed came, and she was delivered of a son so beautiful that he seemed a golden bough; and the first night he was born, a handsome youth entered the chamber where the mother and babe lay, and going near the child, he took him in his arms, and said, 'O my beauteous son, if my mother knew of thee, in a golden bath she would wash thee, and with a golden band she would swathe thee, and if never a cock should crow, never would I leave thy side,' and whilst he was chanting these words, at the first cock crowing he disappeared as quicksilver. The young maid of honour sat near the bedside, and every night she beheld the youth, who came and took the child in his arms, and chanted the same words, and at the first cock-crow disappeared, so she made her way to the queen's presence, and related to her what she had witnessed; and the queen, as soon as the sun, like a clever doctor, had discharged all the stars from the hospital of heaven, bade the crier publish an edict (which was thought by all folk very cruel) that all the cocks in that city should be slain, thus condemning all fowls to widowhood and wretchedness. And in the evening the queen took the maid's place by Luciella's bedside, and waited in great suspense for the youth's coming, and when he came at the same hour, she recognised in him her own son, and she arose and embraced him; and as the curse which had been cast upon the prince by a ghula was that he should wander about in exile far from his home, till his mother should see him and embrace him, and the cock should not crow, as soon as he was in his mother's arms the spell was broken, and the sad term of exile was ended. Thus the mother found that she had gained a grandson beautiful as a jewel. And Luciella regained her husband, and the sisters after a time having knowledge of her happiness and greatness, came with a brazen face to visit her, but they met with the same reception that they had given her when through their wicked rede she had been cast out from the prince's palace; and thus it was rendered to them evil for evil, and they were paid in the same coin, and in great distress of mind they came to know that

Son of envy is the heart's disease.

The Golden Root
(*Italy*)

A person who is over-curious, and wants to know more than he ought, always carries the match in his hand to set fire to the powder-room of his own fortunes; and he who pries into others' affairs is frequently a loser in his own; for generally he who digs holes to search for treasures, comes to a ditch into which he himself falls—as happened to the daughter of a gardener in the following manner.

There was once a gardener who was so very very poor that, however hard he worked, he could not manage to get bread for his family. So he gave three little pigs to his three daughters, that they might rear them, and thus get something for a little dowry. Then Pascuzza and Cice, who were the eldest, drove their little pigs to feed in a beautiful meadow; but they would not let Parmetella, who was the youngest daughter, go with them, and sent her away, telling her to go and feed her pig somewhere else. So Parmetella drove her little animal into a wood, where the Shades were holding out against the assaults of the Sun; and coming to a pasture—in the middle of which flowed a fountain, that, like the hostess of an inn where cold water is sold, was inviting the passers-by with its silver tongue—she found a certain tree with golden leaves. Then plucking one of them, she took it to her father, who with great joy sold it for more than twenty ducats, which served to stop up a hole in his affairs. And when he asked Parmetella where she had found it, she said, "Take it, sir, and ask no questions, unless you would spoil your good fortune." The next day she returned and did the same; and she went on plucking the leaves from the tree until it was entirely stript, as if it had been plundered by the winds of Autumn. Then she perceived that the tree had a large golden root, which she could not pull up with her hands; so she went home, and fetching an axe set to work to lay bare the root around the foot of the tree; and raising the trunk as well as she could, she found under it a beautiful porphyry staircase.

Parmetella, who was curious beyond measure, went down the stairs, and walking through a large and deep cavern, she came to a beautiful plain, on which was a splendid palace, where only gold and silver were trodden underfoot, and pearls and precious stones everywhere met the eye. And as Parmetella stood wondering at all these splendid things, not seeing any person moving among so many beautiful fixtures, she went into a chamber, in which were a number of pictures; and on them were seen painted various beautiful things—especially the ignorance of man esteemed wise, the injustice of him who held the scales, the injuries avenged by Heaven—things truly to amaze one. And in the same chamber also was a splendid table, set out with things to eat and to drink.

Seeing no one, Parmetella, who was very hungry, sat down at a table to eat like a fine count; but whilst she was in the midst of the feast, behold! a handsome Slave entered, who said, "Stay! do not go away, for I will have you for my wife, and will make you the happiest woman in the world." In spite of her fear, Parmetella took heart at this good offer, and consenting to what the Slave proposed, a coach of diamonds was instantly given her, drawn by four golden steeds, with wings of emeralds and rubies, who carried her flying through the air to take an airing; and a number of apes, clad in cloth of gold, were given to attend on her person, who forthwith arrayed her from head to foot, and adorned her so that she looked just like a Queen.

When night was come, and the Sun—desiring to sleep on the banks of the river of India untroubled by gnats—had put out the light, the Slave said to Parmetella, "My dear, now go to rest in this bed; but remember first to put out the candle, and mind what I say, or ill will betide you." Then Parmetella did as he told her; but no sooner had she closed her eyes than the blackamoor,[1] changing to a handsome youth, lay down to sleep. But the next morning, ere the Dawn went forth to seek fresh eggs in the fields of the sky, the youth arose and took his other form again, leaving Parmetella full of wonder and curiosity.

And again the following night, when Parmetella went to rest, she put out the candle as she had done the night before, and the youth came as usual and lay down to sleep. But no sooner had he shut his eyes than Parmetella arose, took a steel which she had provided, and lighting the tinder applied a match; then taking the candle, she raised the coverlet, and beheld the ebony turned to ivory, and the coal to chalk. And whilst she stood gazing with open mouth, and contemplating the most beautiful pencilling that Nature had ever given upon the canvas of Wonder, the youth awoke, and began to reproach Parmetella, saying, "Ah, woe is me! for your prying curiosity I have to suffer another seven years this accursed punishment. But begone! Run, scamper off! Take yourself out of my sight! You know not what good fortune you lose." So saying, he vanished like quicksilver.

The poor girl left the palace, cold and stiff with affright, and with her head bowed to the ground. And when she had come out of the cavern she met a fairy, who said to her, "My child, how my heart grieves at your misfortune! Unhappy girl, you are going to the slaughter-house, where you will pass over the bridge no wider than a hair. Therefore, to provide against your peril, take these seven spindles with these seven figs, and a little jar of honey, and these seven pairs of iron shoes, and walk on and on

---

1 Dark-skinned person.

without stopping, until they are worn out; then you will see seven women standing upon a balcony of a house, and spinning from above down to the ground, with the thread wound upon the bone of a dead person. Remain quite still and hidden, and when the thread comes down, take out the bone and put in its place a spindle besmeared with honey, with a fig in the place of the little button. Then as soon as the women draw up the spindles and taste the honey, they will say—

> *He who has made my spindle sweet,*
> *Shall in return with good fortune meet!*

And after repeating these words, they will say, one after another, 'O you who brought us these sweet things appear!' Then you must answer, 'Nay, for you will eat me.' And they will say, 'We swear by our spoon that we will not eat you!' But do not stir; and they will continue, 'We swear by our spit that we will not eat you!' But stand firm, as if rooted to the spot; and they will say, 'We swear by our broom that we will not eat you!' Still do not believe them; and when they say, 'We swear by our pail that we will not eat you!' shut your mouth, and say not a word, or it will cost you your life. At last they will say, 'We swear by Thunder-and-Lightning that we will not eat you!' Then take courage and mount up, for they will do you no harm."

When Parmetella heard this, she set off and walked over hill and dale, until at the end of seven years the iron shoes were worn out; and coming to a large house, with a projecting balcony, she saw the seven women spinning. So she did as the fairy had advised her; and after a thousand wiles and allurements, they swore by Thunder-and-Lightning, whereupon she showed herself and mounted up. Then they all seven said to her, "Traitress, you are the cause that our brother has lived twice seven long years in the cavern, far away from us, in the form of a blackamoor! But never mind; although you have been clever enough to stop our throat with the oath, you shall on the first opportunity pay off both the old and the new reckoning. But now hear what you must do. Hide yourself behind this trough, and when our mother comes, who would swallow you down at once, rise up and seize her behind her back; hold her fast, and do not let her go until she swears by Thunder-and-Lightning not to harm you."

Parmetella did as she was bid, and after the ogress had sworn by the fire-shovel, by the spinning-wheel, by the reel, by the sideboard, and by the peg, at last she swore by Thunder-and-Lightning; whereupon Parmetella let go her hold, and showed herself to the ogress, who said, "You have caught me this time; but take care, Traitress! for, at the first shower, I'll send you to the Lava."

One day the ogress, who was on the look-out for an opportunity to devour Parmetella, took twelve sacks of various seeds—peas, chick-peas, lentils, vetches, kidney-beans, beans, and lupins—and mixed them all together; then she said to her, "Traitress, take these seeds and sort them all, so that each kind may be separated from the rest; and if they are not all sorted by this evening, I'll swallow you like a penny tart."

Poor Parmetella sat down beside the sacks, weeping, and said, "O mother, mother, how will this golden root prove a root of woes to me! Now is my misery completed; by seeing a black face turned white, all has become black before my eyes. Alas! I am ruined and undone—there is no help for it. I already seem as if I were in the throat of that horrid ogress; there is no one to help me, there is no one to advise me, there is no one to comfort me!"

As she was lamenting thus, lo! Thunder-and-Lightning appeared like a flash, for the banishment laid upon him by the spell had just ended. Although he was angry with Parmetella, yet his blood could not turn to water, and seeing her grieving thus he said to her, "Traitress, what makes you weep so?" Then she told him of his mother's ill-treatment of her, and her wish to make an end of her, and eat her up. But Thunder-and-Lightning replied, "Calm yourself and take heart, for it shall not be as she said." And instantly scattering all the seeds on the ground he made a deluge of ants spring up, who forthwith set to work to heap up all the seeds separately, each kind by itself, and Parmetella filled the sacks with them.

When the ogress came home and found the task done, she was almost in despair, and cried, "That dog Thunder-and-Lightning has played me this trick; but you shall not escape thus! So take these pieces of bed-tick,[1] which are enough for twelve mattresses, and mind that by this evening they are filled with feathers, or else I will make mincemeat of you."

The poor girl took the bed-ticks, and sitting down upon the ground began to weep and lament bitterly, making two fountains of her eyes. But presently Thunder-and-Lightning appeared, and said to her, "Do not weep, Traitress—leave it to me, and I will bring you to port; so let down your hair, spread the bed-ticks upon the ground, and fall to weeping and wailing, and crying out that the king of the birds is dead, then you'll see what will happen."

Parmetella did as she was told, and behold! a cloud of birds suddenly appeared that darkened the air; and flapping their wings they let fall their feathers by basketfuls, so that in less than an hour the mattresses were all filled. When the ogress came home and saw the task done, she swelled up with rage till she almost burst, saying, "Thunder-and-Lightning is determined to plague me, but may I be dragged at an ape's tail if I let her

---

1 A bag with the dimensions of a mattress, filled with stuffing such as feathers or straw.

escape!" Then she said to Parmetella, "Run quickly to my sister's house, and tell her to send me the musical instruments; for I have resolved that Thunder-and-Lightning shall marry, and we will make a feast fit for a king." At the same time she sent to bid her sister, when the poor girl came to ask for the instruments, instantly to kill and cook her, and she would come and partake of the feast.

Parmetella, hearing herself ordered to perform an easier task, was in great joy, thinking that the weather had begun to grow milder. Alas, how crooked is human judgment! On the way she met Thunder-and-Lightning, who, seeing her walking at a quick pace, said to her, "Whither are you going, wretched girl? See you not that you are on the way to the slaughter; that you are forging your own fetters, and sharpening the knife and mixing the poison for yourself; that you are sent to the ogress for her to swallow you? But listen to me and fear not. Take this little loaf, this bundle of hay, and this stone; and when you come to the house of my aunt, you will find a bulldog, which will fly barking at you to bite you; but give him this little loaf, and it will stop his throat. And when you have passed the dog, you will meet a horse running loose, which will run up to kick and trample on you; but give him the hay, and you will clog his feet. At last you will come to a door, banging to and fro continually; put this stone before it, and you will stop its fury. Then mount upstairs and you find the ogress, with a little child in her arms, and the oven ready heated to bake you. Whereupon she will say to you, 'Hold this little creature, and wait here till I go and fetch the instruments.' But mind—she will only go to whet her tusks, in order to tear you in pieces. Then throw the little child into the oven without pity, take the instruments which stand behind the door, and hie off before the ogress returns, or else you are lost. The instruments are in a box, but beware of opening it, or you will repent."

Parmetella did all that Thunder-and-Lightning told her; but on her way back with the instruments she opened the box, and lo and behold! they all flew out and about—here a flute, there a flageolet, here a pipe, there a bagpipe, making a thousand different sounds in the air, whilst Parmetella stood looking on and tearing her hair in despair.

Meanwhile the ogress came downstairs, and not finding Parmetella, she went to the window, and called out to the door, "Crush that traitress!" But the door answered:

> *I will not use the poor girl ill,*
> *For she has made me at last stand still.*

Then the ogress cried out to the horse, "Trample on the thief!" But the horse replied:

> *Let the poor girl go her way,*
> *For she has given me the hay.*

And lastly, the ogress called to the dog, saying, "Bite the rogue!" But the dog answered:

> *I'll not hurt a hair of her head,*
> *For she it was who gave me the bread.*

Now as Parmetella ran crying after the instruments, she met Thunder-and-Lightning, who scolded her well, saying, "Traitress, will you not learn at your cost that by your fatal curiosity you are brought to this plight?" Then he called back the instruments with a whistle, and shut them up again in the box, telling Parmetella to take them to his mother. But when the ogress saw her, she cried aloud, "O cruel fate! even my sister is against me, and refuses to give me this pleasure."

Meanwhile the new bride arrived—a hideous pest, a compound of ugliness, a harpy, an evil shade, a horror, a monster, a large tub, who with a hundred flowers and boughs about her looked like a newly opened inn. Then the ogress made a great banquet for her; and being full of gall and malice, she had the table placed close to a well, where she seated her seven daughters, each with a torch in one hand; but she gave two torches to Parmetella, and made her sit at the edge of the well, on purpose that, when she fell asleep, she might tumble to the bottom.

Now whilst the dishes were passing to and fro, and their blood began to get warm, Thunder-and-Lightning, who turned quite sick at the sight of the new bride, said to Parmetella, "Traitress, do you love me?" "Ay, to the top of the roof," she replied. And he answered, "If you love me, give me a kiss." "Nay," said Parmetella, "YOU indeed, who have such a pretty creature at your side! Heaven preserve her to you a hundred years in health and with plenty of sons!" Then the new bride answered, "It is very clear that you are a simpleton, and would remain so were you to live a hundred years, acting the prude as you do, and refusing to kiss so handsome a youth, whilst I let a herdsman kiss me for a couple of chestnuts."

At these words the bridegroom swelled with rage like a toad, so that his food remained sticking in his throat; however, he put a good face on the matter and swallowed the pill, intending to make the reckoning and settle the balance afterwards. But when the tables were removed, and the ogress and his sisters had gone away, Thunder-and-Lightning said to the new bride, "Wife, did you see this proud creature refuse me a kiss?" "She was a simpleton," replied the bride, "to refuse a kiss to such a handsome young man, whilst I let a herdsman kiss me for a couple of chestnuts."

Thunder-and-Lightning could contain himself no longer; the mustard got up into his nose, and with the flash of scorn and the thunder of action, he seized a knife and stabbed the bride, and digging a hole in the cellar he buried her. Then embracing Parmetella he said to her, "You are my jewel, the flower of women, the mirror of honour! Then turn those eyes upon me, give me that hand, put out those lips, draw near to me, my heart! for I will be yours as long as the world lasts."

The next morning, when the Sun aroused his fiery steeds from their watery stable, and drove them to pasture on the fields sown by the Dawn, the ogress came with fresh eggs for the newly married couple, that the young wife might be able to say, "Happy is she who marries and gets a mother-in-law!" But finding Parmetella in the arms of her son, and hearing what had passed, she ran to her sister, to concert some means of removing this thorn from her eyes without her son's being able to prevent it. But when she found that her sister, out of grief at the loss of her daughter, had crept into the oven herself and was burnt, her despair was so great that from an ogress she became a ram, and butted her head against the wall under she broke her pate. Then Thunder-and-Lightning made peace between Parmetella and her sisters-in-law, and they all lived happy and content, finding the saying come true, that—

Patience conquers all.

The Dark King
(*Italy*)

They say there was once a poor chicory-gatherer who went out every day with his wife and his three daughters to gather chicory to sell for salad. Once, at Carneval time, he said, 'We must gather a fine good lot to-day,' and they all dispersed themselves about trying to do their best. The youngest daughter thus came to a place apart where the chicory was of a much finer growth than any she had ever seen before. 'This will be grand!' she said to herself, as she prepared to pull up the finest plant of it. But what was her surprise when with the plant, up came all the earth round it and a great hole only remained!

When she peeped down into it timidly she was further surprised to find it was no dark cave below as she had apprehended, but a bright apartment handsomely furnished, and a most appetising meal spread out on the table, there was, moreover, a commodious staircase reaching to the soil on which she stood, to descend by.

All fear was quickly overcome by the pleasant sight, and the girl at once prepared to descend, and, as no one appeared to raise any objection, she sat down quite boldly and partook of the good food. As soon as she had finished eating, the tables were cleared away by invisible hands, and, as she had nothing else to do she wandered about the place looking at everything. After she had passed through several brilliant rooms she came to a passage, out of which led several store-chambers, where was laid up a good supply of everything that could serve in a house. In some there were provisions of all sorts, in some stuffs both for clothes and furniture.

'There seems to be no one to own all these fine things,' said the girl. 'What a boon they would be at home!' and she put together all that would be most useful to her mother. But what was her dismay when she went back to the dining-hall to find that the staircase by which she had descended was no longer there!

At this sight she sat down and had a good cry, but by-and-by, supper-time came, and with it an excellent supper, served in as mysterious a way as the dinner; and as a good supper was a rare enjoyment for her, she almost forgot her grief while discussing it. After that, invisible hands led her into a bedroom, where she was gently undressed and put to bed without seeing anyone. In the morning she was put in a bath and dressed by invisible hands, but dressed like a princess all in beautiful clothes.

So it all went on for at least three months; every luxury she could wish was provided without stint, but as she never saw anyone she began to get weary, and at last so weary that she could do nothing but cry. At the sound of her crying there came into the room a great black King. Though he was so dark and so big that she was frightened at the sight of him, he spoke very kindly, and asked her why she cried so bitterly, and whether she was not provided with everything she could desire. As she hardly knew herself why she cried, she did not know what to answer him, but only went on whimpering. Then he said, 'You have not seen half the extent of this palace yet or you would not be so weary; here are the keys of all the locked rooms which you have not been into yet. Amuse yourself as much as you like in going through them; they are all just like your own. Only into the room of which the key is not among these do not try to enter. In all the rest do what you like.'

The next morning she took the keys and went into one of the locked rooms, and there she found so many things to surprise and amuse her that she spent the whole day there, and the next day she examined another, and so on for quite three months together, and the locked room of which she had not the key she never thought of trying to enter. But all amusements tire at last, and at the end of this time she was so melancholy that she could do nothing but cry. Then the Dark King came again and asked her tenderly what she wanted.

'I want nothing you can give me,' she replied this time. 'I am tired of being so long away from home. I want to go back home.'

'But remember how badly you were clothed, and how poorly you fared,' replied the Dark King.

'Ah, I know it is much pleasanter here,' said the girl, 'for all those matters, but one cannot do without seeing one's relations, now and then at least.'

'If you make such a point of it,' answered the Dark King, 'you shall go home and see papa and mamma, but you will come back here. I only let you go on that condition.'

The arrangement was accepted, and next day she was driven home in a fine coach with prancing horses and bright harness. Her appearance at home caused so much astonishment that there was hardly room for pleasure, and even her own mother would hardly acknowledge her; as for her sisters, they were so changed by her altered circumstances and so filled with jealousy they would scarcely speak to her. But when she gave her mother a large pot of gold which the Dark King had given her for the purpose, their hearts were somewhat won back to her, and they began to ask all manner of questions concerning what had befallen her during her absence. So much time had been lost at first, however, that none was left for answering them, and, promising to try and come back to them soon, she drove away in her splendid coach.

Another three months passed away after this, and at the end of it she was once more so weary, her tears and cries again called the Dark King to her side.

Again she confided to him that her great grief was the wish to see her friends at home. She could not bear being so long without them. To content her once more he promised to let her drive home the next day; and the next day accordingly she went home.

This time she met with a better reception, and having brought out her pot of gold at her first arrival, everyone was full of anxiety to know how it came she had such riches at her disposal.

'What, that pot of money!' replied the girl, in a tone of disparagement. 'That's nothing. You should see the beautiful things that are scattered about in my new home, just like nothing at all;' and then she went on to describe the magnificence of the place, till nothing would satisfy them but that they should go there too.

'That's impossible,' she replied. 'I promised him not even to mention it.'

'But if he were got rid of, then we might come,' replied the elder sisters.

'What do you mean by "got rid of"?' asked the youngest.

'Why, it is evident he is some bad sort of enchanter, whom it would be well to rid the earth of. If you were to take this stiletto and put it into his breast when he is asleep, we might all come down there and be happy together.'

'Oh, I could never do that!'

Then they took her back to the dining-hall, where the staircase was seen as at the first, and when they touched the ceiling, it opened, and they pushed her through the opening, and she found herself in the place where she had been picking chicory on the day that she first found the Dark King's palace.

Only as they were leading her along, she had considered that it might be dangerous for her, a young girl, to be wandering about the face of the country alone, and she had, therefore, begged the servants to give her a man's clothes instead of her own; and they gave her the worn-out clothes that she had seen the little old hunchback sitting crosslegged to mend.

When she found herself on the chicory-bed it was in the cold of the early morning, and she set off walking towards her parents' cottage. It was about midday when she arrived, and all the family were taking their meal. Poor as it was, it looked very tempting to her who had tasted nothing all the morning.

'Who are you?' cried the mother, as she came up to the door.

'I'm your own child, your youngest daughter. Don't you know me?' cried the forlorn girl in alarm.

'A likely joke!' laughed out the mother; 'my daughter comes to see me in a gilded coach with prancing horses!'

'Had you asked for a bit of bread in the honest character of a beggar,' pursued the father, 'poor as I am, I would never have refused your weary, woebegone looks; but to attempt to deceive with such a falsehood is not to be tolerated,' and he rose up, and drove the poor child away.

Protests were vain, for no one recognised her under her disguise.

Mournful and hopeless, she wandered away. On, on, on, she went, till at last she came to a palace in a great city, and in the stables were a number of grooms and their helpers rubbing down horses.

'Wouldn't there be a place for me among all these boys?' asked the little chicory-gatherer, plaintively. 'I, too, could learn to rub down a horse if you taught me.'

'Well, you don't look hardly strong enough to rub down a horse, my lad,' answered the head-groom; 'but you seem a civil-spoken sort of chap, so you may come in; I dare say we can find some sort of work for you.'

So she went into the stable-yard, and helped the grooms of the palace.

But every day the queen stood at a window of the palace where she could watch the fair stable-boy, and at last she sent and called the head-groom, and said to him, 'What are you doing with that new boy in the stableyard?'

The head-groom said, 'Please your Majesty he came and begged for work, and we took him to help.

Then the queen said, 'He is not fit for that sort of work, send him to me.'

So the chicory-gatherer was sent up to the queen, and the queen gave her the post of master of the palace, and appointed a fine suite of apartments and a dress becoming the rank, and was never happy unless she had this new master of the palace with her.

Now the king was gone to the wars, and had been a long time absent. One day the queen said to the master of the palace that very likely the king would not come back, so that it would be better they should marry.

Then the poor chicory-gatherer was sadly afraid that if the queen discovered that she was a woman she would lose her fine place at the palace, and become a poor beggar again without a home; so she said nothing of this, but only reasoned with the queen that it was better to wait and see if the king did not come home. But as she continued saying this, and at the same time never showed any wish that the king might not come back, or that the marriage might take place, the queen grew sorely offended, and swore she would be avenged.

Not long after, the king really did come back, covered with glory, from the wars. Now was the time for the queen to take her revenge.

Choosing her opportunity, therefore, at the moment when the king was rejoicing that he had been permitted to come back to her again, with hypocritical tears she said,

'It is no small mercy, indeed, that your Majesty has found me again here as I am, for it had well-nigh been a very different case.'

The king was instantly filled with burning indignation, and asked her further what her words meant.

'They mean,' replied the queen, 'that the master of the palace, on whom I had bestowed the office only because he seemed so simple, as you too must say he looks, presumed on my favour, and would have me marry him, urging that peradventure the king, who had been so long absent at the wars, might never return.'

The king started to his feet at the words, placing his hand upon his sword in token of his wrath; but the queen went on:

'And when he found that I would not listen to his suit, he dared to assume a tone of command, and would have compelled me to consent; so that I had to call forth all my courage, and determination, and dignity, to keep him back; and had the King's Majesty not been directed back to the palace as soon as he was, who knows where it might have ended!'

It needed no more. The king ordered the master of the palace to be instantly thrown into prison, and appointed the next day for him to be beheaded.

The chicory-gatherer was ready enough now to protest that she was a woman. But it helped nothing; they only laughed. And who could stand against the word of the queen?

Next day, accordingly, the scaffold was raised, and the master of the palace was brought forth to be beheaded, the king and the queen, and all the court, being present.

When the chicory-gatherer, therefore, found herself in dire need and peril of life, she took out one of the hairs the Dark King had given her, and burnt it in the flame of a torch. Instantly there was a distant roaring sound as of a tramp of troops and the roll of drums. Everyone started at the sound, and the executioner stayed his hand.

Then the maiden burnt the second hair, and instantly a vast army surrounded the whole place; round the palace they marched and up to the scaffold, and so to the very throne of the king. The king had now something to think of besides giving the signal for the execution, and the headsman stayed his hand.

Then the maiden burnt the third hair, and instantly the Dark King himself appeared upon the scene, clothed in shining armour, and fearful in majesty and might. And he said to the king,

'Who are you that you have given over my wife to the executioner?'

And the king said,

'Who is thy wife that I should give her to the executioner?'

The Dark King, taking the master of the palace by the hand, said,

'This is my wife. Touch her who dares!'

Then the king knew that it had been true when the master of the palace had alleged that she was not guilty of the charge the queen had brought against her, being a woman; and seeing clearly what had been the malice of the queen, he ordered the executioner to behead her instead, but the chicory-gatherer he gave up to the Dark King.

Then the Dark King said to the chicory-gatherer, 'I came at your bidding to defend you, and I said you were my wife to save your life; but whether you will be my wife or not depends on you. It is for you to say whether you will or not.'

Then the maiden answered, 'You have been all goodness to me; ungrateful indeed should I be did I not, as I now do, say "yes."'

As soon as she said 'yes,' the earth shook, and she was no longer standing on a scaffold, but before an altar in a splendid cathedral, surrounded by a populous and flourishing city. By her side stood the Black King, but black no longer. He was now a most beautiful prince; for with all his kingdom he had been under enchantment, and the condition of his release had been that a fair maiden should give her free consent to marry him.

510: Cinderella and Peau d'Âne

Cinderella; or, The Little Glass Slipper (*France*)

Once there was a gentleman who married, for his second wife, the proudest and most haughty woman that was ever seen. She had, by a former husband, two daughters of her own humor, who were, indeed, exactly like her in all things. He had likewise, by another wife, a young daughter, but of unparalleled goodness and sweetness of temper, which she took from her mother, who was the best creature in the world.

No sooner were the ceremonies of the wedding over but the mother-in-law began to show herself in her true colors. She could not bear the good qualities of this pretty girl, and the less because they made her own daughters appear the more odious. She employed her in the meanest work of the house: she scoured the dishes, tables, etc., and scrubbed madam's chamber, and those of misses, her daughters; she lay up in a sorry garret, upon a wretched straw bed, while her sisters lay in fine rooms, with floors all inlaid, upon beds of the very newest fashion, and where they had looking-glasses so large that they might see themselves at their full length from head to foot.

The poor girl bore all patiently, and dared not tell her father, who would have rattled her off; for his wife governed him entirely. When she had done her work, she used to go into the chimney-corner, and sit down among cinders and ashes, which made her commonly be called Cinder-wench; but the youngest, who was not so rude and uncivil as the eldest, called her Cinderella. However, Cinderella, notwithstanding her mean apparel, was a hundred times handsomer than her sisters, though they were always dressed very richly.

It happened that the King's son gave a ball, and invited all persons of fashion to it. Our young misses were also invited, for they cut a very grand figure among the quality. They were mightily delighted at this invitation, and wonderfully busy in choosing out such gowns, petticoats, and head-clothes as might become them. This was a new trouble to Cinderella; for it was she who ironed her sisters' linen, and plaited their ruffles; they talked all day long of nothing but how they should be dressed.

"For my part," said the eldest, "I will wear my red velvet suit with French trimming."

"And I," said the youngest, "shall have my usual petticoat; but then, to make amends for that, I will put on my gold-flowered manteau, and my diamond stomacher, which is far from being the most ordinary one in the world."

They sent for the best tire-woman they could get to make up their head-dresses and adjust their double pinners, and they had their red brushes and patches from Mademoiselle de la Poche.

Cinderella was likewise called up to them to be consulted in all these matters, for she had excellent notions, and advised them always for the best, nay, and offered her services to dress their heads, which they were very willing she should do. As she was doing this, they said to her:

"Cinderella, would you not be glad to go to the ball?"

"Alas!" said she, "you only jeer me; it is not for such as I am to go thither."

"Thou art in the right of it," replied they; "it would make the people laugh to see a Cinderwench at a ball."

Anyone but Cinderella would have dressed their heads awry, but she was very good, and dressed them perfectly well. They were almost two days without eating, so much were they transported with joy. They broke above a dozen laces in trying to be laced up close, that they might have a fine slender shape, and they were continually at their looking-glass. At last the happy day came; they went to Court, and Cinderella followed them with her eyes as long as she could, and when she had lost sight of them, she fell a-crying.

Her godmother, who saw her all in tears, asked her what was the matter.

"I wish I could—I wish I could—"; she was not able to speak the rest, being interrupted by her tears and sobbing.

This godmother of hers, who was a fairy, said to her, "Thou wishest thou couldst go to the ball; is it not so?"

"Y—es," cried Cinderella, with a great sigh.

"Well," said her godmother, "be but a good girl, and I will contrive that thou shalt go." Then she took her into her chamber, and said to her, "Run into the garden, and bring me a pumpkin."

Cinderella went immediately to gather the finest she could get, and brought it to her godmother, not being able to imagine how this pumpkin could make her go to the ball. Her godmother scooped out all the inside of it, having left nothing but the rind; which done, she struck it with her wand, and the pumpkin was instantly turned into a fine coach, gilded all over with gold.

She then went to look into her mouse-trap, where she found six mice, all alive, and ordered Cinderella to lift up a little the trapdoor, when, giving each mouse, as it went out, a little tap with her wand, the mouse was that moment turned into a fine horse, which altogether made a very fine set of six horses of a beautiful mouse-colored dapple-gray. Being at a loss for a coachman,

"I will go and see," says Cinderella, "if there is never a rat in the rat-trap—we may make a coachman of him."

"Thou art in the right," replied her godmother; "go and look."

Cinderella brought the trap to her, and in it there were three huge rats. The fairy made choice of one of the three which had the largest beard, and, having touched him with her wand, he was turned into a fat, jolly coachman, who had the smartest whiskers eyes ever beheld. After that, she said to her:

"Go again into the garden, and you will find six lizards behind the watering-pot, bring them to me."

She had no sooner done so but her godmother turned them into six footmen, who skipped up immediately behind the coach, with their liveries all bedaubed with gold and silver, and clung as close behind each other as if they had done nothing else their whole lives. The Fairy then said to Cinderella:

"Well, you see here an equipage fit to go to the ball with; are you not pleased with it?"

"Oh! yes," cried she; "but must I go thither as I am, in these nasty rags?"

Her godmother only just touched her with her wand, and, at the same instant, her clothes were turned into cloth of gold and silver, all beset with jewels. This done, she gave her a pair of glass slippers, the prettiest in the whole world. Being thus decked out, she got up into her coach; but her godmother, above all things, commanded her not to stay till after midnight, telling her, at the same time, that if she stayed one moment longer, the coach would be a pumpkin again, her horses mice, her coachman a rat, her footmen lizards, and her clothes become just as they were before.

She promised her godmother she would not fail of leaving the ball before midnight, and then away she drives, scarce able to contain herself for joy. The King's son who was told that a great princess, whom nobody knew, was come, ran out to receive her; he gave her his hand as she alighted out of the coach, and led her into the ball, among all the company. There was immediately a profound silence, they left off dancing, and the violins ceased to play, so attentive was everyone to contemplate the singular beauties of the unknown new-comer. Nothing was then heard but a confused noise of:

"Ha! how handsome she is! Ha! how handsome she is!"

The King himself, old as he was, could not help watching her, and telling the Queen softly that it was a long time since he had seen so beautiful and lovely a creature.

All the ladies were busied in considering her clothes and headdress, that they might have some made next day after the same pattern, provided they could meet with such fine material and as able hands to make them.

The King's son conducted her to the most honorable seat, and afterward took her out to dance with him; she danced so very gracefully that they all more and more admired her. A fine collation was served up, whereof the young prince ate not a morsel, so intently was he busied in gazing on her.

She went and sat down by her sisters, showing them a thousand civilities, giving them part of the oranges and citrons which the Prince had presented her with, which very much surprised them, for they did not know her. While Cinderella was thus amusing her sisters, she heard the clock strike eleven and three-quarters, whereupon she immediately made a curtsey to the company and hasted away as fast as she could.

When she got home she ran to seek out her godmother, and, after having thanked her, she said she could not but heartily wish she might go next day to the ball, because the King's son had desired her.

As she was eagerly telling her godmother whatever had passed at the ball, her two sisters knocked at the door, which Cinderella ran and opened.

"How long you have stayed!" cried she, gaping, rubbing her eyes and stretching herself as if she had been just waked out of her sleep; she had not, however, any manner of inclination to sleep since they went from home.

"If thou hadst been at the ball," said one of her sisters, "thou wouldst not have been tired with it. There came thither the finest princess, the most beautiful ever was seen with mortal eyes; she showed us a thousand civilities, and gave us oranges and citrons."

Cinderella seemed very indifferent in the matter; indeed, she asked them the name of that princess; but they told her they did not know it, and that the King's son was very uneasy on her account and would give all the world to know who she was. At this Cinderella, smiling, replied:

"She must, then, be very beautiful indeed; how happy you have been! Could not I see her? Ah! dear Miss Charlotte, do lend me your yellow suit of clothes which you wear every day."

"Ay, to be sure!" cried Miss Charlotte; "lend my clothes to such a dirty Cinderwench as thou art! I should be a fool."

Cinderella, indeed, expected well such answer, and was very glad of the refusal; for she would have been sadly put to it if her sister had lent her what she asked for jestingly.

The next day the two sisters were at the ball, and so was Cinderella, but dressed more magnificently than before. The King's son was always by her, and never ceased his compliments and kind speeches to her; to whom all this was so far from being tiresome that she quite forgot what her godmother had recommended to her; so that she, at last, counted the clock striking twelve when she took it to be no more than eleven; she then rose up and fled, as nimble as a deer. The Prince followed, but could not overtake her. She left behind one of her glass slippers, which the Prince took up most carefully. She got home but quite out of breath, and in her nasty old clothes, having nothing left her of all her finery but one of the little slippers, fellow to that she dropped. The guards at the palace gate were asked: If they had not seen a princess go out.

Who said: They had seen nobody go out but a young girl, very meanly dressed, and who had more the air of a poor country wench than a gentlewoman.

When the two sisters returned from the ball Cinderella asked them: If they had been well diverted, and if the fine lady had been there.

They told her: Yes, but that she hurried away immediately when it struck twelve, and with so much haste that she dropped one of her little glass slippers, the prettiest in the world, which the King's son had taken up; that he had done nothing but look at her all the time at the ball, and that most certainly he was very much in love with the beautiful person who owned the glass slipper.

What they said was very true; for a few days after the King's son caused it to be proclaimed, by sound of trumpet, that he would marry her whose foot the slipper would just fit. They whom he employed began to try it upon the princesses, then the duchesses and all the Court, but in vain; it was brought to the two sisters, who did all they possibly could to thrust their foot into the slipper, but they could not effect it. Cinderella, who saw all this, and knew her slipper, said to them, laughing:

"Let me see if it will not fit me."

Her sisters burst out a-laughing, and began to banter her. The gentleman who was sent to try the slipper looked earnestly at Cinderella, and, finding her very handsome, said: It was but just that she should try, and that he had orders to let everyone make trial.

He obliged Cinderella to sit down, and, putting the slipper to her foot, he found it went on very easily, and fitted her as if it had been made of wax. The astonishment her two sisters were in was excessively great, but still abundantly greater when Cinderella pulled out of her pocket the other slipper, and put it on her foot. Thereupon, in came her godmother, who, having touched with her wand Cinderella's clothes, made them richer and more magnificent than any of those she had before.

And now her two sisters found her to be that fine, beautiful lady whom they had seen at the ball. They threw themselves at her feet to beg pardon for all the ill-treatment they had made her undergo. Cinderella took them up, and, as she embraced them, cried: That she forgave them with all her heart, and desired them always to love her.

She was conducted to the young prince, dressed as she was; he thought her more charming than ever, and, a few days after, married her. Cinderella, who was no less good than beautiful, gave her two sisters lodgings in the palace, and that very same day matched them with two great lords of the Court.

The True Sweetheart
(*Germany*)

There was once on a time a girl who was young and beautiful, but she had lost her mother when she was quite a child, and her step-mother did all she could to make the girl's life wretched. Whenever this woman gave her anything to do, she worked at it indefatigably, and did everything that lay in her power. Still she could not touch the heart of the wicked woman by that; she was never satisfied; it was never enough. The harder the girl worked, the more work was put upon her, and all that the woman thought of was how to weigh her down with still heavier burdens, and make her life still more miserable.

One day she said to her, "Here are twelve pounds of feathers which thou must pick, and if they are not done this evening, thou mayst expect a good beating. Dost thou imagine thou art to idle away the whole day?" The poor girl sat down to the work, but tears ran down her cheeks as she did so, for she saw plainly enough that it was quite impossible to finish the work in one day. Whenever she had a little heap of feathers lying before her, and she sighed or smote her hands together in her anguish, they flew away, and she had to pick them out again, and begin her work anew. Then she put her elbows on the table, laid her face in her two hands, and cried, "Is there no one, then, on God's earth to have pity on me?" Then she heard a low voice which said, "Be comforted, my child, I have come to help thee." The maiden looked up, and an old woman was by her side. She took the girl kindly by the hand, and said, "Only tell me what is troubling thee." As she spoke so kindly, the girl told her of her miserable life, and how one burden after another was laid upon her, and she never could get to the end of the work which was given to her. "If I have not done these feathers by this evening, my step-mother will beat me; she has threatened she will, and I know she keeps her word." Her tears began to flow again, but the good old woman said, "Do not be afraid, my child; rest a while, and in the meantime I will look to thy work." The girl lay down on her bed, and soon fell asleep. The old woman seated herself at the table with the feathers, and how they did fly off the quills, which she scarcely touched with her withered hands! The twelve pounds were soon finished, and when the girl awoke, great snow-white heaps were lying, piled up, and everything in the room was neatly cleared away, but the old woman had vanished. The maiden thanked God, and sat still till evening came, when the step-mother came in and marvelled to see the work completed. "Just look, you awkward creature," said she, "what can be done when people are industrious; and why couldst thou not set about something else? There thou sittest with thy hands crossed." When she went out she said, "The creature is worth more than her salt. I must give her some work that is still harder."

Next morning she called the girl, and said, "There is a spoon for thee; with that thou must empty out for me the great pond which is beside the garden, and if it is not done by night, thou knowest what will happen." The girl took the spoon, and saw that it was full of holes; but even if it had not been, she never could have emptied the pond with it. She set to work at once, knelt down by the water, into which her tears were falling, and began to empty it. But the good old woman appeared again, and when she learnt the cause of her grief, she said, "Be of good cheer, my child. Go into the thicket and lie down and sleep; I will soon do thy work." As soon as the old woman was alone, she barely touched the pond, and a vapour rose up on high from the water, and mingled itself with the clouds. Gradually the pond was emptied, and when the maiden awoke before sunset and came thither, she saw nothing but the fishes which were struggling in the mud. She went to her step-mother, and showed her that the work was done. "It ought to have been done long before this," said she, and grew white with anger, but she meditated something new.

On the third morning she said to the girl, "Thou must build me a castle on the plain there, and it must be ready by the evening." The maiden was dismayed, and said, "How can I complete such a great work?" "I will endure no opposition," screamed the step-mother. "If thou canst empty a pond with a spoon that is full of holes, thou canst build a castle too. I will take possession of it this very day, and if anything is wanting, even if it be the most trifling thing in the kitchen or cellar, thou knowest what lies before thee!" She drove the girl out, and when she entered the valley, the rocks were there, piled up one above the other, and all her strength would not have enabled her even to move the very smallest of them. She sat down and wept, and still she hoped the old woman would help her. The old woman was not long in coming; she comforted her and said, "Lie down there in the shade and sleep, and I will soon build the castle for thee. If it would be a pleasure to thee, thou canst live in it thyself." When the maiden had gone away, the old woman touched the gray rocks. They began to rise, and immediately moved together as if giants had built the walls; and on these the building arose, and it seemed as if countless hands were working invisibly, and placing one stone upon another. There was a dull heavy noise from the ground; pillars arose of their own accord on high, and placed themselves in order near each other. The tiles laid themselves in order on the roof, and when noon-day came, the great weather-cock was already turning itself on the summit of the tower, like a golden figure of the Virgin with fluttering garments. The inside of the castle was being finished while evening was drawing near. How the old woman managed it, I know not; but the walls of the rooms were hung with silk and velvet, embroidered chairs were there, and richly ornamented arm-chairs by marble tables; crystal chandeliers hung down from the ceilings, and mirrored themselves in the smooth pavement; green parrots were there in gilt cages, and so were strange birds which sang most beautifully, and there was on all sides as much magnificence as if a king were going to live there. The sun was just setting when the girl awoke, and the brightness of a thousand lights flashed in her face. She hurried to the castle, and entered by the open door. The steps were spread with red cloth, and the golden balustrade beset with flowering trees. When she saw the splendour of the apartment, she stood as if turned to stone. Who knows how long she might have stood there if she had not remembered the step-mother? "Alas!" she said to herself, "if she could but be satisfied at last, and would give up making my life a misery to me." The girl went and told her that the castle was ready. "I will move into it at once," said she, and rose from her seat. When they entered the castle, she was forced to hold her hand before her eyes, the brilliancy of everything was so dazzling. "Thou seest," said she to the girl, "how easy it has been for thee to do this; I ought to have given thee something harder." She went through all the rooms, and examined every corner to see if anything was wanting or defective; but she could discover nothing. "Now we will go down below," said she, looking at the girl with malicious eyes. "The kitchen and the cellar still have to be examined, and if thou hast forgotten anything thou shalt not escape thy punishment." But the fire was burning on the hearth, and the meat was cooking in the pans, the tongs and shovel were leaning against the wall, and the shining brazen utensils all arranged in sight. Nothing was wanting, not even a coal-box and water-pail. "Which is the way to the cellar?" she cried. "If that is not abundantly filled, it shall go ill with thee." She herself raised up the trap-door and descended; but she had hardly made two steps before the heavy trap-door which was only laid back, fell down. The girl heard a scream, lifted up the door very quickly to go to her aid, but she had fallen down, and the girl found her lying lifeless at the bottom.

And now the magnificent castle belonged to the girl alone. She at first did not know how to reconcile herself to her good fortune. Beautiful dresses were hanging in the wardrobes, the chests were filled with gold or silver, or with pearls and jewels, and she never felt a desire that she was not able to gratify. And soon the fame of the beauty and riches of the maiden went over all the world. Wooers presented themselves daily, but none pleased her. At length the son of the King came and he knew how to touch her heart, and she betrothed herself to him. In the garden of the castle was a lime-tree, under which they were one day sitting together, when he said to her, "I will go home and obtain my father's consent to our marriage. I entreat thee to wait for me here under this lime-tree, I shall be back with thee in a few hours." The maiden kissed him on his left cheek, and said, "Keep true to me, and never let anyone else kiss thee on this cheek. I will wait here under the lime-tree until thou returnest."

The maid stayed beneath the lime-tree until sunset, but he did not return. She sat three days from morning till evening, waiting for him, but in vain. As he still was not there by the fourth day, she said, "Some accident has assuredly befallen him. I will go out and seek him, and will not come back until I have found him." She packed up three of her most beautiful dresses, one embroidered with bright stars, the second with silver moons, the third with golden suns, tied up a handful of jewels in her handkerchief, and set out. She inquired everywhere for her betrothed, but no one had seen him; no one knew anything about him. Far and wide did she wander through the world, but she found him not. At last she hired herself to a farmer as a cow-herd, and buried her dresses and jewels beneath a stone.

And now she lived as a herdswoman, guarded her herd, and was very sad and full of longing for her beloved one; she had a little calf which she taught to know her, and fed it out of her own hand, and when she said,

> *Little calf, little calf, kneel by my side,*
> *And do not forget thy shepherd-maid,*
> *As the prince forgot his betrothed bride,*
> *Who waited for him 'neath the lime-tree's shade.*

the little calf knelt down, and she stroked it.

And when she had lived for a couple of years alone and full of grief, a report was spread over all the land that the King's daughter was about to celebrate her marriage. The road to the town passed through the village where the maiden was living, and it came to pass that once when the maiden was driving out her herd, her bridegroom travelled by. He was sitting proudly on his horse, and never looked round, but when she saw him she recognized her beloved, and it was just as if a sharp knife had pierced her heart. "Alas!" said she, "I believed him true to me, but he has forgotten me."

Next day he again came along the road. When he was near her she said to the little calf,

> *Little calf, little calf, kneel by my side,*

> *And do not forget thy shepherd-maid,*
> *As the prince forgot his betrothed bride,*
> *Who waited for him 'neath the lime-tree's shade.*

When he was aware of the voice, he looked down and reined in his horse. He looked into the herd's face, and then put his hands before his eyes as if he were trying to remember something, but he soon rode onwards and was out of sight. "Alas!" said she, "he no longer knows me," and her grief was ever greater.

Soon after this a great festival three days long was to be held at the King's court, and the whole country was invited to it.

"Now will I try my last chance," thought the maiden, and when evening came she went to the stone under which she had buried her treasures. She took out the dress with the golden suns, put it on, and adorned herself with the jewels. She let down her hair, which she had concealed under a handkerchief, and it fell down in long curls about her, and thus she went into the town, and in the darkness was observed by no one. When she entered the brightly-lighted hall, everyone started back in amazement, but no one knew who she was. The King's son went to meet her, but he did not recognize her. He led her out to dance, and was so enchanted with her beauty, that he thought no more of the other bride. When the feast was over, she vanished in the crowd, and hastened before daybreak to the village, where she once more put on her herd's dress.

Next evening she took out the dress with the silver moons, and put a half-moon made of precious stones in her hair. When she appeared at the festival, all eyes were turned upon her, but the King's son hastened to meet her, and filled with love for her, danced with her alone, and no longer so much as glanced at anyone else. Before she went away she was forced to promise him to come again to the festival on the last evening.

When she appeared for the third time, she wore the star-dress which sparkled at every step she took, and her hair-ribbon and girdle were starred with jewels. The prince had already been waiting for her for a long time, and forced his way up to her. "Do but tell who thou art," said he, "I feel just as if I had already known thee a long time." "Dost thou not know what I did when thou leftest me?" Then she stepped up to him, and kissed him on his left cheek, and in a moment it was as if scales fell from his eyes, and he recognized the true bride. "Come," said he to her, "here I stay no longer," gave her his hand, and led her down to the carriage. The horses hurried away to the magic castle as if the wind had been harnessed to the carriage. The illuminated windows already shone in the distance. When they drove past the lime-tree, countless glow-worms were swarming about it. It shook its branches, and sent forth their fragrance. On the steps flowers were blooming, and the room echoed with the song of strange birds, but in the hall the entire court was assembled, and the priest was waiting to marry the bridegroom to the true bride.

Cinderella
(*Italy*)

Once upon a time there was a man who had three daughters. He was once ordered to go away to work, and said to them: "Since I am about making a journey, what do you want me to bring you when I return?" One asked for a handsome dress; the other, a fine hat and a beautiful shawl. He said to the youngest: "And you, Cinderella, what do you want?" They called her Cinderella because she always sat in the chimney-corner. "You must buy me a little bird Verdeliò." "The simpleton! she does not know what to do with the bird! Instead of ordering a handsome dress, a fine shawl, she takes a bird. Who knows what she will do with it!" "Silence!" she says, "it pleases me." The father went, and on his return brought the dress, hat, and shawl for the two sisters, and the little bird for Cinderella. The father was employed at the court, and one day the king said to him: "I am going to give three balls; if you want to bring your daughters, do so; they will amuse themselves a little." "As you wish," he replies, "thanks!" and accepts. He went home and said: "What do you think, girls? His Majesty wishes you to attend his ball." "There, you see, Cinderella, if you had only asked for a handsome dress! This evening we are going to the ball." She replied: "It matters nothing to me! You go; I am not coming." In the evening, when the time came, they adorned themselves, saying to Cinderella: "Come along, there will be room for you, too." "I don't want to go; you go; I don't want to." "But," said their father, "let us go, let us go! Dress and come along; let her stay." When they had gone, she went to the bird and said: "O Bird Verdeliò, make me more beautiful than I am!" She became clothed in a sea-green dress, with so many diamonds that it blinded you to behold her. The bird made ready two purses of money, and said to her: "Take these two purses, enter your carriage, and away!" She set out for the ball, and left the bird Verdeliò at home. She entered the ball-room. Scarcely had the gentlemen seen this beautiful lady (she dazzled them on all sides), when the king, just think of it, began to dance with her the whole evening. After he had danced with her all the evening, his Majesty stopped, and she stood by her sisters. While she was at her sisters' side, she drew out her handkerchief, and a bracelet fell out. "Oh, Signora," said the eldest sister, "you have dropped this." "Keep it for yourself," she said. "Oh, if Cinderella were only here, who knows what might not have happened to her?" The king had given orders that when this lady went away they should find out where she lived. After she had remained a little, she left the ball. You can imagine whether the servants were on the lookout! She entered her carriage and away! She perceives that she is followed, takes the money and begins to throw it out of the window of the carriage. The greedy servants, I tell you, seeing all that money, thought no more of her, but stopped to pick up the money. She returned home and went up-stairs. "O Bird Verdeliò, make me homelier than I am!" You ought to see how ugly, how horrid, she became, all ashes. When the sisters returned, they cried: "Cin-der-el-la!" "Oh, leave her alone," said her father; "she is asleep now, leave her alone!" But they went up and showed her the large and beautiful bracelet. "Do you see, you simpleton? You might have had it." "It matters nothing to me." Their father said: "Let us go to supper, you little geese."

Let us return to the king, who was awaiting his servants, who had not the courage to appear, but kept away. He calls them. "How did the matter go?" They fall at his feet. "Thus and thus! She threw out so much money!" "Wretches, you are nothing else," he said, "were you afraid of not being rewarded? Well! to-morrow evening, attention, under pain of death." The next evening the usual ball. The sisters say: "Will you come this evening, Cinderella?" "Oh," she says, "don't bother me! I don't want to go." Their father cries out to them: "How troublesome you are! Let her alone!" So they began to adorn themselves more handsomely than the former evening, and departed. "Good-by, Cinderella!" When they had gone, Cinderella went to the bird and said: "Little Bird Verdeliò, make me more beautiful than I am!" Then she became clothed in sea-green, embroidered with all the fish of the sea, mingled with diamonds more than you could believe. The bird said: "Take these two bags of sand, and when you are followed, throw it out, and so they will be blinded." She entered her carriage and set out for the ball. As soon as his Majesty saw her he began to dance with her and danced as long as he could. After he had danced as long as he could (she did not grow weary, but he did), she placed herself near her sisters, drew out her handkerchief, and there fell out a beautiful necklace all made of coal. The second sister said: "Signora, you have dropped this." She replied: "Keep it for yourself." "If Cinderel-la were here, who knows what might not happen to her! To-morrow she must come!" After a while she leaves the ball. The servants (just think, under pain of death!) were all on the alert, and followed her. She began to throw out all the sand, and they were blinded. She went home, dismount-ed, and went up-stairs. "Little Bird Verdeliò, make me homelier than I am!" She became frightfully homely. When her sisters returned they be-gan from below: "Cin-der-ella! if you only knew what that lady gave us!" "It matters nothing to me!" "But to-morrow evening you must go!" "Yes, yes! you would have had it!" Their father says: "Let us go to supper and let her alone; you are really silly!"

Let us return to his Majesty, who was waiting for his servants to learn where she lived. Instead of that they were all brought back blinded, and had to be accompanied. "Rogue!" he exclaimed, "either this lady is some fairy or she must have some fairy who protects her."

The next day the sisters began: "Cinderella, you must go this evening! Listen; it is the last evening; you must come." The father: "Oh let her alone! you are always teasing her!" Then they went away and began to prepare for the ball. When they were all prepared, they went to the ball with their father. When they had departed, Cinderella went to the bird: "Little Bird Verdeliò, make me more beautiful than I am!" Then she was dressed in all the colors of the heavens; all the comets, the stars, and moon on her dress, and the sun on her brow. She enters the ball-room. Who could look at her! for the sun alone they lower their eyes, and are all blinded. His Majesty began to dance, but he could not look at her, because she dazzled him. He had already given orders to his servants to be on the lookout, under pain of death; not to go on foot, but to mount their horses that evening. After she had danced longer than on the previous evenings she placed herself by her father's side, drew out her handkerchief, and there fell out a snuff-box of gold, full of money. "Signora, you have dropped this snuff-box." "Keep it for yourself!" Imagine that man: he opens it and sees it full of money. What joy! After she had remained a time she went home as usual. The servants followed her on horseback, quickly; at a distance from the carriage; but on horseback that was not much trouble. She perceived that she had not prepared anything to throw that evening. "Oh!" she cried, "what shall I do?" She left the carriage quickly, and in her haste lost one of her slippers. The servants picked it up, took the number of the house, and went away. Cinderella went upstairs and said: "Little Bird Verdeliò, make me more homely than I am!" The bird does not answer. After she had repeated it three or four times, it answered: "Rogue! I ought not to make you more homely, but..." and she became homely and the bird continued: "What are you going to do now? You are discovered." She began to weep in earnest. When her sisters returned, they cried: "Cin-der-ella!" You can imagine that she did not answer them this evening. "See what a beautiful snuff-box. If you had gone you might have had it." "I do not care! Go away!" Then their father called them to supper.

Let us now turn to the servants who went back with the slipper and the number of the house. "To-morrow," said his Majesty, "as soon as it is day, go to that house, take a carriage, and bring that lady to the palace." The servants took the slipper and went away. The next morning they knocked at the door. Cinderella's father looked out and exclaimed: "Oh, Heavens! it is his Majesty's carriage; what does it mean?" They open the door and the servants ascend. "What do you want of me?" asked the father. "How many daughters have you?" "Two." "Well, show them to us." The father made them come in there. "Sit down," they said to one of them. They tried the slipper on her; it was ten times too large for her. The other one sat down; it was too small for her. "But tell me, good man, have you no other daughters? Take care to tell the truth! because his Majesty wishes it, under pain of death!" "Gentlemen, there is another one, but I do not mention it. She is all in the ashes, the coals; if you should see her! I do not call her my daughter from shame." "We have not come for beauty, or for finery; we want to see the girl!"

Her sisters began to call her: "Cin-der-ella!" but she did not answer. After a time she said: "What is the matter?" "You must come down! there are some gentlemen here who wish to see you." "I don't want to come." "But you must come, you see!" "Very well; tell them I will come in a moment." She went to the little bird: "Ah little Bird Verdeliò, make me more beautiful than I am!" Then she was dressed as she had been the last evening, with the sun, and moon, and stars, and in addition, great chains all of gold everywhere about her. The bird said: "Take me away with you! Put me in your bosom!" She puts the bird in her bosom and begins to descend the stairs. "Do you hear her?" said the father, "do you hear her? She is dragging with her the chains from the chimney-corner. You can imagine how frightful she will look!" When she reached the last step, and they saw her, "Ah!" they exclaimed, and recognized the lady of the ball. You can imagine how her father and sisters were vexed. They made her sit down, and tried on the slipper, and it fitted her. Then they made her enter the carriage, and took her to his Majesty, who recognized the lady of the other evenings. And you can imagine that, all in love as he was, he said to her: "Will you really be my wife?" You may believe she consents. She sends for her father and sisters, and makes them all come to the palace. They celebrate the marriage. Imagine what fine festivals were given at this wedding! The servants who had discovered where Cinderella lived were promoted to the highest positions in the palace as a reward.

510B: Peau d'Âne

The She-Bear
(*Italy*)

There lived, it is said, once upon a time a King of Rough-Rock, who had a wife the very mother of beauty, but in the full career of her years she fell from the horse of health and broke her life. Before the candle of life went out at the auction of her years she called her husband and said to him, "I know you have always loved me tenderly; show me, therefore, at the close of my days the completion of your love by promising me never to marry again, unless you find a woman as beautiful as I have been, otherwise I leave you my curse, and shall bear you hatred even in the other world."

The King, who loved his wife beyond measure, hearing this her last wish, burst into tears, and for some time could not answer a single word. At last, when he had done weeping, he said to her, "Sooner than take another wife may the gout lay hold of me; may I have my head cut off like a mackerel! My dearest love, drive such a thought from your mind; do not believe in dreams, or that I could love any other woman; you were the first new coat of my love, and you shall carry away with you the last rags of my affection."

As he said these words the poor young Queen, who was at the point of death, turned up her eyes and stretched out her feet. When the King saw her life thus running out he unstopped the channels of his eyes, and made such a howling and beating and outcry that all the Court came running up, calling on the name of the dear soul, and upbraiding Fortune for taking her from him, and plucking out his beard, he cursed the stars that had sent him such a misfortune. But bearing in mind the maxim, "Pain in one's elbow and pain for one's wife are alike hard to bear, but are soon over," ere the Night had gone forth into the place-of-arms in the sky to muster the bats he began to count upon his fingers and to reflect thus to himself, "Here is my wife dead, and I am left a wretched widower, with no hope of seeing anyone but this poor daughter whom she has left me. I must therefore try to discover some means or other of having a son and heir. But where shall I look? Where shall I find a woman equal in beauty to my wife? Everyone appears a witch in comparison with her; where, then, shall I find another with a bit of stick, or seek another with the bell, if Nature made Nardella (may she be in glory), and then broke the mould? Alas, in what a labyrinth has she put me, in what a perplexity has the promise I made her left me! But what do I say? I am running away before I have seen the wolf; let me open my eyes and ears and look about; may there not be some other as beautiful? Is it possible that the world should be lost to me? Is there such a dearth of women, or is the race extinct?"

So saying he forthwith issued a proclamation and command that all the handsome women in the world should come to the touch-stone of beauty, for he would take the most beautiful to wife and endow her with a kingdom. Now, when this news was spread abroad, there was not a woman in the universe who did not come to try her luck—not a witch, however ugly, who stayed behind; for when it is a question of beauty, no scullion-wench will acknowledge herself surpassed; everyone piques herself on being the handsomest; and if the looking-glass tells her the truth she blames the glass for being untrue, and the quicksilver for being put on badly.

When the town was thus filled with women the King had them all drawn up in a line, and he walked up and down from top to bottom, and as he examined and measured each from head to foot one appeared to him wry-browed, another long-nosed, another broad-mouthed, another thick-lipped, another tall as a may-pole, another short and dumpy, another too stout, another too slender; the Spaniard did not please him on account of her dark colour, the Neopolitan was not to his fancy on account of her gait, the German appeared cold and icy, the Frenchwoman frivolous and giddy, the Venetian with her light hair looked like a distaff of flax. At the end of the end, one for this cause and another for that, he sent them all away, with one hand before and the other behind; and, seeing that so many fair faces were all show and no wool, he turned his thoughts to his own daughter, saying, "Why do I go seeking the impossible when my daughter Preziosa is formed in the same mould of beauty as her mother? I have this fair face here in my house, and yet go looking for it at the fag-end[1] of the world. She shall marry whom I will, and so I shall have an heir."

When Preziosa heard this she retired to her chamber, and bewailing her ill-fortune as if she would not leave a hair upon her head; and, whilst she was lamenting thus, an old woman came to her, who was her confidant. As soon as she saw Preziosa, who seemed to belong more to the other world than to this, and heard the cause of her grief, the old woman said to her, "Cheer up, my daughter, do not despair; there is a remedy for every evil save death. Now listen; if your father speaks to you thus once again put this bit of wood into your mouth, and instantly you will be changed into a she-bear; then off with you! for in his fright he will let you depart, and go straight to the wood, where Heaven has kept good-fortune in

---

1 Butt-end.

store for you since the day you were born, and whenever you wish to appear a woman, as you are and will remain, only take the piece of wood out of your mouth and you will return to your true form." Then Preziosa embraced the old woman, and, giving her a good apronful of meal, and ham and bacon, sent her away.

As soon as the Sun began to change his quarters, the King ordered the musicians to come, and, inviting all his lords and vassals, he held a great feast. And after dancing for five or six hours, they all sat down to table, and ate and drank beyond measure. Then the King asked his courtiers to whom he should marry Preziosa, as she was the picture of his dead wife. But the instant Preziosa heard this, she slipped the bit of wood into her mouth, and took the figure of a terrible she-bear, at the sight of which all present were frightened out of their wits, and ran off as fast as they could scamper.

Meanwhile Preziosa went out, and took her way to a wood, where the Shades were holding a consultation how they might do some mischief to the Sun at the close of day. And there she stayed, in the pleasant companionship of the other animals, until the son of the King of Running-Water came to hunt in that part of the country, who, at the sight of the bear, had like to have died on the spot. But when he saw the beast come gently up to him, wagging her tail like a little dog and rubbing her sides against him, he took courage, and patted her, and said, "Good bear, good bear! there, there! poor beast, poor beast!" Then he led her home and ordered that she should be taken great care of; and he had her put into a garden close to the royal palace, that he might see her from the window whenever he wished.

One day, when all the people of the house were gone out, and the Prince was left alone, he went to the window to look out at the bear; and there he beheld Preziosa, who had taken the piece of wood out of her mouth, combing her golden tresses. At the sight of this beauty, which was beyond the beyonds, he had like to have lost his senses with amazement, and tumbling down the stairs he ran out into the garden. But Preziosa, who was on the watch and observed him, popped the piece of wood into her mouth, and was instantly changed into a bear again.

When the Prince came down and looked about in vain for Preziosa, whom he had seen from the window above, he was so amazed at the trick that a deep melancholy came over him, and in four days he fell sick, crying continually, "My bear, my bear!" His mother, hearing him wailing thus, imagined that the bear had done him some hurt, and gave orders that she should be killed. But the servants, enamoured of the tameness of the bear, who made herself beloved by the very stones in the road, took pity on her, and, instead of killing her, they led her to the wood, and told the queen that they had put an end to her.

When this came to the ears of the Prince, he acted in a way to pass belief. Ill or well he jumped out of bed, and was going at once to make mincemeat of the servants. But when they told him the truth of the affair, he jumped on horseback, half-dead as he was, and went rambling about and seeking everywhere, until at length he found the bear. Then he took her home again, and putting her into a chamber, said to her, "O lovely morsel for a King, who art shut up in this skin! O candle of love, who art enclosed within this hairy lanthorn![1] Wherefore all this trifling? Do you wish to see me pine and pant, and die by inches? I am wasting away; without hope, and tormented by thy beauty. And you see clearly the proof, for I am shrunk two-thirds in size, like wine boiled down, and am nothing but skin and bone, for the fever is double-stitched to my veins. So lift up the curtain of this hairy hide, and let me gaze upon the spectacle of thy beauty! Raise, O raise the leaves off this basket, and let me get a sight of the fine fruit beneath! Lift up that curtain, and let my eyes pass in to behold the pomp of wonders! Who has shut up so smooth a creature in a prison woven of hair? Who has locked up so rich a treasure in a leathern chest? Let me behold this display of graces, and take in payment all my love; for nothing else can cure the troubles I endure."

But when he had said, again and again, this and a great deal more, and still saw that all his words were thrown away, he took to his bed, and had such a desperate fit that the doctors prognosticated badly of his case. Then his mother, who had no other joy in the world, sat down by his bedside, and said to him, "My son, whence comes all this grief? What melancholy humour has seized you? You are young, you are loved, you are great, you are rich—what then is it you want, my son? Speak; a bashful beggar carries an empty bag. If you want a wife, only choose, and I will bring the match about; do you take, and I'll pay. Do you not see that your illness is an illness to me? Your pulse beats with fever in your veins, and my heart beats with illness in my brain, for I have no other support of my old age than you. So be cheerful now, and cheer up my heart, and do not see the whole kingdom thrown into mourning, this house into lamentation, and your mother forlorn and heart-broken."

When the Prince heard these words, he said, "Nothing can console me but the sight of the bear. Therefore, if you wish to see me well again, let her be brought into this chamber; I will have no one else to attend me, and make my bed, and cook for me, but she herself; and you may be sure that this pleasure will make me well in a trice."

Thereupon his mother, although she thought it ridiculous enough for the bear to act as cook and chambermaid, and feared that her son was not in his right mind, yet, in order to gratify him, had the bear fetched. And

1 Lantern.

when the bear came up to the Prince's bed, she raised her paw and felt the patient's pulse, which made the Queen laugh outright, for she thought every moment that the bear would scratch his nose. Then the Prince said, "My dear bear, will you not cook for me, and give me my food, and wait upon me?" and the bear nodded her head, to show that she accepted the office. Then his mother had some fowls brought, and a fire lighted on the hearth in the same chamber, and some water set to boil; whereupon the bear, laying hold on a fowl, scalded and plucked it handily, and drew it, and then stuck one portion of it on the spit, and with the other part she made such a delicious hash that the Prince, who could not relish even sugar, licked his fingers at the taste. And when he had done eating, the bear handed him drink with such grace that the Queen was ready to kiss her on the forehead. Thereupon the Prince arose, and the bear quickly set about making the bed; and running into the garden, she gathered a clothful of roses and citron-flowers and strewed them over it, so that the queen said the bear was worth her weight in gold, and that her son had good reason to be fond of her.

But when the Prince saw these pretty offices they only added fuel to the fire; and if before he wasted by ounces, he now melted away by pounds, and he said to the Queen, "My lady mother, if I do not give this bear a kiss, the breath will leave my body." Whereupon the Queen, seeing him fainting away, said, "Kiss him, kiss him, my beautiful beast! Let me not see my poor son die of longing!" Then the bear went up to the Prince, and taking him by the cheeks, kissed him again and again. Meanwhile (I know not how it was) the piece of wood slipped out of Preziosa's mouth, and she remained in the arms of the Prince, the most beautiful creature in the world; and pressing her to his heart, he said, "I have caught you, my little rogue! You shall not escape from me again without a good reason." At these words Preziosa, adding the colour of modesty to the picture of her natural beauty, said to him, "I am indeed in your hands—only guard me safely, and marry me when you will."

Then the Queen inquired who the beautiful maiden was, and what had brought her to this savage life; and Preziosa related the whole story of her misfortunes, at which the Queen, praising her as a good and virtuous girl, told her son that she was content that Preziosa should be his wife. Then the Prince, who desired nothing else in life, forthwith pledged her his faith; and the mother giving them her blessing, this happy marriage was celebrated with great feasting and illuminations, and Preziosa experienced the truth of the saying that—

One who acts well may always expect good.

All-kinds-of-fur
(*Germany*)

Once upon a time there was a king who had a wife with golden hair, and she was so beautiful that she had no equal on earth. It happened that she fell ill, and when she felt that she would soon die, she called the king and said, "If you want to remarry after my death, take no one who is less beautiful than I am and who does not have such golden hair as I have; you must promise me this." When the king had promised her, she closed her eyes and died.

The king could not be comforted for a long time and did not think of taking a second wife. At last, his councillors said, "There is no other way, the king must remarry, so that we may have a queen." Now, messengers were sent far and wide to seek a bride who would be the equal of the deceased queen in beauty. But there was none to be found in the whole world, and even if they had found her, there was none with such golden hair. So, the messengers returned home without having achieved anything.

Now, the king had a daughter who was just as beautiful as her deceased mother and also had such golden hair. When she had come of age, the king looked at her one day and saw that she was in all respects like his deceased wife and suddenly felt an intense love for her. Then he said to his councillors, "I will marry my daughter, for she is the image of my deceased wife, and otherwise I cannot find a bride the like of her." When the councillors heard this, they were horrified and said, "God has forbidden that the father marry his daughter; nothing good can come from sin, and the kingdom will be dragged along into ruin." The daughter was even more horrified when she heard her father's decision, but hoped to dissuade him from his plan. Then she said to him, "Before I fulfil your wish, I must first have three dresses, one as golden as the sun, one as silver as the moon, and one as brilliant as the stars; furthermore, I demand a cloak made up of a thousand kinds of pelts and fur, and every animal in your kingdom must contribute a piece of its skin to it". But she thought, "It is quite impossible to come by this, and I shall thus turn my father from his wicked thoughts." But the king did not give in, and the most skilful maidens in his kingdom had to weave the three dresses, one as golden as the sun, one as silver as the moon, and one as brilliant as the stars; and his huntsmen had to gather up all the animals in the whole kingdom and strip off a piece of their skin; from this a cloak of a thousand kinds of fur was made. At last, when all was ready, the king sent for the cloak, and spreading it before her, said, "Tomorrow shall be our wedding."

When the king's daughter saw that there was no hope of moving her father's heart, she decided to flee. In the night, while everyone was asleep, she got up and took three of her treasures: a golden ring, a golden spinning-wheel, and a golden reel; she put the three dresses of sun, moon, and stars into a nutshell, put on the cloak of all kinds of fur, and blackened her face and hands with soot. Then she placed herself in God's hands and set forth, and journeyed all night till she came into a great forest. And being tired, she sat down in a hollow tree and fell asleep.

The sun rose and she slept away, and was still asleep when it was already broad daylight. Then it happened that the king who owned the forest was hunting in it. When his dogs came to the tree, they sniffed, ran all around, and barked at it. The king said to the huntsmen, "See what kind of game is hiding there." The huntsmen obeyed his command, and when they came back, they said, "In the hollow tree lies a strange animal, such as we have never seen before: on its skin is a thousand kinds of fur; it just lies there and sleeps". Said the king, "see if you can capture it alive, then tie it to the cart and take it with you". When the huntsmen took hold of the girl, she awoke in terror and cried out to them, "I am a poor child, abandoned by my father and mother, have mercy on me and take me with you." Then they said, "All-kinds-of-fur, you are good for the kitchen, just come with us, there you can sweep up the ashes." So, they set her on the cart and drove her home to the royal castle. There they gave her a little stable room under the stairs, where there was no daylight, and said, "Little furry animal, you can live and sleep there." Then she was sent into the kitchen, where she carried wood and water, stoked the fire, plucked the poultry, sorted the vegetables, swept the ashes, and did all the dirty work.

So, for a long time All-kinds-of-fur lived in poverty. Oh, you beautiful princess, what will become of you! But one day a feast was celebrated in the castle, and she said to the cook, "May I go up for a little while and take a look? I will stand outside the door." The cook answered, "Yes, go ahead, but in half an hour you must be back here and carry out the ashes." Then she took her little oil lamp, went into her room, took off her fur coat and washed the soot off her face and hands, so that her full beauty was again revealed. Then she opened the nut and took out her dress which shone like the sun. And when this was done, she went up to the feast, and everyone stepped out of her way, for none knew her, nor thought that she was anything but a king's daughter. But the king came to meet her, gave her his hand, and danced with her, thinking in his heart, "My eyes have never seen one so beautiful." When the dance was over, she curtsied, and while the king looked around, she disappeared, and no one knew where. The guards who stood outside the castle were called and questioned, but no one had seen her.

But she had run into her little stable, quickly taken off her dress, blackened her face and hands and put on her fur coat, and was once again

All-kinds-of-fur. When she came into the kitchen and was about to set to work and sweep up the ashes, the cook said, "Leave that until tomorrow and cook for me the king's soup, I want to have a look upstairs for a bit, but don't let a hair fall in, otherwise you won't get anything to eat in the future." Then the cook went away, and All-kinds-of-fur cooked the soup for the king, and made bread soup as well as she knew how, and when it was ready, she fetched her golden ring from her room and put it into the bowl in which the soup was served. When the dance was over, the king had the soup brought to him and ate it, and it tasted so good to him that he thought he had never eaten better soup. But when he reached the bottom of the bowl, he saw a golden ring lying there and could not understand how it had got there. Then he ordered the cook to come before him. The cook was frightened when he heard the order, and said to All-kinds-of-fur, "You must have dropped a hair into the soup; if so, you will get a beating." When the cook came before the king, he was asked who had cooked the soup. The cook answered, "I cooked it." But the king said, "That is not true, for it was cooked in a different way and much better than usual." He answered, "I must confess that I have not cooked it, but that little furry animal has cooked it." The king said, "Go and bring her before me."

When All-kinds-of-fur arrived, the king asked, "Who are you?" "I am a poor child who no longer has a father or a mother." He went on to ask, "Why are you in my castle?" She replied, "I am good for nothing but to have boots thrown at my head." He asked further, "Where did you get the ring that was in the soup?" She replied, "I don't know anything about the ring." So, the king could not find anything out from her and had to send her away again.

Some time later there was another feast, and All-kinds-of-fur asked the cook for permission to look on, as she had done before. He replied, "Yes, but come back in half an hour and cook the king the bread soup he likes so much." Then she ran into her little stable, washed herself quickly, and took from the nut the dress that was as silver as the moon, and put it on. Then she went upstairs and looked like a princess; and the king met her, and was glad to see her again; and as the dance was just beginning, they danced together. But when the dance was over, she disappeared again so quickly that the king could not notice where she went. But she jumped into her little room, and made herself into a little furry animal again, and went into the kitchen to cook the bread soup. While the cook was upstairs, she fetched the golden spinning-wheel and put it into the bowl, so that the soup was served over it. Then it was brought to the king, who ate it, and it tasted as good to him as the last time; he sent for the cook, who this time also had to confess that All-kinds-of-fur had cooked the soup. Then All-kinds-of-fur came again before the king, but she answered that she was only good for having her boots thrown at her head, and that she knew nothing at all about the golden spinning-wheel.

The third time the king gave a feast, it was no different from the last. The cook said, "You are a witch, you little furry animal, always putting something into the soup so that it becomes so good, and tastes better to the king than what I cook." But because she asked, he let her go look in on the ball at the appointed time. Now, she put on the dress that shone like the stars and entered the hall with it. The king danced again with the beautiful maiden, and said that she had never been so beautiful. And while he danced, he put a golden ring on her finger, without her noticing it, and ordered that the dance should last for a long time. When it was over, he tried to hold her tightly by the hands, but she tore herself away and jumped so quickly among the crowd that she disappeared before his eyes. She ran as far as she could to her little stable under the stairs, but because she had stayed too long, for more than half an hour, she could not take off her beautiful dress, but instead threw her coat of fur on over it, and in her haste, she did not cover herself entirely with soot, but one finger remained white. All-kinds-of-fur now ran into the kitchen and cooked the king's bread soup, and as soon as the cook was gone, she put in the golden reel. When the king found the reel at the bottom of the soup, he sent for All-kinds-of-fur and saw the white finger and the ring he had put on her finger at the dance. Then he seized her by the hand and held her fast, and as she tried to unloose herself and get away, the fur coat opened a little, and the starry dress shone forth. The king seized the cloak and tore it off. Then her golden hair spilled out and she stood there in full splendour and could hide herself no longer. And when she had wiped the soot and ashes from her face, she was more beautiful than anyone had ever seen on earth. And the king said, "You are my dear bride, and we will never part again." Then the wedding was celebrated, and they lived happily ever after.

Rashen Coatie
(*Scotland*)

At an early period, when a plurality of kings reigned in Scotland, it chanced that one of them had lost his queen; and one of the queens had lost her husband. These two, the widow and widower were married, each of them having had a daughter in their first marriage, it caused a good deal of dissention and strife, particularly as the king's daughter was a perfect model of beauty, and the queen's daughter as much so of deformity; but the king willing to indulge his queen as much as possible, and for the sake of keeping peace in his own house, he often winked at the bad treatment his daughter received from her stepmother, all because she was more handsome and fair than her beloved but ugly daughter. Her treatment was however so very bad, that she was put to herd her father's cattle; while the queen's daughter wallowed in all the luxuries of a court endowed with peace and plenty. Rashen Coatie, (for so shall the king's daughter be called), having her meat, which was of the coarsest fare, brought her by the queen's favourite daughter daily, she had learned from some kind fairy how to charm her asleep when partaking of her food, which she did on her immediate arrival, by repeating the following words:

> *Lay down your head upon my knee,*
> *And well looked after it there shall be,*
> *Then sleep ye one eye or sleep ye two,*
> *Ye soon shall see what power can do.*

These words had the desired effect of lulling her sound asleep, which no sooner took place than a genie in the shape and form of a calf brought her meats and dainties of every description, of which she partook heartily, unknown to all but her favourite calf.

The queen being now wearied with trying all the arts that mischief could devise, to bring Rashen Coatie's beauty to a level with her daughter's; or to raise her daughter's beauty to that of Rashen Coatie's; thought she must have some hidden means of subsistence, as all the stratagems she tried were always attended with want of success.

On consulting her henwife, who was a witch, how she should behave in this critical juncture; the witch said she would give her an eye in her neck, by which sight she would be able to discover many things, particularly how Rashen Coatie was fed and maintained without her perceiving it. Accordingly the queen went next day to the castle to discover Rashen Coatie's friends, and discovered how she was fed, owing to an omission of Rashen Coatie's. She found that it was the calf that fed her, which made her long to get it destroyed.

The king though loath to deprive his daughter of her only companion, her favourite calf, he was obliged to comply with the queen's imperious demands, in order to suppress the wrangling and strife which were daily taking place among his domestics, particularly by his queen. Rashen Coatie having discovered the queen's intention, mourned over her ravenous appetite, with streaming eyes and bleached cheeks. The calf having the power of speech, requested her not to be alarmed at what was to take place, but to gather together all the bones into one mass, and place them beneath a particular stone, and in a short time they would revive and come to life again. This having been done as commanded, everything came to pass as predicted by the calf; and the malicious queen having partook of the entrails of the calf, lingered and died of a disease hitherto unknown in that part of the country. Her daughter now became of contempt, despised and hooted by everyone.

Rashen Coatie's sun now began to shine in meridian splendour; she was gentle and mild, humble to everyone, which gained her the esteem and good will of both great and small. Her beauty having kept pace with her virtue, her father took such a liking to her as to wish to marry her; but this being quite contrary to her principles of sound morality, she grew melancholy, every day more and more, and lingered out a weary existence, till having met with her calf, she asked it what was best to be done under such pressing difficulties.

The calf advised her to ask from her father a gown and petticoat made of the rashes that grew on the bonny burn side, in which she was to be drest. This having been accomplished; she then requested of him to give her a dress composed of all the colours of the birds of the air. This also having been given her; she demanded a new suit of variegated colours, composed of all those appearances that float in the air, and in the earth beneath. Having obtained all these varieties; she had now no excuse but to comply with her father's wishes, which were to accompany him to the altar, where all things were ready for the marriage ceremony.

Having thus far complied with his wishes, she went, but on arriving at the place appointed, she started back, exclaiming that she had forgotten her marriage ring. Her father, to prevent her returning home, said he had one which would answer the purpose perfectly well; but she insisted on having her mother's ring, and must needs return for it, but promised to be back in a few minutes.

Again, she had recourse to the advice of her calf, which was to dress herself in her rashen weed, and to leave her father's kingdom with all speed. This was accordingly done, and she wandered far till she came to a hunting lodge, kept by the prince of that country. Here she made free to enter, and go to the prince's bed to rest her wearied limbs, which had undergone much toil and fatigue in the course of a long and laborious travel. When the prince came to his lodge, he was surprised to find a sleeping beauty in his bed, as it was in a sequestered part of his kingdom, where few inhabitants were to be found.

She soon made her escape from him, and went to his father's palace, where she asked a place as a menial servant, which was granted, and thereby put into the kitchen to assist the cook in turning the spits which groaned with the weight of the meat that was roasting for their majesties' dinner. Here she continued for some time, doing all the drudgery of the meanest servant. Christmas, however, came on, when great preparations were made for church.

Rashen Coatie also wished to appear among the rest, but was denied permission by the master cook. But it so happened that, on the first yule day, when all were gone, and she left alone in the kitchen to attend the meat, she said to the spits, peats, and pots, to do their duty till she returned; which was accordingly done. The words of the charm which she made use of on this occasion were as follows:

> *Every spit gar[1] another turn,*
> *Every peat gar another burn,*
> *Every pot gar another play*
> *Till I return on good yule day.*

These did as desired; when she went and dressed herself in rich attire. On arriving at the church, she placed herself in a conspicuous part of the seat, nearly opposite to where the young prince was sitting. He caught more of the flame of love than of the minister's spiritual exhortations, and could scarcely contain himself from making enquiries during the sermon. She went in the same manner all the holy days of yule, but every day more and more superbly drest. The prince at length determined on discovering her rank and place of abode, if possible, little thinking that it was his own menial, Rashen Coatie, as her history seemed to be a mystery to everyone.

The term of her secrecy seemed to be now at end; for hurrying home on the last day, she dropped one of her shoes, which were so completely fitted to her feet that it was supposed it would suit no one else. The prince, on having found the shoe, which was of pure gold, caused to be proclaimed throughout all the regions of his father's kingdom round about that everyone should have free liberty to try on the shoe, and whomsoever the shoe fitted best, was to be his bride.

Many trials were made, but all to no purpose, till the henwife's daughter caused her heels and toes to be pared; by which process she got it forced on her foot. Agreeably to the proclamation, it therefore became the prince to marry her, with which he was to comply, but with a heavy heart.

On their way to the marriage seat, a small bird fluttered over their heads, crying as they went:

> *Clipped heels and pared toes.*
> *They're in the kitchen the shoe on goes.*

The prince hearing the voice of the bird, requested to know its meaning, when it was explained. With joy he returned to his father's castle, much against the henwife's inclination, when it was found that Rashen Coatie,

---

1 Make.

who hurkled[1] in the kitchen, had not got an opportunity of trying on the shoe. On presenting her with the shoe, it went easily on, but what was more to their surprise and astonishment, she pulled out its fellow, and put it on before them. They, of course, we need not add, were immediately married, and lived long and happy. Shortly after the marriage, they paid a visit to her father's court in great pomp and grandeur, by whom they were most cordially received, and his kingdom, at his death, bestowed on them.

1 Huddled.

710: Our Lady's Child

Our Lady's Child
(*Germany*)

Hard by a great forest dwelt a wood-cutter with his wife, who had an only child, a little girl three years old. They were so poor, however, that they no longer had daily bread, and did not know how to get food for her. One morning the wood-cutter went out sorrowfully to his work in the forest, and while he was cutting wood, suddenly there stood before him a tall and beautiful woman with a crown of shining stars on her head, who said to him, "I am the Virgin Mary, mother of the child Jesus. Thou art poor and needy, bring thy child to me, I will take her with me and be her mother, and care for her." The wood-cutter obeyed, brought his child, and gave her to the Virgin Mary, who took her up to heaven with her. There the child fared well, ate sugar-cakes, and drank sweet milk, and her clothes were of gold, and the little angels played with her. And when she was fourteen years of age, the Virgin Mary called her one day and said, "Dear child, I am about to make a long journey, so take into thy keeping the keys of the thirteen doors of heaven. Twelve of these thou mayest open, and behold the glory which is within them, but the thirteenth, to which this little key belongs, is forbidden thee. Beware of opening it, or thou wilt bring misery on thyself." The girl promised to be obedient, and when the Virgin Mary was gone, she began to examine the dwellings of the kingdom of heaven. Each day she opened one of them, until she had made the round of the twelve. In each of them sat one of the Apostles in the midst of a great light, and she rejoiced in all the magnificence and splendour, and the little angels who always accompanied her rejoiced with her. Then the forbidden door alone remained, and she felt a great desire to know what could be hidden behind it, and said to the angels, "I will not quite open it, and I will not go inside it, but I will unlock it so that we can just see a little through the opening." "Oh no," said the little angels, "that would be a sin. The Virgin Mary has forbidden it, and it might easily cause thy unhappiness." Then she was silent, but the desire in her heart was not stilled, but gnawed there and tormented her, and let her have no rest. And once when the angels had all gone out, she thought, "Now I am quite alone, and I could peep in. If I do it, no one will ever know." She sought out the key, and when she had got it in her hand, she put it in the lock, and when she had put it in, she turned it round as well. Then the door sprang open, and she saw there the Trinity sitting in fire and splendour. She stayed there awhile, and looked at everything in amazement; then she touched the light a little with her finger, and her finger became quite golden. Immediately a great fear fell on her. She shut the door violently, and ran away. Her terror too would not quit her, let her do what she might, and her heart beat continually and would not be still; the gold too stayed on her finger, and would not go away, let her rub it and wash it never so much.

It was not long before the Virgin Mary came back from her journey. She called the girl before her, and asked to have the keys of heaven back. When the maiden gave her the bunch, the Virgin looked into her eyes and said, "Hast thou not opened the thirteenth door also?" "No," she replied. Then she laid her hand on the girl's heart, and felt how it beat and beat, and saw right well that she had disobeyed her order and had opened the door. Then she said once again, "Art thou certain that thou hast not done it?" "Yes," said the girl, for the second time. Then she perceived the finger which had become golden from touching the fire of heaven, and saw well that the child had sinned, and said for the third time "Hast thou not done it?" "No," said the girl for the third time. Then said the Virgin Mary, "Thou hast not obeyed me, and besides that thou hast lied, thou art no longer worthy to be in heaven."

Then the girl fell into a deep sleep, and when she awoke she lay on the earth below, and in the midst of a wilderness. She wanted to cry out, but she could bring forth no sound. She sprang up and wanted to run away, but whithersoever she turned herself, she was continually held back by thick hedges of thorns through which she could not break. In the desert, in which she was imprisoned, there stood an old hollow tree, and this had to be her dwelling-place. Into this she crept when night came, and here she slept. Here, too, she found a shelter from storm and rain, but it was a miserable life, and bitterly did she weep when she remembered how happy she had been in heaven, and how the angels had played with her. Roots and wild berries were her only food, and for these she sought as far as she could go. In the autumn she picked up the fallen nuts and leaves, and carried them into the hole. The nuts were her food in winter, and when snow and ice came, she crept amongst the leaves like a poor little animal that she might not freeze. Before long her clothes were all torn, and one bit of them after another fell off her. As soon, however, as the sun shone warm again, she went out and sat in front of the tree, and her long hair covered her on all sides like a mantle. Thus she sat year after year, and felt the pain and the misery of the world. One day, when the trees were once more clothed in fresh green, the King of the country was hunting in the forest, and followed a roe, and as it had fled into the thicket which shut in this part of the forest, he got off his horse, tore the bushes asunder, and cut himself a path with his sword. When he had at last forced his way through, he saw a wonderfully beautiful maiden sitting under the tree;

and she sat there and was entirely covered with her golden hair down to her very feet. He stood still and looked at her full of surprise, then he spoke to her and said, "Who art thou? Why art thou sitting here in the wilderness?" But she gave no answer, for she could not open her mouth. The King continued, "Wilt thou go with me to my castle?" Then she just nodded her head a little. The King took her in his arms, carried her to his horse, and rode home with her, and when he reached the royal castle he caused her to be dressed in beautiful garments, and gave her all things in abundance. Although she could not speak, she was still so beautiful and charming that he began to love her with all his heart, and it was not long before he married her.

After a year or so had passed, the Queen brought a son into the world. Thereupon the Virgin Mary appeared to her in the night when she lay in her bed alone, and said, "If thou wilt tell the truth and confess that thou didst unlock the forbidden door, I will open thy mouth and give thee back thy speech, but if thou perseverest in thy sin, and deniest obstinately, I will take thy new-born child away with me." Then the queen was permitted to answer, but she remained hard, and said, "No, I did not open the forbidden door;" and the Virgin Mary took the new-born child from her arms, and vanished with it. Next morning when the child was not to be found, it was whispered among the people that the Queen was a man-eater, and had killed her own child. She heard all this and could say nothing to the contrary, but the King would not believe it, for he loved her so much.

When a year had gone by the Queen again bore a son, and in the night the Virgin Mary again came to her, and said, "If thou wilt confess that thou openedst the forbidden door, I will give thee thy child back and untie thy tongue; but if you continuest in sin and deniest it, I will take away with me this new child also." Then the Queen again said, "No, I did not open the forbidden door;" and the Virgin took the child out of her arms, and away with her to heaven. Next morning, when this child also had disappeared, the people declared quite loudly that the Queen had devoured it, and the King's councillors demanded that she should be brought to justice. The King, however, loved her so dearly that he would not believe it, and commanded the councillors under pain of death not to say any more about it.

The following year the Queen gave birth to a beautiful little daughter, and for the third time the Virgin Mary appeared to her in the night and said, "Follow me." She took the Queen by the hand and led her to heaven, and showed her there her two eldest children, who smiled at her, and were playing with the ball of the world. When the Queen rejoiced thereat, the Virgin Mary said, "Is thy heart not yet softened? If thou wilt own that thou openedst the forbidden door, I will give thee back thy two little sons." But for the third time the Queen answered, "No, I did not open the forbidden door." Then the Virgin let her sink down to earth once more, and took from her likewise her third child.

Next morning, when the loss was reported abroad, all the people cried loudly, "The Queen is a man-eater. She must be judged," and the King was no longer able to restrain his councillors. Thereupon a trial was held, and as she could not answer and defend herself, she was condemned to be burnt alive. The wood was got together, and when she was fast bound to the stake, and the fire began to burn round about her, the hard ice of pride melted, her heart was moved by repentance, and she thought, "If I could but confess before my death that I opened the door." Then her voice came back to her, and she cried out loudly, "Yes, Mary, I did it;" and straightway rain fell from the sky and extinguished the flames of fire, and a light broke forth above her, and the Virgin Mary descended with the two little sons by her side, and the new-born daughter in her arms. She spoke kindly to her, and said, "He who repents his sin and acknowledges it, is forgiven." Then she gave her the three children, untied her tongue, and granted her happiness for her whole life.

The Lassie and Her Godmother
(*Norway*)

Once on a time a poor couple lived far, far away in a great wood. The wife was brought to bed, and had a pretty girl, but they were so poor they did not know how to get the babe christened, for they had no money to pay the parson's fees. So one day the father went out to see if he could find anyone who was willing to stand for the child and pay the fees; but though he walked about the whole day from one house to another, and though all said they were willing enough to stand, no one thought himself bound to pay the fees. Now, when he was going home again, a lovely lady met him, dressed so fine, and who looked so thoroughly good and kind; she offered to get the babe christened, but after that, she said, she must keep it for her own. The husband answered, he must first ask his wife what she wished to do; but when he got home and told his story, the wife said, right out, "No!"

Next day the man went out again, but no one would stand if they had to pay the fees; and though he begged and prayed, he could get no help. And again as he went home, towards evening the same lovely lady met him, who looked so sweet and good, and she made him the same offer. So he told his wife again how he had fared, and this time she said if he couldn't get anyone to stand for his babe next day, they must just let the lady have her way, since she seemed so kind and good.

The third day, the man went about, but he couldn't get anyone to stand; and so when, towards evening, he met the kind lady again, he gave his word she should have the babe if she would only get it christened at the font. So next morning she came to the place where the man lived, followed by two men to stand godfathers, took the babe and carried it to church, and there it was christened. After that she took it to her own house, and there the little girl lived with her several years, and her foster-mother was always kind and friendly to her.

Now, when the lassie had grown to be big enough to know right and wrong, her foster-mother got ready to go on a journey. "You have my leave", she said, "to go all over the house, except those rooms which I shew you"; and when she had said that, away she went.

But the lassie could not forbear just to open one of the doors a little bit, when—POP! out flew a Star.

When her foster-mother came back, she was very vexed to find that the star had flown out, and she got very angry with her foster-daughter, and threatened to send her away; but the child cried and begged so hard that she got leave to stay.

Now, after a while, the foster-mother had to go on another journey; and, before she went, she forbade the lassie to go into those two rooms into which she had never been. She promised to beware; but when she was left alone, she began to think and to wonder what there could be in the second room, and at last she could not help setting the door a little ajar, just to peep in, when—POP! out flew the Moon.

When her foster-mother came home and found the Moon let out, she was very downcast, and said to the lassie she must go away, she could not stay with her any longer. But the lassie wept so bitterly, and prayed so heartily for forgiveness, that this time, too, she got leave to stay.

Some time after, the foster-mother had to go away again, and she charged the lassie, who by this time was half grown up, most earnestly that she mustn't try to go into, or to peep into, the third room. But when her foster-mother had been gone some time, and the lassie was weary of walking about alone, all at once she thought, "Dear me, what fun it would be just to peep a little into that third room." Then she thought she mustn't do it for her foster-mother's sake; but when the bad thought came the second time she could hold out no longer; come what might, she must and would look into the room; so she just opened the door a tiny bit, when—POP! out flew the Sun.

But when her foster-mother came back and saw that the sun had flown away, she was cut to the heart, and said, "Now, there was no help for it, the lassie must and should go away; she couldn't hear of her staying any longer." Now the lassie cried her eyes out, and begged and prayed so prettily; but it was all no good.

"Nay! but I must punish you!" said her foster-mother; "but you may have your choice, either to be the loveliest woman in the world, and not to be able to speak, or to keep your speech, and be the ugliest of all women; but away from me you must go."

And the lassie said, "I would sooner be lovely." So she became all at once wondrous fair; but from that day forth she was dumb.

So, when she went away from her foster-mother, she walked and wandered through a great, great wood; but the farther she went, the farther off the end seemed to be. So, when the evening came on, she clomb up into a tall tree, which grew over a spring, and there she made herself up to sleep that night. Close by lay a castle, and from that castle came early every morning a maid to draw water to make the Prince's tea, from the spring over which the lassie was sitting. So the maid looked down into the spring, saw the lovely face in the water, and thought it was her own; then she flung away the pitcher, and ran home; and, when she got there, she tossed up her head and said, "If I'm so pretty, I'm far too good to go and fetch water."

So another maid had to go for the water, but the same thing happened to her; she went back and said she was far too pretty and too good to fetch water from the spring for the Prince. Then the Prince went himself, for he had a mind to see what all this could mean. So, when he reached the spring, he too saw the image in the water; but he looked up at once, and became aware of the lovely lassie who sate there up in the tree. Then he coaxed her down and took her home; and at last made up his mind to have her for his queen, because she was so lovely; but his mother, who was still alive, was against it.

"She can't speak", she said, "and maybe she's a wicked witch."

But the Prince could not be content till he got her. So after they had lived together a while, the lassie was to have a child, and when the child came to be born, the Prince set a strong watch round her; but at the birth one and all fell into a deep sleep, and her foster-mother came, cut the babe on its little finger, and smeared the queen's mouth with the blood; and said:

"Now you shall be as grieved as I was when you let out the star"; and with these words she carried off the babe.

But when those who were on the watch woke, they thought the queen had eaten her own child, and the old queen was all for burning her alive, but the Prince was so fond of her that at last he begged her off, but he had hard work to set her free.

So the next time the young queen was to have a child, twice as strong a watch was set as the first time, but the same thing happened over again, only this time her foster-mother said:

"Now you shall be as grieved as I was when you let the moon out."

And the queen begged and prayed, and wept; for when her foster-mother was there, she could speak—but it was all no good.

And now the old queen said she must be burnt, but the Prince found means to beg her off. But when the third child was to be born, a watch was set three times as strong as the first, but just the same thing happened. Her foster-mother came while the watch slept, took the babe, and cut its little finger, and smeared the queen's mouth with the blood, telling her now she should be as grieved as she had been when the lassie let out the sun.

And now the Prince could not save her any longer. She must and should be burnt. But just as they were leading her to the stake, all at once they saw her foster-mother, who came with all three children—two she led by the hand, and the third she had on her arm; and so she went up to the young queen and said:

"Here are your children; now you shall have them again. I am the Virgin Mary, and so grieved as you have been, so grieved was I when you let out sun, and moon, and star. Now you have been punished for what you did, and henceforth you shall have your speech."

How glad the Queen and Prince now were, all may easily think, but no one can tell. After that they were always happy; and from that day even the Prince's mother was very fond of the young queen.

The Goat-Face
(*Italy*)

A peasant had twelve daughters, not one of whom was a head taller than the next; for every year their mother presented him with a little girl; so that the poor man, to support his family decently, went early every morning as a day labourer and dug hard the whole day long. With what his labour produced he just kept his little ones from dying of hunger.

He happened, one day, to be digging at the foot of a mountain, the spy of other mountains, that thrust its head above the clouds to see what they were doing up in the sky, and close to a cavern so deep and dark that the sun was afraid to enter it. Out of this cavern there came a green lizard as big as a crocodile; and the poor man was so terrified that he had not the power to run away, expecting every moment the end of his days from a gulp of that ugly animal. But the lizard, approaching him, said, "Be not afraid, my good man, for I am not come here to do you any harm, but to do you good."

When Masaniello (for that was the name of the labourer) heard this, he fell on his knees and said, "Mistress What's-your-name, I am wholly in your power. Act then worthily and have compassion on this poor trunk that has twelve branches to support."

"It is on this very account," said the lizard, "that I am disposed to serve you; so bring me, to-morrow morning the youngest of your daughters; for I will rear her up like my own child, and love her as my life."

At this the poor father was more confounded than a thief when the stolen goods are found on his back. For, hearing the lizard ask him for one of his daughters, and that too, the tenderest of them, he concluded that the cloak was not without wool on it, and that she wanted the child as a titbit to stay her appetite. Then he said to himself, "If I give her my daughter, I give her my soul. If I refuse her, she will take this body of mine. If I yield her, I am robbed of my heart; if I deny her she will suck out my blood. If I consent, she takes away part of myself; if I refuse, she takes the whole. What shall I resolve on? What course shall I take? What expedient shall I adopt? Oh, what an ill day's work have I made of it! What a misfortune has rained down from heaven upon me!"

While he was speaking thus, the lizard said, "Resolve quickly and do what I tell you; or you will leave only your rags here. For so I will have it, and so it will be." Masaniello, hearing this decree and having no one to whom he could appeal, returned home quite melancholy, as yellow in the face as if he had jaundice; and his wife, seeing him hanging his head like a sick bird and his shoulders like one that is wounded, said to him, "What has happened to you, husband? Have you had a quarrel with anyone? Is there a warrant out against you? Or is the ass dead?"

"Nothing of that sort," said Masaniello, "but a horned lizard has put me into a fright, for she has threatened that if I do not bring her our youngest daughter, she will make me suffer for it. My head is turning like a reel. I know not what fish to take. On one side love constrains me; on the other the burden of my family. I love Renzolla dearly, I love my own life dearly. If I do not give the lizard this portion of my heart, she will take the whole compass of my unfortunate body. So now, dear wife, advise me, or I am ruined!"

When his wife heard this, she said, "Who knows, husband, but this may be a lizard with two tails, that will make our fortune? Who knows but this lizard may put an end to all our miseries? How often, when we should have an eagle's sight to discern the good luck that is running to meet us, we have a cloth before our eyes and the cramp in our hands, when we should lay hold on it. So go, take her away, for my heart tells me that some good fortune awaits the poor little thing!"

These words comforted Masaniello; and the next morning, as soon as the Sun with the brush of his rays whitewashed the Sky, which the shades of night had blackened, he took the little girl by the hand, and led her to the cave. Then the lizard came out, and taking the child gave the father a bag full of crowns, saying, "Go now, be happy, for Renzolla has found both father and mother."

Masaniello, overjoyed, thanked the lizard and went home to his wife. There was money enough for portions to all the other daughters when they married, and even then the old folks had sauce remaining for themselves to enable them to swallow with relish the toils of life.

Then the lizard made a most beautiful palace for Renzolla, and brought her up in such state and magnificence as would have dazzled the eyes of any queen. She wanted for nothing. Her food was fit for a count, her clothing for a princess. She had a hundred maidens to wait upon her, and with such good treatment she grew as sturdy as an oak-tree.

It happened, as the King was out hunting in those parts, that night overtook him, and as he stood looking round, not knowing where to lay his head, he saw a candle shining in the palace. So he sent one of his servants, to ask the owner to give him shelter. When the servant came to the palace, the lizard appeared before him in the shape of a beautiful lady; who, after hearing his message, said that his master should be a thousand times welcome, and that neither bread nor knife should there be wanting. The King, on hearing this reply, went to the palace and was received like a cavalier. A hundred pages went out to meet him, so that it looked like the funeral of a rich man. A hundred other pages brought the dishes to the table. A hundred others made a brave noise with musical instruments. But, above all, Renzolla served the King and handed him drink with such grace that he drank more love than wine.

When he had thus been so royally entertained, he felt he could not live without Renzolla; so, calling the fairy, he asked her for his wife. Whereupon the fairy, who wished for nothing but Renzolla's good, not only freely consented, but gave her a dowry of seven millions of gold.

The King, overjoyed at this piece of good fortune, departed with Renzolla, who, ill-mannered and ungrateful for all the fairy had done for her, went off with her husband without uttering one single word of thanks. Then the fairy, beholding such ingratitude, cursed her, and wished that her face should become like that of a she-goat; and hardly had she uttered the words when Renzolla's mouth stretched out, with a beard a span long on it, her jaws shrunk, her skin hardened, her cheeks grew hairy, and her plaited tresses turned to pointed horns.

When the poor King saw this he was thunderstruck, not knowing what had happened that so great a beauty should be thus transformed; and, with sighs and tears he exclaimed, "Where are the locks that bound me? Where are the eyes that transfixed me? Must I then be the husband of a she-goat? No, no, my heart shall not break for such a goat-face!" So saying, as soon as they reached his palace, he put Renzolla into a kitchen, along with a chambermaid; and gave to each of them ten bundles of flax to spin, commanding them to have the thread ready at the end of a week.

The maid, in obedience to the King, set about carding the flax, preparing and putting it on the distaff, twirling her spindle, reeling it and working away without ceasing; so that on Saturday evening her thread was all done. But Renzolla, thinking she was still the same as in the fairy's house, not having looked at herself in the glass, threw the flax out of the window, saying, "A pretty thing indeed of the King to set me such work to do! If he wants shirts let him buy them, and not fancy that he picked me up out of the gutter. But let him remember that I brought him home seven millions of gold, and that I am his wife and not his servant. Methinks, too, that he is somewhat of a donkey to treat me this way!"

Nevertheless, when Saturday morning came, seeing that the maid had spun all her share of the flax, Renzolla was greatly afraid; so away she went to the palace of the fairy and told her misfortune. Then the fairy embraced her with great affection, and gave her a bag full of spun thread to present to the King and show him what a notable and industrious housewife she was. Renzolla took the bag, and without saying one word of thanks, went to the royal palace; so again the fairy was quite angered at the conduct of the graceless girl.

When the King had taken the thread, he gave two little dogs, one to Renzolla and one to the maid, telling them to feed and rear them. The maid reared hers on bread crumbs and treated it like a child; but Renzolla grumbled, saying, "A pretty thing truly! As my grandfather used to say, Are we living under the Turks? Am I indeed to comb and wait upon dogs?" and she flung the dog out of the window!

Some months afterwards, the King asked for the dogs; whereat Renzolla, losing heart, ran off again to the fairy, and at the gate stood the old man who was the porter. "Who are you," said he, "and whom do you want?" Renzolla, hearing herself addressed in this off-hand way, replied, "Don't you know me, you old goat-beard?"

"Why do you miscall me?" said the porter. "This is the thief accusing the constable. I a goat-beard indeed! You are a goat-beard and a half, and you merit it and worse for your presumption. Wait awhile, you impudent woman; I'll enlighten you and you will see to what your airs and impertinence have brought you!"

So saying, he ran into his room, and taking a looking-glass, set it before Renzolla; who, when she saw her ugly, hairy visage, was like to have died with terror. Her dismay at seeing her face so altered that she did not know herself cannot be told. Whereupon the old man said to her, "You ought to recollect, Renzolla, that you are a daughter of a peasant and that it was the fairy that raised you to be a queen. But you, rude, unmannerly, and thankless as you are, having little gratitude for such high favours, have kept her waiting outside your heart, without showing the slightest mark of affection. You have brought the quarrel on yourself; see what a face you have got by it! See to what you are brought by your ingratitude; for through the fairy's spell you have not only changed face, but condition. But if you will do as this white-beard advises, go and look for the fairy; throw yourself at her feet, tear your beard, beat your breast, and ask pardon for the ill-treatment you have shown her. She is tender-hearted and she will be moved to pity by your misfortune."

Renzolla, who was touched to the quick, and felt that he had hit the nail on the head, followed the old man's advice. Then the fairy embraced and kissed her; and restoring her to her former appearance, she clad her in a robe that was quite heavy with gold; and placing her in a magnificent coach, accompanied with a crowd of servants, she brought her to the King. When the King beheld her, so beautiful and splendidly attired, he loved her as his own life; blaming himself for all the misery he had made her endure, but excusing himself on account of that odious goat-face which had been the cause of it. Thus Renzolla lived happy, loving her husband, honouring the fairy, and showing herself grateful to the old man, having learned to her cost that—

It is always good to be mannerly.

TALE TYPES BY MIGRATION

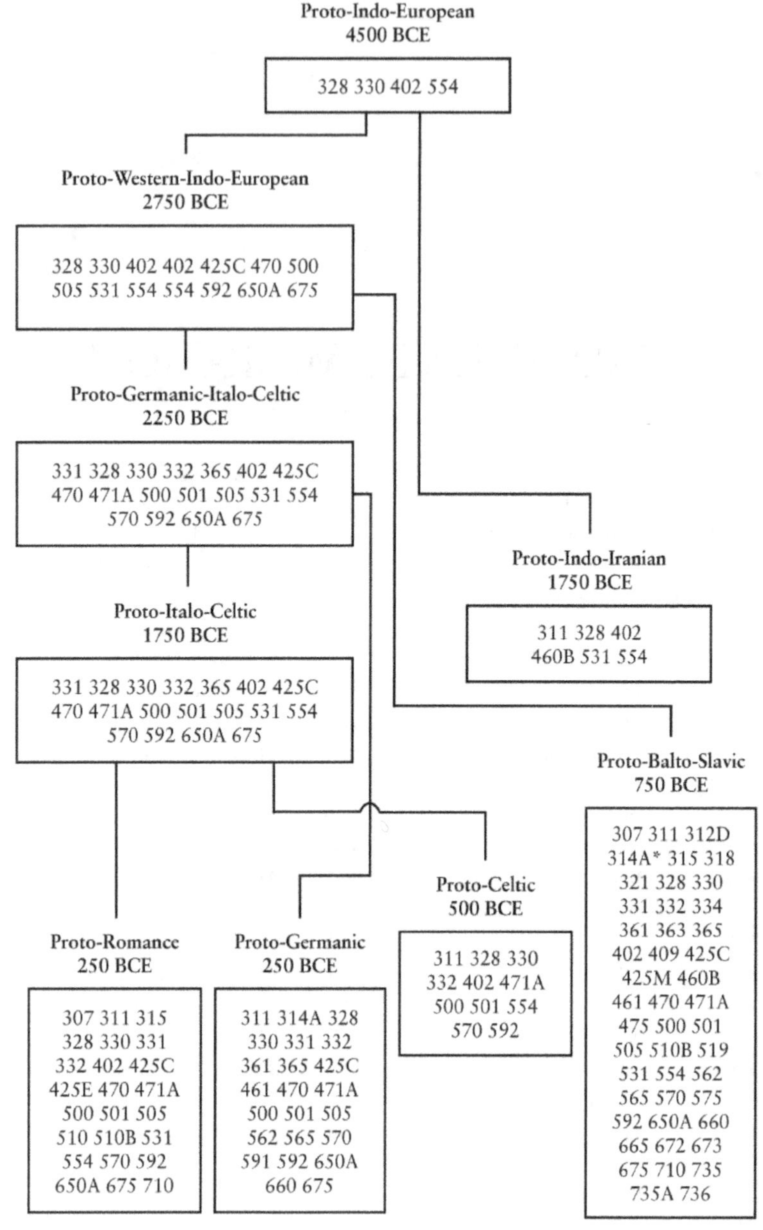

Estimated dates for Indo-European migrations are taken from the study cited by Silva/Tehrani: Chang et al. *Ancestry-Constrained Phylogenetic Analysis Supports The Indo-European Steppe Hypothesis*, fig. 2, p. 200. In *Language* 91 (Baltimore: Johns Hopkins University Press, 2015).

SOURCES AND EDITIONS

SOURCES FROM OTHER ANTHOLOGIES

Addy, Sidney Oldall. *Household tales with other traditional remains, collected in The Counties of York, Lincoln, Derby, and Nottingham* (London: D. Nutt, 1895).

The Small-Tooth Dog

Anonymous. *Gesta Romanorum or, Entertaining Stories Invented by the Monks as a Fire-Side Recreation; and Commonly Applied in Their Discourses from the Pulpit., Vol. I*, tr. Charles Swan (London: John Camden Hotten, 1824).

Of Concord

Anonymous. "Princess Frog." *Russian Crafts*. December 7th, 2021. https://russian-crafts.com/russian-folk-tales/princess-frog.html

The Princess Frog

Arnason, Jón. *Icelandic Legends*, tr. George E. J. Powell and Eiríkur Magnússon (London: Richard Bentley, 1864).

The Deacon of Myrká

Asbjørnsen, Peter Christen; Moe, Jørgen Engebretsen. *Popular Tales from the Norse*, 2nd ed., tr. George Webbe Dasent (Edinburgh: Edmonston and Douglas, 1859).

The Master-Smith
Doll i' the Grass
The Old Dame and Her Hen

True and Untrue
Princess on the Glass Hill
The Three Aunts
The Widow's Son
Why The Sea Is Salt
The Lassie and Her Godmother

Asbjørnsen, Peter Christen. *Tales from the Fjeld*, tr. George Webbe Dasent (New York: G. P. Putnam's Sons, 1908).

Death and the Doctor
Friends In Life and Death
Little Freddy With His Fiddle
Boots and the Beasts
Osborn's Pipe
The Golden Palace That Hung In The Air

Bain, R. Nisbet. *Cossack Fairy Tales* (London: George G. Harrap & Co., 1916).

The Story of Little Tsar Novishny, the False Sister, and the Faithful Beasts
The Story of the Unlucky Days

Bain, R. Nisbet. *Russian Fairy Tales from the Skazki of Polevoi* (London: A. H. Bullen, 1901).

The Enchanted Ring
The Story of Marko the Rich and Vasily the Luckless

Basile, Giovanni Battista. *Il Pentamerone; or the Tale of Tales, vol. I*, tr. Burton, Richard Francis (London: Henry and Co., 1893).

The Padlock

Basile, Giambattista. *The Pentamerone, Or the Story of Stories*, 2nd ed., tr. John Edward Taylor (London: David Bogue, 1850).

Corvetto
Peruonto
The Serpent
The Golden Root
The She-Bear
The Goat-Face

Baumbach, Rudolf; Helen James Bennett Dole. *Summer Legends* (New York: T. Y. Crowell, 1888).

The Adder-Queen

Bechstein, Ludwig. *The Old Story-teller: Popular German Tales* (London:

Addey and Co., 1854).
   The Monk and the Bird
   The Three Presents
   The Hare-Keeper

Black, G. F., Thomas, *Northcote W. County Folk-Lore, vol. III: Examples of Printed Folk-Lore concerning the Orkney and Shetland Islands* (London: David Nutt, 1903).
   Peerifool

Blumenthal, Verra Xenophontovna Kalamatiano de. *Folk Tales from The Russian* (Chicago: Rand, McNally & Co., 1903).
   Woe Bogotir

Bogoras, Waldemar. *Tales of Yukaghir, Lamut, and Russianized Natives of Eastern Siberia* (New York: Anthropological Papers of The American Museum Of Natural History, 1918).
   The Girl and the Evil Spirit

Buchan, Peter. *Ancient Scottish Tales: An Unpublished Collection Made by Peter Buchan, with an introduction by John A. Fairley* (Peterhead: Buchan Field Club, 1908).
   Rashen Coatie

Busk, Rachel Harriette. *The Folk-lore of Rome; Collected by Word of Mouth from the People* (London: Longmans, Green and co., 1874).
   The Dark King

Campbell, J. F. *Popular Tales of The West Highlands, vol. II* (London: Alexander Gardner, 1890).
   Fearachur Leigh

Chodsko, Alex. *Fairy Tales of the Slav Peasants and Herdsmen*, tr. Emily J. Harding (London: George Allen, 1896).
   The Journey to the Sun and the Moon

Crane, Thomas Frederick, tr. *Italian Popular Tales* (Boston and New York: Houghton, Mifflin and Company, 1885).
   Thirteenth
   The Gentleman who Kicked a Skull
   Fair Brow
   Don Firriulieddu
   Cinderella

Curtin, Jeremiah. *Myths and Folk-Lore of Ireland* (Boston: Little, Brown, and Company, 1890).

Oisin in Tir Na N-Og

Curtin, Jeremiah. *Myths and Folk-Tales of the Russians, Western Slavs, and Magyars* (Boston: Little, Brown, and Company, 1890).

The Three Kingdoms

Djurklou, Nils Gabriel. *Fairy Tales from the Swedish of G. Djurklou* (London: William Heinemann, 1901).

Lars, My Lad!

Dulac, Edmund. *Edmund Dulac's Fairy-Book: Fairy Tales of the Allied Nations* (New York: G. H. Doran, 1916).

The Friar and the Boy

Erben, Karel. *The Strand Magazine* (London: George Newnes, 1894).

The Three Gold Hairs of Old Vsevede

Erdélyi, Janos. *Hungarian Popular Tales* (1855).

The Princess' Curse

Fillmore, Parker. *Czechoslovak Fairy Tales* (New York: Harcourt, Brace and Company, 1919).

Grandfather's Eyes

Garnett, Lucy M. J. *Greek Wonder Tales* (London: Adam and Charles Black, 1913).

The Snake-Prince

Gask, Lilian. *Folk Tales from Many Lands* (New York: T. Y. Crowell & Company, 1910).

The Monk and the Bird of Paradise

Geldart, Edmund Martin. *Folk-lore of Modern Greece: The Tales of the People* (London: W. Swan Sonnenschein & Co., 1884).

The Goat-Girl

Griffin, Gerald. *Holland-tide, or, Irish Popular Tales* (London: Saunders and Otley, 1827).

The Brown Man

Griffis, William Elliot. *Dutch Fairy Tales for Young Folks* (New York: Thomas Y. Crowell Company, 1918).

When Wheat Worked Woe

Grimm, Jacob; Grimm, Wilhelm. *Grimm's Household Tales, vol. I*, tr. Margaret Hunt (London: George Bell and Sons, 1884).

Brother Lustig
Gambling Hansel
The Three Feathers
The Queen Bee
Godfather Death
Rumpelstiltskin
The Three Snake-Leaves
Frau Trude
The White Snake
The Three Spinners
The Devil With the Three Golden Hairs
Our Lady's Child

Grimm, Jacob; Grimm, Wilhelm. *Grimm's Household Tales, vol. II*, tr. Margaret Hunt (London: George Bell and Sons, 1884).

The Sea-Hare
Ferdinand the Faithful
The Young Giant
The Devil's Sooty Brother
Second Tale of the Snake
Iron John
Bearskin
The Blue Light
Sweet Porridge
The Three Army-Surgeons
The True Sweetheart

Groome, Francis Hindes. *Gypsy Folk Tales* (London: Hurst & Blackett, 1899).

The Three Girls
The Vampire
The Snake Who Became the King's Son-in-law
The Winged Hero

Grundtvig, Svend Hersleb, Bay, Jens Christian. *Danish Fairy and Folk Tales, tr. Jens Christian Bay* (New York and London: Harper & Brothers, 1899).

The Three Pennies
The Coffee Mill Which Grinds Salt
The Wonderful Pot

Hunt, Robert. *Popular Romances of the West of England; or, The Drolls, Traditions, and Superstitions of Old Cornwall*, 1st series (London: John Camden Hotten, 1865).

The Specter Bridegroom

Jacobs, Joseph. *English Fairy Tales*, 3rd ed. (New York: G. P. Putnam's Sons, 1902).

Jack and the Beanstalk
Tom Tit Tot
Childe Rowland
The Fish and the Ring

Jacobs, Joseph. *Europa's Fairy Book* (New York: G. P. Putnam's Sons, 1916).

Beauty and the Beast

Jacobs, Joseph. *More English Fairy Tales* (New York: G. Putnam's Sons, 1922).

Habetrot and Scantlie Mab

Jones, W. Henry; Kropf, Lewis L. *The Folk-Tales of the Magyars* (London: Elliot Stock, 1889).

The Lover's Ghost

Keightley, Thomas. *The Fairy Mythology, Illustrative of the Romance and Superstition of Various Countries* (London: George Bell & Sons, 1892).

Rhys at the Fairy-Dance

Lang, Andrew. *The Blue Fairy Book* (New York: Longmans, Green and Co., 1889).

Little Red Riding Hood
Cinderella; or, The Little Glass Slipper

Lang, Andrew. *The Pink Fairy Book* (New York: Longmans, Green and Co., 1897).

How the Dragon Was Tricked
The Princess in the Chest
The Flying Trunk
The Troll's Daughter
Don Giovanni de la Fortuna

Lang, Andrew. *The Violet Fairy Book* (New York: Longmans, Green and Co., 1901).

Mogarzea and His Son
Jesper Who Herded the Hares
The Story of the Three Wonderful Beggars

Lang, Andrew. *The Crimson Fairy Book* (New York: Longmans, Green and Co., 1903).

The Gifts of the Magician
Lucky Luck

Lang, Andrew. *The Yellow Fairy Book* (New York: Longmans, Green and Co., 1906).
The Grateful Beasts
The Tinder-Box

Mackenzie, Donald Alexander. *Wonder Tales from Scottish Myth and Legend* (New York: Frederick A Stokes Co., 1917).
The Story of Michael Scott

MacManus, Seumas. *Donegal Fairy Stories* (Garden City: Doubleday, 1900).
The Snow, the Crow, and the Blood

Magnus, Leonard A., tr. *Russian Folk-Tales* (London: Kegan Paul, Trench, Trubner & Co. Ltd., 1915).
The Enchanted Tsarévich
The Dun Cow
The Legless Knight and the Blind Knight
Donotknow
Never-Wash

Mason, Eugene. *French Mediaeval Romances from the Lays of Marie De France* (1911).
Lay of the Werewolf

Mawr, E. B. *Roumanian Fairy Tales and Legends* (London: H. K. Lewis, 1881).
Handsome Is As Handsome Does

Metsvahi, Merili. *The Woman as Wolf (AT409). Some Interpretations of a Very Estonian Folk Tale* (University of Tartu, 2013).
The Wolf's Daughter

Mijatovies, Csedomille; W. Denton. *Serbian Folk-Lore* (London: W. Isbister and Company, 1874).
The Bear's Son

Olcott, Frances Jenkins. *Wonder Tales from Baltic Wizards, from The German And English* (Longmans, Green And Co., 1928).
Luck, Luck in the Red Coat!

Ralston, W. R. S. *Russian Fairy Tales: A Choice Collection of Muscovite Folk-Lore* (New York: Hurst & Co., 1887).

Baba Yaga
The Fiend

Ransome, Arthur. *Old Peter's Russian Tales* (London: Thomas Nelson and Sons, 1916).
Prince Ivan, the Witch Baby, and the Little Sister of the Sun

Spence, Lewis. *Legends & Romances of Spain* (London: G. G. Harrap & Company Ltd., 1920).
Cleomades and Claremond

Steele, Robert. *The Russian Garland* (London: A. M. Philpot, Limited, 1916).
Sila Tsarevich and Ivashka with the White Smock
Emelyan the Fool

Straparola, Giovanni Francesco; Waters, W. G. *The Nights of Straparola, vol. I* (London: Lawrence and Bullen, 1894).
Fortunio and the Siren

Thoms, William John. *Lays and Legends of Various Nations: Illustrative of Their Traditions, Popular Culture, Manners, Customs, and Superstitions* (London: George Cowie, 1834).
The Legend of Paracelsus

Thorpe, Benjamin. *Yule-Tide Stories: A Collection of Scandinavian and North German Popular Tales and Traditions, from the Swedish, Danish, and German* (London: Henry G. Bohn, 1853)
The Girl Who Could Spin Gold from Clay and Long Straw

Webster, Wentworth. *Basque Legends*, 2nd ed. (London: Griffith and Farran, 1879).
The Cobbler and His Three Daughters

Wheeler, Post. *Russian Wonder Tales, with a Foreword on the Russian Skazki* (New York: The Century Co., 1912).
Vasilissa the Beautiful

Wratislaw, A. H. *Sixty Folk-Tales from Exclusively Slavonic Sources* (London: Elliot Stock, 1889).
Fate
The Pale Maiden

Zingerle, Ignaz. Sagen aus Tirol 2nd ed. (1891).
The Grass Snake of the House

TRANSLATIONS ORIGINAL TO THIS EDITION

Anton Rieutskyi

The Magic Shirt, "Чудесная рубашка", from Afanasyev, A. N.; ed. Gruzinsky, A.E. *Народные русские сказки, vol. II*, 3rd ed. (П. Д. Сытина, 1897).

Two Kinds of Luck, "Две доли", from Afanasyev, A. N.; ed. Gruzinsky, A.E. *Народные русские сказки, vol. II*, 3rd ed. (П. Д. Сытина, 1897).

Edward Maxwell III:

Dr. Urssenbeck, Physician of Death, "Gevatter Tod", from Holczabek, J. W.; Winter, A. *Sagen und Geschichten der Stadt Wien*, vol. I (Vienna: Verlag von Carl Graeser, 1886).

Hans Dumb, "Hans Dumm", from Grimm, Jakob; Grimm, Wilhelm. *Kinder- und Hausmärchen, vol. I*, 1st ed. (Berlin: Realschulbuchhandlung, 1812).

The Spirit in the Glass Bottle, "Der Geist im Glas", from Grimm, Jakob; Grimm, Wilhelm. *Kinder- und Hausmärchen, vol. II*, 1st ed. (Berlin: Realschulbuchhandlung, 1815).

The Three-legged Pot (re-telling)

The Full Jar, "Van Kannegien vul", from Boekenoogen, G.J. *Nederlandse sprookjes en vertelsels. In Volkskunde* 14 (1902).

The Three Doctors, "Les trois médecins", from Duine, François (H. de Kerbeuzec). *L'Hermine* No. 24 (1901).

All-kinds-of-fur, from "Allerleirauh", Grimm, Jakob; Grimm, Wilhelm. *Kinder- und Hausmärchen, vol. I*, 7th ed. (Göttingen: Verlag der Dieterichschen Buchhandlung, 1857).

Karl S.

The Serf as Hell's Stoker, "Teomees Põrgus Katlakütjaks", from Karel Dreifeldt (1894). December 10th, 2021. https://www.folklore.ee/pubte/muina/antoloogia/68.html

Saskia K.

Death in a Bottle, "Surm Lähkris", from Gustav Mägi (1906). December 10th, 2021. https://www.folklore.ee/pubte/muina/antoloogia/57.html

Simon H.

The Chursusissa, "Die Chursusissa", from Hahn, Johann Georg von. Griechische und albanesische Märchen (Leipzig: W. Engelmann, 1864).

INDEX BY COUNTRY

Estonia

> *Death in a Bottle*
> *The Serf as Hell's Stoker*
> *The Wolf's Daughter*

Finland

> *The Gifts of the Magician*

France

> *Beauty and the Beast*
> *Cinderella; or, The Little Glass Slipper*
> *Lay of the Werewolf*
> *Little Red Riding Hood*
> *The Three Doctors*

Germany

> *All-kinds-of-fur*
> *Bearskin*
> *Brother Lustig*
> *Ferdinand the Faithful*
> *Frau Trude*
> *Gambling Hansel*
> *Godfather Death*
> *Hans Dumb*
> *Iron John*
> *Our Lady's Child*
> *Princess on the Glass Hill*
> *Rumpelstiltskin*
> *Second Tale of the Snake*
> *Sweet Porridge*
> *The Adder-Queen*
> *The Blue Light*
> *The Devil With the Three Golden Hairs*
> *The Devil's Sooty Brother*
> *The Hare-Keeper*
> *The Monk and the Bird*
> *The Queen Bee*
> *The Sea-Hare*
> *The Spirit in the Glass Bottle*
> *The Three Army-Surgeons*
> *The Three Feathers*
> *The Three Presents*
> *The Three Snake-Leaves*
> *The Three Spinners*

Wales

Rhys at the Fairy-Dance

BIBLIOGRAPHY

SURVEYS AND OVERVIEWS

Grimm, Wilhelm. **Preface** in *Children's and household tales*, 3rd ed. (London: George Bell, 1856).

Lang, Andrew. **The Method of Folklore.** In *Custom and Myth* (London: Longmans, Green Co., 1884).

Ashliman, D. L. **Fairy Lore: A Handbook Greenwood** (New York: Greenwood Press, 2005).

FOLKLORISTICS RESOURCES

Ashliman, D. L. **A Guide to Folktales in the English Language: Based on the Aarne–Thompson Classification System** (New York: Greenwood Press, 1987).

Thompson, Stith. **The Types of the Folktale: A Classification and Bibliography** (Indiana University, 1961).

Hans-Jörg Uther, **The Types of International Folktales. A Classification and Bibliography**, 3 vols. (Helsinki: Folklore Fellows Communications, 2004).

Haase, Donald. **The Greenwood Encyclopedia of Folktales and Fairy Tales**, 3 vols. (Santa Barbara: Greenwood Publishing Group, 2007).

INDO-EUROPEAN MYTH AND FOLKLORE

Silva, Sara Graça da, and Tehrani, Jamshid J., **Comparative phylogenetic analyses uncover the ancient roots of Indo-European folktales**, in *Royal Society Open Science*

(The Royal Society Publishing, 2015).

West, M. L. **Indo-European Poetry and Myth** (Oxford University Press , 2009).

Watkins, Calvert. **How to Kill a Dragon: Aspects of Indo-European Poetics** (Oxford University Press, 2001).

Tylor, Edward Burnett. **Primitive culture: researches into the development of mythology, philosophy, religion, language, art, and custom, vol. I** (London: John Murray, 1920).

CONSERVATISM IN CULTURAL TRANSMISSION

Henrich J., Boyd R. **The evolution of conformist transmission and the emergence of between-group differences.** In *Evolution and Human Behavior 19* (Amsterdam: Elsevier, 1998).

Anderson, Walter. **Kaiser und Abt: die Geschichte eines Schwanks.** In *Folklore Fellows' Communications 42* (Helsinki: 1923)

Collard, Mark et al. **Branching, blending, and the evolution of cultural similarities and differences among human populations.** In *Evolution and Human Behavior* (Amsterdam: Elsevier, 2006).

Bartlett, Frederic C. **Remembering: A Study in Experimental and Social Psychology** (Cambridge University Press, 1932).

ILLUSTRATIONS

Rackham, Arthur. **The Arthur Rackham Treasury: 86 Full-Color Illustrations** (Mineola: Dover, 2005).

Bilibin, Ivan I.; Chandler, Robert. **Russian Folk Tales** (Boulder: Shambhala, 1980).

Dulac, Edmund; Menges, Jeff A. **Dulac's Fairy Tale Illustrations in Full Color** (Mineola: Dover, 2004).

Helen Stratton; Brothers Grimm. **Grimm's Fairy Tales: With Many Illustrations in Colour and in Black-nd-White by Helen Stratton** (Pook Press, 2013).

Gustave Dore; Perrault, Charles. **Perrault's Fairy Tales, with illustrations by Gustave Dore** (Mineola: Dover, 2015).

Mare, Walter de la; A. H. Watson. **Told Again: Old Tales Told Again** (Princeton University Press, 2019).